The Adventures of Elizabeth Stanton Series

Volume 2 The Great Messiah

Vic Broquard

Published by:
Broquard eBooks
http://Broquard-eBooks.com
author@Broquard-eBooks.com
103 Timberlane
East Peoria, IL 61611

Artwork by Crooked Willow Studios

For Morgan and L. Ron Hubbard

Table of Contents

Chapter 1 Beginning Confusions

My name was Elizabeth Stanton and my dearest friends used to call me Bethany — at least it was Bethany until a few days ago. Now I find that they want to call me Madelyn Adid. I never dreamed that picking up a new infant body could be this confusing to everyone, including me! If you are confused, join me.

You see, I, like you, am a being, an immortal spirit. I've lived in many bodies and will have as many more as I desire, assuming the world, our playground, is not destroyed. A few years ago, I was part of a group of like-minded people, the druwids. In my group, I was revered as the Wid Bethany — the title which I took nearly nine hundred years ago now. I am Truth and Knowledge. Yes, you may call me a witch, a demon, or a heretic, but in doing so, you mark yourself as just another Blind One. I chose this road — this path I follow — knowingly and willingly. I do it for all mankind, even you.

I guess I ought to back up and explain my life up to this point in time — to try to undo the confusion. For me, it all began in 550 AH (After Hodhekansis, the legendary twins and founders of Megalos) in a small village called Uru in the northern part of the rolling green hills of the Greenway here on Tarra. Who I was and where I've been before coming to Tarra are blocked in my memories. Believe me; I've tried to crack that black veil, which hides more of my past from me. The earliest memories I can see are running and playing tag with other children in Uru one spring morning.

Uru at that period in history was one of the first farming settlements on Tarra as far as anyone knows. No written records date from before 558 AH. We know that writing was invented by the great artist and philosopher Niccolo Helios, who lived in the land called Megalos. Geography plays a vital role in understanding what has happened to me and to so many others, so let me begin properly with a description of the planet we all call home, Tarra.

Tarra is a blue-green world about eight thousand miles in diameter consisting of vast oceans and one enormous continent shaped much like a dog bone — that is, the two huge continents we call Eastern Tarra and Western Tarra are physically joined by one long, narrow, nearly impassable desert region that is some two hundred miles wide and three hundred miles long. Where this narrows joins the roughly circular lobes of the two continents, two towering mountain ranges block any passage into this desert region that goes by the name of the Desert of Desolation. On our side, Western Tarra, the blocking eighteen thousand foot range is called Kathas, while on the Eastern side, the similar range is named Helios Grande after the great Sun God himself. None of us really knows what lies in Eastern Tarra because no one has been there and returned, though I have heard tales of some who have tried.

Straddling the southern side of the Desert of Desolation is a huge, rocky island, Megalos, which is four hundred miles long but only one hundred miles at its greatest width. Here on the Western Tarra side, Megalos nearly touches the continent. The Sallow Firth, as it is called, is two miles wide yet only three feet deep at low tide! Yes, horses and people often walk across the Firth, but there are ferries for those with money and passes from the Emperor of Megalos. The eastern side of Megalos is some twenty miles from the rocky coast of Eastern Tarra, but here treacherous tides thunder against many hidden rocks in that wide channel. From the dawn of time, Megalos and Western Tarra share the annals of history, both good and bad.

Now Western Tarra is roughly divided into halves by the great Med Sea, which opens onto the ocean at the western most part of the continent. This pale blue sea is nearly eight hundred miles long; its width varies between fifty and a hundred miles. Along the northern shores of Med Sea lie the principalities of the Seven Sea Princes. On the eastern shore of the Med Sea, abutting the Sea Princes, is the arid land called Juda Arad stretching all the way to the Kathas mountain range. I am currently living in a small town in Juda Arad, but more on that in a moment. All across the southern shore of Med Sea lies the giant Red Desert uninhabited and proven unpassable. South of the Red Desert lay the Southlands with rich, rolling green savannahs and forests, rich in animal life but with few, dark-skinned inhabitants. The Southlands and Megalos share a close relationship as far back as anyone can remember, though not necessarily a good one.

North of the principalities of the Seven Sea Princes is a mountain range known as the Appian Way. These spectacular eight thousand foot tall, granite peaks stretch nearly across all of Western Tarra dividing the continent in half. The lands above the Appian Way are divided by nature into three roughly equal sized areas. At the far north lies the cold but timbered lands called Volksholm whose people are called the Axemen. To the east is the Northern Steppes, an arid land home to nomadic horsemen called the Galts, while to the west lies the Greenway, a land of contrasts. Greenway consists of heavily forested, rugged hills interspersed with lush green valleys. My original village of Uru lies in the north central portion of the Greenway.

Many islands both large and small dot the lengthy coastline. However, of note is the large island called West Reach, which lies some ten miles off the coast of the Greenway. It is a large island kingdom unto itself. Though largely unpopulated, it plays a role in this story.

The world at this time is roughly divisible into three political camps. Megalos, rumored to be the cradle of civilization, has great marble-stone cities, is very hot during summers, and has produced the first great thinkers, including the great artist and inventor Niccolo Helios, who I met a few years ago. The principalities of the Seven Sea Princes are the feudal city-states of wealthy men who sail the Med Sea trading there, as well as up and down the coastline of Western Tarra. Finally, all the lands above the Appian Way, are inhabited warring hunter-gatherer groups or primitive farming communities. However, everywhere, rule is by the strongest sword and the mightiest forces, of which the Megalos Centurions are reputed to be the best at this time in history.

Megalos is an old civilization dating back well over five hundred years and currently has the highest level of civilization of any land, though of technology might be a better statement. Emperor Titus, a young man recently placed into power by the Church of Sol, rules them. Yes, these people worship the Sun God. Originally, their Senate made the laws of the land, while the Emperor carried them out. However, over the centuries, the Senate became an ineffective ruling institution, and the Emperor became all-powerful. Their previous Emperor Hiro turned the entire empire into a promiscuous brothel, at least from my point of view. When the Emperor drugged me and tried to rape me, I killed him, forcing a change of power. The Church of Sol took on more power and placed Titus on the throne. Thus, for the last few years, it is really the Church of Sol that wields the true power in Megalos, a change that I had hoped would be for the better.

However, for many years, Megalos has been attempting to bring their version of civilization to the barbarian lands. Definition of barbarian lands: any land not theirs. Long ago in the depths of history, they conquered the Southland, at least the eastern sections. Their soldiers are called Centurions and are bronzed-skinned, carry enormous shields, and fight often with spears and short swords. Some even ride war chariots into battle. They fight in tight formations and have been unstoppable in their forward march across all the lands. Now in the Southlands, they operate wealthy gold and gem mines, and have taken many dark skinned natives back to Megalos as slaves. Today on Megalos, there are many second generation slaves who know only of life as a slave and nothing of their original homeland or people.

Perhaps some thirty years ago, the Centurions conquered the land adjoining the Southlands, Juda Arad, taking its vital port on the eastern edge of the Med sea, Al Barq. Next, they proceeded to attack each of the Seven Sea Prince cities or sectors or principalities, one by one, beginning with Zargarb and ending with Velona. Their style of assault was interesting because they built a straight, level, paved stone roadway from where they currently were located right up to the next city to be attacked. Once that city fell, they resumed their road construction toward the next target. Thus, they were assured of rapid supply and movement of soldiers.

My original land was the Greenway, north of the Appian Way, a land of farmers and hunter-trappers, and sparsely populated. In contrast to the cities of a hundred thousand or more in the Lands of the Sea Princes, our largest city, the port of Calgary, only boasts some thirty thousand people. Only one other town in the middle of the Greenway, Brownsville has a population over ten thousand. Most of our towns and villages have only a few thousand, while we do have numerous hamlets of fifty to a hundred inhabitants.

Yes, all this does tie together. In the Greenway, several hundred years ago, one man, Alabaster Benjamin Crowley, founded a special group of people, called the druwids. We are usually trained from about the age of six to become a part of this group, because it took ten full years of study to learn what was required. The druwids are organized into Circles of seven members, each with their own specialties. The Protector is a highly skilled fighter whose task is to defend the others. The Loremaster is wise about Nature, plants and animals. The Planner is skilled at design and construction of buildings and such. The Judger is both a conjurer and an arbitrator of justice. The Communicator is skilled with telepathy and acts as the communicator between members of the group and other Communicators in other groups. Thus, distance plays no part in holding us together. The Healer is highly skilled in all aspects of healing the sick and injured. Finally, the Wid is the wisest and the leader of the Circle because the Wid is always seeking to know all about everything in the world. Wids are the rarest of all the druwids and hardest to become. I was a Wid in my Circle, the Lightning Circle, before my untimely death a week ago. Now every druwid is skilled in healing, it's just that the Healer has far more skill than the rest of us.

The entire purpose of the Alabaster's druwids is to protect and serve all the people of the Greenway. To that end, most of the druwids live out among the small towns and villages, protecting, healing, arbitrating disputes, and helping with new constructions. We live to help our people and our lives are dedicated to helping them. As an aside, every druwid is a being, just like all the others on Tarra, but a druwid is not located in their body's head, but rather some distance from it. Most of the people on Tarra are stuck solidly in their heads. Druwids derogatorily call them the Headers, a disgusting word rarely spoken.

Further, because of our intense study and total love and devotion to Nature, yes, you may say that we worship Nature; we have developed powers that many find remarkable. We can bring into existence fire, ice, and lightning. My specialty is lightning. Given a cloud in the sky, I can create a bolt to strike where I desire. However, the druwids only use these intense powers to protect our people from the raiders. Frequently, Galts from the Northern Steppes leave their horses behind and form into raiding parties, sacking our villages. To date, the Galts have been the biggest problem of our small eastern villages. Occasionally, Axemen from Volksholm raid the northern villages. Personally, I've never seen one of those.

Now several years ago, Alabaster sent Isabel and several others from her Circle to the Sea Princes both to spy on the Sea Princes and to monitor the invading Centurion army. You must understand something about that land. There, Nature had become horribly unbalanced between men and women. In the Greenway, men and women are treated as equals in all things, save the men do the heavy chores and the women bear the children. In the Sea Princes, this Holy Balance of Nature went awry long ago. Women are less than second-class citizens! They cannot speak unless a man gives them permission. They are abused both physically and mentally. Speaking without permission results in one's tongue being cut out. Fathers routinely rape their daughters! I just could not believe the atrocities being committed there when I visited that land.

Into this mess, defiled women banded together into the Sisterhood.

Under their guidance, these battered, tortured women were taught how to fight and fight well, among many other things. Each sector, that is, each city-state, has its own band of the Sisterhood. Among the population of the Sea Princes, these amazon women were derogatorily called the Abominations. They were highly respected for their fighting skills, for none of the guards of the Sea Princes could ever best a Sisterhood warrior! Thus, these women survived on the edge of civilization. It was into this mess that Isabel came a number of years ago, bonding with these women, providing guidance as she could, though keeping her true identity as a druwid of the Greenway hidden.

When the Centurions attacked the first of the Sea Prince cities, Zargarb, the Prince threw all of his guards as well as all of the fighters he could find or make at the enemy. The results were a couple of casualties on the Centurion side and thousands of dead on the Prince's side. Yes, I personally witnessed this happening at another city sometime later. Finally, as a very last resort, the Sisterhood chose to make a last stand to defend Zargarb, after all else had failed. Isabel and another druwid joined them. The result was spectacular and had far reaching impacts, even in Juda Arad!

A hundred Sisters took on an army of thousands of Centurions. Isabel summoned a huge thunderstorm of immense proportions. In the downpour, the Sisters took their toll: five hundred Centurions died that day, as did the hundred Sisters. However, Isabel, the last defender standing on the battlefield, brought lightning bolt after bolt down upon them. Only a Herculean effort on their part eventually subdued her. The General ordered her not to be slain but instead cut off both her hands that she may never kill another Centurion again, raped her, and left her to die humiliated upon the battlefield. You have to understand, from the Centurion point of view, Isabel was given a high honor to be thusly treated.

During the Great Battle, two other Sisters who were not fighters arrived and watched unseen from a distance. During the night, they rescued Isabel and secreted her away, trying to save her life. For over a year, they devoted their entire existence to keeping Isabel alive. My Circle eventually found her and healed her. Now, Isabel and her two Sisters live in Calgary and Isabel was promoted to a Wid.

However, everyone, including the Centurions believe that Isabel was taken by Tur, the Sea God worshiped by the Sea Princes, healed by him, and now is his personal bodyguard! In other words, the Sisterhood struck immense fear into the Centurions, the only fighters ever to have caused them the slightest problem!

Once a city or land is captured, a Governor takes control of the occupied territory and administers it, bringing civilization, as Megalos sees it, to that land, in return for one tenth of the profits of that city. A few months later, my Circle intervened at another city and forged an agreement placing the Sisterhood in charge of helping to restore law, order, and survival to the conquered city. As a byproduct, the Sea Princes and the Church of Tur were ordered to cease all of their mistreatment of women. As the Governor proclaimed, "anything that happens to a woman I shall personally see that it happens to you." That forced a major change in their treatment of women! However, many Sisters migrated to the Greenway to seek a new and better life, a new chance at life, in fact.

Of course, the problem we in the Greenway faced was the simple fact that we were next on the Centurion's assault list! Our people are farmers and hunters not fighters. We do not even have a central government as such. Hence, Alabaster had sent us to visit the Sea Princes, Juda Arad, the Southlands, and even Megalos in an attempt to find out their strategies and tactics and find some way that we might defeat them. Yes, we managed to find ways to delay their immediate plans on the Greenway by several years. Unfortunately, just as we were returning from our more than year-long excursion, Alabaster's body died unexpectedly. He was, after all, over two hundred fifty years old. For many years, it had taken immense power of his being to keep the aged body alive. At last, he could do so no more.

Even more surprising, when we returned to Calgary, we discovered that his last orders had been to place our Circle, the Lightning Circle, as the leaders of all the druwids! His reasoning was sound; we were the most likely people to be able to find a way to avoid the Greenway in a war with the Centurions. None of us wanted to see the horrors of war, the devastation, come to our people. In fact, we did find an acceptable alternative to war and slaughter. We created a mutual treaty in which the Centurions came and built their paved road system across the heart of the Greenway, provided security and guidance, along with iron farming implements. In return, we provided yearly ten boat loads of grain and food supplies and saw that the new Governor had his own fancy stone residence. Actually, for several years, this arrangement did work out well. The new road system allowed our people to get their produce to market come harvest time almost twice as fast as before. Incidentally, the Centurions still do not know the true nature of the druwids, believing them just to be the local healers in the villages, so our secrets are still safe.

For several years, we relaxed and enjoyed a normal life. Roy, our Protector, and I were happily married and we had three lovely children. I could not have been happier. I was living a dream life at last. Unfortunately, that came to an abrupt end for me.

Far to the east in the Greenway, King Randolf, who was building his own empire, made a treaty of some kind with our enemy, the Galts. Nearly a thousand of those raiders joined his cavalry and foot soldiers near his wooden fortress at Redun. We were not certain what his true intentions were, however. Just north of his lands are those of Erline Herbiscus, a renegade druwid, that is, she knew how to control the weather and bring down fire and lightning, but refused to be a part of our group, preferring to be her own master. Her forces were arrayed opposite the King's army and the Galts. Worse still, the Centurions, thousands of them, were building the new road system nearby and would likely be caught between the warring factions. Hence, a civil war was about to break out and, because of Erline and her "magic," all druwids were in jeopardy. Further, we already knew just what the Centurions would do to all sides if a civil war occurred. They would just bring in thousands more troops and attack both sides. Those that they did not kill, they would ship off to their salt mines as slaves until they died.

This we could not let happen. Thus it was that Roy and I rode into the conflict, meeting with Erline and getting her agreement not to start the conflict. Here is where I made my fatal mistake. I believed that you could reason with an insane man. Under the universal white parley flag, we rode into the King's land in an attempt to meet with him and get him to see reason. As we approached the King, we received a welcoming volley of arrows. One hit me right in the middle of my forehead; my body died instantly.

Into that confusion on that dark and stormy day, Alabaster appeared. Yes, he was there, a being alone, for he still had not chosen to acquire a new infant body. Together with Erline, he and I let loose a tremendous volley of over a thousand lightning strikes, eliminating the King and most all of his forces, including the Galts. To all outsiders, especially the nearby Centurions, it appeared as if another one of the freaky storms of Nature had occurred.

Once the enemy had been eliminated and the druwids and the Greenway were safe once more, Alabaster helped me over my intense grief. After all, I had just lost my body, my husband who I loved dearly, my children, and my dearest friends. All were gone from me the instant that arrow pierced my head. He helped give me a new purpose, a new thing I could do to help the land that I loved, the Greenway.

To grasp its significance, you have to understand side events. Back at the battle of Zargarb, when Isabel unleashed an incredible storm, the side effects were unknown and yet vitally critical to the people of Juda Arad. These devoutly religious people had originally lived somewhere in the Southlands and had been conquered and driven from their homelands by the Centurions many years ago. Now they eked out a bare existence in this arid land, still occupied and controlled by the Centurions. These people had both prophets and messiahs. The prophets continuously spread the word of God, helping the people keep their faith. The messiahs, though deeply religious, were more like religious zealots and attempted to carry their fight for freedom from the infidels, their word for the Centurions. They attacked Centurion supply trains, humiliated city guards. In short, they did everything in their power to convince the Centurions to leave their land.

However, all of their prophets spoke of the coming of the Son of God, the Great Messiah, who would one day be born among them and free them from the infidels, driving the Centurions out of Juda Arad. One of their great prophets, Jamil Tamil, told us, "The signs are said to be three. The first two have already occurred. It is said and predicted by all prophets that first shall come a great thunderous rain, rain in great quantity unlike any rain we have ever seen before. That occurred some time ago, shortly after Zargarb fell to the infidels. The second sign has also appeared. Great fields of desert flowers shall bring forth massive blossoms where before only stark grasses grew. We only await the last sign of the birth of our savior, the Great Messiah, son of Jehosa. It is said that on the night of his birth, a new bright star will appear in the heavens where none shone before. It shall shine for seven days and then fade away, marking the cycle of fleshly life. Our bodies are born, grow to adulthood, then gradually fade, and then die out. The star marks the passage of the son of Jehosa as he is born, grows to maturity and then fades and dies, as do all of our fleshly bodies."

Naturally, when we heard all this, we felt rather guilty, for we knew that Isabel had caused both of the first two signs. Her massive storm moved on eastward from Zargarb into Arad! We all knew that Nature, given this huge rainfall, would respond with a massive new growth. So can you imagine our surprise that night when we, along with Prophet Emil, spied the new star appearing in the constellation of Drago? Instantly, Emil rushed off to the sacred city, where the son of Jehosa was being born, to protect his Great Messiah. Yes, the city of his birth was a secret among the prophets, and yet we found out that it was in fact the very city we had visited, Jerilum.

Alabaster, as did we, wondered about the coincidence of the first two signs. How could these prophets have known many, many years ago that we would be creating the first two signs of the coming of their Great Messiah? Without Isabel's storm, the first two signs would not have occurred! What possible connection could their One God, Jehosa, have to do with us druwids? Alabaster and I were both Wids, meaning we have this incredible urge to learn all that we can, to understand all, to know all. Here was something we both thought incredibly interesting. Besides, Alabaster pointed out to me, we needed to know how this Great Messiah would be able to drive the Centurions from their land. Perhaps we could learn from him and use the same thing here in the Greenway.

This is why Alabaster asked me to go to Juda Arad, to find this Great Messiah, and to monitor the situation closely. He promised to contact me many years later, both to find out what I had learned and to help me get back to my beloved Greenway. I accepted the challenge. How could I not? Here was something I *had* to know.

I floated down to Zargarb and over to Jerilum and discovered the location where the Great Messiah was being raised in secret by the prophets, a tiny village called Bethel. My guess was that their Great Messiah was now about five years old.

Bethel was a small rural village of some five hundred people in total. Most depended upon their small herds of sheep. It didn't take me long to locate their Great Messiah. He was the only child among the many children running around in the streets who had an adult constantly watching over him, protecting him from unseen dangers. What dangers? I could not see any. This village was remote and in the far eastern portion of Juda Arad. No Centurions were here and none was ever likely to come here for that matter.

Now all I had to do was find myself a new baby body to occupy. None of the women seemed with child just now. For a moment, I panicked, wondering if they would ever have more babies here in this village. I bided my time, content with watching the young messiah run and play. To me, he was just an ordinary child, save one thing. He, like I had been, was not in his head. He was always at least five feet above and behind it. If nothing else, he was prime druwid material, I thought.

Again, some time passed. As I have said before, I am a poor judge of time when not in my body, or in this case, a body. Maybe it was a month. A young five year old girl was running and playing in the street and accidentally ran into the side of a wagon that was bringing supplies into Bethel. Instantly, she fell down, unconscious. I moved closer, my natural instincts to heal rising to the forefront, though I had no idea how I could do anything without myself having a body with which to do it. She had taken a nasty bump on the head, but that was all. I looked further; one characteristic of a druwid is that we are trained to observe what actually is. I did so. Oh no, it wasn't a simple bump! When she had fallen to the ground, she had landed on a very surprised viper, who had struck out in retaliation! I spied it slithering away, its back nearly broken.

A crowd of people gathered around the unconscious girl. Much to my amazement, the being whose body it was decided that it was now as good as dead and rose up out of the body, paused a moment, and then shot like an arrow off toward the Appian Way. Here was my good fortune: a body already made and ready to go, except that it was dying from a viper bite that the well-intentioned people did not see. I watched helplessly as the adults did nothing!

I had to take action. I spied their Great Messiah trying to get a look between the legs of the adults. I placed the concept into his mind: *She has been bitten by a viper. Tell the grownups.*

Surprised, he looked all around for me, but, though not spotting me, then did as I asked, yelling "Viper bite! Viper bite!" Sure enough, words spoken by their Great Messiah carried great weight among these people. I filed that detail away for future reference. Soon they had located the telltale bite mark on her right arm. However, they all stood, stared, and said their prayers, but actually doing nothing. Finally, one elderly gentleman arrived and was told what had happened. He moved the others out of the way and examined the girl. Now I noticed what had to be her parents. They were crying furiously in the background, being comforted by several other adults. I watched as the old man took out a knife, made the necessary cuts, and began to suck out the poison. I cringed a bit, because he did not even boil the knife first! This was my first clue that healing in this land was in its infancy at best.

Sometime later, after he had sucked all he could out of the wound, he began to bandage the small wound without even putting any herbs on it to further leech any residual poison out! Clearly, these people were in desperate need of a true healer! I looked around and found what I would have put on it, given the austere village. Then, once more, I placed that idea into their Great Messiah's mind and had him speak it to the old man. Once again, I was doubly impressed with the results. Literally, anything that he spoke was carefully marked by the adults! Further, this time, he spotted me, slightly above the unconscious body. Then, I felt the touch of his mind, and a great, peaceful feeling came over me. Soon, I had the wound properly bandaged to my satisfaction. Only then did I make the solid connection with the body, latching onto its head. I felt the headache from the bump and the dizziness, nausea, and paralysis from the bite. I figured the body would survive. As an extra incentive, I gave this new body an order: *live!* I felt the body jerk in response to my command. Then, slowly my vision turned off, as I slipped more fully into this new body, which was now in a deep sleep.

I felt my body being carried lovingly some distance, placed into a warm bed and covered up. I felt someone kiss my forehead. Ah, I was loved already. *Success. I have a new body about the same age as their Great Messiah. Now I'm all set to see what goes on. First part of my new mission accomplished! Now I think that I'll go to sleep for a while. I seem to be so very tired.* And I slept like a baby. The date was September 1, 564 AH.

The massive confusions began when I awoke, presumably the next day. Of course, I was speaking my language, that of the Greenway. To these people, I probably sounded as I was bedeviled, speaking in tongues! My parents had a shocked, horrified look upon their faces, exclaiming that I was possessed by demons! In fact, my mother began shrieking and wailing. Okay, this goof I quickly recognized and remedied. During my journey through Juda Arad some five years ago, I had learned the basics of the language, so I began speaking their tongue. "Morning, I feel awful. Am I going to be okay? My head hurts so." That did the trick. The wailing died at once, and still crying, mom hugged me. They passed the whole thing off as the effects of a nasty bump on the head. Since they were satisfied with that assumption, I didn't try to correct them.

"Oh Madelyn, dear, yes, yes, you are going to be just fine. You have the Great Messiah to thank. He saved your life. He spied the viper bite. When you're able to go out and play, you must thank him. Promise me that you'll thank our Lord, Madelyn," she insisted.

"Who's Madelyn?" I asked confused. I'm Bethany, of course. I regretted my words even as I spoke them.

Mom was shocked again, "Why, you are dear, you are Madelyn Adid, our eldest daughter. Don't you remember your name?" She had a frightened look on her face. Dad shook his head solemnly; I could read his thoughts: "Head wounds often cause forgetfulness."

"No, I'm Bethany," I protested. I was certainly not going to be called this horrid name. Who ever heard of Madelyn anyway?

"No, you are Madelyn, dear," mom kept insisting.

"Aline, she has had a bad head wound. If she wants to be called Bethany, let her. In time she will recover her senses I hope," dad stepped in to help me out.

Now in my own defense, I can only say that my head hurt so I couldn't concentrate at all well; besides my system still was under the influence of the viper poison. Now I grasped the situation. Their daughter had been called

Madelyn. In effect, I had taken over her body when she departed. Actually, the bond between these parents and their daughter had been severed. I was now their daughter, same body, different being in it, different personality — well you get the picture. I diplomatically offered, "How about me being called Bethany Madelyn Adid? Is that acceptable to you?" I spoke as I was last — a highly educated Wid in her middle twenties, but the words were coming from the mouth of a five year old girl! I watched as both their mouths waggled over the incongruity of such a speech coming from their young child. I'd blundered again.

Mom recovered first, "Yes dear, you can be called Bethany Madelyn; I can't guarantee that I'll always remember to do so. We will try, if it will make you happy, Madelyn, I mean Bethany, won't we Tarzig?" Ah, so my mom was called Aline and dad was Tarzig. I tried to memorize the names, for it would be another blunder to forget my parent's names! This was getting so confusing so fast.

Just as dad was agreeing, a small boy, younger than I, poked his head from behind mom's long dress, trying to see too. "Me see. Me see Madee." He was trying to see me. Oh no, I thought, I have a brother!

Mom lifted him up so he could properly see my lying in my bed. To me she said, "You recognize your little brother?" My face turned red. I know it did because it suddenly felt very hot! Of course, I had no idea I had a brother, let alone his name or how our relationship was — I mean was I supposed to be friendly with him as I would automatically desire or did the real Madelyn not want anything to do with him as I had seen some sisters do?

I smiled at him, saying, "Don't worry. I'm feeling better today." I did feel better physically, but not mentally. Memories of how worried my own brother and sister had been when I was almost killed some twenty years ago came unbidden to mind. This was so similar. I did my best to put him at ease.

To my utter relief, mom said, "There, Jamal, see, I told you she is going to be just fine in a few days. Now off you go and play." Jamal, I committed that name to memory along with Aline, Tarzig, Adid, and Madelyn. *Do I have other brothers and sisters? Oh no, what about all the other relatives? Madelyn probably knew all their names. This is going to be trickier than I thought!* Yes, I was near panicking about now. Fortunately, they insisted that I get more rest, and they left me alone to sleep some more.

However, as I lay there, my grief, long put into the back reaches of my mind, surfaced with a vengeance. I had just lost my body, my loving husband, my children — I would not see them grow up — I would not be there for them — they would hardly remember me. I lost my dearest friends. I cried and cried and cried. Of course, this only spooked my new parents even more, because I sobbed uncontrollably for the next two days!

Poor Aline, she tried to console me, wiping my bruised head with a cool cloth, even holding me in her lap. The worst part of it all was that I could not, dare not, even explain why I was crying. How can you explain to parents that their little girl, the being, the personality that knew as Madelyn, had gone and that I, who had just lost everything, now had her body? This they would not understand and, if they did, might not want to keep me around. After all, I was now an imposter. Perhaps picking up Madelyn's body, when she left it for dead had not been such a good idea!

Worse still, I found myself having to withhold all of this, the true situation, from my new parents. I observed that, as I intentionally withheld telling them who I was and what I had done, I began to feel separate, distant, from them. Instead of the close bond of a child to parent, this was driving a wedge between us. In some back portion of my mind, which seemed impervious to my grief, I took note of this fascinating observation: if you withhold something from another, that action tends to separate you from the other, distancing yourself, making yourself separate from that other. Not a good move, if the others are your parents upon whom you are going to be dependent for ten more years!

However, not in a million years would I have guessed what would happen next. When I was still crying the second day, my folks brought in several of the local prophets, who said various prayers over me for my safe recovery. These were a deeply religious people. More importantly, the Great Messiah had come with them. Later when the adults were off whispering among themselves, presumably about me, he came up to me and took my little hand in his little hand, which got my full attention, naturally. Looking me directly in the eyes, his were so blue I remember, and said so that only I could hear, "Bethany, I understand. I completely understand what happened. It is all right now. You are all right." It wasn't his words that communicated, more it was the total intention behind them. In that brief instant, I knew that another person completely understood what I had done and why I was also crying. From their Great Messiah, I could not and did not withhold. For an instant, we two beings were very close. I stopped crying; my grief melted away.

I whispered back, "Thank you. Unexpected loss is very upsetting." His bright eyes showed me he understood. All this from a pair of five year old children!

Within a few minutes, the adults realized I had stopped crying. Upon seeing their Great Messiah standing beside my bed, they immediately proclaimed he'd just performed another great miracle. The next ten minutes were filled with proclamations of such; my parents alternated praise upon the Great Messiah and religious supplications of thanks.

Once the others had finally departed, I spoke to my new mom, "Sorry about all the fuss. I think that knock on my head has rather scrambled my thoughts. If I don't seem to remember things, don't worry. Just show them to me again or tell me about them once more. I promise to learn quickly."

"Madelyn, I mean Bethany," she stumbled, "dear that is okay. I'm just so glad you're recovering. That is all that matters. The knock must have improved your speech because you're talking so much clearer now than you ever have. Perhaps all this is a blessing, honey." I smiled at her. I know, I told her a half-truth; yes, my mind was rather scrambled. This way, I had bought myself time to learn what Madelyn already knew and to adapt without causing continuous upsets. Now they would just expect that it was simply a result of that nasty bump and not give it any further thought.

During the next few days, I really found out just how much I had to learn and learn quickly! I knew where nothing was at in my new home, not even where the bathroom was located! I didn't know what chores were expected of me, but fortunately, not many were; I was only five years old now. That first week I was more or less confined to stay in the house, and I rapidly learned where everything was to be found. Also, many of my new relatives came by to see how I was doing; some even brought some get well pastries, which I shared with everyone.

Yes, these first few weeks were the hardest on me, mentally and emotionally. Had I not been a Wid with keen powers of observation and recall, I would have made a complete mess of everything, bumbling from one goof to the next. However, the one thing in my favor was that Madelyn had only been five years old. Much had not been expected of her as yet. Also, that I was not fluent in their language was not a problem because a five year old is not expected to have a complete grasp of the spoken word.

The next problem I faced occurred when I was finally allowed to go outside. I didn't know where anything was located! Imagine waking up in a town that is totally unfamiliar to you. It's very spooky to find yourself in the middle of a town and not know where anything is at, and yet everyone else expects that you do! However, Bethel is a very small village — only about five hundred people all told.

It is located in a valley of a mostly dry creek bed, called Zira Creek that came down from the higher country closer to the eighteen thousand foot Kathas mountain range, which I was told lay some hundred miles further east of us. The village had several dozen homes roughly spaced along each of ten streets and sported a large central water well and common park area squarely in the center of the village. The homes were uniformly made from adobe bricks, handmade by one middle-aged man whose home shop was at the edge of the village. The commerce of Bethel supported three blacksmith shops, one on each end of the village and one in the center. Most of the people depended upon their flocks of sheep that grazed in and around the surrounding countryside.

However, I learned that my father actually ran the only trading shop in Bethel. All trade goods came through his store. Half his income came from barter and the other half came from coins exchanged for goods. I didn't know it at the time, but Tarzig Adid was the wealthiest person in Bethel, a fact that would play a critical role in later events.

Additionally, as you might expect, Bethel had more prophets in residence or visiting than any other town in all Juda Arad! At least ten were always present, sometimes more. I learned that the Great Messiah lived in the next block. Our house opened onto the central plaza while his was on the opposite side and further down the street.

Thus, once I had gotten myself acquainted with the town somewhat, life finally became routine, and I relaxed and began to enjoy just being a child once more.

By the time that I was six, I shocked both my parents by willingly helping with chores I knew I could handle. Around the house, I cleaned and helped with the usual domestic duties, as was fitting for a woman in their society. Of course, I knew what needed to be done, and without her asking, I went ahead and did those that I was certain I could do. She was most grateful for my assistance and was always validating me by saying that I did so much to help her. Actually, I learned later that I was doing chores that many of the other children at ten would do only if so ordered by their parents!

I didn't stop there. Once I was familiar with dad's store, I began helping there too as best I could. I swept the dust and dirt out at least three times a day and helped organize goods whenever he got in a new shipment of items to sell. I found he had no system for accounting or keeping track of goods and his income and expenses. By the time I was eight, I invented a bookkeeping system for him. Actually, I just adapted the writing skills I had learned from Niccolo Helios of Megalos to this new language. Yes, I kept it very simple, phonetically spelling each name so dad could easily sound out the name. That simple invention for him got me heaped with praise, not only from dad but also from many other adults in the village. Using this record keeping system, he claimed he doubled his profits in one year's time by reducing waste and errors. After that, he swore I was his little genius.

Thus, all my helping about the family home and dad's shop bought me the freedom to be somewhat eccentric for a young Arad woman. Let me explain. Here women were expected to run the home and generally stay home. Most wore their hair short and all wore long, heavy dresses that had to be overly hot in the heat of this arid country. As I discovered, the women looked after their men, even to a ritual washing of their husband's feet with oil when they came home for the evening. It was vastly different from what I was used to in the Greenway, where men and women were equals in all things. At least here, women were not abused as in the Sea Princes.

Of course, I didn't choose to fit in to this at all well. I love long hair and still had not cut it since I was five. An occasional trim, yes, but by now it was really long and light brown. I loved it. I refused to dress in their heavy dresses; instead, I wore the lighter, more expensive, cotton dresses that also were much cooler. Later, I learned that my type of dress code and preference for long hair were really those used by prostitutes of the larger cities! I had to fight that stereotype from the get-go. I would have preferred to wear pants, but that was strictly forbidden to women in Arad. Hence, my compromise. In other words, because I was so helpful to mom and dad, and others as well, they forgave me my idiosyncrasies, which they assumed I would eventually grow out of, but never did.

One day when I was six, the Great Messiah, who I played with every chance that I had, took me aside for a significant chat. "Bethany Adid, you and

I are very much alike in many ways. Please stop calling me the Great Messiah. I'm called Jes Amir. My father is a blacksmith and my mother weaves wool. My older brother is called Josh. Please just call me Jes." Naturally, I agreed.

He added, "I'm just like you. We're spiritual beings in small bodies at the moment. You and I are not in the bodies, are we?" I smiled and said of course not. He went on, "We both have things to do for all people. First, we must watch others and learn all that we can. Then, one day we shall be called upon to do great things for our people. So, Bethany, learn all you can." Of course, I totally agreed with that point of view.

Over the next few years, I watched him as he paid close attention to all that the prophets had to say, committing all to memory. He would observe the people of the village, and especially those that came visiting from other places. With these, he would often enter into lengthy discussions, learning about life and the situations in these other places.

I, on the other hand, at first spent a great deal of time watching his father, the blacksmith. In the Greenway, a true ironworker was an extremely rare person. Actually, in my life there, I had never met one personally. His father, Josephus Amir, never tired of taking the time to explain his art to me or answer my seemingly endless questions. In return, I did many small chores around his shop, such as cleaning. In the end, I had a good theoretical knowledge of smithing, but knew that I could never really utilize it; I had not the strength to wield the hammer upon the anvil.

When I was ten, a singular event occurred. One day, a strange man walked into town, Brother Jackal was his name. He had come to train the Great Messiah in the fine arts of combat. Just as soon as I heard about his arrival — news travels fast in our small village — I scurried over to watch their first lessons. Brother Jackal was bronzed skinned, rather like the Centurions, bare chested with strong muscles. He wore soft leather pants and boots. His hair first attracted my attention. The top of his head was shaven as if someone had cut out a bowl-shaped section, yet the sides were perhaps five inches long. He had deep brown eyes that did not miss a thing; he even noted my arrival at the sidelines of their practice area, a section of the central park. I was just in time.

Lying beside the side of an adobe house lay his backpack and a light linen shirt. Also many weapons were there, several swords, a spear, and a short bow with a quiver of arrows. What appeared to be a walking stick lay askew against the wall. Wiping the black from his hands, Josephus came out of his blacksmith shop to assist. Brother Jackal spoke softly but commandingly, "Jes, your father and I will give you a short demonstration of the skills you must master. Josephus, please pick up any sword of your choosing." I watched as the big man examined each and picked the largest and heaviest sword. "Now I want you to attempt to attack me with that sword. Please, don't worry or hold back; as you shall both see, you'll not be able to do so." It took several minutes for Brother Jackal to convince Josephus to do it. For heaven's sake, one actual hit from that big sword and Brother Jackal would be very seriously wounded! Naturally, I watched fascinated, as did Jes and his brother Josh.

Brother Jackal spoke truly. No matter how hard the blacksmith tried, no matter how he swung the sword or thrust it, he deftly maneuvered his unarmed body out of the way. Finally, puffing, the blacksmith gave up, though grinning. Even he was impressed, as were Jes and I, for that matter. Next, he had the blacksmith stand twenty feet from him and attempt to hurl the spear into his chest. Naturally, with an efficient movement that didn't even require replacement of his feet, Brother Jackal avoided the spear. At last, he handed the bow and an arrow to Josephus. "Now I want you to take aim and try to shoot me in my chest. Do not worry. I will catch it before it strikes." Ah, now this I had seen Roy and others do, a skill that, considering how I had just gotten my body slain — an arrow in my forehead — I most desperately wanted to acquire! Indeed, just as Roy had often done, Brother Jackal caught the arrow only inches from his chest. Yes, Josephus and Jes were highly impressed, but neither expected what came next.

I ran up to Brother Jackal, "Please sir, please, can you teach me how to do this? I just have to know how to defend myself from arrows and spears. Please, I promise to be a good student and do whatever you want of me, please, please!" Yes, I admit it. I was begging.

"Brother Jackal is here to teach Jes and Josh," protested Josephus, as only an adult can toward a child and as if that would end all such thoughts on my part.

Brother Jackal looked me squarely in my eyes, which I kept riveted upon his, "I have never taught a girl before. Have you any skill in combat?" This effectively quieted Josephus, but Jes watched me closely too.

"Not with a sword. I detest them. I would like to be able to avoid sword strikes, though. I once could shoot an arrow and manage a staff fairly well. I only resorted to a dagger if there was no other way to avoid an attack," I explained without thinking of how these words coming from a ten year old girl would sound. No sooner had I explained this than I realized my goof, and my face flushed red.

Josephus stifled a laugh, adding to my embarrassment. Brother Jackal did not; he, as did Jes, both looked at me closely for a moment. "I am called Brother Jackal. And you are?"

"Bethany, Bethany Madelyn Adid, sir," I replied.

"Well, Bethany, let's see how you do." He fetched his staff, which I had thought was his walking stick. He flexed it showing us that it was supple and strong. Handing it to me, he said, "Now Bethany, see if you can actually hit me with the staff, please. It does not have to be a hard hit, just a hit." I took the staff in hand. It felt smooth and I detected the loving care that it has always received. I tested its balance, perfect, though it was somewhat heavy for my smaller size.

Now I was on the spot. It was over ten years ago that I last fought with a staff, and I was encumbered with this fluttering dress instead of my druwid leather pants. As I circled and feinted this way and that, my old skill slowly came back to me. I relaxed and observed my opponent as he dodged, detected his pattern, feinted, and struck but missed. Undaunted, I observed how he had avoided the strike and repeated the same action only this time, landed my strike where his body would be after he dodged. It worked; my staff thumped him on the side of his leg. Naturally, this brought a huge gasp from Josephus — here this young girl had actually hit Brother Jackal! How awful! Immediately, the blacksmith intervened seeking to make sure that this revered brother was unharmed. He was; it was only a light touch; with my small body and this heavy a staff, I don't think I was capable of a really damaging hit.

To our amazement, Brother Jackal completely ignored Josephus, speaking directly to me and Jes, "Excellent, Bethany. Well done indeed! Here you have seen your first lesson, Jes. How was it that Bethany was able to actually land a blow on me?" Oops, now Jes was on the spot! I had not intended that.

He fumbled and squirmed a bit, digging his toes in the soft, dry dirt. From the corner of my eye, I saw that Josh appeared relieved that he hadn't been asked. Finally, Jes said, "Well, one answer would be she got lucky, but I don't believe that answer is acceptable. So I will go with she must have some skill. That's how she managed to land a blow when dad couldn't with any of those other weapons." He had a satisfied look on his face, figuring he'd answered it properly. I knew instinctively from all of the training I had so many years ago that his answer wasn't going to be accepted, not if this man was a true teacher.

"Unacceptable, Jes. Your father also has skill. How is it that he missed? Is it because Bethany here who is about your age has more fighting skills than your grown father?" Jes's face reddened slightly. He hadn't reasoned well or thought his answer through. Most importantly, I felt, he instantly recognized it.

"Yes, you are right, Brother Jackal, that isn't the reason. Let me think more on it." While many other teachers might just launch into an explanation, Brother Jackal had the patience to wait and let Jes, his pupil, work it out. Thus, my opinion of him as a teacher rose. One learns best by just observing.

After a few minutes passed, Brother Jackal spoke quietly, "Watch, Jes; we will do it again for you. Bethany, attempt to strike me once more. Please use the same motions and actions you used before, but this time, that same move will miss. Once it misses, go ahead and do anything you can to hit me once more. Jes, you watch carefully, for once she hits, I will ask you how that was possible once more."

With Jes and his father and now several other prophets, who had gathered to see this spectacle, watching both of us, I began the same circling and feinting that I had used, well at least as close as I could come. Then, I tried the same maneuver that I had used before to hit him. This time he was ready for that move, and my strike merely landed in the dirt. Now I was once more on the spot; I had to hit him! This time, it took me a lot longer to plot out his reactions to my attempted strikes before I found his new pattern. Then, I made use of that predictability and landed another blow on his right leg. I relaxed with a great sign of relief; I had done it! I shudder to think what would have happened if I would have been unable to ever hit him a second time! I'd look like the fool.

"Now, then Jes, why is it that she was able to strike me?" came the calm voice of Brother Jackal. I heard the hushed murmur of the prophets discussing this as well behind me and caught a few words, "But she's a girl!" Jes paid them no mind; he knew that he had to get it right this time.

"She knew where your body would be and so placed the staff there," was his reply.

"Ah, now we are getting somewhere, Jes!" he said encouragingly. "But that is merely the result. How was it that she knew where my body would be so as to place the staff there?"

Suddenly Jes understood! "Ah, she studied and watched your movements and so could make a good guess where to aim the blow."

"That is correct, is it not Bethany?" Brother Jackal replied, turning to me. I simply said yes. "That is the most important lesson of all, Jes. Always observe and watch your opponent. Everyone fights somewhat differently. Each, you must carefully notice, or they will be able to harm you instead."

He then turned to me, "Bethany, if your parents approve, I will accept you as a student. In fact, to train Jes properly, we need a sparing opponent of about his size. Josh is much larger and will give you both a challenge." Josh smiled; he was several years older and at least a foot taller than we two were. "If you are willing to learn and accept the bruises that come with it, you may join us." I was elated until I wondered how I would ever convince my parents to let me do this.

Jes came to my aid whispering into my ear, "I shall so order it, Bethany." We both knew what that meant. Anything that he said, the adults followed slavishly; he was their Great Messiah. Thus, at the supper table, my parents actually brought the subject up; they had been informed that the Great Messiah had requested that I be his sparing partner and learn the art of combat. In fact, they were more worried that I wouldn't accept this or want to do this thing. When I eagerly said that I'd love to, they were quite relieved. Inwardly, I wondered how and why these people would accept anything that Jes said without question.

That night safely in my bed in the dark, I reasoned it out this way. These people were deeply religious. All had a tremendous belief or faith in their God Jehosa. According to all the prophets, Jes was the Son of Jehosa, in human form. Thus, anything Jes said must be of or from their God. Anything he did must be the divine will of Jehosa, not to be remotely questioned. Such is the power of faith. I wondered, can such faith make one blind instead?

So for the next two years, daily, except for Saturday, their holy day, Jes, Josh, and I spent hours with Brother Jackal, sweating, straining, and learning to fight. I was grateful that Brother Jackal spared me from sword combat. I still hated using a sword. At these times, Josh took my place, giving Jes even harder training with the sword. Yes, after two years, I can now say competently that I, too, can catch spears thrown at me, as well as snatch arrows mid-flight. I also got very competent with the staff. Further, to Jes's complete amazement, once I became quite competent at avoiding the flying objects, Brother Jackal proceeded to teach me how to avoid sword strikes. In fact, often I would stand unarmed before Jes, whose task it was to strike me with his sword. True, until I learned how, Jes only used a wooden sword. Finally, he had to use the real thing, and he was truly impressed at how deftly I continually avoided his strikes. Even Josh was, for that matter.

During this time period another thing occurred that became very important in the village. Occasionally either Jes or I would actually get hurt, a wound. Not having forgotten all of my healing skills, I quickly demonstrated my physical healing skills. Actually, I found the whole thing very interesting indeed. For example, one time I didn't avoid a thrust and took a sword cut to my arm. I immediately worked my healing on it, sewing it up and properly bandaging it. Both Brother Jackal and Jes complimented me on just how good my skills actually were. Then, Jes would take my arm in his, close his eyes, say something that I did not understand and when he was done, my wound was gone, fully healed. I thought what he did was a miracle, but they thought what I did was a miracle. Soon word spread through the entire village that Bethany, too, had miraculous skills in healing. By the time I was twelve, at least once a week a villager would seek me out for help, being afraid to go and ask for such from their Great Messiah.

As you might expect, Jes and I became very close friends. From my point of view, we were actually a lot alike. I still did not know what to make of all this Son of God business, though there was no doubting the miracles I saw him perform, miracles from my point of view as well as the villagers. This very topic came up one time.

Jes and I, during a quiet time, took a walk around the village; we were twelve years old. He explained, "You see, Bethany, our task right now is to learn all that we can. Then, one day I will be expected to go into action here in Juda Arad. Before then, I must know all that I can."

"Are you really the Son of Jehosa? Does this one God really exist? I see Nature all around me. She is real to me," I asked the provocative questions I had long pondered.

"We are all sons and daughters of Jehosa. We are all spiritual beings. Only very, very few actually realize that. Can you actually see Nature or just her products?"

"Well, no, I can't see Nature. I see her effects and conclude she exists."

"Not seeing her, does that lessen her any in your eyes?"

"No, not really, why?"

"Can you see spiritual beings?" He was leading me toward something, but I had no idea what.

"Yes, usually fairly easily," I replied, remembering all those I had observed.

"Ah, but the being. Did you see the being or did you see some physical manifestation, such as an energy field, a mind, pictures, or such created by that being?"

"Oh I see what you are saying. You are right, energy fields. I usually spot energy fields that people have, though sometimes minds."

"Beings are not of Tarra. We have no substance, no solidity such as a wall, but we can create energy, pictures, solidities, and forms to be perceived. You see, beings are not made of anything of which everything else on Tarra is made. If we didn't have energy fields around us, we might not even be visible to one another. I say once more, we are all Sons of God."

"But you can perform miracles — like healing that sword cut in my arm. It just healed up as if it never happened," I protested slightly.

"You could do that just as easily as I, if you just knew how, allowed yourself to do it, believed that you could do it, and then just did it," he countered. "But it seems like a miracle to me when you perform your healing magic. To me it is a miracle that with a needle, thread, and all those herbs you find, the person is healed in a little time."

"That is just a learned skill. Anyone could do it if they only studied a while," I replied. "It is no miracle." Then, I got his point, "Oh, I see. My mom thinks it is a miracle because it is way beyond her skills, just as I think your touch healing is way beyond my skill. Could I learn to heal by touch alone?"

"Yes, Bethany, that is precisely what I'm saying. Yes, you could learn to heal by touch alone, but first you have to have the complete and utter certainty you can do it."

"Jeesh! I'll never have that!" I replied quite daunted.

"Quite true. As long as you say that, that will be the truth of the matter," he replied. Now I wondered about all this even more!

We walked along is silence, each lost in their own thoughts. Jes broke the silence, "I never have properly thanked you for helping me learn so much. So thank you, Bethany, you are a terrific help." I blushed and smiled.

"Soon, I'm going to have to spend a lot of time learning all that the prophets have to teach me of our past, all about our religion, and what is expected of me. If you want, you can learn along with me, unless the tight-lipped prophets forbid it. I don't know if they will let a girl hear about all that they know. All the prophets seem to be men."

I thought about this. True, I have never seen or heard of a woman prophet. This arena of knowledge seemed to be the province of men alone. Perhaps they would be very upset if I attended. I explained my feelings to Jes, and he promised to see what he could find out and arrange. Alabaster's words echoed in my mind, "Religion is a touchy, personal subject."

Chapter 2 Religion

In Juda Arad, since the dawn of memory, holy prophets have been the keepers of the faith and the voice of the One God, Jehosa. These wise men minister to the needs of the faithful of Arad, attempting to keep them on the path to righteousness in the eyes of Jehosa. Additionally, these same men pass on the history of the people. Naturally, that tradition is an oral one, though at this point in time I learned that the prophets have adapted the writing of Niccolo Helios to their language and are now writing down their lengthy history and teachings on scrolls. Apparently, Bethel was chosen as the site for this work.

Just about the time that Jes was to receive his religious education, prophets began to come to our village for extended stays in order painstakingly to write down their words of lore and wisdom. In fact, one entire home next door to Jes was set aside for these men to do just this. A byproduct of their stay was the formal instruction of their Great Messiah. Thus, over the course of the next four years, every prophet in Juda Arad was called to Bethel to dictate their knowledge and pass that on to their Great Messiah, Jes.

If one were a religious historian, attending this singular, four year event in the history of a people would be a monumental learning experience. Here in a relatively short space of time, all viewpoints of the history of their civilization were carefully explained in full along with all of their religious doctrines. I do not know of this type of situation having ever occurred before or since.

It was the summer of 572 AH. Jes and I were twelve going on thirteen, when the prophets answered the summons to set down their lore and teach Jes. As he promised, Jes attempted to get them to allow me to sit in on his learning sessions. For the very first time, a suggestion from Jes was not instantly honored! Women were strictly forbidden to be prophets here in Arad. At first, they attempted to reason with Jes, but he kept doggedly insisting I at least have a chance to attend. Most of their arguments went this way, as Jes later told me.

Prophet In Charge: "Women are not permitted to be prophets."

Jes: "Why?"

Prophet In Charge: "They bear the initial sin against Jehosa, who thus cast us all from his dominion to dwell eternally here on Tarra until we redeem ourselves."

Jes: "All the more reason for a woman to understand fully."

Prophet In Charge: "Nay, Lord, we cannot allow this; it goes against all our teachings."

Jes: "But I insist."

Prophet: "But you must not, Lord."

After a couple days, Jes finally succeeded at least partially. He explained, "I finally tried a different approach, Bethany. You see, the plan is that when each of the prophets talks, three scribes will write down precisely what he says. Afterwards, another scribe will carefully compare all three copies and make a master copy from them. They claim that at least two of the three should always agree on the exact words spoken. Once the master has been made, another copy of the master will be written. Then, the three originals and one master copy are to be secreted away in some safe, dry place as an eternal archive. The remaining copy will then be duplicated many times, and the copies will become publically available for purchase at a small price. The coins received are to cover the entire expense of creating the written legacy in the first place. I think that their plan has great merit."

"But how do I fit in?" I asked unable to see how this would help me.

Smiling and almost teasingly, Jes answered, "Ah, they only have two scribes who can write down the words fast enough at the moment. So I nominated you for the third scribe position. I know you can write fast. This way, while you'll not be allowed to speak at all, you'll get to hear everything, though I expect you'll get a work out with all that writing. At least you can share in what all I learn."

"Perfect, Jes. Thanks!" I acknowledged, relieved that I could at least hear the information. I wasn't overjoyed at having to work so hard at all the writing, but I would do it. I also noticed that Jes had a proud, satisfied look on his face as I thanked him. I also took note in the subtle change in his treatment of me. This was the first time he had really paid close attention to my needs. True, we had become close friends, but this was a subtle shift in respect for me. He was looking out for me, perhaps as a brother would. Or was it something more? I put such thoughts out of my mind.

The next morning after all chores were done, the first of many transcribing sessions began. As instructed, I entered the building by the side door and quietly took my place. In the front of the room, four comfortable chairs were occupied by Prophet Azir, Jes, his brother Josh, and the officiating Prophet Tamiz, whose idea it was to write down their entire history and religion. Perhaps six feet from them were two tables occupied by two scribes. Piles of scrolls, quills, and ink pots lay within reach of each. My table was located just inside the door as far from the proceedings as they could place it and as close to the door as possible. I slunk in and quietly took my place, examining the mountain of blank scrolls, quills, and ink. I was to work and not be seen. Indeed, only Jes took notice of my entrance; the others, particularly the prophets completely ignored me as if I did not exist, and then the session began.

Since I am not a religious historian, I won't tell you in detail everything that was said during these four years of sessions. Actually, from prophet to prophet, the stories varied a remarkably small amount and then only in small details mostly. However, as I soon discovered, each prophet put his own slant, his own viewpoint, onto the significance or meaning of the events. That is, the interpretation of what happened was subject to change, not the actual events in question.

Instead, let me present an overview, my summary of the history, culture, and religion of Juda Arad. In fact, I will relate only what is relevant to your understanding of what happens here in Arad during my subsequent years among these people. Indeed little of what happen in this land will make any sense to you if I don't.

Uniformly, the prophets say that originally, the Arad people lived in the Kingdom of Jehosa, which may be likened to a form of heaven. They had not bodies as we know them. However, they are quite vague on details. Apparently, life was eternal bliss in his Kingdom. Then, came the First Sin, committed by Jaleene Amir, wife of Amal Amir. She had accepted the fruit of life from Lucifer, disguised as a man-sized snake. Lucifer is the archenemy of Jehosa, representing all that is dark, foul, and evil. They were quite vague about what this fruit of life actually was or even her motivation for accepting it. No allowance was made for the deceit of Lucifer. Men. This so angered Jehosa that he spent his rage building a world in exile, Tarra. Once done, he exiled all the Arad people to Tarra, giving them bodies with which to learn right from wrong. Only when one has purified himself will Jehosa accept him back into his realm. Hence, the overriding religious goal from these ancient times until now is to live one's life in such a manner that Jehosa will accept you back into the gilded realm once more. Incidentally, no prophet ever mentioned anyone who had successfully been accepted back into Jehosa's Kingdom.

Now once on Tarra, the Arads took up residence in a land called Anuir, which lies to the south and west of Juda Arad. Geographically, by comparing all their discussions of Anuir, I place its location somewhere near the western edge of the Red Desert, now totally uninhabited. If one merely walks in the desert, he'll contract the rotting disease relatively rapidly, and it is always fatal. The date of their arrival on Tarra is pure speculation, probably centuries ago.

For many years, the castouts lived a peaceful life under King Amal Amir's rule. Then King Angmar, the Tyrant, bronzed-skinned warrior king of neighboring Tyree, invaded their lands, killed King Amal, and enslaved the people of Arad. It is said that, so angered was Jehosa at the enslavement of his people, that he sent fire from the sky to destroy Tyree. In the chaos, his people fled to Juda Arad.

Now here, I must digress. Have you noted the similarity of names? Jes's family surname is Amir. I admit that hundreds of families in the Arad are also called Amir, descendants perhaps of King Amal. I had also heard that name, Amir, before, though it took me nearly a month to recall just where. Many years ago when my druwid Circle journeyed across the Red Desert, well actually under it, we encountered an underground people, known to the outside world as the Moon people, because they were only seen at night. They called themselves the Children of Amir. In one of their underground chambers, a great fresco outlined their ancient history. After the angry, fiery outburst of Angibus, who scorched their land turning it into a desert of death, Amir alone saved their ancestors. Legends say that most of their original people perished either in the fiery blast or from the rotting sickness that followed shortly thereafter. Father Amin invented the Code, and all those who chose to follow his code survived. To this day, the faithful still follow his Code, for failure to do so results in the rotting disease and death.

Could their father Amir be related in any way to the Amir line of the Arad people? Were the Moon people the ones who conquered and enslaved the Arads? Was the Moon people's god Angibus, in fact, Jehosa? If so, why would an Arad Amir save those that had conquered his people? I had many questions and no answers, only speculation. Fascinated and curious, I kept my ears open for anything that might shed more light on these early times.

According to the prophets, the people lived a number of years in freedom here in Juda Arad. They built the city Al Barq from scratch, even designing and building a small fleet of ships to sail along the coastal areas of the Med Sea, establishing trade with the Sea Princes. Then the Centurions invaded from the Southlands. Like the Greenway, Juda Arad had no form of centralized government. Each village pretty well ran itself. Either the prophets or the messiahs settled disputes of a wider nature.

Definition: a prophet is a religious teacher and keeper of the holy ways of Jehosa. Additionally, all claimed some ability to foretell future events. Though there were nearly a hundred prophets all told now, most foresaw the same major events as if they had all been taught the same things. However, in smaller matters, from my point of view at least, much of their daily prophesying was really just observing Nature and predicting what would occur next based on knowledge of Nature. For example, if you plant a seed in July, it may sprout but will surely wither and die before bearing harvest.

Definition: a messiah is also religious in nature, but rather like a religious zealot or fanatic, who took up armed conflict to resolve differences or disputes. That is, they are looked upon as liberators or deliverers and are usually skilled guerrilla fighters. At this time, all are possessed of a Messianic zeal to liberate their people from the yoke of Centurion oppression. In short, they fight for the freedom of all Arad using any methods available to them short of an actual battle campaign. A messiah would never consider marching his forces in a battle line against the enemy lines. Their ways were indirect, such as raiding Centurion supply wagons.

The prophets constantly reminded the faithful of the Decalogue of Jehosa, as they were called. These were ten commandments that a follower of Jehosa was obligated to follow. According to the prophets, the Decalogue of Jehosa was given to Prophet Helas Amin by Jehosa himself during the time that Helas led his people on their flight from Anuir to Juda Arad. I looked upon these more as a moral code to follow so that people could get along with their neighbors.

The Decalogue of Jehosa, as told by Prophet Emil Tamir, is as follows:
There is no god but Jehosa.
Do not worship any other god but the One God, Jehosa.
Do not build statues of Jehosa, for Jehosa has no form.
Set aside the Holy Day, Saturday, from your labors and worship the Lord that

day.

Respect and serve thy mother and thy father, for they have labored long in your raising.

Do not kill another who worships Jehosa.

Do not steal from another who worships Jehosa.

Do not commit adultery.

Do not lie to another who worships Jehosa.

Do not desire another's house, possessions or wife, if he worships Jehosa.

With each of these, each prophet had many parables illustrating what could happen if it was not followed. Some examples were distinctly more graphic than others were. Still, if these were followed, Jehosa followers had a good chance of getting along with each other in relative harmony. Still, I found it most interesting that most all were qualified with "if he worships Jehosa."

Obviously, these actions would be permitted if the other was not a follower of Jehosa, namely the Centurions, who worshiped Sol, the Sun God. In fact, the messiahs did kill Centurions when any such opportunity arose. It was commonplace for anyone to outright lie to their invaders; this was acceptable conduct. Further, given any chance, they would steal from the infidels.

In fact, late one evening Jes, Josh, and I got into a big discussion on these very points. Both men were explaining to me just how vital these three points were for their people. I'm a follower of Nature and could not just "let this pass."

I said, "Look, Jes, these three commandments are only half-truths." I watched as both men ridged and tensed up; I was attacking their sacred commandments. "The real command, if commands we wish to label them, ought to be: Do not steal from another. Do not kill another except in self-defense and there is no other way. Do not covet another's house, possessions, or wife."

Well, as soon as I uttered that, the arguments flew! If one followed these that I proposed, why, there went everyone's actions against the infidels, the invaders, the Centurions. None of what these people did on a daily basis would be valid. As I said before, religion is a touchy subject, highly personal, but I would not just let it be.

"Okay guys, let me illustrate this whole thing," I interrupted their volleys of protest. "Suppose that you stole a valuable item from your neighbor, violating your holy Decalogue. What would happen if that neighbor found out that you did it? Would not that action bring, at the very least, strife between you, if not worse?"

They both completely agreed, with Jes saying, "That is why that is forbidden in the Decalogue of Jehosa." Josh agreed with him completely, a satisfied look on both their faces.

Now I knew I had the both of them. "Okay, fellows, now suppose that the one you steal from is a Centurion. Would he like to have that happen to him any more than your neighbor does? Absolutely not! What would happen if that neighbor, the infidel, found out that you did it? Would not that action bring, at the very least, strife between you, if not worse?" I watched both their faces fall and knew that I had gotten them to see the truth of the matter. "People are the same everywhere; no one wants to be robbed, killed, or lied to about anything. They resent it and protest against it, just as a follower of Jehosa would do so. Your Decalogue is fine for interpersonal relations among followers of Jehosa, but if you do these things to others not of your faith, you pull into yourselves the very things that you are trying to avoid by following these commandments. Stealing is stealing the world over. Killing is killing and lying is lying. You cannot condone it against one person and forbid it against another, for you get back the result of what you do, unless you desire the backlash that you receive."

Both men looked very pale at this point; they realized that I spoke truth. However, I had just shaken one of the foundations of their beliefs to its root. I knew I could not just leave it at this. I went on, "Look guys, just eliminate that recurring clause 'if he worships Jehosa' and you end up with something far more workable." I believe Jes saw immediately what I was suggesting.

Suddenly, I realized that this also tied into something I learned just after I had taken up residence in this new body when it was bitten by a viper. I added my observation, "Imagine this, fellows. Suppose that you, Jes, steal some of Josh's coins. You needed them, he had them, and you took them. He doesn't know how he lost them, but they are vital to his survival — you know, he needs the money. Jes, how would you feel after doing that to your brother? You see him having a very hard time trying to make up for their loss. Would you not feel like you had to withhold from Josh that you were the one that stole his coins? Naturally, you would. But, and here is the critical point, would you now feel as close, as loving toward your brother as before? Or would you feel more distant from him, sort of separated from him?" Now I was doing well with this concept, "In fact, wouldn't you attempt to say that Josh here had done something to you such that he deserved having his coins stolen by you? Because wouldn't you feel justified in stealing his coins if he had done something to you, so that in your mind he deserved it?"

"Bethany Madelyn Adid, you are a very wise woman," Jes enthusiastically pronounced. "Just two days ago, I saw this very thing happen here. I watched as one young lad came walking down the street eating some candy. Another boy, slightly older, asked him for a piece of it. The first refused. The second insisted and physically took the candy from the first boy. The first boy punched and kicked the second boy. The second boy dropped the candy on the ground and began hitting the first, knocking him to the ground. The first boy went home crying, but a prophet intervened and gave both boys a lesson about the Decalogue of Jehosa. But you know only the day before, I saw these boys playing together having lots of fun. Now they do not speak to each other and avoid one another. While this justifies the Decalogue, I now see that the very same thing would have occurred if the first boy was a young infidel lad and not of our village. I say again, Bethany Madelyn Adid, you are a very wise woman."

I smiled back at him and answered, "Observant would be closer to the truth."

The next interesting fact that I learned was that there are four different sects in Juda Arad, each with their own prophets and messiahs, their own slant on Jehosa, the religion, and its application to its followers. The first of these, the Qaams, were the organizers and caretakers of this entire action of committing everything to scrolls. They are followers of the old ways, insisting upon a slavish, literal interpretation of Jehosa's commandments. Most wore long bushy beards with equally long hair, for they did not believe in cutting hair or even shaving. They believe and insist that their fall from Grace is due solely to the First Sin committed by the woman Jaleene Amir. Thus, they respect women far less than men, for women were their downfall. Fortunately, Qaams are in the minority and often looked down upon as fanatical worshipers of the past, extremists in their beliefs.

The second group, the Hessonites, consists of those who least believe in Jehosa. They are worldly in their outlook and have accepted their lives on Tarra for what is. They live them to the fullest and are prone to other sins, such as lewdness, thievery, drunkenness, and deceit. They also have the closest relationships with the infidels, preferring a peaceful co-existence to that of strife. Sometimes, they are called traitors to Jehosa by the Qaams. They excuse their practices as being totally practical about everything, especially fleshly delights.

The third group, the Hamadanites, by far the largest group population-wise, consists of the traders, merchants, and craftsmen of Juda Arad. For them, the most important factor is to get along with all people; otherwise, trade would suffer, and thus their purses. Thus, the other groups look upon them as moderates For many years, the Hamadanites have been the controlling factor, the stabilizing force, in Juda Arad, especially since the coming of the infidels.

The fourth group, the Amirites, trace their ancestry to that of the legendary King Amal Amir. They see themselves as being the rightful rulers, the rightful caretakers of the religion. In short, just the Rightful. As you might expect, many of the messiahs of Juda Arad belong to the Amirite sect. Still, they hold with the ancient traditions, attempting to bring or lead their people along the righteous path so they may be worthy of rejoining Jehosa's kingdom. Jes and his family are Amirites. Yet, Amirites are often looked upon by the other sects as religious zealots.

Each of the four sects have their own worship temples, often all four in the same town, if it is large enough. Rather I should say that nearly every town has a Hamadanite temple. Most have a Hessonite temple and an Amirite temple. Only the larger towns also have a Qaam temple. Because Qaams believe in an austere lifestyle, they often live in their own rural villages or communities.

Thus, the Qaams are only likely to associate with the Amirites, because they do grant that many of Amirites can trace their lineage back to King Amir. Qaams have little to do with Hamadanites, considering them too worldly; they actively condemn the Hessonites, believing that they are perpetuating the First Sin.

The Amirites interact with all others, valiantly trying to rule and control everything, to be the leaders that their distant ancestor had been.

The Hessonites, with their worldly outlook and passion for earthly delights, look upon the Qaams with contempt calling their rituals archaic, but they do suffer the Amirites because of their ancestry ties. Hessonites get along well with the Hamadanites, as one might expect.

The Hamadanites attempt to get along well with all the other sects, though they like least the Qaams. In short, it is a mess.

Prophet Tamiz, perhaps the highest ranking member of the Qaam sect, discovered the benefits of writing some time ago when he received a shipment of grain from the Greenway, via Velona in the Sea Princes. Per my orders years ago, when I was a Wid there in Calgary, all outgoing cargo had to have a written manifest of its contents. Thus, when the grain shipment arrived along with the attached document, he was able to prove that someone had stolen a quarter of the grain during the lengthy delivery process, much to the consternation of the shippers, who had to make good on the delivery. Prophet Tamiz immediately recognized the value of the written record, and had arranged this entire documentation project. His view was that if the entirety of their religions beliefs were written for all to read for themselves, the better the chances that the reader would reform their sinful ways.

Jes and his family could trace their lineage all the way back to the original King Amir. Proud was the day when Josephus Amir taught their heritage to his sons. I had Jes once recite it for me. It was a very lengthy series of this Amir begat that Amir, all the way down to Jes and Josh. Vitally more important was that their long heralded Great Messiah, Jes, was to be born of the direct line of King Amir and under the sign of a new star in the sky.

From the different prophets, I attempted to determine just what this Great Messiah was actually supposed to do. First, he was the Son of Jehosa himself and had come to Tarra in this fleshly body as Jehosa's representative. Of course, I immediately took issue with this. I did not doubt that there could be gods. As a worshiper of Nature, I knew we are all spiritual beings not of this earth, but inhabit one of Nature's gifts, a human body. A few of us, like Jes and me, resided just above and behind the body's head. However, most people were unfortunately stuck in their heads or worse. I had been free of a body just after it had been killed by that untimely arrow to its forehead. As a free being, I had helped Alabaster bring down thousands of lightning bolts to destroy King Randolf and his Galt allies. I'm well aware that a being can act powerfully when free of a body. Indeed, had someone been watching that day, they would have sworn that the Lightning God had struck these men down. Yes, I certainly didn't doubt the possible existence of their God Jehosa, or that he was very powerful, compared to us. No, what I objected to was that a "being" could have a son. Did that imply that I could somehow divide myself into separate pieces? Or could I make a new spiritual being? If so, out of what and how? Or was that action in the province of God? Or — well, the list goes on and on. I tried in vain to recall how I as a being came into existence but came up totally blank. The earliest memory I have is walking in the dirt street of Uru as a child of six.

Second — I bet you forgot that there were more of these — their Great Messiah would have the purpose to set men free. That was the literal translation. Immediately and uniformly, the Prophets qualified this to apply only to those in Juda Arad, who were true believers in Jehosa, and pure, ready for the ascension into Jehosa's realm.

Third, the Great Messiah was to deliver his people from the influence of the infidels. However, this also was immediately presumed to mean that somehow the Great Messiah would drive out or slay all the Centurions in Juda Arad, thereby freeing his people. This alteration, of course, was very palatable to the common man, who was suppressed under the yoke of Centurion occupation.

Fourth, the Great Messiah was to teach everyone the righteous path so that they might regain the Kingdom of Jehosa that they had lost so long ago. Naturally, this aspect endangered the Prophets, whose task had always been just this. They said very little about this purpose and did not elaborate or embellish it.

One night when I was fifteen, Jes and I took a long stroll around the edge of Bethel. Earlier that afternoon, Brother Jackal had finished our fighter training, saying that he had taught us all he knew. We thanked him profusely, and after dinner, he departed as suddenly as he had come. Both of us felt saddened a bit by his departure, he and his tough training sessions had actually been fun and provided relief from all the transcribing during the morning and early afternoons. We walked arm in arm, and I admit that I really enjoyed feeling his solid, muscled, strong arms around my shoulders. For some time, neither said anything, but noticed the dark hills in the distance. Finally, Jes said, "What's on your mind, Bethany Madelyn? I can tell something is troubling you. The departure of Brother Jackal, perhaps?"

"Well, perhaps that," I answered. "Well, no, not really. I've been doing a lot of thinking while writing all that these prophets say."

"Yes, so out with it, my pretty," he teased. I knew I could not hold back from this man.

"It is what they say about you. Are you really the Son of Jehosa? I mean, Jehosa must be a free being, that is, one who operates fully without the need for fleshly bodies."

"But you understand all this, do you not?"

"Well, one thing troubles me. At least once, I have operated effectively without a body. Granted. But how can one being make a new being? I mean how can Jehosa *have* a son?"

He thought for a moment before he explained, "Language can be a barrier to the communication of an idea. One day you will marry, and you will have a son or daughter, but your son or daughter is really another being who has taken up residence in the new fleshly body that you have created. You create the form, but not the being. Yet you say that this is your son or daughter."

It didn't fully answer my questions, but I agreed that language posed a problem. I asked another question. "You are supposed to set men free, but the prophets altered that to mean believers of Jehosa. Which is your purpose?"

He laughed, "Bethany Madelyn, nothing escapes your astute eyes and ears! So you too caught that. Yes, my purpose is to set men and women free, not just those who believe already. It is a tall order indeed."

I smiled, relieved that he too saw what I saw. I explored further, "You are to deliver his people from the *influence* of the infidels. They took that to mean that you are going to somehow kill or drive all the Centurions from this land. True, that would fulfill the purpose, but honestly, there are other ways, especially if you believe in the Decalogue of Jehosa and not to kill another."

Again, he laughed, impressed with my observations. "Suppose, my dear, that I am able to take a being that is stuck inside their body's head, those who firmly suppose that they are just a body, and show them that they are really a spiritual being, not a body. Would that not begin to get them on the path of delivering them, the being, from the influence of the infidels? Yes, there are many ways to do this. However, it does not say that one should not defend his life. Only a fool would stand by and do nothing, while an infidel slaughtered his family and burned down his house. It may be, Bethany, that some force will be needed; then again, maybe not. Time will tell."

"Well, that I grant, one must stand up for what is right. But are you going to then go around and teach all the people in Juda Arad? That would be a lot of traveling, almost a full time job."

"When the time is right, yes, Bethany, I will preach and attempt to show others the truth and the path. You are right. If one is to travel and do only this, one needs helpers and a source of funds. I don't think it fair to live off of the generosity of the people."

"I — I would really like to watch you when you do all this, you know, see how it can be done — freeing beings, I mean!" There, I had said it. I had no idea whether Jes would allow me, a woman, to travel with him or not. At least, I had to try. If I could learn how to get a header to understand fully that they were a spiritual being, the ramifications — well, I just had to. So many people on Tarra needed to grasp this and alter their lives. I just had to. Besides, I really liked this Great Messiah. I couldn't imagine what life would be like without having him around me. I blushed as I suddenly realized that I had felt this way when I had fallen in love with Roy so long ago.

As if reading my mind, Jes said, "I cannot imagine traveling without you by my side." He said nothing more, though, which left me wondering and imagining, as a young woman will.

Chapter 3 Of Solace and Miracles

It was 580 AH and the hot summer arrived with a vengeance this year. The religious transcriptions had been finished five year ago now. For the last few years, various local messiahs had visited Bethel and held long discussions with Jes, whom they looked to for guidance. Always, Jes told them to carry on, for now was not his time. Then, last year, Jes took me aside one night to tell me that it was time for him to wander off alone and commune with his father. This was something he had to do alone. He had learned all that he could from the people of his land, and now armed with that information, he needed to speak with Jehosa, one on one.

"Do not worry one pretty long hair of yours, dearest Bethany. I will be safe. After all, you better than anyone else, save perhaps Josh, know that I can defend myself. Brother Jackal taught us well. I will be completely safe. This is something that I have to do."

"I will really miss you," I said, a tear formed uncontrollably in my right eye. I tried in vain to suppress it. "Promise me you'll be safe."

"I will, you know that."

"Yes, but. Please tell Jehosa hello from me," I added as an afterthought. "Don't worry about anything here in Bethel. I'll look after things."

He smiled, "I will. I'm sure he already knows about you, Bethany. I know that you will look after the people here. After all, you have become our local healer. Don't they come to you before even me?"

Now it was my turn to smile back, "Well, yes, but you know that they're reluctant to bother you. They're almost ashamed to have to come to you to ask to be healed."

That was almost a year ago now. For a year, I felt so empty, like I had been somehow robbed of half of my life. I longed to see Jes, but that didn't stop me from fulfilling my obligations and goals.

During these last five years, I had reorganized my father's business. Now he was able to make far more profits because his business had expanded four-fold. He still called me his little genius. Further, because I was very close to the Great Messiah, he held me in even higher respect. That I was the undisputed village healer, reflected upon him and his fortunes as well. Yes, my father was extremely proud of his eldest daughter.

Long ago, my mother had finally stopped trying to convince me of my proper womanhood place in Arad society. She even stated that she liked my beautiful long hair, which was difficult for her to admit. Out of respect for my family, I did manage to devote a small amount of my time to learning the womanly ways that were expected of an Arad woman. I still disliked washing men's feet as they enter the front door. Since they compromised a great deal, I did so in these smaller domestic duties.

However, life was far from bliss during the year that Jes was gone. In fact, he left at an opportune time. Shortly after he departed, three Centurions arrived. One was a tax collector; the other two, his bodyguards and enforcers. Hector Thallios was a thin man, bronzed-skinned as were all those from Megalos. He had a keen eye for finances and no tolerance for the poor. Just as soon as they arrived, they took over the entire dining hall of Bethel's sole inn. One by one, he called in the head of every household in Bethel. His speech was identical to each, well-rehearsed, cold, and uncaring. "How many people are in your household? Each year at this time, the Megalos Tax Collector, that's me, will come to collect your just and fair tax. I have written your name and the amount that you owe on my lists here. That will be one gold ducat, displaying the likeness of our Holy Emperor Titus on it, per person. Failure to pay your taxes results in your family being taken back to Megalos as slaves. Men spend the remainder of their lives working in our mines. Women are for our pleasure. That will be. . ." He spouted out the numbers for the man who he had just listed on his list.

Of course, nearly every man balked, protested, or swore that he did not have such coins here in Bethel. Hector turned a blind, calloused eye to any such comments. He'd heard them thousands of times before. He would just add, "You have two days to bring them to me before we depart, taking your family back to Megalos with us." I snuck in the back way and stood behind the serving door so I could hear some of this. Then, I rushed back to my dad's store.

"Dad, we *have* to do something! No one has these Megalos coins. They will make slaves out all of us!" I must have looked awfully worried, because my dad stopped what he was doing and ushered me into a back storeroom. He was equally serious. In fact, I cannot ever recall him being quite so tense.

"Bethany Madelyn, this is for your ears alone. Promise me you'll not say a word of this, except maybe to the Great Messiah, should he return," he looked so stern, so grave. I knew this must be terribly important. I promised.

"Don't ask how. For some time now, we knew that this was coming. I have prepared for it. I have secreted away enough of these foreign coins to pay for everyone's taxes. Most of these infidel coins have come to me from our messiahs. Don't ask how. When it is my turn to face the infidel, I will explain to him that the others in Bethel have entrusted me with their coins and that I'm to give him all the needed coins. I am certain that he will go along with this instead of having each man come with his few coins. Any moneychanger would. I don't think this infidel is any different. Please, don't worry about this. It has all been arranged. Now go and watch the store, while I go and see this infidel tax collector." I kissed him, gave him a big hug, and rushed back into the store proper.

As I watched over the store, memories from my last lifetime came back to me. I recalled how my Circle of druwids had helped one of their messiahs take out an infidel supply train. The funds that we took off the defeated infidels were put in a pouch and delivered to a nearby town. Now I made the connection. This meant that the messiahs were still active, and more importantly, they were able to steal sufficient ducats to pay the taxes in each village. How ironic I thought that these infidels were being paid back their own ducats. However, I also realized that if the messiahs ever should not be able to steal sufficient ducats, the local villagers would be in dire trouble.

Dad came back about an hour later sporting a big grin. I knew instinctively that it had gone his way. "Help me count out five hundred six of these ducats, Bethany. I don't want any counting errors." From a concealed safety box hidden under the floor, he took out a large sack of the infidel's coins. While we counted he explained, "This Hector fellow was very eager to handle it this way. I think it means that he can leave Bethel days earlier than planned. I say good riddance."

"Good going, dad," I complimented him. "I know that the messiahs have been stealing these ducats from the infidels themselves. What I worry about is what happens if they cannot get enough of them. What do we do then?"

Dad nearly dropped a handful of coins in surprise. "How — how do you know that? It is a secret. Never mind," he chuckled, "I ought to know better. Nothing escapes the observant eyes of my Bethany Madelyn! Don't worry too much about that. I have been secreting away every ducat that I get in trade. If we run out of those that the messiahs provide, I'll use my stash. The others here can pay me back in trade goods. We always need more stuff to sell. You've gotten my business almost too large." We both laughed. I was proud that my father would take it upon himself to provide for such an emergency for everyone in the village. I realized that we were all in this together against the infidels. Each helped in ways best suited to themselves. Who better than the village's top merchant to handle the vital ducats.

"We've got barely enough," dad finally pronounced with relief. "Two ducats left over. I sure hope the messiahs obtain more for us. We have been very fortunate that the tax collectors have only now gotten to Bethel. I've heard that Jerilum has been paying taxes for many years now." He left once more carrying the heavy sack and returned in a few minutes carrying the signed paper indicating everyone had paid their taxes in full. Of course, he could not read the scroll.

"Can I have a look at it dad?" I asked, curious to see if I could remember how to read Centurion. It had been nearly twenty years since I had last read a letter from Niccolo Helios in Megalos.

"But how dear child, can you possibly read the infidel's script?" dad protested slightly, but he handed the scroll to me. Slowly and carefully, I sounded out each word. It read, "The following household heads have paid their taxes." Following this was a lengthy list of each family name and the number of coins collected. At the very bottom it was signed Hector Thallios, Head Tax Collector, Eastern Province, Juda Arad.

"How?" Dad just stared at me. I thought his eyes might bulge out of their sockets. "Yes, it seems correct. That is what he said it said. But how? How can you read the infidel's writing?"

Oh brother! Now I really had gone and done it, opened my big mouth once too far. How could I explain to him that I learned it last lifetime? *Think fast, Bethany!* "Well, I spent all those years as a scribe for Prophet Tamiz. Our writing is rather similar. I'm a bit slow with it though." It was a half-truth. Certainly, the script we used here in the Arad was similar to that invented by Niccolo Helios of Megalos. I had spent four years transcribing their spoken words. Really, I was using my knowledge learned some twenty years before.

"Ah, then it is not so magical, Bethany. Yes, I had forgotten about that. So our writing is similar to the infidels. A curse upon that! I guess that cannot be helped. For a minute there, you sure had me wondering!" We both breathed a sigh of relief, but for entirely different reasons!

"Come on; let's go home; close up early. It's been an exhausting afternoon, Bethany Madelyn, my child," dad said. It was unlike him to close the store early; on the contrary, often he would stay late. Either this business with the tax collector had somehow upset him or there was something else troubling him. I couldn't tell which. Quickly, I closed the doors and put the X sign on the front door. It was only about four in the afternoon as we strolled arm in arm the short distance to our adobe home.

Mom was as surprised as I was to see him home so early. "Oh, I'm so sorry, Tarzig. I was not expecting you so soon. I don't have the oil warmed yet to bathe your feet." She too looked somewhat worried over dad's unexpected behavior.

"Never mind that, Aline, please. Make us all a hot cup of tea would you, mother? Are the other children out playing?" dad replied in a serious tone of voice, which also held just a hint of worry. While she hastened off to comply, she hollered back that they were. "That is just as good. Come Bethany Madelyn, come sit by me. I've something I want to talk to you about." Taken by complete surprise, I complied thinking rapidly and wondering what I had missed. Something was definitely on his mind and it was serious.

Presently, mom brought in the steaming copper pot along with three clay mugs. She knew I liked my tea strong, so she poured hers and dads first. Thus, my cup also had some of the tea leaves in it, just the way I liked it. We sipped in silence, waiting for dad to explain. Still, I had no notion what it was, and this bothered me considerably. In a way, I felt like I was also looking after them and their well-being — this from their eldest daughter now twenty-one.

"I don't know where to begin, my darling," he sighed. "You are now twenty-one and should be married. Perhaps I have failed in my duties as a father and should have pushed you in that direction some time ago. You are so strong willed, and now, now there might not be time."

"Father!" I pleaded, "You know that I'll marry when I find the right man. I want to marry the man I love. I'm not going to be an old maid, if that is what you are worrying about." I realized that indeed they had been extremely considerate in this matter. I had observed that most other parents either arranged their daughter's marriages or cajoled and pushed them into marrying just as soon as they turned twenty-one. The religious teachings all insisted that couples never marry until both have turned twenty-one. Thus, most couples were the same age. Only if one's mate passed away could another be arranged and even then, the two ought to be close in age. Why this was so, I hadn't the faintest clue.

He sighed, sipped at his tea, perhaps unsure how to continue. "I shall be entirely frank with you, my child." He took a deep breath, "War is coming. I can feel it in my bones. Real war. Death and destruction. It is nearly upon us." I nearly choked on my tea. Mom actually did. I had absolutely no idea that war was eminent! How could I have been so blind to have missed this? "It is prophesied. The Great Messiah shall come and drive the infidels from our lands. We've heard this since we were little children. Now it is actually coming. I can sense it in the mood of the men even here in Bethel. It is far more pronounced in those who come to trade from other towns. I think everyone knows that our Great Messiah approaches twenty-one. No one expected him to take any action before he reached that age."

"But father, why worry? We have only seen three infidels here in Bethel since I was a little girl. Surely, we should be safe here. We are so far away from everything else," I tried to think this through. Now that he mentioned the reasoning, I could have kicked myself for not having seen this coming. It was obvious. I had been living in a dream world all these years. Perhaps this also had something to do with Jes needing some time alone, if indeed he was alone.

"Jamal, as you know, is betrothed and will marry next year just as soon as his bride reaches the age. He'll begin his own family and my responsibilities to him thus end. I have you and your younger sister, Ilene, to think of yet. She is only eighteen, but does have a boyfriend. What I'm very much afraid of is that, when war comes, I may be killed. Bethany Madelyn, I want your solemn vow that if something should happen to me, you'll see that Ilene, your mother, and yourself are looked after properly according to the Holy Decalogue. Even if by some miracle you marry before that time, I bind you to look after them."

Mom began crying, but I kept my composure. He went on, "Normally, I would trust this to my eldest son, but, if he is married, he'll have his own family to consider. Besides, you are a genius, a healer. He, bless his soul, is neither; he'll have all the responsibility he can handle with his own family. It is entirely possible that he too may be slain; men are the ones who fight the wars; men are the ones that die. I want to leave the well-being of my family in your hands. Will you accept this added responsibility?" He looked pleadingly at me, "I know I'm asking a lot, and I have tried not to ask you to do things you don't want to do, well most of the time. Also, there is this to consider. We are the wealthiest family in Bethel. I owe that solely to you, Bethany, and your genius. Under no circumstances do I want that fortune to fall into the hands of the infidels. I have divided it into quarters so my children and my wife can survive well if I'm gone. If something happens to me, I want you to give each their portion. Promise me that you will."

I leaned over and hugged him, "Dad, you can count on me. Yes, I will look after them all. It isn't a burden. I really don't see how you would be killed.

Surely, the war will not come here. Besides, you are too old to go off and be a holy warrior. You are a merchant not a fighter. I think that you are worrying too much." I kissed him on his forehead.

Sighing with relief, he hugged me back. He whispered in my ear so mom could not hear, "Who do you suppose finances wars and handles needed supplies?" Suddenly, I saw a much larger picture! Though not a fighter, he would nevertheless play a crucial role in the upcoming war. Now I understood my father far better.

That night I couldn't fall asleep. I kept wondering just what Jes would actually do. It was now more than obvious that the average person fully expected a holy war at any time. I knew that was really a perversion or alteration of the actual prophesy! The real freedom would be recognition of what they actually were, spiritual beings, and a release from being stuck in and dependent upon a fleshly body, that they might then rejoin the Kingdom of Jehosa. Okay, I'll admit I too prayed that the actual prophesy would come true, even for myself. Look, if a spiritual being could operate fully and not be dependent upon an earthly body, how could anything of the flesh ever have control over them again? I imagined a world full of free beings; Centurions who were stuck inside their heads seemed more like ants scurrying about the dry dirt. In my opinion, this was a goal worthy of God Jehosa. On the other hand, I hadn't the faintest idea how any of it could come about. Then again, I wasn't the Great Messiah. Just as I fell asleep, I vowed to do everything that I could to help Jes achieve that goal, for it was also my goal.

Days turned into months as I waited along with all of Juda Arad, waited for the Great Messiah. However, after my father's warnings, I began to take close note of what people were discussing on the side. My father's supply wagons always seemed to be bringing in more swords than we had ordered or could reasonably be expected to sell. Yet, they always disappeared nearly as fast as they arrived. I suspected that my dad was building up a horde of weapons, but he said nothing, probably for our safety if he were discovered.

Bethel had been spared any visits from the infidels until the Tax Collector came for the first time. Now, I noticed a band of Centurions twelve strong occasionally made unannounced visits to our village. Although they only looked around and did not harass us, I did overhear them making inquiries about the whereabouts of Jes. Of course, we all told the same story; he had left nearly a year ago, and no one knew where he went or when he might come back.

Yet, this began to bother me. Infidels apparently knew something about Jes. Did they know that he was the Great Messiah? If so, would they plan to kill him to thwart any possible rebellion, because rebellion was just what was likely to happen? More and more, these scary thoughts entered my mind. I found them hard to dispel. Though I did not know it fully, all Juda Arad was like a firecracker ready to go off, awaiting only the ordained signal from Jehosa. How could the infidels not also sense this? Yes, fear began creeping into my mind.

It had been over a year since I said goodbye to Jes. My brother had now gotten married and moved into a newly made adobe house near the edge of Bethel with his new bride. Unlike his father, Jamal felt a kinship with sheep and open spaces. He became a shepherd; dad saw to it that he began with a sufficiently large herd so that he and his new daughter-in-law might not want. Ilene, now nineteen, was impatiently waiting for her twenty-first birthday. We four were eating dinner just around dark when a surprised knock sounded on our door. Times being what they were, dad and I were both more than a little anxious as he went to the door.

Can you imagine our relief and joy when Jes appeared and came inside? Whether it was allowed protocol or not, I rushed to his side, hugged him tightly; he me. Then, minding my manners, I quickly anointed his feet using the warm pot of oil beside the door. He smiled and kissed me on my head. At last he spoke. Had his voice been so deep? Somehow, he sounded differently. "Tarzig Adid, it is time. I have come to see you as befitting the Holy Decalogue. I seek your permission to wed your daughter, Bethany Madelyn — that is, of course, if she will have me."

I nearly choked. My mouth utterly failed to operate. My heart raced. I couldn't catch my breath. My father got down on his knees before the Son of Jehosa, "My Lord, you do me the greatest of all possible honors. Yes, yes, I gladly, willingly give her hand to you if she shall have it." He bowed low, his head nearly touching the floor and the feet of the Great Messiah.

Instantly, I felt all eyes were upon me. From the corner of my eyes, I could see Ilene holding her hands tightly over her mouth, praying that I would say yes. No one seemed to breathe as they awaited my reply. How I found the strength to move, let alone say anything is beyond me. I faintly heard a squeaky voice say excitedly, "Yes, oh yes!" I felt his strong arm steading me; my knees shook, and I could hardly walk back to the table.

Mom said graciously, "Please Lord, take supper with us, but I'm afraid we have already eaten much of it. If you can wait but a few minutes, I will prepare more. Tonight calls for a Holy Feast in celebration." I noticed she scarcely dared look Jes in the eyes. He had an unusual radiance about him I had not seen before.

Jes waved his free hand in the direction of our table, saying, "Look, Mother Aline, thy table is already prepared. We have more than enough food for tonight." We looked back at the table. Sure enough, the wine pitcher was now full. The leg of lamb, which was nearly gone, was now full. The plates of vegetables and fruit overflowed.

Now it was mom's turn to lose her voice; dad, likewise. Ilene exclaimed, "A Holy Miracle!"

As we sat down, Jes said, "All this and more yea may do for yourself, as you enter the Kingdom of Lord Jehosa." With that, we all said lengthy prayers to Jehosa. Then, Jes ate hungrily. My guess is that he had not eaten for some time.

Finally, sipping the evening wine that washed the grease off our pallets,

Jes spoke once more. "I don't want to cause hardship in this matter, but I feel that Bethany and I should be Holy Wed just as soon as possible. It isn't safe for me to remain long in Bethel any more. I don't want to bring trouble needlessly to our village. Our wedding shall be small; no one outside of the village is to attend, for safety's sake." Turning to me, he added, "Besides, I don't want our Holy Day, Bethany, to be spoiled by countless others coming to bear witness nor do I want it turned into a spectacle. Our bond is a holy one, just between you and me." With the briefest discussion, we all agreed to conduct the ceremony in two days, just enough time for everything for the ceremony to be prepared.

Then, Jes had to leave to go to his parents and brother. Unfortunately, Arad customs dictate that the bride shall not see her husband until the ceremony, presented as a holy virgin unto him. While I had hundreds of questions for Jes and longed just to be with him, I had to comply with customs. I settled for a very loving goodnight kiss at the door. He whispered, "I love you Bethany Madelyn. Thy patience for yet another two days shall be rewarded." With that, he disappeared into the dark street and I, like a moon-struck child, ambled back to the table.

There I found my family talking very fast, excited beyond words. I was almost in a trance. Though I heard their words, I was rather in my own world. One thing was certain: my entire family felt as though they had just had the highest honor possible bestowed on them. I, their eldest daughter, would be the bride of the Son of Jehosa, the Great Messiah. Looking back on it just now, I believe they thought that their family name would become famous because I would be the wife of their Lord. Funny how things that one believes should be do not end up quite as predicted.

Arad customs usually have the bride and groom moving immediately into their new home on their wedding night. Because of the normally lengthy courtship, there was sufficient time to build a new adobe home. The groom was responsible for their new living arrangements. However, knowing what the purposes of Jes would likely be, I figured that we would be traveling frequently, never staying long in a single location. The infidels most certainly would soon, if not already, be looking for him. Suddenly, memories of my experiences with the messiah Jackal and his wife Missa from over twenty years ago came back into my mind. They were constantly on the move, ambushing infidel patrols wherever they could find them. When they entered a town or village, some of the locals would put them up for the few days that they stayed. I assumed that my life with Jes would be similar to theirs.

The next day was a very busy one. A wedding dress had to be sewn for me, and the plans for the wedding celebration worked out. Again, it was customary for the bride's family to provide food and entertainment for those that attended the ceremony. In this case, we knew that the whole village would turn out, over five hundred of them. This was not an ordinary wedding. Their Great Messiah was marrying. Hence, my father arranged for the very best food and drink in the village to be provided in abundance a befitting this auspicious occasion.

When I was not either fitting the dress or helping with the sewing, I sorted out my meager possessions, preparing them for travel. My old druwid training came back to mind. By the evening, I had my gear down to just two sacks, which would fit on horseback nicely. If we walked, I was sure I could carry one but I wasn't too sure about both.

That night, dad came to my room and asked me to follow him. It was late and the house was rather dark. The others were asleep. We stole quietly into the dining room. Whispering, he said, "I must show you the secret safe." On the floor against one side, he brushed the dirt aside, revealing a hidden compartment in the ground. He opened it and inside I saw four large pouches. In the dim lantern light, I could just make out the small labels he had written on them. Bethany, Jamal, Ilene, and Aline — one for each of us. "Each month, I count my profits and divide it into quarters, placing each share into these pouches. I will continue to do so as long as I am able. Whenever you need funds, help yourself to what is in your pouch here. Remember, if something happens to me, use these to help the others as you promised. Only you and mother know of this secret hiding place."

"I don't know what to say, dad. Thank you very much!"

"Dear, you have more than earned your share. Because of you I am now the wealthiest man in Bethel and perhaps several other village as well. It is the least I can do for you and your new husband. I suspect that you will both be traveling around a lot and that likely means you will need these coins. So in a way, I am doing my part in helping the Great Messiah accomplish his enormous task. One other thing, if you are in some other town and have need, send word to me here and I can forward some coins to you, somehow. I'll find a way. But if anything happens to me, please come back here and retrieve everything. Aline and I are sworn to take the location of our stash here to our graves. I'm sure you will know what to do with these sacks after that."

"Father. . ." I protested, but could find no other words to say. He put his finger to my lips to silence my protests.

"Come, it's back to bed for us. Tomorrow is a very big day." He carefully closed the compartment and smoothed the dirt back over it. If one did not know the precise location of this stash, he could not readily find it. Quietly, we stole back into our bedrooms.

The next day, October 1, 580 AH, Jes Amir and I were married before the whole village of Bethel. Prophet El Bantam of the Amirites sect officiated, primarily because Jes and his family belonged to that sect. I won't bore you with the details of the ceremony or the gay festivities that followed all that afternoon. Suffice to say, this was one wedding that everyone in Bethel would remember forever.

That evening, I went into my room for the last time to gather my two sacks. I found that dad had already put some coins into a small pouch for me. He thought of everything! Jes carried them in his strong hands as we walked over to his father's house. Tonight, Josephus Amir would put us up in his home, Jes's room to be precise. After a supper and small celebration with his parents, his brother, Josh, and his wife, Milla, we retired to Jes's room. Finally, we could be alone!

After a loving embrace, Jes said, "Before we bed, we need to talk. You have come prepared for travel. I knew that you would think of that, so I didn't say anything. Yes, we must travel around a lot. I've really missed you this past year. I think nights were the worst for me; I'd sit and just think of you. I know you must have a lot of questions to ask of me. Already, Josh has filled me in on what's been going on around here. I did make the opportunity to personally thank your father for his part in handling the Tax Collector. What you might not know is that a messiah attacked him and relieved him of all the coins before he could deliver them to his master. Those very same coins I have given back to your father for next year's use."

I could not help but smile, "I rather figured that would happen. I'm not really surprised by it, just glad that no one in Bethel will have to suffer to make the taxes next time. You are right. I have accumulated a pile of questions to ask you, my love. Only just at the moment, I cannot think of a single one. I just want to hold you and be with you. They can all wait until later. How soon do we leave?"

"Tomorrow morning. Come then; let's be together tonight, the first of our lifetime of nights together, my love." We put out the lantern and laid down upon his bed.

Chapter 4 The Gathering of the Disciples

After breakfast the next morning, we both said our farewells to our parents and family. To my surprise, Josh and his wife, Milla, accompanied us. The men led a pair of donkeys, which carried our sacks. Milla was with child and rode when she tired. Initially though, we four walked along, each carrying a stout staff. I would use it if we were attacked, but we all used it as a preventative viper stick, should we encounter any snakes along the dirt road. We said little until we had left Bethel behind us.

Jes began, "Just so that everything is perfectly understood here at the very start, I want it known to us all that Josh is going to help me fulfill our purpose. He is older and wiser about many things than I, especially the geography of Arad. I trust him to lead us from place to place. Josh also knows many key people who may help us from time to time. Milla is an excellent cook and wants to help us with meals; that will be her task, to see we are provisioned properly. Bethany, you are to be my closest advisor, my eyes and ears to the world and people. Above all others, I have come to trust your keen powers of observation. Indeed, never have I encountered anyone as good as you are, my love. I will depend heavily upon you, I'm afraid. Thus, if Bethany advises us on some course of action, we should endeavor to follow it." Here, we stopped and let the donkeys graze as they might, giving Jes our full attention.

"When I left last year, I sought the solace of the distant mountains far to the east. I needed to free my mind of all thoughts and then tackle how best to accomplish the goal of Jehosa. You three must know subjectively that goal and have a personal reality of it. Josh and Milla, you two likely do not, but I know Bethany already has both. Let me explain. We are all in fact spiritual beings, not bodies. We occupy and live within these fleshly bodies, which have somehow entrapped us. No longer can we operate as a free being unattached to a body; we have become first dependent upon our bodies and now trapped within them. Of this, Bethany already is very much aware, though she has, at times, been able to operate while not attached to her body." Both Josh and Milla looked at me as if they had never seen me before! I blushed.

"Thus, before I can continue, this must become totally real to you both." Jes placed his hands upon Josh's head and said a soft prayer. I couldn't hear the words. Instead, I assumed that somehow Jes would have to free Josh from his head and so I began to observe. I smiled as I spotted Josh move out of his head and up above his body some distance. "Bethany, keep an eye on him while I do the same for Milla." I did so. Soon, I detected Milla floating up above her body. Jes then took my hand, and with a slight nudging on his part, we too floated up to join them.

Jes continued his explanations, "Now look about you. See the world. Look down at your bodies. You are indeed spiritual beings, not those fleshly bodies. This is the form our ancestors had while they yet lived in Jehosa's realm. This is the form we must regain if we are to once more enter the Kingdom of Jehosa."

"I — I feel as though I am a god!" exclaimed Josh.

"Me too," squeaked Milla.

"You are the sons and daughters of Jehosa. This is your true state. Bethany, explain to them what this has to do with the prophesy of the Great Messiah."

Oh no, I was on the spot again. Was this a test? No, I suddenly realized Jes's true intention. I would explain it all, and thus, both Josh and Milla would have a true respect for me borne from their own observations. "The Great Messiah shall come to set men free, just as you are free right now. The Great Messiah is to deliver his people from the influence of the infidels. I ask you, if you could be as you are now as well as do everything you desired to do without the need of your bodies down there, how could any infidel possibly have the slightest influence over you? On the contrary, with a thought you could make the infidels' bodies jump through hoops. For are you not godlike at the moment? It is my opinion that the prophets, stuck in their bodies, have twisted this to mean that the Great Messiah would drive out or slay all the infidels in Juda Arad, thereby freeing his people. I can understand how they must think this, if they consider themselves to be nothing but fleshly bodies subject to all the pain of the world. Finally, the Great Messiah is to teach everyone the righteous path so that they might regain the Kingdom of Jehosa that they had lost so long ago. At the moment, we are much closer to that path, are you not?"

"Precisely stated, my love," Jes commented, backing up my observations.

Again, both Josh and Milla looked at me as if they had never seen me before. "Are you, is she, I mean, is she from Jehosa too?" Josh fumbled for words to ask what his mind desired to know.

"She, like me, like you two, like all of us, are children of Jehosa, cast out to here on Tarra, now forced to reside in a fleshly body to survive. Can you see now why I have chosen Bethany, above all others, to wed?"

"Never, my Lord, have I ever doubted your words, even as a child. But now I pledge never to doubt her words as well. When but a child, I dedicated my life to helping you achieve Jehosa's great goals. Then, I pledged my life to you. Now, I also swear and pledge my life to Bethany, to keep her safe, as well as you, my Lord," Josh swore. Little did I know just how vitally important this pledge to me would become!

"Thank you, Josh," I replied meekly.

"Now, let us move back down behind our body's heads that we may continue our journey. I have many plans to discuss with you." I watched as we all did so. I smiled as I saw both of them stop a few feet behind their heads, whereas just a few minutes before, both had been solidly stuck inside them. I knew that both had just had the revelation of their lives.

"I cannot go around and do what I have done for you two to every person in Juda Arad. It is just not possible. Though I admit, for months, I tried to think up ways that I could. It takes time for each action. By the time I had visited everyone in the Arad, why, I would have to start over again, because so many new babies would have been born in that time. Thus, I prayed to Jehosa, my father, for guidance. The answer I found is that I must preach the truth to everyone, perform such miracles as may be, and get the common man's knowledge of himself raised to a higher level, at least to having faith that he is an immortal spiritual being. Others can then spread my words, my teachings, and so like a wildfire, the truth arrives throughout all Juda Arad. At least that is the first step we have to accomplish on this road."

"All this we cannot hope to do alone. Hence, Jehosa has suggested I find those that may care to assist us — the Holy Disciples of the Great Messiah they shall be known, and ten shall be their number. Thus, my friends, our first action is to wander the Arad and find these Holy Disciples. Any questions?"

Ever practical, I spoke up, "How do find these men? What is the criterion used to choose who ought to be a disciple? And what about the normal person's mistaken ideas that you are leading a Holy War against the infidels? What about the other messiahs? If you don't lead a revolution, won't they be rather disillusioned? And. . ." I didn't get to finish rattling them off; Jes interrupted.

Laughing, he said, "Yes, but let's take one question at a time while we continue our walk. You are right, my love, Arad is about to explode. One word from me and vast numbers of our people would take up arms against the infidels. Because of this, I just had to get away from it all and reflect. No, I cannot allow Arad to go to war because of me. Bethany, you know full well what would happen should we take up arms against these infidels."

"Absolutely, and whew, I was worried war might be in the planning," I replied. To the others, I explained, "Do not ask me how I know this, but if Arad openly attacks the infidels, their response, which I have seen before, would be just to pour in soldiers by the thousands, and slaughter every man in the Arad or ship them off as slaves in their salt mines."

Josh and Milla looked at me intensely, he said, "You know this? You have seen this before?"

"Don't ask how unless you are prepared for an unusual answer. Yes, though I'll not say how, I do know the mind set of these infidels, and that is exactly how they would respond — an overwhelming display of force, squashing utterly all resistance. The messiahs thus far have completely avoided this because they only attack the isolated supply caravans. There is no open rebellion to squash. We are safe as long as we don't present a visible target. Give them a target, and they go into action and smash it. I have only known two groups that could possibly defeat these infidels in actual combat."

"Who?" implored Josh.

"One group is the Sisterhood of the Sea Princes. The other I will not name for their safety. They are as yet an unknown force," I answered truthfully. I dare not name the Guardians of the Greenway. However, at the mention of the Sisterhood, Josh seemed satisfied; he had heard tales of that legendary combat over Zargarb.

"My task is complicated by my having to prevent all-out war," Jes continued. "As Bethany has said, we must restrain them from open hostilities and keep the messiahs on their current path of harassing the infidels. It came to me that what better way to keep the eager messiahs in check but to have some of them as my disciples? Many of the ten must be some of the influential local messiahs. However, I must preach and teach the common man so they can understand, as you two have today. My disciples must therefore also be able to relate to the average citizen of the Arad. That is why I did not accept your father, Bethany, though he volunteered."

"What?" I hadn't known of this. So dad had indeed offered to help the Great Messiah. Interesting, I thought.

Jes misunderstood my exclamation, he explained, "He is a very wealthy merchant. If he were to speak to say a lowly adobe brick maker, whose income is at best a twentieth of your fathers, the brick maker wouldn't be likely to believe what your father was saying. Rather, he might say instead, 'That's all well and good for you to say, but you don't have to slave for your daily bread.' Some of these disciples must be able to relate well to the poorest of our people."

"We shall meet the first possibility in two days' time on the isolated hill of El Daka, some hundred miles east of Jerilum. He is called Messiah Jackal and his wife is Missa. They are old warriors and some twenty years ago, successfully invented methods of stopping the infidel's war chariots. He is semi-retired now, though, but he is highly knowledgeable in the ways of the infidels, but the real question is can he preach to others. That remains to be seen."

Jackal! Memories flashed of my Circle's days spent with his band. I recalled how our Planner, Raphael, had actually devised a scheme to take out the dangerous chariots. I smiled as I realized Jackal had accepted the honor of its invention. After all, we had sworn him to secrecy about our involvement. So he still lived! By now, he must be approaching fifty at least. I could see why Jes claimed he was semi-retired. In my excitement, I spoke before thinking, "Yes, I agree, Jes, Jackal would be an excellent choice."

Somewhat startled, Jes said, "You know him? I wasn't aware that you knew of him."

Once again, I had my foot in my mouth. What should I say openly? Jes, I felt certain would totally understand. But would Josh and Milla? An awkward pause followed while I tried to think of the best way to handle this. Right there I realized that if I did not speak the truth or tried to withhold this from Jes, we would begin to drift apart; I would slowly feel more and more separated from him. I wondered if things such as this marked the downfall of some marriages where the two drift apart in life. "Over twenty years ago, my group and I were traveling with him for several weeks. Actually, my group first came up with the hidden trenches that wrecked the chariots when the infidels moved to attack.

Twenty years ago, I'd have nothing but the highest praise for both Jackal and Missa. Together, they seemed an unbeatable pair. However, much may have happened since then. I have no idea whether he could preach as you need."

"But you weren't born yet," Josh interrupted. Milla added her agreement to his protest.

"You are absolutely right, Josh. I had a different body then, before it died due to a mistake on my part. That was before I was born into this body here."

"Then it is true — that when we died, we are reborn in a new infant body?" Milla asked almost in utter awe. "And you can remember who you were and what you did before — before you were born — I mean before this body was born?" I could see her struggling with language. There was almost not even language to describe all this. I sympathized with her; this must seem very strange to her.

Fortunately, Jes came to my rescue. "Yes, Milla. Once we were in the Kingdom of Jehosa before the Primal Sin. When we were cast out and came to Tarra, we took over these fleshly bodies because we no longer could do things directly ourselves. If we could still do these without the need of a fleshly body, why, we could reenter Jehosa's Kingdom, perhaps even at will. Now you see another reason why we need Bethany Madelyn so badly. She has the benefit of having witnessed the infidels through two lifetimes and many places, where you have only your knowledge from your current lifetime." Well, that sure put me into a different light in the minds of Josh and Milla!

Josh still looked a bit puzzled. "My Lord, can you answer another question? Why is it that Bethany Madelyn can remember who she was and what she did from her last lifetime while I cannot remember anything much before I was around five years old, let alone any previous life?" Whoa! What a question! I think my ears must have opened up wide in an instant. I've never been so eager to hear an answer that I can recall!

Jes smiled, "Well, you want the precise answer or a palatable answer?" He looked at all three of us before continuing. "Okay, the precise answer is that you are unwilling to take and accept responsibility for your prior identities or lives. 'It's not my fault' is all too common a reply that I hear. Suppose that you got shot by an arrow and it killed your last fleshly body. Would you not say that it was the fault of the arrow or the person who shot you?"

"Yes, of course it is," replied Josh. Milla nodded her complete agreement.

"No it isn't," I commented. "Jes is intentionally using my own life for this example. It is true that I was shot and killed by an arrow. It hit my forehead just about here," I pointed out the spot. "The body died instantly and didn't even fall out of the saddle. My own death was my responsibility. I made a mistake and believed that you could reason with an insane person. Had I not made that folly, I wouldn't have put the body in jeopardy. No, it's as Jes says; it's completely my responsibility. Come to think of it, I don't recall ever even having the thought that it was the fault of whoever shot the arrow. I never did see who actually shot me. It was just my own folly."

"Hence, you can remember," Jes added, "but what about the life you led before that one, Bethany Madelyn?"

I grinned, "You got me there. A black curtain lies between me and anything earlier. I must not be taking responsibility for what and who I was and did." Of course, now my mind raced along this new avenue. My earlier lives were obscured in my memory because I wasn't taking responsibility for them. If I could take full responsibility for them, my memories, good, bad, and painful, should return to me. Hence, how does one go about doing this? Yes, that is what occupied my thoughts for days.

While I was lost in contemplation, Jes went on, "This explanation may be more palatable to you. Here on Tarra at this time, no one talks about their former lives; the society at large frowns heavily on this. What would you think if the village baker began talking about his former life while you were getting bread from him? Would you think it strange? Perhaps the man is slightly insane — not quite all there?" From the corner of my eye, I caught both Josh and Milla nodding in complete agreement.

"Yes, people don't talk about them; it isn't acceptable to do so. It's a highly unpopular thing to talk about to anyone. This naturally tends to occlude and hide them from your mind. Further, suppose that you did some things that you shouldn't have done that life, things you wish you could undo but cannot — perhaps you cheated on your spouse? Wouldn't you rather just forget about all that and start over with a fresh slate? It is only natural that you cannot remember. The path out of all this begins with a recognition and certainty of just who and what you are, a spiritual being, not a fleshly body. That is the first step toward regaining the Kingdom of Jehosa." Both Josh and Milla responded with large smiles. Yes, they knew that they had taken that very first step today, thanks to Jes. They had experienced what they really were, and it wasn't the bodies they occupied.

We walked on, looking at the beautiful terrain all around us in the distance. Juda Arad has many mesa hills, steep and sheer walls on one side, but with gentle slopes on the opposite side. Our trail naturally followed the lower lands along dry stream beds. Sparse underbrush grew here and there. Occasionally, we'd encounter a grassy area, which often denoted a nearby well or spring. Here we also met a shepherd tending a small flock of sheep. Always, we stopped and chatted with the herder who was very pleased to have someone to talk to if only for a few minutes. I realized that being a shepherd was an very solitary activity.

Yet, all the while, I was puzzling about what Jes had told us. I was really encouraged, because for the very first time, that black veil over who I was, what I had been, and done prior to being a young child in Uru, the Greenway, had lightened. The veil was only dark grey and not a solid black. Perhaps, I had made some headway. Try as I might, no memories appeared.

Then I had a horrible thought. During our travels as a Circle, we discovered when many people died, or rather when their fleshly bodies died, they immediately and without thought went to the three pyramids somewhere out in the Red Desert or to the mountain top in the Appian Way, just south of the Greenway. There, I had seen mantises and strange grey people with three toes do something to these people's minds, somehow scrambling all their memories and issuing a command to go get a new infant body. The highly confused beings instantly followed this command. Could these two mind-altering operations also have something to do with people not being able to remember who they had been? It seemed to me that this messing with one's memories and installation commands would make it very hard for one to accept full responsibility; might this be another factor?

I decided to tell Jes all about what I had observed. I couldn't help but wonder how Alabaster was doing with these strange creatures. When I last left him nearly twenty years ago, he was spying on them. Though he had promised to return to me and help me get back to the Greenway once I had discovered how the Great Messiah was to have freed his people, thus far, I had heard nothing from him. Actually, I didn't really expect to hear from him this soon. However, I resolved to discuss these strange creatures only when I was completely alone with Jes and couldn't be overheard by anyone else. My tale would be just too fantastic to be believed. Perhaps even Jes wouldn't believe me.

The chance came after we camped for the night and had eaten. Once all the chores were finished and before turning in for the night, Josh and Milla wanted to take a stroll together, to spend some time with each other. I took Jes over to a big boulder and we sat side by side in the moonlight. "Jes, I have something to tell you. Perhaps you will not believe what I have to say; it is so utterly fantastic, so unbelievable. After what you told us today, I fell I must at least tell you about it."

"Bethany, what could be so unbelievable? Okay, go ahead." He smiled as always. Soon his smile evaporated completely.

Carefully, I related my story. It took an hour to explain fully everything without compromising any of my druwid friends. I ended with, "I don't know why they are doing this or what their overall purpose might be. Yet, I'm convinced that they are hostile to us. I'm certain they don't want me knowing about them and what they are doing."

When I finished, Jes didn't speak for a while. At last he said, "If you were Josh, I would think that perhaps he had smoked the delirium weed and was merely seeing a delusion. Coming from you, I'm forced to believe that you saw what you say you saw. I admit, I know nothing about this. If what you say is truly happening, that may also be inhibiting our people from knowing what they are and being able to regain the Kingdom of Jehosa and be free of fleshly bodies. It would be very hard for one to take responsibility for having one's memories scrambled like that. Surely, it must occlude all their prior memories. As you say, you did not see if any in the Arad were similarly affected. I will look into it and let you know what I can find out."

"Oh, please be extra careful, Jes, these creatures are horrible and awfully powerful."

"Don't worry one beautiful hair on your lovely head, my love." We embraced lovingly. As we turned in, he said admiringly, "Not a day goes by when you do not amaze me with your knowledge." I snuggled against his warm body and fell asleep totally content with life.

We arrived early at the rendezvous location. El Daka's sheer reddish face reflected the late afternoon sun. From the dry valley, we paused to look at this marvel of nature, pristine, untouched by the hand of man. Miles off every beaten track, El Daka stood proud and tall, the highest point for many miles here in the southeastern section of the Arad. I breathed deep. Odors of scrub bushes, tough grasses, even the smell of sand filtered through my acute senses. I felt very much alive and alert. Here amid Nature was where I really belonged. I think Jes also sensed this, though he said nothing, but paused with me for as long as I did. Finally, we continued around the side and then climbed up the gentle slope of the opposite side of El Daka where Josh and Milla were beginning to setup a campsite.

"You two get to fetch something we can use for a cooking fire," Josh teased, as we arrived and tied up the donkey. "Careful of vipers and scorpions. I think this is an ideal location for them." Jes and I went back down to the valley in search of dry brush.

We were just sitting down for dinner when Josh heard footsteps. We arose and took a defensive posture, just in case. Out here in the wilderness, one ought to be at least cautious. Even in the failing light, I recognized Jackal and Missa, leading their horses up the slope toward us. "Hail and well met, Messiah Jackal, Missa," Josh welcomed them. I could really see now that Josh was looking out for the safety of his brother. For a moment, I mused upon what Josh's viewpoint might be: his own younger brother was the long foretold Great Messiah. Any plans Josh might have had for his own life and future, even for his young wife and soon baby, all had been altered so he could look after the safety of his younger brother. As he spoke to the new arrivals, I fully realized the lifelong commitment Josh had made. Little did I know at this time that my own life would rest in his able hands.

"May Jehosa watch over you, Josh, well met indeed. In time for supper? Oh, I'm sorry, my Lord. I didn't see you," Jackal suddenly saw Jes moving into the light of our fire. Quickly, he got down on his knees and bowed, his nose nearly touching the sandy soil. Surprisingly, Missa did as well. I took this gesture as a sign of immense respect for their Great Messiah, though I hated seeing anyone bow to another.

"Arise and face me, Messiah Jackal and Missa. Your exploits and great service to Jehosa are well known to me. There is no need to bow; I am a man as thee. Partake of our dinner that Milla has so kindly prepared. Ah yes, you know Josh's wife, Milla?" Jes really didn't know if they did and introduced her just in case.

Missa answered, "Yes, but Milla, you are now with child. That is news! Congratulations are in order. When is your baby due?"

Milla, holding her large belly, pronounced cheerfully, "In three months, if all goes well. We haven't decided yet upon a name, so you can give us some suggestions."

"And this is my wife," Jes continued before the women got too involved in their discussions, "Bethany Madelyn." I stepped forward to Jes's side, putting my arm around him, smiling.

"Then, it is true, my Lord, you are of the same flesh as we," Jackal asked. I saw a glint of surprise in his eyes, as the truth of his Great Messiah became real to him. "Congratulations once more. I see you have chosen a beautiful woman," he bowed to me. Okay, I admit that I enjoyed his compliment, though I seldom considered how I looked, beauty wise, that is. "And such beautiful long hair. You know, you remind me of another Bethany I once knew ages ago. She had hair at least as long as yours." I flushed; he was undoubtedly thinking of me when I had traveled with his band more than twenty years ago.

"We've known each other since early childhood," Jes explained. "Brother Jackal trained her in fighting when he trained Josh and me. We were sparring partners. She also was one of the three scribes that transcribed the words of the Prophets. She has a keen mind under all that pretty hair and is my right hand in all things. Nothing is withheld from her." Jes was clearly making my position known at the onset. "But, come, let's eat. I'm hungry, and it's been a long time since lunch." We six gathered around the campfire and Milla served us. Jes, of course, said the traditional prayer before we ate.

I had time now to observe them closely. Streaks of grey lined Jackal's thinning short hair. I could see now why he had cut it. His right arm moved in an awkward manner; he no longer had full use of it. He ate with his left. I spied a distinct scar across the left side of his face. Certainly, he had been in some nasty combat situations since I had left him so long ago. Missa still stood strong and proud, though her hair was now fully grey. She too had a scar on her left arm, probably a sword cut I surmised from its shape. She also walked with a slight limp, I noticed, favoring her right leg. I wondered if it had been hurt when his arm had.

Josh spied me observing our new guests. Perhaps that was what triggered his comment; then again, perhaps it was our conversation earlier in the day. "Say, Messiah Jackal, Bethany said that she knows you — that she traveled with your band for a while a long time ago."

Naturally, the quiet conversations over dinner ceased instantly; Jackal looked squarely at me, as did Missa. I flushed as I realized yet another difficulty arising from knowing fully your previous lifetime. I already knew their reality, and if I said anything, I would be shattering it, but the truth must be said, and Josh had opened the door, perhaps prematurely.

"It's been a long time, Jackal, Missa. Yes, you knew me before as Bethany Stanton. I led a party of six. You remember, we met in Jerilum when Prophet Tamil was giving his speech, the infidels came and spooked our horses, which then trampled several of the infidels. If it were not for you, my party and I would have been captured by the infidels before we could get away." There, I had given them enough details that there could be no denying the truth. I paused to see their reactions.

Missa looked shocked and nearly dropped her plate. Jackal, surprised as well, had the presence of mind to challenge me, "That is known by many. But tell me, what did you teach me later on? Answer that, if you are who you say you are."

"It wasn't me that taught you how to defeat the war chariots; it was my friend, Raphael, our Planner. Everyone seems to be giving you full credit for that scheme. Rightly so, since we still don't want our presence in the Arad known."

Missa's plate did drop with a dull thud. Jackal tried to say something and failed twice before he managed to voice, "But how?"

"We made it home safely, Messiah Jackal. Then I made a mistake and put myself into a nasty situation: took an arrow to my forehead, my body died instantly. I remembered Prophet Tamil's sermons of the coming of the Great Messiah, and so I took a new body here to see for myself. I have an endless curiosity to know, as you well know. So now, here I am again, helping as I can. It is good to see you both once more. I see you have suffered grievous injuries since we parted so long ago." I hoped that this provided enough continuity to allow them to grasp the situation and that I was really on their side.

Jes came to my rescue, "It is as she says. We are all spiritual beings and live in these fleshly bodies. The pattern of life since our fall from Jehosa's kingdom has been repeated over and over. We take a new baby body; we grow into adulthood; we diminish into old age; our body dies; we repeat the cycle once more. Here the only difference is that Bethany has full command of her memories from her last lifetime. This is as it should be, as Jehosa would desire. Why it is not here among our people, I do not know, and Jehosa has not revealed that to me."

"My Lord, I accept your word. Verily, she speaks words that only Bethany could know. She asked us not to reveal their part in the war chariots sabotage. Only my band and hers knows of that." He relaxed, looked at me, and grinned, "You really do love long hair, even if here in the Arad, such is worn only by the women of the night." I flushed; that was true, but I didn't like thinking of myself as a prostitute!"

Dinner resumed, only this time, Jackal explained for my benefit what had happened to Missa and himself. Five years ago, one of their ambushes went wrong. Somehow, the infidels were expecting it. Only half of his band managed to escape alive. His sword arm had been horribly cut as well as his face. Missa had also taken sword cuts to her leg and arm. Neither had ever fully recovered and had since retired from active service. With their lengthy explanation finished, he asked Jes, "So my Lord, both Missa and I have been asking ourselves for weeks now, why would our Great Messiah desire our services? We are both barely able to get around. There are so many good young messiahs. Why us?"

"Wisdom often comes from age and experience," Jes replied. "Your record of service to Jehosa is legendary. But first, I must give you your reward, in the name of our father, Jehosa." Jes gave his now familiar lecture about all of us being spiritual beings and such. Once he had finished, he placed his hands on Jackal's head and then on Missa's. Jes was doing to them what he had done for Josh and Milla, allowing them directly to experience what they actually were, spiritual beings. It was easy for me to see them both now floating about five feet above and behind their heads. Both their bodies looked intensely serene, just as Josh and Milla had.

However, he did not stop here. Instead, he returned to Jackal and placed his hands a second time on his head, praying softly all the while. I watched fascinated, as the scar on his face seemed to vanish before my eyes. Then he did the same to Missa. When Jes finished, he said, "Now stand your bodies up and see how they feel and respond."

Like children testing some new toy, both arose and moved about. Gone was Missa's limp. Jackal's arm moved normally. All traces of their lingering injuries were gone. Both began crying tears of joy. Even Josh and Milla cried as well. Josh exclaimed, "Behold miracles done by our Lord!" All four got down on their knees and prayed to Jehosa, offering them their deepest thanks.

I whispered to Jes, "I sure would like to be able to know how to do that!"

He smiled and whispered back, "Faith, Bethany. Be Faith. I am Faith." I understood the words, but had no idea what he meant.

Humbly, Jackal offered, "How may we sever you, my Lord?"

"I need to find ten Holy Disciples to help me preach the truth to our people. I need a guide that knows all the Arad and the ways of the infidels."

"I am poor with words, my Lord. I would make a poor disciple, but no one knows the Arad better than Missa and me or the ways of our enemy, for that matter. Will you accept our services as guide and counselors then?"

"Absolutely, arise, Holy Counselors Jackal and Missa. From this day forward, both of you shall be known in all the Arad as my Holy Counselors. Keep my fleshly body from falling into the hands of the infidels whilst I and my Holy Disciples travel the Arad preaching the ways of Jehosa; that is your challenge."

"But what of the Holy War?" Missa asked, confusion lining her face. I knew this confusion would be widespread. After all, for untold years, the prophets spoke of the coming of the Great Messiah, and how he would free his people from the hands of the infidels. It was commonly thought that this meant war.

"War is not Jehosa's way," Jes explained. "What if every one of our people knew who and what they are, just as you two now do? What if every one of them could operate as a being without need of a fleshly body? How then could anything that any infidel do harm you? Verily, thou would be free of infidels for all time. Explain it more in their terms, will you Bethany?"

I was intent on catching his every word, and the sudden turn in my direction caught me off guard. "Ah, well, suppose that you could do anything that you could normally do by using your body. Golly, that sounds funny. Okay, suppose that you, as a free, immortal being could wield swords, fly arrows, even punch, all without having to have a fleshly body around to do it. Beings are immortal; we do not die as fleshly bodies do. How could anything that an infidel do harm us in any way? Further, we could harm them without needing a body. We would be free of the influence of any and all infidels forever!" I could see that they were still not completely getting the point. I decided to become more graphic. "Okay, the infidel would see a ghost stabbing him with a real spear, yet all his sword swings would cut through a ghost harmlessly. The ghost could do anything it wanted to the infidel, but the infidel could never do anything to the ghost." Now both of them fully grasped the idea.

"Oh teach us how, Lord!" both begged. I had put it in graphic terms that these two old warriors could understand. Now they most certainly wanted it!

"This is the way back into the Kingdom of Jehosa," Jes said, not really answering their question or request. I wondered if he could teach us how. If so, I had a huge amount to learn. Later, I could return to my beloved Greenway and teach them. I could see the whole of Tarra eventually becoming free. That became my basic purpose. The instant I realized this, that dark grey screen blocking all my prior lifetimes suddenly lightened considerably, to my amazement.

"First, we have to get all our people in Juda Arad to know what you now know, that they really are immortal spiritual beings. That is our first step we must take to regain the Kingdom of Jehosa. However, it is getting late. We should turn in for the night; our fire dies and there is not much deadwood around here." A few minutes later, I laid down on a blanket, snuggling up to Jes. My mind kept drifting off, imagining a world of free beings, though I hadn't the slightest clue how one could be made free.

The dawn came sooner than I desired. Over a light breakfast, Holy Counselor Jackal asked Jes how he was going to find his Holy Disciples. "We wander the Arad in search of them," came the reply. "Actually, I have several possibilities in mind. We will visit them and see. However, I am always on the lookout for just the right people." Thus, off we went, wandering about the country.

It took us a year to find Jes's needed ten Holy Disciples. Rather than bore you with this lengthy search and selection process, I'll just summarize the year. The first problem we faced was that as soon as word got out that the Great Messiah was looking for disciples, many of the existing messiahs stepped up their raids and sabotage of the infidels. Indeed, many now undertook foolhardy attacks hoping to impress Jes! None realized that this was exactly the opposite of what their Great Messiah desired. Life became more and more dangerous, especially in those areas closely patrolled by the infidels.

Six of the chosen disciples were already messiahs, that is, they were leaders of local bands of freedom fighters — okay, religious zealots intent on harassing the infidels anyway that they could. Another eight messiahs were not given this honored position either because they refused to give up their attacks upon the infidels or they were not sufficiently eloquent to be able to communicate well with the common man. In each of these encounters, Jes would first lay his hands upon their heads, showing them who and what they really were. Next, he would explain his purpose. Finally, if the candidate showed promise, he would have the man explain our religion to him, while he pretended to be an ordinary townsperson. Always, before Jes made the final decision, he asked for my opinion of the candidate. To my amazement, several times, he went with my judgment over his own, also surprising the others.

These six messiahs turned Holy Disciples were Hamah Zagros, Rafha Orum, Jamal Mazra, Bandar Dero, Yazi Rigan, and Abu Wadi. All were in their twenties, all fit, all skilled fighters. More importantly, all six had a high charisma and related well to normal people. Most importantly, all six saw that, if Jes were successful, their people would be free from the influence of the infidels. Some were married, and their wives and children traveled with us. However, a few family members wanted to remain in their towns, which was fine too.

Of these, I really detested Yazi Rigan, not because he was unmarried, but because he harbored an intense dislike of all women. I'd already seen enough of that twenty-five years ago, while traveling through the Lands of the Sea Princes. I warned Jes about this, but he overruled me saying that he thought that he could get him to change his views toward women. In hindsight, Jes should have listened to me, because the impact that Yazi ultimately had would resonate through Tarra for centuries to come! But this is getting ahead of the times.

The other four were definitely not fighters. Amar Tarabulus was a thirty-five year old fisherman who lived in a small fishing village called Alcaldus, located some fifty miles north of Al Barq, the city now occupied solely by the infidels. Of all the disciples, Amar had a tremendous affinity for people and for life. I thought that he also would have made a great druwid. In contrast, Jubal Dayr was a simple shepherd, a non-imposing, shy person. Yet, his compassion for his fellow man was enormous. He understood the hardships of life and related exceedingly well to the poor. Des Mandan was a large, burly blacksmith in his late thirties with a homely wife and four children. Des was one of these rare persons who can find a way to make you laugh at life's travails. When Des was around, one felt completely relaxed and at home. When he traveled with Jes, his family stayed at home, and his eldest son ran the shop in his absence.

The last disciple chosen, Ismail Saydah, was a moneychanger. In his early thirties and immaculately dressed, Ismail was snide and quite covert in his comments about others. I didn't like him at all. I told Jes that I did not trust him any farther than I could throw him, which was no distance at all. Jes replied, "I have chosen him for an entirely different reason than all the others.

I believe that a time will come when he will play a pivotal role that none of the others would ever conceive of doing. I understand your view of him and you are correct. Just trust me on this one." I never could get him to explain what he meant. However, we all found out just what Ismail would do much later on.

Now as Jes accumulated his disciples, it fell to me to teach them to read and write. Having witnessed the benefits of the four years that it took to transcribe all the words of the Prophets of Juda Arad, Jes insisted that each disciple keep a journal or log of events that they might one day write of their experiences to teach others. Jes intended to have a written record of his life and teachings for the future generations of Arads. A hundred years from now, one could read the accounts and hear the teachings of Jes, the Great Messiah. This was a new use of writing that I thought would be terrific.

In December of 580 AH, we stopped back in Bethel so that Missa could have her baby. She had a fine son, who she and Josh named Hadid after Josh's grandfather. During this period of relaxation and visiting with my family, I also became with child. For the next few months, Milla stayed with Josh's parents while we continued looking for the disciples.

In September of 581 AH, we again stopped for a while in Bethel so that our son could be born, Ahmad, named for Jes's great-grandfather. Then, again in December, Missa gave birth to their daughter, Ros, named after Milla's grandmother. Not to be outdone, I gave birth to our second son, Emil, in October 582 AH. Thus, either Milla or I was absent for a short while at various times during this gathering of the ten Holy Disciples.

By the start of the new year, 583 AH, the crusade was fully operational. All the disciples could now read and write, the babies were ready to travel, as were their mothers. Following the suggested path outlined by our Holy Counselors, Jackal and Missa, we set out on January 1. By steering clear of the larger towns, we avoided any possible confrontations with the infidels. Besides, it gave us all time to work out the best methods of disseminating Jes's message. If he totally blew it, only a few people would be impacted. It also gave the disciples time to learn as well.

Chapter 5 Spreading the Word of Jehosa

We traveled on foot, leading several donkeys, which carried our meager gear and sometimes the babies when they became too heavy to carry. Wintertime in the Arad brought comfortable nights and cooler days, a welcome relief from the hot, dry heat of the summer. Our pattern was a simple one. As we neared a town, Missa and Jackal would go in ahead of us and scout the village looking for any possible trouble, such as the presence of infidels or their tax collectors. If all was well, Missa would return and our large party would then enter the village. Otherwise, both would return, and we would either wait it out or bypass this particular village.

Our path through the Arad was generally around its outer regions because the larger towns were more centrally concentrated. Besides, the great infidel paved road ran straight up the middle of Juda Arad. Along this road lay the largest concentrations of the infidels. Few ever visited the more remote villages, save the tax collectors and roving soldier bands. We had to avoid any possible direct confrontation with the infidels, because Juda Arad was a powder key lacking only a spark. Everyone believed without question that the Great Messiah would soon lead a rebellion and drive the infidels from the Arad, which couldn't be further from the truth of the matter. Freedom did not lay in yet another war.

The preaching of the Great Messiah varied but little from village to village. We women and children stayed well back of the scene, though I, following Jes's orders, stayed sufficiently close to the action so that I could be his monitor. His disciples always were nearby, working the crowds, getting as many to come and hear the words of their Lord, the Son of Jehosa. I say "worked" because villagers were of two mind-sets. One group had come to accept the infidels and their ways. Primarily the merchants and moneychangers, these people discovered that under the Centurion rule they were prospering. Many even had trappings of luxury about their homes. People in this group had to be coaxed and cajoled into hearing the preaching of the Lord. The other camp detested the infidels and anything associated with them. Given any opportunity for success, these people would rise up in open rebellion. They also steadfastly clung onto their religion, believing utterly in the words of the many prophets, especially those of the Great Messiah.

Hence, Jes was faced with a dilemma. Those that eagerly came to hear his words fully expected the signal to rise up and throw off the perceived yoke of oppression. Naturally, they did not want to hear words of peace and spiritual beings. After Jes would carefully discuss their true nature, one would ask, "So when do we rebel?" It was as if his words were never really heard by these people, who were hearing only what they wanted to hear. On the other hand, those who had accepted the infidels now had a vested interest in doing nothing that would damage their lucrative profits. Stuck in their worldly ways, they cared little for ideas that they were not bodies but beings. Rather, they attempted to glean when Jes would launch the supposed rebellion so that they might somehow avoid or profit from it. Hence, they also only heard what they wanted to hear. At times, I felt sorry for Jes. He was offering them truth and salvation, but they did not hear. Hence his orders to me: listen and let me know when I actually do connect with them and get through to them.

Here was where Ismail and Yazi constantly irked me. Seeing that their Lord was not reaching them, one or the other would suggest openly that Jes perform some miracle so that the unbelievers would see the might of their Lord. Naturally, this led the compassionate disciples, such as Jubal, to second the idea, to heal the sick and injured. Even though I pointed out to Jes that Jubal was asking out of compassion for his fellow man and that Ismail and Yazi had ulterior motives that had nothing to do with compassion for the sick, still he would yield and heal those in need. Of course, afterwards, the crowd sang praises to Jehosa and his Son, the Great Messiah. Jes always felt letdown afterwards because still his message had not gotten through.

After the tenth village with the same reaction, Jes called a meeting that night. We were guests of one of the more wealthy moneylenders of the village, who graciously provided us all with our evening meal with plenty of wine. Hence, his position in the village raised a notch. Jes began, "Our task is a good deal more difficult than I thought at first. As Bethany says, I am just not reaching them with my words."

"What does a woman know of these things? Why do you insist on listening to her and not us, your chosen disciples?" carped Yazi.

"Are we not all spiritual beings? A being of Jehosa is neither male nor female. You are looking at fleshly bodies, Yazi," Jes replied.

"I see with my own eyes," Ismail commented, "that you get their full attention when you perform a miracle of healing. Don't you think that you should do more of that?"

"But isn't that rather like having to prove yourself first?" objected Amar the fisherman. "A competent fisherman merely catches his fish. The baker just bakes his bread. He *is* our Lord's only son. Why should he have to prove himself?"

"Have you all noticed that so many are just waiting for our Lord's word to rebel and throw off the infidel's yoke of oppression?" added Rafha. "Perhaps the rebellion may have to come first before you can talk of spiritual matters." Clearly, this messiah still held out some hope of an armed resurrection. I thought that perhaps he was not alone with this idea.

"Would you then have our holy warriors also slay those Arads who have come under the influence of the infidels?" countered Jes, a rather annoyed look on his face. "There are not good beings and evil beings. There are only good beings and beings who are in deep trouble — who harm far more than they help. I say unto you once more, if you cannot create life, then do not be such a rush to take a life."

"Surely you are not suggesting that we preach to the infidels?" Hamah cried, aghast at the very idea.

"If one should care to come and listen, then I will preach to him," Jes commented softly. Quickly, he added, "But I have not come to preach the word of my father, Jehosa, to the infidels. I have come to save our people. Let us concentrate on our flock before we look to our neighbors."

I felt compelled to correct their impressions, "All infidels are not evil. Granted many are, just as there are among us. I've met some of those in Megalos who are far more like us. Take Niccolo Helios, for example. He is a great artist. He invented writing and he cares deeply for mankind. However, I would agree, most of those that are here in the Arad are intent upon suppressing us."

Yazi glared at me, hatred burning in his eyes. "And how do you know all of this, woman? You've never been to Megalos. I know of you and your family in Bethel. You have never been out of the Arad!" I was not about to tell him about my last life! If Jes wanted to back me up, he could.

He said quietly, "I say this only once. Trust in Bethany. Her words are true. Are you suggesting that I ought to begin with a few miracles and then preach?" I kept a sober face, resisting the temptation to smile back at Yazi; that would only serve to infuriate him further.

After more discussion, the Holy Disciples convinced Jes to try first performing a miracle or two before he preached his message. That night after the kids were sleeping and Jes and I were snuggling, he whispered to me, "Don't worry, dearest, one in every five people will get well if I do nothing but pay attention to them. Haven't you noticed that one in five heal just fine even though what you give them is basically nothing? It's merely their confidence in you or your listening to them that allows them to recover. Of course, they think that it is a miracle or that you healed them. I mean I could just chant gibberish around some and they would get well."

I thought for a moment, before replying, "Yes, a few will do just that. Just be careful with this, Jes. I am worried. If word spreads that you heal anyone, I can foresee that eventually they will line up in the hundreds to be cured of every little ill. They may become dependent upon you for what they should be responsible for themselves. Just go see Jes; he'll fix you up. That sort of thing. Now you take on the responsibility for their well-being instead of them."

"So true, so true. I had better be a bit careful. Perhaps I should really only heal those in dire need. I can foresee a day when they line up in long lines for me to touch and heal them. Jeesh. What a task I have set for myself," he sighed.

The next day our path crossed the paved roadway, which led up the middle of the Arad. We chose our crossing point well distant from any village or town to avoid any possibility of running into the infidels. Instead, we ran into the remains of a messiah ambush. We got word of what was ahead from Missa, who ran back to us. "Halt here. Ambush ahead; many dead and dying men. Keep the children back." At once, Jes and the disciples rushed ahead with Missa. I asked Milla to watch mine; I ran after the others.

Once on the scene, what had happened became obvious, if one looked. An infidel supply caravan had been ambushed by a messiah and his men. Fifteen infidel's had perished, likely the entire group. However, a dozen on our side lay dead, and three more had grievous wounds. Both sides had wiped the other side out, except that the leader, the messiah, was nowhere to be seen. The three wounded men displayed hastily rigged bandages. My conclusion was that their leader had done what he could and then left to get some help. I caught up with Jes, as he knelt beside one of the wounded men. All three were unconscious. "What do you think?" Jes asked me.

Carefully, I examined this man. "He is dying. His body functions have already begun shutting down. Probably only a few minutes of life remain. I really can do nothing for him. Had we been here much sooner, I might have been able to staunch the heavy blood flow. As it is, he's lost so much blood that there is nothing I can do. I'll check the others."

Together, we looked over the other two that were still alive. One actually passed away as Jes held his head up. I whispered, "Jes, can you see him, the being? Watch what he does, where he goes." I watched the being rise up out of the dead fleshly form, pause as if getting his bearings, using long unused senses, and then tear off at lightning speed toward the west and the Appian Way.

"Watch over me," Jes commanded. I knew immediately what he meant. Jes intended to follow him. If you look into someone's eyes when they leave the body, you can tell that the being is not there, that you have just a body sitting there. It happened so fast that I did not even get the chance to tell Jes to be careful.

As the other disciples came over, I whispered that Jes was praying and not to disturb him. Hamah, a messiah himself, quickly suggested that we bury the dead. Perfect, this gave the disciples something constructive to do. From the corner of my eyes, I spied the messiahs carefully searching each body, forming a pile of valuables. Others searched through the two supply wagons for anything valuable or useful. Fortunately, many graves did not have to be dug; the original hiding places of the ambushers, shallow pits hollowed out at the side of the road, were filled with the infidel bodies and hastily covered. Graves were properly dug for the fallen Arad men, however.

During this time, I felt a jerk from Jes's body as he returned and connected back up to it. He rose, pale-faced. I knew he had seen what I suspected and had seen happen many years ago. The Arad man had gone to the strange grey creatures, which somehow scrambled his memories before sending him off to get a new infant body. However, seeing Jes rise, Yazi called out, "See Lord, the work of the infidels. Shall we not slay all the infidels first? Here fifteen good Arad men perished before they could hear your freedom words. Is this not a time for action, not words?"

Amar, the fisherman, asked, "Were these three beyond even your miracles?"

"Yes, Amar, their bodies were beyond my ability to save them. I would have to raise them from the dead, a resurrection."

Amar's eyes grew wide, "My Lord, can you do that? Raise the dead?"

He did not answer him directly, saying, "Many things can Jehosa do."

Just as the last man was laid to rest, six riders came galloping up, the leader had returned with help, five women. All had just lost their husbands and had been crying as they rode. While the disciples led them to the newly marked graves so that they could morn their loved ones, the leader came up to Jes, pale and sober faced.

"All praise to Jehosa that you came to help us! I am Messiah Ahmed. Are you not the Great Messiah? I have heard that you were in this area." The man was probably twenty-five with the characteristic long hair and beard that many messiahs sport.

"Yes, I am he. What happened here? My disciples have sorted out the valuables. Please dispense the gold as usual to the nearest village to help pay their taxes. Perhaps divide the rest of the spoils among those who lost their loved ones here today."

"Accursed infidels! Daily they dream up some new trick by which to deceive us. We surprise attacked what we thought was the caravan only to discover the other half of their forces concealed within the supply wagons!" He went on and on about how this disaster was entirely the infidel's fault.

Missa, standing back beside me, whispered, "He chose a really bad location for a surprise ambush. That is more likely the reason for this disaster." Looking around, I could only agree with her.

Ahmed went on, "Lord, see how much we really need your divine guidance. Had you been here, this disaster could have been prevented. How soon will you be leading the rebellion to drive the infidels from the Arad?"

I spied all of the other disciples suddenly paying very close attention to the conversation. Jes replied quietly, "Ahmed, now is not the time. The time is not yet right. Patience, please." Yes, I thought that Jes was very good at giving plausible non-answers to critical questions! The messiahs-turned-disciples also did not like his explanation.

Since there was nothing more that we could do, our party returned to our women and children and led them a mile further north before we crossed the roadway. None of us wanted our children exposed to the bloody remnants of the ambush. Some of the men whispered what had happened to their wives who were curious. In fact, I overheard Jackal and Missa uttering condemnations of the messiah Ahmed for getting his whole group killed except for himself. I knew on a tiny scale that this massacre was what lay in store for any rebellion. I sincerely hoped that I would not become involved in any such rebellion. I am not fond of burying dead bodies, even strangers.

Our subdued group arrived at the next village by midday the following day. Again, I watched the crowds from a distance, as Jes first healed a man with a bum leg. Yes, the whole village heaped praise, thanks, and blessings upon Jes and Jehosa just as expected. All were now enthusiastic. However, once Jes began his preaching, explaining how they were spiritual beings and capable of many miracles themselves, I watched clouds form over their eyes. It is fine to explain to a person who is convinced he is his body that he is a spiritual being, but in fact, that often is far beyond anything that is real for him. He had terrific success when, one on one, he could move a person outside of his head for a short while; that made the experience quite real for the person. However, the spoken word did very little. True, they kept saying, "yes, yes," but I felt that they were being socially polite more than anything else. Nevertheless, they believed him. Perhaps in the end, that is a start — that they *believed* that they might not be just a body. Naturally, I wanted to study the long term effects and see if they changed in anyway, but we always moved on to the next village because to stay in one location too long might allow the infidels to find us.

By March of 585 AH, we had visited all of the outlying towns and villages, spreading the word of Jehosa. The disciples had filled many scrolls with the teachings of Jes as well as documenting the many miracles he performed. Our children were growing up. Ahmad, our eldest, was three and a half and always underfoot exploring the world. His brother, Emil, a year younger, was now walking on his own. Both boys were quite bright, indeed, both beings were seldom in their heads — possibly prime druwid candidates, I thought. Both loved to play with Josh's children, Hadid, now over four years old, naturally dominated the other three. Dominated is a harsh word, more like he came up with the ideas and the others followed him. Their daughter, Ros, was about the same age as Ahmad. Indeed, Milla and I had our hands full looking out for them, as they played hard every evening, when we stopped for the night. More than once, I regretted not having a permanent home for them instead of being constantly moving from place to place. However, because our children were accustomed to being constantly on the move, they adapted readily to what happened later on.

Here in March, Jes allowed us to spend several weeks in this remote village near the border with the Zargarb sector of the Sea Princes, a town called Florintine Junction. I had visited this town perhaps thirty years ago, when my druwid Circle passed through here. However, during that time, much had changed. New buildings replaced old ones and the town had grown. Yet it remained a border town, a crossroad between the two countries — between the two cultures. Here, Jes sought news. Actually, he was awaiting news. Via messengers, he had called for six local prophets and six messiahs from the central towns to visit him here.

One by one, they came and held private talks with Jes. Often, I was allowed to listen in, though from the most distant corner of the room so as not to offend these men. They might not be comfortable discussing these pressing matters with a woman present, Jes presumed. Old traditions die slowly, especially among the Qaam sect who clung to the old ways, long gone. The news was not good, none of it.

Rebellion was now openly discussed even by the common folk, all except the Hessonites, who preached against rebellion and now openly supported the infidels. The Qaam representatives went so far as to give Jes an ultimatum: launch his attacks to drive the infidels out of the Arad now, or they else would. They gave him two weeks to begin or forever hold his peace. Even the Amirites, Jes's own sect, pleaded with him to do something. Infidel atrocities had slowly escalated. In the larger towns, not a day passed without some new harm befalling its citizens, except those in the Hessonite sect, naturally.

What bothered Jes the most were the reports of more and more infidel soldiers arriving in each of the major towns along the paved roadway. During the last year, fewer and fewer infidel supply caravans were attacked, because the infidels finally found a way to move supplies around without being attacked and looted. They simply marched fifty soldiers along with the supply caravan. This was sufficient strength that no messiah dared ambush them. The result was each citizen of the Arad now had to pay their own taxes. Before, the messiahs looted the supply caravans and gave half of the coins to the nearest village to help them cover the oppressive Centurion taxes. Now, those funds had been exhausted and with almost no supply caravans ambushed during the last year, people had to pay from their own meager funds, a great hardship on the poorer of Arad.

That night after we had the children put to bed and led the communal prayer session for the town, Jes met with Josh, Milla and me. He began, "Bethany, you know the real reason the rebellion is almost upon us is those infernal taxes that they are levying against our people. If they had only not taxed us, most wouldn't be talking of rebellion. Their attempts to install their religion of Sol here have only met with limited success; a few Hessonites have forsaken Jehosa for this new god of the infidels, Sol. No, it's those darn taxes that are affecting everyone. I'm running out of time."

Josh added, "No, I think you *have* run out of time. What can we do in two weeks' time? That's all the Qaams have given us."

"We must begin to preach in the larger towns along the infidel's paved roadway," Jes explained. "We must reach more people faster. I can see no other way."

"But surely the infidel soldiers will cause us problems," Milla replied, thinking of our children. "Will we be safe if we visit these larger towns? Should we maybe stay behind somewhere safe?"

"If the rebellion comes, no place will be safe in Juda Arad, not even in the wilderness," I replied. Jes and Josh concurred with my observation.

Jes sighed, "These are desperate times we live in. Desperate measures are called for. The only way I can see to stop this rebellion is for me to die. After all, everyone is convinced that the Great Messiah has come to liberate them. If I am gone, perhaps they will try another way than open war."

I gasped! Die! "But you can't die on me! What about our family, the children? They need a father. All the Arad needs you," I protested. Milla

61

simply gasped, putting her hand over her mouth, staring wild-eyed at Jes.

"Don't panic!" Jes attempted to quiet us down. "Die is a relative term. The Great Messiah needs to die, not necessarily Jes Amir. Besides, you forget the other prophesies: the sons of the Great Messiah shall be kings on Tarra. No, my children and yours, Josh, carry our family's bloodline, which goes back to the original King Amir. No, our children must somehow survive and thrive so that they may inherit their birthright."

"I've given this much thought, Bethany, Milla. If open rebellion comes, as I am now convinced it may, then you must take the children and leave Juda Arad. I've talked in secret to Josh about this. I have his solemn word that, when I ask him, he will forsake all else and devote his life to getting you and the four children out of the Arad, safely to a new land where you can live in peace that they may grow and train and one day proclaim their rightful place as bloodline Kings. You may not know this, but over the years, many of our people have fled the Arad, establishing colonies throughout the Sea Princes and perhaps beyond. If the rebellion comes, Josh is honor bound to get you all safely out of here."

"But what about you?" I fought hard to hold back my tears. His words sounded awfully like he would not be coming with us.

"I will join you, if I am able. Once the Great Messiah has died, I can't be seen here in this land any more. However, there may be other things that I can do to help our people. It is too soon for me to speak further. Trust me, Bethany. I dearly love you and my children. I'll join you if I can. I'll not forsake you unless something vitally important arises. I hold my duties to my people above even that of my family. Thus, the prophets spoke of the Great Messiah. I can't destroy centuries of history, but I'll try to join you if I can."

"If I'm unable to join up with you all, Bethany, promise me that you will personally see that these four children are raised properly — that they are trained to be able to fight for what is right and just, that they are given the wisdom to lead other men, and that they may be honorable and just Kings when they assume their thrones. You, more than any other person I have ever met, can fulfill this request. Promise me that you will do this, Bethany, please."

"Of course, I swear that I'll train all four to be great kings of which you would be proud." Then, I realized Ros was female. Did that mean that she would be a ruler or perhaps a queen instead?

"Come. Let us all four join hands in prayer. Let us spend this time we have together in peace of mind." We did so, and Jes helped Josh and Milla back out of their heads. All four of us joined in a serenity of union. All worries, all cares melted away, leaving a serenity of mind in its place. I needed this; so did the others. In the back of my mind, I still wondered just how Jes could manage to get Josh and Milla out of their heads. I still didn't have the slightest clue how to move a being out of their heads, excepting when their bodies died, of course.

Chapter 6 General Theos Lacerta

General Theos Lacerta reined in his horse atop the last hill of his long journey from the Southlands. Here, he surveyed the beginnings of Juda Arad and the city of Al Barq with the practiced eye of a supreme commander. He watched smoke clouds curling into the hazy blue sky and heard the distant clanking of hammer upon anvil. This seemed to be altogether a peaceful land, but looks are often deceiving. He knew this land was a hotbed of resistance to the expanding empire of Emperor Titus. It had taken him a year of steady persuasion, but at last, he had his marching orders, direct from the High Priest himself, countersigned by Emperor Titus.

He smiled as he imagined his first meeting with Governor Thrax Nicon, the legendary baby killer. Yes, this Governor would always be remembered as the man who ordered all the new born babies in Al Barq slain in the night because of some silly rumor that the Arad's Great Messiah had just been born. "Nicon is a fool," he thought, "but a clever one." For two decades, this Governor had made up excuse after excuse for why this arid wasteland could not be brought under the iron rule of the Centurions — why he needed more of this and that. In fact, the General's own research and tallies finally caught the eye of His Holiness. He had carefully examined the entire supply records for the Arad. Yes, the expenses the Governor needed for running the Arad were well over twenty times that of all the other conquered lands combined! He patted his orders safely tucked into a belt pouch lovingly. The orders were simple and direct. The Governor was relieved of his duties and to be sent back to Megalos to explain. The General had total authority to do what was necessary to get the situation in Juda Arad finally under control.

He had waited long enough on the hill. Behind him, six legions of Centurions marched in step. Precision drilling instilled by this tough General formed these men into the best fighting legions in the entire Centurion army! Behind the neatly arrayed rows of men came two dozen newly built chariots and then the usual supply wagons. Yes, General Lacerta was a man of war, of action, not of politics. He had not the slightest religious temperament, but he put up with the Church of Sol and their aged High Priests solely because they acted when necessary. His twenty-five years also made him one of the youngest Generals in Megalos. Now he had only one remaining goal: to become the Supreme Commander of the Centurion Armies, second only to the Emperor himself. He smiled to himself as he thought, "Fixing this Arad Problem in short order will gain me a further foothold on that promotion." He nudged his horse onwards, heading down this last hill, making for the southern entrance gate.

The city of Al Barq was bustling with activities; Sea Prince ships docked nearly every day bringing in supplies, taking on other supplies, as well as soldiers and armaments. Al Barq had become the northern hub of their empire, everything going north funneled through this city. Perhaps the single good thing that came from the Governor's baby killings was that all remaining Arads fled the city. For the last twenty years or more, Al Barq was occupied solely by the bronzed skinned men from Megalos. Here the Governor lived in the total safety of Al Barq. The general chuckled as he added to himself, "Used to live." His assumption was that Governor Thrax was in fact a coward, which is why he never ventured out of Al Barq. "Well, now things are going to change around here and mighty fast!" His horse neighed as if he understood the General's order.

As he approached the gate, he spied the three gate men. Two were engaged in a card game, while the Sargent dozed idly, leaning his back against the massive wall by the wooden gates. One of the players spied the general riding up toward them. Hastily, he got up and grabbed for his spear, knocking over the beer keg on which their cards were laying, sending the other player sprawling on the ground, which aroused the Sargent. Seeing a general approaching, the Sargent jumped up and tried to remember where he had laid his spear. Not finding it, he decided to stand at attention instead.

Keeping his voice low and extremely angry, as if he had never seen any conduct so utterly disgraceful, he spoke, "What is going on here? You call yourselves guards? Never have I seen such a disgraceful performance. You three are on report. For the next three weeks, you are relieved of all duties, save latrine digging and cleaning. After that, you go out on patrol until you demonstrate you are worthy of being gate men! Now where is the Governor's Mansion?" All three men's faces were beet red. If they could have stared at the ground, they would have. Instead, they strained their bodies to be stiffly at attention, scarcely breathing. The Sargent finally found his voice and gave him the necessary directions. As the general rode past them, he called back, "Report to the Captain, who will arrive here shortly. Have him find three replacements for yourselves."

"Yes, sir!" all three barked. General Lacerta, entirely forgetting these gate men, rode on into the city. Before he even set foot in this land, he had already decided that security and discipline here in the Arad were lacking. They had to be, in order to account for the vast loss of men and equipment here during the last two decades. He was not surprised to find it so. Instead, he was thinking about the approaching meeting with Governor Thrax . "I think that I will have some fun with him before I actually relieve him of his duties," General Lacerta smiled.

Governor Thrax Nicon's Ruling Mansion was impossible to miss. Occupying a square city block, the Mansion Complex was opulent, even by Megalos' standards. Now approaching fifty-five years of age, he had spent his lifetime building up his governing estate with every luxury he could beg, confiscate, import, or invent. His grandiose estate made up for the forlorn state of affairs elsewhere in the Arad. That was his reasoning, at least. General Lacerta reined up before the hitching post at the main entrance. He tied his mount to the imported teakwood rails, estimating that this extravagance must have cost an entire month's pay. He dusted himself off, straightening his otherwise immaculate uniform, patted his pouch with its critical document, and walked up the polished marble walkway to the gilded front doors.

A doorman opened the door in an elegant, regal manner, more befitting the Emperor than a mere Governor. "May I help you, sir?" he said formally.

"General Theos Lacerta to see Governor Thrax Nicon immediately," he said using a brevity of words on this lackey. His eyes caught the subtle motions of the doorman attempting to shut the door, and he countered him by deftly and swiftly stepping inside the opened door, leaving the doorman somewhat taken aback.

"Ah, this way, General. I will find the Governor. I am sure that he is in an important meeting at the moment. Please help yourself," he added as the General had already begun pouring himself some wine he spied as he entered the opulent tapestry-lined waiting room with its mahogany chairs and tables neatly arranged.

As an afterthought, the General added, "I'll give you one minute to present the Governor to me or I will find him myself." Unused to such brash orders, the doorman fumbled with his collar; straightening a nonexistent flaw, he rushed out of the room. It was a bluff; the General knew that if he had to search this entire unfamiliar complex for the Governor, he'd spend a considerable amount of time. He also knew from experience that servants treated in this manner often made haste to carry out the orders.

Several minutes later, a breathless, somewhat overweight, greying Governor Thrax rushed into the room. His hair was wet and his clothes hastily donned. The General deduced that the important meeting was with a bathing area, probably with women in attendance. "Welcome to Al Barq, the northern metropolis of Megalos. I am Governor Thrax Nicon. How may I be of service, General?"

General Lacerta studied this man carefully. Here was the renowned baby killer himself, a pompous ass, he thought to himself. "I hear that you are having some trouble here in Juda Arad — something to do with fanatical hoodlums no doubt."

"Ah yes, these Arads are a most barbarian people, totally uncultured, religious fanatics and lunatics. No respect for law and order, no respect for the Church of Sol! Sol knows how hard I have tried to educate these outcasts of humanity that live here. The fools believe utterly what their prophets preach about the coming of a Great Messiah who will set them free. I've had to deal with such utter nonsense for a quarter of a century now. Still they cling to such silliness. I swear that all the Arads are insane. You cannot even get them to do a competent day's labor without fouling it up some way. Let me give you a word of advice, General," he lowered his voice and leaned toward the general as if telling him something both secret and of immense value. "During your stay here in the Arad, do not ever dole a task out to an Arad. If you do, expect it to be botched."

"You don't say?" the General taunted, playing him along. "How do you ever manage to govern these savages?"

Using greatly exaggerated gestures, Governor Thrax said, "Only with my steel will and constant supervision. Just look at the wonderful taxes we have been collecting all these years. I've got every citizen paying their fair share gold ducats!" This he viewed as his crowning glory.

"Ah, gold ducats, ducats from Megalos. Yes, I've seen the reports and accountings." Here, the General lowered his voice, leaned close to the Governor, and asked, "Tell me, haven't you found it a little strange that even the poorest Arad is paying with our own gold ducats? Where in heaven's name did that man ever get one of our coins, if he is so poor that he only herds sheep?"

General Lacerta spied beads of perspiration trickling down the Governor's forehead. He watched the man squirm like a pig in a pen. "Well, I — I, ah — well, I force them to pay in ducats. Royal edict. Accept no payment, save in ducats. My decree. We don't have to bother weighing local coins to see if they have the requisite gold content. Saves us a ton of money in the long run."

"Ah, I see," General Lacerta pretended to accept this reasoning. He asked, "And how do you account for needing an almost equal amount of ducats from Megalos as you collect in taxes? Are you giving them the coins so that they can turn around and give them back to you?"

The Governor definitely did not like the insinuating attitude of this General. He often made excuses for the brashness and crudity of the soldiers, but this one here was almost disrespectful. I am the Governor, he thought to himself. "We've had a lot of supply caravans attacked en route. If only the powers would send us caravans that are sufficiently protected, we would have no problem at all. Weakly armed supply wagons are easy pickings for all the thieves and outlaws around here. I don't know how many times I've asked for a stronger Rear Guard force. I've even begged Megalos for them. But no, they are sent off to the Sea Princes, though I can understand why. That plague was just awful. I'm sure glad that we did not have it here. You have heard about the plague?" He attempted to change the topic to events some twenty-five years before.

The General tired of playing with this buffoon. "You will have to come up with answers far better than these, ex-Governor." He purposefully said no more, letting his pronouncement sink in to the man's mind.

The pallor evaporated from Thrax's face. It was all he could do to mutter, "Ex?"

"Yes," he ceremoniously and slowly withdrew the document from his pouch at his waist. Smiling, he handed the parchment to the Governor, whose hands began trembling. As he read the brief orders, they shook so badly that he could scarcely read the paper. He looked up at the General completely dumbfounded, speechless.

"You are hereby relieved of your commission. Juda Arad is now under martial law, my control. You are to report at once to the Emperor. See if you can explain all this to him. I warn you, you had better have a far better story for him. You leave for Megalos at dawn tomorrow. I suggest you get to packing pronto."

The Governor stared at the parchment. His worst nightmare just came true; both the Emperor and the High Priest signed the orders! Doom had arrived. He handed the paper back to the General. Without saying a word, he walked out of the room to find his wife. He knew that come dawn tomorrow, the General would send him on his way whether he was packed or not. Come what may, he had accumulated many valuable things that he desired to take back with him — a small fortune in gold and gems. Secretly, he clung to the hope that he might somehow buy his way out of this mess. Emperors and Priests always needed money; money he now had in abundance.

General Lacerta found the doorman, who had eavesdropped on the conversation. "I am now in control of this mansion. Expect my majors to arrive during the next twenty-four hours. Show them in when they arrive. Now direct me to the bath. I have spent days in transit and wish to wash the dust off." Quickly adjusting to the change in management, the doorman escorted the general to the elegant bath.

The huge room was tiled from floor to ceiling in blue tiles, trimmed in gold fillet. The bath proper was white marble. The water, scented and warm. Quickly, the General took off his trail stained clothes and slowly slipped into the water up to his neck. It had been years since he had had this kind of luxurious bath! About a half hour later, an older woman, though still beautiful, entered and walked over to him. "I just wanted to personally thank you, General. You have made my life-long wish come true at last. Ever since Thrax brought me to this heathen land, I have longed, yearned, and begged to return to Megalos. I even thought of leaving him, but that would be too unseemly. Tomorrow morning my wish comes true, and I just wanted to personally thank you!" She leaned over, kissed his forehead, rose, and left.

The General never said a word. "How ironic," he whispered to himself after she left. "Things are about to change in this so-called heathen land, starting tomorrow. Just now, I am due for a long, relaxing, well-deserved bath."

The next morning the ex-governor and his wife left without ceremony, even before the General rose. Humiliated once, Thrax quietly left Al Barq very early; only the gate men saw him leave, driving a heavily laden wagon. No one suspected the vast wealth Thrax was taking back to Megalos. He felt certain that he had sufficient funds to make any "problems" with either the Emperor or the High Priest evaporate.

The mansion staff had breakfast waiting for the General, who was quite unaccustomed to this kind of service. "There will be six more for breakfast. Is there a conference room in this complex?"

"Would the General like a guided tour of the mansion?" the butler inquired formally. Still munching on breakfast rolls, General Lacerta got his first expansive look at the opulent lifestyle of the ex-governor. Staking out a large stately room for his staff meetings, he ordered the rest of breakfast to be served here and drew open the shades on the south side, which opened onto a central courtyard. Around the other three walls, enormous tapestries that depicted scenes from the history of Megalos covered the magnificent mahogany paneled walls. Beautifully carved oaken furniture complimented the wall hangings. The general arranged the chairs so that he sat at the head as fitting his position.

Within an hour, his six majors arrived. Three had traveled here with him, and he knew and trusted them. The other three were in charge of the Rear Guard Legions stationed here in Juda Arad. Once they had assembled and the formal introductions handled, General Lacerta spoke, "Gentlemen, the first thing I must know is this: what precisely is the military situation in the Arad? I warn you, I want the facts as they really are, not as the ex-Governor might have wanted them. Should I find out otherwise, you will be shipped back to Megalos as well. Things are about to change here, that I promise you. So let's have it."

The ,ajor in charge of Al Barq trading spoke first. Essentially, the local Megalos workers, the shipping contracts, and the security of this city were his responsibility. He commanded only one legion of Centurions, mostly those who were over thirty years old. His report was the only encouraging one of the day. As far as this city went, all was on target and safe, but that was because Al Barq was now just another Centurion city. No Arads lived here any longer.

The reports given by the other two majors were scathing. Both saw this as their first chance to reveal the military truth of the situation, which the ex-Governor had forced them to hide for two decades. On the average, counting all major towns and cities along the paved road, which stretched from Al Barq here in the south all the way to the northern border, ten supply caravans attempted to travel between locations. Of these, at least five would be ambushed and four would be a complete loss. He explained how the ex-Governor continually hid these staggering losses. General Lacerta insisted on a thorough explanation of the tactics being used by these rebels, and the majors were very willing to comply.

The tale was repeated over and over. A caravan would be walking along the road, when suddenly arrows came raining down from a nearby hilltop. From concealed pits dug beside the roadway, rebels sprang at their rear, while the men's attention was on dodging the hail of arrows. "Okay, gentlemen, here is my first order of the day," General Lacerta took command. "From now on, when a supply caravan is ready to depart, thirty of my men will march just out in front of the caravan with another thirty trailing behind. Let's see these rebels take out sixty of my highly trained assault troops!" His majors smiled, but the other two breathed a sigh of relief. Long had they argued with the ex-Governor, who listened to their suggestions, but never did anything about them.

One said, "You do not know how wonderful that sounds to my ears! We've been under political leadership for a quarter of a century. I've had to send countless men to their deaths because of the governor's refusal to follow my suggestions!"

"Now then, who are these rebels anyway? Where do they come from? And what is this Great Messiah person anyway?" the general asked.

"Before the Arads left here long ago, you know, after that mess with killing the babies, I used to chat with one of their prophets," the Supply Major spoke up. "As I understand it, for at least a century, all their prophets predict that one day the Great Messiah, son of their God, will be born. He will lead them to freedom, driving us out of their land. I believe Governor Thrax was terrified of that happening. What is really weird, Sir, is that the common people *actually* believe *utterly* this prediction."

"And you think that this Great Messiah fellow has already been born?" the General queried.

"Yes, Sir. Everyone I have come in contact with since the night of the baby killings swears by it."

"Did the Governor take any steps to find this Great Messiah and remove him?"

"No Sir, he never found out anything. When the Arads abandoned Al Barq, he sort of dropped it."

"Okay, then the Second Order of the Day is this: find out who this Great Messiah is, where he lives, what town. Then, arrest him."

"But how?" asked a befuddled Major.

"Look, I know that you all prefer a straight fight to all this subterfuge and political posturing, but we have to find this supposed savior of theirs and take him out of the political picture, so to speak. I guess the starting place is to find where he was born, find his parents. He must have had parents. Someone must have raised him. Someone must know what we need to know. Surely not all the Arads are totally against us, are they?"

"No Sir. Many of the merchants, moneychangers, and even tax collectors are Arads, who say they belong to the Hessonites sect. For a price, I think we may get some to speak."

"Great! Third Order of the Day: I want signs posted in all major towns and cities offering a reward of one thousand gold ducats for information that leads us to this Great Messiah. I've never seen any situation in which money did not speak louder than religious beliefs. See to it."

"Yes Sir!"

"Now let us prepare to march in two days' time. I want my legions to have a few days to relax from their long journey from the Southlands. We will march our forces down the length of the road. I want to see the territory firsthand. Make a strong show of force. Major, in addition to your supply duties, I am giving you command to oversee all of the tax collectors. Make sure that they are not skimming funds off the top. Behead any that do. No, belay that. Crucify any that do. Nail them to a cross out in full view of the public. Let's make a public statement that crime will be punished no matter who commits it."

"Yes Sir!"

"Now, major, how about giving me a tour of the city, while the others see to the implementation of the Orders of the Day?" Thus, General Lacerta took immediate charge of affairs in Juda Arad.

All told, the general spent two months touring the length of central Arad. In fact, the weakness of their northernmost forces troubled him the most. Should the Galts, the nomadic horsemen of the Northern Steppes, decide to attack, the local garrison could easily be overwhelmed. He issued orders that, once these rebellious people had been put in their places, the army would concentrate on fortifying the northern border.

Ten weeks later during his return to the central city of Jerilum, his efforts to find out information on this Great Messiah began to pay off, compliments of Major Markus Slavius. Markus, the youthful leader of the Tenth Assault Legion, had vast ambitions for one so young. He'd joined the Centurions when he was just sixteen and rapidly worked his way up to major. His daring on the practice field was legendary, which he assumed was the reason General Lacerta had chosen him to lead one of his assault legions. Thus, on the long march from Sud in the Southlands to Juda Arad and Al Barq, Major Markus had kept his two hundred men looking sharp, marching in a well-disciplined manner. This had not gone unnoticed by the General upon whom Markus now depended for further advancement.

After posting the monetary rewards for information leading to the capture of the Great Messiah, Markus Slavius had not been content to sit back and wait. On the contrary, he had obtained permission to remain in Jerilum while the rest of the legions marched on up to the northern border and back again. His reasoning was sound: many of the ambushes on their supply caravans happened within fifty miles of this central city. He would take charge and eliminate such. What he did not say was that he would also see if he could find this elusive Great Messiah. Markus was neither a fool nor just a fighter. All Centurion soldiers were trained to do many other skills, as witnessed by the engineering feats of roadway construction. Markus had cross-trained as a merchant. Why? Merchants know how to bargain and obtain the best deals. They have a wide knowledge of where certain items are located or made so that they can make advance deals to sell them. In other words, in these times, a merchant more than any other person knew what was actually going on in an area, the real goings on. You might also call it spying, but Markus did not. He dealt with "information."

The second day after he took control over the Centurion forces in Jerilum, he donned a native robe and head covering, put on native sandals, and stole out of his garrison to mingle as a native in the bustling city. After a week, one fact had made an impression on him — more so than all the others that he had uncovered. These Arads, though devoutly religious, were not all of the same bent. So far, he had determined that there were at least four different sects all vying for favor among the population.

The Qaams were followers of the old ways, insisting upon a slavish, literal interpretation of Jehosa's commandments. Most wore long bushy beards with equally long hair; they did not believe in cutting hair or even shaving. Markus determined that the Qaam sect posed the greatest threat to the Centurion rule. With these people, there could be no compromise. Fortunately, Markus concluded their actual numbers were small. The Hamadanites, by far the largest group population wise, were the traders, merchants, and craftsmen. For these people, as Markus expected, the most important factor was to get along with everyone, otherwise trade would suffer, and thus their purses. Markus decided that the Hamadanites had been the stabilizing force, in Juda Arad, since the Centurions came here.

The Amirites traced their ancestry to that of the legendary King Amal Amir and saw themselves as being the rightful rulers, the rightful caretakers of the religion, in short, just the Rightful. Markus learned that the people attacking their supply caravans were in fact called messiahs. He had no doubt that many of them belonged to this Amirite sect. Putting clues together, he reasoned that because of this ancient tradition, this Great Messiah must belong to the Amirite sect. Yet, Markus took heart in that he learned that the Amirites were often looked upon by the other sects as religious zealots.

It was the last sect that really caught his attention, the Hessonites. Worldly in their outlook, they have accepted their lives on Tarra as what is. They live them to the fullest and are prone to other sins, such as lewdness, thievery, drunkenness, and deceit. They also had the closest relationships with the Centurions, preferring a peaceful co-existence to that of strife. Markus saw that the best line of approach would be to work through the Hessonites, who were plentiful here in Jerilum.

Each of the four sects has their own worship temples. It was not hard for the disguised Markus, pretending to be a Hessonite from the south, to ask for directions to their particular temple. He slipped inside, hood concealing his head so that only his eyes were visible. Markus was not a religious man, though he tacitly believed in Sol. He'd never seen any worldly intervention by Sol or heard of any, for that matter. What concerned him was what was here and now on Tarra. He was sure that Sol would not mind his entering a pagan temple; his goals were pure.

He listened, though he understood little of the Arad language, he managed to begin learning some basic words spoken in the temple. More importantly, he memorized faces of some of the attendees. After a week of this, he made over a dozen possible contacts. He knew better than to approach these people on the street dressed in his Centurion major outfit. Disguised as a local, a disguise that he knew would easily be seen for just that, a disguise, he might not call undue attention to those he met on the street. At least that was his plan.

For a week, he circulated among his "contacts" trying to drum up interest in the monetary reward that had already been posted about the city wearing his major's uniform. However, while they might not be the most religious Arads, still the Hessonites were not outright traitors. None paid any attention to the reward offers. Markus was stalled only for a few days, until he realized that they might be more interested if they talked to him while he was disguised. It would not be so obvious that they were talking with the infidels. Thus, the next week, dressed like a local, he continued to walk the streets. To each of his contacts that he met, he dropped subtle hints that he would pay for information on this Great Messiah.

A week later, it began to pay off. One man took him aside, and while attempting to show him a vase for Markus to purchase, whispered, "One hundred ducats gets you the name of the city where he was raised."

Without the slightest hesitation, Markus said, "Excellent vase. I'll take it." He handed over a pouch with the ducats.

"Bethel," came the whispered reply, followed by, "Jehosa be praised. Thank you for your purchase." Markus walked home carrying the vase.

Over the next few weeks, the information trickled in bit by bit — a word here, a word there. Independently, none connected. Taken as a whole, the picture slowly emerged. The father's name was Amir. Somehow, Markus was not at all surprised by this datum. He was married. Wife's parents were Adid. Travels around a lot. Has children. Sometimes he is home. Particularly when his wife is having a baby. Has two children. Accompanied by ten Holy Disciples. Some are fighters themselves. Trained as a fighter. Supposed to lead a rebellion to drive the infidels out of the Arad. Is preaching not to fight the infidels now. These last two data Markus did not fully grasp. While it seemed to him that this Holy Messiah fellow ought to have the purpose to lead the rebellion, that he was not doing that made no sense to him.

It was early March 585 AH and General Lacerta had just returned to Jerilum, his inspections and familiarization with the central Arad complete. He had drawn careful maps of the roadway, watering holes, and the towns adjoining the system. He had even made notations of the size of each town, which to his mind, dictated the number of soldiers he might have to deploy to defend that town from the rebellion, should it come to blows.

Markus gave the General a day to relax from his journey before he requested a private audience with him. Major Markus Slavius walked into the General's room briskly and stood stiffly at attention. He followed perfect military protocols. Nothing was going to detract from his coup. "At ease, Major," General Lacerta ordered, slightly annoyed at the stiff protocol because that meant that he too had to follow it, and just now, he was not in the mood to do so. For one thing, there was no one else present to impress with it. "You have something to report?"

"No one has taken up your direct offer of a thousand ducats for the capture of this Great Messiah," Major Markus began, watching the effect his words had on his boss. Just when the General's reaction was greatest, he deftly continued. "So I took matters into my own hands. I've spent only a thousand ducats and I believe I have sufficient information on which we may act."

Naturally, the General's reaction was most favorable. He stopped fiddling with his papers and gave the Major his full attention, "Do go on." The

Major carefully explained the details he had uncovered.

"While we do not know precisely where this Great Messiah is located at this moment, we do know where his family resides and where he sometimes returns. The question is what do we do with this information?" Major Markus knew what he would do, but protocol dictated that this was the realm of his boss. Carefully, he gave not the slightest hint of what he would do if he were the General.

If all my majors were as creative as Markus here, why, we could conquer the entire universe in no time, thought General Lacerta. "Excellent, major, splendid! You shall receive my highest commendation for your work. Very well done indeed." He watched the major closely and spied the surge of self-pride rise in the man, just as he intended. He knew that the major was bucking for a promotion, and both knew that this would count heavily in favor of just that. However, what to do about it remained to be decided. General Lacerta paced back and forth, "What to do about this Great Messiah? What to do with this information? Major, that is the real question. It is one thing to meet the enemy upon the open battlefield and quite another the way it is going here. What would you suggest?"

General Lacerta had the major just where he wanted him. Lacerta already knew just what he would be doing, but this was a prime opportunity to test Major Slavius. Did he hold the same opinion, as did the general — that was the critical knowledge that Lacerta needed to know. It would mark the major for certain promotion or for a wanna be.

Markus realized he was being tested — what he said now would make or break his case for promotion. "If I may speak frankly, Sir, until such time as this Great Messiah chooses to meet us on the field of battle, we are doomed to these innumerable and costly small skirmishes of our caravans. Now, we could take a legion of solders to this Bethel place and hang out there waiting for him to return. Of course, the locals will see us and very likely let him know we are there waiting his arrival, and so he would never return to Bethel. On the other hand, suppose that we go there and interrogate these parents. Perhaps we can learn the whereabouts of the Great Messiah from them. I am not above a little *forceful* persuasion. Even if we get nothing out of them, we will have delivered a strong message to this fellow that we are on to him and that it is just a matter of time before we find out where he is at and capture him. I don't think that we should destroy the whole village though; that might just start an avalanche of rebellion."

A cold, alien voice spoke into his mind, *Kill them. Kill all of his family.* For a moment, he was quite startled; he knew it was not his thought, his idea. His eyes darted about the room looking for another presence who could have spoken to him. Seeing no one other than the general who was looking quite pleased with Markus' answer, he dismissed the random thought.

General Lacerta relaxed, his major was worthy of promotion. "Yes, we think alike, major," he acknowledged his junior. It was the least he could do. "We cannot raise the village; that would only incite riots elsewhere. However, we can put pressure on his family; and as you say, even if nothing material comes from it, we still have sent him a powerful message and warning. Take a sufficient force and see to it, major. Use whatever *force* you deem necessary; just don't give us a rebellion in your wake. Where is this Bethel place anyway? It is not on my maps."

Beaming from ear to ear, Major Slavius leaned over the general's maps and pointed out a spot way east of Jerilum near the forbidding mountains. "Somewhere out here, Sir."

"That isolated? Okay, take three squads of cavalry with you. That ought to be sufficient a force, don't you think? Even if you should by accident run into them, you will still have three to one odds. Always, major, attack with at least three to one odds, never less. That way you always win." The major accepted this bit of wisdom.

"Aye, Sir. I'll get the men together and leave today." He saluted and left in a hurry, confident that his star was soon to be his — Assistant General at the very least, maybe even a full general if he managed to run into this messiah and capture him.

Once the major departed, General Lacerta chuckled to himself. "Now we are getting somewhere. Markus proved himself worthy. Now if he just doesn't blow the actual campaign, I'll give him the command of the northern troops. Good, competent help is so hard to find nowadays." He poured himself a glass of wine and sat down to relax.

Two weeks later, Major Slavius reported on his mission. "Sir, mission accomplished. We found both sets of parents as expected. We roughed them up considerably, but none really talked. We burned those two homes to the ground and that did get us some more information from some others in that tiny hamlet. He has a brother that is traveling with him — an older brother, who also is a trained fighter. We missed capturing them by about two months. They were there over the winter. We have now sent a very clear message to this Great Messiah, Sir. Oh yes, his name is Jes Amir."

"Excellent, Assistant General Slavius, excellent!" General Lacerta grinned and waited for the predictable reaction as Markus grasped the meaning of his words. Markus stood even more rigidly at attention; he had succeeded! He had his long sought promotion.

"Thank you Sir!" he said.

"Tomorrow, I'll hold the ceremony. I'm giving you complete command of all northern troops. I really am far more worried about the Galts of the Northern Steppes. They are the real threat here, not these puny Arad religious zealots. With this promotion comes a grave responsibility. I'm putting you directly on the front lines, so to speak. I see you have ridden hard. You are dismissed. Go take a well-deserved bath, Assistant General." Both men saluted, and Major, or rather Assistant General, Slavius marched out, head held proudly.

"Now we are getting somewhere," General Lacerta commented to his room. He often spoke to his room. He found it far safer to talk to than men.

For one thing, the room never talked back, and for another, the room never repeated what he had said to it. "Check, Messiah Jes Amir. Your move."

Chapter 7 Confrontations

The next morning, the serenity of our union last night evaporated. We were resting here in Florintine Junction and gathering information. First, in the early morning Jackal returned from a visit to Jerilum. His report only confirmed what the various prophets had already reported to Jes. A newly arrived General Theos Lacerta, who had declared martial law throughout Juda Arad, had sent the Governor home. He had brought many more Centurions (infidels) along with him and had just finished deploying them throughout the central towns of our land.

This General certainly knew what he was doing, I thought, because he immediately increased the number of guards with the supply caravans. Now it would be nearly impossible for one of them to be successfully ambushed by the smaller messiah forces. This posed a severe problem because now our own people would have to use their own meager funds to pay the annual taxes; before, the messiahs robbed the caravans and gave half the funds to the towns to use to pay its citizen's taxes for them.

Further, if an open rebellion occurred, he had significant forces that could be brought to bear quickly anywhere along the more populated length of central Arad. The half dozen Holy Disciples, who were originally messiahs themselves, quickly pointed this out to Jes. His face told me just how serious he thought this action was. Our rebellion forces would be slaughtered eventually.

We had just finished digesting all these developments, when a young cousin of Jes and Josh rode hard into our camp. His tattered, worn clothing mirrored his grim facial expression and emotion. I knew instantly that something was very wrong. "Thank Jehosa that you left a few of us word on where you were staying. I have some very bad news to you two — and you, Bethany as well."

"Come, Jamur, dismount and have some water. You look like you have been through the mill," Jes said, offering his cousin a water flask.

"Thanks." He immediately took a long drink before speaking further. "Yes, I have been riding hard for a week now to get here as fast as I could. My poor horse is nearly done in, I'm afraid, but I bear really bad news."

"Well, sit down here by our fire and begin at the beginning, Jamur," I said, adding, "By the way, it is good to see you again."

He complied, but he looked utterly exhausted. "Your families, your parents, Jes, Josh, and yours too, Bethany. Your houses." He began crying; the burden he carried was almost too much for his fourteen years of age. Jes laid his hand on Jamur; I could tell he gave his cousin the strength to deal with the tragedy. "The infidels came to Bethel. Somehow, they have found out who you really are and who your parents are. They came into town and stormed into your house, Jes, and yours, Bethany. They beat up both your parents something fierce, demanding them to tell where you are at right now and all sorts of other things about you. Naturally, none said anything. Then, they burned both houses to the ground!"

Jes's face turned white. Josh smashed his fists into the water flask, breaking it and sending water all over the place. As calmly as I could muster, I said, "A house can be rebuilt. How are our parents? What of the other family members?"

"Bethany, you father didn't make it. I think your mom might not either. Your mother died of her beatings, Jes. Your dad was still breathing when I left, but only barely. I think Ilene may have been in your house, Bethany, when they burned it. But Jamal was out tending his sheep and may have been spared. I just don't know. When I saw what happened, I rushed to Josephus; he whispered to me that I should come get you as fast as I could. I left right away. I don't know much more than this. It was awful."

"Curse these damned infidels. We should be slaying every one of them," Josh cried out. A cacophony of similar expletives came from the Holy Disciples as well as vehement calls for revenge, drowning out all other words for several minutes. Quietly, Jes took my hand and pulled me away from the howling throng. Silently we walked around the outer perimeter of Florintine Junction. I felt the welling grief growing in me; I knew Jes had to be struggling as I was. I waited for him to speak first. "I'm sorry that I have brought this ill down upon your house, Bethany. I should have foreseen something like this might be occurring."

"No, you have far greater concerns. My dad always recognized the honor and the danger of being your father-in-law. I doubt that either of our families would have moved into hiding, even if you had asked them to do it. I am glad that you got us away from the others just now. I just cannot deal with my grief while listening to talk of revenge."

"That's the problem, dear. Look what the news of this has done to my Disciples who supposedly know my methods, my teachings. Think of what may occur when others hear of this atrocity? This may be the straw that broke the donkey's back. How am I going to keep our people from open rebellion now?"

"Do not try to reason with an insane man," I counseled, remembering my own fatal mistake a quarter century ago. That brought a smile to his face.

"Dearest, you have, as usual, brought me back into the present time. No, I won't. I promise you that. However, what I am about to ask of you is critical, and I do not ask it lightly." His tone now became serious. I stopped walking and faced him squarely, looking deep into his eyes.

"I want you to take Milla and all our children and even Missa. Go to Bethel and see what can be done. You are a healer; see if any more lives can be saved. I have a premonition that you will not be in time to save the others, but at least see they are given proper burial ceremonies. Make whatever arrangements you deem suitable, for we will never again be returning to Bethel."

That certainly gave a finality to my visit. He continued, "Meanwhile, I will lead the others into Jerilum and see what we can do to prevent open rebellion. It may be beyond my powers to prevent, but I must at least try one last action. So when you finish in Bethel, come to Jerilum in *secret*. We will be staying with the blacksmith friend of Jackal's — I think you were there last life during your journey to Jerilum. In any case, Missa knows the way."

I remembered the place, though not actually how to find it. He went on, "However and this is one huge however, my love, do *not* believe anything that you hear about me. Instead, *pretend* that you do believe it. Because, if I cannot prevent this rebellion, then it is of the *utmost* importance that we and our children somehow safely evacuate Juda Arad. Remember, our children are destined to be the rightful *kings*; they must be protected at all costs. I want you to place all your confidence and trust in Josh. Believe *only* what he tells you, follow his lead without the slightest question. No matter how horrible it all may seem or how awful Josh may outwardly appear, follow him slavishly. *Play along* with the others, but *believe* only Josh. I know the magnitude of what I am asking of you, my love, but honestly, Bethany, there is no other woman or man I have ever known that I could ask this of and have any confidence that it would be followed. I am placing our family's safety and future *completely* in your hands. Will you accept this trust, this responsibility?"

I gave him a hug and kiss before speaking, "Of course I will. Only, don't you go getting yourself killed by trying to reason with an insane man. If you do get yourself killed, realize that I will be forced to educate our kids that their father was a blind fool." I managed to get in a playful tease, which really hid my gnawing, deep-felt fear that this might be the last time I ever saw Jes alive!

"Thank you, my love. Let's head back. When we get back, you see to the purchasing of the horses you'll need and any supplies. You probably ought to pack enough for two to three weeks. I'll talk to Milla and Missa, first, so they can join you. When you get everything together, just quietly leave, without even announcing it. I will have my hands full with the others and I don't want them to know what you are doing until you've actually left. Some of them might want to go with you and I cannot allow that. I need them here with me." I agreed.

As soon as we re-entered the town, I headed off to get a number of quality horses. This would be tricky. Three women and four children, ages five, four, four and three. Hadid, Josh's five year old, probably could ride a short distance by himself, maybe. The others would have to ride in front of us. If his cousin returned with us, then we could seat one child with each of us. That left only the matter of supplies. Hence, I purchased five horses, all stout, trail worthy, but not particularly tall — horses more for smaller men and women. By the time I was leading them back to our little encampment at the eastern edge of town, Missa and Milla were leading the children and Jamur towards me, looking for me. Both women had very solemn looks on their faces. "Don't worry. I'll get us there safely and back again," I said encouragingly. I also knew that I had to take charge, or let Missa do it, though I knew that she preferred to let Jackal issue her orders for her; she did not like being the center of focus. "Okay, Jamur, you go buy us ten water skins. Missa, Milla, you two go get us trail rations for a couple weeks. Don't forget to get at least a couple sacks of grain. We might not find sufficient grass for the horses. I'll stay here and watch the horses and children." I handed them each several coins with which to make the necessary purchases. I knew that Missa would know just what food supplies to acquire, since she had been doing that all her life.

While they were gone, I let the children hold the horses, while I began teaching them some basics about horses. Then I explained, "As you all heard, the grandmothers and grandfathers have been hurt really bad by the infidels. We are going back to Bethel and see if we can help them. Daddy wants us to try to help them if we can."

"But Aunt Bethany," Hadid spoke up worriedly, "won't the bad men hurt us too when we get there?"

"Nope, they won't. I will not allow anyone to hurt you children!"

"But you are not a messiah," he protested. "How can you stop the infidels?"

"No, Hadid, I am not a messiah. I am a true fighter, the likes of which these infidels have never seen. If they so much as try to hurt us, you will be the first ever to see your aunt go into action! That's why Jes has put me in charge; he knows I can protect us all."

"Is mommy a fighter too?"

"No, she is just a really good mommy. I am the wife of the Great Messiah, so I have to be more than just a good mommy."

"You can beat up a *man*?" asked Ros in awe. Clearly, she had never considered this was within the realm of possibilities. Always here the messiahs were men.

"Sure, so can Missa; she's killed many of the infidels. But enough of this talk. First, we must make a long, hard ride to get back to Bethel just as fast as we can. It is not going to be a fun ride as we have been doing. This time we must get there as fast as we can. Your grandparents really need our help." This seemed to satisfy their immediate concerns.

An hour later, supplies packed, we mounted up. I took Emil, my youngest, in front of me. Missa took Ahmad, my eldest, with her. Ros sat in front of her mom, Milla, while Hadid gaily rode with Jamur, who also had to lead the packhorse. "Okay, we ride two abreast. Jamur and I will lead. I have never traveled this route directly, so I am depending on Jamur and Missa to get us to Bethel straightaway, but bypassing towns where the infidels may likely be found. If trouble occurs, let me handle it. If I cannot, Missa will back me up. If we cannot handle it and fail, Jamur, you get the others away to safety somehow. I know that is a tall order, Jamur. Take heart, I doubt very much that I will not be able to handle any confrontations we may run into, I hope."

He looked at me with a rather funny look, so I added, "You've never seen me get angry before have you? Well, let's hope you never see me get angry!" I patted my staff, which was slung across the side of my horse, but I knew that I would not likely be using that weapon. Missa, on the other hand, already had her light crossbow cocked and armed, slung across her back. She could fire a bolt in short order, if need be. After that, I knew she would resort to using her short bow. So here in the middle of March 585 AH, we set out across country bearing nearly due east, heading for Bethel, which lay hundreds of miles ahead of us.

What a miserable week's travel this turned out to be. Imagine trying to ride as fast as possible while carrying a young child perched in front of you, and you'll get the picture. None of the children was used to sitting on a horse for the entire day! Yes, the first few minutes were fun. After that, it was awful. "Mommy, I gotta go pee. Mommy, can we stop now? Mommy, are we there yet? Mommy, how much longer is it? Mommy, I'm hungry. Mommy, I'm scared I'll fall off. Mommy, my legs are hurting. Mommy, my butt is getting sore. Mommy, when can we play?" I began to wonder seriously if daddies ever had the patience to deal with this! I felt rather sorry for poor Jamur; at fourteen, he was getting a major lesson in raising children.

It took us nine days to get to Bethel, much longer than Jamur had taken to get to us. I was actually surprised to see that it was only a few days longer! Yes, we were torn between a dire need for all speed and the need to bring the children along with us. The compromise reached was to ride for a few hours and then stop to let them run about and eat. That cycle was repeated from dawn until nearly dark. We always camped out in the open, rather than in a secluded location. That way, we could not be taken by surprise.

When we neared Bethel, Missa suggested that we circled around and entered the town from the northeastern track. This bypassed any possible infidels who might be watching the road that led westward out of Bethel toward the central part of the Arad. This east-west track carried the most traffic to and from the town. It was a very wise decision. We learned later that a squad of Centurions was indeed watching the main road.

Bethel is a small village; coming in from the north down the main street, we could see the burned out ruins of our two homes. I felt more than a bit sick at my stomach — queasy actually. I suspected Milla was too. "What happened to grandpa's house?" asked Hadid.

Milla answered, "The infidels burned it to the ground."

"Why did they burn it down?"

"Because grandpa refused to tell them where your father is."

"Why did he not tell them?"

"Because if he told them, the infidels would come and kill your father and us as well. Grandpa died trying to save us from the infidels."

We dismounted in the street and looked first to the right and then the left; both houses were crumbling shells. Jagged walls, three feet tall to six feet, outlined the location where the homes once stood. Ezir, the elderly neighbor of the Amirs, and his wife came rushing out of their house to greet us. Within minutes, the village turned out to see us and watch our reactions. Most took note that neither Jes nor Josh was with us. Ezir came up to us and said, "T'is a sad day. After the infidels left, we took them all into our home. I'm afraid we are not the healers you are. One by one, each died from their injuries. We've buried the five of them together along with your brother's wife. Let the children go with the misses and I'll show you."

She beckoned to the kids, who needed no further encouragement to go run and play. "Thank you, Ezir, thank you," I replied holding back my grief as much as possible. Milla was doing better at it than I, actually. We walked a short distance to just outside the village. There, five freshly dug graves were clearly visible. Ezir had clearly marked each grave with a wooden plaque with the name carved in to the wood.

"Your parents — they were beat up pretty badly. I'm sure they all had broken ribs because their sides were all caved in, and they heaved up plenty of blood." Slowly, he related the sad news. Thirty-some infidels rode into town, asked directions to the Amir and Adid residences. They split into two groups and dragged the four adults out into the street. They kept asking where we were and similar things. When they refused to answer, they began beating and punching the women, believing that would make the men more likely to talk. When that failed and the women fell unconscious, they did the same to the men. Still they got nothing from any of us here. In disgust or malice, they then set fire to the two homes. They did not know that Ilene was still hiding inside. By the time that she shrieked in terror, the home was a raging inferno, and no one could rescue her even if the infidels would have let them. My younger brother's wife tried to rescue Ilene and perished in the blaze too. Satisfied the homes would be destroyed, they then mounted up and left.

Ezir had gotten others to help carry the four into his home and several others all tried to help save their lives, to no avail. Jamal, my younger brother, had been miles out of town tending his ever-growing flock of sheep when this happened. Thus, he had been spared. Ezir sent word to Jamal and told him not to come into Bethel, fearing the infidels were still near at hand. However, a couple days later, he snuck into town late at night and got to say his farewells. Ezir said. "Something changed in him that night when he said goodbye to his young wife. He's different now. He left word that as soon as you get here, he wants to meet with you, Bethany Madelyn. Shall I send word to him tonight?"

"Please do. How can we ever thank you for watching over our parents?" I asked.

"You already have done so, child. Just think of all the folks around here that you have healed while you lived here. Golly, just about everyone was helped at some time or other. I just hope Jes can put an end to these infernal infidels. There is not an ounce of human decency in any of them!" he declared. Now, I couldn't but agree, at least around here anyway.

"Oh, I nearly forgot, Bethany. Your father's last words to me were, 'Tell Bethany, remember funds.' I don't know what he means; but I think I got his words straight, he was barely able to speak."

"I know what he means. Thanks." Milla went back to Jes's home and poked around the ruins to see if anything was salvageable. She gathered up some metal items and blacksmith tools. These she gave to the other blacksmiths of Bethel. Meanwhile, I poked around the ruins of my home. Specifically, I searched for dad's secret compartment hidden in the dirt floor. I had to move a bunch of fallen timbers and adobe blocks and other rubble out of the way, but I did find the hidden hole. Inside were five large sacks, each nicely labeled by dad. One was for me, one for Jamal, one for Ilene, one for mom, and one for the town. However, the town's sack now held only a handful of infidel ducats; most had already been used to pay last year's taxes. These I gave to Ezir to give out to those most in need. Good old dad. The other remaining four sacks were nearly equal in size and contents. My intention was to give two to my brother and keep the other two.

I also told Ezir to spread the word that if anyone wanted to salvage anything useful from our home, just go ahead and search. I didn't want anything. I don't think I could really have taken anything, for that matter — not without a total breakdown. Just now, I could not afford to be crying uncontrollably.

That night, after dark, Jamal snuck into town and met me. Ezir graciously let us spend some time alone in his bedroom where we could talk privately. He was changed. Gone was the youthful, laughing face. Stern, somber eyes pierced mine. Then we hugged. Before I could say anything, he began, "Glad you got here so fast. I've reached a decision, sis. I am, or rather I have, joined the Qaam sect. I am moving my flock further up toward the distant mountains near their isolated village. They have accepted me and promised to teach me the old ways. Once I leave here tonight, I will never be coming back. I know you are constantly moving around, but if you ever need to reach me, just contact the village way up there. The Qaam's will know how to reach me. I will be a communal Qaam shepherd now, maybe more."

"But are you sure you want to do this thing? Your wife died an honorable death, I am so sorry for her and for you."

"Yes, the old ways were good enough for our ancestors. They are good enough for me. I cannot take living like this anymore. Death to all the infidels, a slow, torturous death, as drawn out as we can possibly make it, full of as much pain as possible, full of as much torment as we can inflict. Even that is too good for them!"

I would have cursed, but he would not have understood, so I cursed mentally. He was reacting, not thinking. It never occurred to him that possibly it was the old ways that got us into the current mess. "Here, dad wanted you to have this. He kept salting away money and gems for us just in case something like this should happened to him. He asked me to see that all four of us got an equal share. With mom and Ilene gone, we'll split it in half." I handed him his bag and Ilene's.

"Oh my!" he said as he opened his and began estimating its contents. He stopped counting when he got into the thousands. "Bethany, this is just too much for me. I really don't need even half of all this."

"But a rainy day might come and then dad's gift might save the day."

"But he's already helped me build up my flock so that I've got the second largest one around here. This is way too much for my needs. I have no family anymore and no likely prospects. No, you keep some more of it. You and your kids are going to need it much more than I do, sis. Look, you are always traveling. You must have expenses to pay. Besides, it was you that helped dad expand his business so much that he could make all this money. You've earned it. I'll take about half a sack, how's that? You take all the rest. Who knows, we might never see each other again, alive, that is. We might all be dead tomorrow."

"Hold it, Jamal. You are not your body. We are immortal spiritual beings. Only our bodies die, we cannot."

Apathetically, he replied, "Yea, so they say. My body is what is real to me. Guess I'll worry about the rest after it dies." I desperately wanted to do to my brother what Jes had done for his disciples and others, to lay my hands on his head and somehow move him outside so that he could see the truth for himself. Alas, I still had no idea how Jes managed to do this. I let him put back what funds he did not want, until he had an amount that he could accept. "I best be getting out of here soon, sis." We hugged tightly, both suspecting this would be the last time we would see each other.

After he left, I took some time to go outside and walk. In times of stress, I find that if I just walk, eventually the stress, the worry, the loss, leaves me. In a little while, I realized that truly there was nothing further I could do for my brother. He had to walk his own path through life. Withdrawing to the end of the world to herd sheep on the slopes of a forbidding mountain range that marked the end of the habitable world was not my idea of effectively handling the situation. Then, I was not my brother, nor was I his keeper. I had done all that I could for him at this time. Maybe later, I can reach him, I told myself.

The next day, we packed up our things and prepared to head back to rendezvous with our husbands. This time, I decided to hire a wagon to transport the children, our food, and water. When he heard of my plan, Jamur instantly volunteered to drive the wagon for us. I accepted his offer, as long as he accepted payment for his services. After all, he had already spent three weeks or so coming and going on our behalf. Driving a wagon would be even slower, though Jerilum was only half the distance we had come. He agreed to my terms.

Just after lunch, we finally headed out of Bethel. We three women rode our horses, while Jamur drove the wagon loaded with the four children and with the other two horses tied to its rear. Unfortunately, taking a wagon back forced us to follow the main track that led westward from Bethel toward Jerilum eventually. Our speed was slow, but the children sang songs and Jamur told them stories as he directed the wagon team. The sky slowly grew overcast as March slowly ended. During April, we often got our rain sprinkles that helped new crops begin to grow. April is our rainy season, if rain you can call it. The raindrops might come a bit early this year, I thought. Missa and I rode out front, while Milla followed behind, keeping an eye on the children.

We had gone perhaps some five miles, when eleven infidels sprung out onto the roadway. They all had short bows pointed at us. Missa spoke a curse and spat on the ground as she reached for her bow. I cautioned her not to reach for it, but instead to slowly fall back and protect our rear where Milla was. I dismounted, letting my horse drift back toward the wagon and the others behind me. Missa, used to attacking from the safety of a hilltop, readily complied with my orders.

The Centurions formed into two rows of five, with their leader out in front of them. They were about two hundred feet from us, slowly walking our way. I had to stall. *Concentrate, Bethany.* "You would shoot unarmed women and children?" I called out. Suddenly, mental pictures flooded into my mind. I was in a wagon with Ellen and my family. We were moving from Uru to Karka. It was pouring down rain. Then without warning, the king's cavalry began attacking us, attempting to kill all of us including Ellen. Images of me going berserk, calling down lightning bolts swamped my mind so strongly that I only barely heard his reply.

"We have orders to kill the Great Messiah and all his family. Are you not they? Of course you are. We aren't sure which of you is his wife, so we'll kill everyone. Ready. Load."

Before he could say fire, I interrupted him. So strong was my intention that his final command word could not be uttered. "If you do this, it will fail. I will not hesitate to kill every one of you. Civilized human beings do not wantonly kill women and children. If you fire, you show me you are not human. Your choice."

Behind me, I barely heard the wailing and crying of the frightened children. "Mommy what's happening? Don't let them hurt us? Are these the bad men that killed grandpa and grandma? Why do they want to hurt us?" Poor Missa and Milla, they valiantly tried to respond to the children, forcing them down behind the sacks of food and gear, knowing at any moment a hail of arrows would likely pierce everyone.

For an instant, I looked deep into their leader's mind. I realized that here was a totally beaten man, operating completely on orders from above. He had repressed his own personality, his own self almost completely, hiding in some dark shadowy place in his mind. I was talking to a mechanical robot, really. I heard him finally say "Fire!" As the twangs broke the stillness, I became a whirlwind of action; my many hours of practice paid off. In a blaze of action, I knocked down or deflected nine of the ten arrows and landing on my feet, I solemnly caught the tenth with my left hand just before it would have hit my head.

"So be it," I said. I had already made my connection. True, I was very slow in making the connection to the black energy storm clouds. After all, it had been over a quarter of a century since I had last brought down a bolt of lightning. A skill well learned is always there. The first bolt shattered the leader's head, knocking the body far off the road. The deafening peal of thunder that struck shortly thereafter was music to my ears, though it scared the living daylights out of absolutely everyone else present. Boom. Boom. Boom. Nine more times it came before the last sound echoed off in the distance, bouncing back from the tall cliff of a mesa. Then, dead silence. I could not hear much of anything for some time.

The horses spooked but I rapidly entered their minds sending images of a quiet pasture full of grass. Missa rapidly got them under control after that. I mounted up and signaled the others to move out. We rode up to the scene of the slaughter and then on past it. I glanced behind to see how the children were taking all this. Their faces were absolutely white — pale beyond description. Thankfully, they said nothing, but their eyes took in everything — every vivid detail. Only Missa, who had seen me do this once before in another lifetime, seemed to recover rapidly. Still, even she was pale and very quiet. If she still had any doubts that I was the Bethany that she had known, they were completely dispelled.

When we were a couple miles away from the carnage, I halted. My hearing had finally returned. I figured we were safe. As I rode up to the wagon, I called out in jest, "*Never* threaten a mother and her children. Never *underestimate* a mother." Jamur looked at me and suddenly burst out laughing. This was the absolute last thing he had expected to hear. It was contagious. Missa and Milla began laughing hysterically as well, and the kids joined in, though not quite understanding the humor.

"All praise to Jehosa!" exclaimed Milla. "I had no idea you could do that. You stopped all ten arrows! Jehosa had to be watching over us. Did you see that freak lightning storm?"

"My doing, Milla. I brought each bolt down from the sky directly onto each one of them. Jehosa had no hand in it, unless he inspired me."

"But, how, but," she fumbled, her reality completely shot. Then, I saw an idea form in her mind even before she uttered it. "If you can kill ten in no time like that, if you are around Jes, you and you alone can protect him. My god! We have to get you back to Jes at once. I had no idea you had this much power. Does he know you do?"

"Yes, he does, though he has never seen me do it. Perhaps that is why he allowed us to go to Bethel; he knew that I would allow no harm to come to us, but won't the other disciples protect him, Milla?" Suddenly, I became afraid. What if something terrible happened while I was away from him, unable to protect him?

"Maybe, but not like this," she replied meekly. "Maybe the ten of them might be able to fight off six of the infidels, but there were ten here. I'm getting a really bad feeling about all this, Bethany."

"I am too, Milla. We had better press on and go as fast as we can."

"I'll go back and search them," Missa volunteered. "Never can tell what useful items we might scavenge. I'll catch up with you in a short while."

"Leave the bodies for the vultures!" declared Milla.

Ahmad tugged at my sleeve, "Mommy, can I learn how to bring down lightning like you do?"

"Me too," put in Emil.

"Me too," added Hadid. "I want to catch arrows like you did! How can you catch them? They came so fast!"

"Me too," squeaked Ros; she didn't want to be left out either. I heard her say, "Besides, she's a girl like me. You are all guys. Maybe this is only something we girls can do." I smiled at her sincerity.

"All of you can learn to catch arrows. It just takes a lot of practice and confidence, but if you want to bring down lightning, you are going to have to spend at least ten years of hard study and practice to make it do your bidding. Catching arrows is much, much easier to do." That seemed to satisfy them all. They began gaily chatting among themselves about catching arrows and casting lightning bolts. Their sudden terror began evaporating, thankfully. Even Jamur joined in with their wild speculations and plans. For this small change, Milla was grateful. She was still quite frightened by the whole episode. Why is it adults take longer to let go of a fright? However, she sensed that something far worse might be happening. Unlike some, Milla did not attempt to suppress her intuitions, but did tend to fret over them. On the other hand, my mind raced with speculations and theories based on what had just happened to us.

An hour later, Missa rode up from the rear. She reported that the lightning strikes had pretty much broken the bows. In any case, no Arad would ever use infidel weapons, so she had broken the arrow shafts, snapped all the short swords in half, and broken off all spear tips. Using her horse, she trampled their three-foot shields, splintering them. On the other hand, she had collected a pile of ducats from the corpses. I suggested that she donate them to the next village to help them pay their taxes. She grinned at me, "Well, I found nothing really useful on any of them, but their ducats will really help a village. Ironic. Jackal and I used to love doing just this!" She smiled, and many fond memories came back to her.

She and I then rode out on front of the wagon, where we could talk without being overheard. "They were waiting for us," I began.

"They knew who we were," Missa interrupted. "How?"

"No one knew we were here until we came yesterday, but then someone may have seen or heard that Jamur had left to tell the Great Messiah what happened here. Still, that would not explain just how they knew we would be coming this way. We came on horseback and only changed to the wagon for the return trip. No, Missa, the only explanation I can conclude is that someone in Bethel must have notified the infidels about us."

"But, but," she turned to stare directly at me, shocked, "that can only mean that one of our own people is working for the infidels. A traitor?"

"Yes, that is the only explanation that fits. Why? Is it so shocking that an Arad should turn on us and their Great Messiah?" I asked. She did not answer, but I could see she was wrestling with this awful revelation. "Look, maybe they picked on one of the Hessonites, threatened him or offered him lots of coins. Perhaps a merchant who would see his profits dry up if war broke out. Is that so farfetched?"

"Well, I guess that I've always been an idealist. I've always believed that all Arads consider them to be the invading infidels who should be driven out. Maybe I've been blind to the real situation here. Now that you voice it, I think you might be right. Many of the Hessonites have seemed very friendly with our enemy. I just ignored that. However, Bethany Madelyn, this puts Jes in grave danger when he enters Jerilum. There are thousands of Hessonites in these larger cities. His life may be in danger even now."

"I know, I think Milla also senses this. It was an eye opener for her to see that these infidels wanted all of us slain — wives and children."

"Yes, it is," Milla replied. She had moved up behind us to talk. "Sorry, but I could not help overhear you two. "Please, don't withhold things from me. I am in this too and my children."

"I didn't want to worry you," I tried to be diplomatic. "You looked pretty scared back there, and I thought you needed some time to recover. You think someone in Bethel gave us away to the infidels?"

"What other explanation could there be?" she answered, though her voice was a bit shaky. "Josh and Jes are very likely in trouble right now. I think that Josh wanted us to come up here thinking it would be safer for us and the children. That only means that they expected even worse when they enter Jerilum, but, Bethany, that is not what has me worried. Can I speak my worst fears? I'll feel better if I can just say it aloud. If you think I am off the mark, let me know."

"Sure thing, please feel free to say anything," I replied, still feeling a bit guilty about leaving her out of our earlier discussion.

"Look, it's obvious to me that even Jes's brother's wife and children are wanted dead as well. If we are not safe in Bethel where we all grew up, why, where else in the entire Arad are we going to be safe? That's what scares me. If we were sold out in Bethel, we would even more readily be betrayed in other places. No place in the Arad would be safe for any of us for any length of time. We are going to be hunted animals, always on the move. How can we continually move around and keep avoiding them? Eventually, we're going to be caught and killed."

"I think that you have gotten it straight. No place here is going to be safe for any length of time," I agreed.

"So what can we do?" asked Missa, "leave?"

"That's what I wanted to ask you, Bethany. You seem to know lots about the wider Tarra. Is there any place we could go where we might be reasonably safe from these infidels?" Milla asked. From her face, I could tell this was really what she wanted to know.

"Yes, I can think of a number of places where we might go to seek sanctuary. When we get to Jes and Josh, I'll speak to them about it."

"We'll both speak to them," she added with emphasis. "I'll not have my children put in danger again if I can do anything about it."

"See, never come between a mother and her children," I playfully added. We all chuckled, easing the tensions. Then, I said, "What we have to decide right away is this: do we continue on the main track to Jerilum with the wagon and risk further encounters with the infidels who may lie before us in waiting or do we try to get there some other way? Compounding this is the urgency I feel for getting to Jes and Josh. I agree with you; I am very afraid something terrible may be happening to them."

"Look, both of you," Missa took charge, "it does no good for us to charge blindly ahead into further ambushes. The prudent thing to do is try a more devious passage that certainly will take longer but holds less danger to us. You all agree?"

"Yes!" we chorused.

"One more thing, Bethany," Missa rubbed her face with both hands and tossed her hair, "this attack on us may well spark massive retaliation, the rebellion. Have you considered this?"

"I've seen just how anxious so many are for Jes to ignite a rebellion, if that is what you mean," I replied, not exactly sure of her point.

"When other messiahs hear that their Great Messiah's wife and children were ambushed by the infidels, then that could provide the spark they need to go to war on *behalf* of the Great Messiah. That is, without his approval, retaliation, that sort of reasoning."

"Is that likely?" Milla asked, but I already knew the answer.

"Yes, I do. This is just the excuse many have been waiting for all along. Jackal and I know many of them and the way they think."

"Well, perhaps we can keep it a secret, only tell Jes and Josh," I suggested.

"No good, Bethany Madelyn," Missa countered flatly. "Look, soon everyone in Bethel will know of the dead infidels along the road. They also know that we passed that way. We did not meet anyone else, have we? Although they would have no idea how we escaped, it is obvious that we were the intended victims. My guess is that within a week, two tops, every messiah in the Arad will know of the attempt on our lives, even if we say nothing."

"So the rebellion is just a couple weeks away? Is that what you are suggesting?" I asked.

"I seldom place wagers, not a gambler as you know. Yet, on this, I would make a bet," she said solemnly, staring right at me. I reflected on her words a moment before replying.

"If we go round about, how soon can we expect to make Jerilum?" I asked the critical question. If we took three weeks to get to Jerilum, total war may have already started, and we would be in the middle of it with no way to protect the children. This bothered Milla and me considerably.

"If we go straight and hope for no further incidents, with the slow wagon, probably eight to ten days. If we go round about, more like twelve to fourteen days. Either way, it will be a close one, but then, we could really push the wagon, swapping horses every so often. We do have two spare ones. I think we can make Jerilum before anything major begins. Know this, both of you.

Jackal and I have spent our entire lives fighting against these infidels. We have pledged ourselves to protecting you. Where you go, we go. We will die before we let the infidels get a hold of you."

"Thanks, Missa." I didn't know what else to say to this dedicated woman. "Let's chance a roundabout way to Jerilum. I got lucky back there with those infidels, primarily because they were slow to act, giving me plenty of time to prepare. I might not be so lucky next time."

Satisfied, Milla fell back to check on the children, and Missa led us off the track, taking the next southern fork or valley between mesas. We rode on in silence. For a time, I weighed the camping options. If we traveled until dark, we would have to risk a night time campfire to cook, alerting many to our whereabouts. In the end, we stopped early while there was still light. Hence, by full dark, the fire was out. We intended to hit the trail at first light, eating breakfast as we traveled. All that day, we saw no one else.

However, the next late afternoon, we came upon a shepherd grazing his flock of some hundred sheep on the only grassy area for miles. As we drew close, he hailed us, "Welcome in the name of Jehosa. You are a long distance from a village and night will come soon. Please spend the night here with me. I've plenty of grass, and there is a water spring behind the mesa. I am called El Dir, the Shepherd." He was an older man, perhaps in his forties. His simple clothing reflected his life. Still, alone out here for months on end, he certainly would enjoy our company for one night.

I introduced ourselves using first names only, saying that we were traveling to Jerilum, but taking our time, showing the children the spenders of the Arad countryside. Quickly, we set up camp and, while we made supper, he showed the children his sheep, letting them pet his wooly creatures. This made the kids' day! I think all children love to pet and play with animals. He even had them help him round them up for the night.

We camped on the sloping backside of his mesa, partway up. Since he would have a difficult time obtaining more food, we insisted that he not share his with us, rather we shared ours with him. El Dir did not ask any personal questions, thankfully. Rather, he just enjoyed our company, especially the children. "The only drawback of herding sheep is that I so seldom get to see my four kids. It seems every time I go home for a visit, why they all have grown six inches! But in another year, my eldest boy will be able to come along with me and help tend our flock. I'm looking forward to it."

Out here under the stars, the infidels seemed a very distant problem indeed. Next morning, as we rode along, Missa brought us back to the reality of our situation. "You know, the next problem we face is: how are we going to actually enter the city gates?"

"What do you mean?" I asked, unsure of what she thinking.

"Well, if the infidels know we were in Bethel and headed to Jerilum by wagon, then they could be waiting for us to try to enter one of the four city gates. As you know, everyone must enter through a gateway and that is a choke point. If they corner us there, we have no room to fight, resist, or flee. We'd be trapped like pigs in a sty. I guess that is the reason for the gates in the first place."

"I see your point. We don't know if word of our travel has actually reached the powers in Jerilum, though. I agree with you, we cannot take that chance. We could abandon the wagon, and let Jamur take it back to Bethel with him. I hesitate to do that; we might need it to escape Jerilum. You have to admit that it sure is a great way to transport the supplies and children, so much better than riding double on horseback, though slower. Say, how about one of us only going in, while the rest of us wait a safe distance away?"

"I have an even better idea, but it means losing the wagon. I know a smelly, but secret way into the town. Jackal and I have had to use it on a number of occasions when we had to make a discrete entrance or exit. We can sneak in through the sewer tunnels and arrive really close to the blacksmith's shop. The sewer grate is really old and decaying; no one wants to fix it, so it should still be in disrepair. Many rats live there; guess the children can handle that. We could sneak in under cover of darkness, being very quiet and using only a little light. The only tricky thing is the exit point. There, we may have to wait patiently until the street is deserted."

"Missa, this is excellent! I can provide a pale blue light that is very focused, plus we can rig up a couple lanterns to cast only a small beam. I like the idea of completely bypassing the entrance gate. It feels far safer to me. I'll go let Milla know about this."

Later while we were relaxing a bit after eating lunch, compliments of Milla, I began to feel very uneasy, almost like a nervous hysteria was creeping up out of my stomach. Milla felt it too, perhaps even stronger. Looking pale with a slight trembling in her hands, she motioned me aside and whispered, "Bethany, I am having an awful premonition. Something bad is happening; I just know it! I'm sick at my stomach. Something terrible is going on with Josh and Jes. How soon are we going to get there?"

"I feel it too, Milla. I don't know," I replied. Relief flooded over her face when she found that she was not alone in sensing it and that I believed her. I motioned Missa over to us, "Something is very wrong with the men. How fast can we get to Jerilum? I think that we need to get there now as fast as we can."

"I'm a little uneasy myself. Let's see," she picked up a stick and began sketching out a map of sorts in the soft, dry dirt. "We are here. I was planning to go this way, bypassing all habitations. If we are willing to risk one small village, we can get to the city by dusk tomorrow. How's that?"

"Let's do it. Perhaps we can go through that village fairly rapidly without stopping," I suggested. For the rest of the day, the panic feeling steadily grew on all three of us. We said nothing to the children or Jamur — no sense in unduly alarming them, especially since we had no idea what the panic concerned exactly. Still, that night, Milla and I found it nearly impossible to sleep. Several times, we got up to stretch, nodding at each other. Comfort in misery, I guess; I knew better than to try to connect telepathically with Jes. He would have his mind fully occupied; a distraction could prove fatal if he was in a fight for his life.

We timed our passage through the village of some five hundred to the first crack of daylight, when few were actually out of bed. Luck was with us, as only a couple men saw us; none gave any sign that they recognized who we were. By the end of the day, as darkness stole over the Arad, we rounded a valley and spied the large city of Jerilum dead ahead. We were now coming towards its eastern gate instead of its northern gate where we would have arrived had we taken the main track from Bethel. The valley we were in ran eastward to the city. About a half mile from the city proper, it met another valley, which ran north-south. Against the eastern wall, carved into the mesa side was the cemetery for Jerilum. Those that could afford an expensive burial site had their remains placed into a small hand-carved crypt in the side of the mesa. Those without the means were placed in rows underground just in front of the mesa. The sewer exit point was near the cemetery. The city execution site was also beside the cemetery.

When the valley opened up at the north-south valley, Missa turned us southward heading toward the cemetery and ultimately the sewer exit. As we passed by the execution site, we could not help noticing that it had very recently been used. The Centurions preferred to use crucifixion as a means of punishment. Seeing an offender dying while publically nailed to a cross put a greater fear of the Centurions into the hearts and minds of the Arad locals — at least that was their stated reasoning. Even in the fading light, we could see a large number of fresh footprints and quite a lot of still wet blood on the three seven-foot tall crosses. It was a garish sight and one that I did not relish explaining to the children, who wondered what all this was and meant. All three of us grew even more nervous and panicky. Could our husbands have been killed here? Were we too late to save them or see them? Were Jes and Josh still alive? You can imagine the horrible thoughts that flashed through our minds!

The sewer exit was located on the side of a dry streambed that ran down the length of this valley. Once we pulled the wagon down into the bed, we had just enough cover to avoid not being seen. Quickly, we dismounted and began to organize our gear. Some we had to carry with us through the sewer; some we could safely leave behind with the horses. Missa explained that we should hobble the horses some distance further south and leave what we could not carry there. Later tonight, she would send some men to fetch the horses and our gear. "It's safe here. No one comes to the cemetery after dark. Too spooky, I think."

Once we were ready, we said goodbye to Jamur, thanking him for all his help. I also gave him a few coins as a special thank you. I knew that a fourteen year old boy could always use a few coins. He was just at that age where he could begin to earn some for himself but was still dependent on his parents, for the most part. He grinned and thanked us. Solemnly, we watched him turn the wagon around and slowly retrace our route. He was ordered to get several miles away from Jerilum before camping for the night. As I watched this brave young man recede into the distance, I got the idea that I would never see him again. Indeed, that turned out to be the case.

Now, with two lanterns and my pale blue light, we pushed aside the rickety grate and went into the stinky tunnel. Of course, the children issued forth a series of euh's and ich's. I had to carry Emil; he was only three. We tied a bit of rope to the other three children and then to me. This way, no matter what happened, the children couldn't be separated from me. Milla with a lantern brought up the rear. I led the children using my blue light spell that I focused with my free hand. Missa, sword drawn, went ahead leading the way. As we began walking half bent-over through the tunnel system, I felt very vulnerable. Tied up as I was, if trouble came, there would be very little I could do about it, save somehow protect the four children. Honestly, I do not recommend leading small children through dark sewer tunnels at night, or any time, for that matter. The only redeeming quality was after a couple minutes, the awful stink deadened all sense of smell and the derogatory comments faded.

Footing was slippery with many small, unidentifiable obstacles underfoot. These we tried to step around. Constantly, we could hear scurrying of many feet just outside the range of our lights. Rats, I was sure. After what seemed an eternity, Missa halted. She was now under the right street grate. Just how she knew her way around this maze I could not guess, save she must have done it many times in the past. "Give me a hand moving this grate aside," she whispered. I sat Emil down and let him hold the globe of blue light. Naturally, that made him the focal point for all four children, who stood beside him, stared, and touched the illusory globe. I knew that when they could talk once more, I would be besieged with "How do you do it? What is it? Can we make one? Can I hold it now? It's my turn."

Together, Missa and I struggled to push the heavy iron grate aside. Our combined strength finally moved it out of the way to one side. I helped her get up and out. She in turn, lowered her hands to help the children up and out. Then I helped Milla up and out. Finally, I struggled to get out. It took the two of them pulling and my jumping to get me out. Quietly, we slid the grate back into place. I lifted up Emil once more and stealthily we followed Missa. True to her word, she led us only a couple blocks to the blacksmith shop. I recognized the building as soon as I saw it. My memories from some twenty-five years before came back to me instantly.

However, as Missa was just about to give the secret knock on the door, she hastily pulled her hand back. Carefully, she let a tiny beam of light flow from her lantern, focusing it on a small marking near the bottom of the door. I distinctly saw a mark that looked like a date tree. She cursed under her breath, whispering to us, "Our safe house has been compromised. That mark is our secret sign not to use this place. Now what do we do? Where have they all gone?"

Panic arose in me again. Here we stood just outside the safe house where we were supposed to meet up with Jes and the others, only to find it was no longer a safe place to be! I had no idea where they might be now. Jerilum held some thirty thousand people! It was huge. "Give me a minute to think. Keep a sharp eye out for anyone coming down the street, will you?" she whispered. I stared ahead while Milla kept watch back the way we had come. The children fidgeted; they were tired, hungry, and more than willing to get safely inside a building to eat and sleep.

Suddenly, I spied a dark form coming down the street toward us. *Observe, Bethany! Don't panic,* I told myself. I spied the form waving its arms. "Missa, someone is coming and is waving at us, I think." I pointed him out. She waved a particular pattern in the air. The form gave that same pattern back.

"It's a friend. Maybe he will have some idea where we are to go," Missa whispered. We all breathed a huge sigh of relief when the form drew close enough for us to see him. It was Jackal himself! Luck was really with us this night.

He whispered, "Thank Jehosa that I found you and that you are all safe. Plenty troubles here. Follow me, new safe house." He said no more. It was entirely too dangerous to speak openly out here in the deserted street. Who knows who is behind what doors spying on us?

Five minutes later, we were led inside a door into an inky black room. Once the door was shut, several lanterns were opened, lighting up the large warehouse. Eyes blinking, I quickly glanced about and saw a number of men and women I had never met, along with Jackal and Josh, who was sitting at a large table across from us. Just as soon as he saw us, he sprang up and rushed over to us, "Thank Jehosa that you are safe! Come. Sit down at the table. Gosh, what is that awful smell?"

Milla gave her husband a warm hug and kiss, "We came in to town through the sewers. We all need a bath fast."

"Where's Jes?" I asked, I did not see him anywhere. To my horror, I spied the Holy Disciple Ismail Saydah tied up in chains against the wall on our left. Gagged too!

Josh did not answer me. "Everyone is out looking for you. I sent some to monitor the four gates, even though they are shut at night, just in case. I have several others out along the track that leads here from Bethel searching for you. I've even sent a couple men that Jackal trusts riding hard to Bethel to find you. Jackal was right, though; he said that he needed to patrol the streets. I guess he knows Missa very well. Come, let's get the children and you washed up and some food in you." He spoke to his eldest, Hadid, "Well, my boy, did you behave and help your mom and aunt?"

"Yes, dad," he replied excitedly. "Aunt Bethany makes blue light in her hands, and she's going to teach me how to bring down lightning bolts from the sky, just like she did to kill all the infidels that attacked us, and she knocked down all their arrows, and . . ." He did not get to finish.

"What?" He looked at me, "Were you attacked? How are my parents?"

"Yes," I replied, wondering how best to tell him the sad news. "They all had died before we ever got to Bethel — your parents, mine and my sister, Ilene. There was nothing we could do, Josh. But where is Jes?"

Josh could avoid my direct question no longer for I literally drilled it into his head this last time. He took hold of both my hands, put his head close to my right ear, and whispered, "Play along with me." Withdrawing, as if he had just given me a welcoming hug, he said aloud, "I've terrible news, Bethany. Ismail betrayed us to the infidels. He sold us out. The infidels raided the safe house and captured Jes. They crucified him two days ago. We sealed his body in a tomb only this morning. At dawn, I will lead you to it." From his eyes, I could tell something was amiss. I remembered Jes's parting words: play along with Josh; trust him implicitly. Jes was dead! Our premonitions were then right on the mark.

I reacted as I would if I had heard Jes, my loving husband, was dead. I wailed, I cried, I protested, I reacted. Missa and Milla tried to comfort me, but then found themselves trying to explain the awful news to Emil and Ahmad, who did not really believe their dad was dead. For a half hour, tears flowed like mad. Then the reality of having four children, who were now full of sewer waste, tremendously tired, and overly hungry, intervened. Thus, we took our attention off our immense grief to deal with these mundane chores of motherhood.

While we were thus occupied, I heard Josh order several men to go fetch the others that were out looking for us. Finally, when the children were fed and put into makeshift beds, we all sat down at the huge table. "What happened to Jes?" I demanded of Josh and the other disciples who had returned.

"I'm sorry, Bethany, but first, it is very, very critical that we know what happened to you. Our safety here may depend upon it. Please forgive me. I must know what happened to you right away. Please." He was begging. I did not know what bearing our tale had on them, but I trusted Josh. I related all that had happened to us. He kept saying, "Not good, not good at all." I wondered what that meant but I think I already knew. None of us was safe anywhere in the Arad any longer. Finally, he told us what had happened here in Jerilum.

Chapter 8 Death and Resurrection

"They are safely off," Jes breathed a great sigh of relief. The women and children were now on their way to check on their parents and thus out of the immediate danger. Josh nodded his complete agreement. "We both know the Arad is about to explode and the main cities are likely to bear the brunt, at least initially." He was talking privately to his brother Josh.

"This sure is a wild scheme you have dreamed up, I will say that," Josh said for the tenth time. "But you know that I'm with you. We have to find a way to save our families. If they were here with us now as we enter the city, I doubt that we could pull this off. With them out of the way temporarily, it just might work. You know that timing is everything? If we flub even slightly, it is your life that is at stake."

"I know, I know," Jes sighed, "but I can see no other way. If only I had more time, I'm sure I could reach our people or at least many of them. Yet, time is the one thing we do not have brother. In the long run, over many years, I can see that this might just work, but now the Great Messiah must die. Josh, I can see part of the future of the Arad. I've always been able to see into the near future, what will be. However, long term, no, I cannot. This way, my message to our people will not die with me; rather it will become perpetuated for all time."

"Jes, I still worry that your message will get scrambled and altered over time, you know that," Josh protested yet one more time. They had argued over this plan for many weeks now. Josh had to voice his concern this one last time before they were irrevocably committed.

"Yes, it may well become perverted, but I am willing to chance it. Come, the disciples are packed. We should be off to Jerilum." The two men joined Jackal and the ten disciples, mounted up and began their fateful ride into the largest city in the Arad. "Jackal, how soon until me make the city?"

"Without the women and children, my Lord, we can make it in five days, if we press hard; seven, if we take it easy. Because it is springtime, we can push the horses. If it was the summer, then no way, heat's too great. So what will it be?" answered the faithful guide and messiah.

"Make it five days. You set the pace, for we are in your hands. Get us there as fast as possible," Jes replied. Jackal nodded and kicked his horse into action, galloping out of Florintine Junction, at the border of the Zargarb sector of the Sea Princes, down the main track that led to the central city, Jerilum.

Jes trusted implicitly this aging veteran messiah. He had to. Water holes between these two locations were scarce and not uniformly placed. One had to time each leg precisely in order not to run out of that precious commodity of life. Jackal had spent his entire adult life charging around the Arad, attacking and harassing the infidels and their supply caravans. No one knew the lay of the land better than this man did. Jes's trust was not misplaced. He sat back and enjoyed the five day ride.

Jes allowed himself time to meditate and examine possible future paths. If he did action A, what would then follow? Carefully and for the tenth time, he traced out the futures that would occur depending upon the outcome of each action he took in Jerilum. Indeed, the only variable, the only wildcard in the entire upcoming events was his wife, Bethany. Her actions, he couldn't safely predict with certainty. She was his wildcard. If she were actually present during all his proposed actions in Jerilum, Bethany could take innumerable alternative actions, many of which would completely sabotage his ultimate plan. He hated having to send her away, especially placing the heavy burden of tending to both of their parents. Yet, he already predicted that they would be dead by the time she arrived in Bethel. Everyone would expect, nay tradition would demand, that he, the Great Messiah, should come to the aid of their parents. Jes was counting on the infidels to believe completely that would be the case. They would not expect him to appear suddenly in Jerilum. *In the end, she will understand*, he told himself. There was only a very slim chance that any dangerous situation would befall the women and children. At least that was his prediction and hope. Little did he know that was not going to be the case. *Besides, even if I am completely wrong about these infidels, Bethany is the sole person in all the Arad that I can count on to rectify my miscalculation. Only she.* This was perhaps the highest compliment Jes could pay to his wife.

Having little else to do, Jes kept an alert eye on his ten disciples. To the last man, enthusiasm reigned, for at long last they were bringing the Great Messiah into the largest city in Juda Arad. With the exceptions of Amar, Jebal and Dez, he could sense bloated pride in the men; they were the chosen ones, and they were about to become very widely known by the masses. Only the three men who came from humble lives did not display this ego. On the contrary, they seemed just a bit uneasy. While the others chatted about the details of where Jes should preach, these three said nothing. Perhaps a bit of trepidation, perhaps a bit of worry or concern radiated from their eyes and minds. Jes knew that these three were quite right in their fears, but he could not acknowledge them because it would likely interrupt his grand plan. *In many ways, these three may hold the future of Jehosa in their written and spoken words. Yes, these three are most likely to spread my true teachings throughout the Arad. The messiahs are more likely to add their own spin to it*, he observed.

However, he had been forced to choose six messiahs to become his Holy Disciples instead of others that might have been better. By choosing six from their numbers, that action had kept many other messiahs from attacking the infidels. Not quite true — it had delayed and slowed their offensive actions, which was what Jes had intended. Still, it had not been enough; rebellion would break out any day now. *If only it holds off just a few more days!*

Five days of hard riding from first twilight until near dark brought them to the western gates of Jerilum near sunset. Because they rode in with the setting sun at their backs, curious eyes within the city could not easily see who they were. The only obstacle would be the gate. Would they be stopped or questioned? Good old Jackal handled this last thorn adeptly. He rode up first, handing the gate man the requisite pile of copper coins, the toll for entering, saying, "Group of merchants from the Junction. Long ride. Glad it is not summer. Evening, sir." The party looked like they could be merchants; they certainly did not look like fighters; thus, the gate man bought the likely story. He was also very hungry, which also may have played a part in their unchallenged entry to Jerilum.

Five minutes later, Jackal gave the secret knock on the blacksmith's side door. Another minute later, the men disappeared into the cavernous warehouse that joined the blacksmith's foundry. Once inside, the arrival of the Great Messiah was announced and suddenly everyone remotely connected to the clandestine operations base from this warehouse insisted on meeting Jes, providing dinner, bathing his feet, and any other actions that would be permitted. Over the long meal, many of the overly proud disciples bragged about the miracles that the Great Messiah had performed around the country. Their stories found very eager ears. Jes sat quietly and patiently while the others talked for hours.

At last, Jes officiated a lengthy ceremony in which he personally blessed each person who had come to meet him. As usual, he also spoke of the path to truth, which the disciples had heard now hundreds of times. When the hour became late and most had left them, Jes took the blacksmith aside for a private word. "Jehosa and I thank you for your gracious and generous hospitality to our cause all these many, many years. I've heard much about it from Jackal." The blacksmith smiled but his eyes dared not meet Jes's.

"Because of your steadfast loyalty, I must ask you to quietly move your family and loved ones from this place. A great evil is about to fall upon this dwelling sometime within the next few days. Jehosa greatly desires that none of this evil should befall either you or your family. For your safety, say nothing of this to anyone. Just quietly take those things you deem valuable and find new quarters a few blocks from here. Say you are moving to more modern quarters, if anyone asks. Will you do this for me and Jehosa?"

"Aye, Lord! Ever am I in the service of Jehosa. If he asks, I will follow. You may count on me, my Lord. No words of this shall pass my lips. Often have I wondered how much danger we were in here, but until now, I could never tell. We will begin moving in the morning. All praise to Jehosa." Seldom had this blacksmith been so animated; he seldom even spoke; he was a private man, but a good blacksmith. Jes breathed a sigh of relief; one down, one to go. His next task was to get Jackal out of the way for a few days.

Later that night, he finally got the old warrior alone for a few minutes; the disciples had gone out in search of a local wine shop to celebrate the coming of the Great Messiah into Jerilum. "Jackal, I have a private, secret mission for you to undertake. It is of the utmost importance and lives hang in the balance." Jackal perked up instantly from his half-sleep; he usually was in bed by this hour. "Tomorrow, I want you and some of your most trusted associates to go to the nearest town south and west of here, one that is on the way to the tiny sea port of Alcaldus. There, rent a couple of wagons and buy supplies for ten people to live on for as many days as it takes to get from here to Alcaldus. Also, get some bedding blankets. A couple of riding horses would be great as well, if you can manage. Bring them to the other side of the mesa on its eastern side so that they cannot be seen by anyone here in Jerilum looking westward. Hide them from prying eyes. Then, return here. Shortly after that, you will be leading a party from here to there in the dark, so remember where you leave them," Jes teased. He knew Jackal would not forget something this important.

"But why, my Lord? Are we taking a trip? I suppose it may take me a couple days to get it all together and in place," he replied rather baffled by such a strange request.

"Breathe not a word of this to anyone one, save Josh. He knows what I have planned. I urge you to take at least three days before you return. For your own sake and that of Missa, please take at least three days," Jes urged.

Jackal frowned, "Aye, three days it is, but I don't understand."

"I know. I don't like having secrets, but in this situation, it is crucial to the survival of ten people at least. If I am right, when you do return, be prepared for a great shock, but do not believe all that you are told. In secret, believe only Josh. Remember, Josh will not be able to talk openly about the events. Play along and trust in me and Jehosa. Can you do this?" Jes held his breath. He calculated that the old warrior could, but he needed confirmation.

"Aye, my Lord. Do you expect Missa and the others to be back here by then?"

"Timing cannot be foretold, but you are right, the wagon is for them. If they are not yet back, no harm will be done. Yet, I feel that they just may. Oh yes, when you do return and finally can see Josh, just say to him, 'Jehosa's will be done.' He will understand that to mean that all is ready to go."

"But where will you be? Or should I not be asking that?" a wry smile crossed his face. He began to sense some intrigue.

Jes returned his smile, "Ah, I will be where I will be. Let's leave it at that for now. In time, all will become clear as the night sky, my friend. Now get some sleep. You've had a rough week getting us here so fast. And thank you, Jackal." He laid his hand on Jackal's shoulder. Then, both men retired for the night.

The next morning, Jes sent his disciples out to scout out likely persons in need of a miracle. He would stick to his successful pattern. As arranged, the disciples would bring the ill and sick to the steps of the church in the nearby square. Jes would heal them and then preach his message to the crowd. Only this time, Jes guessed that the crowd ought to be very large indeed. By now, word should have spread throughout Jerilum — the Great Messiah had finally arrived here. Jes expected throngs of people would gather. If all went well, he would repeat the process at the other churches scattered about the city. The only real question that remained unanswered was just how fast would the infidel leader take to react to this news. Jes was certain that this general fellow would insist on meeting him. Indeed, his plans depended upon a meeting with the one person in command of all the infidels in the Arad.

By ten, Jes stood on the steps of the Church of Jehosa, one of the Amirite sect's, gazing out on perhaps five hundred people. Every available square foot of space held a believer; all had come to see their promised Great Messiah and to hear the message of freedom. Disciple Amar brought a fisherman whose leg had been badly mangled in a boating accident several years ago. It had not healed properly, and the man had moved here to Jerilum to live with his wife's parents. His main livelihood was gone. Jes prayed aloud to Jehosa and laid his hands upon the man's withered leg for several minutes. During that time, utter silence gripped the throng in the square; all stared at the spectacle. Sure enough, when Jes finished, the man got up and walked normally — leg healed. The man thanked him and Jehosa profusely, and the crowd clapped and shouted praises to Jehosa.

Next, Disciple Hamah brought an ill child before the Great Messiah. The child was so weak, that Hamah had to carry him and lay him down on the steps before Jes. Once more, Jes chanted a prayer to Jehosa, laid his hands on the boy's forehead. A few minutes later, all traces of the illness left the young lad, who got up on his own power, thanking Jes, walked back to his mother, who held her arms open welcoming him. Again, the throng cheered and shouted praises to Jehosa. Similarly, Jes healed another two before launching into his message.

"I am the Son of Jehosa. I am an immortal spiritual being, just as you are. I, like you, are residing in one of these fleshly bodies for a time. Jehosa has sent me here to Tarra in this fleshly body to show you the way to return to his realm. Verily I say unto you, even now Jehosa awaits your return to his spiritual realm. This he greatly desires, but you cannot return to his realm in one of these bodies. Worse still, these bodies betray us, convincing us that we are a body, hiding our true nature from ourselves. I say unto you, you are not your body! Follow the Decalogue of Jehosa. Do not give way to the temptations of these fleshly bodies and life here on Tarra. For indeed, what use has an immortal spirit for a body that lives only such a short span of time? None." Here and there, some in the throng nodded agreement, at least on an intellectual level. All listened patiently at first. However, this was not the message that they had hoped to hear, not even remotely. This time, Jes did not need Bethany to tell him that he was not reaching the multitudes.

"Look, the infidels can only harm a fleshly body. They can do nothing to harm you, the spirit. You are immortal and beyond harm by mere infidels! Yet, if you do believe that you are a body, then, yes, the infidels can cause you great damage and suffering almost beyond belief." He continued in this vein for a while longer.

Finally, in desperation or frustration, one Hessonite called out, "So when do we attack and throw off the yoke of the infidels?" As if in one voice, the crowd echoed his sentiments. Jes sensed that most of these people just did not understand his message.

"You want to kill the infidels?"

"Yes!" screamed the throng for nearly a full minute.

"I say unto you, you want to kill an infidel, but would you be willing to experience that yourself, being killed? Of course not. Jehosa says 'How can this be? You would cause something that you yourself would not want to experience? This is the route to slavery; this is not the way of Jehosa! I say unto you, if you cannot give life back to another, do not be so hasty to take life from another. Your salvation lies in regaining the knowledge and certainty of your true nature. Only then can you hope to rejoin Jehosa in his realm!" Jes thought that his message might be getting through to a few. So he continued in this manner a bit longer.

When the crowd did not seem to be accepting this explanation, the Disciples interrupted saying that the Great Messiah had to go to the next church; others were awaiting miracles there and to hear his words. Though there was much grumbling, the throng allowed them to make a reasonable exit. Behind him, Jes heard nearly everyone discussing his words; most comments were not very favorable to him. In fact, many felt betrayed, for their prophets had been telling them a somewhat different tale all these many years.

Thus, it went for the rest of the day. In all, Jes made six appearances and spoke his words to perhaps three thousand of the nearly thirty thousand residents of Jerilum. He had healed some two dozen people, so there was no doubt that he was the true Son of Jehosa. Healing could not be faked. Many personally knew those that he had cured. Still, his true message mostly was ignored; ears desired to hear quite a different message.

Indeed, this was the sole topic over the dinner table that night. Each disciple spoke to Jes of their concerns, their observations of the people who had heard his message that day. Actually, it was more like the disciples laying out their gripes and protests that the infidels were not going to be driven from the Arad. Remember, most had been messiahs before donning a disciple's role. True, everywhere Jes had preached during the last few years, it had been the same way. However, in the smaller villages, the people were not so vocal about their objections, the seeming betrayal of what their prophets had been promising all these years.

Later that night, no one particularly noticed that Ismail ducked out of the safe house for a time.

General Lacerta paced his command headquarters. For an hour now, he had been walking round and round the large room. He always thought and planned better when he was moving. Today, he needed to plan. Word just reached him that the patrol, which his newly appointed Assistant General had left just outside Bethel to capture this Great Messiah, had been mysteriously killed to the last man. Surely, the report could not be believed, he thought. Mangled bodies, burned bodies —none with any combat wounds. How could this be? Some had not a visible mark on their dead bodies. Yet, they were all dead, of that he was certain. What devilry was at play here? Had his enemies devised some new ultimate weapon? Any one of his Centurions was more than a match for these sniveling Arad men. One of his crack soldiers should be able to take out at least three of these opponents at a time. Yet, the entire squad had been slain, and there were no signs of any casualties on the enemy's side. None. Only the tracks of a wagon and a rider left the scene of the carnage. None of the report made any sense. Hence, General Lacerta continued to pace the well-worn path around the room.

Should he sack the man directly in charge of this operation, Assistant General Slavius? This he knew he shouldn't do. Think of the morale of the troops if their new General was sacked so soon. No, he had to find another solution. Sacking Slavius this soon after his appointment, no matter how culpable the man might be, would only make matters even worse. Should he, General Lacerta, intervene? No, he could not do that either, because that would only make Slavius appear foolish or worse in the eyes of his men. "Damn, I wish these infernal Arads would just stand up and fight like men! That, I can handle."

Major Markus Slavius, now Assistant General Markus Slavius after his discovery of the location of the Great Messiah's hometown, paced his own quarters. He had a very big problem, one that threatened his entire career. True, he had gone to Bethel to put pressure on the parents of this Great Messiah. Perhaps he had been a trifle brutal, perhaps, but then he did not get any information from them — stupid barbarians. He knew that what he had done to them would certainly bring the Great Messiah back to his hometown to help his parents and his wife's too. It was reasonable, it was logical. What man would not come to the aid of his parents? Besides, these Arad people had some kind of religious belief that one was supposed to aid their parents. He had counted on that scrap of religious belief when he had taken the actions he did against these people.

He had left his crack squad a few miles outside Bethel. Their orders were simple and not easily confused: ambush, kill this Great Messiah, and all connected to him. No more Great Messiah; no more problems in controlling Juda Arad. The advice that the cold voice planted in his mind had been wise indeed, though he still knew not from where those words had come. Still the plan was simple, effective, requiring minimal efforts on their part. When, however, the squad failed to make their daily report, he had sent a fast cavalry patrol to check up on them. They had just reported on what they had found there just outside Bethel, and this news sent a shock wave through the newly appointed Assistant General. He dreaded having to make this report to his superior, General Lacerta. How could he explain to Lacerta the fact that his crack squad had been eliminated to the last man with no enemy casualties whatsoever? Indeed, the descriptions of the dead only raised more unanswerable questions. None had died from combat wounds. No sword cuts, no axe chops, no blows of any kind were reported. It defied description; it defied any reasonable explanation, any rational explanation, that is. He was left only with wild speculations of the supernatural kind!

As a commander, he knew that the news of this, when it leaked out to the soldiers, would be a complete morale breaker. Receiving casualties but inflicting none is devastating to any troop's morale. This had always been at the center of their attack strategy; no army yet could stand against the mighty Centurions. They had taken all of the Sea Princes in but a year or so by using this very technique. Now, it had come back to haunt them here in the Arad. Somehow, this Great Messiah was using this key military tactic on them! However, the situation was far worse.

Following his instructions, one soldier, dressed as a local Arad, nearly completely covered by a dirty robe effectively hiding his bronzed skin from view, had gone on into Bethel to learn what he could. An hour in the local pub was all that it took. His report was that the Great Messiah hadn't come to Bethel! He sent his wife and children! His spy reported that the women and children had left Bethel by wagon. Now he was faced with the obvious conclusion that his crack squad had attempted to ambush a wagon of women and children, not the Great Messiah! Yet every man was dead, and there was no sign of the women or children. How could this possibly be? It defied all reason! How could he go to Lacerta and tell him that a wagon of women and children had somehow avoided the direct ambush and killed every single Centurion? If he couldn't believe it, how could his superior? No, he had to find a better explanation. Better still, he had to find out what had really happened.

If all this was not enough, the Great Messiah had appeared here in Jerilum this very day! He had been seen briefly at numerous churches about the city, right under the very noses of the Centurions, as if in open defiance of them. Thankfully, he did not have to send word of this to General Lacerta. Every Centurion in the city now knew the Great Messiah was in Jerilum! Word spread like a fire.

Actually, that strange feeling in the pit of General Markus Slavius's stomach was fear, though he would not admit it, even to himself. Fear. If the Great Messiah's prostitute wife — she did have uncommonly long hair and dressed like a local whore — if she could kill an entire squad of Centurions without suffering even a scratch, what then could this Great Messiah actually do? This mere thought triggered the horrible feeling in his stomach, which Markus blamed on the foul dinner he had eaten.

Fear has a way of growing, gnawing at one, especially if it is not recognized for what it is. Markus got no sleep that night. Just as he would doze off, he would awake trembling and sweating, both of which grew steadily throughout the night. Hence, by the wee hours of morning, he was a physical wreck. "Yes, *what* is it?" he bellowed, when someone knocked on his door; the sky was still quite dark.

One of his aides opened the door and peered into his bedroom very hesitantly. "Sir, there is something you should know. I think it is important."

"Well, come on in then. What is so important that you need to wake me up in the middle of the night?" he bellowed. He was angry with himself, yet took it out on his aide.

"Sir, we have just received a message from one of these disciple fellows of this Great Messiah. He says that he will tell us the location where he is staying for one thousand ducats and your word that no harm will come to the disciple."

General Slavius jumped out of bed, forgetting even to grab his robe. *Praise be to Sol!* "Well do it man; see to it at once! Call out the guards, but do it quietly. We need to go about this quietly and not raise the alarm. It won't do to have the chicken flee the coup before we get there. Go man, go!" Quickly, the general began dressing himself, even forgetting to put on a clean shirt. He hastily donned yesterday's garments. Within five minutes, he marched stately and authoritatively to the garrison quarters where his men bunked.

He handpicked two dozen of his most trusted, skilled soldiers for this mission. "Men, we are going on an historical mission this early morning. We are going to capture alive this Great Messiah of theirs." The men cheered, knowing that fame would be their reward. They would be able to tell their children and grandchildren how they helped capture the notorious Great Messiah! While he was issuing his orders, his aide returned. He signaled the general that he had the information. Standing as straight and tall as he could, General Slavius led his men out into the darkened streets of Jerilum.

All was very quiet, save for an occasional dog bark. By the time they reached the blacksmith shop and warehouse, more than one cock began announcing the approaching of dawn. The aide explained that they were housed in the warehouse section, which was accessible only from the inside of the blacksmith shop. The General personally examined the front of the shop and, after walking around to the back, the rear. He decided that the front door could be more easily forced open. He set six men on guard at the rear in case any should attempt to flee, while he took the rest back around to the front.

Two strong men physically forced the door open, and they all charged inside. Finding nothing but total darkness, they began lighting several lanterns and then saw the main doors leading into the warehouse. "Ah ha. Now we have them trapped like rats in a cage. This is the only way in or out. Bust these doors down men!" Eagerly several put their shoulders to the task and the doors gave way.

Startled from their sleep, Jes and the others fumbled to light some lanterns and prepare to meet the intruders, not knowing really what was going on. They had formed somewhat of a defensive line, protecting Jes and Josh, just when the doors gave way and the infidels rushed inside.

For a minute, both sides faced each other, as recognition of the situation registered in the many minds. General Markus spoke commandingly, "Which one of you is the Great Messiah?"

Jes knew that many of his disciples might try to take his place, so he acted quickly before they could martyr themselves on his behalf. Stepping slightly forward, he said, "I am the Great Messiah, Sir. How may I help you this early morning? Do you have need of my healing arts?" *Non-threatening, remember, non-threatening*, he told himself.

"You will come with me for questioning. Bring him men," he ordered.

Instantly, Jes felt the rising reactions of many of his disciples — "Over my dead body!" He reacted faster than they did. "Certainly, I will come with you. I suspect you have many questions for me that I may answer. Holy Disciples, do not be concerned. I'll take Josh with me." Turning to the General he asked, "It is all right with you if I bring my brother along with me?"

"Certainly. Let's go now," he ordered in complete disbelief that taking this Great Messiah could be as easy as this. Yet, his military eyes did not miss the veiled threats that many here felt toward him and his men. He was supremely confident that these barbarians really were not a serious threat to either his men or himself. However, he also knew that if he created an incident here, especially with the involvement of their Great Messiah, that full-scale riots might result. It was one thing to lose a crack squad and quite another to be the catalyst for a riot. Thus, he said politely, "This way please, follow me." He even turned his back to them as a sign of faith.

Jes and Josh fell in behind him, as did the other Centurions, leaving the Holy Disciples and the other men staring in utter disbelief. The infidels had just taken their Great Messiah! Hamah Zagros, himself a former messiah, took charge once the infidels had gone. "How could this happen? How could the infidels know about this safe house?"

"I thought this place was a secret," protested Amar Tarabulus. He was quite confused. "And how come they did not arrest us?"

Rafha Orum declared, "This place was a secret. I know. I've used it before. No, the only way that the infidels could know about it is if someone betrayed us."

Jamal Mazra piped up, "You mean one of us is a traitor?"

"One of us or else one of the others who were here when we arrived. Look, the blacksmith and his family are nowhere to be found," Rafha replied accusatively.

"It's not him," Jebal Dayr said softly, "I overheard the Great Messiah telling him to leave here and take his family with him. I didn't realize this was important until now. Perhaps I ought to have said something to all of you before now. Perhaps it is my fault that our Great Messiah has been taken."

"Nay, it is not your fault," Dez Madan interjected. "What would we have done had we known he had sent the blacksmith away? Nothing. I think that he knew beforehand that something like this was going to occur."

"You mean that the Great Messiah knew he was going to be taken by the infidels?" asked Yazi Rigan incredulously.

"Yes, I certainly do. More importantly, I think that the Great Messiah knew beforehand who was going to betray him. I think that Jes already knows who told the infidels about this safe house. I sure would not want to be in his shoes when he gets back! There will be hell to pay, if you want my opinion," Dez replied, his eyes blazing, which was uncommon for the blacksmith turned

Holy Disciple.

Abu Wadi, the observant ex-messiah, had been studying the faces of the other disciples. Ismail Saysah, the ex-moneychanger, continued to sit against the far corner, distancing himself from the animated others. He looked nervous, not worried, Abu thought, warranting even closer scrutiny. As Dez spoke, Abu noticed Ismail's face grow even whiter. He fidgeted with his robes. Convinced, Abu broke in, "Gentlemen, I think we also know who the traitor was." Naturally, everyone turned to stare at him.

"Well, who? Out with it!" demanded Dez.

"Ismail, you look awfully strange tonight. What have you to say?" Abu grilled the man.

"Honest, I didn't know they'd come and take him, I really didn't!" Ismail protested, defending the guilt written on his face. "They promised not to hurt him."

In a flash, Hamah leaped at Ismail, his strong hands nearly throttling Ismail. "What have you done? Out with it all! Or I swear I will strangle you with my bare hands!"

"They — they — they were offering a thousand ducats just to know where he was staying. Honest, I didn't know they wanted to capture him. They said nothing about that. You must believe me!" Ismail pleaded for his life. His mind was racing. If the Great Messiah already knew that it was he who had betrayed him, why had he not said anything — why had he not taken preventative measures? So far, all was going according to the plan Ismail had devised. Over a year ago, Jes had made it abundantly clear to him that he was not going to lead a rebellion against the infidels as all of the prophets had long foretold. Hence, Ismail considered Jes to be a fake Great Messiah. No, Ismail thought, somewhere around the Arad is the real Great Messiah, and he will come to our aid, delivering us from the infidels. Ismail's plan was simple; get the rebellion started anyway he could. Then, the true Great Messiah would appear, showing Jes to be the imposter. What better way to force the people of Arad to rebel than to have their supposed Great Messiah taken by the infidels. Now if he were actually killed, so much the better; to Ismail, he was just an imposter. None of this, of course, could he tell these other nine Holy Disciples. They believed this imposter. No, he had to stay alive somehow; so pleading ignorance, he put on an effective show. Tears even flowed from his eyes. "Here, here is the money pouch. I figured we could give it to several local villages or even to Jerilum so that they can pay the infernal taxes. You know how hard pressed the local messiahs have been this last year. Our people now face paying this year's taxes from their own funds, not those taken from the infidels. Here, you decide who ought to get this windfall."

Struggling against the choke hold, he managed to thrust the heavy sack into Hamah's stomach. The strong man loosened his grip to catch the sack. "Let him be," Amar interrupted. "It is not for us to judge Ismail — whether for good or ill his actions be. Rather, we ought to decide what we should do next. Obviously, we cannot stay here any longer. It is not a safe house any more.

Should we begin trying to arrange an assault on their barracks to try to free him? Should we try to raise the entire city against the infidels?"

"Yes, yes, we should alert the whole city!" Ismail encouraged, thankful that someone other than himself had mentioned this idea, which was sure to begin the rebellion. What Arad would not insist and demand the immediate release of their Great Messiah. Amar was playing right into his hand.

Bandar Dero, an ex-messiah himself, who had been mostly quiet thus far, spoke up. "Nay, that is the last thing that the Great Messiah, our Lord, would desire. For would not then the rebellion begin? No, I say we keep this to ourselves. Perhaps all they want is to talk to him. Perhaps we should spy on them somehow, find out what is happening. Let's not be the instigators of open rebellion, for that is the complete opposite of our Lord's preaching, his message. Remember, he is trying to save our immortal selves, not the immediate fleshly bodies we occupy. Have we learned nothing from him in all these years?"

"Aye, you are right," conceded Hamah. "We should not jeopardize our Lord's goals. We should not say a word about this to anyone just yet." One by one, the others began agreeing with Bandar. Even Ismail was forced to give his verbal assent; however, this was exactly the opposite of his intentions. He merely began figuring out other ways to spread the news around the city.

One of Jackal's men, who had been sitting quietly near the doorway, spoke up, "First, we need to get you all moved into a new safe house — one that the infidels know nothing about. It is amazing that this place has not been discovered long ago. We have another arranged. If you will bring all your gear and that of the others, I'll lead you to it while there are few prying eyes on the streets." Quickly, they gathered up their things and followed him out into the early morning air. The streets were quiet, and they met only one person emptying out a chamber pot onto the street curb. The new safe house was just a few blocks from the old one.

Once safely in their new quarters, Hamah took charge, "All right, tie the traitor up. We are taking no further chances with Ismail! Bandar, you and I are going to go see what we can find out. The rest of you stay put. Under no circumstances are any of you to leave here, understood?"

The others grumbled, but assented. What else could they do?

Jes and Josh were ushered into the private quarters of Assistant General Slavius. The room was sparsely furnished; the general had no time for fanciness. Indeed, of late, he seldom was here. Besides, his new appointment was leagues away up north by the Galts of the Northern Steppes, a location that offered him the potential for great deeds, fighting real battles with real opponents. Only first, he had to finish the mess he had somehow gotten into here with this Great Messiah. If he did not, his superior, General Lacerta would most certainly sack him, or so Slavius considered. He signaled his orderly to bring them some tea and biscuits. He decided to be civil to his prisoners, at least until he finished questioning them. "Have a seat. Tea will be

106

here shortly." The two brothers took a seat on one side of his small table.

The general waited until the refreshments came, besides he wanted to study his opponents. They seemed harmless enough, maybe even helpful. Finally, he had to begin. "Well, Jes, Great Messiah, we meet at last. You realize that I ought to have you crucified for all that you have done around here."

"And what is it that I have supposedly done, Sir? Only a couple days ago did we get here. I've stolen nothing, attacked no one. We are not what you suppose us to be. We are holy men, not fighters, not revolutionaries. For years, I have wandered the countryside preaching the Holy Word of Jehosa. I have been doing all that I can to prevent others from taking up arms against you," Jes began on the defensive.

"Are you not the Great Messiah of which all of your prophets speak?" he asked in return, fiddling with his tea cup. He spoke in an accusatorial manner, knowing in advance the answer he would receive. He was just setting the barbarian up for the punch.

"Yes, I am the Son of Jehosa of whom they speak," Jes replied.

"Ah ha," the General sprung his trap. "It is common knowledge that this Great Messiah is supposed to free the people of Arad from us, is it not? Why, even I have heard some of your prophets speak these very words. Do you deny it?" He knew he had the barbarian now.

"No Sir, I do not deny my father. However, the prophets and others have misinterpreted the meaning of Jehosa's prophesy. Let me explain. You see, we are all spiritual beings and are currently occupying a fleshly body or perhaps stuck in one might be a better description. My sole goal is to show our people their spiritual nature. If they can regain their spiritual side, why, they would be free from these fleshly bodies and indirectly from your influence. Rising up against you is not the answer; only death and rebirth results, loss all around, and no one gains anything. No one gets free that way. No, fighting you is not the answer, though I will admit, far too many of my people feel otherwise. I have come here to ask your help. How can we work together to prevent an uprising of my people?" Jes had cleverly deflected the main charge against him and had gotten in the very question that he had long wanted to ask. This was the last remaining variable in his overall plan for the redemption of his people. He had to give the infidels one opportunity. He couldn't predict what these outsiders would actually do. Were they really a force of civilization as they claimed or were they just infidels seeking earthly rewards from conquered peoples?

Damn this is hard, thought General Slavius, who hated politics. The man was playing with words. "I ought to just outright kill you," he found himself repeating because he had no other answer.

"You realize what outright slaying of the Great Messiah will cause?" Josh spoke for the first time. "To date, he has committed no crime whatsoever. Thus, if you kill him for no reason, I can guarantee you with total certainty that action will bring Juda Arad into full rebellion against you. Killing him is the one thing you cannot do, unless your goal is to create total war."

Unfortunately, General Slavius knew that he spoke the truth. He knew instinctively killing this man would be the single spark that would ignite widespread rebellion in the Arad. He also knew what that would cost him personally — his newly acquired command. He hesitated, giving Jes an opportunity to interject, "General, just what is it that you really want?" He spoke with such intention that the General could not help but answer, such was the command power of the Great Messiah's voice.

"I just want this to be done so I can go up north and fight the Galts," he muttered, wondering just why he said what he really wanted. How could this man have forced that out of him? It was as if his mind or body was being controlled, forced to answer this man, but it was the truth. "I want whatever happened to my crack squad near Bethel to never happen again."

Jes was prepared for the first statement, but not the second. This was totally unexpected. What was he talking about? He asked for a clarification. The general was quite eager to explain the utter annihilation of his crack squad, at least the meager details that he had been given. Jes pressed him for more information, particularly what the squad was doing there, and who was supposed to be ambushed. Of course, the general would not elaborate; he could not say that he had issued orders for his men to kill Jes or any of his family.

"You are not being honest with me," Jes finally concluded. "However, no matter, you are the one that must live with that on your conscience." He had already guessed the truth and Bethany's role in the ambush. "I am prepared to give you my word to both of your desires. We can end this matter so you can go off to fight the Galts and what happened to your squad shall not happen again. However, we must work together to make this happen."

The extremely nervous general, fighting hard to keep from revealing what he had done against Jes and his family, felt a great relief come over himself. Jes was not pressing him. "What exactly do you mean?" he finally managed to utter.

"As events stand, there is no way out for either of us. Thus far, my preaching has been ineffective at best, though no uprising has yet occurred. However, there is one last action I can attempt in hopes of averting this rebellion. The Great Messiah must die — not me, mind you, only the Great Messiah. My family and I must utterly disappear from Juda Arad. When I am gone, your problem is solved and you can go north. I guarantee you that if this occurs, what happened to your squad will not happen again. On the other hand, if the rebellion comes, the Great Messiah will be forced to lead, and what happened to your squad will occur many times over. I doubt very much that I would be able to prevent such outright slaughter of your squads should a full-scale rebellion break out."

The general grinned as Jes's words sunk in, *So the man is a coward as I initially surmised! He wants to get out of here too, deserting his people. So much for their Great Messiah.* Now, at last, he felt he was on common ground, rather than if he was on the hilltop facing down his groveling opponents. "Just what do you have in mind?" he asked coyly, his strength returning.

Walking briskly back toward the safe house, Josh encountered Hamah and Bandar.

"Are we ever glad to see you, Josh!" exclaimed Bandar. "You are not hurt? Where is our Lord?"

This was the hardest thing Josh had ever had to do; he had to lie to these Holy Disciples and lie effectively or the whole plan was for naught. "He — he — he," he faltered, feigning a great fright, "is to be crucified tomorrow, nailed to a cross and left to die!" Both disciples moaned and cursed in reaction before their anger rose nearly to the breaking point. Josh knew that they would eventually decide to attempt to break Jes out of his imprisonment. This had to be avoided at all costs. "Nay, it is the wishes of the Great Messiah that this shall be! His last words to me were, 'Josh, go now and prepare the way. I shall die before all the Arad and my fleshly body entombed for eternity. Yet I say that three days from thence, I shall arise alive once more, living proof of the power and compassion of Jehosa, that we are all indeed powerful spiritual beings. Tell my Holy Disciples worry not and to prepare a Holy Feast for my resurrection.' Come. We have much to do."

Slowly his words impacted upon their minds. Anger gave way to complete disbelief and then to total amazement. "He, he shall die and then return to life?" asked Hamah not even sure of how to phrase his words. People do not come back to life after they are dead, at least not in this world. This would be the greatest of miracles!

"Yes, my friend, we are about to witness the great power of Jehosa," Josh answered, inwardly rebelling at the lie. "Lead on. Which is the way back to the house? I am not familiar with these streets. Such a large city."

Bandar quickly spoke, "This way, my Lord, we are now in a new safe house. The traitor that gave us away has confessed. Ismail. He sold us out for a thousand ducats! We have him in chains now, awaiting judgment. If the Great Messiah returns, then he shall be the one to pronounce Ismail's doom. This way." The pair led Josh carefully along the side streets, which now were also crowded with people. All three pulled their hoods over their heads in hopes that they would not be recognized as members of the Great Messiah's party.

Josh was relieved to find that their wives and children had not yet returned. Jes had said that Bethany would almost certainly launch a raid to free him from the infidels. Josh now saw the wisdom in sending their families back to Bethel to do for their parents what he and Jes should have done. Carefully, he had to retell the other disciples all that he told Hamah and Bandar; in fact, he had to do it several times before they accepted it.

"The Great Messiah asks you to do one more task for him," he continued putting into play the last of Jes's plan. "He wants you to all go out and mingle amongst our people, telling him of the impending miracle and not to worry, not to take any ill-advised actions. Nothing must mar this greatest of all miracles, nothing!"

Thus, the nine Holy Disciples hastened to follow their Lord's command, rushing from church to church spreading the word. Meanwhile, Josh stayed behind to watch over Ismail who was now visibly trembling in his chains. Not only had his action led directly to the death of his Lord, but also his Lord was returning from the dead and would sit in judgment over his treachery. This was almost more than his mind could handle. He reeked of fear and terror, and Josh had no compassion for him whatsoever.

Meanwhile, Jackal returned bearing an anger Josh had never seen before. On his way here, he had heard the news and was fuming. Josh took him aside where they could not be over heard and spoke with him. A few minutes later, all anger left their guide. "Aye, my Lord, all is prepared as you commanded. Now I see why." From then on, Jackal played along with the game, trusting to the wisdom of the Great Messiah.

"Jackal, I hate to put more burdens on your plate, but I need to have many eyes on the watch for the return of our wives and children. We fear the worst for them. Send out scouts; set watchers everywhere. They must be brought here just as soon as possible."

"I'll see to it, my Lord," the trusted guide volunteered. Josh relaxed; Jackal would be mobile around the city and thus less likely to give away anything. He hated to use his close friend this way, but he had no choice. Everything depended on events coming off as Jes had planned. If only Bethany could be contained before she acted in haste. She remained the sole potential problem.

"Check and mate, Great Messiah," General Lacerta commented once Assistant General Slavius had left. General Slavius had personally reported his capture of the Great Messiah. With his death but hours away, the biggest problem facing Lacerta would be history. Indeed, he sat down to compose the letter back to central command in Megalos praising his newly appointed General Slavius. After all, he had promised the young general that he would report his great success. Lacerta had no qualms validating his young officers, because that reflected ultimately back on himself and his stellar leadership. As a reward, he had ordered Slavius to lead an exploratory expedition into the heart of the Northern Steppes to challenge the annoying Galts. He was to leave just as soon as he had executed the Great Messiah. Lacerta grinned when Slavius had outlined the humiliation he intended to put this Great Messiah through before crucifying him. In chains, he would be marched through the city and out to the graveyard. Thus, all the people would see the just end of their rebellion hopes, and Lacerta could get on with things without further problems.

Later that afternoon, chained and whipped along by two Centurions acting as slave drivers, Jes was forced to march through the streets of Jerilum, a crushed man. Fully a hundred soldiers marched both before and after him with General Slavius leading the way. This huge show of force dissuaded anyone from trying to interfere. It was a wise precaution. With each block, the crowds grew, staring at the spectacle. Many cursed and swore; many wailed; many offered prayers to Jehosa. No one dared offer any resistance to this show of force. Seldom did the infidels parade such a force through the streets of this holy city. An hour passed by before the group finally left the western gate and marched down into the gully, effectively hidden from the view of the city.

Here, General Lacerta ordered his men to take up positions just by the gate to prevent anyone from interfering with the execution. In fact, he sent all the men to garrison duty, telling them that he would personally see to the execution. Only Jes and Slavius remained, standing now beside the three tall crosses where the infidels commonly executed Arad rebels. Slavius unfastened the chains as Josh slipped out from the shadows, placing his strong arms around Jes to support him after his ordeal. Once Jes was freed, Josh stripped Jes of his outer clothes and dressed another dead body with them. With Slavius's aid, he helped him nail the corpse to the cross, making sure that the robe's cowl completely hid the man's face. Once the task was done, Josh slipped a pouch of ducats into Slavius' waiting hands. He hefted it once sensing its weight, smiled, and said, "Now be off. See to it that he holds to his bargain. If he is still around in four days' time, I shall return and finish the job personally." Josh nodded and returned to help Jes to his feet. Together, they made their way further down the riverbed and then over to an empty crypt.

There, Josh had placed food, water, and a fresh set of clothes. "Thank you brother," Jes said weakly. "They really had to beat me in order to make it real to our people."

"Are you going to be alright out here alone?" asked Josh terribly concerned with just leaving his brother out here alone inside a burial crypt.

"Yes, I will be fine. Go help the disciples prepare for my return. Any word about Bethany and Milla?" Jes asked, more worried about their wives than himself.

"None yet. I've got men out searching. Jackal's guess is that, after the ambush, they took to the back roads. Don't worry. We'll find them. Now I got to get back before I am missed. May Jehosa guide us through this." They shook hands and Josh left as the sun was setting. Jes covered up in the blankets to get some much-needed sleep.

General Slavius and his legion of ten squads celebrated his victory over the Great Messiah by drinking as they marched along heading north to the edge of the Arad. In their eyes, they had one of the greatest commanders ever to march out of Megalos. Their spirits were high. Besides, finally after all these years of waiting, they had finally been given the orders to march into the Northern Steppes to tackle the Galts on their home ground. No more of these stinking, occupational patrols suitable only for the Rear Guard units, the older soldiers. Visions of glorious combat victories played in their minds, aided by the wine that they were drinking, compliments of their General.

General Slavius thought, "So what if what I reported as 'the death of the Great Messiah' is only half-true. It has *enough* truth to satisfy the curious. After all, what is truth anyway? As long as this man is gone from the land and no more squad slaughters occur, who cares if the actual man is alive or dead? He is effectively dead now anyway. Problem solved. Only he and I know the truth, and they cannot say anything. I sure as heck won't." He smiled and sang along with his men. The future now looked even brighter than he had imagined. Once more, that cold, alien voice spoke within his mind: *Now go slaughter the Galts; leave none alive.* Shrugging it off as effects of the wine, he marched onward. "Of course, I intend to kill Galts," he commented to himself.

I could scarcely believe my ears. We women and children had been escorted into this new safe house only to hear that Jes had been captured, humiliated, crucified, and entombed! Chaos erupted, as the children and other women began crying, wailing, and cursing. During the commotion, Josh took my hand, pulling me away from the others, who were now all talking at once. Some even spitting on their betrayer, Ismail, who was still chained to the wall. "How could you let this happen?" I shrieked to Josh, my voice full of grief and anger, a wild combination.

Pretending to hold me tight in a comforting manner, he whispered into my ear, "He is alive and well. You must keep up the show. Follow my lead, please." Josh placed all the emphasis he dared on the last word. He could see now why Jes was more than a little concerned about what I might do.

Still holding on to me, he raised his other hand for silence. "I will take her out to his tomb under the cover of the night so she can say her private farewells." Milla and Missa offered to come with me, but I told them I wanted a private time; they understood, tears streaming down their cheeks.

Josh and I walked through the quiet streets; neither of us said a word. I held my breath. Was all this a big hoax? What was going on? Why? How? So many questions flooded my mind, that I took comfort in the quiet walk. Once more, we entered the sewer system, only from a more concealed position that Jackal had shown Josh. Ten minutes later, we emerged back outside nearby where I had led us in only a short while ago. The black crosses now took on an eerie ominousness — people, Jes, had died here. I shuttered. Without any light, we picked and stumbled our way along the dry riverbed, avoiding most of the stones. Josh led me unerringly to the empty crypt. "It's me, Josh," he called out ever so softly. "I've got Bethany with me."

You can imagine the relief when I heard Jes's voice reply, "Come on up and in." Rapidly, I climbed the few steps and entered the dark crypt, which was barely able to hold the two of us. His arms found me and we embraced long and hard.

"Okay, so what the heck is going on?" I finally spoke, more than a little annoyed. Anger, grief, shock — yes, more than a little annoyed. "You've got the others and the children very upset. They think you are dead!"

"You must forgive me this. I would not wish to put either you or the others through this emotional torture, but I had no other choice. My death must be believable or the entire plan will fail. Now it is time for my resurrection. Come. Let's join Josh." While we were walking back to the sewer entrance, Jes explained just a little of what was to come and what my role had to be. "I promise to fully explain everything to all of you, once we are safely out of Jerilum." I began to grasp the basic idea of the effect Jes was attempting to create.

When we arrived back at the safe house, I entered first and played my role as he wished. "Attention everyone. I have the honor to have discovered that our Great Messiah has indeed arisen from the dead. I found his tomb open, unsealed! I give you our Son of Jehosa." I made a sweeping gesture and in stepped Jes. What I found interesting was the yellowish glow around his head. I didn't know that he could create such an effect. Quickly, I grabbed the water basin and oil pot, washed off his feet, and anointed them. Then everyone rushed up to him, especially our children, calling out "Daddy!" I washed off my own feet as well. Walking through the sewer definitely required it!

The impression made upon the Holy Disciples was one of immense awe and respect, aided by this glow about his head. All of them, save the chained Ismail, humbled themselves and kneeled before him. "Arise, my disciples. This is the Holy Night of Resurrection. It is a time to rejoice and feast, for Jehosa has shown you once more that we are all spiritual beings, not fleshly bodies." Hastily, everyone scattered to prepare the celebration meal. Josh had already ordered them to acquire the food and drink, so all that remained was to prepare it.

Meantime, Jes walked over to Ismail, who had betrayed us all. The poor man was nearly hysterical, facing the very man his greed had betrayed to his death. Yet through a miracle above all miracles, the man lived again. Jes unchained Ismail and lifted him to his feet. A hush came over the entire group; all anxiously wondered what Jes would do with this traitor. "I fully understand what you have done." Ismail began to cry, but no words came from his lips. "What I require from you is to hear what you have done. So, Ismail, what have you done to me and the others here?"

Sobbing, the pitiful man described how he had secretly met with the infidels and accepted money in trade for where the safe house was located. I could tell that the man experienced a great deal of relief getting it off his chest. However, I also felt that he was holding something back. You know, when one does that, there is something about his voice tone, his emotional responses, or maybe it is his mannerisms. I sent my suspicions to Jes mentally. Jes followed it up, but I noticed his left eyebrow rose slightly, which I presumed meant that he had not detected it as I had. "Is there more, Ismail?" Jes inquired demandingly.

Hemming and hawing, he finally came out with the fact that he did not believe Jes was the real Great Messiah, primarily because he did not intend to drive the infidels from the Arad. However, the death and resurrection of the Great Messiah now convinced him otherwise.

"Ismail, be it known to all, I do forgive you your sins against me. Will the rest of you give him your forgiveness?" Jes asked. Quickly, I replied that I would, and the others followed suit. I could tell from the smiling expression on his face that Jes was proud that the other Holy Disciples found it within themselves to do so as well. "Then, Ismail, please come and join us at the dinner table. I have only this night to share with you before I must return to Jehosa's realm and work for my father. However, I have much to tell you all. Let us pray and then dine."

We dined on roast lamb with a variety of vegetables topped with a fine wine. Finally, Milla, Missa, and I cleaned up the table so Jes could conduct his business. However, Jes insisted that I sit on his right side and Josh on his left. The other disciples arranged themselves equally on either side of us. "In a while, I will make my final appearance before the people of Jerilum. After that, I will leave you all. I must do my father's bidding." Of course, everyone began protesting.

"Josh and my wife will take my children away to a safe location. I believe that Jackal and Missa will assist them. I will not have what remains of my family subjected to further harm in my absence. It is the least I can do for them." This seemed reasonable to the disciples. Actually, Yazi who still hated me intensely, smiled broadly; he was finally going to be rid of me.

"But you, my devoted, beloved Holy Disciples, my work I leave unfinished in your hands to fulfill. I charge you all to split up, travel Juda Arad and beyond, and spread my teachings to the peoples of Tarra. My death and resurrection should help you convince others that they too are immortal beings and not just bodies. This will be your greatest challenge: to convince others of their spiritual nature. Will you freely accept this challenge?"

One by one, each swore to undertake this mission until death took them. Jes then offered a bit of wisdom, "You have each been keeping a diary of our time together. My advice to you is to fan out to quiet locations in the Arad, and then formally write up my teachings. I urge you to make a copy of it and give it to the Qaams to safeguard along with all the scrolls of the prophets that were done several years ago. In this way, we leave a record for posterity, for the children of our children's children. Once you have done this, travel and preach my words to others. Remember, if you can get our people to realize their true nature, the influence of the infidels will be greatly reduced, if not eliminated."

"I caution you: beware the rebellion. I'm convinced that some of our people will shortly be inciting riots throughout the Arad. If rebellion comes, do not partake of any part of it. For if you do, you will be slain and thus fail me by not spreading my teachings. I know that many of you will greatly desire to aid the rebels, but remember that spreading my teachings is a far, far more important goal. Do not succumb to your emotions; do not go to war."

Next, the disciples asked many questions and Jes answered as best he could. When they had finished, he personally gave each disciple a hug and a personal blessing. At last, he said, "Will someone walk with me to the Amirite Church? There I will make my last appearance here in Juda Arad." Hamah volunteered and together they left. The other disciples followed, intent on witnessing this final appearance of the Great Messiah.

Meanwhile, Josh took me aside and said, "Okay, time to depart while it is still dark. Get everything together as quickly as possible, and we will be off." I had not time to protest. The children were now sleeping, exhausted from the long day and night. However, Josh and Jackal carried the larger boys, while Milla and I carried the younger. Missa carried our many sacks. Once more, we entered the sewer and an hour later, we were walking slowly south down the dry riverbed out of sight of everyone. When Jerilum lay about a mile north of us, Jackal turned due west. At first light, we had slowly walked over the far western band of mesas completely out of sight of the town. Next, we walked on down this valley. By now, we were walking zombies. However, just ahead, I spied a wagon and horses, and knew that we would be stopping soon.

At the church, Jes climbed up onto its roof and stood silently waiting the rising of the sun. Slowly, people began appearing in the early morning, many dumping chamber pots. However, with the sun behind him standing on the roof, Jes was quickly noticed. Dumbfounded, people began to stare up at him. More and more people congregated in the square before the church, talking in hushed voices. Finally, when the square was fully packed, Jes spoke in a booming voice. "I have arisen from the dead. Jehosa, our father, wants you all to know that you are just as immortal as I am. Regain belief in yourselves so that you may join us in Jehosa's realm. Follow the teachings of the Holy Disciples. Then you will never again be the effect of the infidels. May Jehosa watch over you. I bless you all."

With that, he suddenly disappeared. He swung down the bell rope causing the bell to sound repeatedly as if it acknowledged his parting words. Behind the altar, he found the bundle of clothes Josh had stowed for him. Two minutes later, completely disguised, Jes walked out the rear door of the church. Ten minutes later and without any fanfare, he walked through the west gate and out onto the track that led westward. An hour later, he climbed into the large wagon and laid down beside me, putting his arm lovingly around me. Though asleep, I smiled and felt more secure than I had in a long time.

Chapter 9 Revolution, Invasion, and Escape

The Great Messiah officially died on March 20, 585 AH and was resurrected on March 23. We all slept long after the sun rose on the 24th.

On the 24th, General Lacerta smiled as his aides left to implement his latest edict. Now that his newly appointed general had handled the Great Messiah's threat to his rule and authority, he intended to tighten his grip on any dissidence. There would be no gathering crowds. Any resistance would be met with instant arrest. Further, the taxes would be doubled for the next three years to compensate Megalos for all the supply losses incurred over the years. He, General Lacerta would show everyone back in Megalos just how it is done and in just a few months' time too.

That same day, General Slavius mounted his horse, pivoted in his saddle to inspect his troops. Ten squads of crack foot soldiers, a cavalry squad, and a full squad of war chariots. *Impressive*, he thought. *Now this is more like it.* "Okay, men, let's go smash some Galts!" he called out to his troops, who echoed with a chorus of yeh's. For years now, the Centurions here in the northern border of Juda Arad had been subjected to frequent Galt raids from the Northern Steppes. Now it was payback time. General Lacerta had issued the orders that his predecessors had been too timid to issue. Slowly, but with enthusiasm, the columns moved out and onto the Northern Steppes. Again, that cold voice spoke into his mind, "Kill every Galt!" He did not need further encouragement.

That same day, in their secret mesa-top fortress at Al Tarm, the top messiahs of the Qaam sect met with the highest prophet of their sect, Hama Damar. Pacing the room, which held the twenty well-armed men, he spoke angrily, "Well, we gave him two weeks and then some, and look what he did with it! Went and got himself killed without even putting up the slightest fight! Just like an Amirite. Men, now it is our time. Too long have we put up with these meddling infidels! It is time for us to revert to the old ways. Fight back!"

The men stamped the floor in unison and yelled, "Fight to the death! Death to all the infidels!"

"Messiahs, here is the plan. Ride like the wind to all towns and villages that have infidels in residence. Rouse all the people. Tell then to attack precisely six days from now. Show no mercy. Slay every infidel in each town and city! If they refuse to fight, burn them out! Eight days from now, not a single infidel will be left alive in all the Arad! Freedom will be ours!" More cheers and shouting erupted. "Go now. Show the people of Arad that we, the Qaams, know how to fight for our freedom!"

The men, still cheering jubilantly, rushed out, mounted up, and dashed off to their respective headquarters in the major towns and cities of Juda Arad. After so many years of waiting, they finally got the okay to do what they had wanted to do all this time — fight back — kill the infidels! They needed no further encouragement. Each would garner what additional support he could muster from others not in the Qaam sect. Then they would wreak havoc on the infidels. These men were more than ready! None had any doubts that in eight days they would be free of all the infidels!

We finally woke around noon that day, mostly because the children were up and about and had to be watched and fed. "Daddy, daddy," Ahmad exclaimed as Jes woke up, "mommy killed the infidels with lightning. You should have seen it!"

Hadid, Josh's eldest, added, "Yes, sir. She did! We all saw it. They were shooting arrows at us. She even caught one in her hands! It's true! Aunt Bethany says she will teach us how to catch arrows!" Ah, the excitement of children. Jes smiled and took it all in, putting his arms around both children.

Not to be left out, Ros, Josh's young daughter, inserted, "It's all true. Aunt Bethany is a messiah too. She can fight!" I did not appreciate all this talk of fighting, though.

Jes replied to all of them, "Children, there are times to fight and times to avoid fighting. Fighting is not always the best answer to life's problems. I'm sure that your mother did what she had to do to protect you. Either she fought or the arrows and men would have killed you. She really didn't have any choice. You should be proud of your mother for having spent so many years training to defend us."

"But why are you not going to fight the infidels, daddy?" asked Ahmad. "All the other kids say you are supposed to fight them and drive them from our land so we can be free." My mouth dropped! In all this mess, I had completely forgotten the children and their viewpoints! I think that we all did. I wondered how Jes would answer this tough one.

"Assume that you are a mouse. Just pretend that you are a field mouse. You have a nice hole in the ground and plenty of food nearby. Life is grand, but then a horse moves into your land. He steps on your grass, tramples your hole, and even threatens to step on you if you don't look out. Now, life is not so grand is it?" All the children agreed. Jes made his point. "So would you, the mouse, now go attack the horse so that you can be free from the horse's trampling?"

"No! How can a mouse hurt a horse?" Ahmad replied, the other children echoed his exclamation.

"Precisely. That is what is going on here in our land right now. We are the mice; the infidels are the horses. True, mommy can slay many of them, but if she were to fight all of them, she would very likely be killed, just as the mouse can be stepped on and squashed if there are many horses running around. A mouse might run and avoid one or two horse's feet, but with so many horses about, surely, it would quickly find itself under a hoof. Yes, on a very small scale, we can defeat a few infidels. Remember, for every one we see here now, there are probably a hundred more that could be ordered to come here to help defeat us. If the people of Arad rebel right now, I'm afraid that many, many of them will be killed and still the infidels would remain in control." Their four faces were downcast; the situation seemed hopeless.

"Now suppose that the mouse learned to be more like our God, Jehosa, and learned how to use his god-like powers, much like mommy has. Ah, now the story has a different ending. What I was trying very hard to do was to help our people become more like Jehosa, so that they may be free, so that infidels could not harm them."

"Did you do it?" asked Emil, our youngest, who was trying to follow everything.

Tears glazed over his eyes. "No, Emil, I believe that I have failed Jehosa. True, I have stalled the inevitable rebellion for several years now, but I have not yet succeeded. That is why I tried the last thing I could think of — the Great Messiah died and was resurrected by Jehosa. Now the Holy Disciples will spread my teachings throughout the Arad. Maybe in time, our people will come to understand. Maybe in time, I will have succeeded. Right at the moment, son, I have failed."

Hadid asked, "Does that mean there is going to be a rebellion soon? I've heard other children talking about it."

"Yes, Hadid, it is coming, though I cannot predict how soon, but soon, very soon. That is why we must get all of you out of the Arad to safety in a distant land. If not, once the rebellion is squashed, the infidels will hunt you children down like rabbits and kill you because your only crime is that you are my sons or Josh's. You four are the rightful heirs to the throne of Juda Arad. In time, you four ought to become Kings of our land."

"Can a girl become king? Hadid says I can't because I'm a girl," Ros asked, looking huffily at her older brother.

"You would be the queen. The male rulers are kings; the female rulers are the queens. Yes, you may become the queen, Ros. It is your heritage — one that traces back to the original King and Queen of our people, Jaleene and Amad Amir. Of all the people in the Arad, you four are the nearest descendants of them, except Josh and me, of course."

Their questions satisfied, Jackal interrupted, "My Lord, we must get traveling, for we are still way too close to Jerilum. Anytime a scout might find us." Thus, a half hour later, we began moving westward, slowly putting distance between the city and us. Of necessity, we traveled back byways, even going across country, dependent totally on Jackal and Missa, who knew where to find the watering holes. Unfortunately, with the two wagons, progress was pitifully slow. By nightfall, we had covered only five miles at most. The terrain was very rough for wagons.

That night once the children were asleep, Jackal wanted a conference with us all. He began, "Just wanted you to know that I purchased these wagons and supplies in a nearby town. I did not go all the way to the small fishing port of Alcaldus. It would have been too far to go. What I need to know, so that I may guide you the best, is the plan you have."

"Since the Great Messiah is now officially dead, I cannot afford to be recognized anywhere in the Arad," Jes answered. "I made a pact with General

Slavius that I would leave the Arad in secret and that what happened to his ambush patrol would not happen again. Temporarily Bethany, no more lightning devastation," he teased me.

Jes continued, "I really have not planned too far ahead, Jackal. We must get everyone safely out of Juda Arad. Where to go, though, is the question. It is common knowledge that ever since that Night of the Baby Murders in Al Barq, some of our people fled to the Land of the Sea Princes. We know that at least in the major cities there, small groups of our people have made a new home for themselves, though they still follow our ways."

"Will your families be safe in that land? There are infidels controlling those lands as well," Missa pointed out.

"The objective is to travel until we do find a land where it will be safe to raise the children and preach the gospel of Jehosa to others," Jes explained. "There is something that I've not told you, except Josh here. I possess a gift from Jehosa to see into the near future. Actually, possible futures based upon what actions I take. For example, while I was on my solo hermitage wandering in the wilderness, what I was actually doing was experimenting with actions that I might take and the possible future that would bring. For every action, there is a predictable reaction."

I interrupted him, "I'd say for every Cause there is an Effect." Jes nodded his agreement.

He went on, "It is of the utmost importance that our children be raised properly so that they may eventually take the throne of Juda Arad when the time comes. Though I must admit, I cannot see that happening; it could well be their children who eventually accede to the rulership. I cannot tell for sure. In any event, I'm placing the ultimate survival of our children under his leadership, with Bethany and Milla at hand, of course. However, I, myself, cannot yet say whether or not I will be always with you." My heart skipped a beat! Jes might not stay with us!

Before I could protest, he continued. "There remain two events that demand my attention. I have not yet made my decision on how to respond to them. You have the right to know what they are. First is this rebellion. I sense that it is very close. The Qaams will be the instigators of the rebellion. They have not the wisdom or knowledge to foretell what damage this will have on Juda Arad, but Bethany and I both know. Our people will be slaughtered, probably in the hundreds or even thousands. The other situation only Bethany and I know about, and it is almost too terrible to discuss, too unbelievable."

Jackal insisted, "Yea, my Lord. I must know all if I am to be of optimum service. Tell me and let me decide whether or not to believe it."

Jes thought a moment, deciding whether to reveal it. "Truth shall set us free. Yes, though you may not believe, I will tell you. We are immortal beings, spirits, that inhabit these fleshly bodies. When a new baby is born, we move into it and accept it as our fleshly body. When it dies, we move out and go in search of another baby. All this ought to be done of our own free choice, our own free will. Our lives ought to be our own, our decisions, ours. However,

Bethany has discovered something beyond all horrors of horrors, perhaps Lucifer himself dwells here on Tarra! High in the mountains north of the Sea Princes dwell a strange people, unseen by all the rest of us, totally unknown to nearly everyone on Tarra. They have grey bodies and are very tall. Their bodies are not human-formed."

"It is not the existence of this strange race that is the problem, but rather it is what they are doing to us! It seems that when our fleshly bodies die, they have some strange device that summons us, the spiritual beings, unto them! There, their device scrambles all our memories, orders us to go back, and acquire a new baby body. Even if I manage to get one of our people free, as soon as their fleshly body dies, they are forced back into another one, instead of being allowed to rejoin Jehosa in his realm! Any successes I have here promptly gets undone by them! Could this be Lucifer's interference?"

"But it is even worse than this," he went on, "Bethany also knows of another even stranger group out in the Red Desert. These creatures are doing much the same with the infidels. Yes, they too are spiritual beings. Once their fleshly bodies die, they are similarly forced to go to this group, their minds are likewise scrambled, and then they are sent back to get a new baby body. You see, even the infidels are as trapped into this never-ending cycle as we are. They are as much a victim as our people."

Jackal cursed and said quite surprisingly, "Many years ago, I talked to an old merchant trader who had traveled throughout the Sea Princes. He spoke of a fairy tale that some of the locals tell their children. Something about 'Do not go into the mountains or the grey monster will get you.' I wonder if the monster and your creature are one and the same? Interesting."

A sudden thought struck me, primarily because I had never talked this openly about these creatures before. "What if interfering with our people when they are between fleshly bodies is not *all* that they do? What if they are interfering directly in our lives, in the choices that we make? One of my certainties, with which you all might not agree, is that for two people actually to fight, there has to be another person behind the scenes fomenting that conflict, directly causing it. Someone had to be behind those infidels who attempted to ambush us, but I have no idea who. I had no desire to harm those soldiers. I did not even know them. I did not hate them. Yet, they attempted to kill us without question. Why are these people from Megalos so intent on subjugating us, when mutual trust and aid could create booming, thriving economies where all could prosper? This open conflict, this continuing hostility is doing just the opposite."

Jackal stared at me, as did Josh, Missa and Milla. It was as if they had never really seen me before. Josh muttered, "Long ago, Jes told me that you, Bethany, were his equal counterpart. Until this moment, I really did not understand what he meant. I do now, and I swear to you that I shall never underestimate you again!" He bowed to me, took my hand, and kissed it, highly out of character for an Arad.

Jackal exclaimed, "We are fighting the wrong targets! We ought to be fighting these devils in the mountains!"

Milla simple stated, "I'm scared to death. If Lucifer is there, he is so powerful. If he finds out we know about all this, he will not hesitate to slay us all!"

"We've got Bethany's lightning bolts," Missa attempted to console Milla.

"No we don't," I added. "I hate to say it, but I encountered them long ago, and my bolts did not do anything to them."

More curses followed my statement, but I'd rather that occur than for them to have a false sense of security. However, all this talk about the strange beings brought back to my mind Alabaster Benjamin Crowley, the founder of the druwid movement. When I last saw him, he was off to spy on these very creatures. I hadn't heard from him all these years. What had happened to him? My mind generated all sorts of horrible images. It took me some time to flush these nightmares out!

Missa commented, "What a fine pickle we are in — we cannot stay here. The infidels will come after us in time. Wherever we might go in the inhabited world, the infidels control, except those areas that we would not want to go to anyway, where the tyrant Galts live. Wherever we do go, these strange creatures may be after us as well. Doom is upon us! By Jehosa, I'll not give up without a fight!"

"Nor I either!" declared Jackal. "What should we do?"

"That is what I need to determine," Jes said softly. "I must meditate and think this through. Meantime, Jackal, get us safely to the port unseen. However, Bethany, I need a disguise. Do you think that you can cut my hair short and help me get rid of my long beard? Make me look like a Sea Prince merchant, perhaps?" So the discussion ended, and I gave him a haircut and shave, trying to style it similar to the way men had it in the Sea Princes when I was last there so many years ago in my prior body. I had no idea if their customs had changed in all this time, but it really didn't matter, for Jes wouldn't be so easily recognized anymore. He looked very un-Aradish now. Actually, I preferred his new look. I really don't like beards, and still don't, but that's just me.

We had about two hundred miles as the crow flies between the small fishing village on the edge of the Med Sea and us. However, because of the mesa terrain, any straight-line travel was impossible, unless you could fly. Worse, all the normal tracks that crisscrossed the western Arad had to be avoided, because we couldn't risk being spotted by either our own people or an infidel patrol. If this was not enough, water is a scarce commodity in this semi-arid land. Wells or springs are not uniformly located. Besides, often a town or village lives around them. Hence, Jackal and Missa had an almost insurmountable task facing them, trying to navigate a safe route. Compounding the problem, we were driving two wagons, which made it all the more difficult.

Result: progress was painfully slow. Yet, this suited the families. For the first time ever, both families had the time to just be with each other and play together with no outside duties interfering. For ten splendid days, we all relaxed and enjoyed the pure pleasures of family life. After all that we had been through, this was heaven, in spite of being on the road, so to speak. Then, it all ended abruptly.

Though we transported many pots of water, the next leg forced us to go through a small village for two reasons. We needed more supplies, and without restocking our water, we would never make the next watering hole. Jackal had no real choice but to take us through Meda, home to some thousand people. Worse still, we had visited this town several times during the years that Jes was preaching, so we stood a great chance of being recognized.

"My Lord," Jackal explained as he halted our small caravan about two miles from Meda, "we must resupply here. Surely, you and your families will be recognized if you set foot in Meda. Missa has an idea. Let's put all the children into one wagon and then you four take the horses and the wagon and go wide around Meda. Missa and I will drive the empty wagon into town and resupply. We can then rejoin a couple miles west of town."

I gave his some coins for the purchases, while Josh and Jes surveyed the terrain for the best route to take. The problem was that the town was cradled between two mesas; the one on our left had a sheer face, while the one on our right sloped gentle to its peak. If we went left around the town, we would pass dangerously close to the outskirts of Meda. On the other hand, stubble grass grew on the sloping side, and we could see several flocks of white-grey sheep herds scattered about the slope. While Milla handled moving the children and most of the gear, I joined the men surveying the land ahead of us.

It was nearly noon, smoke curls rose from several areas in the town, probably the blacksmith shops or bakeries. Clouds hung heavy in the sky, April sprinkles were likely later today. While just observing the tranquil setting, I caught slight movement off to the right near the slopes and the grazing area. My attention naturally focused on what was moving. From this distance, I could not tell what it was. Then I spied a slight flashing of light, not a bright flash, the day was overcast. As I watched, several more dim flashed appeared on either side of the first.

"Hold everything," I called out. "Something is not right. Something is reflecting light way over there." While the others stared where I was pointing, I was trying to figure out what could cause this flashing. I had the feeling that I ought to know what it was. In a flash, a memory appeared in my mind: I was watching the Centurion army assault the forces from one of the Sea Prince's cities. "Centurions!" I called out, forgetting that here they were known as infidels. I quickly corrected my pronouncement, "Infidels ahead. Those are their shields flashing. They must be on the move or in combat!"

Several curses resounded. Instantly, Milla and the children looked up and stared toward the town. "I can't see them mommy, where, where?" cried Ahmad.

While the men attempted to decide our next move, I decided this was as good a time for a real life lesson as any. "Okay, kids, all of you come and stand here beside me." Naturally, all four enthusiastically clamored out of the wagon and joined me. "Now what I want you to do is just observe what is there off to the right of the town. Just tell me what you can actually see, not what you think you see, no conclusions. Just what can you see." It felt rather good finally to begin to train someone as Loremaster Ellen did for me so many, many years ago.

Eventually, all four began to see the light flashes and did describe them accurately. I sketched a picture of the infidels and their shields in the dry dirt, and explained how movement could cause the intermittent light flashes. Meanwhile the men still had not decided on the best course of action to take. One thing was certain, we could not just ignore this town; we were running low on food and did not have enough water to make any other well than here in Meda. Worse still, we could not stay here on this east-west road into Meda. Someone was more than likely to come our way.

The men thought that at least someone ought to circle around and get closer to find out what was actually happening. Naturally, Jackal volunteered. However, that was vetoed because he was the only man who could safely go into Meda to purchase our needed supplies. We simply could not risk anything happening to him. "Look, guys," I interrupted them, "We certainly cannot risk Jes or Josh going either. So it is up to Missa and me. We'll take a couple horses and go see what's happening. The infidels are not too likely to attach any significance to a pair of women out riding. Remember, they think that only the men of the Arad are fighters. We should be safe enough. You guys get the wagons off the road here — say back there in that dry wash we passed back there. Stay hidden. We'll be back in a short while."

Honestly, I did not give the men any chance to argue about it. There really was no other choice; Missa was used to scouting as I, in my own way. They grumbled but assented. I gave Jes a hug and kiss as well as the two boys, mounted up, and Missa and I rode off northward.

"I say let's circle wide around and take up an initial position high on the mesa slope, that way we have the benefit of height," Missa volunteered. "Disadvantage is that the noon sun will be behind them and we'll be easier to spot." We rode hard toward the north and then veered upwards on the leading slope of the mesa, staying approximately two miles from the town. Conveniently, we spied some larger boulders, tethered the horses out of sight behind them, intending on edging our way closer on foot. We would be less likely to be spotted on foot.

A half hour later, we had crawled up to within a mile of the action, and action we saw, combat. A dozen infidels were in a life and death battle with a group of Arad men, a messiah band, we assumed. Time for observations, I thought to myself, and concentrated on examining all that I could see. Missa did likewise; she had spent her lifetime doing just this. After a couple minutes, we compared our conclusions.

The Centurions, as I would have predicted, stayed close together, shields nearly touching, forming a united front against the Arads who outnumbered them two to one. However, the infidels were slowly moving eastward, driving the Arads backwards. Behind them, we saw two wounded or dead Centurions and at least a dozen of our men lying on the dusty ground. We detected some body motions from a couple of these, so perhaps they were not yet dead. Clearly, the Centurions were slowly winning this battle. Memories of the earlier Centurion battles that I had witnessed when I was a druwid came back to me. Their battlefield tactics had not changed in the quarter century that had passed.

Now some of our fighters attempted to flank the line on both sides, but they responded by simply pulling their end soldiers back at right angles forming a three sided defensive position, which only resulted in another two of our men becoming wounded. Missa whispered to me, "I recognize some of them. They are Qaams. I think that man there is a Qaam messiah, but at least half of our forces are inexperienced beginners or are townsfolk. I'd guess the latter. Qaams aren't known for fielding raw recruits."

I concluded, "That means the rebellion must have already begun, if they have gotten some of these villagers to take up arms against the infidels."

"If they win the field," Missa noted, "surely they will lock this village down tighter than a drum head. I doubt that we'll be allowed easy access to the water well, at least not allowed to draw as much water as we need. It would be way too suspicious. Further, buying as much trail rations as we need will also raise their curiosity. Curses. Just getting our supplies is going to be extremely risky."

"Do you or Jackal know the most likely trader who could sell us what we need?" I asked, the very beginnings of a plan began forming in my mind. True, we couldn't interfere in the battle, though at this long range, I still probably could bring down lightning bolts. They sky certainly was in prime condition for doing just that. However, Jes had given his word; I would not break it except if we were in dire peril.

"Assuming he is still alive and still in business, yes," she answered. "Why?"

"Could you find this man at night in a storm and make the trade under cover of darkness? Would you be able to convince him to open up his store late at night just for you?"

"Probably, there are many ways to convince him."

"Okay, then let's get back to the others. I have a plan. I've a way to end this battle. Come on." We cautiously crawled our way slowly back up the slope to our horses. We waited for a while to see if we had been detected. Below, the men were locked in a life and death battle and took no notice of us. "Missa, you ride back to the others and tell them the situation. Make darn sure the wagons cannot be spotted by accident. I have some preparations to do here before I return. I'll be following you in a little while."

"They'll have my skin if I leave you behind!" protested Missa.

"No they won't. Tell them that I ordered you to return. I'll be perfectly safe. I'm only going to need maybe a half hour at most to begin. Hurry up now." Reluctantly, Missa obeyed. Once she was on her way, I began chanting. I had not attempted to control the weather for over a quarter century or more. At first, I doubted that I could remember all the proper steps, as it is one of the most difficult actions a druwid can perform. I needed this time alone and uninterrupted if I was to have even the slightest chance of success. A half hour later, I felt sprinkles falling. Far off to the west, thunder rolled. Perhaps it was working. I mounted up and rode back toward the others.

By the time that I finally reached the wagons, I was completely soaked. Unnaturally heavy rains were falling, nearly wiping out the wagon ruts that led me to the others. Jes had erected a tarp over the wagons, and everyone was huddled tightly together under it, staying partially dry. I tied the horse to the other wagon and slipped under the tarp, sopping wet.

"Are you all right?" Jes asked. "That was foolhardy of you to send her back without you."

"I needed time to bring this rain," I replied calmly. "I haven't done anything like this for a very long time. I needed absolute quiet so I could concentrate."

"Mommy, it is *really* raining!" exclaimed Ahmad.

"You did this?" asked Jackal.

"How?" added Josh.

"Yes, it is really raining. I had to find a way to stop that battle and give us some protection. In simple terms, Josh, it was already going to sprinkle. I just got the clouds to move closer together, denser, so the rain becomes more concentrated in one area instead of widespread sprinkles, somewhat like collecting all the sprinkles together and having them fall in one small spot. It sure is working. Both sides gave up the battle, retreating into the town, heading for cover. Tonight, Jackal and Missa can go into Mesa, find the shop owner, and get our supplies. It will probably still be raining heavily and everyone else will be indoors."

"I say it is another miracle of Jehosa," exclaimed Jackal.

"But Aunt Bethany, why didn't you just use lightning bolts to kill all of the infidels like you did before?" asked Hadid.

Josh tried to hush up his son. Jes fumbled for an explanation, but I replied first. "Several reasons. One, Jes gave his word that I wouldn't do that again here in the Arad. Two, those infidels are not threatening either you or me. Three, I don't know who is in the right in this battle; I don't know who started it; perhaps the infidels were attacked by the Arad men. Four, don't be so hasty to take life from another unless you can create life in its place. However, Hadid, I most certainly did stop that battle!"

Jes roared with laughter, adding, "You should be the preacher, not I! Very well said, very!" His laugher was contagious, and the other adults also joined in, but the children did not see the humor, but smiled anyway.

Ros interrupted us, "But aren't the infidels evil? How come it matters if they were in the wrong, Aunt Bethany?"

"Go ahead and answer that one, Aunt Bethany," Jes teased me.

"Well, the Great Messiah might differ with me on this one. Nevertheless, suppose that you came walking down the street and saw two boys fighting each other. One boy you know and the other boy you know but don't like. You have no idea why they are fighting each other. Would you just dive in there and beat up on the boy you didn't like solely because you didn't like him? If you did, what happens to you when the fight is over and you discover that the other boy just stole some money from the boy you didn't like? You see, the one you didn't like was just trying to get his money back from the thief, and you just helped out the thief! You helped the wrong boy. Now you are guilty of aiding a thief."

"But they are the infidels," she added in slight protest, as if this somehow made a difference.

"Indeed they are the infidels. But with the two boys, how would you feel afterwards when you found out that you had just helped a thief, that the boy you beat up was innocent? Pretty crummy. So hurting others unjustly causes you harm. They may be infidels, but if they were in the right, I would feel awfully bad about killing them unjustly."

"I never thought of it that way, Aunt Bethany."

"Don't feel bad, Ros," Jes commented, "I didn't think of it either." The others agreed with him. "As I said, perhaps Bethany should do the preaching," Jes jested once more, but I detected a subtle hint of truth in his voice and wondered what that might mean. He did not elaborate.

By the time darkness fell, the rains continued unabated. Perhaps I had overdone it. Still, the downpour was certain to keep the villagers indoors, which was precisely where I wanted them to be. Jes gave the signal and Missa and Jackal climbed into the nearly empty wagon and headed back to the road or track into Mesa. Meanwhile, we all followed some distance behind them. Our horses were tied to the rear of the wagon and Jes drove with Josh riding lookout. Both quickly became drenched. The rest of us huddled under the tarp, only half soaked. Our plans had now changed. Jes circled the town on the left side, near the steep sided mesa, avoiding the battlefield side. With everyone indoors, we ran little risk of being spotted. With the rain and darkness, they had a very tricky task of navigation.

Three hours later and two miles on the other side of the village, Missa and Jackal caught back up with us. Jackal's greeting words said it all, "Total success. Much news." We did not stop. Instead, we intended to put more miles between the village and us before stopping. Fortunately, the rain soon subsided to sprinkles and then stopped altogether. The stars began appearing and soon the late quarter moon gave us some much-needed light. We stopped for the night in a side canyon, safely out of sight from the road. Tomorrow we would have to leave the road, once more heading across country on little traveled paths.

First order of business was a fire with which to dry out and cook supper. We were all quite chilly wearing soaking clothes at night. The men soon found some firewood, but could not get the wet wood to take a spark. Jesting and shivering, I said, "Stand back, this is woman's work." The men did as I asked, but not without some parting teases. I chanted a bit, brought a wall of flames into existence just above the wood, and slowly let it descend onto the wood. Shortly with sizzling and popping sounds, the wet wood dried and ignited. This, of course, brought many praises to Jehosa, "look at that's," and "can you teach us how to do that's." The men looked at each other in complete surprise. The children were most excited about this new trick I'd done. I smiled and said, "Now let Milla cook us up something warm! I'm starving."

While she cooked, we took turns warming and drying around the fire, but being careful to stay out of her way. None wanted to delay supper. Once supper was done and the children put to bed in the wagons, the adults gathered around the embers to hear all that Jackal and Missa had learned.

"You were right, my Lord," Jackal began, "the rebellion began several days ago. The Qaam sect is leading it. Apparently, they sent out word to all towns to launch simultaneous attacks on the infidels three days ago. From what we've heard, that first day, they took the infidels by surprise, killing a fair number, but it is just as you predicted, my Lord. The infidels have already begun to strike back. Here in Meda, they have just about wiped out all resistance. Today's battle has reduced our forces to just a few, and they have scattered in all directions to escape the wrath of the infidels. Many young men of Meda are either dead now or have fled for their lives."

Missa added, "Our men are being slaughtered, just as you predicted. We just don't know how bad it actually is. In my opinion, even worse is that before this started, the infidels tripled the annual tax! Three gold ducats will be nearly impossible for most people to pay! If they don't pay, they'll become slaves, and if they do pay, they'll likely starve during the winter months. Juda Arad is doomed. Whatever will we do now? If the numbers of our young men being lost are true, old men and women will have to fend for themselves. Frankly, I've never been this scared of the future!"

"She speaks for me," Jackal vented! "My merchant contact estimates that Meda has lost nearly a quarter of its population in the last three days, most of its able-bodied men, or the younger ones anyway."

I looked at Jes and saw something I've never seen — a grown man weeping. He had seen this coming, done everything in his power to prevent it, and now had to live with his complete failure. This man had uncommon compassion for his people, more so than any man I had ever known. All I could do was put my arms around him and comfort him, support him.

Josh, on the other hand grew violently angry, cursing and stomping about our campsite. "Vile swine! May Jehosa see that they all rot in the eternal fires of Lucifer!" Milla simply cried quietly to herself. In time, Josh's anger gave way to grief, and he too sat down beside his wife and together they cried. No one said anything for an hour, each of us lost in our own thoughts of the massacre, the doom of the Arad.

General Lacerta was polishing his boots when his aide frantically burst into the room. "Sir, they are attacking us! The rebels!" He was breathless from having run all the way across Jerilum to notify the general.

Carefully, Lacerta finished polishing and then calmly said, "Report, please," in stark contrast to the near panic in his aide.

"The whole city is in rebellion! Our patrols have been slaughtered!"

"Whoa, slow down. The whole city cannot be in rebellion. Since when would a woman or child attack one of us? Now be reasonable. How many patrols? How many men? Where?"

The aide took a deep breath and tried to state the facts. When the morning patrols began their daily march through the crowded streets of Jerilum, suddenly and without warning, armed men sprang from all sides. Taken by total surprise, every man in every patrol had been lost. Lacerta quickly estimated the total might exceed a hundred men, a small amount, though significant. He was not worried about a hundred men. No, in fact, he was exceedingly cheerful. "Now we are getting somewhere. Finally, the barbarians choose to stand and fight. Good. Now we can put an end to them once and for all. Rouse the entire garrison!" The aide raced to carry out his order, while the general looked in a mirror and made last minute adjustments to his uniform. It would not due to look disheveled in the slightest. Not today. He must inspire his men to glorious combat!

His men scrambled into squads on the parade grounds of the barracks just as fast as they could. General Lacerta walked out onto his balcony high above his troops, an impressive figure. "Centurions of Megalos, the time we have been waiting for has finally arrived. The Arad fighters have finally chosen to fight. Let's show them how it is done properly. Cavalry, your task is to ride to all of our other towns and garrisons. Undoubtedly, you will find them under siege as well. My orders are clear. Wipe out all resistance to the last man. Show no mercy. Slay any young man that they feel might pose a threat to us. Report to me on a daily basis. Ride hard, cavalry of Megalos! Legions, your orders: form up into triple squads. Fan out from here across the entire city; slay any who oppose you. Kill any man who even looks like they might be a fighter. I leave all such discretion to your commanders. Show no mercy. Let's clear Jerilum of all rebels in twenty-four hours! To victory! To Megalos!" The men cheered and shouted. Quickly the squad leaders issued their orders. Within ten minutes, triple squads began issuing forth form the garrison here in the center of the city. Lacerta watched them go. Shortly afterwards, fully two hundred cavalrymen galloped out of the garrison onto the crowded streets. All gave way to the charging horses.

General Lacerta climbed to the highest room of his mansion to look out upon the city to get a bird's eye view of the action. Ten aides followed him, ready to relay any orders he might have. Since he still could not see well, he climbed out onto the roof. "Ah, much better." He sat down to watch the action on a nearby street.

"Ah, performing admirably!" he commented to an aide that had crawled up onto the roof with him. Below in the square where two cross streets met, his legions formed into a tight line, setting up a shield wall. Spears to the front, they marched into the barbarians. However, because of the wall of shields, the barbarians could not hit his men, while slowly the ever-advancing spears skewered the rioters. "Brilliant move!" he called out as one squad pivoted to meet a flanking assault, slaying six of the barbarians. *Now I can completely clean up this land!* he thought to himself.

At dinnertime, his commanders reported on their progress. Ignoring the hundred soldiers that perished in the initial rebellion, only six had been slain with ten wounded during the cleansing of the city. The rebels lost in the thousands. So many had fallen, that the Centurions simply piled them up outside the city on the cemetery grounds, not even bothering to bury them. The locals could dig the graves for their own fallen, but the city was by no means secured. They had only swept the major thoroughfares. Mopping up would take several days.

Scout riders returned from the closest towns to Jerilum that night, reporting pretty much the same thing. Morning patrols were ambushed, but, following General Lacerta's orders, the local garrisons responded brutally. However, Lacerta knew that the more distant towns and villages would require reinforcements from Jerilum. Indeed, less than a squad patrolled some of the smaller villages. Those would most likely have been wiped out, but he would send in full squads just as soon as he could spare them from here. That night, to celebrate his smashing victory, he opened the finest bottle of wine he could find.

Assistant General Slavius, now three days deep into Galt territory, felt frustrated. Some forty miles into the Northern Steppes, he had found no roads, no towns, no villages, no people, only this location, which appeared to have been inhabited fairly recently. It was no more than a trampled area of grass with holes in the ground where tent poles may have been.

This land was very different from Juda Arad. Once one crossed the Barrier Teeth, a rocky protrusion of stone that separated these two lands, the semiarid, near desert mesa land of the Arad, which gave way to gently rolling grass covered hills. Scattered deciduous forests dotted the hillside here and there. Each hill rose several hundred feet only to drop down into yet another basin. Creeks trickled and bubbled as they meandered from valley to valley, flowing toward the north, not south to the Arad which could greatly benefit from the water. Here was a lush land, one worthy of adding to the dominion of Megalos. Slavius wondered why they had not invaded the Northern Steppes before now.

His problem, of course, was no Galts. His orders were clear: attack the Galts, take the raiding into their lands for the first time. The voice in his mind suggested he kill all Galts, but so far, no Galts.

For nearly a half century, the Galts had been raiding the northern-most towns and villages of the Arad. Why? In the north of Juda Arad, iron mines, smelters, and forges predominated in the local economy. Megalos was quick to exploit these raw materials by encouraging production of many weapons, predominately swords, spear tips, and arrowheads.

General Slavius surveyed the surrounding land. The Northern Steppes were perfect for his army and assault tactics. He could apply textbook tactics with ease, if only he could find these Galts. His aides returned from a closer examination of this site. Definitely, Galts had been here, but where were they now? While he ignored the many hoof prints in the soft turf, his aides didn't. These Galts were known to be horsemen and often raided and fought while mounted and charging. One aide estimated that perhaps a hundred horses had been stationed here. Did that mean there were a hundred fighters?

Assistant General Slavius wasn't stupid. His invading force had sufficient food supplies for a week's excursion before they would have to return. He ordered his columns to follow the trail left by the horses when they had abandoned this location, calculating that they must be somewhere just ahead. He also ordered his cavalry squad to fan out on his flanks and search for the enemy's location. Mounting his war chariot, he signaled the slow advance.

The next noon, he was rewarded. Scouts returned reporting a small Galt village about two miles ahead. After getting a situational update directly from the scouts, he issued his battle plans. Eight squads, shields locked, would make the main frontal assault, while the other two would deal with any flanking action. If none, they would begin an encirclement action. The cavalry and the war chariots, as standard procedure dictated, would be held in reserve, to deal with any hot spots or breaks in the main line.

An hour later, cresting a hill, he saw firsthand the Galt village, if a village one could call it. Three dozen hide covered domed huts, leather stretched tight by bent poles, sat on the lush grass at the valley floor. Nearby, perhaps fifty horses were tethered in neat lines. Smoke from cooking fires twisted into the clear blue sky. The colors were rich, deep blue sky, deep green grass, and dark brown huts, picturesque. He spied a frantic rush of people preparing to meet his forces. He had taken them by complete surprise, a sure sign of victory.

By the time that his ground forces reached the edge of the village, fifty men had mounted and ridden hard to encircle his forces. The majority of the Galts formed into a line to protect the village. To his utter amazement, he saw women wielding swords as well. He signaled the flank squads to pivot back to begin to form a protective line from the enemy cavalry, while he moved his cavalry, outnumbered five to one, into the center of the rear of the main line. All the while, the main line marched in unison toward the enemy. At his signal, another pair of squads on the left and right flanks slowed and pivoted so that now two squads defended each flank from the enemy cavalry.

Finally, the battle was joined, spear into flesh, sword upon shield, in a cacophony of sounds. The cavalry charged into his rear flank guard squads, twenty-five on either side. Rather than divide his single squad, riding in his war chariot, he led them in a charge to meet those attacking on the right flank. Twice, the spinning blades, protruding from the chariot's wheels, disabled horses that came too close, throwing and wounding their riders. It was a classic cavalry versus cavalry clash. Both galloped through the other's line, riders swinging their swords this way and that. Half the Galts fell on the first pass along with a few of his. The second pass eliminated the remainder of the Galts and still more of his. His squad was now seriously weakened. Still he turned them to face the other half of the enemy cavalry, which had charged into a line of spears hastily setup by the two flanking squads. Twice they charged through the line; twice their numbers were reduced; twice many holding the line fell wounded. Finally, the charging war chariot and the remaining cavalrymen managed to drive the few Galt cavalry away from the battle. They were last seen galloping over the crest of the next hill.

Meanwhile, the main assault line had literally crushed the haphazard Galt line of defense and were now marching through the village mopping up. By the time that the general rode victoriously into the village, few remained alive. Only the old, pregnant, nursing women, and children had not fought. However, as his men rousted them out of these domed structures, in vain, these people frantically picked up any weapon or stick they could find laying around to attempt to defend themselves. When the battle finally ended, only a dozen children younger than five remained alive. All had sacrificed themselves rather than surrender.

"What do we do with all these children?" asked an aide.

The cold, alien voice spoke in his mind once more, *Kill them.*

"If we leave them, they will starve and die. Show them mercy. Kill the children too. Search the huts," ordered the General. While his men followed orders, he returned to assess his wounded soldiers. Right on cue, his supply wagons crested the hill. One by one, each wounded man was bandaged. Those that could not ride were given a seat on one of the supply wagons. All told, he had twenty men dead, and it took them an hour to bury them properly.

His aides reported that there was nothing of any real value in any of the huts save only a few coins. This meager loot the general gave to his men. Two hours after the battle started, the victorious Centurions began to retreat the way they had come. Mission accomplished. Now came the long walk home, some sixty miles. They still had plenty of food and water. Once more, he formed his legions into marching squads, and the long line marched in step back the way they had come. Assistant General Slavius knew that he had taught these Galts a lesson they would not soon forget!

Dawn brought circling vultures! I spotted them while getting the kids up for breakfast. "Jes, look at that." He rubbed the sleep from his eyes and faced the grim, sober day. Cradled in this box canyon just off the main track leading eastward from Meda, we could easily be trapped. However, the rains had effectively washed out any signs of our passage into this picturesque canyon between two mesas. Ordinarily, I would have enjoyed the scenery, but the vultures only added to the heaviness that we all still felt from the news we heard last night. Jackal and Jes decided to go investigate, while mommy tried to answer the children's questions about the meaning of the big birds circling round and round, less than a mile from where we camped.

They had not gone but a few feet when Jes turned and asked me to come as well. "Someone could be still alive but hurt," Jes explained as I hastily joined them. A few minutes later, we met the west track and hurried on down it to the west, estimating the location from the birds. Sure enough, we came across the remains of a small battle. The bodies of five Centurions lay scattered about, along with five horses wandering about the area munching on the scattered grass tufts. There leaning against a boulder was an unconscious man. Jes recognized him immediately, "It's Brother Jackal, our old fighting monk!"

Quickly, Jes and I rushed to his side. He stood back as I began my observations of his wounds, which were several. Jackal came up shortly and said quietly, "The infidels are long dead." Jes had him search the bodies and destroy their weapons. Jackal also decided to confiscate their horses because they appeared to be of Arad breeding, probably acquired from us. Five more horses might prove useful in trade.

"He's alive, barely," I reported to Jes, "I've not seen anything quite like this. He ought to have already bled to death from these severed arteries here in his leg and arm, but the opposite is occurring. Somehow, he has slowed all of his bodily functions way down. I'm going to make use of that and see if I can sew him up. Can you boil me some water?" I got out my emergency kit and set to work. Jes managed to get a fire going, though now I wonder how with everything being so wet from the rain last night. Using makeshift pots, he brought me a cup of steaming water just in time for me to use on the needles. He watched as I used the tiniest stitches to carefully mend the arteries and then close the wounds. It took me nearly an hour to get it just right. "Now comes the hard part. We don't have any bandages. I need to go back for all my healing herbs."

Jes smiled, "No you don't. Now that you have repaired the body damage, I can heal it, permanently finishing the process you did. I think that between us, we have been able to save his life." I stood back and watched him as he said prayers to Jehosa then laid his hands upon the monk's head. He still wore that silly hairstyle, rather as if someone put a bowl over his head and shaved off any hair that was visible. When Jes stood up, I looked closely at the two nasty wounds, and right before my eyes, they healed. It was as if I was watching perhaps a couple weeks of natural body healing occur within seconds. Suddenly I realized that might be a clue to how Jes could heal, by speeding up time. I made a mental note to ask him about this later on. Now came the problem of transporting him back to our camp.

Jackal already had foreseen that and had one horse ready to bear him. We gently placed the still comatose man across the horse, and we led them and the four remaining horses back to our camp. Bringing up the rear, Jackal left the five infidels lying where they had fallen. "Vultures also have to eat," he muttered.

When we returned, Josh had everyone ready for a quick get-away, if that was needed, though our breakfasts remained ready for us to eat, thankfully. "That's Brother Jackal!" Josh exclaimed, as we took him off the horse and laid him in one of the wagons. "Is he alive?"

"Yes, between Bethany and me, he will live to fight another day. It appears that he killed the five infidels who attacked him, but he was severely wounded in the battle."

Jackal looked very worried, saying, "My Lord, we best be getting out of here. No telling how soon those men will be missed, and a scouting party will come looking for them. Have you decided where we should go?"

Josh answered, "Get us off the road and out into the wilderness. Head more northeast. We must not be discovered at all costs. No, we have no idea where we are going yet." We moved out of the box canyon onto the road for about a half mile before angling up another valley generally northeastward, out into the desolate landscape.

As we walked along, we discussed our options. Going straight to the fishing village now seemed far too dangerous. With the rebellion in full swing, the infidels would more than likely have even this village under their direct control. As expected, once he knew our thinking, Jackal had an idea. "How about we make for a small fishing village further up the coast in the cedar forest region? That area is quite isolated from the rest of the country. We can hide easily within the dark forests and spy on the village to see if it is safe before we enter. Are you planning to travel by boat from there? I have always assumed so, since you told me to get you all to Alcaldus."

No large Med Sea worthy ships docked along our northern coastal lands north of Al Barq, but numerous fishing boats plied the waters off shore. Many traveled close to the shore from here all the way up to Zargarb in the Sea Princes. We decided to see if we could book passage from one of these small ports to Zargarb and from there take a sea worthy ship further westward. We all agreed on this.

Then, Ahmad called out to us that the monk was waking up. We stopped to check on Brother Jackal. "Am I alive?" he muttered as he slowly sat up, examining the large scars, which had been bleeding death wounds last night.

"Good thing we came along when we did, Brother Jackal," Jes teased our old teacher. "Yes, your wounds have been healed compliments of the Amirs, Bethany and me. We found you nearly vulture bait."

"All praise to Jehosa and the Amirs! I'm forever in your debt. Why, I seem to be fully healed! But oh, I'm so weak! I know. I was losing lots of blood."

"Yes, you need plenty of liquids. Ordinarily, I would recommend liver soup, but we have none. Milla and I will see what we can rustle up," I explained. She and I rummaged through our supplies to see what we could fix him, while the children surrounded him and asked him volleys of questions.

A short while later, while he was sipping a hot broth Milla fixed, he told us what happened. "The rebellion came, everywhere at once, like it was planned somehow. No place is safe now. I decided that this old man had better get out of the Arad for the time being. I was just walking down the road in the rain last night, wondering why it was actually raining. You know I don't know when I have ever seen it rain so much in this land. Oh yes, excepting sometime before you were born, Jes. Then five riders came up on me from behind. I could not see who they were, so I stood aside. I did not want to be run over by horses. Well, when the infidels saw me, for reasons best known to them, they drew their swords and charged at me. Oh my, were they ever surprised when I dodged their strikes. I believe I got a bit angry with them; five to one odds is hardly fair, so I taught them a lesson or two. Killed them all with their own blades, once I disarmed them, one by one. However, I took a couple nasty wounds. I couldn't heal myself, and so I decided to place my future in Jehosa's hands and put the body into a suspended state — you know, slowed everything down so I wouldn't bleed to death for quite some time. And so it is that you found me. Praise Jehosa."

"But I thought that you were supposed to be dead, resurrected, and gone to his Holy Kingdom? How is it that you are out here in the wilderness?" Brother Jackal asked.

"The Great Messiah is dead, resurrected, and gone to the Holy Kingdom. Jes Amir is still very much alive, though fleeing the Arad. I'm trying to find alternative ways to help our people, but I must do it from elsewhere than here now. So the rebellion finally came," Jes sighed.

"Aye, it did, and it has gone just as I predicted it would go. While the first blow went in our favor, the retaliation has been severe to say the very least. Why is it that so few ever listen to their fighting instructors?" Brother Jackal complained. "Now if we had a thousand fighters trained as you three have been, or five, sorry I forgot you two," he apologized to Jackal and Missa, "then we would have a chance at a real victory."

Jes nodded and had an idea. "Say, Brother Jackal, do you have a current assignment?"

"Well, not actually. I was planning to make myself rather scarce around the Arad, if you take my meaning," the old trainer replied. "Why?"

"Well, I offer you a new assignment, one that will occupy you for the remainder of your years. Come with us and train our four children as you trained us. All expenses paid — all earthly desires fulfilled, well, within reason," he added in jest.

"You give an old man purpose yet. Indeed, you're the savior of your people, though many do not realize such. I accept. After all, how can I refuse? I owe any remaining years of life to you two." Jes and Brother Jackal shook hands. He then asked a very strange question, "Tell me one thing, Jes. Has the Yellow Butcher come yet?"

I looked at Jes with raised eyebrows. I'd never heard of a Yellow Butcher. I had no idea what he was asking. Evidently, Jes did, for he said, "Not yet that I know of." He seemed greatly relieved, but since he was now very tired, we let him go back to sleep while we resumed our slow cross-country travel.

As we rode along, I asked Jes what Brother Jackal meant by the Yellow Butcher. His reply filled me with trepidation. "Brother Jackal belongs to a Holy Order of Fighter; they travel Tarra teaching the art of combat to those they find worthy. My dad told me this in confidence one night. Members of his order have long predicted that one day, a Galt, whose skin is slightly yellow, will unite all the warring clans of the Northern Steppes and lead them south to conquer all Tarra. These people have no religion as we know it; they only worship their horses. His order believes that others will view them as butchers. He once told me about the threat they pose, but to date, I've never found anyone who believe these tales. I think he is just overly delirious from his battle last night. Pay it no mind."

Memories of the Galt attacks on Uru came back into my mind. That was over fifty years ago, and I was only six at the time. Their skin did have a slightly yellowish hue to it, as I recalled. As I remembered the Galts, they were not even in the same league as the Centurions. Galts in my memory were just a band of ruffians. I put it out of my mind. I should not have.

Chapter 10 Mikhailovich and Zdlenka Strokova

Zdlenka and her brother had been on their own since they were babies. The twins lost their parents in a raid by a rival clan shortly after they were born and had no memories of their father or mother. As was customary, others in the Strokova clan raised them. Now twenty-one, they were of age and still they were inseparable. The bond between them had allowed them to survive the harsh realities of life on the Northern Steppes.

The numerous clans of horsemen were nomadic by nature, never staying in anyone location for more than half a year. No need to, actually. During three-fourths of the year, the sea of lush grass was more than abundant. Only in the snowy winters, did the clans settle down in one place to wait for the spring melt and the renewal of the grasslands. Here horses meant everything related to survival from transportation to the very hides out of which their domed huts were made. They were superb horsemen, talented riders; their children were taught to ride almost before they could walk.

Their society had clearly defined roles. Men hunted the plentiful game, providing food for the clan. Men were consummate fighters and inner-clan warfare was normal, which was how their parents had been killed. Women, on the other hand, while still masters of their horses, built and maintained the domed huts, wove the leather clothes, did the cooking and rearing of the children. However, their best skill lay in the breeding of their horse stock. The woman who bred the best horses in her clan became the clan breda, a very high honor indeed, second only to the clan ruler, who was the best fighter, which also meant he was the best rider as well. All combat took place from horseback.

Each man was highly skilled with the short bow and could ride at a gallop, load, and fire, controlling the horse with their legs only. The very best could shoot a quiver of arrows in less than a minute, placing most of them into the dummy targets or their opponent, as the case may be. Once the initial assault of projectiles was complete, they resorted to using their curved swords, striking from horseback while at a gallop. These men were fierce fighters; they had to be in order to ensure the survival of their clan from attacks from other clans.

The clan leader, the proven best fighter, had absolute authority over all clan matters. His rule was undisputed. In fact, the clan leader could do absolutely anything he desired, and often did. After all, it was in the clan's best interests to keep him happy and content so that they could depend upon him when raids came. And raids did come. Often a clan had to defend at least twice a season and chose to launch retaliatory raids as just frequently. The object of the raids was both for prestige as well as for horses and women. To the victor went the best two horses of that clan as well as any woman the opposing clan leader desired.

Indeed life was harsh out there on the Northern Steppes. Actually, the only clans that had any kind of semi-permanent residences and were not subject to raids were the metalworkers. There were only seven of these particular clans, located widely spaced about the lands, but always near iron deposits and forests. Yes, small groves of trees grew at widely spaced intervals; so in fact, it was not all a sea of rolling hills and grass. These metalworking clans produced all the arrow tips and swords for all the Galts, and were highly paid, often in gems and jewels found in the rocky streambeds in the more northern portions of the steppes. It was customary for any clan to spend a portion of the year up north, scouring the beds for wealth or raiding other clans for theirs.

Zdlenka and Mikhailovich were outcasts, dependent on the other clan members for their training and survival, a fact that altered both of them during their childhood. Teased by the other kids for having loser parents, both hated the humiliation that was cast upon them daily, but it hardened them both, if not drove them. Because of their low status in the clan, both received only the barest of training from the other adults. If left at that, both were doomed, and they knew that intuitively even at the age of five. As is often the case, if deprived of respect and training, other senses and abilities become enhanced, and that was the case with the twins.

They first noticed it when they were five; each always seemed to know what the other was thinking, and they used it to their advantage. Over the years, that bond grew and strengthened. At puberty, it blossomed into complete telepathic ability. Each could place thoughts in the other's mind and receive them; distance and sight played no part in it. Slowly, they began to use it to its fullest, giving them an advantage over the others, who continually tried to put them at a disadvantage.

As Mikhailovich began to learn the art of combat in earnest, Zdlenka would sit astride her horse some distance away and watch. When he was threatened from the rear, she would send him word of it. She became his overseer, so to speak, eyes that watched his back. From there, it escalated to full-fledged partner in his successes. In fact, by their late teens, Mikhailovich had already made a name for himself as an almost unbeatable fighter, because any threat that came his way he already knew about, thanks to Zdlenka's watchful eye and mind messages. Others thought that he had eyes in the back of his head, for often when someone tried to ride up behind him to strike at his back, he wouldn't even turn to look and see, merely striking out to the rear with his sword at just the precise moment needed to undo the oncoming rider. While Zdlenka could never become a fighter, still she took immense pleasure and satisfaction in watching and helping her brother.

On the other hand, she was always planning. Once she had seen that together, they were unbeatable on the practice field, or rather Mikhailovich was, she then turned her attention to her own situation. She hated doing women's work and did her best to avoid it as much as possible. Mikhailovich gave her a way out — become the breda of the clan. Zdlenka spent all her free time studying and learning the art of horse breeding. She became uncommonly good at it. How?

Each fall before the snows come and each spring after the snow melt has begun, the troka festival takes place. At these two times each year, clans put aside their rivalry and meet somewhere out on the vast steppes in a week-long festival. Besides fun, games, and much mead drinking, the trading of goods replenished needed clan supplies. Zdlenka always shunned the fun and games. Instead, she spent long hours discussing the breeding of horses with the other bredas. She would spy on them, listen in on supposed confidential chats, and in short, do anything to get information. Yes, she and Mikhailovich had to work twice as hard as anyone else; but then as I said, both of these twins were driven persons.

In the end, after fifteen years of very hard work and self-sacrifice, both had made it. Mikhailovich was now the clan leader, while Zdlenka was their breda. She made it because the horses that she bred were reputedly some of the fastest, hardiest horses in the steppes. At twenty-one, her horses commanded top price at the trokas, though few did she sell. He succeeded because of her aid. During one raid on the Strokova clan, their clan leader was slain. Instantly, Zdlenka seized the opportunity to raise their fortunes. She got him onto his horse and, while she mounted and watched from a safe distance, she directed him as he rode singlehandedly into the entire invading force, who was celebrating their success prematurely. With her aid, he slew seven raiders including their leader. Because of this startling twist of fate, the Strokova clan elected Mikhailovich as their new leader. By the time of the next troka, many other clans had heard the tale of his incredible counterattack. Slowly their fame grew.

This was not enough for Zdlenka, not by a long shot. Periodically, for several years now, a cold voice appeared in both their minds, often late at night: *Unite the clans. Conquer all Tarra.* Naturally, this advice appealed to both of them, and she, the planner, set to work. In secret, she accumulated a vast quantity of gemstones. Then, from information gleaned from many trokas, she and her brother visited one specific weaponsmith. Rostov Rondol was his name and he made the finest blades in the Northern Steppes. The two rode to his permanent abode near the northern edge of the steppes, where the towering teeth of the Volgost mountains rose up forming a nearly impenetrable boundary between the Galts and the land of the Axemen, Volksholm. Here in an isolated valley surrounded by steep sided walls and rich in ore veins, Rostov made his home. At fifty-five, he was making few weapons, preferring to instruct and assist his many apprentices. Indeed, his foundry sported fifty makers and their families — a thriving enterprise.

For the right price, he agreed to see the twins in private. "Thank you, Zdlenka," he smiled as he pocketed the gems. "To what do I owe this expensive visit? I rarely see anyone anymore. If you just want a blade, why not just purchase one from our store?"

"We want to commission the making of the finest blade on all Tarra, one that is fast and unbreakable in combat, one that captures the soul of Mikhailovich," she said coming directly to the point of their visit. "You see, we're going to conquer all Tarra. We want an enchanted blade with which to do just that. Yours are the best there is." It must be pointed out that the Galts are a very superstitious people. No attack on a neighboring clan is made if the omens are not right. The camps are not moved until the moon is right. Rostov was the very first person to hear Zdlenka's ultimate goal. She knew such a move could not be done unless the omens were right, and what better way to influence the omens than by obtaining an enchanted blade, one that could be used to inspire warriors to excel to great feats, one that could not be doubted by others, one whose possession guaranteed leadership.

Taken aback by this highly unusual request, the old man pulled on his beard, reflecting, "And you, Mikhailovich, she speaks for you?" Women seldom spoke for men in this land; it was a sign of weakness.

His quiet reply was stranger still, "Aye, for we are one, she and I. Rostov, we have a vision. We and we alone are going to unite the clans into one unconquerable fighting force, a sea of brown horsemen let loose to conquer all the lands of Tarra. Is it not pointless that we spend our days fighting one another, taking from one clan only to have it taken from us at some later date? Folly, I say. Though we try to visit other lands, always we are driven back here. No, rather, we should be taking our just due from other peoples, not from other Galts. Once we unite our people and go forth conquering the world, we, all the clans, will be the most respected fighters on Tarra. We will have wealth beyond measure. However, I cannot unite the clans without an enchanted blade."

"There is wisdom in what you say. These petty raids on neighboring clans are such an incredible waste, but no one listens to the weapons maker. I'm only supposed to provide them. Yet, to provide them so that the clans may extend our dominion, now that is an interesting proposal. You two think you can do this?" He looked long into their eyes; Zdlenka and Mikhailovich looked unflinchingly into his eyes.

Zdlenka spoke, "Name your price; we are prepared to meet it." She was a woman of action and used to getting her way. If nothing else, Rostov saw that these two would not take no for an answer, but the price, now that was another matter. He named a figure. She countered, "And does that include every possible enchantment you can forge into this blade? We want only the finest blade in the entire world."

Such a woman, Rostov had never met, so strong willed, so forceful, so cunning, so dominating, and so intent on getting precisely what she desired. He hesitated a moment, giving the blade's construction some thought. Then, he replied, "Double that amount and it shall be done. Payment ahead of time, of course. Plus, I will need Mikhailovich here briefly, from time to time, during its forging." She didn't waver, as she produced a large sack of gems, dumping them on the table, counting out five and returning those few into her own purse tied at her waist. Rostov's eyebrows rose in surprise. The figure he stated was high, higher than any commission he had ever before accepted, said in part in hopes to dissuade these two.

He smiled, "How soon do you want it? I assume as soon as possible?" Both grinned, knowing that they had succeeded in this phase of their plans. Mikhailovich shook hands with Rostov, sealing the deal.

It took fully six months for Tov's forging — that was the name given to this magical blade. Twice, Mikhailovich had to visit Rostov and intentionally cut his sword hand on the newly forged blade, blending his blood into the body of the weapon, thereby guaranteeing that this blade was enchanted to him and to him alone. It was as if Mikhailovich were transmuting part of his own life force into this magical blade. Rostov forged Tov to be the perfect blade for Mikhailovich, specially designed for this man's height and weight. Heavy enough, yet still light enough to be quick of motion, Tov was indeed an enchanted blade when wielded by Mikhailovich. Only in his hands would Tov achieve its maximum potential, his, or another whose body was identical to Mikhailovich.

The day the weapon was finished and delivered unto Mikhailovich, everyone in Rostov's village witnessed the presentation ceremony. Zdlenka, at her brother's side, smiled as the master craftsman, with the proper ceremony befitting such a momentous occasion, presented him with Tov. Of course, it was only done on a day that the omens predicted was right. As they rode back to their village that day, she commented to him, "Now it begins." He understood, for they were of one mind. "Pleasure me tonight. I've earned it," she coyly commented.

Normally, by their age, they should have been married; yet the two shared the same hut as a man and wife would, though they both remained virgins. When others in their clan commented openly to them about this, Zdlenka replied, "You teased and belittled us all our years until now. How could we 'love' one of you? Besides, clan leader can do as he pleases, as can the breda." This effectively ended all such open discussions, but never the gossip, especially among the women of the clan. Much speculation about what went on in their hut at night filled many ears, but Zdlenka never became with child, which stopped some rumors and fueled others.

She had very long, silky black hair and was exceedingly fair. Mikhailovich was tall, well-muscled, and handsome. She performed wifely duties as needed for him, such as shaving the sides of his head so only the traditional long ponytail flaring back from the top of his head remained. Mornings, she, as a wife normally did, would brush his hair and tie the topnotch, preparing him for the day's action. In all customary ways, Zdlenka did for him as a wife would, save bearing children. Likewise, he did for her all things customary for a husband to perform. Yet within a year, there was not a person in all the steppes that would ever dare cross either of these two!

Now Galts held faith in two gods: Luminka, the Moon Goddess, and Balinkov, the Horse God. Luminka influenced fertility and harmony with nature and was worshiped mostly by women. She was a nurturing goddess.

Balinkov created strong, powerful, swift horses with equally strong and cunning fighters to ride them. Men put their trust in him before battles that they might be victorious over their opponents, but women and bredas also worshiped Balinkov as well, and similarly men also prayed to Luminka to get a strong family unit with many children. In short, the Galts prayed to whichever was appropriate to bless their current needs.

The twins began the uniting process at the next troka. One by one, the twins met with each clan leader in private. After displaying Tov and its magical properties, Mikhailovich commanded, "Join with me now for there is no force on Tarra that can withstand us. Follow us and all Tarra is yours, riches beyond belief, more women than you can please and fame beyond. All on Tarra shall fear your names! Think about it, for untold years we plunder ourselves. Now it is time that we conquer the world, not ourselves! From each town that we conquer and plunder, we will take only what she and I can carry in our hands. All the rest shall be divided among my mighty warriors. In only a little while, you shall be richer than you can possibly imagine!" Both knew that appealing to their greed would be the deciding factor. Self-interest was always in the minds of these clan leaders.

Yet, these leaders were also cautious. Most agreed to supply a number of fighters for one season. When the winter troka came, they would re-evaluate their participation. Both twins knew that that meant they would see how much profit they made and the cost in their clan member's lives.

Zdlenka was no fool; indeed, she had a keen mind for battle logistics, exceeding even that of her brother. Back in their domed hut late at night, she would explain her long range plans. Mikhailovich would listen and suggest minor changes here and there. The first target had to be the northern section of Juda Arad, because here the major production of weapons for enemies occurred. True, they considered all other makes of weapons inferior to those made by their own weapon smiths of the north, save perhaps those of the Axemen. Of course, those made in the Sea Prince lands were the most inferior. Those crafted in the north of the Arad were far better. Hence, the first target was the confiscation of that production.

This meant tackling the Centurions head on, for they controlled the Arad. In fact, since the Megalos soldiers controlled so much of Tarra, the Centurions would have to be eliminated first nearly everywhere. Hence, the twins had spent many hours observing them during their teenage years, while safely just across the border. When another clan would raid the northern Arad towns, the twins snuck along behind them and watched from a safe distance. They concluded that these foot soldiers were well-disciplined, trained to fight together as a team effort. Indeed, on several occasions, the twins watched as one single Centurion bested many opponents. It was as if a single Centurion represented his entire company — rather like all the soldiers coming from the same mold, acting as a single unit.

Zdlenka pointed out to Mikhailovich one day while they were watching, "See, the individual, rebel fighters, acting independently of their own mind?

They are no match for the rigidly held form of Centurion combat. To defeat legions of these Centurion machines, we need a different strategy."

"Yes, Zdlenka, I can see with my own eyes that this is true, but our warriors are all free acting, independent fighters. They cannot be trained into a machine mold as the Centurions. How can we defeat them? We do have speed and mobility on our side."

"Yes, speed and mobility are key. If our fighters are to be successful, they must never stand in one place and fight. Gallop in, strike swiftly, and ride out. Reach, hit, and withdraw, all at galloping speed, like a storm's lightning bolt. That is their weakness. True, brother, but there is another factor that we can use."

"Okay, I give up, what?" he chuckled, knowing she saw another aspect that he did not.

"Fear, fear of us. Our attacks must cause fear in the minds of the Centurion soldiers. This will weaken them, even before battle is joined," she replied.

"I like the sound and implications of that," he replied, imagining how fear of the Galts might affect the outcome of a battle. "How do we accomplish this?"

"Beheading," she replied calmly. "Every Centurion that is killed or wounded is simply beheaded, and the heads cast back at the surviving garrisons. Think of the mental impact on a soldier when he sees the severed head of one of his companions. It cannot but instill fear and terror of us."

Mikhailovich smiled, "Zdlenka, you have a wicked mind! I love it. Take no prisoners; behead all. Clean and simple. Even if the action raises their anger, still fear and horror are always going to be in the back of their minds, gnawing away. Over time, their effectiveness cannot help but diminish. What a pair we make: I, with superior fighting skills, and you, with superior field tactics. Yes, sister, we're about to conquer all Tarra — lay it all bare to our rule — to our control. The world will be ours to command!"

He paused a moment and added solemnly, "Yes, my sister, before long, all Tarra will know the name of Strokova."

While blowing out the lantern, she added in a whisper, "And fear it!"

True to their pledge, after the spring troka, many clans sent fighters to Mikhailovich. On the average, twenty warriors per clan arrived during the week that followed the celebrations. He and Zdlenka were prepared for the new arrivals, having built many more domed huts and stockpiled food supplies. All told, he fielded an army of five hundred Galt cavalrymen. Fully a month was spent working with the men, organizing them and preparing them to act as Mikhailovich desired.

The Strokova clan made its camp this year fairly close to the border of Juda Arad. Only the Gorno clan set their huts closer to the border. All considered it safe enough, since the Centurions had never ventured into the Northern Steppes. However, one sunny spring day while the men were finishing up their practice attacks, several riders galloped toward them from the south at top speed. From the haste and panic visible on the young riders' faces, Zdlenka suspected the worst.

The first lad to arrive and dismount, cried out, "Strokova, they are killing our clan! Even the children! Centurions!" Dropping everything, Mikhailovich galloped over and dismounted. Taking both the young boy's hands in his, he looked him squarely in the eyes, a sign that he considered this boy to be a man worthy of delivering a message. It gave the boy some confidence, as three others from his clan finally arrived and dismounted. They let Kutzik Gorno do the speaking for them. Zdlenka could see the horror in their eyes, as she walked up and listened intently as did many of the new warriors who arrived and dismounted.

Kutzik explained that out of nowhere, a band of Centurions appeared over the hill of their camp. They marched into their village and proceeded to kill everyone, fighters, women, and children. His father, leader of the clan, ordered him to ride for help, while he and his fighters mounted a charge into the enemy ranks.

Mikhailovich needed no further information. He yelled at the top of his voice, "To war, mighty warriors. First, we come to the aid of Gorno. We have Centurions to kill. Mount up; let's ride! Form up into your command groups." Hastily, he swung easily into his saddle. Zdlenka handed him his bow and two quivers of arrows. He already had Tov slung across his back. Other women did the same for the five hundred warriors.

"Please, sir, can we come with you?" pleaded young Kutzik. His three friends begged as well.

"You aren't yet warrior trained, but, yes, ride with Zdlenka and protect her with your lives." Cheering, all four mounted their horses, just as Zdlenka appeared leading her horse, one of the very fastest horses in all the steppes. She had bred her mare for speed and endurance. She carried no weapon, save a dagger for self-defense.

"But why are you going?" asked Kutzik; he had never seen a woman in battles. She seemed out of place, especially since she was not armed.

"I am the eyes of Mikhailovich," was all that she said. The tone of her voice told all four never to ask her that question again or even mention it! She watched the five hundred cavalry fall into ranks and gallop up the side of the hill heading southward, following the trail made by the boys. After the last group had crested the hill, she kicked her horse into a canter to follow, and the four boys did likewise. She looked impressive as she rode like the wind, long black hair flowing behind her, leather clothes matching the leather saddle and the color of her mare. She was one with the horse, moving across the sea of green. She loved riding like this more than possibly anything else.

No one, not even Zdlenka, was prepared for what they found as they crested the last hill overlooking what had been the Gorno clan's huts. Devastation lay everywhere; not one person had been spared. Smoke curled from several burning huts. The four boys gagged and nearly fainted. Zdlenka knew what had to be done. "You four are now the Gorno clan. Kutzik, you are appointed the leader. First action will be to dig graves for all and see to their proper burial, according to our customs. I'll see to it that Mikhailovich leaves several men to help you. I'll be back to help once the vile animals that did this are no more." She sent a message to her brother, telepathically. To the boy's surprise, fifty riders peeled off, circled around, and returned to help them with this ghastly task. She knew that giving the boys a new purpose, a new goal immediately, was the only thing that would keep them from total collapse. Once she repeated her instructions to the men, she galloped off after the small army.

An hour of hard riding brought them success. Mikhailovich crested a hill and spied the marching lines of the Centurions near the bottom of this valley. "A blind child could have followed this trail," one of his men muttered. Quickly, Mikhailovich surveyed the situation, and a plan emerged in his mind from Zdlenka. He formed the men into companies of fifty cavalrymen. His force numbered ten companies, but one left to tend to the burials at Zdlenka's insistence. She was probably right, he thought. He reached out his mind and felt her coming up behind him. He sent her his battle plan; she Okayed it.

He then executed it, crying out, "Let no Centurion live. Every one of these animals is to be beheaded, neatly and cleanly. Companies One, Two, and Three: circle wide to the right, and hit them from the right front. Companies Seven, Eight, and Nine: circle wide to the left, and hit them from the front left. The rest of you, follow me; we hit them straight on, giving the others time to get into position. Arrows only. Save the swords until their numbers are reduced or they route. Ride to victory! For the Gorno clan; revenge!" He yelled a war cry and charged down the hill galloping at top speed; Four hundred fifty others followed suit, all yelling and screaming wild cries.

Assistant General Slavius was not a fool. Seeing the outnumbering cavalry arrive on the hilltop behind him, he assumed that they would charge. Quickly, he issued orders for the few remaining cavalry and his war chariot to assemble in the center, and his squads of foot soldiers formed a square box around him. Should his line weaken, he or the few cavalry could quickly close the gap. It was a tight box.

Like wild men, the enemy came upon the Assistant General's force. Never had they heard such screaming and yelling; it tended to unnerve these warriors. "Now we shall have a real fight, men. Let's show these barbarians how true soldiers fight. Slay them all!" he yelled out his orders, supremely confident of total victory in spite of the overwhelming odds against him. For a moment, he regretted not having brought more squads with him. He would have, had he known that the Galts had such a large war party in the vicinity.

As the charging cavalry approached, the squads, acting as one unit and on command, placed their shields on to the ground, spears protruding outward through the wall of protective shields. However, these wild men didn't close to striking distance, or even spear throwing distance. Rather, while galloping at them, they used their hands to shoot volley after volley of arrows. Slavius marveled that they could even stay on horseback while doing this. He had never thought such was remotely possible! These men all acted independently, shooting their arrows at whomever they chose, in a seemingly random pattern!

While the large shields could totally protect their wielder from a frontal barrage, especially if they ducked down a bit, leaving their bronze helms to protect their heads, many arrows overshot their marks and struck into the rear of those forming up the line from behind. Mikhailovich clearly took advantage of the square formation that the enemy used; his men galloped in from all sides, firing off at least five arrows with each pass. Assistant General Slavius suddenly remembered one of the cardinal rules that General Lacerta had drummed into his head. "An army taking damage without inflicting any is doomed." He felt slightly sick at his stomach as he watched his men begin to fall, arrows protruding from their backsides. Though one may fall, still the Centurions knew from long training what to do; they just closed ranks making the square slightly smaller.

Slavius issued the slow march order. He intended to have the square move slowly back toward the Arad and safety, while still defending from these maniacs. Mikhailovich marveled at how these men could march in such perfect order, some walking sideways, some backwards. Still, the square continued to grow smaller and smaller, as fallen men began to litter the countryside behind them. Mikhailovich knew it was only a matter of time before they would have to resort to sword strikes. He was out of arrows and saw that many others were as well. He sent a note of this problem to Zdlenka, who began to think of a solution for the future. For both twins, this would be an ongoing learning experience, for no one had ever conquered all Tarra.

When the ranks of the Centurions had been cut nearly in half and the square now quite small, Mikhailovich, brandishing Tov before him, ordered the next phase of the assault. Galloping in, they would make one swinging pass with their blades and then pass on by only to circle around and hit them again. With cavalry riding wildly all over the hillside, there always was space available for a rider to swoop in to deliver his crushing blow and get way almost as fast as he swooped into the square.

The Centurion lines quickly crumbled, leaving Assistant General Slavius standing alone in his war chariot. All around him, his men lay wounded or dying. Now the barbarians backed off, leaving this one for Mikhailovich, personally. He slowly rode into a charging position and saluted the general. Quickly, Slavius grasped the situation; he was being challenged to personal combat, perhaps with the barbarian leader. His war chariot was still in perfect condition. Grabbing a spear in one hand and his reins in another, he urged his team into an all-out charge toward the barbarian leader who now did likewise, heading for him. The two Centurion horses galloped at top speed toward the lone rider who rushed even faster at them. Hooves thundered into the soft ground, mud and grass clods flying from their hooves. As they approached, Slavius thrust his spear in a forward motion toward the barbarian, hoping to skewer him. Mikhailovich made a circle swing with his sword at the neck of his opponent.

Slavius received the sensation of his spear missing, striking only air. The next instant, he was floating above the battlefield. Below him, he saw his team galloping at random across the beautiful grasslands. Then he spied his headless body lying on the ground; its head had rolled like a child's ball some twenty feet from it. If he would have had a stomach, he knew he would have vomited at the sight, so it was comforting that he found himself just floating above it all, wondering what was going on anyway. From some dark corner of his mind, a command rang out loudly in his mind, spoken by a strangely familiar, cold, alien voice: "Report back to here when the body dies!" So powerful was that command in his mind that he had no choice but obey. Without knowing how or why, he found himself flying like mad across the land at hundreds of miles an hour, heading for the sands of the Red Desert. He had no idea where he was going; he felt he had no choice.

The warriors cheered their victory and toasted Mikhailovich long and loudly. When they quieted down, he ordered, "Okay, I want each man beheaded cleanly, collect their spears, one for each head. Pack them into bags. Mound all bodies here; we'll leave them for the jackals. As soon as all heads are gathered and bodies piled, we ride for Al Dun. Tonight, we shall give them back their army, heads impaled on their spears. At dawn our enemies will see their ghost legion!" The men roared with laughter and talked among themselves of this brilliant response. They also confiscated any valuables they found on the bodies, just as Mikhailovich said they were entitled.

Meanwhile, Zdlenka joined her brother assisting the binding of two fighter's wounds. Two men had taken spear puncture wounds to the chest. There were no other casualties, just piles of dead Centurions. The twins grinned at each other; their plan was working even better than they had hoped. Zdlenka now wondered about healers; clearly, they would be in great need of healers. Where could they find enough? She hadn't thought of this detail.

The next morning in Al Dun, Major Titus's aide pounded on his door awaking him far too early for breakfast. "Major! Get up! It's horrible; Assistant General Slavius has returned, dead. My god, come at once!" Pulling on his pants and hobbling first on one foot and then the other, not even bothering with a shirt, Major Titus clamored after his aide. They walked to the edge of the small town. As they walked, other men and villagers joined them, while others, white-faced and gagging, hastily headed back into town. At the edge of town was Assistant General Slavius and his entire legion — well, at least their heads were there, resting atop their spears, which were stuck vertically in the ground, nicely arrayed in proper columns and lines. Major Titus vomited on the spot.

Quickly, he recovered from the shock, "Okay, take those heads down, and bury them at once. Dispatch riders: follow me! Sound general quarters; men, we are at war!" Hastily, he headed back to the safety of his barracks. Within minutes, he wrote out several identical dispatches and sent the six riders on their way. Five went to the neighboring towns and villages here at the edge of the Northern Steppes, and one went all the way back to General Lacerta.

The local Arad people knew immediately what this meant. War with the Galts was eminent. By late afternoon, many fled the border towns in wagons, on horse or donkey back, and even on foot. They didn't need to be a genius to realize that the Galts would return in force and very soon. Thus began the exodus of Juda Arad.

Chapter 11 War Comes to Tarra

General Lacerta sipped a cup of tea and nibbled on a biscuit. It was April 1, 585 AH, and he had just sent in his weekly situation update report to the Emperor back in Megalos. It had been a stellar report. True, the barbarians had indeed rebelled; revolt had come. However, he had handled it perfectly. The entire rebellion was totally squashed in just three days. Well, it would take a few more days, perhaps a week, to get the outlying towns completely cleaned up, for they had not yet built paved roads to these more obscure, remote places.

Of course, he found life almost at once falling back into utter boredom. For three days, he had felt completely alive and invigorated. Dealing with the rebellion had been quite exciting. Lacerta was a man of action, not complacency. With the report sent, the last traces of excitement faded, like a marigold in the first snow. "I wish the Emperor would give me the go-ahead to invade the Northern Steppes; then we would surely see some exciting combat," he muttered to himself. He knew those orders very likely wouldn't be coming anytime soon. Emperor Titus was more inclined to shoring up all the occupied territories than expansion.

Suddenly his top aide knocked on his door and entered bearing a mail pouch. "Sir, this is marked exceedingly urgent; top priority. Comes from Major Titus of Al Dun. Isn't that where Assistant General Markus Slavius is at?"

"Aye, let's have it," the general commented. He had never received a top priority dispatch from the field. He opened it and read; the more he read the more excited he grew. "Eureka!" was his first comment. Then, he handed it to his aide and sat back to reflect upon the news. His aide read the following:

General Theos Lacerta: Today, we're at war with the Galts. General Slavius took a company of Centurions into the Northern Steppes and was returned to us today by the Galts. Sitting outside Al Dun, the head of every man was stuck to a spear, which were arranged in a perfect marching order. Ghastly sight. No idea where their bodies may lie. Suspect an all-out attack here on Al Dun shortly. Size of enemy force is unknown, but must be large to have killed Slavius' entire force. I sent word to the other nearby towns along the border. Will defend Al Dun to the last man unless I receive other orders. Send reinforcements before it is too late. Signed: Major Titus Karnus, now Acting Commander, Al Dun.

The aide paled, "Sir, does this mean that over a hundred thirty men were beheaded by these Galts?"

"Yes it does. Must have been a grisly sight indeed. Looks like we are in for some exciting action! Spread the word; we're now at war with the Galts. I'll post the Emperor and then address the men. Oh, and get me an accounting of just where our forces are currently located. We have much planning to do!" His aide rushed out to carry out his orders, while a grinning Lacerta wrote a lengthy dispatch to the emperor. His boredom had completely evaporated. As he wrote, a cold, alien voice spoke into his mind: *Kill all the Galts.* He paid it no attention, because that was already his intention.

However, he lacked information, key data. How large was the attacking forces? What kind of soldiers were they? He suspected cavalry. Where was the opposing army located? What was their next likely objective? Where were all of his forces? More than half had been sent out to put down any vestiges of the rebellion in the outlying towns and villages. These, he would have to recall immediately. He thought about relaying the message to the other generals in occupied Sea Prince lands, but decided against doing so just yet. It was too early to assess the situation properly. Perhaps this was just a retaliatory strike by the Galts; maybe they had no intention of actually invading Juda Arad. "Time enough for messages; I don't want to sound like a fool if nothing should come of all this," he muttered to himself. "Besides, remember the first rule of war: assess the situation. Assess the enemy. Assess your forces."

An hour later, Lacerta had the figures he needed. All told, he now had remaining two thousand five hundred and six Centurions under his direct control, counting officers as well. The untimely loss of Slavius and his hundred thirty or so men paled in comparison. However, figures can be deceiving. Three quarters of his legions were Rear Guard units, meaning they were older soldiers, not front line troops. Well, they would soon become front line troops, he thought. It would take at least a week to pull in all of the Centurion soldiers that had been sent out to the more remote sections of the Arad, meaning east or west of the single paved roadway that ran north-south the full length of the country. A spur road connected it to the port city of Al Barq.

Along with his aides, he studied maps of Juda Arad. One thing became clear to Lacerta. Under no conditions could the entirety of the Arad be allowed to fall into the enemy's hands. Al Barq was the main port of entry and communication with all their forces in the Sea Princes. If this port city fell, the entire garrisons in the Sea Princes would be nearly completely isolated from Megalos. Only a few coastal ships could make the exceedingly lengthy voyage around the entire southern continent to reach the Med Sea. Such a voyage took over six months! Therefore, the loss of Al Barq would be a devastating blow to Megalos, one that he had to avoid at all costs. Perhaps he was being overly pessimistic, maybe nothing much more would come from the Galts. Secretly, he hoped not.

By that evening, he had written out extensive orders to be delivered to every Major under his command. The next day, he personally led a force of seven hundred of his crack troops in a long convoy north from Jerilum heading for Al Dun. He was confident that within two weeks, his thousands of men would be properly placed. The vast majority were to be stationed in and around Jerilum. Should the Galts actually invade, he wanted them completely and utterly stopped no farther south than this large city, centrally located in the Arad.

It took him six days of forced marching to reach Al Dun. During this time, no further dispatches came from Major Titus. However, when they were still a day out of Al Dun, he already knew what he would find when they arrived. The road was flooded with refugees, Arad locals, fleeing for their lives. Many were questioned as they passed. The day after the heads appeared, the Galt cavalry army surrounded the town. The following day, the town fell to the barbarians. Every single Centurion was killed along with many of the local Arad men as well. Women had been brutalized; children killed. The town was in flames; all the weapon smith shops destroyed. The town had been thoroughly sacked and pillaged. He estimated his losses at about two hundred soldiers.

When they actually arrived at what had been the border town of Al Dun, Lacerta's forces were greeted by Major Titus and his men — at least their heads greeted them. Once more, the heads were stuck atop spears stuck in the ground, laid out in a perfect marching order just at the southern edge of town. Smoke still curled skyward from the burned out homes and shops. Dead bodies lay strewn where they died. The stench of death was overwhelming. Not a single alive person was here. Al Dun was now a ghost town.

"Clean up this abomination!" was Lacerta's first order, followed by many more. He sent his fifty cavalrymen out on patrols, half riding north, half riding south. He needed information on the enemy, so they were ordered to scout only, not engage under any circumstances. He needed more that the eyewitness accounts of these invading, screaming wild men on horseback. However, all this beheading business was starting to take its toll on his men and himself. "What incredible barbarians these Galts are!" he commented to his aides. "We should have conquered them twenty years ago!" None disagreed with him; the sight was revolting to say the very least.

Two days later, he had a better assessment of their situation. Scouts reported that the army, if this rag tag band could warrant such a description, was still located safely within the Northern Steppes. Clear trails showed that they rode out of the steppes to attack and then retreated the same way they'd come. The towns immediately north and south of Al Dun had met the same fate as Al Dun, though the loss of soldiers was not nearly as high, for the largest concentration had been here where the roadway had ended.

His scouts also reported that other border towns further away were being rapidly deserted by the local Arad population. Only the hardy or foolish remained, along with the small Centurion garrison forces. He also worked out a time line. Two days after Al Dun was attacked, the western town was sacked. Two days after that, the eastern one next to Al Dun was laid to waste. All three had been major armament suppliers for the Centurions.

"Ah ha," General Lacerta commented to his staff, "now I see their strategy. I'll bet anything that they are taking out all our northern armament factories, all of which lie along the northern borderlands. This makes sense. Their leader thus does have some predictability here. I see his intentions. In fact, that is what I would do if I were invading."

An aide commented, "By the way, Sir, we now have a name for this barbarian leader. Apparently, he left specific orders with one Arad survivor to relay his name to us. He is called Mikhailovich Strokova."

"Heck, I can't even pronounce that name!" cursed Lacerta. "I'll just call him 'Kova!' Well, Kova, you and your men are doomed! Crucifixion is too good a death for you! I swear I'll have your head before long!" However, Lacerta had a small problem: which town would this Kova strike next? If the pattern held and his prediction valid, Kova would be attempting to eliminate all weapons production facilities here in the north of Juda Arad. Kova first took Al Dun where their speedy roadway ended. Next, he went to the town east and then west of Al Dun. Would he go after the next in the east or west or pick an entirely different one? Lacerta had only enough forces to defend one town at a time.

While his aides went in search of a friendly, knowledgeable Hessonite or possibly a Hamadanite who was friendly with the Centurions, Lacerta studied his relatively incomplete and crude maps of this area. Several hours later, after some discussions with a local man and his aides, Lacerta cast his hook. He ordered the majority of his forces eastward to the next major production center in a town called Kaan. Why Kaan? To the west lay rugged country where the mesas merged with the barrier granite protrusion that formed the natural barrier between these two lands. Horses would have a harder time negotiating this terrain, but to the east, once over the protrusion, the land was much less rugged. At last, Lacerta made his prediction and moved his forces.

Two days later, they arrived at the outskirts of Kaan. Here the town was protected by a surrounding adobe wall. Mine tunnels burrowed into the sides of the granite protrusion, while two smelters still belched thick black into the blue sky. Around the huge work area lay piles of iron ore and coal. A line of smithy shops were neatly arrayed opposite the mine entrances, while the village homes were behind these. Today, however, half of the population had already fled deeper into the central regions of the Arad. Only a few weapon makers remained and virtually no miners. Two smelter operators were in the process of shutting them down, hence the thick acrid smoke. Even as they smartly marched into Kaan, locals were leaving, carrying their possessions and supplies on their backs. All other means of transportation had been already taken.

However, even as they set themselves up in Kaan, one of his cavalry scouts returned to tell General Lacerta that another town had fallen to the west. Undaunted, he setup his forces for an attack. He was confident that one would come here eventually. This time, he would personally eliminate this Kova barbarian! They would take advantage of the natural defense offered by the ten-foot tall adobe walls. Of course, the four wooden doors were the weak link. Hence, he kept the bulk of his force mobile within the town to cover any possible door. The rest he armed with short bows and had them man the walls in such a manner so that anyone approaching the doors would be caught in a cross-fire of arrows.

Confident his men were in position, he confiscated a vacant building for his headquarters and ordered up tea and biscuits. It was just a matter of time now. This Kova would eventually make his appearance.

Early the next morning, the earth shook from the thundering hooves of five hundred galloping cavalry. Mikhailovich Strokova had arrived to take Kaan. Cavalry flowed over the granite barrier rocks and onto the sandy land of the Arad quickly encircling the town. Mikhailovich halted with his company on the highest point of land overlooking the town. The sheer number of Centurions defending was more than obvious to him; sunlight reflected off their bronze helms. Thus, he did not give the attack signal; instead, his men screamed their wild attack cries as they galloped around the outer wall, staying just outside of bow distance.

Zdlenka, a lone rider, pulled up behind her brother. "I got your message that the Centurions have decided to place their forces to defend this town. We knew eventually they would put all they have into one of these weapon making locations, so Kaan it is."

"Yes, we predicted rightly once again, sis. Are we still agreed on the action to take?" he replied.

"I think so. We could bash down the doors, but the advantage would lean very heavily to the defenders. Our losses would be too great. We must not lose many men; the clan leaders are watching us closely on this detail. So yes, we go to the starvation plan," she replied.

Mikhailovich gave the orders to his aides who galloped off to the encircling companies of cavalry warriors. Slowly, the vast majority of the warriors retreated the way they'd come, disappearing over the granite barrier protrusion. However, a hundred formed into garrison positions, blocking all avenues of escape from the doors in the adobe protective wall. "Don't forget to keep them guessing," Zdlenka whispered to her brother, who smiled back at her.

"Nope, Tram is on the way," he countered. Tram was the name they had given to the massive door-buster he'd invented. Essentially, it was the trunk of an oak tree fitted with a metal tip hauled on a wagon, which could be used to ram into a door and bust through. As yet, it was untried. "But first, well use the fire arrows. Let's see if we can perhaps get some of the roofs burning. That will lower their morale."

"We think of everything," she smiled at him. "I'll go back to the field camp. Let me know if anything happens; I can be back here monitoring in perhaps fifteen minutes." He nodded and she galloped off into the sea of green to their temporary encampment. She had to make sure that the women were preparing the meals for five hundred hungry warriors.

That evening, once the roof fires had been put out, General Lacerta met with his majors and aides. Half of the buildings in the town were now no longer habitable from the fires. This posed little problems for the Centurions who were used to camping on long journeys. The real problem was assisting the locals whose homes had been burned. "Gentlemen, the situation here is not to my liking. I had hoped that we could have one decisive battle and end this Galt threat, but the cowards show no sign of battling it out. Rather, they are adopting a siege mentality. Burn us out. Starve us out. We're definitely not going to play by their rules. We'd be cut to pieces. Never go into a combat at less than three to one odds, if you can help it. Our estimates put the enemy force at perhaps five hundred, give or take; all cavalry. We've not seen even one foot-soldier. That makes it just over one to one. Gentlemen, I'll not put you in that kind of jeopardy."

Everyone cheered in relief. Most had figured that the general would order them out of the city to take on the charging horsemen. None particularly liked that option, as it seemed a sure way to get injured. He continued, "It is also obvious that our opponents are not completely ignorant. They have planned on methods to take a walled city, as witnessed by that big door-smasher that they are showing us just on the other side of the granite protrusion. True, these puny doors anchored to the weak adobe walls are certainly no match for that contraption. Remember, men, if they choose to come storming in through the doors, they'll be playing straight into our hands. Our city defense will raise our odds to that of three to one, which is much more like it! Since they have not yet used it, perhaps it is there just to let us know that they could opt to use it."

He continued, "Here's what we do. Nothing. Sit tight and wait. Let them make the first move, the first mistake. Let them come to us. They can burn down all the roofs. Little matter. Let's see just what they do. We've plenty of supplies and a good well here in town. Sit back and relax. Let the troops know. Keep a careful watch at night, though. We don't want any sneak attacks. That'll be all for now." Satisfied, his commanders left to spread the orders. All were quite happy with the general's grasp of the situation and his handling, thus far. Besides, only a few barbarians could be seen riding around, just out of bowshot range.

The Strokova twins sat in their domed hut, one oil lantern provided dim illumination, just enough so that they could see each other's faces. He said, "Their leader is a crafty one. I had hoped he would bring his lines of soldiers out to face us. If so, we would have wiped them out to the last man. No, he his holding up. I think we've burned half of the roofs, and the rest I don't think we can reach without endangering the shooter."

Zdlenka commented, "You need to take these troops when they are on foot? Correct?"

"Yes, tomorrow, I'll take most of the men and go on to the next village. I'll leave maybe fifty back here to harry them. If they attempt to leave, my orders are to let them, but notify me at once and follow them, but do not attack. Once they are on the move, then we can safely attack them. How have you fared with the couple of Arads we captured?" At the last town, they had taken two merchant types prisoner, hoping to get useful information from them.

She grinned wickedly, "A little persuasion was all that was needed. I threatened to drive needles under their fingernails. Their tongues wagged when they saw I wasn't kidding around. For one thing, the Arads absolutely hate these infidels; that's their name for those from Megalos. In fact, I think without much trouble, we could get their isolated fighting bands on our side to help us. We're right in assuming that there is no army, no organized fighting force in Juda Arad; the Centurions wouldn't permit it. Apparently, there are many irregular bands harassing them. Anyway, using them is a possibility we might consider, but then what to do with them once we have taken their country? That becomes a problem. However, they have recently attempted a widespread rebellion against the Centurions, and many have been slain already, so their numbers are probably not large."

She added, "The other thing is most interesting. I can see that we as a people have not been too observant of the world outside our steppes. Our constant infighting focuses attention to within the steppes when it should've been placed outward. Fools. I learned some interesting things, if they are true." Her brother sat up very alert, listening to her every word.

She smiled and explained, "The Centurions have mostly what's called the Rear Guard here in the Arad, plus the newly arrived attack troops we're seeing here in Kaan. The Rear Guard troops are older, not as fit soldiers. They also have taken control of all the principalities of the Sea Princes and are garrisoning them with more of these Rear Guard troops. What I found exceedingly interesting is that the entire supply line for all of the Sea Princes is out of Al Barq, the southernmost city of Juda Arad."

"I'm beginning to see what you mean," he interrupted. "If we take Al Barq, then we've cut their main supply line. Can they send ships around the Southlands?"

"I would presume so, but that must be a very long way to travel. The Southlands is huge, isn't it?"

"I think so, but who knows. We've been too long looking inward as a people. That we, sister, are changing once and for all! After we render their weapons production useless, we should drive to this Al Barq and take it. Is that what you are thinking? Cut their supply lines, cripple their ability to retaliate?"

"Indeed, just what I was thinking. We could then sweep across all the Sea Princes, taking that whole country before turning our attention southward toward the heart of Megalos. If we go after the Sea Princes next, there is sure to be plenty of booty to keep our warriors completely satisfied."

"What about those amazon women fighters there in the Sea Princes? We've heard lots of rumors about their skill," he mused.

"Well, we did hear that a group of them nearly wiped out a legion of Centurions a long time ago. Who knows if they still exist? Maybe they all perished in that war. If not, heck, just bypass them. They aren't cavalry, so sweep past them and ignore them." This seemed like a good way to deal with the amazons, should they even exist anymore. Lack of reliable information outside of the steppes was now their biggest problem.

"Maybe we should make an end sweep down the western edge of the Arad toward Al Barq now," he thought aloud. "Already, these border towns are nearly empty. We've taken all the larger ones. Perhaps, I could send half the force on an end run."

"I like that, but won't we need all of them to deal with these Centurions that are holding up here in Kaan?" she countered.

"Oh yes. Then, there is the water problem. I hear that it is very scarce out in the mesa lands. We do need a lot of water for the horses," he added.

"I have an idea," Zdlenka brightened up, "why not send, say, only a company on the flanking ride. They can scout out the water holes before the heat of summer comes. Very likely, there aren't going to be very many real towns out there. It's so isolated. Have the Captain tell the villages to send a quarter of their yearly produce come first snow to us or we'll return and wipe out the entire village."

He chuckled, "My sentiments exactly. Besides, we would only have to wipe out a couple villages before all the others got wise. I'll see to it in the morning. Sis, this sure is going a whole lot easier than I first imagined. I don't see anything that can possibly stop us from conquering the entire known world!" Both grinned at each other.

We moved off the road and behind a mesa where we couldn't easily be seen. We needed time to sort things out, make our plans, and let Jes make his own. Based on Brother Jackal's spooky reference to the Yellow Butcher, we sorely needed more data. What was going on? Jackal and Missa decided to do some reconnoitering on their own. The children appreciated a few days of camping in one spot and had fun exploring the mesa and countryside. However, we were a long way from the nearest watering hole.

By dusk, Missa returned with unsettling news. The infidels were definitely up to something. They spied above normal messengers and troops moving on this track, which should have nearly none. Perhaps had we known that so many infidels would have been sent this way, we might have opted to head more north or south. Missa added, "Jackal is going back into the town seeking news. We saw the infidels cutting down our rebels, but the weird thing is that now they're not taking advantage of that victory to shore up the town. Many appear to have left. Makes no sense. Always the infidels take full advantage of their successes. We've spotted four infidel messengers going by already today. Jackal says that this is highly, highly unusual. We are so far away from their main paved road."

"How many should we be seeing?" I asked out of curiosity.

"None on a daily basis; perhaps one every week or so. Then maybe the rebellion is the culprit. Hope so, anyway. Say, you don't know of any other trickery these infidels might have up their sleeves, do you?" Missa asked, remembering that I had some dealings with them many years ago.

I thought about it before answering her, "Always, when trouble arose, they sent in large numbers of soldiers to deal with it in short order. If the rebellion was a coordinated thing, you know, happening on the same day in every town, then they might be scrambling to get a grip on things. I'm sure they don't have enough soldiers in our land to do as I once saw. That might account for the increased message traffic." We left it at that.

Late that night, Jackal returned, sneaking back into our camp, testing our defenses, which proved nearly non-existence. After we all had a laugh over it, our scout reported what little he had learned. "Today, at dusk, I saw the weirdest thing. A squad of infidels came marching into town. Only a few minutes later, a messenger came riding in at top speed. With only a few minutes to eat, the squad began double time marching back the way they had come. What do we make of this? I surely don't know. I chatted in the pub. Most all the younger, fit men have been killed in the valiant uprising. All were expecting a strong edict from the infidels to be coming in response, but none has yet come! Could it be that our rebels have been more than successful somewhere else?" He sounded so hopeful. Jes did not share his optimism, though, nor did I for that matter.

"Okay, I've reached my decision," Jes announced. "Tomorrow, we must head for the sea coast, find a small fishing village that has no infidels in it, and book a ferry passage to Zargarb or the closest coastal village in that Sea Prince Sector. I will go too. It is just too dangerous to stay here. Because of the rough terrain further south and the lack of watering holes, which will put the coast at least two weeks away, let's cross the road and head more northerly and enter the cedar forests. There we ought to find game to catch and water in abundance, so we don't need to risk getting more supplies. The only tricky thing is crossing the road unseen."

The next day, we made the road in the late afternoon. Jackal rode to the top of the nearest mesa for a long look in both directions. We didn't want to make a mistake. When he gave the all clear signal, we ventured out onto the track and a little while later, I was relieved as we veered once again out into the northern valley. I could see only the faintest signs that this route was used. It certainly could not be said to be a high traffic trail. Probably shepherds used it, I presumed. Jackal was a long time in catching back up with us. He had taken the time to hide the wagon tracks heading into the track and then out of it. Hopefully, no one would find signs of our passing.

The next week of travel, though slow, was actually enjoyable. We met four shepherds tending their flocks here in the back areas of northwestern Arad. All were most friendly, and none recognized Jes, who pretended to be a merchant moving his family to some new town. Once more, the children got to pet sheep and enjoy themselves. Our conflicts seemed far removed.

Suddenly, that all ended. The next day, as we were about fifty miles from the cedar forests, Jackal spied dust clouds coming our way. That could only mean riders galloping swiftly. We were out in the open, traveling the valley between two mesas as usual. With the slow wagons, we had no place to hide and no chance to move quickly out of their way. Jes calmed our rising fears, "It cannot be the infidels. They're ignorant of these parts of our lands. It is probably a band of our messiahs. It is imperative that we not be recognized. Josh and I will hide under the canvas. The two Jackals and Missa can deal with them." I figured that they might also recognize me, so I quickly donned a hooded robe and hid all but my eyes, hunched over, and pretended to be an apathetic wagon driver. Brother Jackal and Milla drove the other wagon, while Jackal and Missa rode just out in front of us. The remaining horses were tied to the wagons and followed along.

Soon five riders appeared slowly growing in size. I admired the way the clouds of dust rose just behind them. It was picturesque. As the lead rider drew close, Jackal called out, "Hail. What news?" No Arad could help but stop and gab if directly asked. The lead rider slowed and motioned the others to ride on past us.

"We're at war! That's what's up. You are messiah Jackal, are you not? I recognize your face. It's the Galts. They have invaded Juda Arad!"

"What?" cried Jackal.

"They've pretty much demolished the northern blacksmith towns, at least the larger ones. The infidels are taking the brunt of it. At Al Dun, they beheaded every infidel and stuck their heads on their spears. They even arranged them in marching lines of heads. It was the most hideous sight anyone has ever seen! Fortunately, most of our people were allowed to escape, fleeing here to the backcountry. When I left, I saw a huge bunch of infidels marching north on their road toward Al Dun. So what the Great Messiah couldn't achieve, it looks like the Galts just might do! Drive the infidels from the Arad."

"But what do they want of us, I wonder?" Jackal mused, unable to fathom the Galts as being friendly to us.

"Messiah Al Mir joined us yesterday, fleeing from his northwestern village. It seems that some of the Galts are headed down this way, the western edge of the Arad. He heard that they were ordering the villages to send a quarter of their yearly produce to the steppes or they would return and wipe the village out. I have to get going. We have to warn as many as we can. If you are wise, Jackal, get your people out of here fast!" Jackal nodded and the young rider galloped off to rejoin the others.

Brother Jackal merely said, "Ah, so now comes the Yellow Butcher. All is right in the world."

"Huh? How is this all right?" I asked him.

"My order has long predicted that one day the yellow men will finally stop their infighting and direct that hostility outwards. Long have we known of their brutal natures. Hence, we predicted one day the Yellow Butcher would arise and strike. Who else to bear that first strike but Juda Arad? That is one reason we have spent so many years in this land training worthy fighters. Now all Tarra shall be tested." He would say no more, which simply raised my curiosity level even further. Who were these monks? Where were they stationed? Why had the druwids not known of them? What were their numbers? Were they all spread out across Tarra, like Brother Jackal, or were they capable of forming a counterstrike force?

Jes and Josh climbed out of the rear wagon and joined us. Jes, with a distinct tone of worry in his voice that I'd never heard before, said, "How soon can we make the relative safety of the cedar forests?"

"Two days, tops with the speed of the wagons," he replied. "My Lord, concerning the gravity of the situation, may I offer the suggestion: perhaps it is time to abandon the wagons and flee on horseback. We can make the safety of the cedars in one day."

"Ah, we need poles, plenty of poles," Brother Jackal commented to no one in particular. He was quite prone to talking to the air.

"What?" exclaimed Jes, rather confused.

"Poles. Poles to use to knock the yellow raiders from their horses. Many poles. Poles do break."

"You think we should abandon the wagons, Brother Jackal?" Jes asked, trying to make sense of the pronouncements of our old fighter-training master.

"Some decisions may not matter," was all that he would say, and he walked off in search of scarce wood that he could turn into poles.

"Jes, with this clear sky, I'm not likely to be able to bring down lightning to help us. I might be able to drop fires on them, though. I'm getting really worried. We have the children. We can't fight from wagons. We can't fight from horse back with children riding double with us either." Of course, the children, who had heard everything, now began to ask endless questions, interrupting us.

Brother Jackal walked back to us looking forlorn. "No poles. No trees. No wood. No good."

"That settles it!" Jes pronounced. "We abandon the wagons. Everyone, load up the horses as fast as you can. We have enough horses for us adults and one spare. Pack the spare with as much gear as possible. The children really got excited and worried, but I was creative in my orders, and soon had ours and Josh's helping us pack, stow our spare clothing, cooking ware, and food supplies. Children love to help, if only we let them do what they can. We abandoned much of our water supply, because once into the relative safety of the cedar forest, I assumed that water would be easy to find.

However, with the horses unhitched, saddled, and sacks tied to the saddles, Brother Jackal exclaimed in glee, "Poles! We have poles!" At once, we saw what he meant. Each wagon had a pole to which the horses were hitched. Also each had four axles that would serve as poles. The men helped Brother Jackal dismantle our wagons. A half hour later, we had seven usable poles; we tied one end to the saddles, letting the other end drag along behind us. I really had no idea what Brother Jackal had in mind with these poles, but since he was now very happy, I was too.

Soon we were off once more, this time making significantly faster progress. By very late afternoon as the sun was beginning to sink, we spied the signs of the cedar forest ahead. We were heading nearly due west now, but our luck ran out. Jackal spied a huge cloud of dust far off to our right, coming our way from nearly due north. From the size of the cloud, one could guess many riders were headed toward us.

"Hold the pole vertical between you and them so that their sword swings cannot strike you. When the opportunity arises, plant one end in the ground and use the other to knock the rider off using his own momentum," Brother Jackal explained.

"What if they use a hail of arrows?" I asked, suddenly reminded of Galt attacks many years ago in the Greenway.

"Over there," Missa called out, "good defensive spot. We can keep the mesa wall to our rear and present only one front. They can't ride past us and encircle us." We followed her suggestion, raced for the mesa wall, and dismounted. We tied all the reins of the horses together so that one person could hold them. That was Missa's task. Milla's was to cradle all four children. The men took up a front line formation in a semi-circle around us. Each had a pole at the ready along with their swords. I had my staff and a pole as well. I quickly dropped the pole. If the Galts broke through the men, I was the last protection for the children. A pole was the last thing I wanted. Dusk was coming. Perhaps they would just ride on by and leave us alone.

They didn't. A group of fifty yellowish-skinned cavalry galloped into view. My first thought was that these Galts looked slightly better dressed, more fit than the one's I had seen long, long ago in my Uru Greenway village. Their leader spoke something, though none of us understood a word he said. We didn't speak their language. We said nothing. The riders all carried wicked looking curved swords and had short bows with many quivers slung across their backs. Their horses pranced and pawed the ground, panting from their long exertion. The leader snickered some additional comments or perhaps orders, and he, and forty or so, galloped off in the direction they had been heading, leaving ten staring wickedly at us. One spoke and they charged our men.

As they closed, each raised their poles to fend of sword swings that were aimed for decapitation. All thudded harmlessly into the poles. At least two lost their swords from the force of the unexpected defense. They swung awkwardly around and made a second pass with the same net result. It became clear to me that they would change tactics now and resort to their bows, for which we had no defense. I envisioned the children being struck by flying arrows as I had been last lifetime. No way was that going to happen to my children, not if I can help it! Necessity sometimes drives me. It did this day. I had to stop the hail of arrows. Visions of my old druwid mentor, Ellen, came back to me. The first time I saw Ellen in action in Uru. She threw up a wall of ice and then of flames to stop the Galts. Ice! That was it! Though it had been some thirty years since I last did it, I began my chants, carefully outlining the effect I wanted to create. A small part of my awareness spotted the Galts reaching for their short bows. I could sense Milla's growing fear, as she forced the children in as close to her body as she could, intending physically to protect them from a rain of arrows at the cost of her own life.

Simultaneously, my wall went up before me entirely protecting me and those behind me. I couldn't get it out in front of the four men because of the distance — they were too far apart. I heard the twang of ten short bows loosened and spied the thuds of arrows as they struck the wall of ice. I saw Jackal go down from a hit. Jes dodged successfully, but Josh took an arrow to his right arm. Brother Jackal merely caught two mid-flight. I watched as they reloaded. Now the second part of my chant detonated. Above the Galts a sheet of flames appeared. I let go of it and gravity took over, dropping the wall of flames upon the startled Galts. Hair singed on man and beast; their leather clothes caught fire. Screaming wildly, they cantered off after the others, which was the wrong thing to do if one's clothes are on fire. One should drop and roll in the dirt to put it out. Instead, riding hard, they fanned the flames. We watched, as one by one, still flaming, they fell off their horses. I let the wall of ice fall to the ground and begin melting.

Missa and I rushed to the men. Jes beat us both. After a cursory glance at Josh, he pointed me to him and went to the fallen Jackal first. An arrow had pierced his chest, puncturing his lung. Blood oozed from his mouth, and he was coughing. I motioned for Missa to tend to Josh and joined Jes, pushing him aside. "Jackal, the arrow has to come out. Brace yourself. This will hurt," I said quickly. Before he could do anything, I grabbed hold of the shaft, positioned myself properly, and gave a mighty pull. Out it came, and in reaction, I went sprawling over backwards. He cried in pain and passed out, as I expected he would.

I got to my feet and went to examine him carefully. A puncture wound needs to bleed out any foreign matter. Unfortunately, his lung was filling up with blood. I looked at Jes; he me. "My turn. I know your prognosis," Jes said quietly. We both knew that Jackal was in grave peril with this wound and that there was little else I could effectively do for him. Jes, on the other hand, could and did. Once more, I watched him say a prayer to Jehosa and lay his hand on his friend. I watched the wound close before my own eyes. He would live, but he would have a devil of a time coughing up all the blood that had seeped into his lungs. I then went over to Josh.

Missa looked at me anxiously, "He'll be just fine. Good, you have the arrow out. I'll work on it now; we need to make it bleed a bit to make sure nothing is in it. Can you fetch my healing pouch?"

"No need," Jes came up behind me. He knelt down beside his brother, spoke that same prayer, and touched Josh. Once more, I watched fascinated as the wound closed before my observant eyes. It healed as a normal wound would heal. Rather, it was the time factor. I swore two weeks of time passed in but two minutes. Did Jes somehow have control over time? If so, that would explain how he could heal these wounds. I made a mental note to ask him about this when we had an opportunity to chat privately.

"Best go now," Brother Jackal spoke up. The children took this as a signal for them finally to talk. Honestly, I think we have some of the bravest children on Tarra. They stood quietly all the while the attack took place. Even when they saw their dad fall with an arrow in his arm, Josh's children said nothing. All four watched closely while we did the healing. Only now with

Brother Jackal's pronouncement did they decide it was no longer time to be quiet. They bombarded us with many question and comments. Though Milla tried her best to hush them, I let them talk all they wanted, all the while directing them to get ready to ride out. I figured that the best way for them to confront the whole situation was to talk, and talk they most certainly did.

Soon we were riding into the long shadows of the cedar forest. "Mommy, what did you do? What was that bluish thing that melted? What is ice anyway? Did you make the fires? How do you do that? I didn't know you could make fires. Can I make fires too? Can you teach me how to do that too? How does daddy heal them? Can we do that too? Why can't you heal like daddy?" You get the picture? Now try answering them as rapidly as they ask them! Honestly, it takes a lot of love to be a good parent. One has to answer them as accurately as possible; they are going to remember what you say years afterward. Tell a lie now and pay most dearly for it later on.

Finally, I had enough war talk. "Say can you smell the forest? Smell the cedar? What a gorgeous odor it has. And it is now so cool."

"Mommy, it is so dark!" exclaimed little Emil. Well, you can't win them all, I rationalized. Jackal had been through these woods once before many years ago. None of the rest of us had ever set foot here. We let him guide us deep into the woods before stopping for the night. Lighting only a few oil lanterns and having a cold supper, we feared to light a fire, which might give our position away. None of us wanted the Galts to return.

When morning came, we hit the trail before eating breakfast, despite the protest of hungry children. Jackal wanted to put many miles between the Galts and us. An hour later, he let us stop to eat and admire the forest. Besides the heady aroma of the cedar, I also thought I could smell the ocean air. We had to be close. Actually, I had never seen a cedar forest, and I took the children for a walk-about. We noticed the forest floor, the trees, the odor, and the quiet. Emil's comment was simply, "Mommy, I like it here. I wish we could live here."

We rode the rest of the day slowly navigating between the trees until we found a logger's trail. Here the forest didn't look so pretty; the land was denuded of these magnificent trees. Trees were dragged down to the coast, bunched together, and sold. By late afternoon, we arrived at Salem's Beach, a very small logging village of perhaps a hundred or so people, who made their living selling cedar logs. From the well-built wooden buildings with lanterns affixed to each door, these people definitely made a good profit.

We stayed at the only inn in the village. In fact, our party took over all three rooms! Jackal, Missa, and Brother Jackal had to double up. For the first time in a long while, we all slept in a soft bed with real sheets! The next day, we bathed in the Med Sea; it was a bath long overdue. While the men went to arrange ship passage, I took the children to the only store and got them some new clothes, a candy treat, and bought myself a well-crafted cedar sea chest. After all, if we were going on a long sea voyage, a sea chest to store our clothes would be more practical than carrying numerous sacks, which could get wet.

That night we ate well in the dining room of the inn. Josh arranged for our passage on the Night Song, which was due to dock in a few days. It was on its way back from Zargarb, having delivered a load of cedar logs. I noticed that Jes seemed a bit quiet or reticent to talk much. Something was on his mind, and I had a hunch that he might not come with us.

After the children were asleep, Jes finally opened up. "Bethany, you know how much I love you, how much I respect your keen wisdom. I have a problem, if you haven't noticed." I'd noticed, but encouraged him to explain it fully. Essentially, he felt a strong obligation to find out what the strange grey creatures were doing in the Appian Way, and an even more pressing obligation to assist our people now with the Galt invasion. Since the ill-fated rebellion, so many younger men were lost, so many of our fighters gone, our people were in dire jeopardy. Still he could not reveal his identity. Think of what people would conclude if they found out that their Great Messiah had not died and gone to the revered kingdom of Jehosa.

"Look, I believe there are Seven Aspects of Life," I counseled him. "A person is attempting to flourish and do well for himself, for his family, for the groups to which he belongs, to all mankind, to all the plants and animals, to the physical universe itself, and to the spiritual realm. We've talked about this before. As I see it, the right decision is that decision, which helps more of the Aspects than it harms. I can understand your intense desire to help our people, especially right now considering all that has happened. Think about it for a minute. If the Arad is overrun by the Galts, we change one master for an even worse one. Will not our people get wise and flee to at least the Zargarb sector? If I were in such a situation, I would quietly exit the Arad rather than to live as a slave to the Galts. No big production, just get up and leave. Surely, many will do so whether you plant the idea or not. You risk far more by going back into the Arad. All it takes is one person to recognize you, and all your good works will become undone."

"You hit the mark, my love. Are you sure that you aren't Jehosa in disguise?" he jested.

"Er no, not by a long shot. As far as those grey creatures, they are way too powerful for us to attack openly. Look, none of my special effects even fazed them. Unless you can perform some attack miracle, you are only likely to get yourself killed or worse."

"Probably so, but ought I to try?" he asked.

"You don't have to make that decision until we are near Velona. From there, you would have the most direct route to their base high in the Appian way."

"Okay, you win. I will stall that decision until we are close enough to make an attempt," he agreed. "I think you are right, many will flee. Perhaps I ought to establish a Church of Jehosa in Zargarb for the benefit of those fleeing there. If I do, then I promise you that later on, I will find you and join you when I can." I accepted his pledge; I cringed, thinking of life without him, but then I couldn't be an albatross around his neck. A person must be allowed to pursue their own goals in life. When the last goal of a man dies, so does the man. I resolved to enjoy thoroughly what days we had together.

The ship finally arrived, but boy was it ever small, compared to the only ships I had known, those of the Sea Princes. The two brothers owned and sailed the Night Song; again, we had to keep our identity a secret from them. Thus, we spoke little and just enjoyed the ride in the open, shallow-draft ship with a single sail. For four days, we watched the tree-lined coast of Juda Arad pass by and then the sharp change in terrain as we entered the Sea Prince sector. The cedar forest disappeared, replaced by rolling hills. Grape vineyards and olive groves dotted the landscape. At last, the huge city of Zargarb came into view.

While I had never been to this city, I had been in several others in this land, so I wasn't surprised by the sight. However, all the others were completely in awe at the incredible size of the city, the huge docks, and the throngs of tall buildings. Soon we could see large numbers of people walking in the streets. Here was a city that was home to over a hundred thousand people, larger than anything in the Arad.

Once we docked, a new problem arose. Only Brother Jackal and I could speak the local dialect, and mine was very rusty and rudimentary. It had been more than thirty years since I spoke it. Hence, we ended up relying upon Brother Jackal. While the children stared and gaped, we walked to an inn catering to incoming passengers; at least that is what Brother Jackal had asked directions to. Once we had rooms, Josh, Brother Jackal, and I went to book passage to Velona. I had no idea whether women were now being treated with more respect or not. I intended to take no chances. Josh would make the arrangements, with Brother Jackal and me handling the translation.

I was completely surprised how swiftly we accomplished our goal. We booked passage on a ship that was leaving tomorrow! I paid for our passage using several large gems, which reminded me of my father. His generosity was saving our lives. On our way back, Josh was jubilant that we had been so successful and with no problems. However, as a man bumped into him, I spied the strings of Josh's small change money pouch being deftly cut and the pouch falling into the man's other hand.

Suddenly, all of my city street-smart training came back to me. Amazing how I had completely forgotten all about the many hours my druwid Circle had spent training for just such a situation. I acted quickly, placing my finger on the back of the man's head, "This knife will end your days if you don't hand that pouch back to that man immediately." I spoke softly and quietly with no hostility, but with total sincerity. The pickpocket took only a couple seconds to decide before his hand slowly held the pouch out to Josh, who took it flabbergasted and totally surprised. "Now just walk on down the street," I commanded and quickly pulled my hand behind my back so the thief couldn't see that he had been tricked. He did as ordered, and we resumed our walk back to the inn.

"Thieves. I had forgotten all about them. These large cities are full of them," I explained.

"But how did you know he stole it? I didn't feel a thing!" Josh wanted to know.

"Lady has keen eyes," Brother Jackal commented to himself.

"But you didn't even have a knife at his neck," Josh protested. "That was a dangerous move."

"Not really, raising a hue and cry and attracting the attention of the local guards is far more dangerous. Notice that I didn't seem at all upset, angry, or antagonistic to him. I simple spoke normally as if nothing of importance had just happened. That was the thief's tip off that if he followed orders, then nothing more would come of his botched attempt at stealing your purse."

"Man, you are good, woman!" Josh declared, shaking his head, still in disbelief. "You surprise me at every turn. I thought I was supposed to be protecting you! Here you continually protect me!" We all chuckled at his humor.

The next day, we boarded the Fickled Winds, a two masted, large sailing ship bound for Velona with a cargo of oil, wine, and cedar logs. As we walked onto the gangplank, I told the children, "Now here is a sailing ship! This ship can sail the entire length of the Med Sea and beyond. Actually, the children were not the only ones dutifully impressed with the sheer size of the ship. Only I was not. The Fickled Winds was about the same size as the Lucky Lady that I had sailed on twice some thirty years before.

What a difference thirty years makes in ship design, though. This trip, we actually had a forward cabin with real bunk beds! Albeit the space was barely large enough, and we had to adopt a practical manner of getting into bed because we all couldn't fit inside at the same time if we were standing. So pairs would enter and climb into their bunks, and then another pair would squeeze in and follow suit. Getting out posed similar problems. However, we spent most of our time either watching the children playing amongst the cargo or else on deck.

Everyone got seasick that first day, save the children and me. However, I had the requisite herbs with me in my healing pouch and acted swiftly at the first signs. None had a very bad case of it, thankfully. I found that I rather enjoyed being at sea once more on a long voyage. Somehow, I missed it. "Someday, I ought to be a sea captain myself," I mused, while pouring the herbal tea remedy into cups. In fact, my decision did come true many years later, but that is another story.

We had fourteen days of smooth sailing with only two squalls that raised the children's excitement levels. During this relaxing time, Jes, Josh, and I held long talks about our future and where we should go to raise our families. I knew that Jes would probably leave us for a time when we got to Velona. He just had to find out about the grey creatures for himself. I just hoped and prayed that he would hold to his promise to return to me soon.

We needed a safe place to raise the children, where they could learn to fight, and learn all the necessary skills to be competent and just kings, as was their birthright. Of prime importance, as far as Jes and Josh were concerned, was that place had to be free of the infidel's rule. Both wanted their children to be completely safe until the time was right for them to claim their rightful positions. If any infidels were around, their safety would always be in doubt, however so slightly. I had pushed for going to the Greenway and the safety of the druwids, but the infidels were there, and besides, it bordered the Northern Steppes and might soon be invaded itself.

For days, we discussed the possibilities, but every place failed to pass their standards. The infidels had conquered most of the known world. Those areas they did not control were inhospitable to us, namely the Northern Steppes and Volksholm, where the Axemen lived. For a while, I was beginning to think that we had made the trip for nothing; there was no place we could settle down in total safety from the infidels or Galts.

Then, one day it struck me: the offshore island of West Reach! It is a huge island, several hundred miles long and at least a hundred wide, full of the richest, most beautiful green lands and forests I had ever seen, though only from a ship at sea. I had no idea if the island was occupied or by whom if so. Everyone thought this was the most workable idea we had, so when we got to Velona, I decided to look into it further.

In the meantime, I asked our Captain, Marcella Bleu, if he knew anything about West Reach. Boy did I get lucky.

"Aye, Missy, been there myself a couple o' times. Metal utensils fetch a high price there, they do. Not many people there as far as I know, though they seem friendly enough. Kind of hard to understand their lingo — never have gotten the hang of it yet. I just show them some cargo and show them some gold coins, and we take it from there. Barter is a common language across all peoples." He went on and on about the folks that lived there and their strange customs.

When I relayed what I had learned, Jes and Josh both kissed me in thanks. Both said that I sounded funny speaking the Sea Prince dialect with our captain. They hadn't understood one word. Brother Jackal had paid no attention to me; he was on deck watching the world go by, thoroughly enjoying this boat ride. "That settles it!" Jes proclaimed greatly relieved. "We move to West Reach!" Next, we had to explain all this to the children so they would understand better where we were ultimately headed.

With our destination finally firmed, I discussed this with Captain Marcella. For a few more gems, he agreed to take us there, once he had unloaded his cargo in Velona and loaded cargo bound for Calgary. He expected we'd be in Velona at least a week and then at least another week before we would get to our destination. Hence, we ended up spending an entire month aboard ship.

Now you can imagine an entire month aboard a cramped ship with four young children. Well, if you cannot, you're indeed lucky! After the newness wore off in two days, the bored children began to be bored children, if you know what I mean. However, I decided this was a good time to start their training, and it would give them something to do and occupy their minds, keeping them out of mischief. Remembering how Ellen had begun to teach me when I was but a girl of six back in Uru, Greenway, I decided to follow her methods. The first and foremost ability they needed was the ability to observe the plainly obvious, not what you think you see, no conclusions, just what you actually do perceive. I remember how hard I found it at first; my children were no exception.

In fact, after the first hour of instruction, I discovered that Jackal and Missa wanted to learn too. Josh and Milla joined in, just as soon as I permitted our two guides to join in — suddenly, I had eight students! I also spent part of the time teaching them the little I knew of the Sea Prince dialect. Our captain, when he heard us trying to learn his language, was gracious enough to give us far better lessons. Thus, I turned the long voyage into a fun learning session.

Immediately, another aspect that I had not considered before raised its ugly head. Thirty years ago, I was the leader of my druwid group, the Lightning Circle. Each of us had spent ten years in nearly constant study to learn and master our skills. However, the druwids were a secret group dedicated to helping our people of the Greenway survive better. Now that I had a new body and a new life, an Arad woman's body, did I still retain my druwid position?

I mean, was I still considered a member of that group even though I now had a different body and life elsewhere? I had sworn my total allegiance to the druwids. Yet, now I, for the time being, had a different life style. Alabaster had promised to come for me when the time was right, presumably to help me get back into the Greenway and into a proper new baby body so that I might continue to help them. You see my dilemma — because of my prior lifetime's allegiances, do I right now consider myself a druwid or am I an Arad person? Just when can one stop being one thing and become another? I had made strong vows to the druwids, and yet in this current life, I had made many pledges to Jes to see to the education of our children so they might be qualified to become rightful kings of Arad. Eventually, these two activities would come crashing together in a conflict of responsibilities.

I now realized that the simple expediency of "forgetting" everything about the life one has just led as its body dies allows one to begin fresh with the new one, except that is not true. Just because one chooses to "forget" doesn't erase those agreements, those decisions one has made. If one lived many lifetimes, the confusion of decisions would become utterly overwhelming! Could this play a role in a person becoming a header, that is, totally stuck inside a body's head, believing utterly that they are this body, this identity? Interesting idea worth exploring, I thought.

I knew that I couldn't teach my children how to bring down fire and lightning bolts, not without getting Alabaster's permission first. Of that I was certain, but there were many lesser skills that I certainly could teach them, none of which would be considered a breach of confidence. In short, the teacher had much to ponder and learn herself!

In Velona, we stayed aboard the ship. To my utter happiness and total relief, Jes announced that he would continue to our new homeland with us. "After I have built you a proper home and can guarantee your safety and survival, then I can return here and find out more about these grey creatures as well as help the Arad people. Until then, I really ought to let the ten Holy Disciples have their chance to make an impact. It's only fair to them." I gave him a hug and kiss to validate his choice. Now life would be fun and enjoyable once more. I can't tell you how much having a stable home pleases me after all those years of constant wandering from here to there. I could not have been happier!

Not even the breaking news that our captain brought us about the war dampened my spirits. He told us that word of the invasion of the Galts had reached the Centurions here in Velona. All their soldiers who could be spared were being sent to the Zargarb sector to help keep the horde of barbarians from turning their attention onto the land of the Sea Princes. In fact, we were very lucky to have already paid for passage westward from Velona. Had we not, we would have been stuck here for some time. Every available ship that was not currently chartered was being commandeered by the Centurions to help transport troops to Zargarb!

Two weeks later, the emerald green isle of West Reach grew steadily larger on the horizon, our new homeland. Except for me, none of the others had ever seen a land so green, so full of life. The harsh survival of the Arad was about to give way to a lush one.

Chapter 12 The Scattering of the Holy Disciples

The final departure of the Great Messiah was dutifully observed by his ten Holy Disciples, and all were filled with nearly overwhelming grief and sadness to see him depart. Without saying a word, they filed back into the new safe house, at a loss for words and for what to do next. They had their final orders from Jes: write up all his teachings and then go forth and spread the word.

Amar Tarabulus broke the solemn silence, "I am going to return to my fishing village. There I shall spread our Lord's words to all who will listen." He picked up his few belongings, shook everyone's hand, and quietly left.

Dez Madan and Abu Wadi decided to go straight for the Qaam settlement in the far northeast. They wanted peace and quiet around them with no distractions so that they could do their very best writing. Both wanted to be as accurate as possible. Shortly after Amar left, these two followed.

Jebal Dayr, the shepherd, decided to return to his home village in the far southeast. He had missed tending his flock as well as his family life. "I am the least eloquent of us all. Perhaps being at home will inspire my writing." He too left, around noon.

Hamah Zagros and Bandar Dero were both former messiahs; they knew very well that a full-scale rebellion would happen soon. Further, they now believed completely in the words of their Lord — that it was wrong to join that fight. Hence, both decided to head for Florintine Junction. It was out of the way, and if war came, they could easily move into the Lands of the Seven Sea Princes. Besides, both knew that a great many of their people had already fled there years ago from Al Barq, after the Night of the Baby Murders. In the backs of their minds, the idea of disseminating the Great Messiah's teachings to their countrymen in exile appealed to them. Thus, by nightfall both left on horseback.

The four who remained in Jerilum, Rafha Orum, Jamal Mazra, Yazi Rigan, and Ismail Saydah, had been former messiahs, except the moneychanger Ismail. Ismail, who still doubted that Jes really had been the Great Messiah, held out hope that another would arise and would lead them to victory over the infidels. He said, "How close do you think we are to a rebellion? The Qaams gave us a time ultimatum. Do you suppose that we will have some advance warning of it?"

Yazi replied with an air of certainty, "Absolutely. If they are going to have any chance, they need a coordinated strike. Hit all the infidel garrison forces at the same time, reduce their numbers. Yes, I expect we will get word. You still think he was not the One?"

Ismail smiled coyly, "Well, we aren't free of the infidels by any standard, spiritually or physically, are we?" Maybe others will catch on, he thought to himself.

"He left the education of the world to us," Yazi countered. "If the rebellion comes here to Jerilum, are any of you going to take up arms?"

"Hey, I'm not a fighter!" Ismail chuckled. "I'll find a cozy corner to hide in. I don't want to get killed. There are many infidels in town here of late, far more than there used to be, in fact. I'd be shocked to see a surprise attack kill all of them. That new general fellow — he's too smart to be easily taken. I'm afraid that an awful lot of people will die. I don't aim to be one. After all, we're supposed to spread the Gospel of Jehosa. How can we do that if we are dead? No, I say do whatever you can to stay alive."

"Religion or not, if the good fight comes, I will be very hard-pressed not to help," Rufha added. "So many of our friends look up to us as their messiahs. Some have supported us for many years. How can we turn aside in their hour of need? No, I will aid as I can. How about you, Jamal? You have supporters here in Jerilum, don't you?"

"Yes, yes, I do," he replied, "I know we've pledged our word to the Great Messiah, but I will be under enormous pressure to lend a hand when the fighting breaks out. Without Jes here, it will be doubly hard not to aid them. We would lose face, credibility. After that, no one would pay us much attention; he didn't even help in the rebellion. No, I'm afraid that I'll have very little choice but to aid. However, guys, I suppose we ought to get on to the challenge of writing everything up. At least, we can do that much for the Great Messiah before the rebellion comes." These four spent the ensuing days finishing up their journals.

However, the next night, Ismail and Yazi went out to a nearby pub for some relaxation and a change of pace. It had been years since either had the opportunity to spend an evening drinking, singing, and making out with the barmaids. Around ten, Ismail, rather drunk, left to return back to the safe house. Yazi stayed on, involved in a challenge match of throwing darts. True, he had seen several men talking to themselves, pointing at Ismail from time to time. Subconsciously, he knew that these men had recognized Ismail. He thought nothing much of it at the time. He ought to have, especially when the five men got up and left just after Ismail left. When he finished the dart game, he decided that they had been very suspicious, and he left following the direct route back to the safe house that Ismail was likely to follow.

He came upon his fellow disciple bleeding to death in the street! He knelt down to help Ismail, "By Jehosa, what happened to you?"

His voice was faint, "They attacked me — said I was a traitor — said I turned in the Great Messiah to the infidels. I did, you know." His body relaxed as his last breath exhaled. Yet, Ismail was at peace; he accepted his fate. No one was there to witness it, but he attempted to find Jehosa's realm, intending on seeking entrance. He realized he had no idea where it was located. Then, an old thought, or command rather, forced its way back into his mind. "Come here when the body dies." So forceful was the command, that he felt he had no choice. He took off heading toward the Appian Way.

Yazi picked up his fellow disciple and carried him back to the safe house. While the others handled the burial details, Yazi went through Ismail's belongings. He found Ismail's scrolls and an idea formed in his mind. When no one was looking, he added them to his pile. Now he had not only his own scrolls outlining the religion as preached by Jes, but Ismail's as well. He smiled and confiscated the eating utensils last used by Jes, along with some discarded clothing Jes had worn.

Several days later, word came that the rebellion was on for tomorrow morning at 10 AM. All day long, various men came by the safe house to talk things over with Jamal and Rafha. Strategy was discussed, tactics were bandied about, but always they were asked if they would help. While they hedged a direct answer at first, by evening both men had agreed to assist as they could. When the last of the visitors had left that night, Rafha grew concerned. "Yazi, we know this is not your town, so you don't have to fight. Look, if anything happens to us tomorrow, our scrolls of The Great Messiah's teachings must be copied and taken to the stronghold of the Qaam. Will you take this burden for us? If something happens to us, take our scrolls to safety. Above all, they must survive."

Yazi could not believe his great luck! He already had Ismail's. Now he could get these as well, making four in all! "Absolutely! I swear to take great care of them. I will guard them with my life; I am a messiah and well suited to protect them." Both men entrusted their precious scrolls to Yazi. Then, he mused, "Say, if the rebellion comes tomorrow and all goes poorly, I might not be able to get out of the city if they lock down the gates. They might go door to door, you know."

Jamal had an immediate answer, "Yazi, I think it best if you can depart the city yet tonight. Get the scrolls away to safety before the rebellion. If we survive the conflict, we'll head to the Qaam fortress and retrieve them there. Just drop them off, and we will get them back later on if we are able. If not, the Qaam scribes can copy them as Jes requested. Thank you, Yazi, thank you!" The three men shook hands, sealing the pact. Little did the two know that they would never see their scrolls again.

However, Yazi left behind the second copy of each of the four sets. He only needed one copy. Yazi calmly packed the four sets of scrolls in a watertight bag. Then, he packed several bags of trail rations and two water pouches. At last, he saddled a horse and said farewell to his two companions. He dutifully left by the east gate, just in case these two should ever inquire after him, he was last seen heading in the promised direction. He rode past the cemetery and the three crucifixion crosses. He turned and headed south down the dry river valley out of sight of the walls of the city.

He thought to himself, "After all, the rebellion is doomed to failure. Any fool can see that without some great messiah to lead us, they are only going to be killed. Look, after all these years, we messiahs have been attacking the infidels, where has it gotten us? The infidels are still here and perhaps even stronger now than they used to be. At least their numbers are greater. No, it is but a Qaam daydream that a rebellion led by them can be victorious. I'll bet the Qaams will get themselves wiped out and all the sacred scrolls with them.

No, I have a better plan and four of the ten sets of scrolls. The Great Messiah told us to go forth and spread the word of Jehosa and his teachings to all of Tarra. That is what I intend to do. I'm going to go to Megalos itself and convert all of them from Sol worship to the worshiping of our Jehosa. Won't that be a strange irony, the words of the Great Messiah end up conquering Megalos!"

He headed south avoiding the larger towns and villages, stopping only at isolated watering holes that were off the beaten track. Ten days later, he entered a small hamlet near the southern edge of Juda Arad. Here he traded his horse for a donkey and his sword for a walking staff. He retained his dagger, for self-protection, though. Looking the part of a prophet of Jehosa, he entered the lands completely controlled by the Centurions, following their paved roadway southward. He stopped in the first town he encountered for desperately needed supplies and for news. He got both. Yes, as he predicted, the rebellion was squashed in only three days. However, he also learned that the Galts had invaded from the north. All of the Arad was now at war with the barbarians from the Northern Steppes. "What irony," he thought as he left, continuing his slow southerly journey.

Soon, he joined up with a Centurion merchant who was driving an empty wagon back to Sud. Yazi offered him a gold ducat to let him ride with him and took the opportunity to learn to speak the language of the infidels, or rather Centurions, as he corrected himself. To be successful, he knew that he had to be able to speak their language fluently. He, Yazi, intended to pull this off; he was going to be tremendously famous, once he had converted the Centurions to the worship of Jehosa!

Thus, two weeks after the Great Messiah passed away, only seven disciples remained, scattered over the land, though none remained in the more populous central regions.

Chapter 13 The Retreat of General Lacerta

A week passed and still the barbarian cavalrymen watched the Centurions trapped inside the burned out shell of Kaan. Following orders, they stayed out of Centurion short bow range. Occasionally, one or two would gallop toward the walls of the town and fire off several flaming arrows, intent on minor mayhem and enhancing their own egos. Thus far, there had been no casualties on either side.

General Lacerta played the waiting game. He knew that his messengers were not able to get to him, and he regretted not knowing what was going on elsewhere in the Arad. However, he implicitly trusted his majors to deal with the situation where they were located. His problem was determining whether this was just an isolated band of Galt raiders or whether an all-out war had broken out. Actually, that was his prime goal: raiders or invasion — which of the two was this? Thus far, except for that first day, he'd seen only perhaps five hundred or so barbarians. Most had left that very same day. These remaining fifty appeared to be only keeping watch on them. Yes, they had a door smasher device that they could press into service to force their way into the town, but that would be just what General Lacerta hoped for — that action would nullify the distinct advantage the cavalry had over his foot soldiers. Forcing house-to-house style combat would raise the odds closer to the three-to-one ration he loved. After a week now, still they showed no signs of doing that.

Now the mayor of Kaan had asked to speak with him, and General Lacerta waited for the mayor to arrive. However, he already suspected what the man wanted. His aide opened the door and presented Mayor Almartz. The general's keen eyes sized up the man before him. Almartz was tall and had the usual Arad brown skin tones. He was impeccably dressed, and the fragrance of fresh oil followed him as he entered. Lacerta hated smelly men, considering it an effeminate trait. Now with women, that was a different story. He scowled at Almartz, "What is it that you want?"

"Sir, I'll be brief. I know you must have lots of pressing matters which demand your attention," he began, knowing that the general probably had very little to do, penned up like an animal in the town. "What are your intentions on long term protection of our town? As you know, already half of our population has fled. Those that have stayed have done so primarily because you and your superior forces have come to our timely rescue. Yet, it has been a week now and still the Galts have taken no action. The question on everyone's lips is, 'When will you charge outside the walls and drive these few Galts out of here?' Only then can we begin the rebuilding process." He didn't add that most townsfolk thought the infidels were scared of the handful of Galt cavalry.

"If we march out the gates, these barbarians will simply ride off from us. Foot soldiers can't go after them. I don't have my cavalry with me just now. Since they aren't attacking us, I've decided perhaps we should pull out of Kaan and head back to Jerilum. It would be clever if there was a backdoor to this town, so one night we could all disappear in secret, leaving the Galts wondering where we have gone."

This, of course, was definitely not what the mayor wanted to hear, that the infidels were abandoning Kaan to the Galts. However, the general's statement was what Almartz fully expected. "Disappear in secret?" he followed up; this caught his curiosity.

"Well, yes, imagine the confusion in the enemy ranks when they find one day that we aren't here anymore. They'd have no idea when we left or where we're headed. Confuse the enemy is a good policy," the general explained rather didactically.

"Ah, I see," the mayor said coyly, "and you would then be heading for Jerilum. May I offer a trade? We can get you and your men all out of Kaan in secret. In return, allow those of us who so desire to travel with your force back to Jerilum." He saw the sudden flicker in the general's eyes and knew he had a done deal.

"Protection, yes, we can provide that, but there is, then, a secret way out of Kaan?"

"Yes, one of the mine tunnels had an unfortunate cave in several years ago. Seems the miners dug too closely to the surface and it caved in. No problem, they simply made that point an entryway and continued with the tunnel. It opens about a mile from Kaan, around the northern mesa. Any egress from that point wouldn't be observable from any spot around here. When do you wish this plan put into action?"

"Hum, how about tonight? Would that be acceptable?" It was and the mayor left quickly. He had many details to handle. Likely the remainder of the town would also evacuate as well, though only himself and a few others would likely head to Jerilum with these infidels. The mayor had been secretly suspecting this might be the plan of action, ever since the infidels did not counter-attack that second day.

Once the mayor left, Lacerta signed, "Thank Sol for our timely rescue! I hate being boxed up like this. If I attacked openly these few barbarians, the remainder of them might come back at any moment, and that I simply cannot allow. They would have a distinct combat edge. No, I'll not put my foot soldiers up against mounted cavalry, even if they are just a barbarian horde." He called for his aides and relayed the plan.

They wouldn't be able to take their supply wagons with them. This meant that the remaining twenty-five horses, save those for himself and his aides, would be loaded as pack animals. Plenty of water had to be carried, because he still had little knowledge of where to find water in this arid land, save along the well-marked paved roadway. He studied his crude maps and marked out an overland path that headed out cross-country, from his point of view anyway, some distance before cutting back onto the paved roadway.

A new moon cast its thin outline just above the horizon as the sun set ruddy red in the west. One by one, the soldiers and townsfolk walked across the plaza, ducking into the Mine Tunnel #5. Once inside, a few candles provided the only illumination for the first five hundred feet. This was not a problem for the tunnel was tall and wide here as it began its long burrowing underground. The idea was to completely disappear without a trace; hence, the total secrecy. Everyone, from the individual soldiers to the townsfolk, knew that their best hope of escape from the barbarians lie in stealth and mystery. Thus, no one grumbled as they groped their way down the mine tunnel in the near darkness.

Once beyond a bend, lanterns were lighted. Only sufficient lanterns existed for one in every twenty-five people, so still, it was a march in near darkness. A group of miners led the way, with the general and his staff following close behind. Next, groups of three squads marched. Some five hundred townsfolk brought up the very rear, led by the mayor and his family. Progress was indeed slow; an hour passed before the night sky appeared to their right. Here, the tunnel had caved in and the practical miners had just turned it into a side exit. General Lacerta took a deep breath of the cool arid, fresh air. He hated being in damp, dismal mines, he decided.

A quick survey of the land brought him some comfort. A mesa now lay between them and the valley in which the town sat. The same mesa separated the encamped barbarians from them as well. Quickly, he formed his legions into marching order as trios of squads appeared from the dark tunnel. These he sent marching off to the southeast, following the valley floor that lay between the two mesas. Once all of his men had exited and headed off after the others, General Lacerta and his staff mounted their horses, while others led the numerous packhorses. Quickly, he overtook the lead squads and resumed his leadership role on this march. He cared little how the Arad people fared. Indeed, he did not even bother to wait for any that intended to travel along with the Centurions.

Hence, he didn't see until the morning that only about fifty locals were actually traveling along with them at their rear. What happened to the other four hundred-fifty never entered his mind. Perhaps it should have. With the sunrise, his force was now about twelve miles south and somewhat east of Kaan. The paved roadway lay several miles to the west past a couple mesa lines. Here they paused for breakfast, but only for a half an hour. The general still felt that they were far too close to Kaan and the barbarian cavalry. Anytime now, the barbarians would realize that the town was unoccupied. He counted on them entering the town and ransacking it, giving the Centurions more time to put distance between the two forces. Whether the barbarians would find the tunnel and its exit or not would probably not be a factor. Certainly, the horde would fan out in all directions searching for the Centurions. He took it as an absolute certainty the enemy commander would quickly be informed of their hasty exit.

The real question was would the barbarian cavalry horde come looking for them, and, if so, would they attack the foot soldier formation? The farther they were from Kaan, the better and the less likely they would be found.

Hence, General Lacerta preferred to force march the rest of the day, though he never did discover whether the enemy discovered their location. In fact, they did. None of the party spotted the lone rider high atop a distant mesa patiently watching their movements for a half hour.

In fact, when General Lacerta arrived in Jerilum a week later, tired and dirty, he and his entire group felt that they had successfully made a completely secret get-away from Kaan. He never guessed at the real reason his small force had been spared an assault from the barbarian horde.

Sitting astride her horse high upon the sloping side of a mesa, Zdlenka studied the assault upon the small village below. Mikhailovich Strokova and his band were wrapping up the conquering of yet another small mining and smelter facility here in the extreme northeast of the Arad. The town offered nearly no resistance whatsoever to the horde on horseback that thundered chaotically through the town, beheading anyone who even looked like they might offer any resistance to them. "This is just too easy!" she thought.

Hence, she was the first to spot the incoming rider from the west, riding hard, an indicator of major trouble. She neck reined to face the messenger, waving to him the signal to approach. As the rider approached, the well-lathered horse with deep panting told her at once that something very serious had occurred. "Hail, what news?" she called out.

The young lad quickly dismounted leaving his horse to wander and cool down, a very atypical action. Spent horses critically needed to be cooled down, watered, and later fed. She knew that his report must be very bad indeed. The lad also knew that any message for Mikhailovich ought to also be delivered to Zdlenka, though they never knew why, but accepted her. "Doubly bad news. During the night, the entire town, every last person in Kaan, just up and disappeared! Vanished without the slightest trace! We watched them cook their evening meals. Come morning, Kaan was too quiet, so we closed to harry the defenders and found nothing. We broke down the entrance doors and rode into the town, but it's empty, totally, completely empty. What devilry, what magic is this? How can this be? How can the enemy and the entire town just vanish in the night? We had sentinels placed close enough that none may sneak past us. Indeed, by day, we can see no signs of their passing outward from the town on the dusty ground." The lad was completely confused; that was more than evident.

"Were scouts sent out in all directions?" Zdlenka asked coldly, pondering the significance of this news.

"Yes, per your standing orders. Still no trace. That is the smaller problem. Gastov originally sent me to report on the action down the western side. Zdlenka, I'm to report to you that evil witches are here in the Arad!"

"What?" Zdlenka startled at the statement. Her eyes pierced the young boy.

He saw that she was paying full attention to him. His face flushed momentarily before he regained his composure. Now he was on familiar ground, relaying the message for which he was originally sent. "Gastov's band was nearly halfway to Al Barq, when out in the middle of nowhere, they came across a small group of what appeared to be Arad locals: three women, four children, and four men. He left ten men to harass them and continued his southerly ride. However, when the ten moved in to attack them, the evil witches acted! While their four men vainly attempted to stop our ten, the witches conjured a wall of ice protecting them from the hail of our arrows. The arrows just bounced off the ice. They described it as taking the layer of ice on a pond and raising it up, standing it on edge as a barrier. Next, the evil witches conjured a wall of fire burning in the air above the ten riders, and then let it fall onto our men and horses!"

"With their clothes, hair, and horses on fire, they galloped away in terror. Five died from their burns! Two others are not doing well. Three are nursing burns but can still fight. Naturally, one caught up to Gastov and reported what had happened. He turned the war party around and headed back to deal with these evil witches. When they arrived, the party had vanished into the smelly forest. Gastov told me to tell you that where the wall of ice had been reported to exist, he found a thin line of wet earth, so presumably it was real ice that melted. His men are now terrified of the evil witches, refuse to go further south, and refuse to enter the woods to go after them. I was told to report this to you or Mikhailovich and ask for orders."

"You have done well. Now go take care of your horse. I'll let my brother know, and we'll give you orders, but not until tomorrow. They must finish taking this village first. Go now," she ordered. The lad did as instructed, while Zdlenka sent a mental message for her brother to come join her now, leaving the mop-up action to the others.

Five minutes later, he came galloping up to her position, a worried look upon his otherwise victorious face. Never before had she called him out of a combat situation, so this had to be critical. She quickly related what the messenger had told her. "What? Witches in Juda Arad? How? I thought that the evil witches were only found in the Greenway? What does this mean, sister? Do other lands have witches too?"

"It would appear so. The report described the women as typical Arad women, brown of skin, not the pale white of those in the Greenway. I conclude that these were not Greenway witches somehow down here in the Arad. These witches must be locals. This is most alarming, to say the very least. These witches wiped out ten of our men without taking any losses themselves. This will crush our morale. It already has. Gastov and his men refuse to go further south or even to go after the witches."

"This is not good, sister, not good at all. How is it that we have never before heard of evil witches in the Arad? This puzzles me. One of the reasons we chose to attack to the south instead of the west into the Greenway is to avoid these demonic witches. The total destruction of Maak's thousand some thirty years ago is legendary and casts fear into the very heart of any Galt. We were going to save the conquering of the Greenway until last anyway just for this very reason — well, also because they generally don't have anything really worth taking anyway except food."

"I suggest that we go more slowly — capture me some more locals; let me interrogate them and find out more about their witches. How many are there? Where are they located? You know, find out all we can. I can persuade even the tightest-lipped Arad to babble out what I want to hear," she volunteered.

"Agreed. Your wish is my command," he teased attempting to lighten their tensions. "Let's talk in depth tonight." She nodded, and he rode slowly back down the mesa to observe up close the raping of this village. He issued a few orders to take several hostages whom he deemed might have the knowledge they sought.

That night the wails, cries of terror, and intense pain pierced the still darkness, as Zdlenka worked to gain the information she desired. Held down by four men, she pushed sharp nails into fingers just under their nails. She had a natural bent for getting information without really harming too badly her victims. However, she did not hear what she expected and kept increasing her means of persuasion, until at last two of the four men her brother had brought her actually died. Only then did she relent.

"Well?" he said, as she coldly washed the blood off her hands and entered their domed, hide-covered hut. "Do you really like torturing them, the captives?"

"No, not really, Mik — rather turns my stomach," she replied honestly. "But we need this vital information from our enemies, and one of us has to do it. It wouldn't be wise for you, the obvious leader, to dirty your hands. They all look to you as the master; let them think what they will of me."

Mikhailovich teased, "Well you're going to scare any possible suitors away, you know. At this rate, you'll wind up an old spinster." She poked him in the ribs.

"I'm sure you will find one of these slave women more to your liking," she bandied back. He smiled at her jest. "Seriously, Mik, I'm convinced that these four Arads know nothing about witches. Two died insisting that no one can make walls of ice of bring flames down from the sky. I'm now convinced that they are telling the truth, at least as they know it."

"What does that mean?" he asked, not grasping her meaning.

"Too many possibilities, that's what it means. This is going to be harder to figure out than I first thought. Maybe we need to revert back to the original idea we had way back when we were first dreaming of all this, you know, send out scouting-raiding parties throughout the land whose task is really to probe defenses and weaknesses so that we have the knowledge we need to accurately plan the real invasion."

"But to answer your original question, it could be that their witches operate in total secrecy from the villagers. It could be that the very existence of their witches is a closely guarded secret, a secret weapon to be sprung upon us when the need is great. Since we haven't run into any witches before now, not even while taking all these northern towns, perhaps there are no witches here in the north. The ones that Gastov encountered lay far to the south and west. It could be we have here a Greenway witch disguised as an Arad woman who is down here on some secret mission of her own."

"I see, so perhaps there are only a very few of these Arad witches," Mikhailovich added, catching on to her way of thinking. They continued inventing plausible speculations until they had about two dozen entirely plausible explanations for the occurrence of this witch.

He then concluded, "I see. We must delay and stall our plans somewhat so that we have time to begin to rule out all these possibilities, one by one. If the clans get word that there are evil witches here in the Arad, our plans to unite them and form a massive army to conquer the world will evaporate in a puff of campfire smoke! We will have to be very cautious about our investigations; not a word of this to our forces. Surely, they will balk and insist on returning home immediately. We're not yet ready to take on these evil witches, that's certain."

"Right, buy me some time to narrow this down. First, let's go visit Gastov and interview the survivors personally. We must find out precisely what really did happen there. Let's have a standing order to bring me one person to question from every town and village we take," Zdlenka added.

"Changing the subject, sis, but you were right. We are going to need a lot of wagons to be able to haul all the booty we are getting back to the clans. I'll issue the orders tomorrow. Half of my men now have so much stuff piled onto their horses that they can barely ride! Besides, when the clans see the vast bounty arriving that can only make them want more and give us more warriors."

She laughed; she had long ago foreseen this development. Only now that the reality appeared did her brother agree with her. "What about the vanishing of the Centurions in Kaan?"

"Oh, I nearly forgot about them. That is another mystery, easily explained if they, too, have evil witches in their employ. Perhaps the witches that Gastov's men encountered were in fact Centurion witches. Can a witch make an entire population vanish? That must have been well over a thousand people!"

"We should look for ourselves. Let's ride to Kaan on the morrow and see what we can see," she suggested. "Now pleasure me. I'm beat."

The next day, Mikhailovich held a conference with the leaders of ten companies of fifty men each. He issued orders for five companies to return to their clans with the bounty thus far confiscated and see if more warriors could be recruited. One of these was the ill-fated one that had encountered the evil witch. Another four were given free rein to scout and probe where they chose in the Arad. However, he sent along one translator with each group, for most of his men understood not a word of the Arad language. The remaining company rode with him to Kaan to see firsthand the reported witch's magical vanishing act. There they would join the encirclement band, which he intended to be one of the five to return to their clans. He planned to take both his group and the other group accompanying him on to join up with Gastov's group, find out more about the evil witch's fatal attack on Gastov's men, and then send the two companies home.

Tracking is comparatively easily done in the dry, soft dirt of the semi-arid Arad and much more difficult within the grasslands of the Northern Steppes. However, the total ransacking of Kaan by his men obliterated any signs of the mysterious passage of over a thousand. Thus, Mikhailovich and Zdlenka found themselves riding in wider and wider circles around the town until at last a half mile distant they finally found relatively undisturbed ground. "Ah, now sis, we can at last see where they exited the town. Let's ride this circle and keep our eyes peeled. A thousand men cannot help but leave an observable trail."

As they rode along, keeping to this distance as much as possible, a scout rider came galloping up from the south. "Hail, Mikhailovich! I've found them!" Quickly, the scout described how he had ridden to the tops of mesas to gain a clear view over the vast distances. From one, he spied the Centurions marching along a valley about a mile away.

"You've done exceedingly well. Go get your share of the booty, and then I want you to come and join my band. You've earned that promotion!" Mikhailovich rewarded this scout, who had forgone sacking of Kaan in order to find where the Centurions had gone. He took an instant liking to this young man.

"Do we go after them, sis?" he asked, though he already knew what her answer would be.

"No. Remember, they could be the possessors of the witches. Rather, let us see how these Centurions managed to elude our encircling forces. We must dispel any ideas that it was a witch spell, if possible," she relied, thinking clearly.

"We cannot go any further at this distance from Kaan, the mesa bars our way," he countered.

"True, let's go down the valley, around it, and see what is on the other side. Perhaps they used the mesa to block our view of them," she offered. An hour later, Mikhailovich pointed to the unmistakable, well-trodden trail left by the feet of thousands. It ran nearly north-south. Of one mind, both turned north to follow it back to Kaan. Soon they discovered the tunnel entrance.

A half hour later, to the utter amazement of some hundred men who were relaxing and sorting out their confiscated booty from Kaan, the pair led their horses out of the mine tunnel into the sprawling center of town! "No magic involved," Mikhailovich yelled, "they simply walked out right under your very noses!"

Zdlenka, not wanting to see the men entirely invalidated, added, "Probably they left during the night, when you couldn't see them all heading into the tunnel. It comes out far behind yonder mesa where you would not be able to see them emerge and leave." The men grumbled and cursed, but they knew that they had failed Mikhailovich. However, Zdlenka had wisely given them a way to save some face, and several eyes glanced her way by way of "thanks." She accepted their intention.

"Okay, men, one mystery dispelled. No magic here, just bad luck. Now we ride hard to join up with Gastov's band." Still grumbling over their blunder, the men mounted up as best they could, while hauling so much stolen goods. Four days later, the hundred plus joined up with Gastov's group, who were now slowly retreating toward the steppes. The spooked commander was very glad so see Mikhailovich arrive.

"You didn't tell us that there were evil witches here in the Arad!" he bitterly complained. "Five are dead and two are on stretchers."

"We don't know that there are witches here, Gastov. We need to speak to the three that are in fairly good shape," he ordered, taking command of the situation before more word of witches spread.

Gastov was camped by a small watering hole under the shade of a grove of trees that grew close to the water's edge. Mikhailovich and Zdlenka picked an isolated spot for their interrogations, and Gastov brought them something to eat and drink. Soon after, three men joined them. Their hair was now very short; burn sores covered patches of their heads, arms and hands. A soothing salve had been administered; they would survive. The two on stretchers were badly burned and, if they survived, would not fight any more this year.

The two had all three describe the confrontation with the supposed witches and their party: three women, four young children, and four men. From the descriptions, the men certainly were fighters. Zdlenka concluded that they were probably some of the local messiah fighters. One woman apparently was looking after the children and didn't appear to have done anything. The two learned that one other woman had been holding onto the entire group of horses. She concluded that action would completely occupy her; she could not be the witch. Further, the men were indeed struck with the hail of arrows, and the warriors thought that one was likely killed and another wounded. Mikhailovich found this encouraging, for it meant that these messiah fighters would be no match for his cavalry hordes.

"So it comes down to only one possible woman; she must have been the single witch present," Zdlenka concluded. "Now describe her to us, every detail!" The three tried to remember as best they could, but at the time, their attention was more on the four men than her.

She was relentless in asking probing questions of these three until at last she felt satisfied. "I agree with you. This one was an evil witch. From the color of her skin, she had to be an Arad witch, not a witch from the Greenway. The Greenway women are pale skinned; this one was brown and indistinguishable from the other Arad women present. She had to be Arad. Further, Mikhailovich, she is Arad, not Centurion. Thus, our real opponents, the Centurions, do not count evil witches among their arsenal. That is vital."

"Well, I'm greatly relieved to hear that!" Mikhailovich replied, seconded by Gastov. "But does that mean we will be facing more Arad witches?"

"That is what we must discover," she answered. "In fact, finding this out is now our highest priority. I have an idea. These people are crazy about the worship of their god. We know that there are also holy men who wander the country preaching. Find one of their prophets and bring him to me alive and in good shape. I want to question him personally. If anyone knows anything about a secret band of witches in this land it would be these holy men." Mikhailovich gave the orders and made it so.

Gastov was allowed to return to his clan with the piles of stolen goods he had confiscated thus far. It also gave his men time to recover, and the two badly burned men a chance to survive their burns, if such would happen. The other group of fifty was sent out to find and capture one of these wandering holy men, while Mikhailovich's band headed back to their main encampment just inside the steppes to await delivery of said holy man.

Two weeks passed slowly, but Zdlenka had much to do with her horses. One day, she took Mikhailovich aside to present her gift to him. "He's ready now, Mik. I give you Troska, the Fleetfoot. He's the finest stallion I have ever bred. He should be the fastest horse in all the steppes! I will ride his twin sister, Nonka, the Silver Moonbeam. It is fitting that we two ride twin horses, the two finest in our land!" Both were brown with black feet; each had a black diamond on their foreheads. Troska stood about a hand taller than Nonka; each was very high-spirited and, after accepting their masters, would permit no other to ride them.

Not to be outdone by his sister, Mikhailovich presented her with a specially made saddle and bridle, with silver ornamentation. He had a matching set. Of course, both had already known what the other had intended to do, but both were pleased. Now both would ride into battle, the twins upon twins — steeds worthy of the conquerors of all Tarra!

At the end of two weeks, a holy man was finally brought before the twins. As usual, Zdlenka did the questioning. This time, she did not need to threaten or use physical pain to get the truth from the man. When she finally communicated what a "witch" was and could do, the horrified look on his face convinced her that these people did not have evil witches as a secret weapon. The man was allowed to return to Juda Arad.

"What does this mean?" asked Mikhailovich. "Surely that was a witch that attacked Gastov's men. It fits precisely what we have heard in the stories from those that venture into the Greenway. Evil witches there control fires, lightning and ice, just as this one did here."

"I believe that it means they do not have witches as part of their normal defenses. Look, if they did, why would not they have used them against the Centurions, particularly recently when they all rebelled and were putdown? No, I think that if there are witches in Juda Arad, they are isolated and keep to themselves. I now believe that their holy men would highly frown upon witches; I think such would go against their religion. Did you see the look on his face when he finally understood what a witch could do? No, the witches in the Arad must be few and keep to themselves. While we may run into some, my best guess is that they will be few and isolated. That's how I feel, anyway. However, it would be prudent to exercise a bit of caution around Arad women. Just don't immediately assume that here is another wench to ravage. If she shows any signs of being a witch, slay her before she can cause damage."

"Makes sense, though it will be hard for the men to implement. You know how lustful they become once the battle is done. Yet, I will issue the order. I think you are right. There may not be very many witches. We only encountered one among all these towns and villages we have thus far sacked. Still, one was too many for my liking. Think hard on it, Zdlenka; come up with a way to defeat the evil witches of the Greenway, for one day we will have to take that land." She smiled and he knew she would eventually come up with a diabolical plan. She always had, thus far.

Changing the subject, she smiled coyly and asked, "So how many wenches have you ravaged thus far, my handsome brother?" It was a tease. She already knew the answer. These two were mentally attuned to each other.

He flushed at the insinuation, "None as yet, but you already knew that, sis. I suppose that we ought to get some children coming — you know, heirs to our dynasty and all that."

Zdlenka sighed, finding a man she could consent to bed, let alone bear his children, still caused her intense turmoil. She needed a man such as her brother, one she could look up to in all respects. Yet in all her brief life, only her brother filled all her criteria. She also knew that Mikhailovich held similar views, though not so strongly; he did not have to bear the children, only raise them. She had long figured he would eventually marry someone, if only to create heirs. She wanted more. She wanted a deep love, one that came from mutual admiration and respect, not just a release of lust. There had to be more, though she was unable to find anyone. "I know," she sighed once more after a long pause, "we should. It's a whole lot easier for you, though." He knew instantly what she meant by that; a twinge of red heated his cheeks. He had no effective reply.

After an even longer pause, he whispered, "I guess this is the biggest difference between us. Still, we ought to try. We do want to pass on the conquered world to our children and not just some other warrior from our clan." She nodded her full agreement. "I'll keep my eyes open for the both of us. You don't mind my making some suggestions for you, do you?"

"Of course not," she smiled. "I will look for you as well. I already know you want a tall, gorgeous woman."

"Ah, well said, one similar to you, though no one is ever likely to be as beautiful as you are, dear sister! Your soft, incredibly long black hair, thick lips, firm body, ah, what else could a man want, save you not being their sister!"

She smiled back, thinking "How true. How true." She said, "Maybe I should try to grow long nails to match my hair. What do you think? Would you be turned on if I had nice long claws to match?" His response was immediate; he gave her some well-deserved pleasure, though again, nothing indecent, for both knew that unions between family members often gave rise to malformed children. Their heirs, the heirs of the world, could not be freaks.

Pacing the room of his war room, General Lacerta studied the new map he had drawn up and nailed to the wall. The elegant tapestry, which had hung in its place, was now heaped in a pile in one corner. His aides sat quietly at the long table along with his majors. Yes, he had successfully gotten all his men safely back to Jerilum. Yes, couriers had been sent to the garrison generals in the seven sectors of the Sea Princes requesting immediate aid. Yes, couriers had been sent all the way back to Megalos also demanding additional troops and support. But no, nothing had arrived yet. Only two weeks had passed, much too soon for any real aid to arrive, especially here in Jerilum. Making matters worse, daily he had to listen to the pleas of the mayor requesting and demanding protection from the barbarian horde from the north. He had no troops to spare to send to any outlying towns. In fact, sending any would merely spell their doom.

"I need cavalry, lots of cavalry!" he angrily pounded on the table, "not foot soldiers."

"Perhaps some will come from the Sea Princes," offered one aide in a hopeful tone.

"As I always say, 'wish on one pot and piss on another and see which fills first!' No, they are not likely to send any." He corrected himself, "Rather not very many. Courier types, perhaps, but not a major cavalry detail. Gentlemen, we are up against a huge army composed entirely of chaotic barbarian cavalry. They will make mincemeat of mere foot soldiers, unless we can field three or four times their numbers."

"What about archers? Wouldn't that help out?" asked another aide.

"That's the *only* thing in our favor! We have some, but not nearly enough. If I had the wherewithal, why I would equip every soldier with a bow and plenty of arrows, but as you well know, we have only perhaps a hundred bowmen in our ranks and only perhaps fifty spare bows in the supply train. Arrows, we have at least enough to supply them for three small battles — not nearly enough for this war, I'm afraid. Well, at least we have enough food and water."

"Does that mean we could withstand a siege here in Jerilum?" asked one of his majors.

"No, look at the map, son, look. Here we are right smack in the middle of the Arad. If we had ten thousand soldiers, then we could safely form a solid line and stop the horde in its tracks. We have but a fifth that number. If we stay holed up here like a rabbit, the horde will just sweep on around us and let us starve into submission. I'm sure that the barbarians do not care if it takes us a year to succumb to starvation and surrender. No, if we stay holed up here in Jerilum, we are going to be doomed. We would be utterly dependent upon some other general coming to our rescue. By Sol, I will not be rescued!"

On hearing this declaration, everyone in the room smiled; all feared that they would be forced to defend this largest city and be trapped. That the general had no such inclination pleased everyone present.

"Gentlemen, it is the political fallout that has me most worried. Militarily, the strategy is simple, fall back, and defend Al Barq and the road of supply leading south. From there, we can get a constant supply of men and supplies. Once we have built up enough forces, we march northward, driving the barbarians back into the steppes. Then, we drive into the steppes and eliminate them once and for all. Militarily, that makes perfect sense, and I wouldn't hesitate a moment in implementing it, except there is the cursed political side to consider."

"What do you mean?" asked a major.

"For nearly a half century, all the Arad is supposed to be under Centurion control and protection. We've been accepting taxes to help pay for all this, in spite of the dubious source from which the money was actually paid. I suspect much of it was our own ducats coming back to us from the local raiding messiah bands, no thanks to the former governor. Politically, the mayor has every right to insist and demand that we provide the protection that they have been paying for all these years. If we do not, then they can easily make the argument that they are allowed to form their own army to protect themselves, and we would then be facing ultimately two armies, not one. Further, there is the Emperor back home to consider. What will he think if we just give up all the Arad to these barbarians without even putting up a fight? He'll have my head in an instant if I do that! Politics! I hate it!" Once more, he pounded his tightly clenched fist on the oak table, jarring several water cups.

No one said a word for several minutes. Finally, one aide spoke up hesitatingly, "Sir, perhaps the actual number of barbarians is not large. We only have seen perhaps five hundred at one time. Maybe that is the entirety of their army. Surely, we can find a way to deal with so few, even if they are cavalry."

"Hector, you do have a valid point. Perhaps, I'm over-exaggerating this threat. You are correct, five hundred at most." Lacerta calmed down. "Okay, let's assume that this is the correct estimation of their force. How can we deal with them, remain politically correct, and yet be in a position from which we can safely retreat to defend what absolutely must be defended at all costs, Al Barq and the southern supply roadway? That is the real question which we must deal with, and deal with at once." He turned to study the large map for the hundredth time.

"Okay, we must prevent the encirclement of Jerilum or we cannot retreat if the situation changes. Here is an idea. Suppose that we place four legions of a hundred men each atop each of these mesas, two on either side of Jerilum and keep another legion within the city walls. Split our archers up into five groups as well to aid in the defense of each group. If the horde attempts to close to battle with any of the groups, we gain the advantage of height; they have to fight up to us. Further, from the mesa tops, one has a commanding view of the surrounding lands. Any attempt the barbarians might make to outflank us can be spotted, and we can begin an orderly retreat."

"Now let's place another ten legions strategically along the roadway south to Al Barq and another five at the southern border crossing and all remaining legions, five I think, in Al Barq proper. At least if they attempt a flanking action, our force will match theirs, if in numbers alone. You know that we need three to one odds. We will not go on the offensive until we attain that edge. This is a critical point when facing an all-cavalry army."

"Brilliant!" exclaimed the old major who had spent his life guarding Al Barq. "When the new troops arrive, whether from the homeland or the Sea Princes, I can funnel them on up the roadway into Jerilum. Once you have sufficient numbers, you can then go on the offensive. I like it."

"Good Pax. Say, you've dealt with these other generals in the Sea Princes. What do you think the odds might be that they will actually send me significant numbers of cavalry?" General Lacerta asked. He had his own suspicions, but to be prudent, he remembered that Pax here had long dealt with these other generals.

Pax shrugged, "Not very likely. They tend to look out for their own welfare, if you take my meaning." The general did.

"Okay, then it is settled. We stay put here and set up our defenses. Keep everyone ready to evacuate on an hour's notice. I will not be forced to stay within a besieged city! Sol help us if the barbarian's numbers grow! Personally, gentlemen, my prediction, and you can quote me on this one, my prediction is, before this is over, we are going to face thousands of barbarian cavalry!" This certainly cooled any enthusiasm the aides felt with the current planning. Little did Lacerta know that his estimate was far too low by an order of magnitude.

Chapter 14 The Fall of Juda Arad and the Rise of Jehosanity

Holy Disciples Dez Madan and Abu Wadi finally finished setting down all the teachings of Jes Amir, Holy Son of Jehosa. They'd brought a number of other disciple's scrolls with them too. The early summer heat bore down on the Qaam fortress there at Al Tarm, situated high atop a tall mesa. Actually, it was the last mesa, for its eastern slope blended uniformly into the foothills of the impassable Kathas Mountains. Al Tarm was located somewhat north and way east of the central Arad city of Jerilum, far off any beaten track. There was no destination beyond Al Tarm, just the rocky, sparsely vegetated, steeply rising foothills suitable for the grazing of sheep in the summer months. After spending so many months here as guests of the Qaam, both men began to look like locals. Long, uncut hair and beards grew with wild abandon, and they had taken to wearing the simple homespun clothing that all Qaams wore.

Qaams believed in the old ways, the simple ways, simple times, believing this path through life led them towards a purification of the spirit, and that one might rejoin Jehosa in his Holy Realm. Both men had watched the Qaam inspired rebellion come and go, total defeat in but three days. Also, the men knew of the initial invasion of the Galts from the Northern Steppes. Indeed, many of the Qaams who lived in the towns and villages that bordered the steppes had fled to Al Tarm when the Yellow Butcher conquered their towns. They brought with them tales of horrors and atrocities too numerous and too vile to discuss openly. Further, both men heard about the arrival in Kaan of the great infidel general and his army and of their sudden retreat in the face of the yellow horde.

Into all this chaos, the two men began to preach the teachings of Jes Amir. All told, the population of Al Tarm averaged some three thousand. I say averaged because many came and others left over time. The two realized that Jes had predicted the utter failure of the Arad Rebellion and used this as a lever to promote his other teachings. The crushed Qaams slowly began to believe much of what they had to say and promote: that each was an immortal being. Both men attempted to stay as true to Jes's teachings as they could. They also found that hardly anyone really knew what they meant by "immortal being or spirit," but the townsfolk readily grasped the miraculous healings that Jes had performed. More often than not, they retold storied of how Jes healed this person and that one.

Hama Damar, the Elder Prophet and ruler of the entire Qaam sect, graciously permitted the two disciples to remain in Al Tarm and even supplied them with their daily needs. He too, had a vested interest in having all Jes's teachings committed to scrolls and then safely stored in the secret underground tunnel complex dug deep into the foothills of the tall mountains.

He saw the original wisdom in getting all of the prophets' tales written down so many years ago, preserved for posterity.

Now that so many messiahs and even some prophets had been wantonly slain in the ill-fated rebellion, he saw just how vital it was to have it written for posterity. Thus, he considered it a fair trade — the teachings of Jes Amir for food and shelter. With his copy of their scrolls safely stored deep inside the concealed vaults, Hama rested easier knowing that priceless information would not be lost to future generations.

No, Hama was far more concerned with the present, crumbling situation in Juda Arad. It became obvious that the infidels would not protect any of their towns and villages. Only Jerilum and those towns on the paved roadway south to Al Barq were under the control and protection of the infidels. All the rest of the land was left to the barbarians from the north. Worse still, the Arads had not been allowed to have any army; only the renegade messiahs and their men were trained as fighters, and they attacked the infidels covertly. Now, even this token resistance had all but ended. During those three days of the uprising, over three-quarters of all the messiahs and their bands had been slain. Precious few remained to help defend from the barbarian horde.

Daily the situation grew more perilous as the barbarians took town after town, raping, pillaging, burning, and stealing, as they came and went all but unchecked. Thus far, Al Tarm had been spared, primarily because it was so far from any other settlements and nothing but rangeland lay behind it. They had chosen this site carefully with just such reasoning in mind. No, to come here one had to intend to come here — it was that far off any trade route.

Thus, during the late spring and early summer, Hama ordered the fortifications strengthen and saw to the stockpiling of necessary supplies that they might withstand a long, protracted siege. The numerous flocks of sheep were moved even higher into the foothills. Water was stored in giant cisterns within the fifteen-foot tall stone walls that surrounded the fortress. He sent forays out to other towns and villages seeking all the arrows and bows they could find or buy, stockpiling them here to be used to repel the yellow horde. His idea was to rain arrows down upon all the barbarian cavalry as they attempted to close to the fortress walls. He would make them pay dearly to take this city! Naturally, the counter move would be to starve them into submission, hence the necessity of stockpiling food and water. Still, they had several secret underground tunnels that led to exits far into the foothills. Thus, they could secret additional supplies into the fortress while under siege. He felt confident that they could withstand any lengthy assault by the Galts.

The real question that he debated now that summer blossomed was whether to signal a countrywide call to arms. Should he order all members of the Qaam sect here to help the defense of this stronghold? The greater the strength here, the better their chances of fending off any assault. However, the greater their numbers, the greater their daily supplies would have to be. In the end, he only suggested that fellow Qaam members come here if they chose to do so. Already the population had risen to three thousand and was remaining constant. More than half were able-bodied men who were being trained in assisting the defense of the fortress. Since this number greatly exceeded the number of cavalry in the invading yellow horde, he felt confident Al Tarm was now secure.

On July 10, lookouts spied a large dust cloud coming their way. A great gong sounded in the heart of the fortress, and all men dropped what they were doing and raced for their defensive positions. Thus, over fifteen hundred men watched the galloping arrival of five hundred Yellow Butchers riding swiftly on proud, swift horses. Like a sea of water flowing over the land, the sea of men and beasts flowed around the fortress, staying all the while just out of bowshot range. The siege of Al Tarm began. Hama Damar would never again set foot outside of his fortress high atop the mesa nor would the two Holy Disciples of Jes Amir.

During this time far to the west in Florintine Junction, Hamah Zagros and Bandar Dero began preaching the Holy Word of Jehosa to the many Arads who fled Juda Arad for the safety of the Zargarb Sector of the Sea Princes. All during the late spring and summer months, families migrated into Florintine Junction, seeking sanctuary. Of course, there was no available housing for the new arrivals, so new adobe homes had to be built, and Hamah and Bandar found themselves the prime organizers of house building and the major players in the resettlement effort. This gave them the prime opportunity to preach the Holy Word to the newcomers. By early June, Amar Tarabulus, the fisherman disciple, joined them. News of their success spread to his small fishing village some hundred miles to the south. With the Yellow Horde riding close to his village, he abandoned it, bringing another hundred folks with him to Florintine Junction.

Thus, the three Holy Disciples worked together to support the ever growing numbers of their people in exile here. Since they were also overseeing the construction of numerous new homes, they built the first Church of Jehosanity in Tarra. Jehosanity was their word for it. Yes, all the Arads were deeply religious with an unshakable faith in their Lord Jehosa. Still, Jes's teachings were living proof of the existence of their God. In order to differentiate their message from that of the traditional prophets, who were now rapidly becoming extinct, they called it the Church of Jehosanity.

At first, they too attempted to stay true to the teachings of Jes Amir. However, from the start, it was obvious that no one who listened to them had any idea of what an immortal spirit or being actually was. All were convinced that they were a body with a mind that can think. None of the three possessed the skill that Jes had — to separate the person from his body and let him experience it first hand, as Jes had done with them. For weeks, the three discussed the many problems they were having just trying to convey Jes's Holy Words.

Late one night, in utter frustration, Hamah suggested, "How about this, guys? Let's say that you have a soul, which is separate from your body. It is your soul that goes to Jehosa's realm. Let's call that place Heaven. To get there, you have to follow both the Decalogue of Jehosa and the Holy Teachings of his son, Jes Amir, who died and was resurrected that we might see the truth and believe in him."

"Hey, I like that!" exclaimed Bandar. "And we can say if you don't follow it, your soul goes to a place called Hell where Lucifer dwells. They all know of Lucifer. Let's give him a place to reside as well. It makes it more real to the populace."

But Amar objected, "We are perverting Jes's words! Aren't we just trying to control them when we say you have a soul? You are your soul; you don't have a soul!"

Bandar replied, "True, but we *are* trying to control them, in fact. We are trying to get them to follow Jes's teachings and the Decalogue. I say that anything we can do to get them to follow both is worth it. Right now, they are dislocated, disoriented, lost their homes and livelihoods, lost family members, and have fled for their very lives. How much worse can it get? If we get them to come together in church services every Holy Saturday, why, we can console them, prop them up, and help them adjust and survive better. So yes, we are indeed trying to control them, but our intentions are pure. Surely, Jes would understand. I've often seen him altering his message, rephrasing it so that the listener might understand his message better. Why should not we do the same?"

"Yes, but this is a total alteration," Amar continued to protest.

"Have you any better idea?" asked Hamah, knowing that he didn't.

Looking downcast, Amar replied, "No, no I don't. I guess we really have no choice. Our people desperately need help, and we three are all that's here to do so. I've not seen any prophet now for over a month. Perhaps they have all been slain as well. It may well be up to us to keep Jehosa alive in our people. All right, let's try it, but if it doesn't work out, let's drop it quickly."

They did not have to drop it; rather the opposite occurred. The desperate people could accept this description and wanted to believe. The Church of Jehosanity took the place of the missing temples that the people had left behind. Being displaced people, they found solace in the company of others and the enthusiastic, optimistic preaching of the three Holy Disciples. In fact, these disciples were the closest many could now come to their Lord, for these three had journeyed with Jes Amir, the Son of Jehosa. Their preaching carried a particularly heavy weight.

By midsummer, well over four thousand people from Juda Arad had immigrated to Florintine Junction, seeking a safe haven from the barbarian horde now ravishing their homeland. In fact, they outnumbered the local Sea Prince inhabitants of the town. Still each week brought ever-increasing numbers flowing into the sprawling town. They brought with them many skilled trades: some were blacksmiths; some, miners; some ran smelters; some wove cloth, some spun wool, some made candles. Many even brought their flocks of sheep. Thus, the town did benefit from the arrival of so many refugees, especially since they bought many items from the local traders.

By early summer, the three Holy Disciples had become the most influential people in this Sea Prince town. Already, they had converted over fifty locals to the worship of Jehosa, who abandoned their god, Tur, who seemed very distant. The Sea God lived in the Med Sea, which was hundreds of miles from here. Many had never seen the Med Sea. This new God appealed to them, especially the Decalogue of Jehosa, which gave them moral guidelines to live by and with which they could agree. Historians would later differentiate this brand of the Church of Jehosanity by calling it the Bandar-Hamah version or simply the Northern Orthodoxy.

A long, slow month had passed as Yazi Rigan approached the outskirts of Sud, the southernmost Centurion city in the sprawling Southlands. Just across the narrow Shallow Firth lay the island of Megalos, his ultimate destination. Most of the way down the long paved roadway, he had ridden along with various merchants, eagerly learning their language and testing theories of how best to convince Centurions that there was only one real god, Jehosa, and how to get them to convert from their religion of Sol, the non-existent Sun God. Yazi had a brilliant mind, both quick thinking and fast to adjust to changing circumstances.

In many ways, Yazi considered himself very like the chameleon he discovered along the way. This amazing animal changed its outward colors to blend in with the environment in which it found itself. Fascinated by this new creature, he kept one for a time as a pet to study its ability to blend in to its surroundings. He decided that he and the chameleon were brothers; both knew how best to fit the circumstances in which it found itself at the time. "We are similar brothers," he spoke to it as he let it go beside the road.

News, he also discovered, traveled rapidly along this single roadway. Messengers rode in both directions and, as they passed by, news was shared, especially the unsavory or ill news. In this way, Yazi learned that the rebellion had been only short-lived, less than three days, for the most part. Just as well, he concluded, because he didn't believe that the Qaams had any right to rule the Arad. That was the sole province of the Amir line, the Amirites. What he found fascinating in the extreme was the news of the Galt invasion from the Northern Steppes!

The commanding general had taken his forces north to put an end to the raids, but found himself instead running from the barbarian cavalry horde! This, Yazi knew, played right into his plans for establishing his new Church of Jehosanity. The Centurion defenders had been forced all the way back to Jerilum, giving up the entire northern half of Juda Arad to the invaders! His casual conversations with the many traveling merchants informed him that they all thought that this was a total humiliation, a disgrace. After all, everyone knows that the Centurion soldiers have no equal on the face of Tarra! Uniformly, all who heard the news were dismayed, a fact that played right into Yazi's plans.

Quietly, he dropped a hint here and a comment there that their Sol god had abandoned them. Yazi was not surprised to find that many began to believe just that. Using his smooth, lilting voice, he would then suggest that the one real God, Jehosa, his God, would not ever abandon his followers. However, as he got closer to Sud and learned more subtleties of this new language, he found out something even more vital to his cause: uniformly, those in power tended to be of loose morals, that is, sexually promiscuous, even to the point of openly flaunting it. His first encounter with such came at a wayside inn. The barmaid served up drinks and herself, pocketing a large sum of coins for one night's work. To his utter amazement, nearly half of the men in the inn took advantage of her and did so openly before everyone else. Many others at least flirted with her nearly constantly. "All this," thought Yazi, "almost guarantees my success!" Yes, he saw a very few men openly disgusted with the behavior of these others. Those would be his first targets; he now came to expect to find these minorities quite ready for a change in behavior. *I shall preach we need a change!*

Yazi began experimenting with those that found all this promiscuity revolting or at least disgusting, explaining the holy Decalogue of Jehosa to them. Uniformly, he found each quite receptive to its guiding principles. So much so, that by the time he reached Sud, he had many suggestions that he should start up a church to spread the word of Jehosa. Several of the merchants even suggested locations for just such a church. Arriving in Sud, Yazi had many leads and ideas with which to work.

In less than a week, he had gotten several of his new followers to help fund the monthly rent on a warehouse to serve as the first Church of Jehosanity in Sud and a place for him to stay as its first preacher and leader. In the Arad, Saturday was traditionally the holy day, but here, the worshipers of Sol chose Sunday. Yazi quickly followed suit, making Sunday the day of gathering in his new church.

Long ago, he had found that people had no idea of what an immortal spirit actually was, no concept at all. Fleshly bodies and minds — those were real. Thus, he began preaching that man has a soul. If that man was not good and following the Decalogue of Jehosa, their soul was doomed to eternal damnation. Of course, he had to invent what that damnation actually was. Since this land was always hot, even in the wintertime, he decided to call it Hell, the land ruled by Lucifer, a land of burning fires and constant pain. One morning he accidentally cracked open a rotten egg, and it inspired him to add horrible odors to his invented Hell, eternal fires filled with the stifling odor of sulfur. If one was lustful and immoral, not following the Decalogue, his soul went to Hell when the body died. This, his new converts believed; its imagery convinced even the skeptical.

Yazi also hated women. A woman was the downfall of man, a fact that he went to great lengths to exaggerate. "Women are the reason that we are here in these fleshly bodies and not in Jehosa's Great Realm, where it is cool with warm waters and abundant food, where a man no longer has to work and slave just to barely survive! Lucifer enters the bodies of all women attempting, through them, to call all we men unto him, steering us away from the path to righteousness and Jehosa's realm. Do not our bodies come from the womb of women? Tainted are we who are born from the womb of a woman that Lucifer has converted. Nay, do not we even let these very same women raise our young until they are old enough to be taken and properly educated? Do not find it so surprising that so many of our people have fallen victim to the wiles and false promises of Lucifer. We have only women to blame and ourselves for allowing them to nurse our children into the ways of Evil."

"Does it not surprise you that so many of your leaders, even the royal court, are so wantonly promiscuous? Even though you may not have known of Jehosa, we are all his children. Jehosa struck down your last Emperor for such wanton lasciviousness, did he not? Massive lightning bolts from the sky killed the worm and even destroyed much of your magnificent marble buildings, I've heard. Were any of you witness to this wrath of Jehosa so many years ago?" Of course, he could count on at least one older person to have nearly firsthand information of that mighty event. "Sure, your priests of Sol told you that Sol was angry. But is that the truth? Look who ultimately benefitted from that pronouncement. Who now controls your Emperor?" Naturally, the crowds would invariably shout out, "The High Priest!"

Thus, Yazi found eager ears for his preaching and lessons. The population definitely needed a change. He was a master of the art of communication or rather the art of convincing communications. During the summer months, his following grew each week. Midsummer found well over a thousand in regular attendance during his Sunday worship services. By summer's end, he had to hold three services each Sunday to accommodate the swelling numbers who had joined his Church of Jehosanity. Incidentally, his personal coffers had also swollen; by any standards, in just these few months, he had become a very wealthy man, or rather, his church had. He did not differentiate.

As spring began to give way to early summer, Zdlenka convinced her brother to send the remaining five companies home. Indeed, all including his clan company had accumulated a sizeable amount of booty. There was no place to store it, so sending them home with the loot made good sense. Besides, just as the twins had predicted, when their home clans saw the amount of booty their fifty men had acquired in the service of Mikhailovich Strokova along with virtually no casualties, greed swayed clan leaders. When the five companies returned a month later, they brought along another fifteen companies. Again, a Galt company was usually comprised of fifty men, including commander and four sub-commanders. Counting those who had not yet returned, their army now numbered close to one thousand two hundred-fifty!

True, these new companies had to be trained somewhat, so that they understood the orders that Mikhailovich Strokova would eventually issue. All were inherently fighters by nature, so the training period was short, mostly convincing them actually to follow Mikhailovich's commands without question. During the early summer months, Mikhailovich Strokova's orders were simple — go forth and take all towns north of the central Jerilum. His scouts had already reported just how the Centurion General had setup his defense line around this location. Mikhailovich still didn't want to besiege Jerilum directly and this general just yet. Zdlenka cautioned him to make sure that all the northern half of the Arad was securely in their hands before striking the killing blow to the Centurions.

One evening the twins were discussing matters in their domed hut after dinner. Mikhailovich asked, "Do you think that we have enough men now to take out their general in Jerilum? We've got over a thousand now."

"Patience, Mik, patience. Undoubtedly, that general has brought up reinforcements from their homeland or from the Sea Princes. Remember, when we strike, we must be able to take Al Bark, their sole line to the Sea Princes. We must cut that line so that the snake is cut into. One half will wither, while the other becomes crippled. As long as they hold onto Al Barq, we cannot go after the rich lands of the Sea Princes because they could launch a counter-strike anywhere along the immense coastline, cutting our forces off from our homeland. No, I say two thousand. Wait until we have that many warriors. Then, we can send half to wipe out their forces at Jerilum and the other can take Al Barq."

"Right as always, dear sister. Whatever would I do without your keen insight?" He meant the compliment.

"You have to worry about leading the men; that is a tall challenge, Mik. As we long ago agreed, it will take us both to pull this off. I plan; you lead; we win." She smiled and gave her brother a loving sisterly hug. She added, "At this rate, we should be ready to launch our assault in less than a month. I predict that by the end of this season, all the Arad shall be ours. Then, during the snowy winter, we can plot our next move."

General Lacerta hated this infernal waiting game more than he hated politicians! For months now, he had been forced to hole up in Jerilum. His legions guarded the nearby mesas. Though the enemy cavalry were sometimes seen at a distance, they never closed to attack. He could not leave these legions just camped on mesa tops indefinitely. Men had needs, so he began a rotation, transferring the legions guarding the city with some on the hilltops.

"If only the Emperor would send me the forces I need to finish these barbarians off. Or if only the Sea Prince generals would send me some of theirs, if only, if only," he cursed. Slowly as the summer came, new legions did arrive, primarily in Al Barq. As predicted, only a token amount of cavalry was lent to him. The wise Sea Prince Home Guard generals would not give up theirs. Five fully equipped legions did come, arriving in Al Barq. These five hundred men he left to guard the town, moving the same number of his original legions closer toward the proposed front lines. One legion joined the others protecting the roadway into the Southlands; another guarded the roadway to Al Barq and was positioned about halfway between the roadway and the city. The other three came on up toward Jerilum, though he wisely left one about halfway in between. It was far too soon to expect any legions to come marching up from the homeland, Megalos, far to the south. That trip on foot would take many months. Still, he was grateful for the support that he did receive and now with his aides began to work out a strategy to go on the offensive.

However, the scouts he sent out northward from Jerilum all returned reporting escalating numbers of the enemy cavalry. He'd learned their basic organizational unit, if they even bothered to call it such, was a company of some fifty men. This seemed to be the basic attacking unit, never smaller. For larger towns, several companies joined, but operated chaotically and independently of each other, which is what he expected of untrained, uneducated barbarians. Thus, any real offensive General Lacerta put on hold for the time being. Besides, he didn't want to go on the offensive in the high heat of the Arad summer. Better wait until the cooler fall temperatures arrived. Besides, by then more legions may arrive up from Megalos.

His wishes were not to be. On July 1, 585 AH, signal fires sprang up on the four nearby mesa tops, the sign that the enemy was closing or at least threatening. His aides called out various confusing situations to him, but he ignored their frantic cries and theories. In times of crisis, a man must see with his own eyes — that was General Lacerta's motto. Ignoring the many calls, he scrambled up the many steps to the very top of his compound's tallest building to see for himself about what all the commotion was. Jerilum is located in the normally dry valley between two tall mesas. As throughout all the Arad, these mesas offered a gentle slope up to their tops from the east and presented a very steep, sharp drop of many hundreds of feet on their western edges. Hence, his view was severely limited even from the rooftop.

Great clouds of dust curled upwards in the far distance, not only coming down this valley directly toward Jerilum, but also on the two adjoining valleys on either side, several miles apart. He could not actually see any riders, too many obstructions, and too far a distance. However, he didn't need to see them to know. "Damned be this day!" he cursed, for he knew well enough what these signs foretold: his doom. In an instant, he saw the error of his troop deployment. What had been an excellent move when facing five hundred was a major blunder when facing thousands. What could he do to rectify the incorrect positioning of his forces in time to save them? Foot soldiers move like snails compared to these barbarian cavalrymen. He yelled for someone to hand him up the light signal mirror.

A nervous aide climbed up to join him, handing him the three-foot polished silver mirror. Carefully, he positioned it and began sending to the troops on the western mesas. Once he got back the proper acknowledgment, he did the same to those to the east. "You mean that?" his aide asked hesitatingly, shocked at the sudden reversal in orders from what they had been.

"Absolutely, mount up; we are abandoning Jerilum. We must be on the move in less than fifteen minutes. Leave anything that isn't critical to our survival! Jump to it man!" he barked and climbed down as rapidly as he could, rushing into his rooms to gather up his personal items. He had just given the orders to have the legions to the west to charge toward Jerilum. That is, those on the nearest mesa would run down the slope and hopefully join up with his forces leaving the city. The legion furthest west was to come down into the valley, move south one mesa before cutting over to form a solid left flank around the retreating legions. Those on the nearest eastern side would have to go down the side going further away from Jerilum, but were to immediately go south and cut over at the next mesa to form a right flank. The eastern most legion was ordered to go even further south before cutting over to the west, joining up with the retreating forces.

He had four full legions quartered here within the city now and a full legion of cavalry — well, almost cavalry. From the Sea Princes, he'd received a token compliment of twenty-five. Attrition of his own cavalry who had been pressed into service as couriers had left him with about twenty-five of his own. Thus, he's picked fifty of the most likely candidates from among the foot soldiers and had them undergoing intensive training. That meant the fifty real cavalrymen had been pulled off all other duties and had spent the last month here in Jerilum training the new fifty recruits. Now General Lacerta had second thoughts about having done that. Normally, he would have had advanced scouts out for miles; today, they would have given him much earlier warning of the oncoming horde.

Fifteen minutes later, General Lacerta took personal command of the cavalry legion, leading them out the northern gates. As he rode through town, the mayor caught him and begged to know what was going on, why were they all leaving? He had no time for politics. Curtly he said, "We ride forth to do battle. I will try to lead the horde south of the city. If we lose the battle, defend your city anyway you can." He kicked his horse into action leaving the mayor's mouth wagging protests. *Today, mayor, it's all yours,* he thought to himself. He was abandoning the city. It wasn't defensible except for a lengthy siege, and he would never get tied down in a siege, not if there was anything else he could do!

Once the cavalry exited the gates, they formed ranks across the valley north of Jerilum, facing the oncoming enemy who still were not yet visible. Meanwhile, his four hundred foot soldiers in complete disarray dashed out the other four gates and formed up into marching lines, heading south along the paved roadway. Using his light signal, General Lacerta ordered his legions into positions. A pair of legions moved out nearly to the edges of the opposite mesas, while the other two took up a position midway between them. He took his cavalry straight down the center where the road snaked its way across this dry, arid, bleak landscape.

Just in time, his scrambling forces got into their positions, and he, his.

As he turned around to face north, the galloping barbarian hordes came sweeping around the edges of the distant mesas and into plain view funneling toward Jerilum. He signaled once more, as his men prepared to fight to the death. He didn't trust the signals to his aides, for there could be no possible mistake or they were more than doomed. Looking from side to side at his five hundred men spread out like a giant snake across the valley from mesa to mesa, he watched the archers among them take their positions slightly behind the front ranks, who positioned their large shields before them to protect from the enemy missiles that were sure to come.

To his amazement, the enemy halted just south of Jerilum, forming into a giant line that also stretched across the whole valley. There had to be at least seven hundred cavalry just waiting orders to attack! However, the barbarians just stood their ground and stared at the Centurions, who stared back. A thousand yards separated the two forces. "What are they doing?" an aide asked him.

"Sizing up the situation," he replied. "It seems our tactical move has them confused. Ah, look there, that must be this Kova fellow. Many keep looking his way." Yelling so that all his cavalrymen could hear him, he exclaimed, "That one there! That is their leader. When we attack, do everything you can to get to him. Kill that one and the rest will scatter like leaves in the wind!" No one saw the lone woman rider some distance behind the enemy line.

Mikhailovich sent to his sister, *It is as you predicted; this general will do anything to avoid being trapped in a city. He has mustered his entire garrison. The city is likely defenseless.*

Yes, they're likely attempting flanking moves with those garrisoning the nearby mesas. Hold a little longer so our other men can get into the desired positions, Zdlenka replied. She looked at the city cradled behind the fifteen-foot tall adobe walls. She saw frantic men rushing along the walls evidently trying to put up some kind of defense should they attack the city itself. *I can't see a darn thing back here. Be my eyes. What are they doing?*

Watching us. No, now they are slowly walking backwards, retreating, he sent to her.

She replied, *Okay, give them some yells and cheers, as if we might just settle for their retreat, giving us the city to sack,* she replied. *We need another five minutes at least.*

He answered, *He has about a hundred cavalry. Where did all those come from anyway? I thought he didn't have many left? The general is with the cavalry, and they are right in the middle where the road goes. Do we change tactics? Cavalry is a threat to us.*

No, wait and see what he does with them. Only a fool would throw a hundred against seven hundred. I don't think this one is foolish. Stick to the plan unless he charges with the cavalry. If he does, then have all our forces circle around them and eliminate all the mounted men. Then, resume the plan, she suggested. He accepted her wisdom. It made sense. This had to be a crushing defeat; everything depended upon this one major confrontation. Lose this one and many of the clans would likely withdraw their allegiance and men.

Caretakers have arrived, she sent. About a hundred women driving wagons pulled up well beyond bowshot range of the city. Their job was the caring of the wounded men. This was her doing. When men go to war, wives stay home, worry, and fret that their husband and children are going to be killed or hurt. Her idea was to have those that had some skill in bandaging wounds drive rescue wagons. Any warrior who was injured was ordered to make for these wagons and get some aid. Hers was an untried idea. Before, men got hurt; men died in battles; that was the way of war. Because of the intense pressure they had from the other clan leaders to wage this war with minimal casualties and maximum loot, she had devised this plan. Today, she would see if it bore any fruit.

"Why don't they charge?" pleaded one of Lacerta's aides in a pitiful tone of voice. He knew instantly this aide had already thought the battle lost. "Are they really going to just let us retreat out of here? Do you think that's what's going on?" The aide tried to sound hopeful, but failed miserably. He was quite frightened; this was his first real combat situation in which the odds were not so totally slanted in their favor so as to almost not even be a battle.

"Idiot! Think man!" bellowed the general totally out of patience with this aide. "The other dust clouds. He is stalling so that those men can out flank us on both sides and hit us from the rear. However, if we have any luck at all, the other four legions are moving into counter-positions to prevent them from circling round and hitting us from all sides. Use your brain, man! Heads up, everyone. Here it comes!" Indeed, Mikhailovich dropped his sword arm violently down and the entire horde kicked their horses into an all-out gallop, charging toward them.

It is said that war is hell, mass pandemonium, and total chaos. To be an effective general, an effective leader, one has to see order in chaos, bring order to chaos, rising above it. The ordinary soldier has spent years practicing his skills, his moves, and his strikes, daily, hour by hour. That is practice only. War is the real thing. An encounter in all likelihood lasts but mere seconds, before one of the two opposing men is down. These Centurion foot soldiers had been drilled and drilled so that, if one goes down, his neighbor immediately fills in the hole. They are like a colony of soldier ants, according to Bethany anyway. Yet a man on foot even with the huge shield and spear is no match for a man on a galloping horse. Even the horse may do him in.

On the other hand, these Northern Steppes cavalry were used to individual fighting and raiding, but definitely not used to working together. After all, they were from warring clans. Each of Mikhailovich's men rode for himself and his clan. Thus, he could barely get them to follow a general, overall plan of attack. This was his weak link, and both the twins knew it fully. Yet, they counted upon the utter chaos these men would wreak to counter the well-organized opponents.

Two miles south of Jerilum amid the stone and sands of the dry streambed and paved roadway, the battle began, nearly eight hundred warriors on horseback, firing streams of arrows, charged toward the lines of the legions. The front line raised their large shields in part to protect themselves, but also the line of their own archers just behind them. However, shooting at a galloping target is far more difficult than shooting at men on foot. While the Centurions launched well-disciplined volleys of a hundred arrows at one time, the cavalry fired independently. While some of the barbarians or their horses received the thudding impact of an arrow, far more of the Centurion archers were hit and knocked out of action. This took place in all of sixty seconds.

As the charging horsemen closed the distance, they swapped their bows for their curved swords. The sounds of horses smashing into the shield line echoed up and down the line, an awful sound of crunching wood and bones, amid cries of pain, and the wild yelling war hoops of the barbarians. Only a bit of steel upon steel followed, as the riders simply rode on past the line and into the smaller group of archers. Swinging right and left, the barbarians cut a path through the men and rode on past them. Once very clear of the enemy, they circled round and came back on slightly different routes. The Centurions had no choice but to attempt to turn and face the charging from the rear, all the while attempting to close ranks where their friends had once stood.

Watching his foot soldiers being cut to pieces, General Lacerta finally committed his hundred cavalry, leading the charge himself. Intellectually, he found it interesting that this Kova fellow chose to ignore him and his few cavalry completely . The enemy leader had chosen to smash through his lines to the right of his cavalry detachment. Lacerta now led his hundred horsemen straight at Mikhailovich and his company of fifty men, intending to encircle the enemy commander and eliminate him. "The best tactic now is to wipe out this Kova fellow and put an end to all this right here," he yelled to his staff as he led the charge. Besides, Mikhailovich seemed preoccupied with attacking the foot soldiers. With luck, he would take him by surprise.

Cavalry in closing on you, Zdlenka sent. Just as Lacerta thought his surprise move would work, suddenly without warning, Mikhailovich and his men pivoted and circled to come at the advancing cavalry from both flanks. In seconds, the cavalry versus cavalry battle joined. Both sides swung at their enemies, as the riders passed within striking distance. Some men on both sides fell, but Mikhailovich deviated from the pattern shown thus far and didn't have his men ride on through. Instead, they chose to rein in and press the attack, catching Lacerta's men off guard. Now it was close quarters combat, rider versus rider, all in a relatively confined space. Repeatedly, Lacerta's men attempted to strike at Mikhailovich from the rear. Miraculously, just at the very last instant, Mikhailovich would thrust his sword behind him at precisely the right spot to eliminate the oncoming rider, taking him by total and complete surprise. Zdlenka was very busy indeed. Later, all Mikhailovich's men swore that their leader had eyes in the back of his head. In fact, rumors that he did and could not be killed began to circulate amongst all these barbarian cavalrymen. This day, their opinion of Mikhailovich was elevated to near godhood, for only a god could have performed as he did.

Five minutes later, down to less than a dozen riders, General Lacerta galloped off the battlefield, heading south rapidly. The expected aid from the legions on his flanks, coming from the nearby mesas, did not materialize. His legions were in total shambles. He rode for his life so that he might fight another day. As the Centurion soldiers saw their numbers shrinking drastically and their general leaving the field, they broke into an all-out run, retreating as fast as they could. Every one of them knew what these barbarians did to their fallen mates: heads on poles. Fear and terror became the emotion of the day, as they ran after their general, hoping that the enemy would not pursue them. It was a vain hope. An hour after the battle began, the last foot soldier was killed, and the blood-splattered surviving barbarians slowly circled round the battlefield, looking for any enemy that still breathed and their own fallen comrades who could yet be saved.

Slowly the rescue wagons Zdlenka had assembled moved onto the body-strewn battlefield. Fifty of the barbarians died that day; another hundred-fifty were wounded but would recover. General Lacerta and ten cavalry escaped along with only fifty of the many foot soldiers.

His legions around Jerilum were almost completely wiped out, but the General was not too concerned, because he had kept about two-thirds of his legions in the south guarding Al Barq and their roadway to the Southlands, some hundred-fifty miles east of Al Barq. He intended to rejoin these forces and make a solid stand on his terms. He just was not yet sure what that meant yet. After all, all this was really the Emperor's fault. He'd been in command of Rear Guard Legions, mostly old soldiers and those who no longer were completely fit. He needed fresh, Assault Legions, not these old men. Perhaps now the Emperor would release them to his command.

Not until two days later did General Lacerta discover that simultaneously the barbarians had attacked Al Barq with at least seven hundred cavalry. On the second day, the enemy had taken this port city, the only Centurion gateway to the entire Sea Princes and the Greenway. When his messenger rode up to the city, he found it ablaze and found the heads of the Centurion legions nicely arrayed stuck to their spears in a proper marching order. He vomited and returned as fast as possible to the general.

An hour after the battle south of Jerilum began, Mikhailovich retreated to his sister's side, and she washed the blood of battle off him. He'd only suffered a slight cut to one arm; a simple bandage handled it. "Any news from the other bands?" he asked her.

"Not yet. Too soon. The key will be Al Barq. If they are successful, then all Juda Arad is ours for the taking," she replied while nursing him. "I wish we could control our men so that we could continue driving to the south and finish off the last of the Centurions, but they have earned their pay and will insist on the lucrative sacking of Jerilum. I expect the wealth to be confiscated there will surpass anything we've taken thus far."

"I agree. If we could only press on the attack — but you are right. The clansmen must have their rewards. Too many have died here today; too many wounded. They must take back sufficient bounty to their clan leaders to offset their losses. After we take care of our wounded, I'll see about the sacking of the city."

"Use some caution, brother. I saw them trying to man the walls with archers — the local citizens, that is. I don't expect they're good shots, though. Hit all four doors at the same time; they can't hope to defend everywhere at one time. We know they don't even have an army or even garrison forces. The Centurions wouldn't tolerate that. However, we should expect that some of their covert fighters, the messiahs as they are called, might yet be within these walls. If they are good enough to inflict casualties on the Centurions, we should exercise some caution. Besides, in a city this large, there are bound to be more of the evil witches. I fear them more than their messiahs; we can handle fighters but not these fire spells."

"Agreed. I think that we can safely rule out the Centurions having any of the evil witches among their numbers. If they had any, I'm sure they wouldn't have hesitated to use them against us today. Conclusion: the evil witches are Arad citizens. So I'll remind the company captains before they assault the city proper. Slay any woman who even looks like she might be about to cast a spell on us."

He glanced at the many wagons. All the fifty wagons had two or three men at them having their wounds being attended. "Say, I must compliment you, sister. Your idea of these recovery wagons is proving most useful. When they finish with the bandaging, can you have them comb the battlefield and recover what arrows can be found, especially the metal tips?"

"Are you going to behead all the dead and line them up?"

"Absolutely, I think that will demoralize those within the city walls. Once the men have finished that gruesome task, have your women scour the battlefield for the arrows. I'll see to the sacking of the town. I promise I'll not get within bowshot of the walls nor will I actually enter the city. It's far too dangerous without you watching my back. By the way, thanks for today. You really saved my backside many times over." He gave her a loving hug. She shooed him off, while she walked to the other wagons relaying the orders to her women caretakers.

Later in the afternoon, four great door-smashers pulled up before the four wooden gates of the city. The men and horses that were bringing them up to the gates were well protected under a canopy of confiscated Centurion shields affixed above the contraption as if it was a roof. The hail of arrows from the few men vainly attempting to stop them did little to slow down their approach. Great smashing sounds of doors rendering were quickly replaced by the war hoops of the charging barbarians who rode into the city, attacking anyone within reach.

The sacking of this once large city was terrible to behold — gruesome and bloody and without mercy. Once home to nearly a hundred thousand Arad citizens, by the end of the next few days, less than half remained alive. Many women were raped and tortured. The conquering barbarians seized anything of value during the house-to-house search. So great was booty, that the men took nearly an entire week to search every house. In the end, all of the wagons plus all that they could find within the city were brimming with goods as the conquering army slowly began retreating northward to the steppes and eventually to their clan's current locations.

Over the next three months, half of those that remained chose to leave the city. Some went to smaller towns and villages nearby. Some chose to make the long journey to Florintine Junction, in the Zargarb Sector of the Sea Princes, seeking asylum. Tales of woe and suffering abound uniformly from all those that finally arrived at the swelling Zargarb town.

Now down to just over seven hundred soldiers, General Lacerta spread them all out across their paved roadway just at the border between Juda Arad and the Southlands. He waited. What other choice had he? Any further help from the Sea Princes would not be coming. His only hope lay with the Emperor, who he hoped had just sent vast Assault Legions northward. Then, he could finally go on the offensive. He waited, expecting any day that this Kova fellow would come charging down the roadway. It would have been just what he would have done had he been in his enemy's shoes. Finish off the remnants of the opposing army quickly. Then, secure the land. The expected final attack never materialized. Long he wondered why, at last yielding to the conclusion that this barbarian Kova was really just that, an ignorant barbarian.

In fact, Mikhailovich's forces spent the rest of this fighting season sacking all the other towns and villages of Juda Arad, taking anything of value back to the clans. During the winter, the tales of Mikhailovich's victories swelled the heads of all the nomads of the steppes. Spring would find him in command of a vast army. He had succeeded in uniting all the clans under a single leadership for the first time ever in the history of the Galts.

Zdlenka and Mikhailovich spent the long, cold winter nights planning their next move when the spring thaw came. Both just knew that they were indeed going to be able to conquer all of Tarra, bring it all under their rule. It was just a matter of time. They had plenty of that.

Still, neither wanted to make a careless move. Their biggest decision was whether to go after the Sea Princes next or to head on south towards Megalos. Long they discussed their decision.

Chapter 15 The Response of Megalos

It was July 585 AH, in Galantas, the imperial seat of power of the Centurion Empire, and hot, very hot. Not only the weather was hot, but tempers were equally heated. News of the incredible defeat of their army in Juda Arad had reached the island, and every senator crammed into the stadium for this special Senate meeting; they had demanded to know what could have possible precipitated this horrendous event. Never had they ever suffered any defeat. Senators wanted answers. Both the High Priest and Emperor Titus were ordered to appear and explain. While the senators often disagreed on normal matters, the defeat solidified them as nothing had before. To say that their tone was furious would be an understatement.

Originally, centuries ago, the Senate made all the laws and the Emperor carried them out. The Church of Sol looked after religious matters. No one quite remembered how things had changed, but by the time of the previous Emperor, the moral fabric had given way to lewdness and debauchery. Free love reigned in the royal court, and the Senators had tacitly gone along with it. Emperor Hiro had executed anyone that dared challenge him. True, Hiro was psychotic, probably quite insane, but no one dared defy him, but that all changed some twenty-five or so years ago.

The High Priest and some senators, notably the late Niccolo Helios, the famous artist and inventor who had invented writing, had clearly demonstrated to everyone that the massive lightning bolts from the freak storm that killed Emperor Hiro had actually came from Sol. Sol, they claimed, insisted on a reformation of moral conduct throughout the land. Thus, the Church of Sol chose a new emperor, Titus, a young man who would do precisely what the church told him to do. Yes, by now, everyone knew that Titus was merely a figurehead for the Church of Sol in Megalos. While much of the lewd conduct was halted, it was still present if one looked for it. Those in court were now discrete with their free love attitudes.

At the same time as Sol struck down Emperor Hiro, he also destroyed the great dam that held back the waters that fed the aqueducts that supplied Galantas with its abundant water. The founders of Megalos had built the dam over five hundred years ago. However, over the centuries, knowledge of its engineering and construction had been forgotten. These days, everything was planned and executed by Senate committee, which, of course, meant that in the intervening twenty-five years, nothing substantial had been done on the rebuilding project, though a new, supposedly temporary, system of hauling water up from the coastal towns was implemented.

Further, money spoke loudly in Megalos. True, the scathing reports that General Lacerta had presented to the Church, Emperor, and the Senate clearly demonstrated that the governor in Juda Arad had been cooking the books. Vast sums of supplies, equipment, and men had been sent to the Arad to squash local resistance. Actually, the excuses the governor made ranged the gamut from lost in transit to incompetently trained personnel. He always had a viable excuse that accompanied every request for more aid. Yet, General Lacerta finally saw through the smoke screen, revealing the truth of the matter. Emperor Titus, after consulting with the Church, had sent Lacerta to Juda Arad to end this mess once and for all.

Yet, when the governor returned, instead of being tried for treason, embezzlement, or complete incompetence, he was given a hero's welcome. Why? He deposited a very large sum of money in the Emperor's personal treasury and, some say, in the Church of Sol's treasury as well. Still, the Senators couldn't agree on whether this was disgraceful or whether the ex-governor should be tried for unspecified crimes. In the end, the Senate committee took no action, and the ex-governor retired to his old mansion high atop a hill far from Galantas.

Then came word of the Arad Rebellion, followed immediately by the magnificent actions of General Lacerta that totally squashed the rebellion in just three days. Everyone felt over-joyed and satisfied that they had the right man at the right place at the right time. Life was continuing as it had always done, save now there would be no more inflated expenses ruling the Arad! The Centurions were bringing civilization to all the barbarian lands as it had been doing for centuries.

Days later, the Grand Picture totally collapsed. The barbarian Galts of the Northern Steppes actually had the audacity to invade Juda Arad! The reports in Galantas of the treatment of slain Centurion soldiers had been embellished and exaggerated. Yet, it was hard to exaggerate seeing the heads of an entire legion of a hundred men held up head-high and stuck on the end of a spear in the ground, in mockery of them. In just a few months, nearly all their Rear Guard army in Juda Arad had been killed, most in the Battle of Jerilum, in which General Lacerta had only barely been able to escape. Currently, he bravely held on to the southern portal, the roadway into the Southlands. He was all that stood between this barbarian horde and Megalos.

Further, with the simultaneous fall of Al Barq, the Centurions lost their primary route to the profitable Sea Princes. Now, any trade had to go by boat around all the Southlands, which added well over six months to the travel time. Thus, Megalos was effectively cut off from its most profitable conquered lands, I mean civilized lands. Translation: money talks, in this case, a sudden lack of money screamed! Thus, every Senator reacted angrily, demanding an accounting. A few Senators ever saw this as an opportunity to strip the Church of Sol from its place of power and control over the Emperor. Some envisioned the Senate becoming the sole power point in Megalos, but this was not agreed upon uniformly, senator to senator.

It was one o'clock and one hundred degrees here in the great Senate coliseum, as the President gaveled the meeting to order. "First, Major Lexault Thavious, one of General Lacerta's aides and one of the few survivors of the Battle of Jerilum, is here to address the Senate. He brings us the Field Report of General Lacerta. Welcome, Major Lexault." A dutiful round of applause greeted the soldier as he stepped onto the raised platform, standing before the senators.

"Good day Distinguished President, Honored Senators. I bring you the field report on how this calamity, this debacle, occurred. As you know, General Lacerta was placed in charge of the Rear Guard Legions in Juda Arad. Just so that there is no mistake, these are not front line, crack troops. Many of these are old fighters, who have given their lives to the army. Many had wounds that didn't heal properly. None could be called assault troops, save those few that he brought with him when he came to Juda Arad. From all previous reports, you know these troops are and were entirely adequate to contain all the Arad, bringing rule of law and order into that barbarian land. Their well-coordinated, well-planned, but vain attempt to rebel against us was put down in record time by these brave men."

"However, for many years now, the northern towns of Juda Arad have been plagued by raiding bands of these Galts of the Northern Steppes. Yet, the ex-governor and both Emperors never took any effective action to stop them or get retribution. Thus, by not invading the steppes in force and conquering that land of vile barbarians, we left ourselves open to invasion. Embolden by their successes over these past thirty or more years, they finally decided to take all the Arad as theirs."

"But take note: they didn't field an army such as ours, foot soldiers. No, they invaded with a horde of cavalry. To date, we have not yet seen even a single Galt foot soldier! And we do not expect to see any. In that ill-fated battle, the enemy fielded perhaps as many as two thousand cavalrymen against our hundreds of foot soldiers. None of you can imagine the lopsided horror of that day. I can. I was there. I witnessed it all and General Lacerta's valiant attempts to throw off the attackers with his rag-tag group of a hundred cavalrymen. Picture our magnificent line of soldiers with their shields and weapons at the ready. Magnificent. But then the enemy comes at them galloping at top speed on horseback, thundering into our lines, smashing shields and bones. How can a man on foot withstand a galloping horse and warrior? He cannot."

"When I last left General Lacerta to bring you this report, he was attempting to establish a defensive line to protect our roadway into the Southlands, there at the southern border of the Arad. If the barbarians smash through his last line, then you may fully expect them to come galloping all the way down to Sud, across the Firth, and sack your homes!" This, the general carefully calculated, brought a huge outcry of emotion and reaction. Fully five minutes were required for the President to regain control.

"What can be done about it? How soon can you expect the barbarian horde to come here? The General doesn't have all the answers. His educated guess is that we still have time, because the barbarians are currently content upon systematically sacking every Arad town and village. Perhaps, they'll not bother expanding their domain until next year. He suspects they'll not fight during their winter. Something about heavy snow, whatever that is."

"General Lacerta knows what he needs to put an end to this barbarian horde. He asks for three thousand assault cavalry, five hundred war chariots, a thousand assault foot soldiers, and two thousand archers. The foot soldiers are to protect the archers. Give him the means to eliminate our enemy before it is too late. Yes, he is actually begging you, the Senate, to give him the men equipped to face this new challenge. Never before has Megalos faced such a serious threat to its very existence! He urges you to act now while there is still time." The major stepped down, satisfied that he had presented his boss's orders as he had been drilled.

The Senate erupted into to furor of discussion. The horrid plague that had wiped out their entire assault legions in Velona, the Sea Princes, twenty-five years ago was still vivid in their reckoning. They had lost nearly all of their best, youngest, and fittest soldiers. It had been extremely difficult to replace losses of this magnitude. Indeed, another generation had to be born into the army. While the cost of fielding such a different type of army was huge, the consequences of not doing so would be far greater. Yet, the Senators had no real idea of just how big the newly rebuilt army actually was. This was entirely the province of the Emperor Titus.

After a brief recess during which water bearers made their rounds, the President recalled the meeting. "And now, the High Priest of Sol and Emperor Titus are here to answer our questions." This time the applause was far softer, just barely acceptable for the welcoming of the two high dignitaries. Both climbed on stage together.

The High Priest spoke first. "You have heard the excellent report from General Lacerta. Neither the Church nor the Emperor wishes to dispute or contradict any part of it." Here, a lot of hushed talk between the senators temporarily interrupted the old, greying man. Many senators expected these two to deny most of the report.

"Yes, the seeds of this doom lay twenty-five years in the past, a past that we cannot undo. Believe as you will, but the original plans of bringing civilization to the barbarian lands would have prevented the current situation. Yes, once Velona had been secured, the overall plan was to move our forces into northern Arad, launching an offensive into the Northern Steppes. But as you well know, all that was destroyed when the plague struck down our entire army in Velona. Until now, there simply has been *no* army that we could have sent there. Emperor Titus will address the current state of the rebuilt army in due course. This is an historic occasion, albeit one that threatens our very existence. Please, let's put aside our differences, and let us all work together to put an end to this most serious crisis, in the name of Sol, I beg you." He left with the most pleading, propitiative tone he could muster.

Emperor Titus moved a step forward, right on cue, giving more than one senator the idea that the two of them had rehearsed this appearance long and hard. "I concur with our High Priest and the eminent General Lacerta, who I hold in the highest respect. Yes, the seeds of this doom do go back to that horrible plague, which destroyed our assault troops. An entire generation of soldiers was wiped out that winter. We have been making do with the older troops of the Rear Guard. Actually until now, that has worked out remarkably well. Do not think ill of those men who gave their lives for us."

"Ever since then, we have been attempting to rebuild the army, but even if today you enlist a thousand men, they still need at the least a year's rigorous training to become an effective fighting force. I'm proud to stand before you today and announce that we now have three thousand trained assault troops scattered around Megalos; they are putting the final polish on their training and are nearly ready to be fielded."

"But Senators, I can't send them north to General Lacerta. Do you really want me to leave all the Southlands and Megalos completely undefended? Esteemed Senators, I cannot and will not do that unless I am overruled by both the Church of Sol and the Senate! Besides, you heard what our best general requires: cavalry and archers in quantity. Somehow, we must create an army of cavalry and archers. The archers, I find a doable request, though time will be required to construct so many bows and the tremendous volume of arrows they demand. But, senators, how will we ever find so many thousand cavalrymen? I think perhaps there aren't that many horses on Megalos, let alone trained riders!"

"I agree with our High Priest. We must all work together to find a way to field and support an army of cavalry and war chariots. I'm sure I can find ways to amass the required archers, but I have no idea how to build such a large cavalry force. I beg you to put your minds together and help us find a way before it is too late. If you simply relegate this to another committee, why the barbarians will surely come knocking on your doors before you have solved it." This was a clear snub and attack on their committee system that seemed to study a problem endlessly without ever actually solving it. Emperor Titus, of necessity, felt he somehow had to force the Senate to take immediate action. While the senators, to the last person, felt more than a bit insulted, they, nevertheless, realized the factual truth of his slam.

Prepared speeches finished, they took the usual few questions, but nothing significant was said, and the two men left the Senate shortly thereafter. Privately, as they walked down the streets of Galantas, the High Priest commented, "Titus, you did very well indeed. My compliments and those of Sol." The Emperor grinned and held his head even higher as they walked toward the palace and Church. Both men felt that they had now placed primary responsibility upon the Senators for the country's recovery from this barbarian invasion. Should the requisite cavalry army not be created and Megalos threatened as a result, blame would fall on the Senators, not the Church or Emperor.

What the two men had carefully avoided saying was that at the moment, fully ten legions, or one thousand men, were stationed about the country to protect the Church and its property, while another forty crack assault legions were under the direct command of the Emperor. Of these, Titus placed ten legions on Megalos just opposite the Shallow Firth, another ten protected Sud. The remaining twenty legions were currently training to be archers as well. Titus planned to send these legions north to General Lacerta within a month's time, and with luck, they would reach the front line by December at the earliest. Titus had spent considerable time watching their progress. "Awesome!" was his constant comment when he watched a coordinated flight of a thousand arrows rain down upon the dummy targets. In his mind, no one could survive such a hail of Centurion arrows. Thus, he really didn't expect the huge numbers of cavalry were actually going to be needed to defeat this barbarian horde. Emperor Titus had never been in the army, though.

Chapter 16 New Allegiances

Mid-May 585 AH, brought the emerald green isle of West Reach into close view. We all stood on deck staring at what was going to be our new home, our new country. Already we spied the telltale signs of civilization, smoke curling lazily into the deep blue sky, touched with giant, white, powder-puff clouds. Captain Marcella Bleu tacked the Fickled Winds toward the southernmost point of land, a port town known as Bregia. All the children were excited, constantly asking unanswerable questions.

Personally, I felt just a bit of anxiety. We were moving here to this land; there was no going back, certainly. I knew almost nothing about the island or its people. Already, the captain had said that the population spoke a strange language, and I wondered how fast language would become a barrier. How would we find a place to stay or, better still, land on which to build a home, or how to put food on the table? I, we were now strangers in a strange land, unable even to say an intelligent "hello." I swallowed hard; there was no safer place on Tarra for this family that I knew anything about. If the children were to be raised safe from harm, safe from the influence of the Centurions, West Reach was the place — the only place. Still, I felt uneasy, slightly nervous. I think the other adults felt likewise, except perhaps for Brother Jackal, the wandering monk who had visited many places on Tarra.

There is something magical about a ship gliding into a foreign port of call. Slowly, yet gracefully, the Fickled Winds slipped across the entrance bay filled with deep blue, but still, waters. Bregia, I estimated, had perhaps a hundred buildings, all made of wood, all one story tall. Unlike the rather crude homes I had seen in Uru, Greenway, in my last lifetime, these were more like log cabins. The walls were logs that had been planed slightly, with mud filling the cracks between them. Each log was about a foot in diameter and its corners notched to accept a cross log. At one end, a stacked-stone chimney rose several feet above the roof. I couldn't tell the construction of the roofs, though, some kind of grey, flat stone. I'd never seen buildings quite like these before. Jes suggested that perhaps five hundred people lived here.

Small fishing craft dotted the wide, tranquil bay. Some fishermen waved as we passed by; the visit of a large Sea Prince ship was obviously a significant occurrence, because one by one, nearly two dozen of these small boats headed toward the docks following in our wake. The actual dock to which our ship was heading was a long board-plank stretching some hundred feet into the water from the shore. The center of town was open, right down to the docks. One by one, the smaller fishing boats pulled into the many smaller docks, though some were more like posts protruding like toothpicks near the water's edge.

Friendly was our reception! As we neared the dock, we saw men, women, and children coming out of homes, filing out into the large central open area, heading down towards us to welcome the arrival of this large ship. I could see their clothes and faces now, and I liked what I saw. Smiles and hand waving, especially from the many children, greeted our arrival. A few older men caught the heavy ropes that the crew threw them, and skillful hands began pulling the boat up snug to the dock.

The clothes! Ah the clothes. We must have looked foreign to these people, dressed in our drab woolens, though I sported my leather shirt and pants. These people wore loose fitting clothes that were extremely colorful. Red, blues, greens and yellows — all vivid and bright — decorated their attire. One could liken it to a patchwork quilt. Each section of the garment was made from a differently dyed cloth. For the larger sections of the shirts and pants, evidently swatches of colored patches had been added. Yet, the designs were not random. Oh no. They were meticulously detailed! Some looked like woven knots; others were interlocking circles and similar designs. We were now close enough that I could see that nearly everyone's clothes sported a large amount of colorfully embroidered designs as well. The amount of workmanship that went into one set of clothes was something to behold. These were proud people, of that I was certain, proud and very skillful. I could hardly fail to notice the consistent motif of numerous interlocking chains. One large circle had another intricately done circle weaving in and out, above and below it. A curious and interesting design, I wondered what its significance was.

Our children waved and shouted back to the other youngsters on shore. However, the language was quite foreign! I couldn't understand a single word, but it sounded more like music than speech. This was a mellow language for sure, one that I wanted to learn, even if I wasn't planning to live here. Just as soon as the ship was securely tied up, the children pleaded to disembark; they'd been cooped up for over a month and wanted nothing more than to run and play. "Don't go too far away," Jes insisted as he let them rush off to join the other children in the center of Bregia. Captain Marcella and his crew carried a number of boxes of trade goods ashore, and we followed them, somewhat taken aback by the language barrier.

Several women brought out pitchers of mead and many cups, offering each adult a glass, which we accepted, smiling, and nodding our appreciation. The captain opened one chest to reveal many metal axe blades. Another held short swords. Another, picks and shovels — all minus the necessary wooden handles. We watched closely as men and women gathered round and began bargaining with the crew. They'd pick up an item and display a crudely made gold coin. Often, the crew member would shake his head and put up two fingers or so, depending on the value of the item. Thus, they were more than able to barter all their trade goods in exchange for gold. Only a handful of precious stones were offered. The crew also accepted several finely crafted silverware items in exchange. We knew at once that there was both gold and silver to be found somewhere on this island.

I kept one eye out on the children, but they were getting along far better than we adults were. All were now involved in a game of kick ball. I began to wonder if every child in Tarra knew that game. Once the major trading session was about done, we unloaded all our sea chests and gear. Now Jes and I began to try to find us a place to stay. I finally managed to get across our intention. Motioning to one of their buildings, I tried to make hand gestures that encompassed all of us, and laid my head to one side on my hands as if I was sleeping. Then, I offered a gold coin and repeated the series. At last, several caught on, smiling, and talking all the while, which was completely not understood by any of us; they led us to an inn. Again, by signs and coin offerings, we managed to find rooms for the night as well as food. I sighed in relief. We'd taken our first steps in our new land.

Captain Marcella shook our hands in farewell, and we watched as he and his crew got back onto the Fickled Winds and cast off. Immediately, many of the townsfolk stared in awe at us, finally grasping that we weren't leaving, but were actually staying here. I hoped that they would be just as friendly in the morning. I needn't have worried about that.

At dinner, while we dined on venison and potatoes with numerous green vegetables, which I did not recognize, a man and his wife entered. True, nearly two dozen locals had dined here, constantly staring at our group and likely gossiping among themselves about these new arrivals. Interestingly, this pair seemed darker skinned. All of the people we had seen today were pale skinned, similar to those that live in the Greenway or the Sea Princes. We, on the other hand, had a darker, yellow-brownish skin color that stood out. These two that just entered looked quite similar to us. They came over to our table and spoke Arad! From their speech patterns, I suspected that they had not spoken our language for some years.

"Welcome to Bregia. You're from Juda Arad, aren't you? So are we. Immigrated here many years ago after the Night of the Baby Murders. Name's Amar, Amar Borum. Wife's Mazri," he said, while she grinned broadly.

Jes did the introductions all around. You can't believe the relief I felt hearing Amar speak! Now we had a translator! My prayers had been answered. "I'm Jes Amir and this is my wife Bethany Madelyn. My brother, Josh and his wife, Milla. My dear friend, Jackal and his wife, Missa. My old training master, Brother Jackal. Are we ever glad to hear your voice! We will be forever indebted to you, if you can translate for us, and help us learn the local language."

"Aye, that you will!" he exclaimed good-naturedly. "We haven't forgotten our first weeks here, have we Mazri? Sure, we will be honored to help you. Are you planning to stay a while?"

"Yes, we have moved to this island. I've no idea where on the island we will finally settle down, but there is no going back for us, that's for sure," Jes explained.

"What is the news back home?" Mazri interrupted. "It's been over a year since we heard anything." Thus, we spent a good hour bringing them up to date on the latest news, just prior to our hasty departure. As expected, both were dismayed with the news of the coming and going of the Great Messiah, though Jes didn't tell them that he was the Great Messiah — the Great Messiah part of him was officially dead now. It was our secret; it had to be for the safety of our children. However, their dismay was far greater when they learned of the invasion of the Galts from the steppes.

"I knew it would come one day," Amar exclaimed, "didn't I always say so, Mazri?"

"Yes, dear, you were right. I'm even gladder that we left when we did. Life's been exceedingly good to us here. We've raised eight children and now have three grandchildren as well. Jehosa knows how few we would have had if we had stayed in that murderous city, Al Barq, I mean. Tomorrow, though, we need to take you shopping and get you some proper clothes. You don't want to look like a stranger very long. I know just the place, Bethany. Say your name sounds more like a Greenway name than an Arad one."

I blushed; little did she know just how true that was. I replied, "Thanks, we do look very out of place. Their clothes are so magnificent, so gay, and so intricate. I have never seen anything like it. Yes, it is a Greenway name. I chose it. I like it. Mom called me Madelyn, but I didn't like it. So you have three grandchildren already. My." I deftly changed the subject.

"Yes, they take immense pride in their clothing. I believe it ties into their religious beliefs somehow, though I have never really inquired," she went on. We chatted until the children began falling asleep in their chairs. As we picked them up to take them to our rooms, the Borums said good night, promising to return midmorning to help us out.

That night, I slept like a log, totally at peace. All my worries had evaporated. In many ways, I felt that we had arrived in Paradise! Okay, a relative paradise at least.

The next morning our crash course in West Reach began, when Amar and Mazri met us at the inn. We wandered around the bustling town, while our children ran and played with the other children of Bregia, making new friends rapidly. Amar and his family had been here close to twenty-five years. They left Al Barq the day after the Night of the Baby Murders, traveling from one Sea Prince sector to the next, in search of a more hospitable land in which to raise their growing family. Always, the presence of the Infidels caused them to reject each sector in turn, until at last, a ship brought them here to Bregia. Here they stayed.

They stayed because not only there were no Infidels here whatsoever, but also because they found the people here were just as deeply religious as they were. Thus, first we learned a bit about their religion. They believed utterly that they were immortal beings, children of God, who were sent here to Cymry, their name for the West Reach, housed in fleshly bodies that they might experience life and triumph over evil and hardship. Only by experiencing true life in totality could they hope to reach complete purity of being. They called themselves the Annwn, meaning in part those spirits housed within mortal bodies. They believe that God is housed in each and every particle that makes up all life and the universe. When they succeed in experiencing life and achieve victory over evil and hardship, they believe that they then leave the fleshly bodies behind and move into the realm called Gwynfyd, a purely spiritual kingdom close to God. This is the primary circle in their ornamental motifs. The other circle, which intertwines in and out, above and below the circle of Gwynfyd, represents their lives, the Annwn, their ups and downs, their constant struggles to triumph over temptation and evil. Now their patterns began to make sense to me. These people celebrated their religious beliefs on their clothes and as decorations on virtually all things that they made. Even tables and chairs had similar hand carvings depicting this eternal challenge of life.

I could see that the Arad people and the Annwn people were not so unlike in their beliefs. Indeed, the druwids of the Greenway would blend in here too. I wondered if Wid Alabaster had ever thought of forming Circles here in the West Reach. Perhaps the impending invasion of the Centurions compelled him to avoid this island for the time being. At least our families would fit right in with the local people.

Next, we learned of the natural and political divisions of the island, which was about two hundred miles north to south, but only a hundred twenty-five east to west. Cymry was divided into five distinct geographical areas. Here in the extreme south, the land was hilly with forests and open grasslands interspersed. It was called Layamon, meaning translators. The best portage for ocean going ships lay along the many protected deep-water bays here in the south. All contact with the rest of the civilized world took place here in the extreme south. Hence, the people who lived here had become skilled in communicating with foreigners who spoke strange tongues. Layamon was also a land of farmsteads; probably more than half of all the grains were grown here.

Angling up the west-central spine of the island rose the Ath Mountains, marking the western border of the highlands known as Ruadan. This central area was filled with rolling, rocky hills that emptied into numerous lochs and moors. Only scrub trees grew throughout the highlands and those were quite sparse. The bogs yielded a high volume of peat, which when dried, was used throughout the island for fires. Burning trees was considered a sacrilege of the natural balance of living things. Trees held life force, just as men. Many mines dotted this sparse, but amazingly beautiful landscape. Most of the gold and silver came from this zone, along with iron manufacturing, as primitive as it was.

To the west of the Ath Range lay the rain drenched, green hills of Tewdwr. A vast landscape of ever-rising hills covered in with thick, rolling grasses helped give the island its green coloration. Here primarily sheep were raised; however, animal husbandry was prized throughout Tewdwr. Some livestock and chickens dotted many a homestead, but sheep dominated. However, one must enjoy dense fog if he or she chose to dwell in Tewdwr, because great fog banks rolled in from the ocean nearly every night. The fog was very dense in late fall and early spring.

To the east of the central highlands lay the dense, dark forests of Moyrath. The river Lir, draining from the highland lochs, flowed wide to the sea, cutting the immense forest in half. From here came most of the lumber for the construction of homes. The sacred wood was lovingly carved with the eternal patterns and symbols of their faith. While no one would consider burning trees for fires, they fashioned the wood into their homes, each one living praise to Nature. The people who lived in the dark forest were either loggers or carvers of great renown.

Finally, the far northern portion of West Reach consisted of the rocky land known as Ruthcroghan. Here only lichens grew upon the vast boulder-filled hills that crept down into the ocean from the northern edge of the Ath range. Few people actually lived in Ruthcroghan; the land was not life sustaining and bitterly cold and wind-blown in the winters.

Thus, the first decision a newly arriving family made was in which region would they settle — a decision based on climate, environment, and job desired. The second choice was the amount of contact a family desired with other people from other lands, who came to trade or visit, though West Reach was not exactly a tourist destination. Those in Tewdwr and the highlands of Ruadan seldom met any strangers from other lands. The fog and treacherous shoals kept all ships away from the western coastal areas, while the highlands were landlocked and isolated. Layamon where we were now was frequently visited by at least the hardier Sea Prince captains.

The third factor was safety. We learned that several times a year, usually from late spring through early fall, Axeman raiders from the far northern land called Volksholm would attack coastal towns and villages. Without warning, their strange long boats would sail along the coast of West Reach and then land. Raiding bands of usually fifty men would descend upon the village or town, wreaking havoc, plundering what wealth they could. Sometimes, they took women back with them, who were never seen again. No one knew their fate, but most assumed the worst. The Axemen struck often along the coast of Moyrath, where they also felled many trees, taking large timbers back to their land, probably to aid in their boat construction projects. However, they also raided towns here in Layamon as well.

Amar and Mazri explained that their children had moved into the central highlands just at the northern edge of Layamon. They had witnessed an Axeman raid once. When their children married, they insisted on moving to a safer area in which to raise a family. He and his wife, unwilling to leave the southern coastal area for fear of missing the arrival of people from their homeland of Juda Arad, stayed behind in Bregia. They spent part of the year with their children and their families and part of the year here in the port town. It was a compromise, one that aided us tremendously, which was why Amar had chosen to split his living arrangements between the two locations.

The religion as practiced here in Cymry had no name. They believed in the One God who went by no other name. I found it to be a curious blend of belief in immortal spirit of man combined with a deeply religious faith in

Nature. In fact, their beliefs were not so different from that of the druwids of the Greenway. So I, naturally, felt very much at home here, more so than the others from Juda Arad, who mostly neglected Nature. Jes confided in me how thankful he was that I had taken so much care to explain my druwid beliefs of Nature to him when we were teenagers. Here, he found himself facing a real need to know and appreciate the viewpoint these people had on God and Nature. Religion would not pose any problem to us.

Ownership of land was another matter entirely. Land ownership was an evolving arena of activity. At first, we were told, one owned whatever land he chose to settle and farm or work. One simply went out into the vast wilderness, chose a spot, constructed dwellings and buildings as needed. If farming, one cleared the land of rocks, piling them neatly into a fence or border around your field. Once done, every person on Cymry respected your property boundaries, no questions ever asked.

However, within the last fifty years or so, things began to change. At first, because of the numerous Axeman raids, strong local fighters banded together, electing one of their members as the Duke. The Duke then assumed the responsibility of protecting his area, whether that was a town or a village or a small settlement. As some of the Dukes were actually successful at fending off the raiders, their powers grew. At this time, Cymry boasted a dozen Dukes, who had grown to become quite powerful warlords. All of these were in either Moyrath or Layamon, where the raiders came.

Using this as a precedent, the highland clans began forming their own ruling groups, the heads of which were called Earls. While the Dukes derived their governing authority from their ability to fight off the Axeman raiders, the Earls, on the other hand, derived their power by being able to keep the peace, settle arguments, and control the local commerce, particularly the storage of food for the long winters and the establishment of semi-permanent, formal trade relationships with other areas in Cymry. Thus, the Earls had an economic hold over their towns, while the Dukes provided protection. At this time, the highlands sported ten Earls, while Tewdwr boasted only five.

Ownership of land now boiled down to whether one wanted to settle on land controlled by a Duke or Earl, in which case you needed their permission, or whether one wanted to settle on uncontrolled land. Naturally, the best locations, that is, locations within or near the larger towns, were all under the control of a Duke or Earl. But West Reach or Cymry or was so large that there was plenty of space into which one could still just move and settle on your own initiative, owing allegiance to no one. Then, of course, a Duke would not attempt to protect you should the Axeman raiders come.

A final aspect came into play when Amar suddenly realized something, "Say, if the Galts are really invading and destroying our civilization, I'll bet many will choose to immigrate to another country, the Sea Princes is the likely choice. But, you know, our people would be far better off coming here to West Reach. No infidels. I ought to have sent a message back to some of my old acquaintances in the Sea Princes, letting them know it is wiser to come here than there. Alas, the boat has already sailed."

Jes replied, "Amar, you do have a point. I expect our people are fleeing the Arad as the Galts take over. We certainly did. How can we put out the word safely without alerting the infidels and other unsavory types?"

The old man chuckled, "You leave that to me. I have ways — secret ways." He would say no more, probably because he did not as yet fully trust Jes. Rightly so, we were just another bunch of newcomers as far as Amar was concerned.

Hence, the final aspect on where we ought to settle down hinged upon the idea that in time, others from our homeland might join us here in West Reach. It would be convenient if we were sufficiently close to their arrival point, perhaps Bregia, and yet in a location where many others could put down new roots without their having to swear allegiance to a Duke or Earl of whom they knew nothing.

That afternoon, Jes and I, children in tow, took a stroll around the town, eventually walking its circumference. Green grasses, green trees, soft earth — I hadn't realized how badly I had missed them! Juda Arad was a land of dry, sandy mesas, picturesque, but with little to offer me. Here, grasslands met interspersed woodlands. I felt relaxed, comfortable, as if home, though this was not my beloved Greenway, it was in fact even prettier! These natives had certainly picked Nature's Haven for a homeland. The others, who had never seen such an abundance of growing, living things, chatted endlessly. Our children talked incessantly about this patch of grass, that tree, the next bush. Yes, they were excited with our choice of a new land, more than pleased. They had the advantage of not feeling uprooted from their friends and familiar home; in the Arad, they actually had neither. Their entire childhood, until now, had really been spent traveling from town to village, while Jes preached. In hindsight, this worked in their favor; none of the four children was the least bit upset with our moving.

During our walk, Jes suggested that we take Amar up on his suggestion. He and his wife were heading north to visit his children and grandchildren in the highlands, and offered to take us with them on a guided tour of Layamon and the lower portion of Ruadan, at least to where they lived. They were leaving within a week and Mazri insisted that we visit her favorite seamstress and get proper Cymry clothing so that we did not look quite so foreign. Ordinarily, I would not bore you with a visit to a clothier but this trip proved quite illuminating about the people here in our adopted land.

When we all walked into her shop, Mazri introduced us to the seamstress, Brea, an older woman with long brown hair and pudgy cheeks with a broad, friendly smile. Brea did not understand a word of Arad, while we spoke only a smattering of her language. Thus, Mazri did the translation. After she told Brea what we wanted, Brea gaily chatted at us and then Mazri translated.

"You see, the clothing is not a problem. She and her assistants need to measure you. What is vitally important is to get the symbolic designs appropriate to each of you. You see, with all Cymry clothing, the designs mirror the spiritual beings wearing them. See my wandering chain pattern that goes all over here?" She pointed out the huge, seemingly endless chain motif that adorned the front of her dress. "It reflects me. I'm a wanderer by nature. We wander all the time from our small house here to the highlands. Brea wants to ask you each very personal questions so she can make designs that mirror you."

I volunteered to go first. This was an intriguing concept: clothing, which mirrored the wearer. Thus, Brea began asking me all sorts of questions. As I answered her, she began sketching intricate patterns. Finally, after nearly a half hour, she beamed as she showed me her creation for the front of my new semi-dress. Interlocking chains formed two trees, which then merged into a dove symbolizing my love of Nature and strong intention to bring peace, knowledge, and wisdom to the universe. Indeed, Brea was most impressed with my outlook on life and the complexity of the mirroring design. However, while here the women wore long dresses, I love leather pants and the freedom of movement that gives. We found a culturally acceptable compromise. I would have a short dress that completely hid the top of leggings. I appeared as a woman ought to look, yet still had the freedom of motion I wanted.

Interestingly the design she made for Jes that of a sun radiating beams of light in all directions. The front of Josh's tunic showed chains that formed a stalwart bear protecting its family. Milla's displayed a design that interwove a pattern of nurturing life. Even more fascinating, Jackal and Missa both ended up with identical patterns! Chains representing a fighting form stood victorious over strange creatures. The design of Brother Jackal, our traveling monk, depicted a man walking over water bearing a cudgel in one hand and a dove in the other.

The children merely picked from a dozen common designs. Since they would out-grow any set of clothes rapidly, their designs reflected merely what they liked. Brea explained that later on, once fully grown, then they would get designs that would mirror them. When we all left the shop several hours later, I took a new interest in looking at the designs on everyone's clothes! How fascinating! Brea promised us that they would be ready before we were to leave with our new friends for the highlands and they were.

About ten in the morning, we had everything packed, mostly supplies, water, bedding, and cooking gear. Each carried something on their back, though the children's packs were quite light. As was the custom here in this land, everyone carried a stout walking stick. We were traveling on foot. Amar and Mazri met us at the inn and inspected our packs. Satisfied, they led us onto a heavily traveled path leading north from Bregia. At first, the trail climbed rapidly with numerous switchbacks to make the going easier for carts and hikers. We had gone barely a mile and were on a hillside switchback overlooking the port when the woods echoed with the sound of gongs being struck frantically. "What is that all about?" Jes and I clamored above the noise in unison.

"Oh no!" exclaimed Amar. "Not now! It's a Axeman raiding party! Look there to sea. See those two long boats. Probably number at least fifty fighters." Down below in the town, people were running in all directions. Mothers gathered up their children and ran off into the woods in all directions from the town. None ran back into their homes. Meanwhile, the men grabbed weapons or what could be used as such. About half held swords, while the others held staffs or what appeared to be pitchforks. One man seemed to be organizing the defense. "That'll be the Duke. Duke Amasis Boyne. He's the self-appointed Duke of Bregia."

"Shouldn't we go lend them a hand?" asked Josh. "After all, I certainly don't want our new friends down there to get hurt or robbed by these raiders."

"Well, we are out of town, so to speak," Amar replied. "Besides, there are the children to think of — you know. No one will think less of us if we just continue on our way." Jes and I both could sense that Amar, not a fighter, was trying to give us a way out of the confrontation.

Yes, this was not our fight, but then, if we chose to live here, it was our fight too. Jes did not hesitate, "Brother Jackal, you stay behind here and look after Milla and the four children. I'm going to go give them a hand." He knew I would not stay behind and neither would Josh. Jackal and Missa, though aging, would also not shrink from a fight with raiders. Quickly, we dumped our packs and readied our weapons. I resorted to using my sturdy staff, naturally.

Perhaps not unexpectedly, Brother Jackal spoke in his usual quiet tone, usually reserved for giving instruction to novices under his training. "Watch the enemy carefully before you make contact. Observe their style before you attack. You have not seen men swinging battle axes before; they move differently. They are most vulnerable at the end of their swings."

"Thanks!" I replied and then joined the others who were now running back down the switchback trail into Bregia. As we jogged along, the two highly unusual boats pulled into the dock area. Both the bow and stern had huge arcs rising upwards from the keel. The square-rigged sail had been lowered. Two men steadied the boat, while the other men leapt into the shallow water and charged ashore. The men had long, disheveled blond or red hair and were both tall and very heavy-set, bordering on obese, in my opinion. They carried large axes and some had small axes and round shields. Most were protected by either leather armor or some kind of ring mail. I thought they all needed a shave and a clean set of clothes; a diet would also help. Such was my first impressions of the Axeman raiders.

By the time we came running into the northern edge of the town, the Duke had formed a battle line across the open area dockside. The heavyset raiders smashed into the line of the defenders. I could now see why their weight was as it was, momentum. As they smashed into the defenders, their sheer weight forced the line back. Though the defenders outnumbered the Axeman raiders nearly two to one, these attackers were all experienced fighters, while the townsfolk were not. Before we could even get to the line, two dozen of the townsfolk had already fallen. My cursory estimation was that the defenders would slowly be pushed back through the town, leaving a trail of fallen men in their wake. It did not look good for us.

While we paused to catch our breaths, Jes ordered, "Let's observe a bit and be prepared to fill in any break in their defensive line." I noticed that four had stayed behind guarding the boats.

Suddenly, I had an idea. "Missa, can you shoot a flaming arrow into each boat from this distance?"

"Yes, but what good will that do? There are two guarding each boat. They'll simply douse the arrows."

"Just do it, and let me coordinate with you," I replied as I began concentrating and chanting softly to myself.

Jes touched my arm, "Bethany, you probably shouldn't use your spells openly here. We do not know how these people will react to them."

True, I don't intend to show my hand, I sent him mentally so as not to break my chanting. From the corner of my eye, I spied Missa tying some flammable bits to the ends of two arrows. She stuck them into a nearby cooking fire and indicated she was ready. "One on the right side first. Now." I called out, ending my chant and carefully pointing my finger to the boat.

Her arrow flew true, blazing flames from its head, and thunked hard into wood just out of view inside the open deck area. At that same instant or just a second later, a horizontal wall of flames appeared engulfing the entire boat, sending the two men diving into the water to escape the conflagration. "Now," I called out, and she sent another arrow into the other boat. Again, flames erupted almost at once turning the second boat into a wall of flames.

Thirty seconds later, the tide of the battle changed utterly. Morale broke as the raiders glanced at the inferno. They had a choice to make and no time in which to make it. Either they abandon their attack and attempt to put out the fires or lose their boats, their only way back home! One redheaded man, their leader, attempted to turn mayhem into order. He bellowed something in a language none of us understood. At once, half of the men retreated to the boats and began to attempt to put out the blazes, while the others formed into a smaller line and slowly retreated toward their boats.

Now, the men joined the Duke's forces and pressed the attack with not quite four to one odds. Actually, this was the balance point. It took four of the Duke's men to have a fair chance with one of these Axeman raiders. Missa and I moved to join our husbands, who were now attacking a pair. Okay, so I did find a new way to fight these men. Certainly, I could not stand and take their heavy axe swings. With my trusty staff, I made solid contact with their groins and private parts. While they reeled from the pain, others would take them down. Jes exclaimed in jest, "Remind me never to get on your wrong side!" All those around us laughed loudly.

Three minutes later, the battle was over. Fifteen Axeman raiders lay dead; the others abandoned the fight, doused the flames, and managed to pole their crippled vessels back out into the sheltered bay. The Duke and townsfolk stood gasping for breath from the strenuous exertion. I looked at the ground and the fallen. Thirty men lay dead or wounded; some were moaning pitifully. "Get some hot water boiling immediately. Get me some sheets and a knife fast." Of course, no one understood my words. I was speaking Arad.

The Duke came over to me as I examined one of the fallen men and said, "Prithey sayest thy words 'gain." Of course, I understood him not; he was speaking Cymry. I placed the three ideas into his mind: a picture of a kettle of boiling water, piles of sheets, and a sharp knife. He nodded and issued orders, though he did stare at me quite startled for an instant when he received my images. Further, I realized that we had not yet discovered the state of healing in our newly adopted land. My hunch that healing was not well known here proved correct.

You know, it takes a lot of confront to face a field of wounded and dying men, to sort out whom you cannot save, prioritizing the rest so that you attend to those that need immediate attention first, saving the lesser wounded for last. I noticed that many of the townsfolk just could not face this mess, including the Duke. Thankfully, my group could and did. Jes did his best to organize the others, who appeared with sheets and other items for bandages. Missa, who was an old hand in battlefield clean up, became my right hand. We put the remainder of our men, along with those few townsfolk, who wanted to help, in charge of sorting out the wounded and seeing to it that the one we worked on next was the one currently most in need of our services. I regretted not having a huge bag of healing supplies and vowed to remedy this when we continued our journey to the highlands.

Battle axe chops to limbs and chest are quite different wounds than sword cuts. Missa had never seen wounds like these nor I for that matter. I had to improvise, based on my extensive knowledge of the healing arts. These were great gashing wounds, limited to about six inches in length, but cleaving often clear into the bone. We had to make sure all bone splinters were washed out before we sewed them up. With two who had taken the axe hit in their chest, the blow had actually severed one or more ribs puncturing their lungs. These were the hardest to repair, and I guessed they might not actually survive their wounds.

During all this, Amar and Mazri arrived, though Milla and Brother Jackal kept the children far out of the way. Both now served as our translators, especially when the wives and family members of the fallen reappeared seeking to find out how badly their loved ones were. Two hours later, exhausted, Missa and I finally finished sewing up the last one.

Five townsfolk were dead outright. We couldn't save another three, try as we might. The other twenty-two would live. While the wife of the last one that we helped took her husband home, we two walked down to the sea and cleaned ourselves up. We were so bloody, that we just waded out and took a swim to clean off our clothes. When we waded back ashore and stood dripping beside the fire, which they had built to provide kettles of hot water, Jes and Josh handed us some towels, and we began to dry off. It was a shame to have gotten our brand new outfits so completely soiled, but they would dry in time.

Duke Amasis Boyne personally brought us each a hot mug of a cider spiked with mead. Grinning in appreciation, I downed mine quickly. He said, "Verily, thee outsiders be'st moost welcome here in Bregia. Thy service doneth 'ere today be'st moost valuable indeedst! Accepth my heart-felteth thanks and thet of my men. I be'st moost honoredth shoudst thou chooseth to liveth here in Bregia. We canst moost useth thy special skills. Thou be'st the greatest healers I hath ever seeneth! Since thou art on a journey, whenst thou gettest back, stoppeth by the seamstress shoppe. I wilst seeth that thou hast new clothes awaiting, since thy new ones be'st soiled by the blood of my men. Thanketh thee once 'gain." He actually shook Missa and my hands!

Well, I was pleased to hear we would get new clothes. I was beginning to grasp their language partially. I answered, "Thankest surely. How ofteneth dost thee getst Axeman raids?"

He smiled at my crude Cymry speech, but I was understandable. "Two times per summer, usually," was his reply. "Yetst, this time, thanketh to the lucky flame arrow shots of Missa, we didst beateth them. Tis the erst time we beatheth them squarely! Thanketh to all of thee!"

Jes broke in, "Yes, I explained to the others that her arrow shots must have hit flasks of oil which caused the massive fires. It seems a reasonable explanation." We smiled knowingly at each other.

"Prithy, be'st all Arad women such great fighters?" he asked. "I seeth thy staff strucketh them in their manhood. Remindeth me not to picketh a fight with thee!" he teased me.

His comment meant that, although he was involved in the fight, he still was their leader and had been watching the rest of his forces as well. That meant he was observant at least, quite a necessary quality for a leader. "Some be'st fighters, though not many. That spot stoppeth any man," I jested back, grinning. He laughed.

Then, using Amar as a translator so that nothing would be misunderstood, he once again offered us the opportunity to settle down here in Bregia. He said that the townsfolk would all chip in and help build us homes where we desired near the current edge of the town. Our new homes would cost us nothing except our allegiance to him and to answer the next raiding party alert. He went on to describe the many benefits of living here in Bregia, especially all of the trade from the visiting Sea Prince ships. Yes, he made us an offer that was hard to resist. We thanked him and told him we would let him know when we returned from our trip to the highlands. Since I said that we wanted to first view this beautiful land, he smiled and accepted our reply.

We resumed our journey. Our children demanded many explanations because they did not believe Jes's explanation that Missa had two very lucky arrow shots. In addition, they were very impressed with all of the healing work that we two performed. They had not seen us doing so much on so many wounded before. As you might expect from alert, curious children, we had to field many difficult to answer questions about what we had done.

Later while we were walking along, Jes and I commented to each other that if we chose to settle in one of the towns controlled by a Duke or perhaps an Earl, we would be forced to change allegiance from Arad to Cymry. For me, it also meant changing from druwid as well. It began to become slightly confusing to maintain a proper balance. We would have to honor Cymry actions without compromising our Arad ways or my own personal druwid principles. Confusing, yes, but it would become ever more confusing as time passed. I resolved to be true to my own self and let the rest come as it may.

Chapter 17 The Happy Years

Mid-May 588 AH, three years have passed, perhaps the three happiest that I've known. Just now, I have an awful foreboding that I may never see Jes alive again. He has just left for the mainland, but I should bring you up to date. After our tour of the southern portion of the island West Reach or Cymry as it is called here, we decided to build our own town in the wilderness of Layamon. Thus, we owe allegiance to no Duke or Earl. New Jerilum was carved out from the wilderness by our own labors.

We chose a spot on the top of a magnificent green hill, one that commands an extended view of the surrounding forests and grasslands for miles in all directions. Located about fifty miles north by west of Bregia, New Jerilum, or Nuadilan as the local people say in their language for that is as close as they can come to pronouncing it, sits close to the river Daneas, which ambles on down to the ocean not too far from Bregia. My design was chosen to follow for its construction, modified by Jes, who still has some ability to foresee the future. Time has shown that he was correct. "Plan for an ever growing town; many other families from Juda Arad will be migrating here to join us in time." He was right. In just three years, Nuadilan has grown to over a thousand inhabitants!

My plan was a simple one. Initially, we built our homes and shops at the very top of the hill, surrounding these dozen buildings with a wooden wall of posts ten feet tall to provide protection from any raiders. I must say that our men were incredibly industrious. Jes and I have a spacious log cabin style home, as do Josh and Milla, and Jackal and Missa. Brother Jackal chose to have a small cabin. Jes built the First Church of Jehosa in West Reach next to our house. We have a large stable for horses and several more buildings for supplies and even several craft shops. Josh has himself a blacksmith store now. A large open grassy area lies at the center of our circle of buildings along with a well or cistern really that is filled by catching rain water. Self-sufficiency was our motto.

We had not even finished the construction when more families from Juda Arad wanted to join us. We expanded by making another circle wall around ours. Nuadilan now has seven circles of walls enclosing the hundreds of buildings. With my plan, as more folks move here, we just create an even larger outer circle around the new buildings. Further, we have also had a fair number of local people move here, though they had to learn to speak a little of Arad in order to get along with us. True, we now all speak Cymry fairly well, especially the children who have picked up the new language far faster than we older folks. Indeed, at this point in time, Nuadilan is a very prosperous town, showing no signs of ending its rapid growth.

On Saturdays, our day of rest, everyone congregates at the First Church of Jerilum for worship services, conducted until this week by Jes himself, who has continued to preach his Holy Words of Jehosa. Now that he has left for the mainland, Josh is taking over the pulpit. We've had to enlarge the church three times now, and still it is not large enough to hold more than two hundred at one time. Thus, on Saturday, we run four services throughout the day so that all who want to come and hear the Holy Words can. Once each service is done, those that desire can stop by the congregation hall for a snack. Milla usually supervises the many women who graciously volunteer to make rolls and tea and other snacks. The children, who eat fast, head out onto the open grassy center to play ball. I look upon Saturdays as a great time to socialize with all our friends.

Jackal and Missa have organized the Nuadilan Defense Force. Every able-bodied person, who wants to contribute to the defense of our town, is trained according to their skill and abilities. Some, such as me, handle the healing of the wounded; others practice putting out fires; others have taken up the use of swords. By far the largest group is archers. Interestingly, we have adopted a local weapon for our use, the long bow. Missa insisted that we do the moment she shot her first arrow from one! She claims it is far more accurate, covers a longer range, and its arrows have a heavier impact on the target.

Following Cymry tradition, we have installed large gongs in each of the seven circles, so that when anyone spots trouble coming, the warning sounds can be made quickly. Now more than ever, this is needed because well over a hundred people work the crop fields below our hilltop town. They need to be able to hear when trouble comes so that they can get back inside in time. Thus far, no trouble has actually befallen us, thank goodness.

In case you are interested in my children, Ahmad is now seven and Emil is six. Last year, we added a daughter to our family, Sarah Elizabeth. Josh and Milla's children have grown as well. Hadid is now eight and Ros is seven. Not to be out done, they added another son in the same month as we, Mac Dez, who is also now one year old. All of the older children are being trained in combat by Brother Jackal, who is very pleased to be able to train a second generation of Amirs. Yes, I know that I promised them that I would teach them what I could of my druwid skills, but circumstances being as they are, compounded by Jes's insistence that they be highly skilled in fighting because they are destined to become kings and queens, they are totally immersed into learning the arts of combat. Hence, for my part, I've only taught them basic survival techniques. Now that Jes has gone, I will teach them even more skills. I've promised him to make them all fit to be kings and queens.

Where has my husband, the Great Messiah, gone? Mainland, Velona, Sea Princes. Why? I've asked myself that question a hundred times. Jes has strong ties to his people; after all, he is the fleshly son of Jehosa. I believe that the real reason lies in the disintegrating situation on the mainland. Gosh! Three years and I am now looking at the world through the eyes of a Cymry native! Mainland. Ah well, I'm adapting.

The Yellow Butchers, as Brother Jackal calls them, the Galts from the

Northern Steppes, continue to conquer land after land. Nothing stops them for long. The Zargarb Sector fell in the summer of 586 AH, along with part of the Solamina Sector. In 587 AH, Pieta and Bonilla Sectors also were overrun, as was part of Vito. Already news has come that Barcella has succumbed this year, 588 AH. Only the Velona Sector of the Sea Princes remains un-invaded as far as we know here. From travelers and immigrants, we have heard such tales of plunder, murder, pillage, rape, and wanton destruction that would make your hair stand on end. What began with Juda Arad has now spread like a plague across much of the inhabited world.

I believe that Jes's intentions are to go to Velona and personally attempt to convince as many exiles from Juda Arad as possible to come here to our newly adopted land. As I said, our town has passed the one thousand-member mark, and we continue to grow. We have staked out another suitable hilltop about five miles distant for an expansion town, when Nuadilan becomes too large. I think Jes has the idea that he can persuade a hundred thousand Arads to immigrate here to Cymry or West Reach, and rebuild their nation. Personally, I have my doubts that he can get that many to abandon everything, come to a new land, and start over.

What of the Centurions, the Infidels? We've heard very little save that they consolidated their forces into the large name-sake cities of each sector, attempting to defend the primary city, letting the rest of the sector to fend for itself. I can only imagine the horrors those people feel. The mighty Centurion army was supposed to protect them from invaders, creating a civilized nation. Of course, they were not allowed to build their own army. So what do these poor Sea Prince people do to defend themselves from the Yellow Butchers? Often, I keep wondering what has happened to the Sisterhood and her amazon fighters of great renown. Are they still an effective fighting force? As I remember, they always were a small force in any one sector, never larger than perhaps five hundred in any one city-state. Still, I reflect on what they might do to oppose these barbarian invaders. It is sheer speculation on my part. To date, I've heard absolutely nothing about them.

Hence, I've repeatedly asked Jes to look into their situation for me. Yes, we have agreed to stay in telepathic contact with each other periodically. He's promised to contact me each night before he sleeps, whenever possible. Here, I've left strict orders that I am not to be disturbed after seven pm each night unless it is a dire emergency. Still telepathic contact is a poor substitute for his physical presence in our bed at night. I'm already missing him and this is only the first night!

Chapter 18 Planning the Conquering the Seven Sea Princes

The winter of 586 AH went well for Mikhailovich and Zdlenka Strokova. True, already they had more wealth than they could spend in a lifetime. Their clan had become one of the richest in all the steppes. Their policy of letting the other warriors claim booty for their own clans had paid off handsomely. At the winter troka, nearly every clan leader spoke with them, promising warriors for the spring offensive. After returning to their winter retreat in the northeastern section of the steppes, Zdlenka commented, "So far, so good. All is working according to our plans. See, I told you that once the clan leaders saw just how much wealth could be acquired with so little effort, all of them would pledge allegiance to us and join our cause."

"True, sister, true. Don't discount the brilliant strategy that actually worked: the taking of Al Barq. That alone has severed the head of the Centurion serpent."

"Do we take out the head of the serpent next or go after the tail?" she mused.

"If the clans provide us with as many men as they have promised, we are going to be inundated with green troops, unused to following a central command authority. That still remains our weakest link. Getting warriors from two clans to agree to follow any order together, especially an order that must be coordinated between them, is almost as hard as pulling a rotten tooth!"

She played with her long black hair and said, "You are the better judge of the warriors. You think we should go after the tail first — to get them used to working together?"

"Yes, not only for that reason but also for riches. We both know that ultimately the clans are uniting under us for the sole reason of gaining riches for themselves without the expenditure of much effort. If we tackle the snake's head, there will be little riches to be immediately had. As I understand it, it is a long, long way down to the Sud town and the island of Megalos, but the vast riches of the Sea Princes are just at hand. I don't see any other way to pull this off without taking over the Sea Princes first."

"Greed. Men! Is riches all you ever think about?" she teased him.

"And women to bed," he teased back. "Don't forget that aspect."

Zdlenka chuckled, "How can I forget that? Men! Say, how come you have not bedded one of the prettier ones?"

Mikhailovich sighed and paused long before answering his sister. "Respect. I do not consider myself an animal. True, so many of our warriors act wild bulls. Perhaps that is why I am the first — we are the first — to ever unite our people. We are not animals. I will bed only a woman I can respect, but how about you? Seen any in the captured towns that you want me to bring back for your pleasure?" He cleverly shifted the focus of the conversation.

Zdlenka would not budge, "Nay, brother, we are in agreement on this point. Respect must come first. Have you not seen all the strutting warriors begging for my attention and bed? Fools, the lot of them. Surely, in the entire world that we conquer, there must be a man and woman that we can respect. I suppose that it just takes time to find them. So it is the Sea Princes that we now attack?"

"Yes, we should begin our planning. Should we perhaps send out advance spies to learn their strengths and weaknesses? More importantly, do they have evil witches in their employ?" Clearly, Mikhailovich was worried about encountering more of the witches. Except for that one instance last year, they had encountered no other witches during their conquest of the Arad. Still, his policy of slaying any threatening woman before she could potentially cast her spells had resulted in at least a hundred women slain thus far. An ounce of prevention was his attitude for he had a deep fear of evil witches. They represented something that he did not understand. Horses, men, swords, of these he was master. Burning men on horseback with magical fires was far beyond his reality.

Zdlenka took her time considering his questions. "A few traveling merchants have ventured into Zargarb over the years. I've been questioning them at every opportunity that I get. The Sea Princes are like seven, independent city-states. None will come to the aid of the others. That certainly is a major factor in our favor. We only need to attack them one at a time. All their strength, such as it is, lies in the principle city of each sector. Probably all the wealth lies there as well. Merchants say that the outlying towns and villages really only exist to make the goods needed by those in the great cities. I don't think spies would tell us anything that we don't already know."

She went on, "As far as the evil witches, no merchant has ever reported seeing or hearing of anything remotely like them. Perhaps, they only live in the Greenway. No, I think the most important factor for us to consider are these amazon women fighters we keep hearing about, you know, remember all the stories we've heard?" He nodded. "Many years ago when the Centurions first invaded Zargarb, remember the stories we've heard — how the official Prince's soldiers were routinely slain and only these amazon fighters were able to hold the field against them? I think these women warriors are going to be our biggest obstacle. Certainly, the Centurions there are old men and easily defeated. Merchants report that these women actually control much of the trade routes and are fierce fighters. Undoubtedly, they'll not give up easily or without a fight."

"You have learned much, sister! Impressive. Okay, let's assume no evil witches. I agree, these legendary amazon warriors are going to give us serious problems. Well, not necessarily," he paused, just remembering something. "Just how many of them are there? If there are thousands of them, we could be in for a major fight. That'll not go well with the clan leaders. Right now, my prime concern is to get them all some easy victories and major loot so they become more solidified in their support of us. That way, when the going gets tougher later on, they'll not withdraw their support. By then, it'll be too late for them to do so."

"Who knows their numbers? From all that I've ever heard, theirs is a secret organization. Perhaps no one knows their true strength," she replied thoughtfully, combing her long hair which she often did while thinking.

"That bodes ill for us, sister. If they are as good as legends say, I'm beginning to get worried about them. Maybe the taking of the Sea Princes will not be as easy as I need it to be."

"One thing is for sure, there is no way we are going to be able to infiltrate their ranks and spy on them," she added with certainty. "Maybe they will not be as good as legends say. Story tellers are prone to exaggeration, you know."

He sighed again, "I guess time will tell. However, I will be especially on guard for them. It's late, we'd best turn in; I've a long day of training the new recruits ahead of me."

On May 1, 587 AH, the Galt army moved out onto the trails southward toward Juda Arad. Unlike last year, from the hilltop, the twins watched in awe as their army began moving. He had organized his army into companies of fifty once more. That had proved to be an effective size last year. Only this year, they watched as two hundred companies began the ride! Five hundred wagons loaded with supplies followed behind them with another two hundred empty wagons bringing up the rear; these were to carry the expected loot back to their home clans. Fully five hundred women and another five hundred support troops manned these wagons. Truly the army was magnificent, a first in the history of the Northern Steppes. Both twins sensed the history they had created as it moved before their eyes.

Their plans for conquering the Zargarb Sector were simple. Split the force into quarters. All roads led eventually to Zargarb, like the spokes of a wagon wheel. Each group would drive down one spoke, all rendezvousing at the outskirts of Zargarb. From there, the city would be attacked from all sides. There would be no way to evacuate, no way for outside help suddenly to intervene. It was a good plan, a sound one.

Each of the quarter of the army, now called a gruppa, consisting of fifty companies, was led by either Mikhailovich himself or one of his most trusted lieutenants, all members of his clan. He and Zdlenka would take the most direct route toward Zargarb by invading the border town of Florintine Junction and then driving straight down the road to the city at the edge of the Med Sea. However, he would delay attacking the border town for two weeks in order to allow his other gruppas to drive deeper into the sector before they too turned down the main roads toward the city. He wanted a coordinated attack on the real target, Zargarb. All else was fluff.

Chapter 19 The Zargarb First Grand Council

A light dusting of snow covered the extensive grounds around Ranchero Paladina, the center of the Sisterhood in the Zargarb Sector. Revered Sister Rosalita Armino, the blonde, thirty year old leader of Fighter Group, nervously paced the floor of the conference room. Mother Sister Aminia Sciota had given her the enormous task to provide total security for this highly unusual, vitally important Grand Council. Already most of the delegates had arrived, including some legendary Sisters! It was late December 586 AH.

"Relax, Revered Sister," the calm soothing voice of the Mother Sister contrasted with the sharp pounding of the younger woman's boot heels upon the pine floor. "They'll be here soon. Nothing will go wrong. You have your best riders leading them here." Mother Sister Aminia was now fifty-five years old, with short greying hair and ruddy complexion. She had never been what might be considered good looking, but she had the type of personality that soothed upsets merely by her presence in the room. For the last twenty-five years she was the leader of the Zargarb Sector of the Sisterhood, founded from the scattered remains of the previous Sisterhood, most of whose members died in the famous defense of Zargarb during the Centurion invasion. Aminia was also an excellent organizer and administrator, able to keep track of many different activities at the same time — a skill needed to run the Sisterhood in its new capacity of Protectors of Commerce.

"Are our other guests comfortable with the lodgings?" Aminia asked Sister Rosalita, intending to get her Fighter Group leader's attention onto something else. Worry would do no good. Everyone had arrived now except the group from the most distant sector, Velona. One might expect slight delays, when traveling six hundred miles, more or less, overland during the winter.

"Well, yes, yes, I've heard no complaints. After all, we are giving them the best quarters we have to offer. There shouldn't be any complaints," Rosalita replied, but immediately began wondering what deeper significance this all had. She always looked for deeper meanings, plots within plots; it was part of her makeup. Well, ever since her ill-fated marriage to a leading politician of Zargarb some twelve years ago. Now, she trusted only her own observations alone, but this worked to her advantage as the leader of the Fighter Group. Thus far, she had managed to avoid all potential clashes by foreseeing them coming and taking a different overland route or changing the overall plan. "Do you suppose that some of our guests will think our lodgings are too squalid? Certainly some of the other sectors are far more wealthy than we. Will they now think less of us?"

This sudden conjecture caused Aminia to chuckle. "By Tur, you find plots even in lodging for our fellow sisters! No, I was just asking if they're all comfortable and resting up. Nothing more, dear child. Nothing more." She began thinking of some other avenue of conversation to get Rosalita's mind to relax, when a loud knock on the door startled both women. Rosalita answered it.

One of her advanced lookouts stood on the doorstep, breathless, having run all the way from the entrance gate. "They're here — they've arrived — Velona. But there is a *man* with them! They are asking for permission for him to enter along with them. I told them to wait while I got permission." Quickly, both women wrapped winter cloaks about them, grabbed a pair of lanterns, and followed the scout back out to the entrance gate. It was late, around nine, and dark. Still, they saw a fair number of horses panting, clouds of steam slowly rising from the noble beasts. Clearly, they had been ridden hard.

"Greetings. I'm Mother Sister Aminia Sciota, head of the Zargarb Sector. This is the Revered Sister Rosalita Armino, leader of our Fighter Group. Welcome, welcome to Ranchero Paladina! I'm *so* glad that you all could come."

Another aging woman spoke for the riders. "Greeting, Sister. I'm Rosita Bellini, Mother Sister of Velona and d'Grange. This is Sister Lucretia Botini, my right hand and Fighter Trainer. We've brought two very special, legendary guests with us." Even in the dim light of the lanterns, everyone could see the immense pride Rosita took in introducing the pair. "It is with the highest honor that I present Simon and Sandy Glaston Donegal, better known," she added with a coy twinkle in her eye and voice, "as Sister Simone." She paused for dramatic effect, hoping that the others would pick up on her subtle clue. Sandy was now forty-one while Simon was forty-two.

Sister Aminia couldn't believe what she was hearing. Yes, the name rang a bell. The entire current Sisterhood owed its very existence to this man, Sister Simone. He had brokered the Sisterhood into its current position of extreme power and respect first in Pieta, and from there, it spread to all the other sectors of the Sea Princes. For Sister Aminia, the appearance of Simon and Sandy after all these years was no more momentous than if her god, Tur, should unexpectedly appear at her gate! For the first time in her life, Sister Aminia was momentarily speechless. Finally, after gasps of recognition of the name from her other Sisters, she found her voice. "Oh my. Oh my. Oh my. This is the surprise of a lifetime! I am almost speechless! Welcome! Welcome! Welcome to Ranchero Paladina. This is the greatest honor I can imagine! Please come in! Follow me. You can stay in my room. That way, you'll have some privacy at times. Wait until the others hear about this!" She began leading the way up the gravel path to the stables. Several Sisters, who had been on guard duty, raced ahead to alert the stable hands.

Sandy spoke up, "Sister Aminia, we wouldn't dream of taking your room. If it's all right with you, Simon and I would prefer to bunk with Rosita and her party, perhaps with a side room, to give the women some privacy."

"Certainly, certainly you may. I think I know just the suite of rooms. Rosalita, go on ahead and get the Banicheri Rooms ready for these guests." Quickly, Rosalita ran off toward the sprawling complex of buildings that formed this huge ranch. "You are the last to arrive, so tomorrow morning after breakfast, the First Conference can begin. Sandy, Simon, does Rosita Rosario and Janisseko Bottellio know that you are here?"

"Wow! They are here?" exclaimed Sandy very excitedly. "We haven't seen them in at least thirty years! No, can you let them know we're here and anxiously want to see them? Oh Simon, this is so wonderful. We've never expected to see all our friends down here ever again. I'm *so* glad you called for this conference, Sister Aminia!"

"I'll tell them, but I'll give you some time to clean up after your long journey." She paused, then added, "You realize that absolutely everyone here is going to want to at least see you, maybe shake your hands, perhaps even get an autograph? We've taken up the writing skills Sister Bethany taught us so many years ago, you know. Simon, you and your group are really legends around here now. I hope you will not be offended at the adulation we have for what you all did for us?"

Simon chuckled, "No, it goes with the territory, so to speak. Besides, we are too old to care much about that. Look at it this way; you have some living legends. That I think is far better than having dead legends." Everyone laughed. Sisters running the stable took their horses as everyone dismounted. Others insisted on carrying Simon and Sandy's packs, as well as those of the other guests. In a few minutes, the Velona party found themselves in a large, spacious, and elegantly decorated living room with smaller private sleeping and bathing quarters attached. After showing them where everything was located and pointing out the huge mess hall, she explained that if they wanted any late night snack, they only had to stroll over there and ask. One Sister was always on duty throughout the night for just such eventualities.

Back in Sister Aminia's living room, Sister Rosalita complained, "Gosh, I had better triple the guards now! Imagine! The real Simon and Sandy — here — at Ranchero Paladina! I must ensure their total and complete safety! You never said that we would have such important guests! You should have warned me! What if bandits should attack? What if the Galts try some surprise attack now? They'd get the entire leadership of the Sisterhood! Woe is me. I have to quadruple the guards! I've . . ."

"Whoa a minute! Slow down. I didn't know about their coming. I think just doubling the guards will be more than sufficient. Besides it is pretty cold outside for much fighting," she attempted to calm the nerves of her overly excited Sister. Quickly Rosalita agreed and left to see to the doubling of the guard. However, within thirty minutes, everyone here knew of the unexpected visit of their living legends! Truly, this promised to be an awe-inspiring conference! And every Sister in the place desperately wanted to get a close look at the two legends.

About ten that night, two old women knocked on Banicheri Rooms. Shortly after they entered, cries of joy echoed throughout the large living room. With tears in her eyes, Rosita cried out, while hugging both Sandy and Simon, "Why, I never thought I would ever see you two again! All praise to

Tur! It is a miracle."

"Same goes for me!" Janisseko added, joining in a four-way hug, of dear old friends. Even Rosita Bellini had to wipe tears from her eyes, though she had already undergone similar reactions many weeks ago when the two had appeared on her doorstep asking if they could come with her to this conference. She knew just how these other two women felt.

Jan asked, "And how are the others, and the young one, Bethany, I think was her name? She was your leader way back then."

"I'm sorry to say that Bethany was killed in a Galt raid only a few years after we all got back home," Simon explained. "But the rest of us, even Thallia — we're all just fine, though our bodies are old and grey and not so limber any more. It was a considerable challenge for us to make the long journey here."

They all laughed. So true. Everyone present in the reunion was at least sixty years old; greying was the least of their worries. Jan had taken a nasty wound to her sword arm many years ago. She had to give up actual fighting as a result, because her right arm no longer worked properly, and now the arm muscles had atrophied considerably. This group talked long into the night. Sandy had to tell them about her many children and grandchildren. She also relayed messages from many of the other Sisters, who had migrated to the Greenway so long ago. Yes, it was a joyous chat for several hours.

When the group went to the mess hall for breakfast the next day, over five hundred Sisters thronged the building, more than three-quarters stood just outside waiting for the appearance of their Living Legends. Both Simon and Sandy were overwhelmed by the sheer volume of admiration and respect shown by so many; tears trickled down both their cheeks. By Sister Aminia's orders, no one bothered them while they were actually dinning. Soon it was time for the actual conference to begin.

One building housed the ornate, yet immense, meeting hall. Mahogany panels covered the walls. Great windows let in the yellow sunlight of the new day. Aminia had the room arranged as follows. A long oval oaken table sat against the back wall. Sixteen chairs were placed facing out towards the rest of the huge room. Chairs had been confiscated from nearly every other building so that there was room to seat another three hundred Sisters, all facing the sixteen. Actually, the night before, it had only been fourteen, but with the unexpected arrival of the two legends, Sister Aminia had added two more.

Quickly the room filled up, though all those who had traveled to get here were allowed entry. The remainder of the chairs, some two hundred, was shared by the Sisters of the Zargarb Sector, who would take turns witnessing the event. At the head table each of the matrons of the Sisterhood in the seven sectors sat, along with their Fighter Group Leader. Simon and Sandy also had a place of high honor, sitting beside their old friends.

Sister Aminia stood and opened the conference, speaking in her soothing, calming voice that could be heard throughout the room. In fact, between words, you could have heard a pin drop. "It is December 21, 586 AH. Welcome one and all to this historic First Grand Council of the Sisterhood.

Yes, this is an historic day indeed, and we are extremely honored by the presence of two of our Greenway friends, who helped us become what we are today." At this point, she had to pause to let the huge round of applause die down.

"Always before, each matron operated pretty well independent of the others, though as you well know, we always shared ideas and information. But this is indeed a first for the Sisterhood. Today, we are all gathered together to act as a single unit, a single entity. First on the agenda will be a sharing of information on each sector's operations and status, so that we all know the true situation in each sector. Then, we will address what we know about the Galts and the likely invasion. Finally, we shall attempt to reach some consensus on how to properly deal with them." Once more, she had to wait until the applause died down.

"I'll go first, and then I think we shall just go on down the line of the sectors. I hope the Velona group will not feel upset at having the last word." She looked at Rosalita who smiled and shook her head. "My name is Sister Aminia Sciota, and this is my right hand warrior, Sister Rosalita Armino." The younger sister stood up for a moment so that those that did not know her could see whom she was. She quickly sat back down.

"As many of you know, the Sisterhood here in Zargarb was nearly wiped out some thirty years ago when we made a last stand in the defense of the city as the Centurions invaded. Thanks to Sister Rosita Rosario and Sister Simone, the agreement they worked out for Pieta actually saved us from complete extinction. Graciously, she sent in her own people to help resurrect our order here. Though not a fighter, I accepted the leadership position and followed carefully the pattern Sister Rosita had established. No words can thank her enough; our entire order owes its very existence to her untiring efforts on our behalf. In fact, none of us would be here if it had not been for Sister Simone — our dearest friends from the Greenway." Again, she had to wait until the spontaneous applause quieted.

"Now for the status of the Sisterhood here in the Zargarb Sector. I must truthfully say that things have indeed changed for the better since you two were here, Simon and Sandy. While women are still not treated as equals, crime and brutality against our sex is drastically lower. In fact, I must add that thirty years ago, I thought I would never see the day when women would not be treated as animals or objects for a man to do with as his whims spoke. But it has happened. We women are now allowed to speak our minds openly without fear of reprisals. Here, most of the crimes against women are committed by their husbands, if you can believe that. However, and more to the point, the Sisterhood has gained the respect of everyone."

"No important convoy of goods or people or even messengers would dare travel without our active participation. We always send at least a pair of fighters on each mission. It is now common knowledge that if a convoy has the protection of the Sisterhood, it is a worthy one, one that is in the best interests of all the people of our land. We have been highly rewarded for our services.

Indeed, our treasury is now a force with which to be reckoned, though probably not as large as the Church or the Prince's funds. One other interesting result that has emerged within the last five years: the Sisterhood is no longer just a place for outcast or ill-treated women. We have gained a great measure of respectability. Every month we have at least fifty women wishing to join us, but only perhaps five of those because of hostile actions by men. Most are now joining because they see it as an opportunity to better their lives and live by their own independent hand. At the moment, our Sisterhood numbers about two thousand strong, but only half are fighters."

"In fact, we now have the means to actually help the old and infirm. This past year, we have a group of one hundred that we call the Helpers, who routinely visit the outlying towns and villages providing all kinds of domestic assistance to those who need it. This program has done much to improve our image and acceptance in the general society." The meeting took an unexpected digression at this point. Many other leaders wanted to hear the full details of this new program. It was quite clear that they would implement the same when they returned home.

"After each of the others report on their status, then I will discuss the Juda Arad situation. So following the arc of our cities, Solamina is next. We are honored to have Sister Mia Fleuora speak next," Aminia explained and gestured for her to stand as she sat down to listen.

Mia rose, tall and blonde; she was about forty-five years old with blue eyes and a stern countenance. She spoke briefly. "This is our Fighter Group leader, Sister Racina Bello. I would love to add my heartfelt thanks to our friends from the Greenway. Though I did not see them when they were here, their incredible impact was felt in Solamina just as it was throughout the Sea Princes." Again, she had to wait for the applause to quiet. Racina was twenty-seven, at least six feet tall and well-muscled, with a fit, tanned body. She, like Rosalita, looked every bit the Fighter Group leader.

"In Solamina, when the invasion of the Centurions came, the Sisterhood chose to scatter to the northern, remote villages to wait it out. Hence, we did not suffer the drastic loss of sisters, as did Zargarb. The conditions in Solamina are much as Sister Aminia has described for Zargarb. We are a thriving, prosperous, and honored Sisterhood now. Our rolls count nearly five thousand members. Again, half of them are fighter trained." She sat down satisfied she had nothing more to add.

When Rosita Rosario of Pieta rose, she received a standing ovation that brought tears to her eyes. Old and grey, her deeply lined face beamed with pride. "Thank you, thank you one and all. Really we ought to be thanking our Greenway friends and Sister Simone in particular." She gestured for Simon and Sandy to stand. Thunderous applause deafened the room for nearly five minutes. Simon and Sandy move to either side of Rosita, and all three put their arms around each other. Three aged people accepted the intense gratitude of so many women. Yes, even Simon and Sandy had water dripping down their faces. Never had they felt such a spontaneous outflow of love and gratitude.

When the noise finally quieted down, Rosita introduced her Fighter Group leader, Janisseko Bugatti, also in her early sixties. She still saw to the training needs of her group, seeking to guarantee each of her fighters stood the best possible chance of winning a fight. Rosita went on, "I have very little to add. The Sisterhood in Pieta is now a highly respected organization and wealthy too. I believe our last tally showed eight thousand members; again about half are fighter trained. "Bonilla, your turn." She sat down.

"Janisseko Botellio of Bonilla," she said as she rose. She was fifty-eight but looked somewhat older. For her, the years had not gone well. Stiff-jointed, she walked with difficulty nowadays. She still had that vibrant, almost domineering personality. "My Fighter Leader, Winea Vino," she gestured to the young woman on her right who was thirty-three. "Sandy and Simon, I thought that I would never see you again. Long have I told others just how incredibly lucky I was to have accompanied you on your travels through the Sea Princes. It is *so* good to see you again!" This, of course, brought a round of whispers and applause from the audience. She had made her mark, letting everyone present know that she also had strong connections with the living legends. That, she calculated, would increase her influence when it was time for decisions to be made. Jan continued to be coldly calculating. "We have a little over seven thousand members in our organization, fully four thousand trained to fight. All else is pretty much what Aminia has said. It seems the Sisterhood is now well respected everywhere. Vito, your turn." She sat down.

A younger woman rose and spoke, "I am Carmina Bunne and this is our Fighter Leader, Sister Ellena Els." Both women were in their early thirties, some of the youngest of the leaders of the Sisterhood. "I am proud to say our rolls number seven thousand five hundred, growing fast. We field thirty-five hundred fighters, which serves our needs adequately. I for one am very glad that we chose to have this conference, for if nothing else, I have learned from Aminia. I promise that we too shall implement a program for the old and infirm. There is much to be said for this sharing of ideas. I hope that we can continue to do this in the years to come. Barcella," and she sat down.

"I am Lucia Lupe, leader of the Barcella Sisterhood and this is my Fighter Group leader, Sister Lana Felini. Our story differs little from yours, save in the plague salvage operations that we performed for those in the Velona Sector. We have now seven thousand members give or take a few. Like Sister Carmina, we have kept the number of fighters constant at thirty-five hundred. We have earned the respect of many people in the Velona sector as well." She sat down; she was forty years old, while her companion was thirty-five. Noteworthy, she did not mention that it was Velona's turn.

Rosita Bellini rose; she was in her middle sixties but still firm of mind. Lucretia Botini, also in her middle sixties stood at her side. A hush fell over the room. "I am Rosita Bellini," she announced in a solemn voice.

"I am Lucretia Botini," her companion added.

Rosita continued very solemnly, "I believe that it is time we shared a bit

234

of history with all of you. I, we, feel that it has a strong bearing on this conference." The room was so quiet that you could hear a feather hit the wooden floor. For years, wild speculation ran throughout the other six sectors about what had happened with the plague. "It is time you hear the truth about what happened some thirty years ago. At that time, Prince Jamil Alverado was a weak, coward of a man and a man-lover. When the invasion of the Centurions finally arrived in Velona, he moved the entire population of Velona out to the surrounding villages and towns. He ordered the plague ship to be brought and docked in Velona. We have found out that his grand idea was to turn the plague loose on the invaders, wiping them out. He would then recapture the city when most of the invaders had perished. The Church of Tur held complicity in this matter and went along with it." Many gasps echoed throughout the room. Until now, it had only been wild speculation that the Prince had caused the plague.

"My esteemed Greenway friend, Bethany or was it Sarah Jane — ah age does wonders for my memory — one of the two once told me that 'plague cares not whom it strikes.' She was right. However, when we heard that the plague was to be loosened upon Velona, the Sisterhood, which had been supporting the Prince and aiding with the mass migration of our people, voted to abandon the Velona Sector entirely. In hindsight, had we not done so, there likely would not be any Sisterhood left in that sector. For my part, I took about half of our sisters and moved into the Barcella Sector to wait it out."

"The results of the plague: half of the entire population of the Velona Sector perished! That fact has been carefully hidden by the Church out of fear that other sectors might try to take over Velona. Actually, the youngest son of Po took over control of both the Princedom and the Church. I think that this is the very first time total power rests upon one man. However, the state of affairs is hardly priestly. The entire economy of Velona was nearly destroyed. In the aftermath, widespread lawlessness became the rule. I think the people were just trying to find some way of surviving it all. The Sisterhood stepped in at the bequest of the Church and the Centurions. Today, much of that wild nature has been curtailed, but bandits still roam the outer lands. I've set up our main headquarters similar to that of Zargarb, about fifty miles north of Velona, our own town, so to speak. Our numbers have reached about twenty-five hundred strong with two thousand of them trained in the combat arts. I'll let Lucretia discuss what happened to the other half of the original Velona Sisterhood." When she sat down, many voices whispered; much of this was rumor and here-say; finally the truth had been told.

Lucretia rose, cleared her throat, "I bid you all welcome from the eight Sisterhood." She paused to let that significance hit. Several gasps told her it had. "Yes, I took about half with me and headed into the nearly impassable northern coastal area. Originally, we intended to at least get to Fortress d'Grange and from there press on into the Greenway. Yes, many of us fully intended to accept our friends' offer of sanctuary in the Greenway. However, when we got to the Fortress, about two hundred fifty accepted the Count's gracious offer to stay with him and help defend it. The rest of us headed on down into the Greenway. Yes, it is a veritable garden of the gods; tis everything they have ever said it was!"

"Once the facts behind the plague became known, the Count seceded from the Velona Sector, forming the d'Grange Sector, which occupies all the rocky extreme northwestern portion of what used to be the Velona Sector. We found him a gracious leader, one who respects women and a man with foresight. Already, he has begun the construction of two more stone fortresses; one will be a port, while the other rises on the hillside opposite the first fortress. The only path any invading army can follow leads right between the two. The crossfire will be unbelievably deadly."

This second fortress is called Fortress Botini. Yes, I'm its commander!" She paused for a few seconds for the impact to reach minds. Thunderous applause and cheers spontaneously arose. This was an unprecedented event! A Sister was actually the sole commander of an entire fortress! The cheering and yelling and whooping did not end for over five minutes. When she could finally continue, she added, "The d'Grange Sisterhood now numbers a thousand with seven hundred fifty fighter-trained. Indeed, we are well paid for our services, and the Count depends upon us to guard all valuable shipments. Oh yes, the current leader is Count Leonardo; his father passed away five years ago."

"One further detail: we continue to maintain extremely close ties with the Guardians of Greenway. We have a mutual defense treaty signed by the Count. If either of us is attacked, the other will come to its aid. Finally, it is my firm belief that the most valuable thing our Greenway friends have taught us is to work together for the common good. That is why I invited their representatives to attend our First Council." She sat down, satisfied that she had made an indelible impression on every Sister in attendance. In truth, she had.

Sister Aminia rose, "Next, on the agenda is the Juda Arad situation. Being the closest sector to that country, Zargarb probably has acquired the most information, though I know that many Arad citizens have migrated to other sectors. I will begin with all that we now know." She took a deep breath to steady her nerves. This presentation had to be perfect. In the end, the survival of the Zargarb Sisterhood hung on this meeting, she was certain of that fact, which is why she had organized this First Council.

"The Galts are now in complete control of all Juda Arad. This observation and conclusion has been verified to our satisfaction completely. The Centurions there have been soundly defeated and now occupy only a small town at the extreme southern edge of the country, where their great south road leads into the Southlands. From what we have learned, the Centurions intend to hold that position at all costs. During the last year, we all know that the Centurions shipped some of their forces from here in the Sea Princes down to aid in the defense of Juda Arad. With the sudden fall of their only port, Al Barq, the Centurions here in the Sea Prince Sectors are now cut off from their homeland and source of supply. True, we know of a very few mariners who have accepted commissions to sail around the Southlands to Megalos directly. They are highly paid, I'm told, but that voyage is exceedingly long and arduous, to say nothing of risky."

"Since the first days of the Galt invasion, we have seen escalating numbers of Arad citizens immigrating to our sector. Uniformly, they ask for asylum here, and it has always been granted. Our northeastern town of Florintine Junction has seen its population swell to nearly ten thousand; nearly all are Arads! Our Prince has attempted to conduct a survey of the total number of Arads within our borders. Whether or not the count is accurate, we cannot tell. The Prince is often prone to exaggeration. His estimate is that they number some fifty thousand strong. I suspect that might be on the high side."

"This is not a bad thing, to have this influx of people, because they bring with them many skills. Especially valuable are metalworking and silver-smithing, to say nothing of common shepherds. We are always in need of people to raise sheep for wool and meat. Yes, the Prince and the Church both see profit in having as many come as possible. Finding housing is perhaps the greatest challenge they face, but employment is easy."

"They have also brought with them a new religion called Jehosanity, which is catching on like a wild fire, even among our people, worshipers of Tur. They claim that the one God who made Tarra sent his son to Juda Arad some years ago to show them the way to freedom. He was called the Great Messiah before he was crucified by the Centurions. He taught that we are all spiritual beings who inhabit fleshly bodies here on Tarra. We believe more important than that message are his ideals for living a good life. Many of our Sisters readily grasp these ideals. Roughly stated, they are as follows:

There is no god but Jehosa so do not worship any other god but the One God.

Do not build statues of Jehosa, for Jehosa has no form just as you do not have.

Set aside the Holy Day, Saturday, from your labors and worship the Lord that day.

Respect and serve thy mother and thy father, for they have labored long in your raising.

Do not kill; do not steal; do not commit adultery; do not lie to another.

Do not desire another's house, possessions, or wife.

You see how women who have been victims of men at one time or another take so readily to these principles? I think that at this point nearly half of our Sisterhood now worships Jehosa. Only in Zargarb proper is Tur still heavily worshiped. This, naturally, has the Church of Tur very worried. However, as long as the Prince, the Sisterhood, and the Centurions continue to allow the Arad immigrants their religion, there is very little the Church of Tur can do about it."

Next, she asked the other leaders to report on the Arad situation in their sectors. None had an exact count, but uniformly most suggested that there might be as many as ten thousand Arads in each sector. The vast majority chose to live in the major city of the sector and chose to live close to other Arads, forming a sub-community within the city. This new religion was not yet noticed in any other sector.

Sister Aminia took a deep breath, for here came the critical portion of the council. "Now the next thing I want to address is what to do about the Galt invasion. Let me begin by saying that, based upon what the refugees have told us, these wild cavalrymen are systematically looting the entire country, carrying off anything of major value, particularly gold, silver items, and gemstones. They rape and pillage as they go. Not a single village has been spared. Now as winter descends, the Galts have retreated into the Northern Steppes. Surely as soon as the spring comes, they will be back. The question is where will they strike next?"

"As I see it, there are only three choices for their next assault: the Greenway, the Sea Princes and us in particular, or to the south and the remnants of the Centurion army. Long have we studied the situation; we've talked to many Arad immigrants. We've even encountered a number of Galt merchant traders and quizzed them for information. From our scanty knowledge of the Greenway — and correct me if I am completely wrong about this — the Greenway does not have much gold and silver, if any. Its wealth lies in the grain that it grows. Based upon the Galts' patterns, it does not seem likely to me that they will next strike the Greenway."

"That leaves us and the Centurions. My gut feeling about these barbarian men is that they are likely to see no profit in attacking the remnants of the Centurions in the extreme south of Juda Arad. What would they gain? As I understand it, Megalos lies hundreds and hundreds of miles further south. I think these greedy bastards will strike the Sea Princes come spring. That makes Zargarb the prime first target." She paused to sense the feelings the others at the large table. Were they of a similar mind, a similar conclusion? From the nods, she concluded the other leaders bought her conclusion.

"I've brought this matter to the attention of the Centurion general in Zargarb, to the Prince, and even to the Church of Tur. The Prince says the defense of Zargarb lies with our conquerors, the Centurions, or even with the Sisterhood. The Church says it will not happen, but if it does, it is the will of Tur. The Centurion general had no comment, but he looked very angry with me for having brought it up. Further, we have been closely monitoring the movements and numbers of the Centurions since the Galt invasion began last year. A pattern has emerged. Our general has pulled nearly all his soldiers back into to Zargarb, abandoning all the outlying towns and villages. Oh, he has done this slowly and on the quiet — two men here; a new one arrives and three leave — a sort of shell game. At this very moment, I dare say there is not a Centurion beyond twenty-five miles of Zargarb!"

"It is plainly obvious what his defense plan actually is: give up all the sector and protect only the city!" Much hushed discussion filled the room, and she paused long enough for some to exchange comments. "It's probably worse than this. Here in Zargarb, the Centurion soldiers are called the Rear Guard.

We know why, having had much contact with them. They are the older men, past their prime or those whose wounds make them unfit for what they call their assault troops. We think that our general is going to try to stop the Galts with about fifteen hundred old or relatively unfit men! Never happen!" Again, the discussion between Sisters echoed around the room. Sister Aminia paused judiciously, giving them time to vent their feelings.

Sister Lucia spoke up, "I can add a little news from Barcella. We've observed that our general has also been consolidating his men. Just this week, several boatloads of men set sailed westward. He has perhaps fifteen hundred men, Rear Guard, as you say. I will keep watch on their actions and send you additional reports on their troop movements. Perhaps they are headed to Zargarb or possibly they are going to attempt to retake Al Barq."

Carmina rose, "Since we are going in reverse order, let me add to what Lucia said. Last week, several ships set sail from Vito loaded with Rear Guard Centurions. How many, I cannot say for sure, several hundred for sure. And yes, we've noted the slow disappearance of Centurions in the outlying towns and villages. The Sisterhood has slowly moved in to maintain the peace in their absence."

Similarly, Janisseko of Bonilla, Rosita of Pieta, and Mia of Solamina explained that they had reports of several legions, of a hundred men each, marching westward from their respective cities. Everywhere, it seemed, the Centurions were abandoning the outlying regions of the sector, consolidating their forces at the key port city. Where the men were ultimately headed and their purpose remained unknown.

Sister Aminia again rose, "So the real question I place before you is this: what should we, the Sisterhood, do about the coming invasion of the Galts? If we choose to stand and fight, I want desperately to avoid what happened to us during the invasion thirty years ago. Too few in numbers, we were nearly wiped out to the last woman. I ask you, if we choose to stand and fight, will each of us stand alone or can we somehow work together? If we all joined forces, might we be strong enough to defeat these evil men?"

"Before you consider this, there is one other minor matter I want to raise. It is a very strange one. From our extensive questioning of those who have immigrated here, we had detected a pattern in the Galts behavior towards the Arad women, one that is most peculiar. You would expect these barbarian men just to rape us. But no, any strong willed Arad woman is slain out-right! Hundreds have been thusly slain — women who have done nothing whatsoever to these invaders. It defies all reason. Those of you, who know me, know that when I encounter a mystery such as this, I just have to solve it. It has taken me months of questioning hundreds of Arads, but I finally believe I have found out. Yet, it makes no sense to me. These Galts are terrified of encountering 'Evil Witches!' Now what on Tarra is an Evil Witch? What is a witch anyway? I've never ever heard of such fairy tales. Can these barbarians just be unbelievably superstitious and ignorant?"

"Are their supposed witches only women?" asked Mia in wonderment.

"Yes, only women as far as I have been able to tell," Aminia replied. Again, everyone began talking among themselves.

"Just what are these Evil Witches supposed to be able to do anyway?" asked Rosita Rosario.

"We are not quite sure," Aminia replied. "Something about casting evil spells sometimes involving fires and lightning storms maybe. Perhaps the stupid barbarians have fabricated Evil Witches to explain acts of nature." No one noticed the slight flush that appeared upon the cheeks of Sandy and Simon, who had been quietly listening to the proceedings.

You don't suppose that the Galts think of us druwids as being Evil Witches do you? Sandy mentally sent to Simon.

I'm certainly tending to believe that might just be the case, he sent back, as the redness slowly withdrew from their cheeks.

"I don't know if this has any bearing on it, but I did chat with a shepherd and his family who were migrating to Florintine Junction early last year just after the invasion began. He and his wife both report coming across three dead barbarians and their horses. They looked as if they had been somehow badly burned to death. There was no signs of a forest fire anywhere around. This was at the edge of the Cedar Forests just south of the Junction," Aminia explained.

Simon, we don't have any operatives in Juda Arad at all, do we? Sandy sent to her husband.

None that I'm aware of — say why not contact Wid Julie and see what she knows or can find out. This might be a critical piece of information. Sandy closed her eyes and reached out with her mind, spanning the great distance to her home as if it were but inches. Once she had established contact, she opened her eyes, so as not to offend anyone by appearing to be asleep at the meeting. However, if one looked, her eyes displayed a distinct not-there look.

A little while later, Sandy sent, *She says that we have had only one druwid in the very north of the Arad last year. He was spying on both the Galts and the Centurions. He reported on the butchering of the Galt encampment and the subsequent retaliation butchering of every last Centurion. After that, he returned home. So no, we don't have any operative here who could have done these deeds.*

Hey, wait a minute! Didn't Alabaster tell you that Bethany was doing fine, that she had picked up a new Arad body and was going to monitor the activities of their Great Messiah?

Oh my! You are right! Bethany! I'd forgotten all about her. You don't suppose that was some of her handiwork?

Timing is the key, Sandy. Let me ask. Simon then rose, which of course got everyone's attention. "Excuse me for butting in on your affairs, but may I ask one question? You might not know the answer to this, but here goes." Everyone had nodded affirmative, so he asked, "When was their Great Messiah supposedly crucified?"

240

"I'm afraid I don't know," replied Sister Aminia.

"I do," came a shy voice from the back of the audience. A young sister rose and said, "The priests at the church say that the Great Messiah died in Jerilum on March 20 last year and was resurrected from the dead on March 23. Does that help?"

"Thank you! Yes, it does," Simon beamed praise her way. She was obviously one of the Sisters who had adopted this new religion. "Sister Aminia, about when did the shepherd find these charred bodies?"

"Ah let me see, I think he said it was early April. Why?"

Sandy instantly saw the connection and knew her husband well. She sent to him, *You have got to say it. We can't let on about the druwid connection.*

Simon nodded his head slightly, signaling his wife he understood. "Well, my own opinion is that the charred bodies were probably an after-effect of the passing of the Great Messiah. Exactly how, I have no idea, but it seems a plausible connection. Do they say that this Great Messiah is still around Tarra in his spiritual form?" Of course, no one had any remote idea of this detail. Simon was very sure that word of this would soon reach the ears of these Arad Priests. He knew that they would make a big deal out of the correlation. Priests were funny that way. However, the highly likely connection that event had to the druwids would remain completely hidden.

This means Bethany is still alive somewhere. Oh I do wish Alabaster wouldn't have ordered me never to attempt to contact her. She was my best friend. I still miss her. Tears welled up in her eyes, hazing her view for a time.

Yes, but we've not heard from Alabaster for what, thirty years or so. Maybe when we get home, we can discuss it with the others and try it. Perhaps Bethany has information that we need to fight the Galts. We can use that as justification. Think Wid Julie will buy into that argument?

No, but it is worth a try.

Sister Aminia rose once more, "We've been at this all morning. Let us take a leisurely lunch break and think about the situation. What are we, as a Sisterhood, going to do about the Galt invasion that likely will come this spring?" With that, the meeting adjourned and people filed out, heading for the huge dining hall. The heady aromas of a feast floated on the air outside the building making stomachs growl and taste buds tingle.

By mid-afternoon, everyone had reassembled in the great hall. Sister Aminia's constant fretting was very atypical for her. Would the Sisterhood unite? Should they fight? So many questions and so many possibilities. She carefully called the meeting to order, though a hint of her worry was in her voice, a note that her companion, Rosita Armino detected. The Fighter Group leader responded by twisting her sash into a knot, unwinding it and re-twisting it. Her hands had something to do.

"Next on the agenda is to decide what to do should the Galts invade the Sea Princes. I think that we all agree that we are the likely next target. What should we do? At the very least, we ought to protect the Sisterhood and our facilities."

Mia suggested, "Look, if we do nothing at all, then history will repeat itself. I swear, one by one, the sectors will fall. Why is it that I believe our overlords, the Centurions, haven't a prayer of a chance of fending off this barbarian horde? Besides, it is their fault we are in this predicament. They won't allow our Prince to build an army for the defense of Solamina. The overlords are only going to defend the city; it's plainly obvious that they are forsaking all the other towns and villages. What are we to do? Should we go to war? I dread taking that action. Only recently have we even gained a slight recognition of our contributions to our country. The Prince would love to see our Sisterhood eliminated as an effective fighting force. I for one am very hesitant to raise a hand in defense, unilaterally."

Carmina added, "I agree with Mia. The burden of the defense of the sectors should not lie on our shoulders. Yes, we have more respect than thirty years ago, but if we lose all our fighters, what then? No, that is playing right into the hands of the Prince. I'll not have Vito's Sisters placed in such jeopardy, fighting a battle that ought to be fought by the Centurions and the Prince. Never!"

Rosita Rosario slowly rose to speak and everyone became quiet. Actually, her opinion carried a great deal of weight. "How can we help but agree with Mia and Carmina? It is the responsibility of our overlords, the Centurions, to protect us and, secondarily, it is a prime duty of each Prince. We aren't strong enough to take upon us the defense of the entire Sea Princes. Such was never our intentions, and I hope never will be, but Sisters, can we afford to sit back and do nothing while our friends and neighbors are attacked, slaughtered, and raped? What will popular opinion of us be, if we sit back and do nothing whatsoever? I think doing nothing will bring us more harm in the end. Mind you, I don't know what we can really do. I just think we ought to do something somehow."

Janisseko commented, "One thing I do know. If we remain as we are, each within their own sector, there will be very little we can do. None of us has the resources to do a whole lot. However, if we were to somehow join our forces together, we would have a better chance."

"Are you saying that we send the majority of our fighters here to Zargarb?" broke in Mia. "That would leave us nearly defenseless!" Murmurs of agreement spread throughout the room.

In the lull, Lucia commented, "Well, we could move all the Sisterhoods all the way back to say Velona or perhaps d'Grange and there make a last stand. By then, the entire Sea Princes would have been totally overrun."

"It has merit," Rosita commented, "but the flaw will be popular opinion. It would appear that we deserted our sector in this time of trouble. Any return might be met with ridicule or worse."

The arguments raged back and forth, with no idea, no plan seemingly workable. Finally, someone called out, "What say our friends from the Greenway? Can they give us any learned council?" Simon already knew that he would have to intervene. At this point, he had no choice. They had come here for just this purpose.

"Dear Sisters, as much as I love and respect all of you, I can't tell you what you should or should not do. That isn't my place. However, I can make some points that seem to me to be the more significant ones raised thus far." The room was utterly silent, hinging on his every word. "United as one Sisterhood, you are far stronger than any of you can imagine. Always keep that in mind. Certainly, if it comes to your very survival, all you are more than welcome to retreat to the Greenway or to d'Grange. You are always welcome, no matter the circumstances. You always have that option. Remember that. Further, there is some truth in each of the arguments placed before us today. I also suggest that you examine the aftermath of any invasion. What is the situation in Juda Arad at the moment?"

"I can speak to that," Sister Aminia answered. "It is complete chaos. There is no central government, no force to maintain law and order. All trading systems have been broken; they are surviving solely by the barter system. There is no security; villagers live in fear of the next time the barbarians ride through their village. Naturally, many have just given it all up and immigrated. Personally, I don't see how things can improve until the barbarians are wholly stopped."

"It is as I thought. Thank you for the update," Simon continued. "So you see, in the aftermath of the barbarian invasion, once more the Sisterhood could reach out and provide the security needed to rebuild. However, that requires the Galts to have permanently left the land, never to return."

"I will, however, offer one piece of advice. Perhaps you can find a way to make a separate peace or truce with the barbarians so that they will give you a wide berth and not harm you. You see, the Galts are really after loot and booty that can be gotten easily. Fighting the Sisterhood yields them very little in the way of a profit. If you can find a way to make them see that fighting you is not worth their trouble, perhaps you can arrange a satisfactory truce. How that might be accomplished, I do not know at this point. If you desire, Sandy and I will remain behind here after the conference is finished and see if we can lend you a hand in finding such a way."

Sorry, love. I didn't ask you first, or our Wid. But this is the least we can offer, don't you think? Simon placed in Sandy's mind.

Damn, you've placed us right in the middle of a war! I bet Wid Julie will tan our hides for doing this! But yes, we have to at least try to help somehow, though I really do not see any way we might be of help without using our druwid spells, she answered back.

Their thoughts were interrupted by wild cheering and applause. They vaguely heard the words, "Honestly, we cannot expect you to stay." "Your lives would be in great danger." Similar cautions reverberated.

The women talked on for several hours. In the end, they did reach an agreement, based in part on Simon's wisdom. Each Sisterhood agreed to send several hundred of their fighters to assist in the defense of the Zargarb

Sisterhood. All realized that if the Zargarb Sisterhood fell, then theirs would surely fall later, once the barbarians got to their sectors. However, each Sisterhood retained sufficient fighters to maintain order in their own sectors without jeopardizing daily operations. It was perhaps the best that Sister Aminia could have hoped for, overall. Yet, for the first time in history, the Sisterhoods had united to fight a common foe. This was indeed a triumph.

Chapter 20 The Enemy Strikes

During the early spring of 587 AH, Ranchero Paladina, the center of the Sisterhood in the Zargarb Sector, was the scene of a great deal of activity. The nearly overwhelming task of training and coordination of all the Sisterhood fighters fell upon the lone shoulders of Sister Rosalita Armino, the blonde, thirty year old leader of the Fighter Group. As promised, the Sisterhoods of the other sectors sent fighters to bolster the Zargarb group. Each day, housing and such had to be found for the new arrivals, but this task went to Sister Aminia, the leader of this sector's Sisterhood. However, that did not lessen Rosalita's gargantuan task.

Once housed and introduced, each new fighter had to be assessed as to her skills, abilities, knowledge level, and actual combat experience. Only then could she be placed into an appropriate combat unit. Even though the reinforcements came in numbers, Rosalita knew that when the barbarian invasion came, they would not have enough warriors to defeat the Galts, who numbered in the thousands at last report from Juda Arad. The defense of the Sisterhood in Zargarb fell directly and only upon her; there was no one else who could fill her shoes. Rosalita was one of those people who had a photographic memory and could recall every detail of everything she had ever seen in her lifetime. She had an uncanny ability to organize others and a personal presence, which made those around her follow her orders without question. Her comrades loved her and respected her almost more than they did for Sister Aminia, a fact not lost on Aminia.

Borne from years of necessity, Rosalita also had a highly practical mind, which had gotten her out of many tight situations over the years, but she had absolutely no sense of humor. To her, life had always been and always would be tough and uncompromising. Her companions often heard her say, "Life is full of tough choices, and you've got to choose and choose the right one. So do it!" Actually, of all the sisters in Zargarb, Rosalita had a knack for always coming up with the best military strategy in any given situation. Of course, this was one of the key reasons she had risen to the leader of the Fighter Group.

On top of everything else, she now faced the task of finding a way to protect the entire Sisterhood from annihilation at the hands of these barbarian warriors. For months now, she had sent her scouts out across the northern portion of the sector in search of those who had seen firsthand the attacks of the barbarians. Many immigrants from the Arad were interviewed in detail. From this, during the winter months, she had devised a defensive plan. There was no way she could stop or prevent the barbarians from overrunning the sector — that was a given. However, her plan was to consolidate all her forces and protect only one area, Ranchero Paladina.

The barbarians attacked in a disorganized, chaotic manner, with little seeming overall control. They operated in large bands of some fifty men. Thus, a highly disciplined and controlled group of sisters, with the right defensive position, could expect to hold their own and with luck defeat them.

First, a defensive line that would stop any cavalry charge had to be constructed surrounding the large, ever growing ranch. Fortunately, the rear of the ranch butted against a steep cliff totally protecting their rear from any kind of attack. Thus, in a huge arc around the outskirts of the ranch, the sisters constructed a wall of wooden "jacks." Each jack was firmly embedded in the ground with numerous sharpened shafts protruding outward. Any horse attempting physically to smash through would be fatally gored in the process. However, the line of jacks could be jumped, so a second line was created and properly positioned behind the first, eliminating any attempt to just gallop up and jump over the barrier.

She knew that the barbarians generally let loose a hail of arrows at defenders before actually closing to sword combat. Rosalita's answer was to organize her forces into units of six women. One woman was the squad leader who gave orders to the other five. One squad was given enormous shields made of small branches tied together. Their task was to so position the five-foot tall shields such that any hail of arrows would hit the shield, protecting the other squads right behind them. Two squads of archers stood behind each shield wall, ringing the entire outer perimeter of the barrier wall. In stark contrast to the barbarian's seemingly random arrow shots, each member of one squad would aim for the exact same barbarian rider, guided and directed by the squad leader. Each leader was trained to focus solely and only on a very narrow zone in front of her squad, leaving barbarians out of her zone to other squads. Their survival depended upon complete teamwork; they were utterly dependent upon each squad doing their precise actions.

Getting all of these Sisters to work together was indeed very challenging. Rosalita found herself repeating over and over how the defense should work. Worse still, most of her fighters were not that good with bows. Thus, the best, strongest of her fighters she organized into ground attack squads. These would remain well back of the archers until the barbarians closed on foot. At such time, the attack squads would simply move out in front of the bow and shield squads to meet the assault.

Finally, the worst of the fighters, the least experienced, the meekest or those who had some healing skills were formed into rescue squads, again with six members each. Their task was to quickly reach any wounded Sister, get her back out of harm's way, and off to the makeshift hospital in the stable. Once safely out of any further danger, they would tend to the wounds as best they could. Both Aminia and Rosalita were very pleased that Simon and Sandy chose to stay on and help with healing. The healing skills of their Greenway friends were legendary, perhaps blown all out of proportion to their real skill levels.

Honestly, the morale boost the women had from knowing that, if they were wounded, they would be immediately and well-tended, was remarkable. Never in the history of Tarra had warriors faced going to war with a medical squad there to back them up. It had never before been done. Rosalita was loathed to lose even one sister to these barbarian men! Yes, she had a distinct, justified hatred of most men, but then so did nearly all the Sisters; that is why the Sisterhood even existed.

As April came, signs of spring and a rebirth were everywhere. Light, pale shades of green dotted the landscape around the ranch lands. Rain showers became more frequent, but the usual rising of spirits did not come this year. No, the coming of spring only foretold the coming of the barbarians was imminent. Rosalita doubled the training sessions all the archers, relenting in mid-April only because now five out five shots from each squad hit the bales of straw where the attackers would be. Still, she reasoned, it is one thing to hit straw dummies and quite another to hit a galloping barbarian in the chaos of battle. Still, she was impressed with their progress. When they first began, at best only one arrow would find its mark. She ordered a celebration to acknowledge her Sisters' progress, breaking out casks of wine.

Her whole strategy depended utterly upon their knowing just when the enemy would be attacking them. For months now, she'd been sending out scouting parties. The ranch was about fifty miles north and west of the big city. To understand travel in the Sea Princes, one must understand the road system such as it is. The city is the hub, the center of all activity and trading. All other smaller towns, villages, and hamlets serve only to provide sustenance to the city. Thus, all major roads lead to Zargarb, rather like the spokes in a wheel. There are seven all told that lead from Zargarb to the edges of the sector, passing through most major towns and villages. However, periodic crossroads dot the spokes, arcing east-west across the sector, some actually entering the neighboring sector or Juda Arad. The ranch lay on the fifth spoke, counting from the eastern edge.

Thus, Rosalita reasoned, the assault ought to come by raiders coming down south along the spoke road or perhaps from the east-west road that also passed by the ranch. She coldly calculated that the barbarians would take the easiest path to Zargarb and not travel cross-country, as the Sisters often did, when they needed an element of secrecy in their travel. Few had the skills to travel in such a manner. She calculated the attack would come either from the east or from the north. She sent out her scouts out in these directions, mainly, though a few were sent in other directions, just in case she miscalculated. Each group of three scouts was under strict orders to hide and spot the approach of the barbarians. Just as soon as they were seen, one rider was to ride as fast as possible back to the ranch to report. The other two would secretly parallel the advancing army. Should the army change directions or such, another would ride back to report. Under no circumstances were these scouts to engage the enemy; they were ordered to flee at once, should they be confronted in any way. Rosalita did not want to lose even one of her scouts; they were her finest horsewomen, perhaps the finest in the entire sector. Besides, when battle was finally joined, she wanted all of her scouts back in the relative safety of the ranch.

On Monday of the last week of April, the first notification came. A scout came galloping in yelling, "They're coming! They're coming! Down the north road!" Daily more reports came in from the other scout groups. The barbarians were not coming in a single large mass. Rather, they had divided their forces into several smaller groups and were systematically riding down the major spoke roads toward Zargarb, sacking every town and village along the way. The scouts reported many horror stories that they had witnessed from their secluded hiding places. These reports, Rosalita did not attempt to conceal from her warriors. On the contrary, she watched as the hatred of men seethed and boiled in them; old memories of their own mistreatment by the hands of men rekindled. She even had to argue with Sister Aminia over this point, for the leader of the Sisterhood thought it was not so wise to stir up these vile memories.

True, a few women suffered a relapse and became mostly useless; their memories, long repressed, resurfaced, and totally overwhelmed them. These, Sandy and Simon attempted to help as best they could. However, Rosalita observed the hatred boil and fester in the others and knew that they would funnel all that anger and hostility out onto the barbarians when the attack came. These women would act like a wild mountain lion, trapped, scratching, and clawing to the bitter end. Inwardly, she hoped that it would be enough.

Finally, by the end of the week, it became quite clear to her that the barbarian group coming down their northern spoke would be the first to encounter the ranch. From all her reports, she estimated that the attack ought to come on May 1. That night, under a quarter moon, she stood alone at barrier wall, looking off into the distance. Sister Aminia came out to meet her, "I know, you are worried, Sister. No one could have done more than you have. Take heart. If we fail, it is through no fault of yours, Rosalita. If the fires come, the fires come. It's life."

Rosalita gasped, "Fires! I completely forgot about fires! Aminia, what if they launch flaming arrows at our buildings? I forgot about that!"

"You think that is likely? That they will try to burn us out?"

"Well, I would, if I couldn't get through the barrier wall!" she replied aghast at her oversight. "We must pull some warriors off and put them on water patrols!"

"No, Rosalita. Let the rest of us handle that. Let me do this one thing for our defense; you've done so much else. I'll organize the others into a fire brigade. You need not worry about flaming arrows. We'll take care of any."

Rosalita heaved a sigh of relief, grateful for this unexpected burden being lifted from her shoulders. "Thank you. I am so sorry that I completely forgot about it. Now I am doubly worried that I forgot about some other aspect that could prove our very undoing! I must think long and hard. I'm so sorry, Aminia."

"Think nothing of it dear child. You have done so much; you have given so much to us all. Don't chide yourself. No second guessing. What comes tomorrow, comes tomorrow. Only Tur knows, or perhaps this new god of the

248

Arads, this Jehosa. I'm not a religious woman, as you know. Tur seems so distant from us, but I will pray for our survival tonight. Don't know if it will do any good, mind you. Yet, I will feel better having done so. How about you?"

"You know me, Aminia, I've lived thirty years, and I've never seen the slightest sign that any god of any kind exists anywhere. I think our mariners are just superstitious! What god would allow such barbarism to exist? If one did, I sure would not want to worship him. Sometimes, I think that our friends from the Greenway have it right — Nature exists, but is very out of balance here. That I can agree with, but gods, no way. You go pray, if it makes you feel better. I think I will stand here and think. If I forgot one thing, I may have forgotten something else."

"Okay, Sister. Promise me one thing, no matter how late it gets. If you think of something else that we need to do, promise me that you will come and wake me. Let me see if I can help remedy it. Promise me this," the matronly leader pleaded.

Rosalita relented, sighing, "Yes, I promise. Now go get some sleep." She watched as the elderly leader walked back to the main ranch house. For a minute, her eyes passed along the huge row of hastily constructed dwellings housing all the sisters. She wondered how many of the sleeping women would not be sleeping ever again after tomorrow. Tears trickled down her cheek, and the remains of her left ear throbbed. An hour later, she walked up the path to her room, nodding to the few guards who stood watch throughout the night. She was proud of these women; fighters every last one of them. She loved them all. She knew that there was nothing she wouldn't do to keep them safe from further harm. Rosalita collapsed on her bed, asleep as she landed.

At the crack of dawn gaily proclaimed by the numerous cocks around the grounds, the sisters arose. This morning, each was given a hearty breakfast, heavy on meat. Indeed, to someone not apprised of the situation, they could swear it was a feast. However, Aminia knew that these women might not get the chance to eat again all day. She wanted them to be as prepared as possible. Rosalita just hoped the attack did not come for several hours; you cannot fight on such full bellies. In spite of feast, the mood of the women, especially the warriors, was anything but festive. Solemn would be more accurate, though fear was the prevalent emotion among the non-warrior women.

Tired night shift scouts slowly rode in as the day shift rode out. Based upon the nightrider's reports, Rosalita estimated the attack would come around ten this morning. She would be ready. It would not do to have all of her warriors arrayed in their positions for hours; she let them enjoy their morning. Though as the morning drew onward, one by one, the squads formed and took up their assigned positions on their own volition. Likely, every warrior had heard the scouting report and could just as easily predict when the attack would come as she could.

"Zdlenka, this is almost too easy," Mikhailovich Strokova commented to his sister as they rode down the dew-covered roadway. Behind them trailed his elite combat group of fifty veteran members of his clan. Far behind them came the endless supply wagons driven by their wives and girlfriends. "Surely they will offer some resistance." He pulled on his newly grown black beard. His long black hair was tied back in a knot as customary for those of his clan.

Today, Zdlenka had not taken the time to braid her hair and her three-foot long, straight black hair fluttered slightly as she rode beside her brother. "If you have a weak force, you concentrate it at the one key defensive position. That must be the strategy the Centurions are using here. Mark my words; there will be a great battle for the city, Zargarb. They are giving us all these outlying towns. I can see why, too. Not much worth taking so far, wouldn't you say?"

"True, true. We got much more of value from the Arads. It appears the real wealth of a Sea Prince Sector lies solely in the namesake city." He signed, "You know, we still haven't heard from these amazon fighters; Sisterhoods, I think they call themselves. What do you make of that?" he asked her, looking for her opinion of these strange women.

Zdlenka poointed out, "They are still spying on us. I saw one on the far ridge line when I stepped out of the hut this morning. We know they have been monitoring us ever since we hit Florintine Junction. So far, they've done nothing but watch from a distance. Still, keen eyes can see that they are women, not men. I still stand by our intelligence I extracted from captives. The Sisterhood is the only effective fighting force in these parts. We know that the Centurions deployed the Rear Guard here in these conquered lands — mostly old soldiers and those who are no longer really fit for combat. However, I still urge caution: they may be old but they are veterans of many battles. I don't think that they will be as easy to defeat as you keep suggesting."

She continued, "What still gnaws in the back of my mind is the history of these women fighters. Legends say quite clearly that some five hundred of them stood alone against thousands of the best Centurion fighters and nearly won the day. How is this possible? I keep asking myself that."

He chuckled. He had asked himself similar questions, but was glad to hear her vocalize it. "And what do you answer yourself?" he teased playfully.

Extending her left foot, she gently kicked his shin in reply, "Nothing! That's just it. I cannot figure it out. Logically, they ought to be easily subdued; they are only women after all. Any one of your men could take any one of us women down in short order. I just do not understand it, but I suspect we will find out. Surely they'll not just let us ride in and take over everything without offering some resistance." Her voice trailed off into silence as a spooky memory replayed for the untold time in her mind.

Images of their attack on Florintine Junction vividly flowed, nearly as real to her as her horse and the road. A week ago, they had sacked the border town, meeting very littlc rcsistance. Yet they were quite amazed to see the huge population of Arads, who had now taken up residence in this town. She concluded that they had fled here from Juda Arad in a vain hope that here they would be safe from the Galts. How silly of them, she thought. As she rode through the conquered town at her brother's side, they passed by a burning home with two older men standing outside. Both had taken some relatively minor wounds. One held onto a bleeding arm and the other, his leg, but as she rode by them, both men stared at her and her brother with the queerest look on their faces! So weird were their stares, that the image had burned itself indelibly into her mind! Try as she might, she could not discard those mental images. She was almost spooked by those two men.

Connected mentally as they were, Mikhailovich sensed what was troubling her. "It's those faces again, isn't it?" He too had been plagued by their strange stares, but not as badly as she had been. When he found out that she was deeply troubled by them, he had ridden back into the town expressly to outright kill both men — to put an end to it once and for all. Even stranger, both men had utterly disappeared and could not be located anywhere. Perhaps this had added to her fear of them, he guessed. She nodded and he said, "Cheer up; they are long gone to who knows where. They are really not any threat to us, really." He tried to make less of the situation, but it had never worked yet.

"Insane, I swear that was the look of totally insane men! Gods, it gives me the creeps! Unnerving to say the very least, Mikhailovich. I am still terribly worried about those two. I just cannot get them out of my mind!" She signed, tossed back her hair, raised her head high, "Ah well, they are long gone. Probably I'll never see them again, but I swear they were insane. That's creepy. I get goose-bumps down my spine even thinking about them."

Al Markesh, holding his wounded arm, cackled with a weird glee. Something within him had just cracked. Last year he had been driven from his home in Juda Arad, when these barbarians sacked his village. He'd been forced to watch as his wife had been slain as a witch and his children butchered, while trying to go to their mother. He fled here to the Junction seeking to start life over at age fifty. His brother, Zeb Markesh, five years younger, had come with him. Together, they had built a new house and begun their pottery making business once more. Now, the barbarians came again, nearly killing them as they tried to stop them from sacking their small home. For hours, he stood dazed, staring into space doing nothing, while his new home burned to the ground, leaving only the adobe walls standing. Beside him, his brother, Zeb, stood, equally silent, equally dazed, and barely able to stand from his leg wound. Then, the conquering general and his mistress rode by them. In that instant, both men cracked. In unison, they cackled in glee, uncontrollably and loudly. Both stared with glazed eyes upon the two riders until the two were out of sight far down the street.

Al, the older, commented, "I, the Old Man of the Mountain, I shall seek the ultimate retribution!" He laughed the laugh of the hideously insane.

Zeb heard not a word, for he babbled, "I shall eat their babies for breakfast! Hee, hee, hee!" Slowly, though still laughing, he hobbled off into the nearby dunes, disappearing forever from his brother. Al, not even noticing his brother's departure, simply walked out of town, back into Juda Arad, heading out into the open desert regions, laughing all the way. His mind was scheming diabolical plots faster than he could vocalize them. Neither brother ever saw the other again.

From the corner of her eye, Zdlenka spied a rider ducking back behind the ridge to her right. That slight motion brought her out of her moodiness. "There, there went another one of those Sisters. They are still watching us."

"Ah, look how the trees now grow close to the road. This would be a perfect place for an ambush. Hold up, sis. Let my scouts go first. We take no chances. These women warriors might try something here. It is a good location." He raised his arm and signaled his men behind him. Quickly six galloped up and around them, heading down the road ahead, searching for any ambush. Soon, they signaled Mikhailovich the path was safe, and the two resumed their ride.

Shortly after ten, the trees suddenly gave way to a vast expanse of grasslands cradled against the side of a steep hillside way off to their right. Ahead was clearly a village of some kind. An east-west cross road lay before them as well. The village was entirely encircled with some kind of pole barrier. An army stood just behind the strange looking wall of protruding poles. Mikhailovich halted his band to survey the scene.

"I think we have found these women warriors at last," Zdlenka commented to herself. As her eyes swept over the defenders, every one of them was female. It was rather obvious even from this distance.

Suddenly, his men also recognized that the entire force they were facing was merely women. Before he could issue any orders, several yelled, "Hey, let's go get them!" "They are only women!" "Hey, we can each have a dozen women!" His combat group chaotically charged toward the defensive position.

"Damn!" cursed Mikhailovich. "You stay back," he ordered Zdlenka, who took her usual observation position far to the rear of the battle. She kept a sharp eye on the action, mentally alerting her brother to any unseen attack on him. He galloped off to join his men in their wild, reckless, disorganized charge.

"Okay, here they come. Steady, steady, wait until their initial volley of arrows are shot," Rosalita called out to those nearest her. Already, the shield squads had raised their makeshift shield barriers, protecting themselves and the archery squads behind them. Rosalita ducked behind a barrier near her position just inside the single entrance point in the barrier wall. Random arrows thudded into the shields as the barbarians shot while galloping. The little she could see told her that all the reports were not an exaggeration. These men could shoot quite accurately while at a gallop. Soon, a flaw in her defense appeared. While the shield squads held up the protective barriers, it left their feet exposed. Several women took errant arrows in their feet.

She watched as the rescue squads moved quickly into action. Even better, one of the rescue squad members had the foresight to take over the vacated position. So the shield wall held without straining the remaining members. Rosalita could not help smiling, pleased that her warriors had the presence of mind to think on their feet! She was immensely proud of them.

Now that the barbarians had closed and were veering off to her right, the shield walls lowered and her archery squads began their zonal firing. As she watched, her fear of poor accuracy against moving targets was borne out. Many flights were missing the fast moving riders. However, one of her fighters behind her commented to her, "Looks like you were right, Rosalita. Having five fire simultaneously at the same target is working. At least one hits! Brilliant plan!" Rosalita smiled in spite of herself; it was working. Several barbarians had actually fallen off their horses. As she watched, the squads then had a stationary target or nearly so. Five arrows found their mark. So far, so good. Now those that had circled around returned, launching another round of arrows. Again, the shield squads quickly raised the barriers. Some were slow to react though, and several in the archery squads were hit. Once more, the rescue squads darted in to aid those that were hit.

Several squads on the far side of the barrier wall, having nothing to do, slowly made their way across the yard to take up the positions vacated by the wounded, maintaining the defensive strength. Rosalita was glad that only a small force was attacking. Had there been a thousand barbarians, they would be in serious trouble. She felt sure that they could handle this small group. Her confidence grew.

Mikhailovich watched as his men slowly succumb to the deadly rain of arrows. Coldly, he surveyed the situation. His darting eyes spotted the single entrance in the pole barrier wall, the ingress/egress point used by Rosalita's scouts. Instantly, he recognized this was the weak point. Yelling to his men, he pointed his magical sword at this exact spot. Then, he charged straight toward it, dodging the arrows coming his way. A half dozen of his men followed right behind him. When he got close, he executed a perfect flying dismount and began to run through the opening, intent on getting inside the barrier wall. Once inside, he could force sword combat and easily defeat this large number of women fighters. They would be no match for his men's heavy swords. His men thought likewise, completely ignoring the fact that there were hundreds upon hundreds of women inside the protective barrier, while their numbers had only been fifty when they began the attack.

Fixed ideas can be the downfall of anyone. In the Northern Steppes, Mikhailovich and his men would have been completely correct in their assumptions. Fifty fighters could easily dispatch a large bunch of women, for their women neither were trained for fighting nor desired it, but they were not in the Steppes; he should have paid more attention to the lessons of history, as his sister routinely did.

Mikhailovich! she mentally screamed into his mind. *What are you doing? These are the Sisterhood fighters! Remember what happened to the*

Centurions when they tried to conquer Zargarb! You are going to get yourself killed!

It was too late now. Rosalita countered his charge; she and her handpicked, elite group of fighters stepped out from behind a shield wall, blocking the entrance. She had set up the entrance with malice aforethought. Six Sisters could completely block the entrance, perhaps just even five. Attackers were also limited to five or six, if they wished to fight in very crowded quarters. Further, if the attackers met Rosalita's numbers, they could only get one-on-one odds. That is, a Sister couldn't easily be attacked by more than one opponent at a time, greatly assisting her chances of survival.

Rosalita had a keen eye for those in charge; she instantly determined Mikhailovich was their leader. Deftly, she positioned herself directly in his path. She would take him on herself. Her assumption was that their leader would be their best fighter; thus, she could not in good conscience let any other Sister battle him. It was her responsibility to face their best. She drew her short sword and assumed her usual wide spaced defensive stance, shoulders curved, back slightly bowed, knees bent, ready for whatever this barbarian might do.

As Mikhailovich closed the distance to the opening, he saw the six fighters cleverly appear, blocking the way. Going to have to fight our way in, he thought. "I've got the blonde one who is out in front," he called out to his men who had joined him. Of course, all of the women were various shades of blondes, but his men knew that he meant the one who stood slightly out in front of the others in the direct center of the narrow opening.

One of his men called out in jest, "We may never get any sleep tonight! There are so many women to bed!" Then, swords met swords and the sounds of steel upon steel echoed. Actually, the women made very little noise at all, grimly facing their tasks. The noise came from the yelling of the barbarians, who thought wild yelling would help break the morale of their opponents, scaring them, perhaps.

Rosalita parried nicely his first arcing slice, deflecting his swing causing him to momentarily fall off-balance. However, she was too skilled to attempt immediately a counter thrust. Without knowing her opponent's skill, that could prove fatal. Indeed, it would have had she done it, for he recovered swiftly and made a counter upswing with his blade as he returned to his stable position. "Nice move," he called out to her, though she understood not a word he said. This time he feigned a thrust to the right and followed with a sharp attack to the left. Though caught slightly off-balance by his motions, she was quick and nimble — and she had some acrobatic moves that he had never seen before. She not only recovered, but also managed to swing a leg up and around, whacking him hard on his sword wrist. A sharp pain shot through his arm, but he did not drop his weapon. "Say, you are pretty good!" he exclaimed. Once more, she had no idea what he was saying.

He heard grunts, groans, as well as cries of pain coming from his men beside him. He dared not look their way, but he knew that they were taking hits from these women. This was most unusual. With few exceptions, every time that his forces had to engage in hand-to-hand sword combat, the melee was over in less than a minute, normally their opponents went down. A minute had passed and one of his men went down, but another stepped over him to take his place. This was not going as planned. Zdlenka screamed into his mind once more, *These Sisters can fight. Get out of there fast! We are going to need the whole army to take these out!*

Zdlenka was entirely correct, but men, especially fighters, have an ego. She realized this even as she screamed mentally to her brother. Their own egos would not let them retreat from a band of women fighters. "Men!" she cursed aloud, but no one heard her. She was powerless to do anything about the situation and had to watch, a sinking feeling of helplessness swelling in her bosom. "Men can be so utterly ignorant. There is no reasoning with them at times like this. He's going to get himself killed and ruin my plans to rule Tarra, I know it!"

Five minutes passed. Never had Rosalita ever had to skirmish so hard so long! Sweat poured down her face in rivulets, in spite of the fact that it was only springtime. Already two Sisters had been hit, but others instantly took over the position of the fallen, while the rescue squads dragged or pulled the wounded sisters out from under foot. Rosalita had a well-trained group under her command. On the other hand, three of the barbarians had been dispatched, though three more had taken their place, stumbling and trampling over the wounded men, in sharp contrast to the sisters.

Ten minutes passed. Rosalita was tiring fast; her opponent's blows where powerful, each one strong enough to knock her weapon from her hands had she chosen to meet the blow squarely. He was starting to catch on to her acrobatic deflection motions too. Three more sisters had fallen, while four barbarians had also been wounded. Still they pressed on, intent on breaking into the barrier wall.

With a mighty swing, Mikhailovich put every ounce of strength he had on this swing. This clever woman kept deflecting his blows so that he couldn't knock her weapon from her hand. This time, he swore, he would make such a swing that even deflected, it would disarm her. When his blade met hers, an awful cracking sound echoed; her sword shattered, throwing her completely off-balance; she began falling to the ground. A grin began to spread over Mikhailovich's face. His tactic worked better than he had hoped. However, as she fell down toward the left, she reached out with one arm, using it as a pivot point, allowed the falling motion to swing her legs into the air in a massive circle kick that caught him completely off-guard. One connected with his sword arm, sending his sword flying out of his hand, landing several feet to his right. Her other foot missed the sword arm and hit his jaw instead, sending him falling sideways and backwards to the ground after his sword.

As rapidly as she could, Rosalita got back up and did her well-practice quick-draw. In the same instant as she finally stood on her feet, both of her daggers that were strapped to her shins were in her hands. She resumed her defensive posture, though with only a pair of daggers with which to defend herself.

She watched as her opponent, though horribly startled by this completely unexpected action, very deftly rolled as he hit the ground, grabbing his sword as he passed over it, and then up onto his feet. However, the motion had taken him about five feet back of where he had stood, fighting her. Never had anyone ever disarmed him! Yet this woman had done the impossible! Still she fought on! Daggers, no less. Would she not ever give up? She was like a cougar in the tall steppes guarding her young. As he stared these few seconds, he heard another woman call out, "Rosalita!" He watched as another woman behind the skirmish line toss another short sword up over the heads of the other fighters toward Rosalita. Without taking her eyes off of him, she dropped her left dagger and snatched the sword mid-flight. With a well-practiced motion, she tossed both weapons to the opposite hands, ready for him once more. "What a move!" he called out, genuinely impressed, but she understood him not, nor really cared to, for that matter. She was out of breath, having narrowly escaped death, and tiring rapidly.

Then the totally unexpected occurred. "Hold, men. Cease all fighting. That's an order!" he yelled out loudly, and instead of stepping forward to continue the attack, he ceremoniously sheathed his own magical blade. Hearing the sound of the blade going back into its scabbard convinced the other Galts also to cease. They were more than ready to end this ill-fated assault. Half of them were wounded, and several were even dying. This had never happened to them before. Their grim faces looked quite stunned; all turned to face their leader.

Since the barbarians appeared to want to end the battle, Rosalita barked out, "Okay. Stop fighting. Stay alert for some new treachery. I don't trust these barbarians. Keep a sharp eye on all of them," she panted, holding her knees, breathing fast and furiously. *If nothing else, it gives me a chance to catch my breath before the next wave hits*, she thought. *Tur, I am eternally grateful that there were only fifty and not the thousands that have flooded into our land!*

Still she kept her full attention on their leader. What happened next, she could never have imagined. Suddenly, between gasps for breath, he began laughing loudly. She sensed that the mirth was not directed at her or the sisters — that much she could feel. Mikhailovich called out, "You are the one for me! I want you to birth my children! Such fighters they will be!" He realized that she could not understand a word he said. He yelled back to the others, "Send for the translator at once!"

Sensing something was going on that she ought to understand, Rosalita called out, "Fetch me someone who can speak the language of these barbarians, please, and quickly. He's saying something that might be important."

Within a minute, she saw another rider join up with the lone woman, who had stayed well back out of archery range, watching the whole battle unfold. Then, the two rode slowly toward the barbarian leader. Four women stepped up to her side from behind. One was Sister Aminia; one was the sister who Rosalita knew could speak this language, for she had been raised up north and had had some contact with these barbarians many years ago. She blushed as she recognized Sandy had also come, along with another woman holding Sandy's hand. She had never seen this other woman before, but she looked almost like Simon!

Rosalita whispered, "He probably wants us to surrender before he brings thousands of the barbarians down on our heads, or something like that." Sandy found her hand and gave it a bit of a reassuring squeeze. Rosalita really needed it. She was not known for parleys. Rarely did she ever discuss anything with her enemies or opponents. She suddenly felt very awkward.

Mikhailovich watched as four more women joined this impressive fighter. Since they bore no obvious weapons, he did not react. Perhaps one of these could translate for this incredible woman warrior. He sensed Zdlenka dismounting and felt her presence as she came to his side along with Boca, a merchant who spoke the Sea Prince dialect.

"Boca, translate please. Go slow; make sure they understand my every word."

"Aye, aye," he drawled and prepared to do his job for which he knew he would be royally paid. This was a much better way to get his share of the massive bounty; he hated fighting, for trading was his thing.

"I am Mikhailovich Strokova, soon to be Emperor of all Tarra, and this is my sister, Zdlenka, soon to be the Empress of all Tarra. What is your name?" He pointed directly at Rosalita so there could be no mistaking whom he was addressing.

Feeling rather embarrassed, she answered, "I am Sister Rosalita Armino, leader of the Fighter Group of the Zargarb Sisterhood. This is our leader, Mother Sister Aminia Sciota," she replied, hoping that this Mikhailovich would now turn his attention onto Aminia, who ought to be doing the parleying, in her opinion.

Mikhailovich bowed to Rosalita and said, "Rosalita Armino, I am more than impressed with your skills. In fact, I want you to bear my children. Such children from the union of the two best fighters in all Tarra ought to be invincible. What price do you require to do this for me willingly?"

Boca choked, recovered, and translated. Hearing the words, Rosalita shrieked completely shocked! Minutes ago, she was fighting for her life against this barbarian. Now he wanted her to bear his children. It was too much for her mind to handle; she shrieked in complete and utter disbelief. The translators repeated it to make sure she grasped his meaning fully.

However, Zdlenka also shrieked mentally into Mikhailovich's mind! *What are you doing? She is the enemy! She nearly killed you! She will kill you while you sleep!* He jerked from the volume of her unexpected communication. However, Sandy, the Communicator of her druwid group and an expert at mental communications, also perceived the wild telepathic communication from the untrained Zdlenka. Suddenly many things became clear to Sandy, including what and why Zdlenka was always present with her brother during battles, but always staying a safe distance away.

Poor Rosalita. What an incredible predicament she found herself now enmeshed. When she was a teenager, oh so long ago, she had had much practice fending off would-be suitors, men begging to get her into their bed. Long ago, she knew what to say so as not to offend but still let them know the answer was unqualified "no." But that was before she was married. That was before her husband had caused her so much grief. That was before her arrival into the sisterhood. Once in the Sisterhood, she never had to deal this way with men again. The men of the Sea Princes still thought them as abominations, though they would never say so aloud any more. Their attitudes were changing, but old ideas take a long time to die out. Tremendously shocked, she found her mouth so dry she couldn't even speak. She felt faint and dizzy. Her head reeled. She found herself clinging tightly to Sandy's hand.

Then, she felt Sandy ease into her mind; she felt a feeling of utter calm and tranquility flow over her entire body, a peace she had never known before. Such was Sandy's mental ability. Simon now spoke for her. "I'm Sister Simone," he began speaking slowly. While he could have spoken in the Galt tongue, he thought better of it. "Your offer has taken Rosalita completely by surprise. She is understandably speechless at the moment. Minutes ago, she was defending the Sisterhood with her life, and now you want her to bear your children. That is quite an abrupt change. We know not your customs, but here in the Sea Princes, it is customary for a man and a woman to first fall in love, then to marry, and set up a home, before embarking on the raising of children. Plus there is the fact that she is in the Sisterhood. You might not be aware of the significance of the Sisterhood. Let me explain. Every one of these women you see here has been badly mistreated by the men of this land. Years ago, many women lost arms, legs, or tongues at the hands of some of the more violent, disgraceful men. However, the situation has improved remarkably during the last thirty years. You see, every one of these women had at least one major reason to hate men; quite frankly, none of us trust men farther than we can see them. You seem to be an understanding man, a trait that the Emperor of All Tarra must have in order to rule. Surely you can understand the position into which you are putting poor Rosalita."

Ah, Simon had not lost his touch. He had had years to hone his craft, that of the Judger, the arbitrator of disputes. Mikhailovich grimaced when he heard the words describing some of the crimes committed against these women. Simon spied that reaction and knew that he had this man just where he wanted him. "Barbarians! These Sea Prince men are barbarians!" declared Mikhailovich, stamping the ground with his boot for emphasis. "Hear yea women, one and all," he spoke loudly, though few could really understand his words. "Let it be known that Galt men never so mistreat our women. If one of us committed such a despicable crime, we would punish him severely — even drive him from our clan!"

Lowering his voice, he continued, "In our land, it is much the same with man and wife. We do court our women, marry, and raise children in our huts. Perhaps our customs are not that different after all. However, I'm Mikhailovich Strokova. I'm conquering all Tarra. One day I will rule all the lands everywhere. It is my destiny and that of my sister. The gods have so agreed. One day when I grow old, I will leave the world to my sons to rule. I must have fit, capable sons, worthy of ruling Tarra. Rosalita, you are a very special woman indeed. There is not a single woman in all the Northern Steppes who could best you in a fight! In fact, there is not a man in all the Steppes who could have disarmed me, yet you, Rosalita, you did disarm me. If your sword had not broken, you might even have had a chance to slay me while I rolled! For this, you have earned my highest, utmost respect. For this reason, not for love, though that may yet come in time, who can say, I wish you to bear my children. With such breeding, they will be fit to rule when I am old and grey. Name your price. I will pay anything within reason," he added quickly as Zdlenka's anger flared, urging him to exercise utmost caution. This woman could ask for more gold than they currently had; neither had been taking much loot, preferring to let their warriors have most of it. It ensured their further cooperation in the conquest of Tarra.

Rosalita found her tongue, thanks to the serenity flowing through her via Sandy. There was only one single thing that she wanted more than anything else. "My price? I only want one thing. Leave the Sisterhood in the Sea Princes alone. Never harm or cause to be harmed one of my sisters. We are easy to spot. We all wear these yellow headbands. Just bypass us on your conquest of Tarra. Leave us be. We will not attack you, unless provoked. We have, as yet, no real quarrel with you, though some of us do believe that you should not be sacking Zargarb. We have not been asked to help defend Zargarb either, for that matter. A truce with us — that is my price. There is no guarantee that our babies would be sons. It is just as likely they be daughters. I am already too old to go on having many babies just to get you a son. Let's agree on a number, say two children. I give you two children. If they are sons, you may take them and do what you will. If they are daughters, I keep them here safe in the Sisterhood, safe from the ravages of men."

Note to the reader: in case you are wondering, Simon, via Sandy, helped her focus her thoughts and speak the right phrases. If you look back over her speech, you can tell her thoughts from Simon's additions.

As the words were translated, a triumphant, broad grin spread across Mikhailovich's face. "A king's ransom you could have, yet you choose this. To your price, I completely agree. From this day on — well as soon as I can get word to all my thousands of fighters — they are scattered all over this land — none of us will ever harm any Sister. It is a good thing that you wear the yellow headbands, so we can tell you apart from other women. You will find that I am really a kind and gentle man in bed. In time, we might form a strong bond, who can say. I cannot make you Empress of Tarra, for that belongs to Zdlenka. Yet as my wife, you would hold immense power and have vast riches."

Zdlenka interrupted her brother for the first time. "Mikhailovich, we can't take her with us across country, even if you want to — think about what you're doing. If she becomes with child, she shouldn't be on the road — especially when her time comes. We don't treat our women that way. We can't take her back into the Steppes just now; she wouldn't be safe there, even if you ordered it. You know that. She is not of our clan. She doesn't know our customs or anything." He knew she spoke the truth; he didn't dare take her along with them and couldn't send her back to the Steppes.

Simone came to the rescue, "Mikhailovich, why don't you, your sister, and I sit down somewhere quiet, have something to drink, and discuss the details. Since Rosalita and you have agreed on this in principle, why don't we sit down and work out how best for you both achieve what you want? I'm sure Rosalita won't mind my working on her behalf, will you?"

"Oh no. Please Simon — Simone, please go ahead. I need to go check on my wounded sisters," she almost stumbled. It was hard for her to maintain the illusion that he was she because she knew she was he. She had never experienced this magical illusionary trick before and was more than a little confused about it, particularly how it was that the others could not see that they were talking to a man, not a woman.

By now, Mikhailovich's supply wagons rolled into the crossroads area, and the women began to see to the wounded men. He led them over to his wagon and ordered some wine. Together, Simone, Zdlenka, and Mikhailovich worked out the critical details. While they were finalizing the plans, Rosalita finally joined them; she had decided she had to tell this man something. Naturally, he was very pleased to have her come and join their discussions, but she kept her distance at first.

Formally, she explained with Simone translating, "Mikhailovich, there is one thing that I feel I must tell you before we actually do this thing." She was so sincere, so somber, that he was taken aback.

"What is it, dear Rosalita?" he said trying to sound as kindly and concerned as he could. He even felt he meant it and that was a first for him.

She paused for a moment, trying to find the right way to say what she knew she had to say. "If you are rough with me, harm, or hurt me, I — I *will* kill. I — I killed my husband. Then, I joined the Sisterhood." There, I've said it. I'm a murderer and now he knows it, she thought.

It took a second for him really to grasp what she was confessing to him. For an instant, he felt some anger, but he realized that she must have had a good reason to do what she had done. Calmly he said, "You must have had justifications."

She pulled back her short hair that covered her ears and displayed what was left of her left ear. "He got drunk one night and cut my ear nearly off. When he passed out, I took his knife and slit his throat, and that was before I ever learned how to fight. So I do mean what I say. I have absolutely no tolerance for being mistreated. Mistreat me and I will kill. I felt you ought to know this up front. I'll leave you to finish the plans." She quickly left while her legs could still function. She felt elated that she had spoken, but also terrified. She would be sleeping with the enemy, the man who was about to conquer, slay, sack, and pillage all of the Sea Princes and have his children as well. She felt sick at her stomach at that thought, but forced it out of her mind in favor of the concept of just having saved the Sisterhood in all the sectors. I hope the other sisters appreciate what I am doing for them, she thought as she walked back to her room.

By now, word of her bargain on the behalf of the Sisterhood had spread to all the women, so she was not surprised by all the stares and whispers behind her back that she got as she walked back to her room. Rosalita was eternally grateful that none of the women tried to speak to her. She just could not handle that right now. She wanted desperately to be alone and find that tranquil feeling that Sandy had induced earlier. Either that or get very drunk.

"Come on in and lay down for a while," the soothing voice of Sandy greeted her as she entered. Rosalita heaved a huge sigh of relief and did just that. Just hearing Sandy's voice helped her relax and bring back the tranquil feeling.

"Rosalita, you have my highest respect for what you are doing. Seldom have I met a person who would make such a huge personal sacrifice solely for the benefit of others in the group. I know in my heart that I couldn't do what you are doing. I just couldn't do it. You have my complete admiration and respect."

She smiled for the first time, "Thanks, coming from you, that means a lot. All my sisters out there — they were staring at me. I could hear their whispers too. You think that they will understand?"

"Yes, dear child, yes. More than likely, they owe their very lives to you because of this. Speaking of which, here is the outcome from today. Fifteen wounded, but no deaths. All will make a full and complete recovery. Only five have serious wounds. I've seen to those personally. You can trust Simon to work out the best possible arrangements for this whole thing. He is a master of getting what he wants out of people all the while making them think that they were the ones suggesting it."

"How does he do what he does? I mean, I saw him as a woman for a split second before I realized it was he. But the others — do they really see him as a sister? How?"

"Simon has spent his whole life learning how to master illusions. As he is fond of saying, 'People see what they want and expect to see, not what actually is.' This is a Sisterhood, so no one would expect to see a man among you. So they do not see. I really don't fully understand what he does either, but then I haven't studied how to do it. I've enough trouble dealing with reality, with what is, without worrying about what isn't!" Both women chuckled.

Feeling a bit freer, Rosalita volunteered, "I'm not proud of what I did — slitting my husband's throat. I ought to have done something else. I just snapped." She looked at Sandy and felt that she should explain. "You see, first I thought I was in love with him, but then on weekends, he'd get drunk on wine and beat me. For months, I kept thinking he would quit; he kept saying so the next day; I kept hoping. That night when he nearly cut of my ear for not listening to him, I just snapped. Looking back on it now, I think that I must have gone insane or mad. I just lashed out at him."

A Sister found me in the street around midnight, blood all over me, all down my left side. She brought me here. Honestly, I was quite crazy at the time; I didn't even know who I was or where I was. So you see, I owe these Sisters my life. Besides," she continued insistently, "we both know that if those barbarians hit us with all their men, we won't have the remotest chance of surviving. Today we stopped what — fifty of them? But they number in the thousands. Even with all the reinforcements that we got from the other sectors, we would still be easily wiped out. If I can somehow do this crazy thing, then all the other Sisters in all the sectors will survive this invasion of barbarians. I just *have* to do it. I *owe* it to them."

"I understand," Sandy replied softly but with certainty. Truthfully, she honestly didn't know what else to say to this brave woman. "There are so many things that can go wrong with a crazy scheme such as this one is, Rosalita, that I think Simon and I will stick around a while longer. He has the skill to make it work out properly. We must trust in him; I'm sure he'll get you the most acceptable way to make this all work out."

"Thanks," the Sister replied, squeezing Sandy's hand.

"We have also learned a very important strategic fact about this conqueror and his sister — all thanks to you." Rosalita looked at her strangely, not at all grasping what Sandy was saying. "Those two, Mikhailovich and Zdlenka, are not only brother and sister, but their minds are connected. They can exchange thoughts and ideas much as Simon and I do. You might call it mental telepathy, just to give it a name. When you were fighting him, she was back at a safe distance feeding him information, as if he had eyes in the back of his head. That fact alone will make it very hard for someone to defeat him in a battle. Now that we know, we may be able to use that against them some day to stop them."

"Interesting. I wondered what she was doing watching the battle," Rosalita commented. "I promise I'll not reveal that we know this to either of them. Maybe this can be used to stop them somehow. I'll leave that up to others, though. I've made my promise; now I have to keep it," she declared stoically.

An hour later, Simon knocked on her door and was let in at once. "Well, Rosalita, I believe we have worked out satisfactory details. Zdlenka was right to be so concerned about her brother's rash decision. You could easily spy on their plans and undermine them. They cannot take you on the road with them for obvious reasons. Therefore, he has agreed to sleep with you here at the ranch. He will try to come by periodically, when you let him know the time is proper. However, for his safety and yours, when you two are alone in a room, there will always be one of his translators and one of yours just outside the door. Also, two of his guards will be posted outside as well as two of ours.

Further, when he does come, he will bring his entire company who will camp outside the barrier wall. That way, it will not give others in this land the wrong impression that the Sisterhood is cooperating with the enemy."

"I got him to agree to keep this union relatively secret; it is in both your interests to do so. If his enemies found out you were having his children, they might come here, and seek vengeance on you and the children in order to get to him. Hence, I agreed that the Sisterhood would always provide top security for both you and any children at all times. He also agreed that if he mistreats you, he gets what he gets," Simon winked at her. She smiled. "If the Sisterhood or any of its members are harmed in the future by his men, you will be informed and can take whatever action you decide is fitting, including ending the birthing of more children. Reluctantly, he did agree to this stipulation."

"Now more importantly, he has agreed to two children, though he hopes both will be sons. The sticky point is just when does he take the children away with him. He knows that he can't really keep them with him until they are old enough to travel. He also knows the trauma that would be caused by suddenly taking a young child away from its familiar home and mother. It seems that those two are orphans themselves. Interesting detail. Anyway, we think it best that he take custody of the children when they are about a year old. What do you think about that?"

She suddenly burst out laughing. Seeing the baffled look on his face only caused her to laugh even more. Finally, she exclaimed, "You got the barbarian leader who is out conquering the known world to agree to all that! Why didn't you get him to agree to end the war while you were at it! You are incredible." Now, all three laughed together.

"I thought of that, believe me, but he didn't want you quite that bad," he jested. "But seriously, are these arrangements acceptable to you?"

"You know they are. As long as our Sisterhood is spared destruction, I'll do most anything. I can't thank you enough, Simon. Honestly, I really mean that. Actually, I must admit that I'm a little flattered that he really desires me. It has been such a long time. I guess I have strange tastes in men," she commented.

"No, you didn't choose him; he chose you," Sandy clarified. "Besides, Rosalita, when this is all over, if you just want to find a good man to love and who will love you properly, why just come to the Greenway. I know lots of men who would love to court you."

"That reminds me, thanks Sandy," Simon interrupted. "Rosalita, if ever anything goes horribly wrong and you need to escape to some safe place, head north to the Paese di Dio. Follow it across all the Sea Prince sectors until you reach land's end. Then head north. You will reach the eighth sector and the stone fortress. There you can find sanctity or you can journey just a little further and reach our lands and our fortress on Mont Blanc. You are more than welcome at any time and under any circumstances."

"Oh yes, one last thing. Sandy and I are going to stick around here a while and make sure all goes as planned. She has already arranged it with our superiors back home, so don't worry about us. Now we'd better let you rest a while and recover from this shock. By any chance, do you have any idea when your next fertile time should come? I'll let him know."

For a moment, she looked slightly embarrassed. Such matters were usually not discussed so openly. She fumbled and muttered, "Next week." Simon nodded and he and Sandy left. Rosalita sank back on her austere bed, hands behind her head. She had lots to think over, but soon exhaustion set in, and she fell asleep, thanks to a slight nudge from Sandy.

Once outside, Simon whispered to Sandy, "There is one other detail I gleaned from the meeting. Zdlenka is extremely jealous of Rosalita. I think those two may be closer than we think."

"You don't suppose they — no, everyone knows that is a recipe for malformed children," she commented.

"No, there would more than likely have been children," Simon replied. "Still, there is something there between them. She could not conceal her intense jealousy from me. We must keep a very sharp eye on her when they are here. I do not trust her." Sandy agreed.

Mikhailovich and Zdlenka led their group on down the road. "Don't *ever* surprise me like that again!" she spit out with a passion!

"I promise, sis. I am sorry I didn't let you know first," he said apologetically, struggling to find some way to appease her. He had never seen her this angry, and he did not like being the target of her spite.

"Apology accepted," she finally muttered. "I do now see the benefit. You cleverly got these fighters completely out of the picture. I told you the Sisterhood would be a major problem. They are the best fighting force we have seen! They make the Centurions look like street urchins. Somehow, I don't think that we even saw all their fighters today. Probably many more held back in reserve. I surely would have."

"I realized that only too late. Well, today, you witnessed my first blunder. I hope I never underestimate anyone else! We were very nearly undone. Think of the repercussions to our plans if I had to call in all the combat groups just to take them out? And for no treasure either! I bet there is hardly a gold coin among them. They certainly have nothing of value for us there. After losing half my forces taking them, we gain no prize worth all that loss. The men would certainly rebel at that. Now taking Zargarb is another story. The loot there will keep them more than contented for some time."

"Say," Zdlenka had an idea, "you don't suppose that there is any way that we could get them to come and fight for us do you? We could send them in against the Evil Witches in the Greenway. Let them deal with all that sorcery."

He thought for a moment before replying, "No, I don't think so. They seem to be focused only on surviving in a hostile land. However, we need to be very alert and see if we can get a good estimate of their total strength throughout these lands. Who knows, one day we may have to deal with them. But for now, I agree, problem cleverly solved. Now, there is nothing to stop us from taking the city and perhaps the greatest wealth to date."

Chapter 21 The Fall of Zargarb

"Well, that's that," General Pax Iona commented sourly. An aide had just brought news that the Galts had finally attacked the Sisterhood forces but had not been stopped by the women fighters. In truth, he did not believe that they would have been able to stop them, although he had not even bothered asking them to try. He had always discounted the legends of the Sisterhood nearly stopping the Assault Troops some thirty years ago, long before he was born. Wives' tales, he considered them or more likely a cover-up of some major battlefield blunder by the then general.

Pax was conducting yet another planning meeting with the Prince and the Mayor of Zargarb. The objective was to put the final touches on their intended defense of the city. Mayor Alonzo Pino took the news rather hard. He was in his mid-thirties, though his premature balding made him look much older. His double chin seemed more pronounced as his disappointment grew on hearing the news. However, he was probably the wealthiest merchant in the sector, second only to the Prince. As Mayor, he was the people's interface between the Prince and the Centurions, usually bringing gripes and complaints before them for resolution. Unlike the General, he had placed all his hopes on the Sisterhood stopping the Galt invasion, though he could not say how they might have done that deed. Of the three men, he took the ill news the hardest, dashing all his hopes that the attack on the city might somehow be prevented.

"So *now* what are you going to do to prevent the city from being sacked?" he demanded of the General and the Prince, impatiently as if this somehow changed their plans.

Pax glared at the mayor, but didn't address him. "Prince, it's time. Let everyone know that the city will be shut off as of this evening. Anyone leaving had better be gone by dark. After we shut it down, no one will be allowed in or out. Is that understood?"

"Yes, sir. I'll get the word out now. How long do you think it will be before they hit us?" the Prince said calmly. He had a hand in the creation of the "plan" and felt that it did have a good chance of success, but there were a lot of if's involved.

While the city was huge, roughly semicircular, and about ten miles across, there were only eight main roads into the city. Buildings would act as a defensive wall. His men had built massive wooden barricades that would be set in place by dusk. Once set, there was no way into the city except to climb over the obstacles or to climb on top of buildings and drop down to the street or to break into a building through outside windows. For months, his men had been going from building to building constructing heavy wooden shutters over any outside facing windows. For the first time in thirty years, the Centurions had given the Prince permission to raise an army for the defense of the city —

more like ordering him to conscript an army. All winter, the Centurions trained the new recruits. The Prince now fielded an army of nearly two thousand men compared to the mere seven hundred Centurions that remained in Zargarb.

At dusk, squads of men led by Centurions would be positioned at each barrier wall. They reasoned that only a few men could hold each position, considering the relative narrow widths involved. However, they fully expected the Galts would eventually break through at some entrance. Ten more fallback barrier walls were manned and ready to be closed. Further, squads of archers would stand on the nearby roofs and rain death on the Galts below them who were trying to penetrate these inner barriers. On paper scrolls, the defense looked formidable.

The Prince, however, still had his doubts that these briefly trained recruits could actually hold these wild men from the Northern Steppes. He refrained from suggesting this to either the General or the Mayor. Instead, he made other plans in secret. Already his private yacht had sailed south carrying his family and much of his transportable wealth. Near the southern continent lay his private islands, the Isla del la Rochas. He had a summer vacation villa there. In secret two days ago, his entire extended family had set sail late at night, arousing no suspicions. This meant that they ought to be docking there this evening, and in three more days perhaps his boat would be back here awaiting his last minute escape from Zargarb, should the need arise. The Prince felt certain that the city could hold out at least that long. Besides, he intended to stay right up to the last possible minute, because if they actually won the battle, he wanted to receive the majority of the credit. Nowhere in the Prince's make-up was there any feeling or compassion for his people and their plight. Everything was about politics and power, nothing else, except staying alive if it came to that.

The Prince left the General's room and stepped outside into the warm April air. Spring had come, but so had the enemy. Nearby, his ten assistants jumped to attention as they spotted him coming out of the General's front door. "It's today," he calmly and impassionedly spoke to his men. "Let the word go forth. Zargarb is closed at dusk until further notice. Garrison forces are to be at their assigned positions by dusk. I will go notify our High Priest personally." The men saluted briskly as the Centurions had taught them and rushed off at once with enthusiasm.

These were all young men who had never seen real combat. The Prince saw that they thought all this as mere "fun." He knew that in a few days their attitudes would be quite changed. He strolled through the crowded streets toward the large Church of Tur complex located not too far from his own palace in the wealthiest section of town. For once, he was glad that they were only about halfway between the docks and the outer perimeter of the city. He would not be locked out of his palace until the fourth barrier walls were needed and set into place.

He arrived at the ornate wrought iron gates of the church grounds. Two young initiates stood just inside. "I'm here to see the High Priest. It is most urgent."

They bowed out of respect for their Prince. "I'll run and fetch him at once," one man said and he took off at a run. The other said formally, "If you will follow me, I will lead you to the meeting room." He bowed and turned to lead the Prince inside.

Yes, it was always this formal here at the mother church. The Prince had come here dozens of times during the last few months and was now familiar with their routine. While he walked behind the young man, he wondered to himself just how long they would be able to operate as if nothing was amiss — he smiled as he thought, "Only days, perhaps."

He was led into a large meeting room, filled with a twelve-foot long mahogany table and matching chairs to seat twenty. Great tapestries hung on three walls, depicting great sailing ships upon the ocean. The outer wall boasted five ten-foot tall windows that let in the bright daylight. He did not have long to wait before the High Priest entered followed by some servants bearing a decanter of fine wine and two golden goblets. "Please be seated," the priest exclaimed. From his demeanor, the Prince could tell that the man had already guessed what he'd come to tell him.

After pouring them some wine, the priest said softly, "So it is time?"

Sipping the excellent red wine, the Prince said softly, "Yes, I came to tell you personally. Dusk. At dusk, Zargarb will become a closed city. May the grace of Tur protect us from the northern barbarians." He felt those were sufficiently pious words for the priest's ears.

The priest, in his late forties with a nearly trimmed black beard and bulging belly from over-indulgence, nodded. "Yes, we heard that the Sisterhood was unable to stop them. I had held out some hope that those poor women would somehow be able to delay the barbarian horde, but they are only women. I hope they were not treated too badly. I still say we ought to have done something to assist them. After all, they have played a vital role in maintaining our security for the last twenty years or so. We owe them something for that."

"They were well-paid for their services," the Prince countered coldly. He still felt uneasy talking about these abominations, these fighter-women. He, the Prince, had been given orders many years ago that if anything bad happened to the women, he would be held responsible. Old habits die hard and, for the first five years, it had cost him over a thousand gold coins to make amends. He still had not forgotten that, though these days, such open violence had pretty much died out. Men kept their feelings more to themselves, and more importantly for the Prince, they kept their hands to themselves. In the last six months, not a single case of woman abuse had been brought before him. He still privately thought of them as abominations, and he had no intention of thinking otherwise.

This old priest, on the other hand, had sided with these women and had risen to be their most ardent defender. The High Priest now brought most of the claims of abuse to the Prince. "You are prepared," the Prince asked.

"Yes, yes as much as can be, I suppose. We have food, blankets, and medicinal supplies stationed at all the buildings you indicated. Two adepts are at each site as we speak. But one last time, I beg of you, before you cordon off another section of the city, please let those that live outside that sector have a chance to get inside. Please do not leave them to the mercy of the barbarians."

"Look, we've been over this a hundred times. At least a hundred thousand people live in Zargarb. If we are forced to retreat deeper into the city toward the docks and all those that live outside that zone retreat with us, why, eventually there will be nothing but a solid mass of people with nowhere to go, sit, or stand. We must be able to fight. Fighting takes room to maneuver. No, when the secondary barriers go up, we can't allow everyone to fall back with us. It's just not possible. War is harsh, High Priest. Besides, the barbarians are not likely to harm the old, the children, or the women; they will be too busy fighting us to bother with them as we fall back. If the very last line fails, then we are all doomed and at the mercy of the barbarians, if they even have such feelings, which I highly doubt." The High Priest knew he was right, but still sighed, thinking of all the suffering and misery about to fall on the citizens of Zargarb.

"Well, thank you for coming to let me know, my son. The Church of Tur will be ready to assist those in need. As we planned, I will round up all the healers in the city and get them to the assigned stations. We must all do our part."

"Yes, we must. If you will excuse me, I do have urgent business elsewhere, as you might expect. I bid you good day," the Prince said, rising to go. The priest rose, blessed him, and watched him leave, guided by the adept, who was waiting for him just outside the door.

"Is it time, Your Holiness?" asked a nervous adept who attended the High Priest.

"Yes, yes, Wilfredo, it is time. Send forth the word as planned. I will be in my sanctuary praying, if you need me." With that, he walked slowly out of the room to his private quarters. He did not intend to pray just yet, because he had plans of his own with which to deal. The church was not without means, not the Church of Tur, the God of the Sea and Mariners. They had one large yacht, Tur's Holy Vessel, still moored at the docks. Quietly and without ceremony, he gathered up all the priceless gems and jewelry from their secure, locked, and secret hiding places. They fit very nicely into one large sea chest, which he locked and then placed inside a larger chest. Once that one was locked, he and four acolytes made their way through the town to the ship. For the last few days, food and water supplies had been loaded aboard the vessel, making her ready for an extended voyage. Once the sea chest had been stowed, The High Priest spoke privately with his trusted ship's captain. He then returned with only two of the acolytes to the church grounds. Yes, the valuables of the church would be safe at sea. There they could remain for six months if need be. If the city fell and the church was sacked, the barbarians would get some gold to satisfy their lust, but the real treasure of the Church of Tur was now out of their reach.

That afternoon, across town, ten men met in secret in a hidden basement of Harri's Tackle Shop. Not ten ordinary men were these, oh no. These men were the heads of the ten wealthiest extended families in the Zargarb Sector. Between them, they owned outright over sixty ships of various sizes and types. For several months now, they met in absolute secrecy. They had to, for they were plotting against the Centurions, the Prince, and the Church — all the current ruling establishment.

Alonso Botecelli, the sixty year old self-appointed ring leader, opened the meeting, "Gentlemen, the city will be closed as of dusk tonight. This will be our last meeting for some time. It is just too dangerous to meet when the city is locked down and under siege." The others uniformly nodded and grunted their agreement.

"Have you all taken the agreed upon preventative measures?" Everyone again nodded or answered softly. "All right then, my ship leaves at high tide, around an hour after midnight, with or without you. Make sure you are there. Remember, only fifty pounds of baggage per person; no exceptions." Again, they nodded.

There were some smaller discussions among the men for another hour. Their basic plan had been set into play months ago. To the man, they were completely disillusioned with the leadership of, the management of, and the protection of Zargarb. For some thirty plus years under the Centurion rule, they had not been allowed to rebuild their army. With the Galts certain to attack them, coupled with the catastrophic losses of the Centurions in Juda Arad last year that had siphoned off many of the better Centurion soldiers, they had no doubts that for the second time in their lifetimes, the city would be sacked and plundered. Only this time, they expected far harsher treatment than they had suffered from the Centurions, who had claimed they were bringing civilization to Zargarb.

In secret over the last few months, these men had sent the majority of their extended families a short distance away, to the Isle of Morovia, where many had summer homes. Along with their families, they also sent much of their vast wealth, leaving a good deal of the heavier gold behind. Not all could be saved on such short notice. Tonight, they themselves would disappear in the night, joining their families at the vacation homes, which by now were very well stocked with supplies.

That was only part of their conspiracy. To the man, they had agreed that if the city was sacked, then, when they returned, neither the Prince, the Church, nor the Centurions would be allowed to rule. Rather, they were forcibly going to take control of the country. In fact, they had already agreed upon the organization. The High Council, as they called it, would consist of thirteen voting members: themselves, the Prince, the Church, and one man representing the skilled trade workers, who had not yet been chosen. Thirteen, so there could never be a tie vote. The Prince and the Church, because many still felt that those should have a say in the governing of the sector despite their shortcomings. The council was divided on whether there should be a Sisterhood representative or a trade worker. They were equally divided on that issue.

Finally, each had selected a dozen men who would confiscate abandoned weapons with which to arm the council enforcers. One hundred twenty men, during the siege, would be gathering up weapons and hiding them in concealed locations. When these men returned, they would be able to arm an effective fighting force and overthrow the Prince's authority as well as the Centurion's, if any remained. Yes, these men were determined to bring positive change to Zargarb. They had enough of this "civilization" and war. Merchants, other than those providing weapons, could not make a decent profit, if the city kept being periodically sacked. Profit for these men was their primary motivation in life.

Mikhailovich and Zdlenka sat on their horses at the edge of a hilltop olive grove surveying the situation below. Five miles away, the great city of Zargarb lay, a giant semi-circle against the blue Med Sea. The last of his fighting groups had finally arrived, and his massive force of thousands looked most impressive, collected here in one place, just outside the city.

"The one thing that we cannot do is starve them into submission," Zdlenka commented, though they had discussed this issue many times. Seeing the vastness of the city and the reality of the sea for the first time with their own eyes, they realized they had been right in their conclusion. "Look, there comes two ships into the city even as we stand here. It's obvious that they can bring in shiploads of food whenever they desire, and there is nothing we can do to stop that."

Mikhailovich commented, "Yes, very true. Very true. The only way in looks to be to smash through those wooden walls between the buildings."

"Either that, or smash through the adobe or wooden walls of the buildings," she said thoughtfully. "Our battering rams are up to either task, aren't they?"

"I think the makeshift wooden barriers would be easier to smash outright. Still, it is going to take time and cost lives. It will not be a pretty sight. What about burning them out? I still think that has some potential, though I must admit that sea sure is full of water. Yet, they would still have to move the water from the sea to the fires."

"Perhaps a combination of the two," she suggested. "Start numerous fires, and while some are occupied fighting them, smash through the barrier walls."

"My thoughts exactly, give them more than they can handle. Tomorrow the siege begins with the promise of vast wealth for all! I'll meet with all the group leaders now and set the stage. See you at our hut for supper." He rode down the hill, collecting the various leaders as he went.

Zdlenka stayed a while longer admiring the sight of so many brave fighters. Never had this many Galts been organized into a single fighting army in their history. Indeed, today was an historic event; she savored it as long as she could.

June 15 Zargarb finally fell; the last of the street barrier walls were smashed, and the barbarians fought their way down to the docks. Even as they stood at the water's edge, a lone ship slowly tacked out to sea carrying the Prince with it. One hundred Galts were dead; another six hundred wounded. General Pax Iona's head sat on a spear at the water's edge. No Centurion remained alive. More than half of the hastily trained fighters of the Prince were dead; the remainder was wounded or had fled, disappearing into the population. Fully half of the buildings had suffered some amount of fire damage, especially to their roofs. At least two thousand civilians had also perished.

The Galts spent an entire month sacking the town, going door to door in the more affluent sections of the city, confiscating things of value or interest to the conquering men. Wagons loaded to the maximum slowly crawled out of town heading north or east. Not until August could Mikhailovich get enough men re-organized to head on to the next sector, Solamina.

Footnote: In June, Rosalita became pregnant. Once confirmed, she was taken under heavy guard north to the Sisterhood's secret safe house, called simply North Point. North Point was actually an enormous cavern complex in the far northwestern portion of the sector, far off any beaten path. Here the Sisterhood raised their children in complete safety. Sandy and Simon accompanied her and stayed with her, along with one hundred fighters. Sister Aminia would take no chances with the safety of Rosalita. Only a handful of the Galts were told of the location, and Mikhailovich did not visit it until sometime after his first son was born.

Illanovich Strokova came into this world in the middle of March 587 AH. His father saw him for the first time later that spring, when he led his army through Zargarb on their way to Pieta and then Bonilla. Late that fall, he stopped by on his return trip and spent time with his son and Rosalita. Early June of 588 AH, Lenkova Strokova was born. He saw his daughter late that fall as his conquering army returned from taking Vito and Barcella. Finally, mid-June of 589 AH, he returned from taking Velona, and this time he took his two children with him. Rosalita had done her part, and he had held to his word. Not a single Sister who wore a yellow headband had been harmed in any way by his forces. However, several had been killed when they were not wearing their identification, but that was acceptable to all.

For three bloody years, the Land of the Seven Sea Princes underwent the ravages of the barbarians from the Northern Steppes. However, the major cities were spared repeated attacks because Mikhailovich led his armies along the east-west roads through the middle of the already conquered sectors. He had discovered that bothering with the outlying towns yielded little of value. He moved his army along the path of least resistance. Yes, each year, despite his losses, the number of fighter groups he fielded grew, as more and more clan members wanted a part of this incredible wealth.

Final note: after sacking Velona, he decided not to push northward toward the unknown eighth Sea Prince sector. First, he did not relish attacking a stone fortress; he had never seen one. Second, he could find no passage through the boulder fields over which he could take his horsemen and their wagons. Zdlenka suggested that they take it after they conquered the Greenway. Perhaps this stronghold would be more readily attacked from the Greenway side.

Chapter 22 The North Point Events

Early July 586 AH, one hundred fighters accompanied the now pregnant Rosalita and her two inseparable companions from the Greenway, Sandy and Simon, on their week's ride to North Point, located high in the hills and only about thirty miles from the great high plains known as the Paese di Dio, the Path of the Gods. This remote section was largely uninhabited, far, far from the Med Sea, around which the livelihood of the Sea Princes depended. Bandit groups thrived in the zone from about fifty miles from Zargarb to one hundred miles inland, but even they ventured no further inland; there was no profit in such outlying villages. Closer to the city, they occasionally raided in the past, but the ever-presence of the Sisterhood, kept them at bay. In fact, in the last twenty-five years, only one band had attempted a raid closer than fifty miles from the city, and the Sisterhood fighters had soundly defeated them.

However, with the coming chaos of war and invading barbarians, Sister Aminia took no chances with the safety of the three most important people she had ever known. Upon Rosalita depended the very survival of the Sisterhood and that of the Greenway guests who were now living legends for the service they had performed more than thirty years before. These hundred fighters were ordered to stay at North Point and guard these three. The week passed slowly and uneventfully.

For days, the trail twisted from valley to valley, but the general elevation continually rose. Rounding a valley curve, North Point came into view. "There lies North Point," Rosalita pointed out the obvious. A large limestone cavern complex opened into the side of the hill. A roughly semi-circular, rock wall some five hundred feet in diameter and four feet tall encircled the black opening into the chambers. As they rode up, numerous children of all ages were playing in the enclosed courtyard under the watchful eyes of a dozen women. One hailed the party and the children stopped their games to stare at the new arrivals. Many other women, old and young, came bustling out of the dark opening to catch a glimpse of the new arrivals. They had known of their coming for some time now and were prepared. Yet the sudden arrival of so many women at one time was a first.

As the group dismounted, one matronly, elderly woman, wiping her hands on her apron, stepped forward. "Welcome to North Point. I am Sister Elena Elbo; I'm in charge here. We are so honored to have you three here. Rosalita, all we sisters cannot thank you enough for what you've done for us all." Rosalita blushed, unused to this much adoration. Elena ignored her discomfort and faced Sandy and Simon. "I'm so honored to have the opportunity to meet the legendary Saviors of the Sisterhood." She bowed low and humbly. "I hope you'll not find our accommodations too crude here at North Point. Please come inside; let me show you around."

Sandy replied, "We didn't even know this place existed. I'm sure we'll love it here. It is so close to the Paese di Dio."

Elena chuckled, as did many other nearby women, "You aren't supposed to know of this place. It is a secret. Here is where all our women with children come to raise them in complete safety. The rock fence is to keep the littler children from getting into too much trouble."

The caverns were huge. Once inside, many lamps provided illumination. The women had built wooden and stone barrier walls, cordoning off sections into "homes" or private living quarters. One section near the entrance provided shelter for the horses, another for their cows, sheep, goats, and numerous chickens. Elena explained that here everyone had assigned chores to fulfill. Once a child could walk, they were given tasks to do that they could perform. At this time, not counting the new arrivals, fifty women were here along with nearly one hundred children, from babies to those who were nearly sixteen. That was the coming of age year here. Once a child reached their sixteenth birthday, they were free to seek their fortune in the world. Most of the young men chose to move to some relatively nearby village, becoming farmers or managers of grape harbors and olive groves. While some of the young women stayed on, a few moved to these villages as well.

To Rosalita, she said, "I'm afraid you might find life here too quiet and boring, from what you are used to having."

"Well, I'll just have to get used to it. I don't want anything to go wrong. There's just too much at stake, but you're right, I think I'll be clawing the walls before this is finished." They both chuckled.

By the next day, Rosalita was completely bored. As the senior leader of the fighters, she began issuing orders for her fighters to scout the area and keep an eye on everything within a twenty-five mile radius of North Point. Her fighters greatly appreciated the chance to get away for long rides, breaking the monotony of their lengthy stay. Periodically, these hundred would be replaced with another group. Each time the current group left, Rosalita truly wished she could be going with them! For a woman of action, this was nearly like being in prison!

Breaking the dull routine, each week sisters would arrive bearing news from distant places. Soon, it was clear to everyone that Mikhailovich was keeping his word. Still, hearing of the chaos and destruction of their homeland was indeed disheartening. Simon held long talks with Rosalita about what the circumstances were likely to be, once the invasion had passed on into another sector. Lawlessness would rule the day. Sure enough by late fall, the number of bandit bands quadrupled, their ranks filled with disgruntled, disappointed, and angry men displaced from Zargarb.

Once more, the Sisterhood came to the rescue of honest merchants. They provided an armed escort for the merchant's caravans so that goods and supplies could be moved from the country to those in dire need in Zargarb. To the surprise and amazement of the merchants, the Sisterhood charged only a fraction of their usual fee, making their services available to nearly all merchants. This was their way of helping to ease the suffering of others in their sector.

In October after the last of the barbarians had finally left the Zargarb sector heading back home for the winter, a number of special ships began arriving at the docks. The wealthiest families returned to the devastated city. Immediately, they put their take-over plans into action. Their operatives had managed to confiscate thousands of weapons from swords to daggers to short bows. Within a few weeks, each of the ten had formed up a sizeable force of men.

However, the one thing they had not counted upon was the impact of the Sisterhood on Zargarb during their long absence. They returned to find recovery well underway, led and controlled by the Sisterhood, specifically by Sister Angelina Torra, a highly practical, middle-aged woman. Thus, when they formally announced the change of power, the merchants and tradesmen refused a position on the council, saying that it rightfully belonged to the Sisterhood to whom they now owed a great deal. The Sisterhood guaranteed daily supplies actually got to the city.

Thus, when the Prince finally returned to his city, he found himself completely out of power and had no choice in the matter whatsoever. Thus ended the long reign of the Sea Prince family rule over the Zargarb Sector. It was a bloodless coup. Further, for the first time in their history, the Sisterhood had a say in the day-to-day running of their country. They had gained tremendous respect for their service to the common man. Finally, these women were accepted into society, not as abominations, but as equals. Yes, Sister Angelina found herself occupying the Sisterhood seat at the new High Council. I will describe how all this came about shortly.

In late September, another event occurred. Rosalita was four months pregnant and quite bored. When an older woman arrived riding a donkey, Rosalita grew interested and accompanied Sister Elena to greet the lady, whose arthritis made her slow in dismounting. "Mrs. Rolfo, how good to see you again. It's been quite a long time," Sister Elena said while shaking her hand. "To what do we owe your visit?"

In a rickety old voice full of sadness and concern, she spoke, "It's my husband, Fredio. You know it is time that we always meet the hermit Antonio up by the Paese di Dio and bring his offering down here to you folks." Since Rosalita had no idea what this was all about, Elena explained that for some fifteen years now, a hermit up in the Paese di Dio provided those at North Point a flock of new goats and sheep. In fact, he had singlehandedly kept all the children supplied with milk and meat via his kind donations. He only asked for some bare necessities in return, some salt and flour. However, he was so shy that he never actually brought his offerings to the Sisterhood. Instead, he was met by the nearby farmer, Fredio, who brought them to North Point and returned with the salt and flour.

"It's Fredio; he is awfully sick and simply can't make the journey this year. I came to ask you if you could not send someone else this year. I'd go myself, but I've got to look after the farm and Fredio too."

"I'm so sorry, Mrs. Rolfo, is there anything we can do to help you out?"

Before she could answer, Rosalita volunteered, "I'll go in his place. The outing will give me something to do. I am so utterly bored here."

Sister Elena started to protest, "You can't — your condition."

"I'm pregnant, not disabled!" Rosalita barked. "Besides, there can't be any danger in riding maybe twenty-five miles up to the Paese di Dio!"

Mrs. Rolfo looked a bit shocked. "But you don't understand. The hermit says he cannot talk to you, only to a man."

"All right, I'll take Simon," Rosalita countered determinedly. That ended the argument. Ten sisters and Sandy accompanied the old woman back to her farm. Sandy went to see if she could do any healing for Fredio, while the sisters went to help bring in the fall harvest. Very glad to get an outing, Simon accompanied Rosalita and another ten sisters to fetch the sheep and goats.

They rode half the distance yet this day and camped under the stars. Simon truly enjoyed the evening out in the open, gazing at the splendid heavens. Around noon the next day, the party climbed out of the last ravine and onto the Paese di Dio. Simon's memories of this magnificent land returned to him; he had last been here in his youth, when his band of Guardians was secretly returning home to the Greenway. The Paese di Dio was a relatively flat land of green grass that rose ever upward to the actual tall mountains known as the Appian Way. More than a mile high, the stars were vibrant and brilliant. It was a desolate land inhabited only by an occasional hermit who raised sheep. Here one definitely felt close to God or their maker.

Just ahead of them, they spied a flock of sheep and goats along with one man standing behind them, waving towards them. As they rode up, he called out, "Hello Fredio! Glad to . . ." He stopped short when he saw that they were all women and no Fredio.

As they dismounted, Rosalita cheerily exclaimed, "Fredio is very sick right now and cannot come this year. I am Rosalita. I've come to take his place." She didn't expect the response she got or had the faintest idea of what to say or do next. The man in his mid-thirties hemmed and hawed around, scuffing at the grass under his feet, utterly unable to face her or say even one word. Though he tried a couple times, nothing coherent came out. To say that he looked ill at ease and uncomfortable would be an understatement. She turned to Simon for help.

He stepped forward, "Hello, I'm called Simon. Can I help?"

The hermit looked completely startled by the appearance of Simon. "I swore I only saw the women. Yes, I can talk to you. Here, I have all the new sheep and goats that I have raised this year. They are for the children and the babies. Please take them back to North Point for me. They will give you some salt for me in return. I'll wait here until you get back. Thank you." He put his full and undivided attention onto Simon, as if the women simply were not present! Simon thanked him and explained that they brought his supplies with him. However, Simon could not help wondering what was going on with this man and his strange actions. Simon loved a good mystery, and here was one staring him in his face.

"We've never met, actually. I'm Simon Donegal. What are you called?"

"Antonio Pazzio, I believe that is what I was called. Yes, it's been a long time since I spoke it. Say, how is it that a man is with the Sisters. I thought they didn't have men with them?"

"Oh, I am a friend of theirs, just here on a long visit before my wife and I head back home. Since I am new here, I really don't know just what the different situations are around here. You know, I'm sort of learning the ropes. That's why I came along with Rosalita here. I've heard that you don't speak with women, only men. No one seems to know just why. If I am prying, why just tell me to mind my own business. I would like to get to know you better, and why you don't want to speak to the sisters, who owe you such a great deal for your generosity. I've met so very few men who have such a level of sincere kindness to these women as you have. I'm sure that they would really like to thank you personally for all that you have done for them, especially the children." Simon had the gift of neutralizing objections to his questions. He stopped talking the instant that he found the right reaction in Antonio.

"I — I can't — I mustn't — I just dare not talk to women — any women, just can't," he blurted out in a disorganized rush, full of fear and sorrow at the same time.

"Tell me about it," Simon said soothingly and softly. "An old dear friend of mine, now long dead, once told me, 'Always speak the truth for only truth can set you free.' I've always followed Bethany's advice; it has served me well."

Rosalita swore she saw tears form in the man's eyes. In her entire life, she had never seen an emotional man who cried, except from pain. It made a lasting impression on her. This man was somehow very different from any other that she had ever known. She strained to hear his every word, wondering how Simon always seemed to know just what to say.

"It's all so utterly confusing. I don't know any more exactly what I did. Never did exactly, for that matter. So confusing." Simon coached him on. "I had a sister once. I got her killed."

Simon, not at all taken aback by his pronunciation, simply said, "Yes, go on."

"I was sixteen and she was a year younger. She was beautiful and so much smarter than I was. I was very jealous of her. She was always besting me in everything I did. I had a gang of fellows that I hung out with in town. Then one day, a good job opened up and I applied for it. Unfortunately, my sister also applied for the same job. That night when we all went out for a drink at our pub, I told my friends about the new job. They congratulated me about applying for it. But I said that I would never get it because my sister would most certainly get it over me. After all, she was pretty and very smart, and I was rather dumb. I think I said that 'I wished she would be out of the way' or something like that. It is so confusing, just what I said. I thought if she would get married and move away or get a different job or go to live with our Uncle in Zargarb — something like that was what I think I meant. Then she would be out of the way so I could do what I wanted to, without her always showing me up. Well, when I went home that night, she was not yet back either. Don't know where she was, probably out with her girlfriends. We shared a room — with a divider between her half and my half. Our parents were rather poor; it was a small house. When I awoke the next day, she still had not come home. I grew worried about her. I did love my sister, though, you see, just jealous of her."

"Well, about midmorning, a guard came by with the news that my sister had been killed in the street last night. He wanted to know if I knew anything about it or where she had been. He kept asking me questions. My face must have been red, because I felt so hot! She was out of the way now! I had the thought that maybe one of my friends had gone out and killed her to get her out of the way. Should I tell the guard this? If I did, my friends would most certainly be interrogated. If I said that I had told them I wanted her out of the way and they did just that, why, I'd be even guiltier than they were! Surely, the guards would declare this just a big conspiracy, and I'd be lynched for being the ringleader. I didn't know what to say or do. I just sat there like a dumb log. I didn't say anything to anybody. After that, I couldn't even look at the faces of my friends. I kept thinking one of them probably killed my sister! And if I said anything, they'd just reply, 'Well you said you wanted her out of the way, didn't you? We all heard you say so last night.' What was I to do?"

"So after we buried her, I just packed a small bag of clothes and left on foot. I just couldn't get it out of my mind. I had gotten my sister killed by just saying words about her. I was so confused. I still am. After many days of thinking about it all, I just decided that I couldn't ever again trust myself to speak to a woman. I'm terrified of saying the wrong thing and getting her killed. I ended up here in the Paese di Dio. Almost no one else is up here. Now there is no way my words can get another woman killed. The Sisterhood is full of women who have all suffered horribly at the hands of men like me. I decided to try to make amends for my horrible crime. I've lost count of the number of years that I have given all my new sheep and goats to them to feed their babies and children. Unfortunately, with each passing year, I feel no better. My shame I will take to my grave and beyond. Every night, in my mind, I still see my dead sister's face — all my doing, by saying the wrong words. I still see the faces of my friends talking among themselves, whispering and such. I knew that they were up to something that night, but I did nothing about it. So I'm responsible for her death. For years, I contemplated returning and confessing my crime and letting them lynch me for it. Then, I'd see the faces of all those children who are depending on me for their milk and meat to see them through the long winter and know that I can't do that either, for their sakes. So I just stay up here where I can't possibly bring harm to another woman and never speak to no woman or about one and raise sheep and goats for all the children."

Simon spoke gently, "Is that all of it?"

"Yes, I just knew those guys were plotting something, and I knew I should have intervened but I did nothing. My sister died because I did nothing." He looked so utterly forlorn that Rosalita could not help but sense his grief.

Simon knew that there was only one possible way out for Antonio. He had to have forgiveness from those he had harmed. However, his sister was dead. He placed a thought into Rosalita's mind, shocking her at first. *He needs forgiveness from you as a Sister.*

For a minute, she was dumbfounded by having Simon's thought in her mind. *But I don't know what to say!* She thought in a screaming effort, fairly blasting Simon's mind. He was not as adept at telepathy as his wife was. It took him a minute to recover from her wham.

Say something like this. On behalf of the Sisterhood and all women who have been harmed by men, we accept your confession of what you did, and we hereby forgive you for your misdeeds so long ago. You need not carry this burden any longer. Simon placed into her mind.

Though the words sounded rather strange to her, she took a deep breath and spoke to Antonio. "Antonio, I speak for myself and for all of us Sisters who have been mistreated by men. We accept your confession of what you have done so long ago. We hereby forgive you for all that you did or failed to do so many years ago. Honestly, from now on, you don't need to carry this burden any longer. You may speak freely among women and about us from now on." She added this last bit thinking that might really be helpful, especially if old Fredio passed away.

"You're — you're — you're teasing me?" he finally said his first words to a woman in seventeen years.

"Absolutely not! Do you have any idea just how much you have helped us? I think not! Over these years, hundreds of children have gone through North Point. Everyone owes you for providing the means for their milk and meat year round! Those women and children who have come to North Point have had all manner of mistreatment, physically, mentally, and emotionally. Some were in such bad shape that they could not even care for their young at first. Your contribution has been lifesaving, Antonio. We owe you a debt that we cannot pay. The very least thing we can give you is forgiveness." She leaned over and kissed him on his forehead. "Honestly, you are completely and wholly forgiven!"

"Really?" he asked still unbelievingly.

"Really!" she exclaimed. Her ten companions, who had heard the whole conversation, chimed in enthusiastically, "Really!"

As they watched him, his heavy burden dissipated. He stood a bit taller; a smile crept into his countenance. He took a deep breath of life. For the first time in seventeen years, he felt no shame, no regrets, and no blame.

"Say, I forgot to thank you for all these sheep and goats, Antonio," Rosalita commented hoping to change the subject. She felt a bit awkward in this man's presence. Why? She could not tell.

"Oh, please don't worry. I will continue to provide as many as I can each year. Children always need milk and meat, if they are to grow strong," Antonio hastily confirmed, afraid that they would think that he might now quit. That reminded him of something that he had been thinking about for over a month, ever since he heard the details from Fredio.

"Say, there is one thing you can do for me, ma'am. I've heard what a valiant, noble sacrifice Sister Rosalita Armino has made to save the Sisterhood from the barbarians. Old Fredio explained it to me. Could you please take a message to her for me?"

Several women smiled and two even squelched a giggle. It was obvious that this hermit did not realize to whom he was talking. It took Rosalita by surprise. *Well, we never gave our last names*, she thought to herself. Antonio flushed; he did not understand what he had said that caused the others to react as if it had been humorous.

Sensing the uncertainty and awkwardness of the situation for Rosalita, Simon explained, "I must apologize, Antonio. I failed to introduce everyone here. This is Rosalita Armino, the very one your message is for. You can deliver it to her personally." Several women didn't attempt to conceal their mirth now.

"Oh, I'm sorry," Antonio blurted, "forgive me. I didn't know."

"So what message do you have for me?" she asked. The moment of awkwardness passed; she now was quite curious about what he wanted to say to her. She wasn't prepared for what he did say.

"I've been up here a long time, here in the Paese di Dio. After a few months of living here, something happened to me, something amazing. For years, I could not explain it to anyone. I didn't understand it myself. Some months ago, a couple of shepherds, immigrants from Juda Arad, passed through. They told me of their Great Messiah and their god, Jehosa, and his teachings. Suddenly it all made sense to me. Their Great Messiah said that we are all spiritual beings inhabiting these fleshly bodies. I swear to you, Rosalita, they speak the truth! After living up here for a few months, I found myself outside of my body, floating just behind its head. I've been there ever since! At times, I feel so serene — I just cannot find words to explain it. I wanted to share that with you. If you ever have a few months when you have no pressing obligations, I would be honored to have you come up here, stay for a while, and see if what happened to me happens to you. If it does, there could be no greater gift I could give you for helping the Sisterhood so selflessly."

Though he paused, Rosalita could find no words with which to answer him. Spiritual matters seldom interested her. That was the province of the priest of Tur, which generally had little to do with the Sisterhood or their well-being. Once more, Simon interceded on her behalf, giving her time to absorb what he said and offered. "Indeed, we are all spiritual beings, just as you have said. In my experience, so few actually realize this fact. I commend you, Antonio, for having discovered your true nature."

"Well, it does tend to put things into a different perspective, I'll have to admit," he replied. "I don't look at things like I used to any more. If I am not my body, why, that casts a very different view on things. Oh yes, Rosalita, one other thing I wanted to say. It's about the children that this barbarian is trying to get. When you can see that each of us really is a spiritual being, not just a body, then you may also see the fallacy in that barbarian's reasoning. He thinks that by joining with you, an especially dynamic woman, that the resulting children will be somehow superior to all others. That is a falsehood. It is the spirit alone that matters. I mean, do not worry that by doing this, you are somehow making two supermen tyrants who will later on dominate the world. That is his thinking, and it is not true. Once you experience for yourself what I am saying, you will understand too. Okay, I've talked to women longer now than I have in the last eighteen years. I will shut up and get back to my flocks. It has been a great honor for me to have met you, Sister Rosalita Armino." He bowed low to her and turned to go.

He had struck a nerve deep within her mind. Late at night, she often debated, wondered if her actions in bringing his children into the world would create, as Antonio suggested, a pair of supermen. She had told no one of this inner fear; it was the one possible flaw in her plan. Was she rescuing the Sisterhood now only to have them be crushed later on by his children? Such nightmares on more than one night had awakened her in cold sweat fits. Now here was this hermit who had guessed at her inner terrors and spoken of them openly! Not another single soul had she told of this, not even Sandy. She had been too terrified of the consequences, if Sandy told her that her fears were well founded!

"Before you go, there is something that I have been meaning to ask someone here for over thirty years. How do you survive the winters up here in the Paese di Dio?" Simon asked, which once more let Rosalita collect her racing thoughts. Besides, he was dying to know, ever since he had passed through here so many years before.

He turned back to face Simon, "Can't actually. Too cold and snow gets too deep. I will sleep with my flocks even through the first light snowfalls, but once the snow gets too deep, the sheep would starve if we stayed up here. In about a month, I will have to drive the flock down this gully here and seek shelter on the leeward side from the winter winds. I make a little hut from fallen brush, and we somehow survive. It does get very cold, but I wear many layers of woolen clothes. Sometimes I cannot get a fire going for a week at a time. Just as soon as the grasses peek through the melting snows in the spring, we head back up there. The sheep can then find enough to graze upon, though I usually lose a fair number during the winter."

"Well, why don't you just bring the flock a little further down the valley to the caverns at North Point and stay with us during the coldest part of the winter?" Rosalita suggested. She was very happy that the subject had been changed. Besides, it was plainly obvious that Antonio and his flocks had a miserable existence throughout the winter. Giving him a warm shelter was the very least the Sisterhood could do.

"I, ah, I would not be imposing upon you Sisters?" he queried uncertain that she really meant it.

"Look, for years you have helped provide for us. Giving you shelter through the dead of winter is the least that we can do for you. I'm sure that Sister Elena would absolutely demand you come and stay, once I tell her about your situation," Rosalita insisted.

"You are sure about this?"

"Right!" she replied.

"Right, then," he echoed, still a bit hesitant. "Look for me and my flocks in about a month, when the heavier snows hit the Paese di Dio. Thank you for me and for my sheep and goats. This means that there will be even more sheep next year," he smiled. Again, he bowed, turned, and began walking back toward his flocks, which grazed about a half mile away.

"What a strange man!" declared one of her fighters.

"Indeed," answered Rosalita, but there was a tone in her voice that had not a derogatory intention behind it. Rather, she found him irresistibly intriguing. Simon also noticed this in her. Soon, they began the long journey back to North Point, herding the sheep and goats along at what she thought was a snail's pace. "A shepherd must have infinite patience," she declared. Everyone laughed.

The next noteworthy event occurred the last week of September 587 AH, when Mikhailovich, Zdlenka, and his group of fifty warriors arrived at North Point. He spent some time playing with the six month old Illanovich Strokova. Of course, he bedded Rosalita once more. Again, they followed the same protocols. Simone and another sister stood guard outside the bedroom, along with Zdlenka and two of his most trusted men.

Sandy, following orders from her Wid, the leader of her Circle, gently touched the minds of both Mikhailovich and Zdlenka. Once she had the faintest tendrils of contact established, she joined with a dozen other Communicators back in the Greenway. Together, they attempted to implant a heavy thought, idea, or concept, one that these two would obey as if they had thought of it themselves.

As the pair said their farewells, promising to return in the spring when he would lead his ever-growing army against the remaining city-states, Mikhailovich said to Zdlenka, "You know, I've had the strong thought in my mind that we really should leave the Greenway until last. I greatly fear those Evil Witches there. They well may be our very undoing."

"My sentiments exactly," she replied. "I keep having this gnawing fear that those Witches can wipe our forces out before we can even get to them. I think we need to figure out a completely different strategy to handle them. Also, I think we ought to leave that rogue eighth Sea Prince city-state go, until after we take out the Greenway. By all reports, there isn't an overland passage for an army to get to them from anywhere within the Sea Prince lands. What do you think?"

"I concur, sis. I've heard that passage there is treacherous even on foot. We cannot afford to leave the supply wagons behind and go on foot. It's probably best if we take them out from the Greenway side. Besides, what wealth could they have accumulated for our taking? Very little, they are just a new rogue city-state. No profit there."

In the spring of 588 AH Sandy and Simon were called home. A dear friend and member of their Circle had just passed away, Roy Ron Randell, their Protector. Thus, they were not present for the birth of Lenkova Strokova in early June of 588 AH. Neither did they witness the transfer of the two children to the Strokovas, when he passed by on his way home in mid-June of 589 AH.

Once the transfer of the children had occurred, Rosalita's obligation was finished. Rather than return immediately to active duty, as she called it, she took some time for herself. On July 1, Antonio watched as a lone rider came up onto the Paese di Dio toward him. She spent a month in his company. Just as Antonio had predicted, she discovered her own true nature. From that point on, her nightmares never recurred. She knew the truth. In December, she asked Antonio to marry her. She would be a working wife, but they had their winter times together. In the end, Rosalita and Antonio found both love and respect from the opposite sex, though neither would have ever thought such possible.

Chapter 23 Counter-Strikes and Survival Measures

Early July 586 AH, an old man wandered into the once proud fortress of Al Tarm, once the center of the Qaam sect of Juda Arad. It was a ruins now. Gone were the thousands that once made this their home, here at nearly the edge of the civilized world, high atop the last mesa whose eastern slope blended uniformly into the foothills of the impassable Kathas Mountains. Long dead were Dez Madan and Abu Wadi, the Disciples of Jehosa. Gone too was Hama Damar, the Elder Prophet and ruler of the entire Qaam sect. Gone were all the hopes and lives of those that believed in the old ways. The old man wandered the ruined streets and counted but a hundred mostly starving survivors, who begged him for food, which he had none to speak of. He had lived off the land in his long journey across Juda Arad.

Al Markesh, his wounded arm now healed as much as could have been hoped, cackled in glee. To the destitute men and women clinging to him, he called out, "I, the Old Man of the Mountain. I am seeking ultimate retribution!" His beard and hair had grown unkempt since he had left Florintine Junction months ago. Now disheveled and looking every bit the part of the crazed Old Man, he looked at but barely saw the sea of human misery about him.

"Food! Can you spare a bit of food?" a voice pleaded with him. The voice sounded like some distant echo in a canyon, far off in the distance. If he even heard them, he made no outward sign of recognition. Not until a young man tugged on his arm.

"Sir, sir, can you help us? I've been trying to feed the survivors, but I cannot do it alone. Can you help? Most are so weak they can barely walk." For the moment, Al returned to the present time, suddenly opening his vision to what was before him. He looked into the eyes of the desperate young man who had pulled him briefly back into the world.

"Is there no food here at all?" he asked the obvious question.

"Nay, long ago eaten. I know where we might find ample, but it is some distance from here, way up in the mountains. We are all too weak to make the journey there," the man answered.

"Opportunity knocks," flashed through Al's mind. "Yes, I will save you all if you promise to always follow me and serve me." Of course, a chorus of "Yes" and "I will" greeted his offer, for these were a starving, defeated people, shorn of their beliefs and faiths, merely attempting to stay alive by any means, though now they uniformly were too weak to even seek out sustenance on their own. Of course, they would agree to anything for a bit of food. "Then, I shall return with food."

A few hours later, Al Markesh returned leading six sheep that he had dubiously acquired from a flock he had passed earlier on his way to Al Tarm. The young man, who was probably in the best condition of the lot, oversaw the butchering, while Al rummaged through the rubble to find firewood. By nightfall, the six sheep had been cooked and eaten.

Relaxing by the embers of the fire, the young man spoke to Al Markesh. "Thank you sir. My name is Jamal Adid, once a shepherd to the Qaam who lived here. I was up in the foothills back there when the barbarians attacked. By the time I got here, they had left. It's pretty much as they left it even now. Most of those who somehow survived fled west. Probably these that chose to stay ought to have fled as well. I still have a flock somewhere up in the distant foothills. If we could find them, we'd have plenty of meat."

"Good man. I am Al Markesh, the Old Man of the Mountain. I am in need of a mountain with a cave that is far, far from any known civilization — a mountain that is defensible with but a few men. You have walked these foothills. You know where I might find that mountain?"

Naturally, this was not how Jamal anticipated the man would reply. He had to think about the request. "Well, yes, the further you go eastward, the more mountains there are. Each one is taller than the last one, until they are so tall that the snows never melt."

"Ah, then tomorrow, Captain Jamal, your task is to wander those mountains and find us our new home — a cavern would be nice, but so would a mountain top that cannot be taken by force. You find us that place, while I forage for food. We must get our people's strength up so that they can make the journey to our new home. I promise you that within a few years, you will be the wealthiest of men on Tarra!"

Part of each day, Al foraged the surrounding countryside for whatever the land had to offer. He found sufficient edibles to continue his newly acquired assistants on the road to recovery. The balance of each day, he poked through the rubble in search of items that would be needed to establish his new fortress town. However, he was keenly interested in finding one key item that he knew had to be here somewhere. On the third day of searching, he let out a shriek, "Here you are at long last!" He'd found the poppy extract that the village healer gave to the seriously ill. "Now we are in business. Well, at least until we can make more of this!" The ruins echoed with his insane laughter for ten minutes.

His searching also turned up a fair amount of valuable items that the barbarians had missed. When Jamal had not returned after a week, Al sent two of the men, who had by now sufficiently recovered sufficiently, to the neighboring town armed with many of the coins he'd found. They were under orders to buy some of the finest cloth available as well as the most expensive scented oils, suitable for royalty or a palace. "Oh yes, and don't forget to buy some fine wine as well," he added, nearly forgetting that detail.

"But why sir?" asked Facquaar. "Should we not buy flour, salt, and food supplies with this?"

"Nay, that we shall get in due time. First, we need the finest cloth, wine, and oils. It is part of the plan." Humbly, both men accepted his orders, though neither had the faintest notion why. While they were gone, he sent two other men in search of a pair of vipers. Naturally, no one had any idea why their crazy man wanted poisonous snakes, but they did as they were told. Vipers are commonplace in the Arad, so they had little trouble finding some. Catching them without getting a fatal bite was another matter.

After dinner, Al proceeded to milk both snakes, carefully catching their venom in small ceramic jars. "I am a patient man. Patience is needed, for it will take days of milking to meet our needs." Still those that watched him had no notion why he was collecting the venom or so carefully preserving it. All that Al would say was, "It is part of the plan, just part of the plan."

Two weeks after he had left, Jamal returned, having found a remote mountain, which also had a cave of sorts on the western side. Though he knew little of defenses, he thought it would serve. Two weeks later, the Old Man of the Mountain arrived at his mountain, along with his followers, one hundred six men and women, all bearing the salvaged gear from the ruins of Al Tarm.

While Captain Jamal and a few other went to round up all the stray sheep and form a communal flock, Al set the rest to work constructing their new town. A month and thousands of adobe bricks later, the rudiments of a village appeared centered on the cavern. However, the cavern was converted into what appeared to be a royal palace, filled with all the luxuries they could find in the nearby towns. For now, it would have to do. No one lived in the palace, though.

On September 1, the Old Man of the Mountain held his first communal conference, outlining his plans. "My good people, if you had all the money you needed and could go on a shopping spree in Jerilum, what would you like?"

His people were expecting to hear great plans. His opening question took them completely by surprise! One woman called out, "A pig and a cow! I've not tasted ham for so long. And milk, what I would give for a small cup!" Soon others added to the list. Al dutifully jotted down their suggestions.

Once they finished, he spoke once more. "Then, before the snows fall, you shall have all that you have asked for, if only you will follow my orders to the letter." Naturally, everyone agreed whole-heartedly. "Tomorrow, I want Captain Jamal and two other strong men to go to Jerilum. Captain Jamal will present a scroll to the city's mayor. The other two will search out a derelict man, one who is so utterly down on his luck and fortunes that not a soul will miss his passing. After dark, give that man one drop from this vial. When he is asleep, bring him here, keeping him asleep all the while. You will need to place one drop in his mouth every six hours. Do not fail to keep him asleep. Meanwhile, our women, your task is to bathe and anoint your bodies with our expensive oils. Make yourselves into princesses for the night. When the others arrive with our derelict, he will awaken in our palace with you women all around him, looking after his every need. Wine him, dine him on our best, tempt him, seduce him, but do not actually bed him. Do nothing that you do not feel comfortable in doing. All the while, tell him that the gods have brought him to the Heavenly Palace so that he may see what his life could be. When he is ready, I will appear and tell him that he can return here forever if he will only do one small deed for us."

From the baffled looks on everyone's face, he knew he had to explain more fully, none yet grasped his plan. "That scroll you deliver says to deliver unto the representative of the Old Man of the Mountain, the following items. I made a list of all the items that you wanted. If he does not comply, his first assistant will be killed the next day. How? Not by our hands directly. Our derelict will do the deed willingly. Think of the mental state our derelict will be in once we are done with him. I will give him a dagger covered with poison and tell him that all he needs to do to return to the Heavenly Palace forever is to plunge this dagger into the assistant. However, he must get his mortal body killed in the process, so that he can ascend to the Heavenly Palace. Drugged, as he will be on our poppy extract, why, he will immediately desire nothing more than to do it as fast as he can. We will put him asleep once more, transport him back to Jerilum let him do as I command. Captain Jamal will return the next day asking the mayor if he has reconsidered. If not, we repeat the process. I assure you that very shortly you will have everything on your wish list here at our home!"

In order to dispel any reservations they might have about all the murders, he went on, "I assure you that we will be targeting our enemies and those Arads who have betrayed us. We'll pick on the Infidels and those who have supported them, those who betrayed Juda Arad, giving her to the hands of the barbarians from the north. Next year, we will even go after those barbarians as well. Soon, we, my people, we, we will control the lands, not our enemies. We will not need to wage war and wreak devastation on our brethren. Soon we will be held in utter awe; our word shall become law." He raised his voice to a high pitch, high volume. His people cheered wildly, including Captain Jamal, who saw that real revenge might be possible to acquire.

Mid-October, just before the first snowfall of the season came, a large caravan made its way up the mountainside. Captain Jamal and two dozen of his men returned from Jerilum with every item on the wish list. It had begun.

Zeb Markesh, the younger brother of Al, and who had suffered a severe leg slice when he tried to stop the sacking of his pottery shop by the barbarians, crawled and slithered along the dusty, dry, sandy ground. Reduced to pulling himself along with his arms and one leg and ignoring the intense pain, he made good his escape. Mentally, he felt no pain, no emotion, just a single burning desire to extract ultimate revenge on these inhuman barbarians. For months, eating only what he could scavenge from the land at ground level, he moved northward. His leg healed poorly; he would never really walk upright again, but that concerned him little, focused as he was on his single goal.

Midsummer, he finally crossed over the barrier rock that separated the arid Juda Arad from the steppes. With difficulty, he eased himself finally onto the soft, grasses of the Northern Steppes. Here the three-foot tall grasses completely hid his form as he slithered along like a snake. In many ways, he adopted the life-style of a snake, hunting as one does, eating what he could catch with his hands or mouth. Crazed, yes, as he bit into a rabbit, eating it raw, his face covered in its blood. Zeb would no longer be recognized as human, for what sane human would act and live in such a manner.

Another month and Snake in Grass, as he now called himself — he had taken to mumbling to himself almost constantly now — finally spied what he had been seeking for so many months. A small Galt village lay in the green valley below him. He was about a mile away as he sat up, parted the tall grass, and watched smoke clouds from cooking fires as they wove their twisting path into the deep blue sky. Flakes of dried blood and refuse flaked from his face as he grinned broadly. He had not grinned since he and his brother departed months ago. Now, like a tiger on a hunt, he waited and watched, studying his prey.

A dozen hide covered domed huts formed this small clan's temporary village. A dozen horses grazed nearby. Women and children moved about doing their daily chores and playing, completely oblivious to Snake in Grass. He spied only two old men in the camp. At last, he saw just what he was seeking. A mother brought out her infant son to give him a bath and some air. His mouth salivated in anticipation, drool streaking down either side of his mouth. "Patience Snake in Grass, patience." He watched and waited, noting very carefully into which hut the baby was carried, as dusk fell across the vast grasslands and distant wooded groves.

Around midnight, Snake in Grass made his move, slithering down the gentle hillside toward the huts. No guards were posted. Here in the Northern Steppes, there were no real threats to humans, save other clans and their internal warfare. Since the coming of Mikhailovich Strokova, the inner-clan fighting had ended. All able bodied men had now joined up, garnering vast riches for themselves and their respective clans. All last year, life here at home had been exceedingly peaceful and quiet. Some women claimed that was because all the men were down south waging war on others. Some said it was because they were now striking back at their eternal enemies. No matter what view you took, life was calm indeed — no need for any guards.

Slowly, he slithered into the outer edge of the camp where the grass had been trampled underfoot. He stopped for a moment by the tack row and grabbed a saddle blanket. Carrying it in his teeth, ever so slowly he made for the hut. He smiled at the entrance; the flap was wide open allowing fresh air to circulate on this hot summer night. He listened for was seemed an eternity before he moved ever so slowly inside. He spied the infant in its cradle. Minutes later, he paused beside the baby, placed the blanket over its head to muffle any noise. Then, gently like a mother, he removed it, placing a tiny effigy he had made in its place. Just as quietly as he came, he left.

So slow and careful were his motions that the baby did not even wake. Snake in Grass did not pause until he reached the safety of the distant woods across the valley, just as a pale red predawn sky bespoke the coming of a new day. He smashed the baby's skull, drank its blood, and dined on its brains, leaving a horrid scene to be later discovered. Satisfied, he slunk deeper into the woods, and then just as a snake in search of bird prey, he climbed up into a tall maple tree, hiding in its foliage. Something inside him demanded that he witness the discovery of the dead body. Quietly, he waited.

Not long after the reddened sun rose above the waving sea of green, he heard the distant wails and cries. He grinned and laughed his sickly laugh, dislodging bits of gore from his face. Yet it was nearly noon before the villagers finally discovered his faint trail and found the ghastly remains at the edge of the woods. The wails and crying, the cursing and swearing were god's music to his ears. He restrained himself from laughing hysterically. "Sweet is my revenge," he whispered to himself, "sweet indeed."

All day he stayed in his snake perch, waiting for dark to descend. He knew that there were no other infants at this camp so it was time to move on in search of another encampment. He hoped that there would be more than one baby at the next one he found.

Later in the year when cooler autumn approached, he found a small cave. From the closest village and over many months he stole food and blankets. When the first snowfall came, he crawled into his hole in the ground, plugged its small entrance, safe and warm inside, he hibernated for the winter, just as he knew a snake would. In fact, several snakes had joined him. Or rather, he had joined them, for this was their winter den. It had been a successful hunt this year; he'd dined upon a dozen infants.

When the Yellow Horde arrived to sack Florintine Junction, the three disciples of the Church of Jehosanity, Hamah Zagros, Bandar Dero, and Amar Tarabulus, had already prepared for the worst. Dried food and other supplies, enough to feed the town for perhaps two weeks, had been collected in the Church's name and secreted away. Having already experienced the destruction of their country, Juda Arad, these disciples vowed to be prepared this time. For months, they had quietly hidden away what they anticipated they might need should the barbarians come here next. In truth, all three fully expected the Galts to come, they just did not know when.

Still weekly, more and more immigrants from the Arad arrived. Building new housing and finding work for the newcomers kept the three men fully occupied. By the time that the barbarians came to sack Florintine Junction, six thousand Arads now dwelled here.

Further, three adobe churches had been built to accommodate the ever-growing numbers, with each of the three disciples running the services at one of the buildings. These Churches of Jehosanity, or Northern Orthodoxy Jehosanity, had already become the central focus for life in this border town. Their preaching consisted of explaining that each person *had* a soul, which was separate from their bodies. Upon death, the soul, if it had followed the Decalogue of Jehosa, went to Heaven, the new name for Jehosa's ethereal realm. Sins were defined as transgressions against the Decalogue. Further, if one sinned, the soul went to Lucifer's realm called Hell. It was a very workable system, especially when it was coupled to the arrival and departure of Jehosa's son, the Great Messiah, Jes Amir, who died and was resurrected so that the average person would see the truth of all this and believe.

Still, Amar objected, claiming that they were perverting Jes's words and that, in fact, this perversion was actually an attempt to control believers. Amar said, "You *are* your soul." Bandar's reply did not dispute Amar's observations; they were trying to control the people to get them to follow Jes's teachings and the Decalogue. The people were dislocated, disoriented, had lost homes and livelihoods, had lost family members, and had fled for their very lives. It gave them comfort in their misery to believe that those barbarians who caused all this were going to Hell. Thus, the disciples were telling their parishioners just what they wanted to hear. Since these three had journeyed with Jes Amir, the Son of Jehosa, their preaching carried a particularly heavy weight.

When the barbarians were sighted heading en-mass toward the town, the Northern Orthodoxy Jehosanity Church was really in total control of the town. Bandar's orders that no one should offer any resistance to these barbarians, letting them ransack their new crude dwellings as they desired, was followed. Virtually no one offered any overt resistance. As the disciple anticipated, the barbarians quickly realized these were the same people they had already robbed last year in Juda Arad. Probably the fact that they still wore the same clothing styles gave them away to the barbarians. After sacking a few houses and finding little of value, save food, the barbarians left the town intact.

The locals were the hardest hit, those who already lived here before the massive influx of immigrants. Their clothing styles gave them away as being true Sea Prince inhabitants. Thus, their homes and businesses were thoroughly ransacked for valuables. In truth, some gold and gems were found. All told, though, the barbarians were very disappointed at the total amount of loot gained. For them, it was just traveling money; nothing to send home. In less than twenty-four hours, they moved on down the road.

However, the next Saturday, the disciples found every single native Sea Prince person in attendance at one of the services at the three Northern Orthodoxy Jehosanity Churches! In one day, they had managed to convert all the remaining Tur believers into Jehosa believers. The fact that the disciples handed out food and supplies to those now most in need, the ex-Tur worshipers, only aided the massive conversion. Work began the following week on three more churches. When the barbarians passed through Florintine Junction on their way home that fall, there were nine churches all told.

Bandar and Hamah had bigger plans. As the reports of the devastation of the other nearby villages and small towns came in to the Junction, they reacted. Bandar exclaimed, "This is our golden opportunity, a gift from Jehosa!"

"What?" Hamah cried out in anguish. "All this suffering? How so?"

"We still have plenty of supplies here. We should send forth emissaries from our church to all these other afflicted towns and aid the stricken. You know, provide what little healing we can do, provide them with a few good meals, perhaps blankets if their homes were destroyed. Say, maybe even man-power to help them rebuild their homes."

"Well, yes, that is what Jehosa would want us to do," Hamah replied, nodding his head, but still not grasping Bandar's enthusiasm.

"Don't you see?"

"No."

"Look, if we come to their aid, they are far more likely to hear our message of Jehosa. Hearing that message, they too will convert! Fully stomachs, warm bodies, and free aid in rebuilding — these will speak in thunderous echoes," Bandar bellowed in high enthusiasm.

"I see, yes. Now it is clear. I agree," Hamah now shared Bandar's excitement. "It might really work!"

"We need to give our church representatives a name," Bandar went on, thinking aloud. After trying several ideas, the two men came up with the "Missionaries of Jehosa." By mid-May, the first six Missionaries of Jehosa were trained and fired off to the neighboring villages. Each missionary drove a wagon loaded with supplies and six volunteer workers with their tools. By August, two dozen sets of Missionaries were out in the field, helping those in need. In return, they also built a new church in each town or village. So it was that the Sisterhood first encountered the Missionaries of Jehosa. Why?

By early June, the missionaries had encountered a serious problem: bandits. As they traveled to towns and villages further from the Junction, they naturally entered the zone controlled by the renegade bandit bands, whose ranks swelled in the wake of the sacking of Zargarb. Of course, the missionaries were stopped, robbed of their supplies, and forced to return to the Junction. After six robberies and much discussion, Bandar learned a crucial fact.

Prior to the Galt invasion, the Sisterhood had provided the sole security for all caravans, which passed through bandit-controlled lands. Normally, the locals explained that there would usually be a couple Sisters present in the Junction, but they had all been recalled long before the actual invasion. No sister had been seen in the Junction since last fall. Naturally, the picture that the locals painted of the Sisterhood was a most confusing one, ranging from abominations of Tarra to sainthood, depending upon to whom one talked. With little choice, Bandar Dero packed his fighting gear with his supplies. He and two companions headed for the only known location of the Sisterhood, a place called Ranchero Paladina located about a hundred miles west and a little south of the Junction.

A few days later, they reined in before an impressive ranch complex with rows upon rows of small buildings, barns, large houses and all surrounded by some kind of wooden pole barriers. Several women were standing guard near the only possible way through the barrier wall. They dismounted, and Bandar gave his reins to one of his followers. "Stay here," he ordered and walked up to the guard women. "Greetings, I am the Reverend

Bandar Dero of the Church of Jehosa in Florintine Junction. I am not familiar with your customs, but I wish to speak to someone who is in charge, please."

"You don't look like a bandit. What is the nature of your business? I must tell her that. Still, she might not wish to see you, you understand. We seldom have dealings with men," she replied.

"I wish to hire some protection for our missionaries, who are attempting to come to the aid of the people in towns that have been raided by the barbarians from the Northern Steppes. The bandits are stopping our aid wagons," he replied truthfully. *Surely, they don't hate all the people in this land?* He began to wonder. The woman looked every inch a fighter, one who could probably give him a tough combat. This detail he took as a good omen. If the others looked as these here at the entrance, then there was hope indeed. Until this moment, he always had reservations about using women fighters to protect his wagons, but then, he recalled that there used to be a few very competent women fighters in Juda Arad before its fall from grace. He watched her walk across the equipment-filled yard up to the largest home built from wood. He liked the way that she walked, but restrained both his budding smile and his eyes as the other two guards glared at him.

Five minutes later, she returned. "Mother Sister Aminia Sciota has agreed to see you. Your men may stay here with your horses. Watch them," she said aside to her two companions. "Follow me, please, Bandar." Quickly he fell into step behind her.

As he entered the large frame home, several other women were quickly clearing various maps and scrolls off a large oaken table. Mother Sister Aminia Sciota beckoned him to enter. Bandar guessed that she might be in her mid-fifties. She had short greying hair and a ruddy complexion. Though not "good looking," she had the type of personality that soothed upsets merely by her presence in the room, which he felt as soon as she opened her mouth. "Welcome to Ranchero Paladina. I am Sister Aminia Sciota; you may call me just Sister Aminia, if you prefer. Come have a seat. Belinda says that you wanted to hire our services? Something about missionaries being robbed?" Bandar took a seat.

From the corner of his eye, he saw that Belinda wasn't about to leave him alone with her. She was evidently standing guard over him. This he thought was a wise measure for them to take and did not take offense with the action.

"Yes, I am Reverend Bandar Dero of the Church of Jehosa in Florintine Junction. I am originally from Juda Arad, where I was for many years a disciple of the Great Messiah. When the Arad was ravaged by the barbarians from the Northern Steppes, I and many others fled to the Junction to start life anew. With the death and resurrection of the Great Messiah, I and two of my fellow disciples have founded a church so that all may seek salvation. Already I count nearly seven thousand among my flock, including nearly everyone who lives in the Junction."

"Yes, I could tell at once that you were or are from Juda Arad. Your beard and clothes give you away. Though we may seem isolated here, we have heard some tales told by travelers about your Great Messiah. It is a shame that he died. Tarra could use more good men; that's the truth. Pray, what does this have to do with us?" she asked.

"Well, you see, we all follow the Decalogue of Jehosa." The blank look on her face told him that she had no idea what he was saying. He elaborated. "Bear with me a moment. Allow me to explain the basics of our faith, and you will see the importance of this meeting." She nodded, so he continued. "Here is the Decalogue; these are our guiding principles."

There is no god but Jehosa.

Do not worship any other god but the One God, Jehosa.

Do not build statues of Jehosa, for Jehosa has no form.

Set aside the Holy Day, Saturday, from your labors and worship the Lord that day.

Respect and serve thy mother and thy father, for they have labored long in your raising.

Do not kill another.

Do not steal from another.

Do not commit adultery.

Do not lie to another.

Do not desire another's house, possessions, or wife.

Do unto others, as you would have others do unto you.

(Footnote: if you detect some slight changes in the Decalogue at this time, you have a keen eye. Bandar insisted on the changes, citing the preaching of the Great Messiah and their own attempts to get their people into the right frame of mind.)

"Each of us has a spiritual soul, which, if we follow the Decalogue in life, will be found worthy enough to enter the Holy Realm of Jehosa, Heaven we call it for short, when our fleshly bodies die. Part of our faith demands that, when we see others in our land suffering as they are from the ravages of the barbarian invasion, we feel it is our holy duty to assist them as we can. To that end, we have sent trained missionaries to our nearby towns. They bring food, supplies, and a half dozen volunteer workers to help them rebuild their homes and businesses. Naturally, the missionaries also spreads the word of Jehosa as we help them. In return, all we ask of the village or town is to allow us to build a Church of Jehosa there. If you wish to verify this, please check with any of the six closest villages to the Junction."

She smiled a wry smile, "No need. We have already heard of your work. I must say that for once I was actually impressed with the actions and conduct of men, but please continue."

Nothing escapes her! What all does she already know? I'd better continue as planned. "We are now trying to send out nearly two dozen more missionary groups to towns more distant. However, we have encountered numerous bandits, who have completely ended all our attempts to help, robbing us, and sending our wagons back home. I must freely admit that I know very little of the Sisterhood. What I have heard is most confusing. However, it is said by all that at one time before the invasion, your fighters provided protection from the bandits for merchant convoys. Is this true?"

"Yes."

"Then, would it be possible for our church to hire your services to protect our missionaries so we can travel to the afflicted towns and do what we can to help them recover?" He held his breath, waiting for her reply. He had no idea of what their circumstances were here or how steep a price she would demand, but at least all was going well so far.

She replied, "These are trying times for us all. We know that Zargarb has just fallen to the barbarians. Even as we speak, they are sacking the town. By the hundreds, city folks are fleeing to the nearby towns seeking safety and have completely overwhelmed those towns' ability to feed and care for so many refugees. We continuously monitor the situation and attempt to help as we are able. At the moment, about all we can really do is to suggest that those, who are able, travel further, and go to the more distant towns and villages. Even those have already been sacked by the barbarians on their way to Zargarb, and supplies are scarce. We have been trying to figure out where food and supplies are located so they could be sent to those most in need. That planning was what we were reviewing when you arrived. I can tell you the situation will become most likely life threatening within a couple of months. It's going to be very grim indeed. I wouldn't be surprised to learn that more of our people died *after* the barbarians left than did *during* their attacks."

"However, it is refreshing to see men wanting to do something to help without an ulterior motive, profit, or political gain. I think we can work out something between us, but you must understand our position. We have worked out a truce between the barbarians and us: if we don't bother them, they'll not bother us. When they first came here to attack us, they only brought one of their combat groups of fifty men. I believe that is the number. We kicked their butts, if you don't mind my expression. However, it became quite clear that if they brought their full army to bear on us, the entire Sisterhood would have been wiped out, just like it very nearly was some thirty years ago, when the Centurion army invaded. Perhaps you've heard tales of the valiant stand the hundred Sisters made against their entire army. We nearly won the field that day, inflicting as many casualties. After that battle, only a handful of Sisters remained in the entire sector, and those had to go underground just to survive."

She went on, "This time, since neither Prince Cassias nor the Centurion General or even the Church of Tur, for that matter, asked us to help in the defense of Zargarb, we felt making the truce with the Galt leader was more than acceptable. We aren't a religious organization; in fact, most Sisters feel that our god Tur, has long abandoned us. Something you must understand about us, Reverend Bandar, every one of the Sisters is here because she has been brutalized, tortured, or badly mistreated by the men of this land. Even I, look at this," she showed her left hand, the index finger was missing. "My husband cut it off one night merely because I tried to point out he had made a bad error in judgment, but that was a very long time ago, when I was a young maiden," she sighed, and long forgotten memories stirred within her mind. Bandar looked entirely outraged. He had no idea that women were so badly mistreated in his newly adopted country.

Before he could vent his outrage, she went on, "That was before the coming of the Centurions. Before they came, women had their tongues cut out for speaking openly before men. Women had fewer rights than dogs in the street. When the Centurions found out about all that, they put a complete stop on such barbaric practices — outlawing it, in fact. So from our point of view, the Centurion invasion was not all bad. Over time, the situation has improved quite markedly, though we still are not considered 'citizens' of this country; outcasts we remain. However, to survive, these Sisters had to learn how to defend themselves, and many became very skilled defensive fighters. We had to be; no one else would look after us, and besides, hatred can be a powerful emotional force. So yes, over these many years, we have earned a living by providing security for shipments and caravans. Every man thinks thrice before attacking a Sister! And right they should! Before the barbarians came, we charged a decent price for our security services. They paid without a second thought!"

She concluded by saying, "Your case is different. We both are trying to help as we can. I will make you this deal, Reverend Bandar; we'll provide an escort for your wagons. We guarantee that you'll not be robbed by bandits and will make good any such losses incurred while under our protection. However, should the barbarians come, we cannot and will not defend you from them — our truce, you see. Yet, there is a good chance that because Sisters are present with you, the barbarians will leave you alone. In return, we want food, supplies, and wagons with which they may be delivered to the needy towns and villages. I would also prefer it if we could coordinate our efforts. Some towns will need far more assistance than others will. Could you afford to give us a wagon load of supplies for every, say, half dozen missionaries that we escort?"

Bandar could scarcely believe his good fortune! "Absolutely, Sister Aminia. "We have been trading with those that remain in the Arad and have been working out means of acquiring as much as we can. The economy was pretty well shattered last year by the invasion, but now those that have stayed are trying to barter what they can for what they need to survive too. Trading is back to the barter system right now. By the time that I return, our churches ought to have about eighteen wagons ready to go out. Each has a missionary and six volunteer workers with their tools. I'm sure that we could also prepare another three wagons loaded with food and such for your payment. I can see tremendous benefits in coordinating our efforts. We are beginning to have difficulty in obtaining many basic food items. If you can locate towns, which have some to trade, perhaps between us we can arrange for its purchase and transportation. If skilled tradesmen are needed, the Junction now has many that would offer to help. The Junction now has a population of well over seven thousand folks."

She inquired, "That many? It used to be but a few hundred. My, how that town has grown. I have not been there in many, many years, I'm afraid. How is it that the Junction was spared the ravages of the invaders?" she asked, a note of curiosity in her voice.

He answered, "The vast majority are immigrant Arads. When the Galts recognized this, they pretty well left us alone. After all, they had already robbed us of our gold last year. Unfortunately, the locals did not fare so well, but we have already assisted them in rebuilding and getting back into operation. Yes, it could have been far worse than it was."

Sister Aminia explained, "I see. Well, then, I will discuss the numbers with my Fighter Group Leader, Rosalita, but I think that we should send a half dozen fighters with each wagon. Normally, we'd send only two, but the bandits are far more numerous and more desperate these days. I'll see what she thinks before I commit them. I'll send four Sisters back with you to help coordinate our efforts. They will relay messages back and forth between us. Within twenty-four hours, the fighter escort will follow you. Is that satisfactory, Reverend Bandar?"

"Most generous, Sister, beyond my wildest hopes!" He offered his hand to seal their bargain. He noticed that she still had a solid handshake.

"You are welcome to come back and visit sometime when you have the time," she replied. "Perhaps more changes are in the wind." With that, Bandar was escorted out, and he rejoined his men. Shortly, four blonde, shorthaired women, bristling with weapons, galloped out of the complex to join them.

"I'm Sister Frieda, your escort and Sisterhood representative," the taller women in her mid-thirties announced. "Shall we be off? To the Junction is it?" She had a tan and looked every bit like a woman who enjoyed the out-of-doors and the trail.

Bandar smiled; it would be good to be riding in the company of knowledgeable fighters once more. His years as a messiah fighting the Infidels came back into his mind; this was before he met the Great Messiah. Somehow, he felt more alive and comfortable being in such company.

"Seven, I want seven to accompany each wagon," Rosalita answered Sister Aminia, who had just finished explaining the unexpected situation. "Do you think that we can trust these men?" She desperately wanted to go along with them, but as she had just become pregnant, she knew the answer would be a resounding no and kept her desires to herself. "Seven of them, seven of us. Even odds, should anything come of it. Besides the bandits are getting more desperate too."

"Very well, seven it shall be. Do we have the hundred fifty sisters available at the moment?"

"Yes, if we delay my departure to North Point a week or so, just until some of the others return from their current assignments. We are spread a little thin trying to assess the damage countrywide. That will still leave over a hundred to protect us here," Rosalita commented. She wanted to put off her departure as long as possible. While here, she was of some use; at North Point, she guessed that her life would suddenly become incredibly boring, monotonous, and sedentary. None of which she wanted, but knew it could not be helped.

"I know you would dearly love to be a part of the wagon escorts, but so much depends upon your health now," Aminia struck close to the mark. "I wish I could offer some other solution, but I can think of none. You have my eternal thanks for what you are doing. Without that, none of us would likely be alive at this time. We owe you so much, but do try to think of this as a much deserved vacation; perhaps with that attitude you won't find motherhood so distasteful."

Rosalita smiled; she hadn't thought of this as motherhood. None of the children would be hers to raise. In many ways, she felt more like a cow or sheep, not a mother to be. Yet, in some small cranny of her mind, tucked away in darkness, she had a faint idea that this Mikhailovich might get killed on the battle field, and the children would then be hers. She dare not let this idea take root. She had fought him and Zdlenka; he would be exceedingly difficult to slay in battle. Just then, two sisters arrived from their scouting mission and needed to report, so Rosalita set about the task of getting her fighters briefed and ready to ride to the Junction the next day.

Chapter 24 Aftermath in Zargarb

"I hate to put you on the spot, Rosalita," Sister Aminia apologized, "but you must be leaving soon. I must ask you: who do you want to take over your position while you are at North Point?" It was early June and Rosalita would soon be leaving her post here at the ranch.

Rosalita dreaded this day, but knew it was coming, ever since she detected that she was finally pregnant with the barbarian's child. She never thought of it as being her child, incidentally; she could not afford that luxury. Going to North Point where the Sisterhood kept all the children and mothers out of harm's way meant that she would have to appoint someone to fill her shoes as their Fighter Group Leader, the second highest position in the Sisterhood, second only to Sister Aminia, their administrator. Without the slightest pause, she declared, "Sister Fiona. I want her."

"What? Her?" Sister Aminia gasped, "Surely you don't mean that?"

"Yes I do! I want her. She is more than qualified."

"But she has only the one arm and a violent temper."

"She can do more with one arm than many can do with two. Besides, I am choosing her because of her violent temper."

"Why on Tarra?" asked Sister Aminia, completely baffled with Rosalita's choice.

"She knows how to command and accepts no questioning or second guessing. She is like a mad dog on the trail of a fox, when she needs to be. Look, when the Galts finally leave Zargarb, the city will be in complete and utter chaos, total lawlessness. All of those who could command law and respect have long ago set sail for the southern islands out of harm's way. Cowards, the lot of them. May Tur sink their ships! She is going to have to go in there and bring some semblance of order. I can think of no one more suited to that task than Fiona."

"Ah, now I see. I hadn't thought of that aspect. I suspect you are right as usual. Fiona it is then. I'll send for her."

A few minutes later, Sister Fiona entered. She had very short blonde hair, stood five-nine, but weighed nearly one hundred eighty pounds, all muscle. Long ago, she had lost her left hand during an argument with her husband; he had lost far more than a hand. That was years ago before she joined the Sisterhood. Fiona was now forty-one, and as she entered, she snapped to attention before Rosalita, her long time boss.

"Reporting as requested, Sir!" she barked crisply, saluting with her right hand. Rosalita had long ago stopped trying to suppress a smile at her formalities. Of all the Sisters, only Fiona addressed her as if she were a general.

"At ease, Sister Fiona," Rosalita said calmly. "You are here because as you know, I must be leaving shortly for North Point. I need to pick a replacement head of the Fighter Group. I've chosen you to lead them in my absence, Fiona."

"What?" a look of utter, complete disbelief and total surprise spread instantly over her face. Never did she dream that she would one day be allowed to take Rosalita's place. No, she had guessed that Rosalita would have chosen one of three other women and had called her here to get her to agree to follow the other's orders, which, of course, she would have given. "You are teasing me?"

"No, you are perfect for the job at hand, Fiona. You are now the Leader of the Fighter Group. If you have any questions or such, you know where to reach me. I have infinite faith in you. However, remember one thing always, Fiona: Never make any decision when you are angry."

"Yes, thank you, Sir! You've told me that many times. I have it memorized: Never make any decision when I am angry. I won't let you down, Sir! I will lead us to victory over what assails us. You can count on me! I shall not fail, Sir!"

Rosalita interrupted her jubilant pronouncements, "Remember, as Leader, you are allowed to choose your own advisors. My last request, not an order, is to consider taking Sister Alena as one of your advisors. She has a very keen eye for deceit in men's words. She will serve you well, as she has me."

"Yes, Sir! I will pick her first. Thank you, Sir!" Fiona could not believe her incredibly good luck. Fighter Group Leader! She!

"That will be all; go now and pick your team. Your biggest challenge lies in Zargarb, once the barbarians leave," Rosalita commented as Fiona stiffly saluted and left. Once the door was closed, both women chuckled. "She takes her job very seriously," Rosalita commented. "She will do well in trying circumstances. If trouble comes, don't hesitate to reach me."

"I told you Hermino, we should have left with the Zuchi family. Now here we sit starving!" Alicia complained openly to her husband. It was early August 586 AH in Zargarb, fully two months after the last resistance had been wiped out. Hermino normally would not tolerate such open criticism from his wife, a woman, but times had changed drastically. He honestly had no idea how even to feed them. At first, he was grateful for the foresight Alicia had shown by stockpiling food before the Galts attacked, though he never told her so. That stockpile had run out several weeks ago. Now they had nothing at all to eat, though water was plentiful still, because the city had numerous wells.

Every day, Hermino went out to scour the city for something to feed his family and search for weapons. The latter had been a duty bestowed upon him by Cecil, one of the wealthiest men in town. Like a fool, he had insisted on payment up front, and now that was gone, stolen by the Galts when they ransacked his home, terrorizing his wife and two children. In fact, his youngest son had protested when a Galt had confiscated one of his toys and kicked the big fighter in his shin. At least the barbarian had not outright slain his son;

rather he bashed in the boy's face, breaking his cheekbone with the hilt of his sword.

Further, he now didn't have to worry about the kids playing inside their home. At first, coming home was a nightmare, because the streets were not safe for the children to be outside. Hence, they had been forced to spend their waking hours cooped up inside their house. He only had an inkling of what Alicia had been though. Now both children were nearing death from starvation, confined to their beds. Neither played at all; his youngest was still in vast pain, and his cheek was swollen and very black and blue. His spirits had steadily fallen, and today even the departure of the last of the barbarians did little to cheer him. "What's the use of trying anymore, Alicia?" he said hopelessly. "No one's got any food. You know that. I've told you; I've tried every place I can think of — there's nothing."

"Well, what do you want us to do? Lie here and die? Some husband you are," she scolded him, hoping nagging would force him out of his utter apathy. "You want me to go out in search of food while you watch the kids?" She taunted him, risking his violent ire.

That did it. She hit his remaining button of male-hood. To stay home and let his wife, a woman, go out into the chaos of Zargarb and forage for food was the ultimate slam against him. "No, I'll go. Only I don't know where to try anymore," he sighed, wiping on his shirt sleeves the first trace of wetness, which formed in his eyes

"Well, it's been months since we could get to the northern sections of town. Try there, maybe the Galts left some stuff untouched there," she tried to suggest somewhere he had not yet been. "You've said that they finally left early this morning. It can't hurt to try. Please find something, I beg of you. The children won't last much longer."

Hermino slowly picked up several sacks as he had done for the last sixty days and left the house. He carried a short sword in one hand and the sacks in another. Out in the streets, it was every man for himself, and had been so for two months. To date, lady luck had been with him; he had managed to avoid all confrontations. Back alleys offered him a safer path to follow than the open, broad streets. Carefully, listening for any sounds of trouble, he began to meander northward.

At the end of each alley, he paused to observe the street he had to cross in order to disappear into the alley ahead. Today, more than the normal number of people was roaming the streets. Many had formed themselves into gangs, safety and power in numbers. He wondered if he should've joined up when he had the chance a couple weeks ago. From what he had seen, though, the gangs fared little better than he in scavenging for food.

As he walked along, passing by a pair of forlorn looking women, he wondered if he should try his hand at fishing from the docks as some did. However, their catch this close to shore was dismally small. Besides, he was a tinsmith not a fisherman. He had no idea how to catch fish. Surely, he thought, with all that have died and have left town, somewhere there ought to be some forgotten food. A half hour later, he finally entered the most northern section of the city, where the bloodiest of the combat had occurred. Nearly every home, he observed had fire damage. Wooden structures were but shells, a few charred timbers thrusting toward the deep blue sky. The adobe buildings had fared better; hence, he began poking his way inside some, hoping against hope to find something edible to take back.

While he was poking around near the top of a tall building that had been a large storage facility for tack, he spied a large convoy of wagons and riders snaking slowly down the north road toward the city. He stared, wondering if the barbarians were returning. No, these were local wagons! Quickly, he made his way down the crumbling stairs and headed to meet them, taking to the main streets, casting safety to the winds. Perhaps someone was coming to help!

Others had seen the caravan coming as well. By the time that he reached the northernmost open plaza, at least a hundred others, mostly men, but also a few desperate women too, had gathered. He pushed, shoved, and managed to get near the front for a better view.

Sister Fiona, riding stiff and tall in the saddle, led her convoy into the northern sector of Zargarb. She had one hundred handpicked fighters with her, and of course, her advisors. She also brought all the spare dried food the Sisterhood had managed to acquire during the last few months. Twenty wagons were filled to capacity, and her troops rode either in front with her or alongside of the wagons, guaranteeing their complete safety. She knew this delivery was critical, but she didn't know just how badly it was needed.

She reined in before the large crowd in the plaza, surveying the destruction around her. "I had no idea it was this bad!" she commented to sisters Alena, Mona, and Monica, her three advisors.

"Have you any food to spare?" a man called out pitifully. Another added, "We are starving." Then others took up the call. In a minute, hundreds of people were begging loudly, trying to be heard above the others.

Fiona rose in her saddle and yelled even louder, "Silence! We bring food. Silence!" She had that aura of command about her. In seconds, you could have heard a pin drop. "That's better. We have brought twenty wagons of dried food for you. Form up into orderly lines. One bag per person."

Instant chaos. She had said the magic word: food! Everyone pushed and shoved to get to the wagons. The fighters, using their horses, forced them into semblances of lines. Hermino was lucky or thoughtful enough to rush toward one wagon near the end of the convoy and so was first in line. "Please, Sister, I need four bags. I've a wife and two sons who are near starvation." The young woman looked deep into his eyes. Adjudicating that he was probably not lying, handed him four sacks. "Thank you, you have saved my family!" he said as propitiatively as he could muster. These were the Sisterhood. Ordinarily, he would never deign to speak to one. Yet, she was handing him back life. He swallowed his pride. As he stuffed them into one of his sacks, a thought struck him. "My youngest son was badly wounded by the barbarians. Are there any

302

healers with you?"

"We didn't think it safe to bring them inside the city until after we have dispensed all the food. Can you bring him back here in, say, an hour from now?" she replied, handing another man two sacks.

"He is too weak to travel. Maybe I can carry him here. Thank you Sister!" he repeated his thanks several times, as he backed away as others pushed in to get their turn. He pushed and shoved to get clear of the throng to get his gift of life home. Suddenly, a burly man moved in front of him. From the corner of his eye, he saw another move behind him.

"I'll take that sack from you," he demanded.

"No, it is for my family. Go get your own. It's free," he protested.

The thug had no intention of standing in line. Instead, he punched Hermino and ripped the sack of precious food from his hands. "Help!" was all Hermino could think to say as his hope faded away in an instant.

Twang! He felt something go by his ear. The man, who had his sack, staggered and fell to the ground, dropping the sack. A quarrel protruded from his back. Quickly, Hermino snatched up his sack and turned to fend off the other gang member, but Fiona was quicker, she simple pulled her horse up behind the man and knocked him on his head with the pummel of her sword. The man dropped unconscious to the ground. She spied other gangs trying similar thefts. Veins at her temples bulged as she bellowed, "That's it! Next time we see someone robbing these people, we will shoot to kill!" The huge volume of anger in her voice made everyone stop what they were doing instantly. No one moved a muscle; all lines, all conversations ceased.

"I said we will do this orderly! The next theft will result in death! Do you hear me?" she bellowed as loud as she could, which was hardly needed over the intense silence. "Once you get your food back to your families, I want to see all tradesmen here in the square at noon time. As you were." She felt like she was addressing raw recruits.

Hermino, his luck still holding, fairly ran the rest of the way home. As he passed others, he told them of their good fortune. Of course, they began running for the north plaza.

"Back so soon?" his wife said demeaning, assuming that he had given up all hope.

He held out his sack, produced the four nicely bundled bags. "You did it!" she exclaimed, her voice filled with awe and surprise. While she opened them and began to fix a much-needed meal, she asked, "Praise be to Tur. How did you ever find so much?"

"Not my finding. It's the Sisters. They arrived a while ago with twenty wagons of food! They are doling out one bag per person. One thug tried to steal mine as I was leaving, they shot him in the back, and their leader smashed the other one over his head with her sword. Can you believe that?"

"I'll believe anything! I'll try to make this last us a few days," she said, mentally rationing their newfound bounty.

"They brought healers too," Hermino added. "I'm to take Michaello to the north plaza in an hour or so. Maybe they can do something for him. I'll have to carry him, though."

"Yes, he is too weak to walk. This will help him, if we can get some of it down. His cheek is in pretty bad shape, I don't know if we can." She had already given up hope for his recovery, but with healers now here in Zargarb, well maybe. Carefully, she made a mush, which she hoped he could swallow without trying to move his mouth and broken cheek too much. The lad did manage to get some down.

Taking no chances, Hermino carried his young son to the northernmost plaza, arriving a bit early. He found all the wagons were now empty, and the sisters were spreading blankets in the wagon beds. "I'll take him, sir," an elderly woman said, reaching out her arms. Not knowing what else to say or do, he complied and watched her lay him on the blankets in the wagon. She adeptly began examining Michaello, asking him if this hurt or that hurt. His moans spoke volumes. Hermino wanted to ask, "Will he be all right?" but bit his tongue instead, fearing to interrupt a healer at work.

At last, she spoke solemnly, "He has a badly broken cheek bone, right here," she pointed to the obvious. "It appears to already be mending, though it will likely leave him slightly disfigured, I'm afraid. I must ask that you leave him with us for a few weeks so we can help him more fully recover. Trust us; we know what to do to save your boy. You can check on him daily, if you like."

Hermino stopped himself from gushing what his heart felt, saying, "But I can no longer pay you for your assistance. Before the barbarians, I could have met any reasonable price, but now, I'm afraid I cannot pay you." He reached out his arms to take his son back home, figuring that would be the end of that. After all, everyone wanted or demanded payment for everything.

"No charge, sir. We don't expect any payment for our help. However, if later on after everyone has recovered, if you have some extra funds, why, we would appreciate any donation you might care to make. Go now. Go listen to Sister Fiona out in the plaza. I'll take good care of your boy." He said many thank-you's and did as she requested, scarcely believing his incredible good fortune. His mind recoiled in thoughts; his father had taught him that these women were the abominations of Tarra. And yet, without thought of recompense, they were here helping to save his son and feeding those in dire need. The two concepts collided in his mind, as he joined the huge throng in the plaza.

Sister Fiona was still on horseback, surrounded by a half-dozen other women fighters. They were positioned in the center, entirely surrounded by hundreds of men. He recognized some of his competitors and friends. That the other fighters were positioned strategically around the edges of the entire plaza did not escape his keen eye for detail, after all, he was a tinsmith. She was beginning to speak, so he stared her way. As she raised her left hand for silence, he noticed it was not there! His benefactor had no left hand; a dagger contraption was in its place. Somehow, he gave her his full attention.

"Greetings. I am Sister Fiona, Fighter Group Leader of the Sisterhood. I bring you greetings and news from the northern towns. I can report to you today that all the outlying towns and villages are now on the road to recovery. Each and every one we have assisted and helped get them back into some semblance of order. It is their food that you received this morning, all that they can spare at the moment. I assure you that no one up north, other than perhaps the bandits, is starving at this point." Cheers spontaneously arose, in part from the relief that many felt knowing that their friends and some family members were probably in better shape than they were just now.

"I also know that you people have borne the brunt of the wrath of the barbarians; many have died in the unsuccessful attempt to protect Zargarb. I know that you are grieving, that your shops have been robbed, even perhaps destroyed, that food is scarce, and that your lives have become a misery, a waking nightmare."

She raised her voice for emphasis, though it was not needed; everyone listened intently to her speech. "The barbarians have gone and will not likely be back. We must get the city functioning once more." Catcalls and "how?" and "not likely" and "impossible" and others defeatist words bounced around her, though no one dared openly defied her.

"So where is the Prince? Shouldn't he be here to bring order and get things going?" she interjected.

Naturally, someone called out that he left by boat months ago. She continued, "Right! Ran away like a coward. All right, then where is the mighty Church of Tur? Could they not lend a hand?" she was on a roll now.

As expected, someone called out "What church? They are all dead or gone too."

"Okay, then let's let the wealthy nobles who normally take care of business — let's let them tell you what to do now," she resisted the temptation to smile, keeping a serious, stern countenance.

"They left even longer ago! Took their whole families with them," yelled back several men in disgust. Much grumbling could be heard on all sides. She knew she had them right where she wanted them.

"Okay. You have but two choices. One: do nothing and die of starvation. I said I brought all the spare food we could find anywhere. Pray that the Prince, the Church, or the nobles return and put things right. Or two: you and we, together, we can get things going in the right direction." As expected, these men were not particularly friendly to the Sisterhood, though none dared call them Abominations any longer.

"Look," she continued slightly angry, which was altogether easy for her to express, "Look. You don't really have any choice. Up north, they are desperate for things that they normally get from the city. Things like wine barrels, for example. Dried fish for another. If you can get yourselves organized and start producing what is desperately needed by your kin in the northern towns and villages, then they will be able to send you what you need most, more food and some trade wine with which to buy more. They are beginning to eat their sheep because they have no fish. It is getting grim up there."

She paused long enough to let that reality sink into their minds. "You have a big enemy: time. It is already approaching mid-summer. If we have not gotten the economy back on its feet by fall harvest time, your winter will be indescribably bleak, and that is putting it politely. By next spring, I would expect to see half of you dead or dying of scurvy or rotting diseases."

"I offer you one chance. We will provide security and help with overall organizational things. You help each other out to get shops back in working order producing. You round up all able-bodied fishermen and get them back to fishing as best they can, lacking any large ships. Get the drying rooms operational. Get crews out foraging for more timber with which to rebuild those buildings that can most easily be repaired. We have very little time to waste before winter comes and does us in."

"Yeh, that's easy for you to say. What's in it for you? We got to pay you royally?" someone yelled out. He conveniently hid behind others so that she could not see him.

"Idiot! Are you an imbecile as *well* as a coward?" she taunted. "We *are* all in this together. If you do not survive, how is the Sisterhood supposed to survive? We are all interdependent upon one another, in the final analysis. Only a man could be *so* ignorant not to see this!" she taunted. "End of discussion. No, we want no payment. We just want to survive too. Except," she added, "we have one option that you do not have: we can leave Zargarb for good and join up with the Sisterhood in the other sectors. Where will you go and on foot? Not far. Now make your choice. Let me know what you decide before dark. If you want to do nothing, great, we will begin making our plans to leave this sector to its doom." She started to neck rein her horse to move out of the center of the plaza.

She had no more than started the motion, when a man in back yelled out, "I say let's give it a chance. If I can get some of you to help me, and get someone to fetch coal, I can get my roofless blacksmith shop back in business yet today."

Another called out, "Aye, I say give her a chance. I know where some old dingys are stored. Not sea worthy, but we can get out beyond the docks where the bigger fish are. Some of us long to get back onto the sea and fish. Only we need the processors to take in our haul."

"Hey, one drying house is mostly intact. We can start drying fish in there, just needs some cleaning up is all," another man added.

It was catching. Everyone began offering ideas and soon no one could hear anything specific any longer. Fiona grinned to her advisors, who grinned back. She gave them a few minutes to volunteer more ideas. When Alena gave her the secret hand signal, Fiona rose tall in her stirrups to get their attention. "Gentlemen," she had never called a man that before, she began to wonder if she were slipping and caught herself. "Gentlemen. Please talk it over and spread the word. I want you to elect one person from each of the trades to be your representative. Have all representatives come here tonight at sunset to help formulate plans. We will camp here near this plaza in these burned out shells of buildings for the time being." Now she did neck rein and carefully moved out of the crowd. The other Sisters who were strategically positioned around the entire edge of the plaza remained in position. Each was armed with a crossbow, fully loaded, and cocked. They continually monitored the crowd, looking for trouble, but saw none, thankfully.

When they reached the wagons now loaded with wounded men, women, and children, Fiona dismounted for the first time today. The others followed suit. Sister Alena commented, "Good job, Fiona. You handled that like a pro. You have them eating out of your hand."

"No, what other choice did they have?" Fiona countered. "None, really. It is go along with us or face a far harsher situation. Who knows when the Prince will return or the nobles, for that matter?"

"Would we really abandon Zargarb, Fiona? I mean if they did not go along — would we really do that?" asked Sister Mona.

Sister Monica answered her, "What other choice would we have? Life is an interdependency among all living things. That's what Reverend Sister Aminia is always telling us. I've heard our friends from the Greenway also saying that too, for that matter. Yes, we'd have to leave."

That night, fifteen tradesmen, skilled craftsmen, and fishermen walked up to the campfire that Fiona was poking. They talked long into the night about what to do first, what was most critical to bring back into operation. Fiona also mentioned that a bunch of new immigrants from the Arad also wanted to come to help, bringing manpower. However, she had told them that she would ask if they wanted the help first before sending for Bandar's missionaries. They replied that any help rebuilding would be most appreciated, so she sent a rider out that night. The next day, ten missionary wagons, each with six volunteer workers arrived to lend a hand where needed.

Slowly over the next week, order was restored, and production, although only a fraction of what it had been, was occurring. The hundred fighters were positioned at all the major intersections on guard duty. It was common knowledge that their standing orders were to shoot first and ask questions later. During this recovery period, the crime rate in Zargarb was practically nil. Such has never been equaled before or since.

What Fiona did not say, however, were where the hundreds of fighters were stationed, those that the other sectors had sent to help defend the Zargarb Sisterhood. True, some had been sent home or to Solamina to assist there, but the bulk of the extra fighters Fiona carefully kept aside to provide secure escorts for their caravans and those of the Jehosanity missionaries. Why?

Banditry had escalated in the wake of the invasion, just as Rosalita, Aminia, Sandy, and Simon had predicted. Within perhaps an arc of seventy-five miles out from Zargarb, any unescorted wagon was highly likely to be raided, anything of value stolen by these most desperate men. Whereas in the pre-invasion times, the Sisterhood would provide two fighter escorts per wagon in the convoy, now at least seven went, sometimes more. In fact, had Fiona needed more than a hundred fighters to secure the city, she would not have been able to get them unless she wished to sacrifice caravans.

Fiona and her three aides along with the fifteen representatives worked wonders in the city. Her aides were excellent organizers, able to keep track of many detailed situations at the same time. All Fiona needed to do was maintain order, a task at which her personality excelled. Quickly the tradesmen representatives dropped any residual prejudice against these women, primarily because of the grim reality of the situation they faced. Fiona's statement "Act now or starve later" became their byword to all those that they represented. Considering everyone had already had a strong taste of starvation, they acted instead.

Within six weeks, fully one quarter of the buildings in Zargarb had been repaired sufficiently to get by at least a winter. Three fish drying warehouses were finally shipping their products to the northern towns and villages. Wine kegs were sent in return and stored, awaiting ships to arrive and take them to other lands in trade. Perhaps even more critically, more and more of the original inhabitants of Zargarb, who had fled to neighboring towns, began returning. While most found their homes in various stages of disrepair, the tradesmen council immediately set them to work in their previous occupations, while directing construction crews to make necessary repairs to their homes. Daily shipments of timber, coal, olives, produce, and such arrived in Zargarb, while shipments escorted by the Sisters left heading northward, some even bound for Juda Arad. In fact, the day that the first wagonload of dates from Juda Arad arrived in the city, a celebration was held. It had been six months since they had last had dates imported; citizens of Zargarb had a passion for dates.

On the last day of July, Fiona, sitting as she usually did, astride her horse, surveying the situation, spied white sails far off on the horizon. Soon, the city was abuzz with the news that many ships were coming to the docks. A large crowd formed at the docks to watch the arrival of life giving ships. The Sea Prince economy depended heavily upon their ships and trade. Fiona commented to Mona, "Well, this throws a crimp in our plans. We've pressed all the dockhands into the general construction labor pool. With all these ships to handle, there goes construction!"

"Well, they had to come back some time," Mona replied.

"Ah, but who is coming?" Alicia added. "Now that is the more important question. If these ships are just bringing in supplies or want to take on shipments, that's one thing. But what if they are bringing the coward nobles and their families back or even the Prince and his staff? It they come back, we had better make a hasty exit. You know how the nobles feel about the Sisterhood! We need to become 'invisible' again."

"It is likely the nobles," Fiona interrupted with a sigh of disappointment. During the last few weeks, she found that she really did enjoy her job of running security of the whole city and acting as the ultimate voice on the tradesman council matters. She'd had a taste of power beyond that of simply the Sisterhood Fighter Group Leader; she discovered she enjoyed it. Never before had she considered that she might actually enjoy working with men. Although she still found their jokes crass and in poor taste, the tradesmen were not all scum. Many actually had some good ideas, which were put into action. Yes, Fiona's viewpoint had shifted, though she would never have admitted that openly.

Watching the sixty-some ships tacking this way and that as they slowly made their way in from the open sea to Zargarb's sheltered cove and docks was enjoyable even for landlubbers. Finally, as several ships drew close, their banners could be discerned: those of the ten noble houses. The ten wealthiest families of Zargarb were finally coming home. "Well, now they will find that they are even wealthier than the rest," Fiona spat on the ground. "Leave the others to be robbed of everything of value, and you return with all your gold — that makes you even richer — damned cowards!" She spat again.

"Wasn't one of those nobles the father of the husband who mutilated you?" asked Monica, remembering something that Fiona had confided in her many years ago. Seeing the noble's ships coming had triggered that distant memory.

"Cecil Armonga's son, Herbito. Yes, there is one man who will not want to see me, Cecil, that is. I killed his son. I know it was a very long time ago, but I doubt that he has forgotten what I did back then. If I had not joined the Sisterhood, Monica, I would have been dead a long, long time ago."

"I hate to interrupt," Alicia interjected strongly, "but these nobles will most certainly take back their control of the city immediately upon landing. I suggest we make our exit now before any confrontations can occur."

"Yes, you're probably right," Fiona commented. "Let's find one or two of the representatives, tell them that we are leaving, and that we will leave behind a few messengers through whom they can contact us as needed to safeguard their caravans and such." Quickly they spied several and relayed Fiona's instructions.

Just as the first noble of Zargarb stepped onto the dock amid some low-keyed cheering by his loyal supporters, the sisters, all but a handful, that is, save some messengers and two healers who still had patients under their care, rode north out of Zargarb, raising a large dust cloud which very few saw.

Alfredo Monsigau, checking that his clothes were still spotlessly arranged, commented to Cecil Armonga as their ship nudged up against the dock. "Well, so far it's all going according to the plan. At the last minute back there, our ships pulled ahead of the Prince's; now he will be unable to dock for at least twenty-four hours. Just as planned; look at our audience! There must be a thousand of them. Some are on rooftops; some are leaning out of the windows overlooking the expansive docks. You got the speech ready?"

"Yes, yes, Al, all according to our plans. This part of the city does not look nearly as bad as we thought it might. Say, the people there on the docks — they don't look like they are in particularly bad shape. I thought that they would be starving by now. Well, here goes, Al." The two stepped onto the planks of the dock; the other eight noble house leaders were right behind them. Additionally, twenty-five well-armed fighters, their security guards, circled out in front of them, forming a barrier wall, preventing those in the crowd from reaching these wealthy men.

The cheering was definitely low-key, not at all what Cecil had anticipated. He heard a couple other nobles behind him muttering comments about just this. He tried to put that out of his mind and concentrate of delivering the finest speech of his career. Everything depended upon his sales pitch. He raised his hands for silence, "We have returned, loyal citizens of Zargarb. We bring shiploads of food to ease starvation in the city." He paused waiting for the expected gigantic cheers of welcoming. None came. Dismayed, though not displaying it, he went on, "All is not lost. Be it known that we have saved the vast wealth of our city from the barbarians and are bringing it back for us all." Again, he paused, expecting a loud round of applause; hearing none, he continued, more than slightly annoyed. This was not what had been expected by any of the dozen nobles.

"We realize the horrific sacrifices that you all have endured." Now he did get a reaction from the crowd, one that was expected. Someone yelled, "You can say that again!" He did and a roar of similar sentiments followed. Relieved that part of his speech was going as planned, he said, "We of the combined Noble Houses of Zargarb have decided to make it right with you." More cheers came as expected. Someone taunted him, "You 'goin ta give us a year's pay?"

Smiling, he replied, "No, no nothing like that." The cheery mood of the crowd instantly dissipated. "We have decided to make some ruling changes in Zargarb. Two invasions, two sackings of our city in one lifetime is two too many. Our Prince has failed us twice. The much vaunted Centurions likewise. They are gone, and I hope they never return." Again, the crowd cheered, echoing his sentiments; Cecil felt that he was once more back on track with his speech.

"We nobles have decided that there are going to be some major changes in the way things are done around here. From now on, Zargarb is going to be run by the High Council of Thirteen, not by the Prince. We ten nobles are on the Council. The Prince and the Church of Tur each will hold another seat. Finally, one of the tradesmen, duly appointed by fellow tradesmen, will occupy the final seat. From now on, the Prince will have only one vote among the ruling council. And you tradesmen shall have an equal voice and vote as the Prince!" He had hoped that the crowd would yell and cheer over the proposed change in management, but they did not. However, a few "Yes!" comments did reach his ears, a hopeful sign.

He stood tall, took a deep breath, and prepared to deliver the all-important punch line that would ensure their total cooperation. "Citizens of Zargarb, we nobles have engineered a plan to stop any further sacking of our city in the future. Yes, we will *pay* for the complete rebuilding of our city. But most importantly, we are going to build a tall stone fortress wall entirely surrounding the city. Once the wall is built, Zargarb will never fall victim to any enemy army ever again! We will even pay to field our own, highly trained, well-equipped army as well. We nobles stand before you today and swear to you who have given so much that we shall not ever let Zargarb suffer the fate it had endured twice in one lifetime. Zargarb shall never be conquered ever again!" Here he raised his voice to a feverish pitch for added effect, just as he had rehearsed it a dozen times. After a bit of a pause as the importance of his pronouncement registered in the minds of his listeners, spontaneously a great roar of approval arose, one that was difficult to quell. No one made the slightest effort to halt it. Instead, the men proceeded to being unloading and other operations, a sign that the meeting was ended.

The Zargarb docks were equipped to unload/load ten ships simultaneously, assuming there were sufficient dockworkers present. At this time, many had fled, many had died, and the rest had been put to work on construction crews about the city. Hence, the critical shortage of hands made the work go more slowly. Five ships carried what the nobles thought would be critically needed food supplies. Enough hands were found to begin unloading three of these; the other two would have to wait. One had ferried the nobles and their guards. One crew was assigned to its unloading. However, the other five carried a number of other armed men part of the household guards and servants of the nobles. Ships carrying their families lay just off shore; they already knew that they would not be allowed to dock until these ten had finished. Beyond security, the primary reason for this delay, besides forcing the Prince to dock even later on in time, was the condition of their homes. None had the slightest doubt that their vast mansions had been thoroughly ransacked by the invaders. So the heads of these families wanted to first survey the situation and then arrange housing accordingly for their large extended families — a wise and safe precaution.

An hour after they docked, the hundred twenty-five guards had fanned out within the city, accompanying the nobles to check on their homes. They had been told to expect to have to perform extensive civilian control; on their arrival, the nobles fully expected a wild, chaotic, and unruly population. However, what they found was completely the opposite. In fact, the order was vastly superior to that at any time in the history of the city.

Their homes and estates, on the other hand, were just as they anticipated — a devastating mess; most were currently not livable with roofs missing or partially burned down. Footnote: the Sisterhood had given no consideration whatsoever to the rebuilding of these mansions, rather they concentrated everyone's efforts at rebuilding the homes in which the survivors lived. Within hours, the nobles were confiscating newly arrived timbers slated for the survivors' homes, rerouting it to theirs, under armed escorts, that is. Half of the guards found themselves helping to rebuild homes instead of patrolling the streets.

By evening, the High Council met in a makeshift room. Their first action was to round up those in their employ who had stayed behind to confiscate any and all abandoned weapons. They sent some of their guards out to locate them and bring any weapons back here. By morning, there was a huge pile of weapons, many in ill repair, with which to equip as many volunteers as possible. The next morning, their guards began going door to door in search of young men who would accept a bag of gold coins to join the Noble Reserves, an armed body of volunteers who would answer any High Council call to arms. So when the Prince finally landed two days after the nobles, already the High Council commanded and paraded on the docks fully five hundred armed men. They wanted the Prince to know from the first moment he set foot in Zargarb that the High Council now held all the power that he formerly held. They intended to drive home the point that it was futile to think otherwise.

During this first meeting, once some guards had left to find the confiscated weapons, the High Council sent for key tradesmen that they knew would be likely to go along with this sudden change in power. From these men, they intended to nominate one to hold the seat on the High Council. By seven pm, two dozen had arrived, though they had to sit on the floor, as there was a distinct lack of chairs. Cecil, as the elected head of the council, spoke first. "As you have heard, the High Council now wields complete power of rule in Zargarb. We have reserved one seat here for one of you tradesmen so that the views of the common worker can have an equal vote and say in the governing of our city. But before we get to that, can some of you answer our questions? What happened here? How did the battle go? How many of our citizens were killed? We could not help by notice the city is over half deserted. And how is it that you have recovered so quickly? We assumed that you would all be nearly at death's door by now, and hence, we felt we could delay our return no longer."

For a half hour, they heard grim tales of the attack on their city and its eventual capture and ransacking. The actual losses were not as great, for many families fled the city as soon as they could dodge the barbarians. All this they took in stride, as gruesome as it was, for this is what they had always anticipated and even predicted.

Alonso the blacksmith then changed the subject, remembering what Cecil had asked about earlier. "Aye, when the Galts finally left, we were starving; food had run out or been confiscated by the enemy. It was terrible. Just as all hope had faded, the Sisterhood arrived with wagons of food supplies and even healers! They were the ones that organized us and got the city back into operation. If it had not been for them, you would have likely landed in a ghost city, full of decaying corpses." Several other tradesmen elaborated on Alonso's words.

Meanwhile, no one really saw Cecil's face turn ashen. This was his worst nightmare, the damnable Sisterhood! None of the nobles foresaw this strange turn of events. All along, most had predicted that these women would have all been slain by the barbarians just as they had when the Centurion invasion came some thirty years before. Cecil's only regret was that they had not been completely and utterly annihilated back then. Now it seemed they hadn't perished but were just as strong as or stronger than before the invasion! In fact, everyone on the High Council knew that the only possible barrier to their taking and securing total governing control over Zargarb would be the Sisterhood. If the Prince somehow acquired their services in helping him regain control, their ill-trained, ill-equipped force would easily be wiped out. They would lose their bid for power and control. More than one noble's face turned ashen.

Finally, Cecil decided to call a short recess. He needed to discuss this horrible turn of events with the others on the council. "Very well done all of you. I am very proud of what you have accomplished. Let us take a short break. While we are gone, please discuss among yourselves who you wish to represent you and take your seat on the High Council. We'll be back in say a half hour." Hastily, all ten men rushed out of the room and headed to the basement, where they couldn't be overheard.

Just as soon as they got the oil lanterns going, Mel exclaimed. "The Sisterhood! We're doomed if the Prince gets word to them and has them come to his rescue. We cannot hope to fight them! What are we going to do? Is this the end?"

Another noble answered, "True, but as yet the Prince has not landed and hopefully knows nothing of our power grab. All we have to do is ensure that he cannot contact the Sisterhood."

"Yes, but my guards reported seeing a few Sisters at the northernmost plaza. We can't hope to block all the streets; we have too few men. Surely, the Prince will be able to slip a message to them!"

Thus the discussion went. Various suggestions were made on how to prevent the Prince from contacting the women. The best idea was to surround the women with their guards, who would decide who could pass by them to the Sisters, but that could only be a very short-term answer; the Sisterhood would not take long to react to such a move. Besides, that would surely tip them off — that something vital was happening. Every noble knew instinctively that very little that went on politically ever escaped the notice of the Sisterhood. They swore that this group had spying eyes everywhere. Yet, these same noblemen depended utterly on the Sisterhood fighters to protect their vital caravans and convoys and would need them now more than ever with the escalated bandit problem.

Cecil pointed out, "Look this is a very touchy subject. We can't afford to get on the wrong side of the Sisterhood. If we do, they'll hit us where it hurts the most, our money pouches. Still, we can't let the Prince make any kind of deal with them or we *are* doomed." A half hour passed with no real resolution of their monumental problem. In the end, they agreed to sleep on the problem and to meet first thing in the morning. They still had at least another twenty-four hours before the Prince would dock.

They rejoined the tradesmen. Cecil asked, "Gentlemen, have you decided who should take the tradesman seat on the High Council?" This would be the easiest item of business with which to dispense.

"Yes, we have, sir, rather in a way we have," Alonso the blacksmith spoke for the group. "We all agree on our choice."

"Great, let's have it. Which of you will it be?" Cecil said, all smiles, looking from face to face. These were all men that he had dealings with in the past. He knew each man well. He was comfortable with any of them sitting beside him on the High Council.

"Sir, we all agree. Our position on the new High Council should be held by one from the Sisterhood." Cecil choked, his face paled noticeably. Many others coughed as well. No one could have ever in their wildest imaginations predicted this turn of events! Alonso took the coughs to mean that the nobles did not approve of their choice, so he quickly began explaining their decision. "Sirs, you have to understand what has happened here while you were gone. When the barbarians left, we, to the last family, we were slowly dying. No food anywhere. Out of the blue, here come the Sisters with food, healers, and other folks to aid us. It was the Sister Fiona, I think she is called, that got us all organized. She got us back on our feet. They helped us with everything, even patrolling the streets. Incidentally, there hasn't been a reported crime since the sisters came. Do you know what they charged us for their selfless assistance?" He did not wait for anyone to reply. "Nothing. Not a single coin! She said that we're all in this together — that if we don't make it, they wouldn't be able to survive here either and would leave Zargarb for good. All of us, every last man, woman, and child that is in Zargarb and all of the outlying towns and villages — every one of us owes our very lives to these women. We are unanimous in our decision. We all think that the time has come for the Sisterhood to have a say in what goes on in our city. We know that they will properly represent us, probably far better than any one of us could. Please accept our decision." He sat back down on the dirt floor, as his fellow tradesmen all called out their total agreement with what he had to say.

Alonso fully expected that Cecil, who now rose, would veto their nomination, offering countless reasons why it was not possible. Some of the tradesmen had heard rumors that the Sisterhood had killed one of his youthful sons many years ago. He figured there was no love between Cecil and the Sisterhood. However, Cecil did not become the wealthiest man in Zargarb by being slow-witted. All the while the blacksmith was pleading his case, his mind raced down the possibilities. True, he hated these abominations, a word he carefully avoided saying in public anymore; the repercussions from the Centurions disabused him of that. Yet, the inkling of a plan began to grow in his mind.

He said, "Alonso, my beloved tradesmen one and all, I think that your generosity toward these women is most commendable, most honorable. Long have these women aided us, even at the risk of their own lives. You have my *full* support and that of the High Council in your request. Please go contact them and let them know about this. Request that they send their representative here just as soon as feasible. Tell them that their representative to the High Council will be *welcomed* with open arms." He specifically avoided saying "with open hearts," for that would have been an outright lie that even he could not stomach saying.

Half of the other nobles immediately saw precisely what Cecil had reasoned out; the other half sat silent with open jaws, completely bewildered. All knew of Cecil's intense hatred of these women, though few shared his hate. This half had not yet seen the wisdom of the move. Quickly the tradesmen left, and some went to carry out his orders. Most headed home; it was getting late, and they would have to be at work early in the morning. Once the tradesmen had gone, Cecil gaily poured everyone a glass of fine wine brought ashore from his ship. "Gentlemen, our problem is solved!" Seeing the baffled looks on many faces, he elaborated, "With the Sisterhood holding a voting seat on the ruling High Council, do you think they will give that up to help return the Prince to power? Not for all the gold the Prince still has will they give up this chance for a bit of power. Mark my words, the Sisterhood will join with us. The Prince problem is totally handled! Let us toast our *total* victory, gentlemen!" Ten glasses clicked together. Some even commented aside to Cecil, "Brilliant, absolutely brilliant!" He felt relieved and happier than he had since he set foot on land.

The next morning, while Fiona was making her full report to Sister Aminia, one of the messengers she had left in Zargarb came dashing into the house, claiming, "I've got an urgent message for Sister Aminia! I've got to see her at once!" She was ushered into the front room. From her disheveled appearance, both women assumed that she had been riding all night to get here.

"Calm down Sister," Fiona said. "I just left there yesterday. What could possibly have happened in so short a time that is this urgent?"

"You won't believe this!" she exclaimed still out of breath and highly animated. She did not attempt to control her emotions.

"Okay, sit down. Tell us all about it from the beginning, dear," the soothing voice of Aminia had its impact.

"The nobles have overthrown the Prince! Yes, it's true. They have formed a High Council of thirteen members who will now rule Zargarb. There are to be ten seats held by the nobles, one for the Prince, one for the Church of Tur, and one for the tradesmen. The Prince doesn't know this has happened yet though. His ship is still awaiting a chance to dock, maybe as soon as tonight. The High Council has said that they don't want to see the city invaded and sacked ever again and promised to build a high stone wall entirely around the city and even form an army to man the walls!"

"Well, this is indeed interesting news," Sister Aminia interrupted. "So they finally came to their senses and ousted the Prince. Well, the timing is right for that, if ever it was. The Centurions are dead or gone. I am not surprised. The nobles, though they managed to save their valuables, nevertheless, they have lost a great deal, especially where it hurts them the most, their pocketbooks. It will cost them dearly to get the city restored. Imagine that, a stone wall around the city! That will cost them a pretty coin! Yes, this is indeed interesting news you bring us. Thank you, Sister."

"But that's not all, Sister Aminia. Here's the best part. Last night, the tradesmen were asked to choose whom they wished to hold their voting seat on the High Council of Thirteen. They insisted that someone from the Sisterhood hold their seat for them!"

Aminia gasped, flushed, and fainted. She would have hit the floor hard had not Fiona reacted instantly and broken her fall. "Water, get some water in here fast!" she barked out orders left and right. Aminia's aides rushed in with a glass, blankets, and fussed over her. By the time a healer arrived, Sister Aminia had awakened and was placed on her bed. "Oh, I'm all right," she protested, testing her limbs hesitantly. Once the healer was satisfied, she said to the messenger, "You are sure you have the message correct? They want us to represent us and them on this new High Council?"

"I'm so sorry, Sister Aminia, I didn't want to cause you harm," the messenger apologized, tears running down her cheeks.

"You didn't hurt me. I was just a little shocked, that's all," she replied. "No, make that completely and utterly startled!" she added with a little chuckle. "Please, can you repeat the entire message for me? I'll stay here on my bed so I won't fall this time," she added for Fiona's benefit.

Dutifully, though more hesitantly, the young woman told her everything that the three tradesmen had told her last night, leaving out nothing. "They said voting member? Equal voting member? Equal to one of the nobles or the Prince?" Aminia asked.

"Absolutely!" the woman replied eagerly.

"Suspect diabolical treachery!" Fiona offered at once. "Do not trust them. You know we can't trust men, especially wealthy men."

"And you say that the tradesmen said that Cecil actually said that the tradesmen had his personal full support in their decision?" Sister Aminia asked, still not believing it.

"He must have some dirty scheme going on under the table. You know how he hates the Sisterhood!" Fiona added. "There must be far more going on than meets the eye."

Sister Aminia was silent for several minutes, then she began to cry, "Do you realize what this means? How momentous this turn of events actually is for us? For the first time in history, the women of Zargarb have a say in the governing of our sector! This is unprecedented! I never in my wildest dreams did I think that anything remotely like this would ever happen, ever! One vote in thirteen, yes, we may always be out-voted; there are ten nobles, but even to have the chance to be heard and actually to have a vote, this is just too incredible to believe."

"Suspect treachery at every step," cautioned Fiona, who still did not trust them, though to have a say would be such a tremendously positive step forward, she was having a hard time retaining her skepticism.

"I know," the messenger said, "and they want our representative to get there and take her seat just as soon as possible."

"Probably because the Prince has not landed and discovered that he has been kicked out of power," Fiona surmised. "They need our support against the Prince, I'll bet anything on that. If we backed the Prince with our fighters, we could overthrow all of their wormy guards."

"Send for Alicia, she is the best one of us to adjudicate the motivations of men," Sister Aminia ordered. "Let's get her opinion. I do see what you are suggesting, Fiona, and I am inclined to agree with you." One of her aides ran out to find Fiona's aide. When she returned, Aminia had the messenger relay the entire message for Alicia's benefit. Next, both women shared their concerns with Alicia and asked her opinion.

"First, this is just fantastic, almost too good to be true. However, I am inclined to go with Fiona. We ought not trust men, until they prove they are worthy of that trust. For Cecil to have said what he apparently has said, supporting us to have a voting seat, there must be some other overpowering reason. He, of all the heads of the noble families, hates us the most. We lack knowledge and information about what is really going on behind the visible scene. I don't think that we have the time to try to find out either. We are going to have to make educated guesses. We can always refine our conclusions later on, when we do manage to find out more," Alicia concluded.

"They've been gone for months. We have no way of knowing what all they have done or decided during that time. Either the Prince already knows about the power change or he does not. I don't think the Church of Tur matters much anymore," she argued her thoughts out loud. The others listened intently to her every word.

"We have to go at this in reverse, lacking any data. If Cecil is supporting a Sister to be a voting member of the High Council, this certainly means that this is a solution to such a huge problem that the solution far outweighs his hatred for us."

"Yes, that would seem reasonable," Aminia commented.

"What is that problem that our presence on the Council solves? That is what we must discover. Now it has to be their problem, not ours. From their point of view, what does the Sisterhood offer that they do not have? The only thing we have ever offered are superior fighters. So this problem he has must involve our fighting strength. By now, he certainly must know that the invasion has not wiped out the Sisterhood, as it did when the Centurions came. He knows we are still powerful. That would seem a reasonable assumption," Alicia continued thinking aloud.

"It would appear he needs our fighters or the potential to call upon our fighters as needed without having to pay for our services. We must ask ourselves, why would he need our fighters at this point in time? The Galts have gone and will not likely return to Zargarb; they've already ransacked it of every valuable item. It could be that the nobles are worried that they will return and try to rob them. If I were in their position, I would not really bring back to

Zargarb all my wealth just yet, not until this new protective wall was built and manned. It's not too likely that we are supposed to protect their wealth. That can't be it. No, the problem that we solve for him must be a far greater one."

"Yes, but what?" Fiona interjected impatiently. She was a woman of action, not of this deep thought.

"What else would he need our fighters for right now? We left the city secure, so it can't be to provide security. It doesn't need it right now. I can't see anarchy breaking out in the streets overnight once we left. They were doing well working together to survive while you were running things, Fiona. That can't be it either. Why does he so desperately need our fighters? You know, the only other thing I can think of is this. What if the Prince doesn't know about this power grab? Suppose the Prince lands and finds out his power has been usurped by these noblemen. If you were the Prince, wouldn't you want to offer some resistance to this and try to regain your power position by getting rid of these nobles? I certainly would, but the nobles are now well organized and have quite a fair number of guards in their pay. The Prince likely only has his personal guards, insufficient to deal with the nobles. I think this line is leading somewhere. What if the Prince came to us and asked us to help him regain his power, his throne, so to speak, by offering us a small fortune? If we have no allegiances, might not we accept his offer? We certainly could use several thousand gold coins. Fiona, your small band could easily take out all the noble's new forces and quite rapidly for that matter."

"I think you have it!" Fiona exclaimed. "The Prince buys our services, and there goes the entire rebellion down the drain! That has to be Cecil's greatest fear, losing this bid for power!"

"Well, I can see no other reasonable explanation for his conduct," Alicia commented.

"As always, Alicia, your mind is a marvel to behold!" Sister Aminia praised her. "You have undoubtedly got it right. It seems so completely real and so simple that I wonder now why I didn't see it right away! You are a dream, Alicia. Thank you!" Alicia smiled; this was not the first time she had used her brilliant mind to unravel the sometimes mysterious conduct of men.

"With these assumptions, I can now make an educated decision on this matter," Aminia said. "Do we reject this offer and accept the Prince's offer, when it comes, to help put the Prince back into power or do we accept the offer and become a voting member of the new ruling body? The choice is plainly obvious. We gain nothing by helping the Prince. With Cecil's offer, we at least have some chance for betterment of conditions in all Zargarb. We accept this offer to be the tradesmen's representative on the new High Council. That is my decision. However, we'll spend a great deal of our resources on searching out the hidden agendas behind the nobles decisions. I'll not trust them just yet, Fiona. I share your skepticism. So having made that decision, it only remains to choose who we send to hold that position."

"If I sent you, Fiona, I would love to see Cecil's countenance when you sit beside him! That would surely be most interesting to behold! But I cannot hold petty grudges nor can I spare you from your duties as Fighter Group Leader, not until Rosalita can return to active duty. We must send someone else."

"Okay, I volunteer," Alicia said with a smile. "Who else is more qualified?"

"Thank you. I accept. However, I'll send a couple of fighters to be your constant bodyguards. I don't trust these men. Promise me that you'll never go anywhere without their presence?" Sister Aminia insisted. Alicia did so. "Go now and get packed. Take what funds you think you will need. We can send more as you need them. As I understand the message, the sooner you can arrive and accept the post, the better. This will be especially critical if the situation is as you have deduced — the Prince knows nothing of all this. Promise me that you'll be extra careful. I don't want anything bad to happen to you, Alicia." She promised and hastened to gather up her things. Within the hour, she was riding back to Zargarb along with the messenger.

However, many other messengers were dispatched, spreading this incredible news to all the sisters who were not here at the ranch, particularly Rosalita, Sandy, and Simon, who were at North Point. This was indeed an historic day for the Sisterhood. Aminia also sent dispatch riders to the other seven Sisterhoods. She wondered how the other Sisterhoods would take this monumental news. Aminia could also not help but wonder if a rebellion was in the offing for the other sectors. She had much to ponder that evening when she finally went to bed.

Alicia arrived in Zargarb late in the day and immediately checked in with the small group of Sisters who had remained in the city. They were staying in a shell of a building whose roof had been destroyed at the onset of the assault of the city. Here, seven patients were being watched over by the two healing women. "Are we accepting?" several asked the instant she dismounted.

Grinning from ear to ear, Alicia acknowledged, "You bet! I'm the representative. But I must first meet with those that have asked us to represent them. We have one final detail to be verified. Is there any way we can meet with them yet tonight?"

An hour later, the messenger sisters had rounded up ten of the tradesmen and brought them there to the northern edge of town. Alicia began her first brief meeting by saying, "On behalf of the entire Sisterhood, we thank you for your generosity and kindness. It is a bit overwhelming and so sudden. Before we can accept, or rather, I can accept this position, I feel that we must understand something up front. My allegiance lies with the Sisterhood. If ever there is a conflict while representing you, I will have no choice but to side with the Sisterhood. Is that acceptable to you?" This really was the key question as far as Alicia was concerned. If she represented them and the Sisterhood by default, then this could be the only source of problems in the arrangement.

Alonso the blacksmith, who still acted as spokesman for the group, said, "Aye, we can accept that. Honestly, if ever there is a difference of opinion between you folks and us, it is us that are probably wrong." Alicia's mouth dropped. Never had she heard a man in the Sea Princes ever defer to a woman; it was unheard of!

After a moment to regain her composure, she said, "Well, then that's settled. The Sisterhood accepts your generous offer, and I, as the representative, will do my very best at all times to represent our interests on the High Council. Now then, if I am to do this, I must know what your interests and such actually are. You must realize that as an outcast woman, so to speak, I have very little knowledge of just what your concerns are."

Several men chuckled. Alonso interrupted her, "Sister, you are teasing us, right. Some of us swear that you know more about our needs than we do!" Several men laughed openly. Alicia blushed, slightly embarrassed.

"Nevertheless, as your representative, I need your input and will need to come back and ask you your opinions on matters that are raised at the Council. We need to organize. Every tradesman in the land must know who his direct representative is so that he can take his concerns, problems, and such to them and ultimately to me. I would like to have you form up a first line group of representatives, one from each of the trades. These I will directly keep informed and often ask their opinions on matters. Each of these can then have as many beneath them that they choose. All I ask is that the simple tinsmith in a shop on Tin Alley knows to whom he can go to ask for help, seek information, plead his case and such, and have his needs ultimately reach my ears."

"Aye, now that would be a first!" Alonso commented. "Imagine that, old Petro can complain to one of us, and his complaint can actually eventually be heard by those that govern us. How utterly extraordinary! This won't be hard to sell to any of us!" All of the men laughed at this understatement.

"Don't get your hopes up too high," Alicia caught their meaning at once. "I have only one vote and that will probably be against the ten nobles. We are rather outnumbered, but at least for the first time those controlling the real power will hear of the ordinary citizen's problems. That's a good start, I think."

They laughed again, with Alonso adding, "We certainly thought so. We understand each other perfectly. It'll probably take a while to get all organized as you want, but we'll get on it. I'm sure that you ought to visit Cecil tomorrow in the morning. He seemed terribly concerned to get a Sisterhood representative on the council just as fast as possible. Maybe they already have made some more big plans. We don't know."

"Thanks for coming on such short notice. I'll check in with him first thing in the morning." The men headed for their homes, while the other Sisters, who had been standing in the corner, came up to her, hugged her, and patted her on the back. None of them could believe their incredible luck. The Sisterhood was actually being recognized as a power in their society!

At noon, Alicia stood tall and proud, the lone woman among the eleven High Council members lined up formally on the docks to welcome the arrival of the Prince and the High Priest of Tur. As she waited and watched the two ships moving slowly toward them, her mind reviewed her first meeting with these men earlier that morning. Yes, they were courteous to her, even thanking her on behalf of the Sisterhood for all that they had done to save the citizens of the entire sector. She felt certain that their gratefulness on this topic was indeed genuine. However, she also detected unseen daggers in their words spoken through smiling lips. It was clear to her that they both despised the Sisterhood and yet respected them as the best fighting force around, even if their numbers were small. Their mixed emotions and feelings were difficult to separate. Alicia knew that she would need to draw on all her skills when dealing with these men, in order to separate fact from fiction, truth from deceit. *Intrigue, that is what this will be about!* She suddenly realized just what the game was that she had now begun to play. A smile appeared on her lips.

The tow lines flew up and out in graceful arcs, caught skillfully by dockhands, who pulled and tied the ships securely to the wooden posts. The Prince, dressed in his finest clothes, with bands of yellow and red, faced the High Priest, who stood opposite him on the other ship. He looked small and pudgy in comparison; his ruddy face stood out in stark contrast to his royal purple robes of office. They nodded to each other and ceremoniously disembarked together. Ever since the founding of Zargarb hundreds of years ago, members of these two families had shared the ruling power over the sector. Alicia wondered if either knew about what was just about to happen when they met the nobles, only to find they were now the High Council. Did either of them have advanced knowledge? If not, what would be their reactions? She watched with a very keen eye and great interest.

The two men walked stately, side by side up to the line of the eleven. "Greetings, Cecil," the Prince said, but nodded to the others. He completely ignored the presence of Alicia. The High Priest mumbled some words, which Alicia could not hear, but shook each noble's hand in turn, though likewise ignoring Alicia.

Cecil, the duly appointed spokesperson for the High Council, broke the news to the two men. "Greetings Prince, Your Eminence. We must have a word immediately. Both of you have been stripped of your power. Zargarb is now ruled by the High Council of Thirteen. Each of you has a seat, as do we eleven you see before you. Thirteen was chosen so that there could never be a tie vote on any matter. Majority rules from now on. Sister Alicia, who you will treat as your equal, is the duly elected representative of all the tradesmen — elected by the tradesmen personally, I might add. We assume that she will also be representing the Sisterhood as well. How could she not? From some days ago onward, Zargarb is ruled by this High Council. All votes are equal. Any questions?"

Cecil delivered his speech in a most serious tone. For him, though this day was an immense victory, not only himself, but all of the wealthy nobles of Zargarb, he dare not show self-satisfaction, not just yet. Yes, he believed that he had thought of every possible eventuality and had taken preventative measures so that nothing could go wrong. Yet, the nomination of Alicia had taken him completely off-guard. That the Sisterhood would have a representative on the High Council had never entered his calculations. Cecil was a careful, methodical man; if he had missed that detail, undoubtedly he had not foreseen others. Besides, there would be nothing to gain by immediately making an enemy out of the Prince by gloating and insulting him. Better to show no emotion and present the situation solemnly.

Alicia watched the facial expressions of both men intensely as they received the news. The High Priest's body sagged, as if some great weight had been lifted from his shoulders. She felt certain that meant the High Priest was greatly relieved no longer to have so much responsibility; he would gladly accept the High Council. The Prince was another matter. She saw several nervous twitches in his jaw. His arms tensed, though he tried not to show it. He stared long at Cecil before he spoke and when he did, it was through clenched teeth. "My great-great grandfather built this city with his own sweat and blood; he gave it life. Today, you have given us the saddest day in all our history, Cecil. You may yet live to regret what you have done here today, Cecil." He paused to let his veiled threat affect the eleven before him.

Interestingly, his fiery eyes slowly went down the line of the nobles, facing and confronting each in turn. However, when he reached Alicia, his countenance changed into a smile, and he reached out his hand to her and said, "Greetings Sister. Forgive my neglecting your presence." He bowed as if she were a noble woman, which she was anything but.

He then said, "I see you have a well-armed force already to back up your actions. So be it. As you know, I sacrificed my entire army, save a few guards, in the defense of the city. At this *time,* I cannot resist your actions." he placed particular emphasis on that word, then went on with a condescending nod, "So be it. When does the Council meet and where? Will I be informed so that I may attend?"

He's taking this rather grandly, thought Cecil. "You are not stripped of all power, Prince; you are just sharing ultimate power and authority with twelve others now. Yes, your vote counts. We will meet say tomorrow noon for a working lunch meeting. I want to give you some time to attend to your affairs. Our homes are in complete shambles. Your palace, likewise. We all have much work to do. Just so you know, it was the Sisterhood who selfishly came to the rescue of our citizens, saving their lives. Because of them, we do have a relatively acceptable place we can meet at Antonio's Diner on Water Street. It has been mostly repaired and is operational. It will do until better arrangements can be made. See you two at noon tomorrow then. In the meantime, as you view the destruction, do not be so disheartened. Everything can be rebuilt, given time. After all, we have all saved our fortunes."

The men bowed to each other; Alicia nodded respectfully. The High Priest actually said thank you repeatedly to the eleven as he moved on by, heading for what was left of his church estate. Alicia felt a little sad for the priest, because she had seen what was left of the largest Church of Tur in

Zargarb. The poor man would be in for quite a shock; so would the Prince, for that matter.

When the two men, their few guards, and adepts were out of earshot, one council member who Alicia could not see commented, "He took that rather well, don't you think?" Another asked, "Do you think he already knew what we were going to do?" More critically, from her point of view, another's comment was far more astute, "What does he mean by 'at this time I cannot resist your actions?' Do you suppose he will be seeking revenge on us?" Alicia detected a trace of fear in the man's voice.

Cecil just said, "Don't worry. The Prince sees that any resistance is futile, that we have the upper hand, and that we control enough fighters to enforce our will if he resisted." His steadfast comments reassured all the men, save one. Words alone cannot supplant fear in one's mind.

During the next two weeks, the High Council met every day at noon. Most matters were routine, such as details on the reconstruction of the city, re-establishing trade, the urgency of acquiring as much grain from the Greenway as possible and so on. During the second week, Alicia was approached by her tradesmen, who gave her their first matter for her to bring before the Council. Since so many of the tradesmen and their families now believed in this new religion, Jehosanity with their Great Messiah who had died and been resurrected to save everyone, Bandar wanted permission to build a large Church of Jehosanity at the northern edge of the city where the destruction of buildings had been the severest. Of course, there was much discussion and protests from the High Priest of Tur, but the nobles saw little advantage in alienating their skilled workers so soon. The vote was twelve to one in favor. Thus, in the early fall construction on the first large Church of Jehosanity in Zargarb began, the first of many such churches.

Footnote: the mariners were unshakeable in their faith in Tur, but the landlubbers now favored the new religion. It offered one thing that belief in Tur did not: sinners would go to Lucifer's realm now called Hell. The average person who had survived the Galt invasion took some comfort in believing that these barbarians would be going to this Hell when they finally died. It had an emotional appeal to the citizens of Zargarb, just as Bandar desired.

After the hectic first two weeks, the High Council decided to take a week's break so that everyone could put their full attention on their own personal matters. Alicia took this time to return to the ranch and brief Sister Aminia on all the events. Because Alicia had a few days to spare before the next meeting, Aminia had Simon come down from North Point so that they could get his opinion on these breathtaking events. They talked together for an entire afternoon. However, one thing still bothered Alicia greatly. "Simon, try as I might, I cannot get the Prince's initial words out of my mind. He said, 'At this *time* I cannot resist your actions," with special emphasis on 'time.' Ever since I heard that, it has troubled me. Always at the meetings, he sits back as if he is more of a spectator than a participant, as if he is somehow aloof from it all. Any ideas? What can he do now?"

Simon thought a moment, "You know, I think you have put your finger on the crux of the matter. What can he do about it? Well, he was in the good graces at the very least with the occupying Centurions. One option he might be contemplating is forming some kind of agreement with them to have a number of Centurion legions come back and retake the city from you. Another option that I can see is that he might be requesting forces from the other Sea Princes, asking them to come and rescue him from the mess in which he finds himself. If he is going to undo what's been done, he must do it by bringing in a force strong enough to defeat the new garrisons that the High Council has created."

"That's what has been scaring me!" Alicia exclaimed, relief flooding across her face. She hated herself when she knew that she ought to be able to identify the source of an ill feeling but could not. "I knew that there was something I was overlooking. That's it. What if the Prince calls upon the other six for help? What if one morning we awake to find dozens of ships have landed bearing a small army from the other sectors? We could be wiped out in a very brief fight and lose everything. I just knew that I felt uneasy about something. Thank you Simon! Do you ever have the feeling that something is amiss and just cannot figure out what?"

He chuckled, "All the time! But you can take steps to avoid such catastrophes. Let's look at each situation, because they have different considerations and likelihoods. First, with the Centurions coming to aid the Prince: the Centurions are in a very weak position, ever since they lost the vast majority of their crack assault troops to the plague in Velona. They've tried to get by using their older Rear Guard troops, who have not thus far been truly able to defend any position. We know that they have siphoned off much of their strength to help defend southern Juda Arad. From all reports, the vast majority of their forces were eliminated last year. Unless they can magically rebuild a new and mobile army, I believe the likelihood that they would openly send significant troops up here to Zargarb is not great. To be honest, I think that they are plenty worried that the Galts will head south into their heartland."

"Well," Alicia replied, "we can set up some outposts to watch the paved roadway leading here from Al Barq. If they do come overland, we would have probably a week's warning. They would be foolish indeed to send what few troops they still have, who are guarding the other major Sea Prince cities. Sisters in other sectors have been reporting on their movements, or lack thereof. If the came by ship, we ought to again have sufficient advanced warning. What about getting other Princes to aid them?"

"Solamina is under siege now, so they won't come from there," Simon observed. "The possibility exists that Velona, which most certainly will not be attacked this year, could send some troops to help the Prince regain control. However, we have going for us the fact that each Sea Prince seems to be independent of the other. From all that I know, they have never really cooperated with each other, but then again, never has one of their princes been usurped. Again, I would have your fellow Sisters in the other sectors keep an eye on any large movement of forces by sea. They could only get here by sailing; overland, they would run into the invasion forces from the Northern Steppes, which I am certain they would never want to do. I guess I'm wondering just how much they will feel threatened themselves by the overthrowing of your Prince. Incidentally, Solamina stands a good change of also becoming free of their Prince's control. Because they were attacked before the Zargarb High Council formally rebelled, why there is a good chance that the Prince there knows nothing of it. The real question that I would like to know the answer to is this: are the nobles of Zargarb in communication with the other nobles in the other sectors? Are they all planning similar overthrows or is Zargarb the exception? I suppose you could ask Cecil, but I would be completely surprised if he answered you truthfully."

She laughed, "Cecil wouldn't; he can barely tolerate my presence, if the truth were told. He puts up a good, amenable facade though. You know, I think that as time goes on and we see what happens in the other sectors, we can answer that question. Once the Galts have left, if all the sectors overthrow their Prince as we have done, surely the nobles of all sectors have been in on the planning. If it is just us and perhaps Solamina, then the nobles probably aren't working together on some grand plan. Makes sense, but I still don't trust our Prince at all. He sits there quietly during the council meetings, as if he is just biding his time."

"What about poisoning the Council?" asked Fiona, who had been seriously contemplating actions that the Prince might take. "He could try to poison all of you."

Simon answered, "Yes that is a possibility. He also might try to make a pact with all the roving bands of bandits and use them to try to retake his seat of power."

"You're right. I hadn't thought of the bandits as being a viable force, but for the right money, I'm sure they'd do just about anything," Fiona replied. Alicia looked crestfallen; here was yet another worry.

"Poison wouldn't accomplish his ultimate objective of getting his throne back," Simon pointed out thoughtfully. His mind was racing down avenues that the bandits might follow. "Poison might be his last attempt at revenge, when all else failed. Perhaps the wise counter would be never to drink or eat anything that you have not brought personally to the meetings. But the bandits, yes, they could be a problem. Because they are so scattered and diffuse, it will be hard to keep an eye on them, besides they'll not take kindly to being spied upon continuously. How about this: have sufficient sisters on watch say within thirty miles of the city reporting on any large-scale moment of bandits toward the city. Might only give you a day's warning, though, and you would have to have a pretty tight net for them not to sneak past you during the night."

Alicia commented, "Well, of all these, the bandits secretly joining forces with the Prince will be the most difficult for us to guard against I think."

"Yes, indeed," Fiona added still thinking the situation over in her mind.

"Ah ha!" she exclaimed a minute later, "Why not quickly present a motion before the Council to get the banditry situation under more control, that is, wipe them out or something like that, you know, eliminate their numbers by some kind of coordinated action?"

Alicia chuckled again, "It would not take much to convince the nobles they have become a major problem to all convoys and caravans! If we act fact, we might be able to curtail them and lessen their potential threat besides making the paths safe for commerce. They will certainly buy into that idea. I'll do it at the next meeting." After further discussions, all were satisfied and went their ways, Simon returned to North Point; Alicia, to Zargarb.

By the time of the next High Council meeting, Galt wagons loaded with the spoils of war in Solamina began snaking their way eastward across the Zagarb Sector. At first, a few bandits attempted to waylay some, but were soundly defeated by the small garrisons that accompanied them. After that, large guarding forces accompanied all wagons trains heading across the sector to the Northern Steppes.

The Council authorized, with a sufficient monetary contribution, of course, the Sisterhood to take an active role in suppressing banditry. Further, they also sent out their first Combat Regiment of newly trained soldiers to also harry the bandit gangs. Pressed on three fronts, many bandits simply deserted and rejoined the population of nearby towns and villages. Thus, by late fall, Alicia could discount bandits as being a viable force for the Prince to somehow use against them.

Solamina fell that fall as well. When the barbarians finally left the sacked town, once again, the Sisterhood took an active role in re-establishing law and order. However, so close to winter, the situation was far more desperate than it had been in Zargarb. This time, the nobles of Solamina returned fairly soon, bringing much needed food supplies. Yet, it was a very austere nine months for that large city. As in Zargarb, the nobles also overthrew their Prince in an almost mirror manner. A somewhat smaller city, the High Council only had eleven members, eight nobles, the Prince, the Church of Tur, and a Sisterhood representative. The nobles from the very announcement of their takeover of power had included the Sisterhood. Thus, Alicia was completely convinced that the nobles of these two sectors had been working very closely together. Having the Sisterhood on the council allowed the nobles to keep a closer eye on their activities and denied the Prince any opportunity to rally the Sisterhood to come to his defense and help him put down the rebellion.

All that winter, Alicia pondered what would happen next spring with the other sectors. Certainly, every other sector now knew of the change of power in Zargarb and Solamina. Even a blind man would be on his guard; the other Princes would certainly take steps to prevent their nobles from overthrowing them. She mused and wondered herself to sleep many nights. For her and her sharp mind, these were exciting times in which to live.

Chapter 25 The Murders

Bandar Dero, head of the Church of Jehosanity in the Zargarb Sector, quietly rode up to Ranchero Paladina, the main headquarters of the Sisterhood in this sector. It was June 587 AH. Pieta had fallen, but that concerned him little. No, he had a much larger problem on his hands and no way to solve it. Although the sisters guarding the entrance of the wooden pole wall recognized him, one asked him what he wanted. "I desperately need to see Sister Aminia Sciota, please. It is a matter of life and death." He added that last to help ensure that she would see him. He really did not understand these women still, but he just knew that he had to see her.

"You look well," Sister Aminia welcomed him into her large living room, filled with numerous scrolls, which tracked all their advanced planning. "She said it was a matter of life and death. Come sit down." As always, she had a way of disarming everyone, making them feel right at home, and completely comfortable talking to her. She smiled as he obeyed; she had not lost her touch.

He managed a flicker of a smile as he sat down across from her. "Now then, what is troubling you, Reverend Bandar?" she asked.

After a deep sigh and mentally composing himself, he began, "I have a grave problem and I don't know where else to turn." She gave him a nod to continue; he said, "It's murder, plain and simple murder. Someone unknown is murdering members of the Church of Jehosanity in Zargarb." The tenseness in his body subsided as he finally uttered the pronouncement, the only real conclusion he had been able to make in the matter. She turned up her eyebrows; murder was nothing foreign to her; she had lived through just such a time in her youth when women of Zargarb were maimed or killed just for speaking to men without their consent, but that was so long ago.

She finished his sentence for him, "And you would like us to help you find those responsible?"

"Aye, madam, if that is at all possible. I'm at my wit's end. People are even afraid to come to church on Saturdays. No longer do they talk openly of Jehosanity. I believe that at least one hundred followers have died thus far; it might be more. Some family members are probably denying that their deceased member had gone to our church out of fear they would be killed next. I tried to bring it to the High Council, but they have done effectively nothing. In desperation, I thought of the Sisterhood. Perhaps this isn't something in which you would want to become involved. If so, I can understand." He wanted to give her a gracious way to refuse him and not lose face. After all the assistance that the Sisterhood had been to his church, he felt it was the least he could do.

"This is serious indeed. Personally, I'm no good at mysteries, Reverend, but I do know someone who is superb at solving puzzles. Let me send for her, one minute, please." She excused herself and went into another room to have a word with one of her aides. She returned a few minutes later, sitting back down across from him.

"You are in luck. Group Leader Fiona has only just returned from a mission, and she will join us presently after she has washed the trail dust off. Meanwhile, let me tell you a bit about Sister Calli — or rather prepare you. Calli has only been with us for about two years now. She was very badly treated by her boyfriend and his gang. Emotionally, she bears the scars, though she is physically healed. She still lives in terror of men; she will appear very shy and reserved in your presence. Do not let her demeanor fool you. Calli has one of the sharpest minds I've known. If anyone can get to the bottom of this mystery it is Calli. But I will have to have Fiona accompany her everywhere she goes for her own safety, mentally as well as physically. She trusts Fiona more than any other Sister." Just then, the door opened, and Fiona ushered in a shy young woman in her mid-twenties.

Calli was a thin woman, perhaps five-five and one hundred twenty pounds. Her face was ashen white, indicative of her terror at having to meet with a man. Her blonde hair was quite curly and cut short like many of the sisters. She had full lips and breasts; the latter had gotten her into trouble with her boyfriend. Although she stared down at the floor as she meekly was led to a seat on the other side from Bandar, her eyes darted about the room, occasionally observing the Reverend. Although terrified, her mind missed nothing.

"Thank you both for coming," Sister Aminia began, "This is Reverend Bandar Dero, head of the Church of Jehosanity in our sector and leader of the church in Zargarb proper." To Bandar, she said, "Sister Fiona, you already know. This is our greatest mystery solver, Sister Calli." Calli felt obligated at least to glance at him; a flicker of a smile crossed her face for an instant before resuming her no emotion appearance.

"Reverend Bandar has a very serious problem or mystery that I believe you, Calli, might be able to solve. Left unsolved, Calli, this problem will seriously impact even our Sisterhood, for I do believe at least half of us now believe in Jehosanity." She said the magic word: mystery. Ever since she was a little girl, mysteries intrigued her. She grew up solving mystery after mystery. No matter what else was happening around her, she always became totally absorbed in solving a mystery. Bandar watch her deep blue eyes suddenly sparkle, as if a light had suddenly turned on in her mind. "I'll let Bandar explain."

"Yes, well for some months now, members of my church have been mysteriously turned up dead. I estimate well over a hundred have been slain. I know that there is crime in any large city. But out right murders?"

Calli interrupted him with a drilling question, "How many murders have there been in the city during the time those victims were *not* known followers of Jehosanity?"

He thought for a moment, "Two that I am aware of, but there could be a few more. I was not watching closely until this past month."

"Then, it is a safe assumption that the perpetrators are indeed, as you say, going after your followers. You are from the Arad, are you not?" He nodded. "And I assume that those who were murdered were also from the Arad?"

"No, that is just it! Well, one was, but all the others were converts from the city, former followers of Tur, I believe."

"Now that is interesting and suggestive," Calli mused. "Were the victims men?"

"About half were men; the others, women. Why? Is that important?" he asked rather surprised by her sudden change in appearance and demeanor.

"It is but one piece of the puzzle. Now, when the victims were found, were they robbed in any way? Did their relatives notice missing money pouches or jewelry?"

"Ah, no, that is what first bothered me. One would think robbery might be a strong motive, you know, the victim resists and is killed for his or her money. But no, rarely do their families claim that anything is missing."

"Now as to the time of death, were they killed in the daytime or night? Any patterns on the time of the slayings?" Calli continued like a hunting dog on the scent of a fox.

"Night, usually after ten. None in the daytime as far as I know."

"Locations of the slayings? Any patterns noticed there?" she rolled onwards.

"Now that you mention it, why yes. Most bodies were found in dark, deserted alleys off the main streets."

"Okay. How were they killed?"

"I see, I see. Yes, most were stabbed in or near the heart. Only a few had other wounds on their body."

"Ah, lots of blood found around their bodies then, I take it?"

"Er, no. Not much. Why?"

"If someone is stabbed in the heart, they are going to bleed profusely all over the place. So that means they were killed elsewhere and their bodies dumped where they were later found. Interesting indeed. All right. Days. Did they all happen on the same day of the week or randomly?"

He thought for a moment. "Yes, random days, I would venture to say. I did not really pay much attention to that early on; only more recently have I become so concerned."

"Good, now social status? Trade? Occupations? Do you know about these with any of the victims?"

"Maria, she was the latest victim, though there probably have been more since I left. She was a loving mother of three boys and generously baked breads for our services on Saturdays. Now another man, he was running a tinsmith shop, I believe. Another man, he was a fisherman; I remember him, he always smelled of fish when he came to the church. One was a potterer, one a gardener, and, yes, one was a seamstress."

She interrupted him, "Okay, safe assumption, all walks of life. How about social status? Were any victims related to the noble houses? Were any wealthy?"

"Well, yes, Fred was a second cousin to Cecil, I believe, but I don't think that any of the victims were what I would call wealthy."

"Their past: were all the victims present in Zargarb when the barbarians invaded? Or were some of them off in the southern islands waiting it out with the cowardly nobles?"

Bandar instantly knew what she thought of the nobles. He had to think before answering this one. "You know, with the possible exception of Fred, I think that all were likely in the city when it fell or had abandoned it and subsequently returned. Why? Is that important? By the way, Calli, you are positively amazing! It would have taken me years just to think of all those questions!" For the very briefest of instants, Bandar saw a genuine smile appear on the still ashen face, though some of her color had been slowly returning.

"One more question about the victims, their wounds. Did the authorities say whether a sword or a dagger caused their fatal wound?"

"Ah my dear, now you have asked me a question that I certainly can answer. In my youth I was a messiah in Juda Arad, a keen fighter, if I do say so myself, that is, before I met the Great Messiah and became one of his Holy Disciples. From those that I have personally seen in the last few weeks, I'd say a dagger was used. Probably one with at least a six-inch blade did the damage. Why?"

"Close quarters. To use the dagger, the perpetrator must be very close to the victim. That is yet another clue, you see. Oh, permit me to ask one other question about the victims: were any of them trained fighters or part of the new army that I hear they are forming? Were any of our Sisters killed or do we know?"

"No Sisters," Aminia quickly spoke up. "We've not lost any for quite some time."

"Yes, I think at least three or four were involved in the new City Guards, as they are being called. Why? Is that important?"

"I know a number of Sisters who have joined your church and some are on guard duty in the city, protecting Alicia. They would be more than likely to eliminate the attacker than become the victim. Yet some of the guards — I find that curious. One would think that a fighter would be less likely to be attacked. Now then, I'm afraid that I know next to nothing about your church organization. What I need to know is this: were all the victims holding what might be called prominent positions in your organization?"

"Well, none of them were adepts or missionaries. So no, none were actually apart of the church organization, but they were prominent members in their areas. As I said, one woman donated bread regularly for our communal dining after the main service. Quite a few were donating some hours each week working on construction of new churches about the city. Our numbers are growing so rapidly that the few churches we've already built cannot handle the numbers of faithful that come for Saturday Service. Helping with construction was, until recently anyway, one of the more popular ways many of our faithful chose to serve Jehosa. At least two dozen of those slain had worked on construction projects at one time during the last six months."

"Fine, so would it be a safe assumption for me to conclude that those that were slain were quite open about their new faith?" Calli asked.

"Certainly, as I said, these were prominent parishioners, who gave from their hearts."

"So that means anyone would easily know that they were active in the church. It doesn't help narrow the field. All right. I assume that these deaths have slowed the church constructions."

"Not really. I've just put more of the immigrant Arad workers on the projects."

"Interesting. Can you think of any enemies that you have made in the city, someone or some group that hates your church enough to want to harm your parishioners?"

"No, we try to help everyone, regardless of their situation or status or wealth. We, every one of us, you and I, we're all children of Jehosa. We've turned our backs on no one that I am aware of — that's why I am at my wit's end. I don't know what to do." He looked very upset indeed.

"Well, someone is your enemy, Reverend," Calli pronounced. "Now then, we have more than one hundred native Sea Prince citizens, both male and female, all prominently known church supporters being killed somewhere by a dagger thrust to the heart at close quarters and their bodies dumped in back alleys. This pattern does not fit with a single person seeking retribution for some alleged crime committed by your church. My bet is that there is some organization or individual that is behind the crime wave, perhaps offering a monetary reward for each person slain. I have never heard of a single criminal who has killed that many people. My guess is that the actual doers of these deeds are several in number, perhaps maybe as high as a couple dozen men. I say men, because I don't believe a woman would ever commit such a crime. Sorry if I offend you with this. Men it must be. Lowlife scum, brigands, and bandits, unscrupulous men — these would be the types who could kill and go on killing the innocent. But no, wait a minute. Such men would be very hard pressed actually to leave money pouches or jewelry on their victims! Ah, we can likely rule such men out! So the circle narrows. We are looking only someone who can kill innocent people and feel not the slightest urge to lift their valuables when the deed is done. Their motivation must be against your church. That can only mean one thing: those that are actually committing these murders must be fanatical supporters of the Church of Tur."

"Reverend, we are looking for radical Tur supporters. Undoubtedly, these murders would be taking other visible actions against you. Have you ever been in public and had someone in the crowd heckle you, taunt your church, curse your church, anything like that?"

"Well, yes, as a matter of fact. But then we have always been persecuted by others; even when I was preaching with the Great Messiah in Juda Arad, someone was always doubting us, rallying against us. Now that you point it out, there are times we do get quite a lot of jeering in public."

"Where are you at in the city when you receive the most outcries against you?" Calli was becoming very excited, like a dog closing in on the fox den.

"Well, I'd have to say that we have the most trouble down by the docks."

"Okay, then, makes sense. Dockhands are a rough lot, and they, along with the mariners and the fishermen, are the most devout believers in Tur. It is highly likely that among those that taunt you and your church are your murders. However, the real question is what lies back of that?" Calli was thinking fast and talking just as fast as she could go. "It is possible that a number of them got together and formulated this plan to murder all — no wait, it fits. Look, they are not killing immigrants from the Arad, only locals. In their eyes, they must be viewing locals who lose faith in Tur and adopt this new god Jehosa as traitors or worse. Hence, they feel their criminal actions are somehow justified. That is how they can go on killing; in their eyes, they are trying to get those that have deserted Tur to reconsider switching gods. It fits!"

Calli continued her deductions, rapid fire. "Now while it is possible that the dockhands worked all this out by themselves, it is highly unlikely. Dockhands are not known for their brilliant minds, just for their brawn. This plot seems too well thought out, too well orchestrated to have been thought up by dockhands. No, I smell a deeper, more sinister plot here. My money is on someone else being the driving force, providing the motivation for the crimes. Ah, yes, has to be. Look, the dockhands spend the vast majority of their time in the dock area. How would they be able to gather the necessary information on the victims — to know who to go after and when that person would be vulnerable — someone has to be gathering intelligence; someone has to be staking out the victims beforehand. When they have enough information, they contact the dockhands who perform the deed. This is getting more and more sinister!"

Now Calli's face was pinkish, her cheeks were flush with life. She was rapidly drawing a noose on the culprits. By contrast, Reverend Bandar's face grew paler. Never had he been involved in such a sinister plot. He had always been an open man, a fighter. He could never stomach all this spying and sneaking down dark alleys. The magnitude of the problem only grew vastly larger in his mind. Someone out there in Zargarb wanted his church to fail. Perhaps it would only be a matter of time before they expanded their hit list and went after the immigrant Arads in the church or even the priests, adepts, and missionaries. He grew paler and paler.

Calli was still talking rapidly, "Now who could be behind this well run organization? That is the question. Someone who is losing, because the Church of Jehosa is expanding. The only opponents who lose are the Church of Tur and/or the Prince himself. They are the only ones who stand to lose anything as your church grows. Both men have lost their shared positions of power over the city. Conclusion: either the High Priest or the Prince or both are ultimately the ones behind this murder campaign. Undoubtedly, they are using one group of men as spies and stalkers and another group to do the actual killing. Case solved!"

Fiona cursed loudly. Sister Aminia grimaced, tightlipped. Bandar's face changed from ashen to red rapidly, as his anger rose. He had a target, his old messiah ways rushing to the fore, supplanting all the teachings of the Great Messiah. Only with great effort could he contain his rage. Sister Aminia calmly said, "Very well done, Calli! I knew you could solve it. Now all we need is to gather the proof necessary to bring charges before the High Council."

Even as Sister Aminia spoke, slowly the healthy color in Calli's face began to wane. Her mental rush was over, as she had solved it to her satisfaction. Real life now called her back. Bandar enthusiastically said, "Yes, well done indeed Calli. You have a brilliant mind, and you look beautiful as well. Thank you very much!"

Poor Bandar was totally unprepared for what happened in the next instant. Calli shrieked, began bawling, got up, and ran into the kitchen. A moment later, the sounds of Calli crying and pounding her head into the wall echoed through the house. Bandar's mouth opened, but he could say nothing. Fiona ran into the kitchen to try to prevent her from hurting herself further and to attempt to calm her down.

Sister Aminia, very ill at ease, tried to explain. "It's not your fault. You couldn't know."

"Couldn't know what? What did I say?" he managed to mutter, still in shock and not certain what was happening.

"You said she was pretty. She blames her good looks for inciting her fiancé and his pals for raping her. Of course, we know that isn't true, but she believes it or wants to believe it. Just suggesting she is pretty, often sets her off. Maybe in time she will recover, maybe."

Compassion awoke within Bandar. He closed his eyes and began praying silently to Jehosa. Never before had he prayed so devoutly, not since the Centurions had captured the Great Messiah so many years ago. He remembered how Jes would lay his hands on someone and heal them. He begged that he might do the same for this woman, who had just possibly discovered the source of the killings. *Jehosa, Father, and Jes, the Son of God and my mentor, hear me, thy humble servant, Bandar, disciple of the faith, I have done as you asked, spread the gospel far and wide. I beseech you; let me help this young woman, who only a minute ago has done great things for our church. Jehosa, Jes, please.*

So intense was his intention to reach Jehosa and Jes that Jes woke up and sat up in his bed in the middle of the night on the island of West Reach. Bethany lay asleep beside him; she had had a busy day. The kids had long ago gone to sleep. Their new home was dark and quiet. Yet, Jes heard his disciple's prayer, almost as if Bandar had been yelling it into his mind. Jes reached out and touched his disciple's mind. *I am with you always. Go now and touch her.*

Shocked beyond words to hear the voice of the Great Messiah in his mind, in his head, Bandar got up and walked almost trance-like into the kitchen. Fiona had gotten Calli to stop pounding her head against the wall. Great black and blue swellings were already growing rapidly on her forehead. She was still sobbing, leaning on Fiona's shoulder. She tried to motion him away with her stub; her good arm was holding tightly onto Calli's body. Failing that, she scowled at him, but dared not say anything for fear of upsetting Calli once more.

Calli saw him reaching out his hand and started to react but he was faster. Gently the palm of his large hand rested upon Calli's shoulder. "Be at peace, Calli," he said. In his mind, he felt the power of Jes flowing outward through his body and into his hand and on into that of Calli. Indirectly, it also went into Fiona. Jes told him what to say, so he spoke as her crying ceased, just as fast as it had begun, "Calli, dear child, tell me what happened that night."

She could not help herself; the words spoken, the memory was burned into her mind complete with the horrible sights and sounds of that rape; she could even smell their odious body odors, wine on their breaths. Like a movie, the scene played out in full within her mind, though she could only describe perhaps half of what she re-experienced. Yet, Jes, and thus Bandar and Fiona, saw the whole series of images in full, ugly detail.

When she had finished, Bandar said quietly, "Thank you," as Jes directed. "Now Calli, did you actually *do* anything there that may have caused them to treat you that way?"

For the first time in her life, she answered truthfully, "No. They were drunk. Honestly, I never did really trust my fiancé — that's why I kept putting off our getting married. I bet that is what really triggered him to do what he did that night. I could never tell him why I was always hesitating about actually getting married. He was frustrated, maybe."

"Very good, Calli. Do you want to be rid of all these upsetting and harmful memories, to end their destroying your life?"

"Yes, yes but how? They are always there when I shut my eyes. Sometimes I lie awake all night just so I don't have to see them again!"

"God Jehosa has forgiven you, Calli, for your actions. If he, our maker, can forgive you, can you not find it in your heart to forgive those men? Just forgive them their sins as Jehosa has forgiven you yours."

"It's so hard; they wronged me. I wanted to kill them. I still want revenge."

"Calli, if you could reach out at this moment and slay them, would you really feel any better about it, honestly? Here, imagine you are standing over their dead bodies. At that moment, would you feel good?"

"No, I guess I'd still feel just as miserable, only now I'd worry about having killed them. Is there no way out for me?"

"Forgive them, Calli. That is the way out."

After a moment's silence, Calli said falteringly, "I — I — I forgive them. They should never have done that to me, but I forgive them. There, I said it."

Another voice spoke into his other ear, "I forgive him." It was Fiona! She was still holding tightly onto Calli so that indirectly Jes was affecting her as well.

"Then by the grace of Jehosa, our spiritual father, your confession and absolution is accepted. Arise and let these memories no longer bother you. Yours as well, Fiona." He felt Jes backing out of his mind and quickly sent, *Praise be to thee, thank you Great Messiah. I will work twice as hard to bring your words of truth to the world.* Then Bandar felt alone once more. Later, he often remembered this evening; he had been touched by his God and the Son of God, and he would never forget it.

"Thank you," Calli said, wiping her eyes and moving out of Fiona's comforting grasp.

"What, what just happened here," the timid voice of Sister Aminia said. She had been standing in the doorway and witnessed the entire event. Awe was in her eyes. No trace of the massive bruises remained on Calli's forehead. There was a light in her eyes and smile on her lips, as she stared at Bandar as if she had never seen him before.

"Oh my!" exclaimed Fiona, who had just raised her stump only to find her hand was there. She fainted. Calli reacted swiftly to arrest her fall, as Bandar got a hold of her, carried her into the living room, and laid her gently onto a soft rug. Calli and Aminia just stared at Fiona's left hand. For a score of years, Fiona had a stump, where now there was a perfectly good hand, one that matched her right hand.

"It's a miracle! No, two miracles," declared Sister Aminia. Fiona awoke, stared up at them, and then at her hand. All three women began to cry tears of joy. Meanwhile, Bandar felt more exhausted, more drained than he had ever felt before. He quickly found a chair and sat down before his wobbling legs failed him.

"Yes, it is a miracle," he finally said now that he was not in danger of collapsing. "Jehosa and his son, the Great Messiah, are living God and Son. They are as real as you and I. For many years, I was one of the Great Messiah's Disciples, who followed him through the Arad. I have seen him perform miracle after miracle, healing the sick, the blind, and the lame. You women have been blessed and touched by Jehosa and his Son, the Great Messiah. If I ever needed proof that Jehosa is the One God of us all, not just Arads, I have it here tonight. You two are living proof that we are all Jehosa's children."

"My hand — it feels like I never lost it!" Fiona interrupted him, moving it this way and that, comparing it to her right hand. Calli was also feeling it just to make sure it was indeed there and not some kind of illusion.

"Thank you, Reverend Bandar," Calli said looking him squarely in his eyes, "for the first time in so long, I can say that my mind is at peace. It truly is a miracle. Thank you."

"No, it is yourselves you have to thank. You accepted Jehosa's forgiveness and forgave those that harmed you. That is what allowed the miracles to happen. That is the Lord's way," Bandar preached.

"How can we ever thank you, Reverend Bandar?" Sister Aminia said humbly, realizing that the Sisterhood now owed him a debt that could scarcely be repaid.

"Oh you already have. Calli here solved the murders of our church members. That is more than enough payment," he proclaimed.

"But it is just a theory, a logical deduction," protested Calli. "We do not know that for sure and besides we have no evidence."

Still twisting her new hand this way and that, Fiona piped up, "Not a problem. We will just have to get the evidence, won't we?"

"But how will we do that?" asked Bandar.

"Set them up and catch them in the act," suggested Fiona. "Catch the killers before they slay another victim and force it out of them." After a slight pause, she added, "Zounds! My anger is gone too! I can be angry, if I want to be angry. Normally, just talking about something like this, my anger rises to an almost uncontrollable pitch. Only Rosalita's training has allowed me to work around it. But now, it is, like, gone!" Bandar smiled; he knew that it went with all the rest of her bad experience.

"This calls for a celebration. Reverend Bandar, would you be so kind as to spend the night here with us? I'll break out our finest wine."

"Thank you. I've a few guards outside waiting for me. I guess they can camp out of doors."

"I'll not hear of it. Tonight, accept our hospitality." She winked at him, "You realize that very, very, very few men are ever allowed to spend a night inside our ranch."

"You are very gracious; I am honored indeed. But please, a really good cup of tea is more what I need at the moment. I want to keep my wits about me. Also, I feel more than a little weak after that healing. My old legs aren't what they used to be, I guess."

While she brewed a pot of their best tea, Calli went to fetch something more solid to eat. Fiona just had to go show her dear friends what had happened to her. No one was going to believe this, and yet she now had the hand to prove it. Both women stepped gaily, light heartedly out of the door, free from their own personal nightmares.

Now that they were alone, Sister Aminia said quietly to Bandar, "I must tell you that in my lifetime, I have only known a few men who I trusted and respected. Tonight, you have joined that list. Thank you. Do you often perform such miracles? I've hundreds of similar cases under my care." By that, Bandar knew she meant the entire Sisterhood.

He chuckled, "Sister, tonight was my first miracle. I've watched the Great Messiah do it many, many times, but I'm not the Son of Jehosa. No, I am merely his humble messenger. Jehosa and his Son performed the miracle tonight, through me. I cannot claim that I did anything; they were acting through my mind and body. To be perfectly honest, that has never happened to me before. Tonight, Jehosa has answered my prayers and for that I will be eternally grateful."

"Well, you certainly made a believer out of me. I suspect when word of this gets around, many the Sisters will want to know more about Jehosa. Might it be somehow possible for us to have a church build here or perhaps nearby for my sisters to attend regularly? If I know my Sisters, they are really going to be impressed and desirous of knowing all about this Jehosanity. We would, of course, help pay for its construction."

"I would be delighted if we could build a church near here, say exclusively for your Sisterhood members. I would have to be extra careful to pick a good pastor, however, one that would be very sensitive the needs of your Sisters. I'm sure, given time, just the right pastor could be found. We are a little short of manpower at the moment, what with all the new construction in Zargarb. Let's say we split the cost."

"Deal!" she exclaimed. They shook hands to seal the bargain.

Just then, Calli and Fiona entered, bearing armloads of cakes and meat patties. Bandar caught a glimpse of a crowd of women standing just outside the door, trying to get a glimpse of him inside. It was a bit unsettling. Calli, now bubbling with enthusiasm, exclaimed, "Fiona has come up with a plan, and I am going to be the bait! We are going to catch them red-handed!" Over the light meal, Fiona outlined her scheme.

Chapter 26 End of an Era

By late June 587 AH, the Sisterhood spread their net, hoping to catch the ultimate culprit behind the rash of murders in Zargarb. A young maiden, who went by the name of Calli, took up residence at a newly rebuilt housing complex not far from the docks and two blocks from the new Church of Jehosanity that was partially constructed. Ten construction workers toiled at the site daily.

Calli often visited the site and began bringing freshly baked bread and drinks to the workers. "I'm *so* glad you are working *so* hard to build this church! I can't *wait* for the new pastor to begin holding Saturday services here," she casually explained to several workers who took a break to enjoy her gift. Half of the workers were immigrants from Juda Arad; half were local men.

"We sure do appreciate your bringing us a midday snack," one younger worker praised her. "Normally, when we're doing construction work, nobody cares what we do, except the boss. Sure seems to be a lot of comradery amongst your church members, Jehosanity, isn't it?" He knew it was, of course; he was just being polite. He was enjoying her talk as well as her pretty looks.

"Oh yes, Jehosa is the one God. I've heard all sorts of tales from their preachers about the wonderful miracles he and his Holy Son have performed. This is a *real* god! After all, how many miracles have you ever heard of Tur doing?" She gaily chatted on about how wonderful this new God actually was. The men chuckled along with her from time to time. Once they finished the snack she had brought, they went back to work. She returned to her new home to bake more bread. For a week, Calli brought the workers a snack twice a day, mid-morning and mid-afternoon.

On Saturday, carrying a large bag full of bread loaves, she walked the ten blocks across town to the nearest Church of Joshanity to attend services and help provide the noon refreshments. Both before and after service, she did her best to talk to as many people about her supposed religious fervor, attracting as much attention as she could. None of this was hard for her to do now. Yet a month ago, she would have positively gone insane being out here amongst all these people, especially the men and would have never in a million years brought snacks to the workers. Truly, she was a living miracle to the divine touch of Jehosa, though she never mentioned this aspect. No, she was playing a role, a coldly calculated one. Yes, she was in fact attempting to duplicate those actions that others had done just before they were murdered.

No one would recognize Sister Calli. Women are the masters of casual disguises, besides she was not fighter trained. However, she did not wear provocative clothing; under no circumstances did she want to "provoke" a man into doing something they would both regret. Had you seen her as Bandar did that day at the ranch and then seen her now, you would be very hard pressed to say they were the same woman. Her disguise was complete, even her Sisterhood friends told her so.

Yes, Calli was being the bait in a scheme that Sister Fiona and she had concocted after both women had been miraculously healed, if that is even the right word, by the Great Messiah through the touch of Bandar Dero. Both knew that whoever was responsible for over a hundred murders of church goers just had to be caught and punished. They were going to see that happen no matter the risk to themselves; this was something they had to accomplish, perhaps their way of saying thank you to their new God and Son of God.

The new home that Calli occupied was specially modified for her use. In adjoining homes on either side, concealed doorways were cleverly installed. Numerous Sisters, also in disguise, came and went from these other two homes, often conferring with Calli, keeping her appraised of what they had discovered. Even on the streets, Calli often spied her friends and was very grateful that she had learned all the Sisterhood secret hand signals. Messages passed between them that could not be overheard.

Besides, Calli loved a good mystery. Although she had "solved" it basically, she still wanted to know who was behind this diabolical, vicious plot: the Prince or the High Priest of Tur. Knowing that would be the last piece of the mystery as far as she was concerned. Fiona only wanted to get her hands on the culprits.

Nothing much happened that first week, but then Calli did not expect to get results that fast. She was sure that she had to make it very convincing, that a Sea Prince woman had completely forsaken Tur for Jehosa. Saturday night, she was in her new home along with ten other Sisters conferring on the day's results.

"I'm sure you were being watched by two men," Sister Ali commented. "Of course, women are always going to be watched by men anyway; we watch men too, especially handsome ones." They all giggled. She added, "As you say, the plotters must be keeping an eye on you to learn your movements and daily habits. Don't worry, Calli; we've now got both those men under observation twenty-four hours a day."

Calli replied, "If my theory is right, one or more of these spies must be reporting to the top man at some time. Whether after that the same spy contacts the actual murderers or whether the top man somehow does, that I don't know."

"Fiona has someone watching both likely top men. You should see our Sisters in action. Anyone going into the Prince's residence and coming out is followed, quite cleverly, I might add. One Sister follows him for a while and then passes it off to another Sister. I swear that there is going to be no way the spies will know that they are being spied upon! Honestly, this is the most exciting thing I've ever done!"

"Just be very careful," Calli cautioned, "we are dealing with utterly ruthless men here. They think nothing of murdering women and men alike.

These are really evil men."

Just then, Sister Fiona entered through the opened concealed door. "Hi'yall! Anything to report?" Nothing out of the ordinary was the uniform replies. "Well, Calli, everything is all set for Phase 2 of our plan. Starting tomorrow night, you are to work on a Church relief effort on Digori Street about four blocks from here. We have it timed right; you go to work just after dark and return here around ten. Now you must, I repeat, must follow this precise path to and from work. Your life will likely depend upon following this slavishly — no variations for any reason." She handed her a crude street sketch.

"I know," protested Calli, "I know. They always murder their victims at night. I assume that the route is down some low traffic side streets, alleys perhaps?"

Fiona grinned, "You betcha. Got you covered every inch of the way. Still, Calli, if they only use a dagger, then that means that the murderer must get very close to you. It's going to be very risky for you. You can still back out of this. You know that another murder took place last night? Another one of our people who converted to Jehosa."

"I heard; it's terrible. No, I want to catch these men and put a stop to it," Calli replied. "Besides, Fiona, you know I have to go through with this. Just don't let the murderer get me, please."

Three days later, Fiona caught Calli in her home before she left to deliver the mid-morning bread to the construction workers. "I think it's going to be today, tonight rather. Be extra careful tonight, probably after work on your way home, my best guess. Gotta run."

During the day, from other Sisters, Calli learned that one of the men who had been following her periodically had visited the Prince the day before. Interestingly enough, Simon was on hand for just such an eventuality, and he accidentally bumped into the man in the crowded streets and lifted his money pouch. Inside was a hundred gold pieces, a fortune for a man who was supposed to be a simple tailor.

Thus alerted, other Sisters followed the Prince later that same afternoon when he went to visit to docks, reportedly on official business. On his way back, he dropped into the Beached Whale pub, a slimy, dockworker's pub, which no noble of the city would ever think of entering. What Calli found most interesting is that the Prince carried a money pouch tied to his belt when he came to the docks, but had no money pouch when he left the pub. Calli's comment: "The inevitable money trail speaks volumes."

Hence, she felt certain that tonight, either going to work or more likely coming home from work, one or more dockworkers intended to murder her. It was sobering to be able to anticipate one's own murder; Calli found it a very strange feeling indeed. The rest of the day, she felt a bit nervous. Things could go wrong. However, she had a deep faith, a powerful confidence in Fiona and her Sisters. Besides, she still had the remnants of that serene peace of mind from the touch of her newfound God, Jehosa. Several weeks had passed since that fateful night of miracles, and still she felt at peace.

Nothing occurred when she went to work just after the sun set, but then she really did not expect anything so early in the evening. Her path to work led her down several back alleyways, which still had a good deal of foot traffic. No there would be too many witnesses for a blatant murder now. It would happen when the streets were more deserted.

At the converted warehouse, she joined about twenty other volunteers. Some men were building tables and chairs for a family in need. She joined several women who were sewing bedding blankets. Time passed quickly, but Calli spied another Sister in disguise entering, taking a position opposite her. At first, the Sister just began sewing as well, but quickly signaled Calli. With hand signals, Calli was informed that the man working on the rugs was one of the spies. After Calli signed back that she understood, the Sister excused herself to use the bathroom. Instead, Calli saw her quietly leave the room.

As the hours drifted by, Calli became more and more excited; the doomsday hour was fast approaching. The closer quitting time came, the more the adrenaline rush she felt. At last, a gong sounded ten. After saying thanks for helping to her women acquaintances, and they, likewise, Calli prepared to leave. The man carefully rolled up the rug he was apparently making and slung it over his shoulder. He timed it right so that he met Calli just at the door.

"Excuse me, Miss, could you hold the door for me? This rug is a bit awkward. It's almost done. I'm sure they will really appreciate it; don't you think so? My name is Anree," he said quietly. Calli detected a hint of covert politeness in his voice, almost like a dagger in her back. "Thank you so much," he said as she held the door for him.

She stepped out into the warm evening and took a deep breath. Anree was right beside her. "It sure is wonderful of you to care about this needy family so much." He was trying to strike up a conversation with her, of that she was certain.

She decided to go along with him, "Same with you. So many are in such need, you know. I'm so glad that I can really help others. Aren't you?"

"Sure. Say, are you all by yourself? You know these streets can be a bit dangerous at night. Mind if I walk along with you? If any trouble comes, why I'll just bop them with this rug here," he made a silly attempt at humor. She could see that he had no weapons on him, though he might have a concealed dagger in his boot.

"Sure, follow me. I take the short way home. No one is in the alleys at night. They are quite safe." Both began walking down the first of the alleys; Calli followed the route slavishly. Anree continued to chat idly with her, and she realized this would easily distract someone. She began to see just how easily the others had been murdered. Two blocks later, they crossed a wide street and entered another back alley. Half way down, she spied a derelict man, probably drunk, lying against the side of a building. He seemed to have passed out. In addition, she noticed several large piles of garbage stacked alongside some of the buildings. None of that had been there earlier when she passed by on her way to work.

Once passed the drunken man, just ahead she saw another man sitting against the opposite side. His leg appeared at a crazy cockeyed angle, as if it was broken. He was moaning softly to himself. As she and Anree approached, he looked up at her and said, "Please, Miss, help me. I've twisted my leg. Can you help me up to my feet, please, Miss? I've been stuck here for hours and can't get up on my own. Please."

Instantly, Calli now saw just how the murder victims had gotten close enough to be stabbed in their hearts. He was playing upon the victim's strong desire to help their fellow man in distress. Surely, if she bent down to help him up, then all it would take is one quick upward thrust to stab her in the heart. All her instincts screamed at her not to bend over. Anree said, "The Decalogue bids us to help him, does it not? I'd help him, but I've my hands full with this rug. Can you lift him? If not, maybe you can take this rug from me, and I'll get him up."

Calli now saw that Anree was making it very difficult for the intended victim, her, to not do this simple task. *These men are good at this. Guess they've had a lot of practice.* Still, she hesitated, knowing that just as soon as she leaned over, his hand would probably plunge a dagger into her chest. Just then, she heard a bird chirp, a Sisterhood signal. "Sure, I'll get you up. Can you stand on that leg?" She leaned over, took his outstretched hand, and began to pull him up.

Naturally, as he began to rise, his other hand, which had been behind him all this time, propping him up, swung around. She saw a dagger coming toward her chest at the same time as she heard a telltale twang and felt the sudden rush of air pass her shoulder. In slow motion, she watched the dagger move to within three inches of her chest, and then saw the quarrel drive squarely into his hand, the dagger dropped to the ground. The man screamed in pain. A dozen Sisters appeared out of nowhere, some dropped to the ground from the roofs above. Some crawled out of the garbage piles. Fiona appeared from under some boxes close beside her, crossbow in hand. It was over in a split second. Sisters pointed crossbows at the heads of the supposedly passed out drunk and at Anree. The drunk was not drunk and began pleading for the Sisters not to shoot.

"Thanks, Fiona. It worked. I admit I was worried there, once I'd finally figured it all out. Now I know how they could get so close to stab their victims in the heart. When helping someone regain their feet, you naturally lean over, and as they come up, their other hand comes swinging around, only with the dagger in it. The victims never had a chance!"

"Okay, Sisters, let's get these three inside our place pronto," Fiona ordered. "If you try anything, you are dead men," she said using a large volume of anger in her voice.

"But I . . ." Anree finally tried to speak. He was still in shock that their murder had failed. It all happened so fast, less than thirty seconds had elapsed thus far. Two minutes later, all three men were shoved into the home next door to Calli's home. Once inside and the door shut, Fiona took charge.

All the windows were covered so that no light could get outside, and no one could see inside either. However, several Sisters were already here with lanterns lighted and had ropes ready to tie up the captured men. Four minutes after the attempted murder, the three were securely tied up, and the quarrel pulled out of the dockworker's hand. Now all three men fully realized how much trouble they were actually in — no one had seen them get captured. They were at the complete mercy of the abominations. Trapped.

Anree tried to plead, "What is going on here? I was just trying to see that this young woman got home safely."

Calli cut him off abruptly. "Shut up. I've already figured out what the rug is for. We know the victims are killed at one location and their bodies dumped at another. What better way to carry a dead body around the city than rolled up inside a rug. No one would be even slightly suspicious. Clever idea. Fiona, I suspect that another man will be coming along shortly probably carrying a keg of water to wash away the blood."

"Twenty are still watching," she curtly answered. "If they show, we'll get them too. Gag them. I don't want to listen to them just yet." Quickly, all three were also gagged. "Keep an eye on them. I'm going back out," she ordered.

She returned a few minutes later, escorting another dockhand. "Tie this one up too; he brought the water, just like you predicted, Calli." Fiona left once more just in case others might show up. After no one else came by the alley for a half hour, she felt confident that they had rounded all them up, at least for this attempted murder. Undoubtedly, others were involved, considering there had been so many murders. She and another dozen Sisters re-entered, joining Calli. Still, she had numerous others outside keeping watch, and many were on rooftops.

"Now then, it is time to get some answers from these fellows." Fiona pulled up a chair and sat in front of the four gagged men and had their gags removed. Next, she spoke in a soft, determined anger tone, "Gentlemen, you are now going to tell me everything about these murders. You will answer all my questions or else." She winked to Calli.

"Or else what?" the snide words came from the dockhand who had tried to thrust his dagger into Calli. He was directly taunting her, even though his hand was throbbing in pain. Pain he could deal with; he was used to physical discomfort.

Fiona glared at the man, "I'll make this simple so you don't tax your brain too much. Each time you refuse to answer, I will cut off a finger. If we run out of fingers, then it will be toes. If we run out of toes, your ears go."

"If we run out of ears," Calli added in jest, "take off his balls, Fiona." All the women chuckled at her joke. The man struggled helplessly, suspecting that they would do just that.

"Okay, dear, last to go will be his balls. If you still don't answer, then we take out your eyes, if you still don't talk, why, you will never talk again. We'll just remove your tongue and deposit what is left of you back on your docks, nicely rolled up in this accommodating rug here. Do I make myself perfectly clear?"

"Can't we start with his balls, please," Calli jested once more. True, she was talking very crudely, but she had noticed that only the loss of his manhood seemed to make a lasting impression on the dockhand. She knew that Fiona probably would not really cut off anything, but these men did not know that.

"You wouldn't dare," he taunted back, half-heartedly. "The Prince . . ." He caught himself as he started to reveal too much and quickly shut up.

Fiona simply drew out her dagger and laid it on the table in front of the men. "Okay, big man, you are up first. Tie his legs apart to the chair legs. Then, we'll open his drawers. Calli, let me know when the staunching iron is plenty hot. I don't want them to die from blood loss." Several women tied his legs apart, and Fiona carefully cut open his pants, though not through his underwear yet.

Shortly, Calli returned holding a red hot rod and said cheerily, "I'm all set. I *do* hope they don't talk. This is going to be *fun*."

That did it! All four men were extremely pale; Anree was terrified, in fact. Seeing the dagger, the remains of his pants, the red hot rod, and the steel determination in Fiona's eyes, the dockhand relented. "Okay, okay. Just don't do this. What do you want to know?"

At noon the next day, Cecil fussed with his official robes of office as he sat down ceremoniously at the head of the High Council. The others took their place following suit. He said seriously, "This special session of the High Council will now come to order. Be it officially known, Alicia has called this meeting on behalf of the tradesmen of Zargarb. Thus, I will turn the meeting over to her." All thirteen members were present, though only Alicia knew precisely what the nature of the meeting would encompass.

"A hundred and five townsfolk have been murdered during the last couple of months," she began. "The victims were tradesmen, craftsmen, husbands, wives — just ordinary folks. However, the one thing they all had in common was their acceptance and support of this new religion of Jehosanity. All were killed because they converted from a belief in Tur to a belief in Jehosa. The Sisterhood was asked to assist in finding their murderers." She paused to let the significance impact with these men.

The Prince immediately commented, "Why it is obvious who is behind them. It has to be the Church of Tur. They are the ones who stand to lose. It's obvious; we don't need a meeting to decide that."

The High Priest immediately protested, "How can you blame these murders on us? We are Holy Men, not cutthroats. I protest these outlandish accusations! You have no proof that we are involved!"

Alicia spoke softly, "Ah, your Holiness, but we do have proof. We have captured several members of the gang of murders, captured them while in the act of attempting to murder yet another young woman." She paused to let this news climax. Carefully, she eyed both the High Priest and the Prince. Both men began to look exceedingly nervous. She continued, "At this time, I would like to present the Sister who made the capture and bring in the guilty men. She can outline this diabolical plot in detail."

Cecil had no other choice but to agree. "See to it, then." He stared at both the Prince and the High Priest; his curiosity was aroused. His mind raced down eventual outcomes. Cecil was a planner and schemer and had gotten exceedingly wealthy because this. He seldom misjudged a situation.

Sister Fiona, along with a number of other Sisters, marched the four men into the dining room where the meeting was held. Briefly, she outlined all that she had learned, dropped the sack of gold Simon had pilfered from Anree after the spy had left the Prince's home. She also produced a short list of the other members, both spies and the actual dockhands who committed the murders, saying, "The council can have these men arrested. You may question each of these men to verify what I have said is the truth. I have promised them that the High Council will show them mercy if they speak the truth now."

With the exception of the Prince and the High Priest, the ten nobles looked positively stunned by the news. The High Priest and the Prince were both angry, but for different reasons. "This is all a big lie," screamed the Prince! "There is not a shred of truth in any of this. The High Priest has put them up to this, not me."

"You lie," the very animated Priest exclaimed. "How dare you try to lay the blame for this on the Church?"

"I'll not put up with any more of this treachery!" screamed the Prince, who got up to leave.

"Sit down, Prince!" Cecil commanded, and for once, Sister Fiona found that she had been given an order from Cecil that she could obey. She forced the Prince to sit back down, glaring angrily at the man. "Someone go fetch the Captain of the Guards for me please."

When the Captain arrived, Cecil gave him the list of others who were involved and ordered him to arrest every one of them. He also requested some Sisters also accompany the guards; it was obvious that he did not fully trust the current skills of his newly recruited guardsmen.

Once the Captain had left, Cecil solemnly turned to the Prince. "I have only one question for you, Prince. Why? I expected you might make alliances with other Princes, the Centurions, heck even the bandits, anything to regain your seat of power. Why this?"

The Prince refused to speak another word. Calli, who had accompanied Fiona along with the other Sisters guarding these four men, spoke up. "Permit me. I believe I can explain his reasoning."

"And you are?" Cecil said sardonically.

"Sister Calli. May I?"

Cecil glanced around the table, seeing no one objecting — rather all his friends seemed more than eager to hear her speak, he said dryly, "Please do."

She took a deep breath and began, "It's rather simple. Since no other

Sea Prince can afford to come to bail him out — they are more than scared of the Galt invasion hitting them next — since the Centurions have been driven out, since you already have an armed group to enforce your rule, the only option left to him was to implicate the High Priest, get His Holiness convicted, and removed from the Council. He probably planned to install one of his men as a replacement here on the High Council. That would give him two votes. I suspect that next he would be going after some of you. By eliminating each of you by various nefarious methods not traceable back to him, such as poisoning, he would slowly get his men or those loyal to him onto the High Council. Eventually, he would find himself back in control once again. I think that you can consider yourselves fortunate that you have not yet been poisoned or killed. Simple really." She finished and retreated to the other Sisterhood fighters.

Pietro Bonellita, a noble who had always supported the Sisterhood in the past, spoke up. "I think that we here owe a great debt of thanks to the Sisterhood for uncovering this nasty plot. We probably owe our very lives to their incredible good work. I move that we highly commend the Sisterhood for their fast action in this matter." It was quickly seconded by nearly all the nobles.

Cecil, who still hated the Sisterhood and Fiona in particular, having never forgiven her for slaying his son so many years ago, found that he had no choice. But he was ever the manipulator, he spoke, "Yes, yes, we are all in agreement. Pietro, draft the proclamation for the Council, please. On behalf of the High Council, we thank the Sisterhood, Alicia." Note that he did not address the thanks to Fiona. He quickly added, "What compensation does the Sisterhood request for this invaluable service that you have performed on our behalf?" He hoped that Alicia would request monetary compensation so that he could use that to make the Sisterhood look like they did everything for a profit, lessening them in the eyes of his fellow council members.

Alicia said quietly, "We only want justice and perhaps compensation for the surviving family members. Some children have lost their mothers; some men have lost their wives, and so on. We feel that the Prince ought to compensate the survivors for their loss. We don't want anything for ourselves, except to see the guilty properly punished."

"Here, here, I'll second that," called out Pietro. "I make a motion that the Prince should pay each of the surviving members of the hundred and five people that were murdered a thousand gold coins. Let's see, that comes to one hundred and five thousand gold pieces. That ought to satisfy our loyal tradesmen." Several others seconded the motion. Cecil grinned. He knew that this would drastically lower the wealth of the Prince and his extended family.

"All in favor?" Cecil quickly took a vote. It passed with only one no vote, the Prince's. "Your Holiness, the Council asks you this: what is the punishment that Tur seeks for someone who has so ordered the murders of one hundred five innocent townsfolk?" He already knew what the High Priest would answer. By having the pronouncement come from the priest, he was off the

346

hook; he was not responsible for it.

The High Priest sighed. He had known the Prince and worked with him for many, many years, sharing the ruling power over Zargarb through good times and bad. He found it most troubling to speak, yet he must. "Gentlemen, ladies, I am afraid that there is only one punishment that would have the slightest chance of appeasing Tur so that he does not cause enormous storms to sink all our ships. His head must be cast out to sea." He lowered his head, knowing that he had just signed a death sentence for his Prince, but there was no other option open to him. This time, not even all the bags of gold would buy another head to be cast out to sea, only the Prince's.

The Prince was livid, "May Tur sink every last one of your ships! My great-great grandfather built this city with his own sweat and blood. Now you are destroying everything he did. I pray Tur goes on a rampage!"

Cecil spoke softly, but solemnly, "Escort the Prince out of here. See that he is locked up securely. Have a dozen men guarding him at all times. Your Holiness, as is the tradition here in Zargarb, we leave the execution of his sentence to the Church. It should be done soon though."

Alicia detected tears forming in the priest's eyes; this man had no choice but to behead his longtime associate. She said, "The Sisterhood thanks the High Council for handling this matter and the High Priest in particular. However, gentlemen, there remains one very serious question."

Cecil and the others looked at her. What else could there be? Alicia continued, "Who is to take the Prince's seat on the Council? We cannot leave our numbers at twelve — could be a tie vote sometime."

Cecil, already had been calculating just this very thing, but he spoke sarcastically, "And I presume that you are recommending that another Sister take his place?"

"Oh no Sir, that would not be fair. Honestly, I think that we must seek another member of the Prince's line to take up this vacant seat. It is only fair that someone in the line of founders sit on the ruling body."

Damn, she is good! thought Cecil. *Positively brilliant. Everyone wins this way. The High Council is seen to be reaching out to that family, not holding a grudge. This woman is good!* "Sister Alicia, my compliments. I totally agree with you. The vacated seat belongs to our founding father's line. All in favor?" The vote was unanimous and the meeting adjourned so that they could see to the execution of all of the motions.

As they disbanded, Alicia comforted the High Priest, who said, "The Church of Tur is forever in your debt, Sister. Do you realize that when I carry out this sentence, as I must, it will mark the end of an era in Zargarb? The end of an era," he muttered as he walked out of the dining room, heading for his church. He was a sad, lonely, old man.

Chapter 27 The Snake Demon

In late June 589 AH, Mikhailovich and Zdkenka Strokova crossed over the Barrier Teeth from Juda Arad setting foot once again on their homeland of the Northern Steppes. His mighty army now some nine thousand strong galloped off, fanning out to their respective clans. The two watched this incredible spectacle, something never before seen in the steppes. Yes, they were the conquerors who now possessed Juda Arad and the entirety of the Lands of the Seven Sea Princes. Once the armada disappeared over the rolling green hills, a vast sea of wagons rolled by, many piled high with loot from the last of the Sea Prince cities to fall. Most of the wagons, however, carried the supplies for such a huge army.

Yet, none of this wealth could match what Mikhailovich brought with him in his wagon. Yes, the twins personally drove this wagon because they had with them his son and daughter, more precious to him than all the wagonloads of treasure the others took. Illanovich was now two and a half while his sister, Lenkova Strokova, was just a year old. Illi sat up on the bench with his father, who even let him hold the reins, well partially. "Look at me, Aunt Zel, I'm drivin," he proudly explained. Zdlenka held his sister so that she could see the rolling green hills of their new home.

Yes, Rosalita had done an excellent job preparing the two children for this day when Mikhailovich would come and take them from her at North Point. Neither child was the least upset at leaving with the twins. It could have been vastly different for Illanovich, except that daily Rosalita kept telling him that his father would come soon to take him to his home in the green grasslands. Although she found it hard to squelch the maternal attachment that she never expected to have with these children, nevertheless, she did not show it when around the children. Thus, both were more than willing to go with the twins when they had stopped by to pick them up on their return trip from Velona.

Yes, Mikhailovich had asked her if she had reconsidered formally marrying him and moving to the steppes, but she kindly declined, saying, "Thanks, but no, my duties lie here with my Sisters. Thank you for honoring our bargain." However, she did watch the children leave until the wagon was no longer visible. Immediately after that, she saddled up her horse and headed up on to the Paese di Dio taking some time off for herself. Yes, she felt the loss of her children, in spite of everything she had done to not become attached to them.

"You like my new title, Czar Stokova?" Mikhailovich asked his sister as their wagon rolled over the grasslands toward their clan's last known location.

Looking up from feeding her little niece, Zdlenka commented, "Great leader. Well, we ought to have predicted something like this. It is only right that the clans should elect you and I to be their first supreme leaders. Czarina

Stokova has a nice ring to it," she teased. "Your kids are doing well. That Sister took good care of them." Something was stirring within her breast that she'd never felt before, a longing for her own children. Of this, she said not a word to her brother, though.

This season, the Stokova clan had stationed itself in the central portion of the steppes. It took the twins nearly a week in the slow wagon to arrive at the thousand huts that marked their clan's summer dwellings. The plan for the campaign to conquer Tarra was not on hold, rather, Czar Stokova had given his army two month's off. The first of September, all the fighters were to be at the Barrier Teeth, ready to sweep through the Arad and tackle the remnants of the Centurions guarding the paved roadway that led into the luxurious Southlands and ultimately Megalos itself.

A week after settling down to enjoy life with his children, the representatives of several clans came riding hard into his camp, demanding to see the Czar at once. Tamboltz of the Kaluga clan spoke, "Czar Stokova, I am here on behalf of the Kaluga clan. We have a serious problem, one that might keep us from sending any more fighters to the campaigns." Instantly, both twins knew something was very wrong and gave him their full attention, letting other clan women take care of the children.

"Come; let us speak beside the fire," Mikhailovich said, leading the way. This was the most formal a setting for a clan meeting, one that denoted great respect between the individuals. "Tell me about it, please, Tamboltz."

"We've aroused the ire of the Snake Demon, that's what!"

The Galts are a very superstitious people, seeing omens everywhere. Although neither twin had ever heard of a Snake Demon, they nonetheless sympathized with Tamboltz; he obviously was terrified of something. "Tell us about it, please!" he ordered.

"Our clan has upset the Snake Demon. The only thing that we have done differently is to send our fighters to help you. It's either that or it disapproves of all the gold we've brought back. Our soothsayer has not been able to divine which has offended the Snake Demon. All this spring, the Snake Demon has been visiting our huts, stealing our babies in the night right out of their cradles. In the mornings, we search and find their lifeless bodies; their brains have been sucked out, just as small snakes suck out the eggs of large birds. The Snake Demon leaves behind these tokens in the empty cradles." He presented the Czar with the latest token, woven strands of grass bundled together tightly in the shape of a snake. The bundle was tied approximately every inch along its foot length with other strands of grass. It was definitely spooky and upsetting.

Ordinarily, Mikhailovich could care less about other clan's problems. However, in this case, it resonated within him; he had just brought his two children here. He and Zdlenka looked at each other, thinking the same thought: What if this Snake Demon kills my children! Quickly the Czar exclaimed, "Tamboltz, I am glad you brought this matter to me. We will ride immediately to your huts, and I will personally see if I can sort out what is happening here."

Two other clan representatives had also come along with Tamboltz, the Yaro clan and the Lochek clan. Both had similar stories; both clans were located fairly close to the Kaluga clan this spring. The Czar took two actions before he left. One, he ordered fifty of his men to guard his children at night. Two, he sent riders off to visit all the other clans to find out if any other clan had babies killed mysteriously.

Next morning, the twins arrived at the Kaluga summer clan encampment of nearly two hundred huts. His first action was to interview all the grieving mothers. Uniformly, he got the same story. Each had put their baby to bed in the commonly used wooden rocking cradles; sometime during the night, the Snake Demon stole the baby, leaving a crudely made snake idol in the cradle; no one heard anything. Always, when they searched the surrounding lands the next day, they would find the dead baby body. Under further questioning, on several occasions the demon left a visible trail across the grasslands, but it always ended just inside the wooded hilltops nearby.

"Why would a demon leave a visible trail?" asked Zdlenka, absorbed in attempting to understand the situation. Surrounded by other clan members, they discussed possibilities. It was hard for Mikhailovich to discount the now commonly held view of a Snake Demon. Yet, if he could not, this alone could derail their entire plans for conquering Tarra. Neither twin had ever allowed for anything like this in their scheming.

Finally, Mikhailovich picked up on his sister's question. "Look, a man leaves a trail. Have we ever seen a trail left by the horse god or the fertility god or the woodland god or any of our other spirits? No. We must be dealing with some demented, evil person. Who would want to kill babies, let alone in this manner? He has got to be a crazy man." While some tended to believe he might be right, most just nodded or grunted, but were far from convinced.

Later the twins took a walk around the outskirts of the encampment so they could talk freely. "Mikhailovich, this is the most serious obstacle we have ever faced to our plans. If this demon continues unabated, the clans will not be sending any more of their fighters. We will have failed just as we are succeeding! We have to get to the bottom of this thing," she stated clenching her teeth.

"You can say that again, sis," he replied. "You know, it is almost as if someone out there," he waved his arms over the landscape, "is actively trying to stop us from continuing to conquer Tarra."

"Say, could it be one of those Evil Witches of the Greenway?" inspiration suddenly struck Zdlenka. "We are in the western section of the steppes fairly close to the Greenway."

"You might be on to something there. The Evil Witches could cast some spell hiding their passage into a hut and snatching the babies. Damn witches anyway!" he cursed. After thinking about it further, he said, "Well, maybe not. How could a woman commit such a crime against a defenseless newborn baby? Even in the Sea Princes, who are notorious for brutalizing women, even they do not kill babies, let alone suck their brains out. That is just plain revolting."

"They'd have to be insane," she commented, "totally crazy. Even so, we've never heard of anyone losing their mind here in the steppes and committing such awful crimes. I think you are right; we are dealing with an insane, crazy person or persons. But how to prove it? How to catch them and slay them? Now that is the question. It is one thing for us to suspect this and quite another for the clans to accept this reasoning. I can see why assigning these deeds to a Snake Demon appeals to them so readily. I cannot even imagine ever killing babies, let alone eating them."

"You are right. We are going to have to catch this demon red-handed and kill it. Otherwise, the clans are never going to believe us and never send their fighters anymore," he commented. "We could send out hunting parties looking for this demon person, but with the vastness of the steppes, it would be like looking for a blade of grass in this sea of grass. No, we are just going to have to be on hand when he strikes again, then track him, and slay him."

This was far easier stated than executed. Two weeks later, all the messengers that the Czar sent finally reported to him here at this clan's encampment. The news was staggering and wholly unexpected. A dozen clans reported babies slain by the Snake Demon. All told, fifty-three babies had died over the span of nearly three years. More importantly, every single occurrence happened when the clan was camped here in the far southwestern section of the steppes. This provided them with the first solid evidence that the demon was only operating in a narrow zone of their country.

"If the demon only operates in this area and if we must catch him, then I've got an idea, Mikhailovich," Zdlenka proposed. "Let's request that all clans, save say this one, immediately move far to the east, completely out of the way. Then, there would be only this one for the demon to stalk and strike."

"Brilliant, Czarina," he teased. "Consider it done. I should have thought of this myself, but then you are better at planning things, sis. I'll issue the orders immediately. Several women are going to be having their babies soon. As much as I hate it, we can use them as bait and with luck catch this demon red-handed before it can kill again." Quickly, he issued the orders to his messengers who galloped off later in the day to deliver the Czar's orders. Meanwhile, the twins settled in for a long wait.

During this lengthy waiting period, Zdlenka made another observation whose significance was huge, though neither recognized the ultimate effect it would have in their land. Already, each clan had an enormous amount of treasure. Women routinely wore expensive jewelry. It was not uncommon to see families eating off golden plates with golden candelabra for light. In fact, there such a volume of heavy gold and silver objects in each encampment, that moving from place to place, as was the historical tradition with the clans, proved very difficult indeed. The people had become weighed down by all the loot that they had acquired. Further, gold and gems were now so plentiful that they almost could not be used as a means of exchange! The importance of this and its impact neither recognized; they just observed it.

Two weeks had passed; Zdlenka felt very uneasy, and still there was no sign of the Snake Demon. Yet, she felt certain that the encampment was being watched. "I feel like cold, evil eyes are staring at me. It gives me goose bumps, honestly, Mik."

"Yes, I feel it too. Something is out there watching and waiting, something very evil," he replied. "It's like it is just waiting for another chance to strike. Maybe it can tell there are two women who are near their time, do you suppose it can?"

"Suppose it comes in the dead of night. How are we going to see it coming in time to prevent another death? How are we going to track it? If we have a roaring campfire, it might not strike. Right now, there is not much moonlight either," she asked with a sense of worry in her voice.

"Perhaps that works both ways; we can't see it, and it can't see us," he offered. "I wonder if it has a keen sense of smell and could smell our presence? Do you suppose we ought to send out scouts to see if we can find any signs of this demon?"

"You've pretty well tried scouts already; they couldn't find anything. If it really is some kind of demon, why it probably can smell or sense us. On the other hand, if it is a demented person, no. If it really is a demon, Mik, our plans to conquer Tarra are completely gone. I'd rather not think on that one, not after all we have done and been through. I hope it is just some insane person. That we can handle. I think we are going to have to deal with it soon, Illi's probably going to have her baby tonight."

"Okay then, I'm going to try and get some sleep during the day. I'm going to be up and awake all night and see if I can catch this demon," he pronounced.

Sure enough, around midnight, a new baby boy was born. Next morning, the proud parents brought their son out to see his new home on the Northern Steppes. Following time honored traditions, the Welcoming Ceremony was held, in which the new boy was presented to the clan and the clan to him, person by person. Zdlenka's sole comment spoke volumes, "If the Snake Demon is watching, it surely knows a baby is here for the taking."

While the ceremony was in full swing, Mikhailovich snuck into that family's hut, hopefully unnoticed. His plan was simple: he would spend all day hiding in the hut. Then, at night, he would stand watch over the newborn. If the Snake Demon made its appearance, he would raise the alarm and attack it. Neither twin said much about what if it really was a demon, though. Of course, the only real problem with the plan is that newborn babies need frequent feedings and sleep only a few hours at a time.

Nothing happened that first night, and the parents had to bring Mikhailovich his meals. He did venture outside to stretch once in the early morning. After a few days, all settled into a routine, waiting for the demon to strike. Half of their fighters began sleeping some during the day and only pretended to sleep at night. At least a dozen men would be ready to answer the call of Mikhailovich, should he spot the demon entering the hut.

Then, heavy rain clouds rolled in late one evening, complete with heavy thunder and lightning. During one flash that illuminated the freaky looking world, Mikhailovich spied something pushing the entrance flap aside. He was hiding behind a large number of sacks and saddles so that only his head was barely visible. Thus, Mikhailovich could see straight at the entrance flap. The newborn's cradle was just beyond the pile to his left, while his sleeping parents were on the right. Panic swept over Mikhailovich as he glimpsed the Snake Demon. It appeared somewhat man-like, except it did not walk; it crawled.

Between lightning flashes, he watched petrified as each flash showed the demon gradually drawing closer to the baby cradle. Just as a hand reached for the baby, Mikhailovich forced his body to do his will. He yelled loudly, leaping up and over the sacks and gear. Startled, the demon moved even more quickly, retreating out of the entrance into the dark, rain-drenched night. Mikhailovich drew his magical sword and ran out into the storm after the demon. He saw a man-like creature slithering crudely across the well-trampled grass of the camp heading toward the tall grasses that lay beyond the encampment.

Both parents were now up; the woman held on to her son while her husband, sword in hand, joined Mikhailovich just outside the entrance. However, the Czar's handpicked men also responded; several threw a lot of wood on the nearly dead fires while the rest ran over to where Mikhailovich was standing. Zdlenka, awoken by the cries, stepped outside to see as well, quickly moving over to her brother's side. "Is this the demon?" she asked fearfully.

"Men, we have our demon. Circle around it so it cannot get to the tall grasses and elude us. Form a circle, but keep your distance. Make sure that it has nowhere to slither away from us!" More men, roused by the commotion, joined their Czar. Within two minutes, they had formed a complete circle around the demon, though none ventured closer than fifty feet from it. More than a little fear was felt during the brief glimpses of the creature when the lightning flashed. The creature saw all avenues of escape had been cut off, and it stopped moving.

Slowly, Mikhailovich, sword raised high over his head ready to strike, took cautious steps toward the demon. Very hesitatingly, other men followed suit. The bonfires finally caught, and the demon became more readily visible. It watched Mikhailovich closely, never taking its eyes off him. It completely ignored all the other men; they refused to get even half as close to the demon as did their Czar. Now he was so close that Mikhailovich could clearly see that this demon was really a pitiful, decrepit man. The Snake Demon suddenly began laughing in an insane, gleeful, hideous manner, piercing the night with his sounds. Even as Mikhailovich moved to within striking distance, he only laughed harder. Now, he could see the drool and blood covered mouth and beard, complete with rotting teeth. Even from this distance, the smell of the man was positively nauseating.

As Mikhailovich swung his magical blade, the Snake Demon continued his diabolical, insane laughter. Only when his head was severed by Mikhailovich's mighty swing did silence reappear. One by one, everyone moved close to see just who and what the Snake Demon had been. Both Zdlenka and Mikhailovich were shocked; both instantly recognized that face. It was the face that had been haunting them ever since they first rode through Florintine Junction on their way to capture Zargarb. It was the face of Zeb Markesh, one of the two faces that had haunted their memories for three years now.

While the clan celebrated the next day, burning the filthy demon body in a huge fire, the twins were sober and moody. Both now realized that the reason they had been haunted by the memories of those two men that day was because they had stared into the eyes of men who had just gone insane, crazy, psychotic. It had riveted their attention and still did. One of the two men was still out there in Tarra somewhere and that filled them both with a very uneasy feeling. True, the Czar sent word to all the clans about the slaying of the Snake Demon, and his fame grew enormously among the clans. Their Czar had single-handedly slain the demon during a storm. While the twins rode back to their camp that day, Zdlenka tried to put a positive slant on things, "At least he will not be interfering with our plans of conquest anymore. The clans ought to send along all their fighters after this." In the back of her mind came the though, *Are we responsible for having driven those men insane?* It was a chilling thought that she could never dispel. At night when she retired and just before she fell asleep, it kept reappearing in her mind. It affected her sleeping ever after; from this moment onward, she always slept poorly.

Chapter 28 From the Ashes of Sol

Spring had just arrived here in the extreme south of Juda Arad in 587 AH. General Theos Lacerta and his remaining seven hundred Centurions had encamped just across the Dakar River that formed a natural barrier between the savannahs of the Southlands and the arid semi-desert Arad. The marvelous Centurion-made paved roadway Y-ed here, one section headed north to Jerilum while the other veered to the northwest and Al Barq. Still the Galts did not attack.

On the contrary, his advanced scouts reported that Strokova was now assaulting the Land of the Seven Sea Princes. General Lacerta just could not believe his incredible luck. As a military commander, had he been in Strokova's position, he would have continued the battle because their small remaining forces ought to have been easily defeated, leaving the entire Southlands and Megalos defenseless and ripe for the taking. Now he had time on his side, if not reinforcements.

He made no move to retake Al Barq, however. That city was destroyed . His scouts reported that only the burned-out adobe shells of the once proud city remained, silent specters of what once had been. Even the docks were gone. Yes, Al Barq would have to be completely rebuilt, requiring significant funds and far more manpower than General Lacerta had. Instead, he concentrated his fortification efforts here just across the shallow river. With only seven hundred men, he could easily be out-flanked on either side. This worried him all winter.

Then one night, in his mind he heard a cold, unemotional voice speak: *Fight a fighting withdrawal. You will know when it is time to counterattack.* More than slightly spooked, he looked around his darkened tent. No one else was present. He wiped the cold sweat from his brow and laid back down on his bedroll. However, his mind rapidly calculated the affect of a fighting withdrawal. If he did not get significant reinforcements, he had no other choice. He had never lost a war yet and had no intention of losing this one. Battles, yes, but the war was far from over.

The serious problem with a fighting a withdrawal of foot soldiers from attacking cavalry was enormous. Speed was everything. Foot soldiers could not hope to outdistance galloping cavalry, a lesson that he had relearned during his horrible retreat from Jerilum. No, the retreat would have to be on his terms, not that of the enemy.

At the staff meeting, he announced his Grand Plan of Retreat. "Gentlemen, when the Galts next attack us, we are going to fight a fighting withdrawal, but on our terms." He emphasized the "our" heavily. "What can stop cavalry? One, an even larger cavalry force; we don't have any, unless the Emperor creates one for us. I've asked, but who knows. Two, natural barriers; we are across the river here, but this shallow river will not stop them for a minute. Once beyond here, the Southlands is vast; natural barriers are going to be very hard to find. Three, a hail of arrows; now this is something that we can do, given enough time for construction of bows and arrows and of course training. Men, we will pick our spots to stand and defend, raining arrows of death until we evacuate that position. Each position that we choose must be chosen for its defensive capabilities as well as ease of rapid evacuation. Also, men, we are going to borrow a tactic that the religious fanatics of Juda Arad used on us: hidden pits to break charging horse lines."

He continued outlining his strategy. "You see, once we choose a defensive position, we will also decide how we are going to evacuate that position. Our evacuation route will be carefully mined with numerous concealed pits that will trip a horse, taking it and its rider out of the picture. Once they charge after us and lose numerous horses and men, they will necessarily stop and move forward very slowly, examining every inch of the ground, while we are running away to the next defensible position. Any questions?" He felt unduly proud of his plan.

"Are we going to have the time to build all these things?" one Major inquired.

"Glad you asked that. Yes, as you all have heard, Strokova is going after the Land of the Seven Sea Princes this year. My bet is that he will be at that task for several years, given that these barbarians do not seem to want to fight in the wintertime. Depending upon how well the cities there hold out, I give us two to three years to prepare. During this time, let us hope and pray that the Emperor sends us all the forces that we need to go on the offensive instead. Take heart men, I have heard that over a thousand new men are on their way even now, with more coming as they complete their basic training. Perhaps, we might even field a sizeable cavalry force — now wouldn't that be just the thing. Men, let us not count on having sufficient forces to go on the offensive. Rather, let us be conservative and establish a continuous line of defenses, all the way back to Sud, if we have the time. I know that is some eight hundred miles, but if we can fight a slow withdrawal, my guess is that we can stall them for perhaps another year, giving the Emperor even more time to field a huge army with which to defeat these barbarians from the north."

Before the Galt attack came in the late summer of 589 AH, fully one hundred fifty defensible fortifications had been built by the industrious Centurions. Each averaged about five miles from the next, stretching in a line more than halfway back to Sud. Given that the likely countermove on Strokova's part, once he'd encountered the first few defensive positions along the road, would be to flank them, say five to ten miles either east or west of the roadway, after the first five fortifications, General Lacerta began placing some on their flanks, at first a few miles from the road, and then even further out. From the eyes of a high flying hawk, these fortified positions fanned out like an enormous arrowhead. However, none was placed further than twenty-five miles from the roadway. These outlying positions were also randomly placed, following no discernable pattern, save they were chosen for their defensive position.

The design of each fort was similar in nature, though always taking advantage of the lay of the land. Wooden posts were set in the ground, protruding some six feet up, behind which archers could safely stand and counter-fire at will. Running off at one hundred twenty degrees from the front wall, the side walls flared out. There were no back walls. All around the sides of the forts, three-foot pits were dug and hidden with mats made from the yucca plant and covered with dirt and bits of grass. The objective was to make the concealed pits look like the normal terrain. Always, there was a safe evacuation route just to the rear of the fort. Several brighter soldiers added their own personal touches to the pits, placing sharpened sticks pointing upwards, designed to skewer anything that entered the pit. To conceal further their safe avenues of escape, parallel trenches were dug on either side of the safe path. These General Lacerta intended to fill with oil and set ablaze as they retreated, giving them a cloud of smoke in which to hide. Sufficient food and water were also stored at each fort for the retreating men. Hence, when retreating, each man could travel light and make the fastest possible speed. Yes, the General was quite proud of his accomplishments, certain that he could fight a fighting withdrawal from a charging cavalry army. Now if he only had sufficient men.

Disciple Yazi was most impressed with the greatest city of Megalos, Galantas. Every day he marveled over the breathtaking beauty of the white marble city. Galantas was the most impressive city Yazi had seen; he suspected there was no finer city on Tarra. It was here in the heart of the Centurion empire that he chose to establish his mother Church of Jehosanity. True, he had been very successful in Sud, creating converts to Jehosanity by the thousands. He had even seen to the conversion of several warehouses into full-fledged churches. He'd personally already trained over a dozen new High Priests of Jehosanity. In fact, so popular had his religion become that he'd personally received a request from the Emperor to visit Megalos and discuss it with him. That was just the signal Yazi had been waiting for these past two years.

Emperor Titus still wore his youth on his face. Though now fifty years of age, his face looked more like he was twenty. His bronzed skin contrasted sharply with his black hair and black eyes, though if one looked carefully, some grey hair was visible. Daily, the Emperor plucked those out, of course. Outlined in his bright yellow robe of office, he still cut a smashing figure; at least all of the courtly women told him so. However, Emperor Titus had been handpicked to replace Emperor Hiro, who had led the country into such a wanton lascivious behavior that Sol had struck him down with a massive lightning strike many years ago. Seizing upon the opportunity to strengthen its control over Megalos, the Church of Sol had chosen Titus, who was a devout worshiper of Sol.

For many years, Emperor Titus was basically a puppet or figurehead for the Church of Sol. Gone were the days when people lived in terror of Emperor Hiro's whims. For many years, the church had led the country without a hitch, even reforming slightly the lascivious ways many citizens had adopted. All that changed when the barbarian from the Northern Steppes, Mikhailovich Strokova, invaded and conquered their occupied country of Juda Arad. At first, Titus believed what the High Priest told him, that Sol had intervened and spared the final sacking of Megalos's greatest living general, Theos Lacerta. However, the Emperor no longer believed that. On the contrary, all reports told of the sacking of the wealthy cities in the Land of the Sea Princes. Even he could see that it was far more lucrative to attack these cities than to chase down the rag tag remnants of General Lacerta's army. Daily, doubts grew in the Emperor's mind. It didn't help that the High Priest should have retired many years ago. The aged priest seldom now seemed to have a firm grasp on situations.

Enter the new religion, this Jehosanity. Yes, the sweeping success it had in Sud attracted the attention of the Emperor. For over a year, he had sent out spies to gather information on this new church and its leaders, especially this man from the Arad, Yazi Rigan. Emperor Titus became fascinated with Yazi, for at no time did any of his spies ever report that Yazi had any inclination to rule the country, quite unlike the High Priest of Sol. Perhaps this more than any other single aspect most intrigued him. At last, he openly sent forth an invitation for Yazi to take the ferry across to Megalos and come to visit him in Galantas.

Yazi, ever thinking ahead, had long ago adopted sky blue as the official colors for his priests. Yes, everyone in this land wore robes or togas as they were known. The color of the robe indicated the status or rank of the wearer. The only bright yellow robe in all of Megalos was worn by the Emperor. His staff wore light yellow togas. Senators wore grey; commoners, white; priests of Sol, royal purple togas; artisans and those in the construction trades, brown ones; city guards, red. Thus, to distinguish his Priests of Jehosanity, Yazi chose sky blue, a color that was most impressive and not easily missed by anyone.

Thus properly attired in his immaculate sky blue toga, Yazi walked into the Royal Palace, accompanied by six attendants in light yellow togas. His extensive research of the Emperor had been accomplished in time for this visit. Hence, he had what he thought was a very good understanding of the man and the office and even the ground layout of the palace. Yazi also knew that he was about to embark on the sales pitch of his life. If he could reach this one, single man, then all of Megalos was his for the taking, religiously, that is.

For this meeting, Emperor Titus had dismissed all of the normal courtiers, who tended to live in his palace. Gone were his advisors; this was to be a very personal meeting, though he stationed numerous guards just outside the entrance to his throne room, just in case of trouble. "Ah, there you are, Yazi Rigan. I am Emperor Titus, how should I address you Sir? High Priest?" He began in a formal, yet pleasant tone.

"Your Excellency," Yazi bowed low as he had been told he must do out of respect for the Emperor. "I am the Holy Disciple of Jehosanity, a Follower of the Great Messiah, before he was slain and arose from the dead to show us the path to Heaven, the Realm of Jehosa. Please just call me Disciple Yazi, Emperor Titus."

"Very good, Disciple Yazi. Please, have a seat near me. Let us dispense with all the normal formalities. Just call me Titus, please; it's simpler."

"Ah then, Titus," he said as he adjusted his toga and sat close to the Emperor facing him, "call me Yazi, please. How may I be of service?"

"Simple, I wish to know all about your religion and your god, Jehosa. Please enlighten me. I've heard many of my people swear by your new religion." There, he could not have made his request plainer. He sat back to listen and to study this man.

"Some accuse me of being long-winded, Titus. Am I under any time limitations? I suspect that you are a very busy man indeed." Yazi was being tactful; he left nothing to chance. He did not want to be only partially done when the Emperor was suddenly called to other duties.

Titus smiled. *An astute observation.* "Yazi, for you, I have cleared my calendar for the rest of the day, if you can talk that long," he jested.

Emboldened, Yazi began. "We, you and I and all of the other people on Tarra, we are all immortal, spiritual beings, made in the likeness of Jehosa. Now days, we all have these fleshly bodies which is inhabited by our soul, that part of us that is immortal, but it was not once so. In the beginning, we were all in Jehosa's realm called Heaven. Yes, we were like gods in Heaven, a place in which nothing is found wanting. All the food, drink, love one can desire; days are cool, not sweleringly hot. Life was eternal bliss in his Kingdom. Then, came the First Sin, committed by Jaleene Amir, wife of Amal Amir. She had accepted the fruit of life from Lucifer, disguised as a man-sized snake. Lucifer is the archenemy of Jehosa, representing all that is dark, foul, and evil. Please, Titus, realize that our downfall from Heaven was entirely the doing of women! It is because of women that we are here today in these bodies!"

"Now this so angered Jehosa that he spent his rage building a world in exile, Tarra. When he finished, he exiled all people to Tarra, giving them fleshly bodies with which to learn right from wrong. Only when one has purified his soul will Jehosa accept the soul back into his realm. Once on Tarra, we took up residence in a land called Anuir, which lies to the south and west of Juda Arad. I believe it is now called the Red Desert. Yet, still women committed more sins, even as they do here in your palace, if I am not mistaken. This continual sinning so angered Jehosa that he sent fire from the sky to destroy all of the Anuir. In the chaos, survivors of that cataclysm fled to all corners of Tarra."

"Yet, Jehosa has given us the Holy Decalogue, which if we follow it, our souls will be purified. These are our guiding principles.

There is no god but Jehosa.

Do not worship any other god but the One God, Jehosa.

Set aside the Holy Day, Saturday, from your labors and worship the Lord that day.

Respect and serve thy mother and thy father, for they have labored long in your raising.

Do not kill another, excepting your enemies and enemies of Jehosa.

Do not steal from another, excepting your enemies and enemies of Jehosa.

Do not commit adultery.

Do not lie to another, excepting your enemies and enemies of Jehosa.

Do not desire another's house or possessions.

Do unto men as you would have men do unto you."

(Note to the reader: Again, note the changes to the Decalogue as modified by Yazi.)

"So you see, it was not Sol who destroyed your sinful predecessor. No, it was in fact Jehosa, just as he has done so in the past. Yes, at this point in our history, Titus, so many of us have totally lost our way. It was true in my original homeland of Juda Arad. Yes, I used to be a holy warrior, a messiah, even attacking some of your Centurions there, but that was long, long ago. That is in part why I am here. I am making amends for my youthful crimes against Megalos. You see, I was chosen by Jehosa to spread his truths. I digress."

"Since we are all so utterly lost, Jehosa sent his only son, the Great Messiah, to us, to live in a fleshly body for a time and teach us the path to righteousness. For years, I was one of his ten chosen ones, the Holy Disciples, following him around the Arad, writing down all of his teachings, watching all of the miracles he did. Yes, he did perform many miracles." Here Yazi spent an hour recounting as many of the more miraculous healings that Jes performed. He knew that this was a vital aspect, if he were to reach this Emperor. Indeed, Titus stopped him many times to ask for details. He was intrigued that so many people witnessed these miracles. Now Yazi knew that he would ultimately "get" Titus.

"Besides healing, he also tried to teach the common man what was needed for their souls to be worthy of reentering Heaven. He even took a traveling companion, a long haired prostitute, around with him showing her and others the true path to salvation, though admittedly, she never followed it — not surprising, as she was a woman, instigator of the First Sin.

"I must point out that never *once* did our Great Messiah ever fight or slay a single Centurion, or any person for that matter. Further, when the others in the Arad were about to rebel against the Centurions, he even let himself be captured and crucified on the cross in Jerilum so that everyone would see him die and then be resurrected from the dead, walking among us again for a short while. He vainly hoped that people would see the path to righteousness."

"Those that do not purify their souls have their souls go to Hell, a horrible place of eternal damnation, run by Lucifer himself. Hell is full of hot fires and sulfur odors, which make a Megalos' summer seem cool and cozy by comparison. Indeed, when these barbarians from the Northern Steppes die, their souls are doomed to spend the rest of eternity rotting in Hell, contemplating their foul deeds."

"Thus, when our Great Messiah finally ascended into Heaven after eating the Last Feast with us, his final command was for we disciples to travel all of Tarra and spread his teachings so that when these fleshly bodies die, the souls may be found worthy of entering Jehosa's realm, Heaven. I took up the challenge. Because of my youthful transgressions against the former Governor of Juda Arad, I chose to come here that I might make amends by helping all of you purify your souls that they may enter Jehosa's Holy Realm."

"Already, thousands in Sud have begun to worship Jehosa and embark their souls on the path to righteousness. However, Titus, as you well know, I may be too late. The Galts are still at war, conquering all the Sea Princes, lands you once attempted to civilize, driving your remaining Centurions from those lands."

Titus looked somewhat ill at ease; he said, "Is there no hope for us then? Do you see none?"

"Jehosa is a merciful God. When he sees that his children, we are all his children, have repented their sins and have begun to walk the path to righteousness, he will intervene on behalf of his children. After all, it is his goal as well, for his children to come to their senses, so to speak, and reenter his realm, Heaven. However, to date, lasciviousness, crudity, greed, promiscuity — all these still run rampant throughout your people. True, I have made a good beginning in Sud, but Sud is but a small part of your lands. Yes, Megalos is still being punished for all its sins."

"What must we do to gain the favor of Jehosa once more, so that he will act to help us here in our hour of most desperate need?" begged Emperor Titus.

"Ah, you ask the very same question that I have asked. Long have I prayed to Jehosa, asking for guidance on this very issue." Cleverly, Yazi said no more.

After seeing that Yazi was not going to say anything further, Titus pleaded, "And did he answer your prayers?" He fully expected to hear something like let Yazi run Megalos.

"Yes, Jehosa answered my prayers. Three things must be done to satisfy Jehosa that you, as a people, are sincere in reforming your ways. One, you must publically state that Jehosanity is now the official and only religion in all of Megalos. Two, you must grant us a small parcel of land somewhere on Megalos proper and allow us to construct a grand Mother Church of Jehosanity from which we can service all the other churches scattered throughout the realm and your colonies. We must be granted total autonomy from all governmental authorities, free to pursue the Holy Path without interference from any governmental decrees and doctrines. Three, I must meet personally with General Lacerta, and if he personally becomes a follower of Jehosanity, then Jehosa will work a miracle on his behalf, leading your forces to ultimate victory over the barbarians."

"I know that this is asking much you, which is why I did not mention it until you specifically asked me. Time is not an issue here. So take your time. Perhaps when things are the darkest, wisdom will come, as well as your miracle."

Titus chuckled, "Well, you certainly ask for most unusual things, that's for sure. You do not want to have any hand in the governing of Megalos? I find that hard to believe. The Church of Sol has always been active in running things here, from the background, mind you. Now your first request will be hard to meet. As for the second request, I will see to it later today. Please stay in Galantas for a few more days; enjoy the sights. I should be able to acquire some land on which you may build your church. A Royal Decree is all that is necessary to ensure your autonomy. As for General Lacerta, I will send him a message, but I cannot guarantee that he will do as you desire. I take it if I ordered him to do it, then that would not count."

"Right, that is why Jehosa has asked that I meet with him personally. I can express my undying gratitude to the land grant. Thousands of followers will also want to thank you as well. You have made a very good first step of three. Thank you Emperor Titus. It is my fondest desire to see Megalos free from this barbarian invasion and your lands renewed." The two chatted further on smaller matters, and then Yazi took his leave.

Later, settled into a room in the finest inn in Galantas, Yazi celebrated his victory over the Centurions. He, Yazi Rigan, had just done what no messiah had ever accomplished. He had personally converted the Arad's worst enemies, the infidels, to a worship of the Arad God, Jehosa. *What irony!* He thought. *I did what Jes Amir could not do.* Well, factually, he only had achieved one of the three steps, but he felt certain that in time the other two conditions would be met.

Emperor Titus also felt most relieved. This new church definitely did not want to have anything to do with running the country, of that he was now quite certain. *How unlike the Church of Sol*, he thought. Yes, he could make a small land grant, for that was one of the things any Emperor could do, just part of his job. He could dispatch General Lacerta, but Yazi would have to meet with the general and do the convincing, not he, the Emperor. Yes, Titus liked this aspect. In truth, the only obstacle was ousting the Church of Sol. This was something he was not yet ready to do, politically or socially. The timing was not yet right, so he would merely delay until that time did arrive. Emperor Titus celebrated that evening with a grand feast; he had gotten all that he had wanted from Yazi and this new religion, this Jehosanity.

By the summer of 589 AH, the Emperor had formed up a sizeable defense force of new legions. Recall that a legion had one hundred soldiers in it. Under pressure to react at once, he had already sent ten legions north to help General Lacerta back in 587. Since then, he had been busy. He stationed ten more legions to help defend the Church of Sol, those legions were mostly deployed where the church desired protection, mostly on Megalos proper. Three out of every ten new legions that he formed and had trained, he kept for his own personal use.

Here in the summer of 589, Emperor Titus had thirty legions under his personal control. Ten of these, he made publically visible, guarding his palace and other key sites throughout Megalos proper. These ten legions he officially claimed to have. The remaining twenty legions he had kept secret even from the Church of Sol and from the Senate. More to the point, of the other fifty legions, he placed twenty legions in and around Sud so that the barbarians could not cross the Shallow Firth and assault Megalos. In the early spring, he ordered the remaining thirty legions to march north to join up with General Lacerta.

Of the cavalry, he had left that aspect to the Senate. He knew the cost of fielding one cavalry man was easily ten times that of a common foot soldier. Besides, horses were at a premium. After three years of debate, committee meetings, conferences, and such, the Senate had finally funded and equipped ten legions of elite cavalry. However, only five legions were sent north to General Lacerta this past spring. The other five cavalry legions had only recently been formed up and were not done with their basic training. Hence, these were stationed outside of Sud and were not expected to be fully operational for yet another season.

It is noteworthy that none of these ten thousand foot soldiers was Rear Guard, that is, none was older men, retired, or not so fit career soldiers. All were youthful, in their prime, and fit, representing the best of the current youth of Megalos. In fact, one legion of cavalry was second generation slaves, blacks tracing their parents back deep into the Southlands. These men wanted to contribute to the defense of their homeland, and the Senate, desperate for good horsemen, accepted them into service, breaking all previous traditions in Megalos. Had all these ten thousand foot soldiers and one thousand cavalry been placed in one position, General Lacerta could have gone on the offensive that summer. However, they were not so placed.

General Lacerta had command of four thousand foot soldiers, five hundred cavalry and his remaining seven hundred Rear Guard soldiers. He knew this was insufficient to stop a charging army of cavalry that may number at least four thousand. Worse still, half of these new legions were not equipped with bows and arrows. Thus, his first action was to so equip them and get them trained. These twenty legions he placed halfway between Sud and the frontier front lines. He kept his cavalry back ready to exploit any weakness in the barbarian lines. Five hundred cavalry would not fare well tackling four thousand cavalry. He divided the remaining forces among the various fortresses, with more being assigned to the forts near the border of Juda Arad and the Southlands. Thus, when the Galts finally came in the late summer of 589, General Lacerta was as prepared as he could hope to be.

Early August of 589, Mikhailovich Strokova halted his vast army of four thousand five hundred cavalry just across the Dakar River separating Juda Arad from the Southlands. His army was impressive, stretching for miles on either side of his position; his burly, seasoned fighters sat watching their enemy hiding behind wooden barricades just across the shallow river. They awaited his order to attack. Just behind them stretched miles of supply wagons as well as empty treasure wagons. Zdlenka sat on her mare beside her brother, gazing at the grandeur of the Galt army. Never in their history had such a huge army been gathered. Both twins felt a surge of immense pride in their accomplishment. No longer were the Galts to be driven like cattle back into the Northern Steppes. Now they could ride out of their land and demand respect of others!

They were now the masters of Juda Arad and all the Lands of the Seven Sea Princes, the upstart eighth Sea Prince did not count. True, they left no men in charge of their conquered territory. There was no need. If they wanted anything from a conquered country, they only needed to send in a company of fifty fighters to get it. No, they chose not to waste even a single clan fighter on such governing duties. They had no desire to govern their conquered lands. In truth, they already had taken what they wanted, anything of value, particularly gold and silver items and useful weapons of war.

Zdlenka commented, "Mik, eight hundred miles further south lies the vast riches of Megalos, which should make all that we have taken thus far seem small by comparison."

"Yes," he replied with a satisfied air, "and all that stands between us and victory are these puny wooden walls with pitifully few defenders. It appears that the Centurions have pulled the majority of their forces back closer to their island. I suspect we will meet their large army as we near their southern town of Sud. Between here and there, from what we have learned, are numerous gold, silver and gem stone mines. That will indeed be a treasure to confiscate."

"Ah, but the finding of them, that will be the challenge. They are obviously not on the main paved road. Much scouting of the lands will be needed to find them. I wonder if the Centurions are leaving large forces to guard their mines?" she pondered.

"Well, I guess we had better get started then," he grinned. He raised his hand high and then brought it down in a sweeping arc. Hundreds of Galts started their traditional wild yelling, and one thousand began the charge across the river to assault this first fortress of the Centurions.

General Lacerta, on his roan mare, rode up and down the defensive line, issuing last minute orders. Here he placed five legions to defend against the initial assault. He was more than gratified to see that only a thousand cavalry rode across the river. He did not have to face the entire army. This factor also was part of his overall strategy. It was physically impossible to get four thousand cavalrymen into the smaller area that his first fortress occupied. True, he could be flanked, but then the surprise concealed pits would take their toll. He had three years to fortify this first defensive position; his men had not been idle.

Here he had deployed three newer legions of young men alongside of two legions of his seasoned Rear Guard units. He wanted a good portion of this initial set of defenders to be familiar with the fighting style of the Galts. He hoped the seasoned older men would offset their liabilities and add a measure of confidence to the untested youthful soldiers who were experiencing combat for the first time. His was a wise decision indeed. The wild yelling tended to unnerve the new soldiers.

The Centurions waited patiently behind their protective wooden walls, bows at the ready. When the barbarians finally closed to striking distance, General Lacerta commanded, "Fire at will!" Hundreds of twangs resounded with a hail of deadly arrows landing among the charging Galts. Horses fell; men fell. Arrows flew back from these seasoned Galt cavalrymen; they were highly skilled at firing from galloping horseback. However, because of the protection offered by the wooden barricades, only one Galt arrow in ten found a mark, whereas nearly four in ten found their marks from the Centurions. For an hour, the Galts charged in close to the walls, launching a volley of arrows at the defenders only to ride swiftly off again. Slowly the deadly arrows took their toll on both sides.

Seeing that they were taking far too many casualties, Mikhailovich ordered two groups of five hundred each to circle around to either flank and hit then from the open rear quarters. He watched in horror as the first wave hit the concealed pits, horses stumbling and crashing down, breaking legs or worse, toppling riders hard onto the ground or into pits just ahead of the fallen horses. Quickly, the remainder reined in and stopped, surveying the catastrophe before them. Several sent riders back to Mikhailovich to inform him of this new treachery. One hundred horses were lost in less than a minute, to say nothing of their riders!

The only tactic the flanking Galts could employ was to dismount and close on foot. However, they too fell into the concealed pits, some landing upon the vertical sharpened posts. Thus, the attackers were forced to move forward very slowly, constantly testing the ground before them. Naturally, this made them sitting duck targets for the defenders' arrows. True, had General Lacerta been able to build one massive fortification here and place his entire army in it, he might have been able to defeat the Galts or at least substantially reduce their numbers. However, that would then have left unguarded the entire route to Megalos, something that the General could never condone.

After an hour of combat, the defender's losses mounted up. Hundreds had been wounded or slain. Thus, when they were no longer as effective as required, General Lacerta ordered the pits to be fired. Suddenly long lines of oil fires began burning, creating an acrid, black smoke that quickly covered the field of battle. Once it was thick enough, General Lacerta ordered the retreat. His men began running down the only safe passage avenue southward toward the next defensive position some five miles further south. As he had planned, the smoke cover completely hid their mass evacuation. The additional concealed pits halted any rapid following by the barbarians.

He had lost about half of his men, but Mikhailovich fared far worse, counting five hundred dead or wounded, including well over a hundred precious horses! "Damn, this is not going well at all. This General has one diabolical mind!" he commented to Zdlenka.

"We must see to the immediate healing of those that are wounded, Mik; that must take priority or the men may lose heart," she replied. "I grieve for the horses. Never have we lost so many so quickly, such a wanton tragedy." She was a breda, after all. She signaled for the healing wagons, while he rode off to inspect the carnage and see firsthand the nasty surprises the enemy had unleashed upon his forces.

Mikhailovich and the other group leaders spent the rest of the day examining the battlefield. The smoke died out in less than a half hour, revealing that the Centurions had indeed abandoned this fortification, leaving their dead behind them along with those that were too badly wounded to escape under their own power. These were quickly beheaded. The Galts showed no mercy; they never did. Quickly, the overall defensive strategy was revealed. The hidden pits were all too effective. In the end, they chose to simply detour a mile around this area to avoid the remaining pits; they were that numerous.

As the army began to move in two waves, one flanking to the east and one to the west, Mikhailovich sent out scouts in a wide fan shape pattern. He did not want to be taken by surprise like this again. By late afternoon, he learned that just five miles further down the road lay yet another of these defensive walled fortifications. Evidently, the survivors had retreated to this position. Some of his field commanders took the initiative and attacked this next position, with nearly the same result. True, they eventually took the fortification, but the cost to men and horses was significant.

Thus after the first day of combat, Mikhailovich held council with Zdlenka on how best to deal with these new defenses. She commented, "The frontal zone is obstacle free, plus a small retreating path. This General is trying to force us to charge toward the wooden wall where his archers can reach our riders. True, it is much harder to hit a fast moving target, but still perhaps there is another way."

"They certainly did not have all these archers the last time we encountered these Centurions," he said with a sigh, he rubbed his sweating forehead. "Guess they learn from their mistakes."

"We should not underestimate these Centurions and this General, brother. Remember, before us, they had conquered much of Terra." After a pause, she suggested, "Perhaps we could bring a shielded battering ram to bear. You know, move it up to smash a hole in the center of their wall. The timbers are not that big in diameter; it should be fairly easy to punch into it."

"I believe you are on to something. If we were on foot, then we lose our decided advantage of being on horseback. Yet, if there was a hole punched, our riders could charge straight into their midst. Further, that would break their line of defense. Great thinking. We can put one crew into action positioning the ram. Once a breach is made, the others exploit it on horseback. I'll go explain this to the Captains and see to getting the battering ram ready. It will be far slower going, but this will save casualties. On this trip, I think that is the most important thing to consider. There's going to be precious little treasure for quite some time, I expect."

By noon the next day, the slow moving ram was finally in position just before the barrier wall at the next Centurion defensive fortification. A giant log hung suspended from massive rawhide ropes. One tip was iron re-enforced, designed to penetrate and shatter walls and doors, particularly adobe ones. A giant canopy of hides covered the engine so that twenty-five men could move it slowly into position. It took a large number of strong arms to pull the huge log back so that its forward swing could do the damage. The hide covering protected the men from the expected hail of arrows.

At noon, Mikhailovich gave the hand signal for the assault to begin. Under the expected hail of arrows from the defending Centurions, his men slowly moved the ram towards the direct center of the front wall. While a few arrows did find their mark, the Galts were relatively protected. After a half hour of trial and error, the men heard the sound of music: snapping timbers. An hour after they began, they had made a sufficiently large hole in the wall for their riders to exploit. Hundreds charged past the ram, as the ram men slowly moved it back.

Futilely, General Lacerta formed up foot soldiers to block the onrushing cavalry. "Aim for the horses, kill a horse as it comes through so it can block the hole!" he ordered above the dim of combat. Here was a battle, bone crushing, as horse trampled into men and shields, steel upon steel, arrows firing randomly into the melee. Within a few minutes, General Lacerta saw that too many of his men were down. However, a lucky shot had brought a horse to its knees blocking the hole temporarily. He chose this as the prime time to order the retreat. Once more, blackish smoke suddenly obscured the battlefield as his remaining men ran for their very lives as fast as they could, heading south toward the next fortification.

'Well, that certainly worked better," Zdlenka commented to her brother as they rode down to inspect the battlefield. His men had just finished making sure every Centurion present was dead. The wagons bringing the aid for the wounded men pulled up beside the battering ram.

"Yes, much. We only had two men actually killed and ten wounded. The Centurions fared far worse. It's just very slow going. I doubt that we can take out more than one of these positions a day. Going to be a long time getting to Megalos and her treasures." Just then, a number of scouts that he had sent out on reconnaissance yesterday returned.

Some did not make it back alive; some had to return on foot. Their report was grim. The whole countryside around the main paved roadway was full of seemingly random concealed pits, designed to take out a horse. Breaking a leg is about the worst thing that can happen to a horse, General Lacerta had explained to his foot soldiers. They responded by digging hundreds of these concealed pits. Apparently, these fortifications were placed somewhere around five miles apart down the main route. However, the further south the scouts ventured, the more additional side forts existed and were well manned. "Well, it seems that we cannot easily outflank our opponent," Mikhailovich concluded.

"Surely they have not had time to build fortifications say fifty miles east of the roadway," Zdlenka thought out loud, "or even a hundred. What about sending say a thousand riders inland a fair distance, then have them turn south for say another hundred before heading west to find the road again. They could then attack any fortifications that far away from the rear. They might have better luck that way, and besides the Centurions would have their retreating path cut off."

"I don't like them attacking without our guidance, sis, no telling what blunders they might make. It could be costly," he countered.

"Mikhailovich, we're talking about clans who have been fighting each other for centuries. I think your captains can handle these little skirmishes. It is not as if they're going to encounter a thousand Centurions at one location. So far, there have been only a couple hundred men defending any one fortification, at most. Surely they can handle that."

In the end, he gave in to his sister's plan. The next day, a thousand of his cavalry headed due east, followed by fifty wagons, bearing food, water and some healing supplies. Meanwhile, the remainder of his army moved slowly down the roadway toward the next fortification.

Two days later, a messenger from that raiding party met up with Mikhailovich bearing some news. "Czar, Czarina, you'll never guess what we ran into heading east! On the second day of travel, the countryside totally changed! It opened up into a vast savannah filled with strange animals. We spied a giant cat with orange and black stripes tearing the flesh off an equally strange horse-like creature, only it had black and white stripes! We saw huge herds of deer animals and some enormous four legged ones with a hugely elongated nose that can move around like a tail and touch the ground. These creatures are ten times larger than our horses, at least. Yes, you were right; water seems to be rather scarce, though by luck we found a watering hole. Oh yes, I'm supposed to tell you that we have encountered no more fortifications or any Centurions."

Over dinner, the twins had the messenger describe in detail all these new animals he had seen. Mikhailovich's comment was, "See, there's a vast world out beyond our borders in the Northern Steppes. We should have long ago gone forth to see all this. Before this is over, I want to go and see them for myself!"

Many days later, while his surviving soldiers were running toward the next southern fortification, the general, high atop his horse, saw that indeed they had been outflanked. The fortification they were making for had already been attacked. Smoke still curled into the late afternoon sky from several fires.

As expected, the men who had been slain here were lined up facing the north — at least their heads were, stuck atop their spears, which were implanted in the ground. These barbarians certainly knew how to strike a terror cord in their enemies, he thought to himself. However, his defensive alignment considered just such a flanking move. After all, if he were the attacker, this would have been one of his tactics to try. Quickly, he signaled his men to head to the east; they would just go to a side fortification instead. They just had to run a little further, that's all. Later, they could retreat further and rejoin other forts further south along the road. His Grand Plan for a Fighting Withdrawal was working perfectly. The enemy was able to make only five miles a day. At this rate, it would take the barbarians over three months to reach Sud. Except that there were not many forts built yet that far south. Eventually, he would run out of forts. However, he did not worry about that yet. That would be in a couple months' time.

Days stretched into weeks and weeks into months. Every day the Centurions were forced to retreat still further toward Sud. Daily, General Lacerta faced the loss of more men. Indeed, men who were not outright killed during the defense of the forts and who could not run away during the retreat, had to be left behind and were summarily executed by the victorious Galts. The continuous loss of so many young men began to drain the heart and soul out of the general. His emotions sometimes at night sank to near apathy or hopelessness.

By November 1, he had retreated back to the last fortification that had been hastily built by the reserves back in Sud. This final fortification lay barely a hundred miles from Sud. Here he pooled all of the remaining soldiers from his initial allotment that he had assigned to the fighting withdrawal phase, some five hundred men. He had long ago given the orders for those men in flanking forts to retreat to Sud in relative safety; those numbered another five hundred at most. His five hundred cavalry, who had previously been relaying messages and handling long-range reconnaissance, he had pulled back here to this last fort. His final idea was to use the cavalry to assist those who needed to evacuate this fort when it was no longer feasible to attempt to hold it. In other words, he still had not committed his cavalry to any combat. The other half of the cavalry, another five hundred, were still back in Sud awaiting orders. Fully twenty fresh legions of archer-foot soldiers also were in Sud awaiting deployment orders. Yes, he had lost over fifteen hundred men in this fighting withdrawal, but he had slowed their advance down enormously. However, once this fortress fell, Sud would be besieged and ultimately Megalos.

The only thing stopping the assault by the barbarians was the weather. Intense thunderstorms blew in from the southwest, sheets of rain fell drenching everyone. Visibility was very poor beyond just a few feet. This was not fighting weather for either side. Since this was considered wintertime down here in the south, General Lacerta knew that these storms sometimes lasted for an entire week. Thus, for once, he welcomed the torrential rains with open arms, hoping that no fighting would occur until the storm passed on eastward.

In the back of his mind, the General entertained the idea that these Galts might just stop fighting for the rest of the winter period, head back to their homeland, and their snow. At least that had been their pattern for the last four years. Yet no snow ever fell this far south, only torrential monsoon rains. Had General Lacerta been in charge of the barbarian army, retreating to the homeland for the winter would never have been an option! To up and withdraw from all that hard fought territory was, in his opinion, the height of foolishness. If the barbarians were to retreat for the winter, why, he would just rebuild all the fortifications and force the Galts to have to retake them all once more. Would these barbarians be so foolish as to retreat when total, complete victory was within their grasp?

In the quiet of his tent, the General took out the personal letter from Emperor Titus and read it for the twentieth time. His liege wanted him personally to visit with the leader of this new Church of Jehosanity. The Emperor almost promised him a miracle if he saw fit to embrace this religion. Right now, General Lacerta needed a miracle. He sighed and summoned two messengers.

Back in Galantas, Pope Yazi I was overseeing the construction of the Mother Church of Jehosanity. The Emperor, true to his word, had issued a royal proclamation giving Yazi fifty acres of land adjoining a small northern port town of Athos, some twenty-five miles north of Galantas. At once, Yazi utilized the skills of his new followers. Some architects drew up initial plans, stone quarrymen began cutting marble blocks, and the work began, nearly all being done by volunteers. This would be the finest church ever built, if half of what Yazi had in mind could be built.

Yes, he took the title of Pope Yazi I. He realized that he needed a unique title as the supreme leader of his new church. High Priest was already in use by the followers of Sol, and he wanted to do everything he could to distance himself from them. Thus, he created three levels of hierarchy for now. He was the Pope, the supreme leader. He chose five of his best priests and gave them each the title of Bishop. Each bishop oversaw another six local Priests who actually ran his ever-growing smaller, makeshift churches. This way, there could be no confusion between the Church of Jehosanity and the Church of Sol.

On November 4, he received the dispatch for which he had been waiting all these months. General Lacerta agreed to see him. True, he had been following the progress of the war, if you could call a slow, continuous retreat a war. The next day, he packed his traveling bag and prepared to let the messenger lead him back to the General's last known position. Just before he left, he received another letter from the Emperor. It was short and to the point.

5 November 589

Pope Yazi I,

Word has come that General Lacerta has agreed to meet with you. For my part, if and only if, said promised miracle occurs on the battlefield, I will make the public proclamation you requested, fulfilling the balance of the bargain. Before I issue said proclamation, would you be so kind as to visit with me once more? I would like to go over its wording with you.

Kindly,

Emperor Titus

Yazi smiled as he read the letter and then put it away for safekeeping. As the sun set amid the heavy rainfall, he and the two messenger riders galloped back across the paved roads of Megalos heading for the crossing at Sud and then north to General Lacerta's last fortification. The two cavalrymen said little as they rode, which suited Yazi just fine. The rain-filled journey took four days.

He had much to ponder. *Only one more crucial step and then complete, absolute, total victory is mine! I've been a messiah myself. I know what it is like to lead men into battle and have them killed, though not on the scale of this butcher. I know at this moment he must be in the depths of depression over his continual losses. What's it been now, nearly three months? And that's not counting his horrible and utter defeat initially, back in Juda Arad. If ever this man would be open to suggestion, it is now! General Lacerta, I have you right where I want you. In just a few days now, the religion that you and your Centurions tried to stomp out of existence with crucifixions and death will have conquered your own country! If only Jes Amir could see me now! I, Yazi Rigan, have done what you, the Great Messiah, could not even do! In a way, I am more qualified to be the Great Messiah, am I not? It is I who is conquering Megalos, not you. What is absolutely hilarious is that they are welcoming me with open arms! They are even building the churches themselves!*

Other ideas flickered through his mind before he settled into another line of contemplation. *Now I will get the opportunity to rectify some crucial details. The first one will be to wipe out all traces of his prostitute wife! Women were and are the creators of the Ultimate Sin. I, Yazi, will see to it that that fact is never forgotten! Ah what better way to keep women from ever interfering again than to make all our priest celibate. Yes, all priests are strictly forbidden from ever marrying. Get married and lose your priestly status and be excommunicated from the Church. This way, women will never have any say or influence over my church or its priests! Brilliant, Yazi, positively brilliant!*

Say, we also need Holy Relics. The few things that the Great Messiah had or used that I brought here with me are in great demand. Everyone wants to see them and pray on them. We could use the crutch of the man whose leg was healed, if only it could be found. I should set about collecting all Holy Relics that I can find or make. I really don't want to go back to Juda Arad, just yet. Maybe later on, I can. If so, I'll bring back wagon loads of Holy Relics. After all, a visible object is real to people and can be prayed upon by the faithful.

Now wait just a minute here, Yazi. Why not get all these others to do that for you? I'll just form up an Order of Holy Knights and give them the Holy Quest to go to Jerilum and bring back the cross upon which the Great Messiah was slain. Or bring back the Vile Spear with which he was slain upon the cross. Some of these men would make it their life's work just to accomplish the bringing of a Holy Relic back here to the Church. Yazi, now you are thinking! Ah, first things first, I think we are here.

Indeed, it was noon the next day, but through the pouring rain, one could not tell. A large number of pup tents dotted the horizon just in front of a wooden palisade wall. The two messengers dismounted, so Yazi followed suit. "This way," one said and led him to the largest tent here. "Wait here," he commanded and he parted the flap and entered. Shortly, he returned and motioned for the rain-drenched Yazi to enter.

"Greetings priest. Welcome to my tent, such as it is. I'm afraid you'ill have to sit on the floor. We have no comforts here that you are probably used to having." General Lacerta, of course, was sitting on his bedroll, which allowed him to sit slightly higher than his guest, indicating his importance over this priest.

Yazi took off his saturated rain poncho, revealing his magnificent sky blue toga and sat down in front of the general. "I am Pope Yazi I of the Church of Jehosanity in Megalos. You may call me Yazi. Thank you for seeing me."

"The Emperor suggested in no uncertain terms that I should see you. I'm General Theos Lacerta. General Lacerta will do. Now what is it that you wanted to see me about that you needed to get the Emperor to speak to me on your behalf? It must be rather significant for Titus to have gone to all this trouble or else you have somehow gotten the favor of the Emperor, the chosen one of the Church of Sol." There, he had cleverly inserted an unmistakable reference to the sole Megalos God.

Yazi's keen eyes missed nothing. After all, he had been a messiah in his youth, a leader of holy fighters against this very same man. The grey bags under his eyes, the slowness of his speech, the doleful sound of his voice — all these and more spoke of the mental state of the general. Yazi guessed that this fortification would be the last stand against the barbarian Galts. He'd seen no others as they rode up the road from Sud. When this one fell, Sud itself would be besieged and then Megalos shortly thereafter. He could sense that this was just what the general was thinking. Further, he knew that the general knew that, unless some miracle occurred and occurred soon, that would inevitably occur. General Lacerta would lose the war, going down into the history books as the first Megalos general actually to lose a war! Yazi knew that he also *had* this man.

"Let me begin by explaining what Jehosanity is all about. I will be brief, no telling when these barbarians will attack next. Please hear me out. If in the end you find you cannot agree, so be it. I will not pester you again." Yazi then made an abbreviated presentation of the history of spiritual beings on Tarra just as he had done with so many others. As with the Emperor, Yazi spent the bulk of his time relating all of the miracles that the Great Messiah had performed, all the while setting up the General for his punch line.

"Yes, all of these many miracles and so many more that I have not the time to relate, he did perform. All were clearly visible to many, many other people. None of these could ever be considered a fake miracle; there were too many observers. Now then, it is clear to me that you yourself need a miracle here on the battlefield, if I am not entirely mistaken. I have spent hours praying to Jehosa, asking what I, his humble servant in Megalos, can do so that you, general, can be blessed with a miracle. None of us wants to see our country, our cities, our families sacked, tortured, and enslaved by these crude barbarians. I want to do my part to help. So I prayed and prayed. Finally, God Jehosa has answered me." Once more, he shut up and said nothing more, forcing the general to inquire.

"Well, out with it, man, what did he say to you? There certainly can be no witnesses to what he has said to you. Gods are not in the habit of speaking out loud so everyone can hear his message to one person," he said with disdain in his voice, doubts too. He wanted to make very sure that Yazi knew that he was clearly drawing a line between "observed" miracles and a god's supposed answer to one's prayer.

"Lord Jehosa told me that three things must be done for him to feel that we are beginning to change our sinful ways. If these three things were accomplished, he has promised to act on our behalf, for it is also on his behalf that we change our ways so that our souls may once again enter his Holy Realm. One," he paused for emphasis. "The Emperor must publically state that Jehosanity is now the official and only religion in all of Megalos. Before I left to come here, I received this letter from our Holy Emperor." He showed the general the letter and watched as the general's eyes twitched in total surprise that his Emperor would actually forsake the Church of Sol! Yazi knew that this definitely made a significant impact upon the general.

Yazi continued, "Two, the Emperor must grant us a small parcel of land somewhere on Megalos proper and allow us to construct a grand Mother Church of Jehosanity, from which we can service all of the other churches scattered throughout the realm and your colonies. This he has done some months ago. Already hundreds of volunteers have begun its design and construction. The foundation is already in place. Thus, you see, the first two requirements are met. The third and final one is that I must meet personally with you, General Lacerta. If you personally become a follower of Jehosanity, then Jehosa has promised to work a miracle on your behalf so that you and you alone may lead your forces to ultimate victory over the barbarians."

"And just how is this God to know whether or not I am a follower? I can say any words I choose, but the words might be a complete falsity," the General astutely replied.

"It is but a simple ceremony, General Lacerta. One simply professes his undying faith in Lord Jehosa and takes a sip of holy red wine, which symbolizes the blood of the Great Messiah as he bled to death upon the Holy Cross. Yet, know this. Lord Jehosa knows what is in your heart and mind. Lord

Jehoas is everywhere, sees everything, and knows all. There is no place you can hide from his countenance — no thought you can conceal from our Lord. He will know if you speak sincerely. Only if you truly convert to Jehosanity will he then perform the miracle that all in Megalos are praying for daily. Think it over, General Lacerta. *All* Megalos is praying that you make the right decision, so that Jehosa will act on our behalf before we're all overrun by these evil barbarians, who are doomed to go to Hell when their fleshly bodies finally perish."

"Take your time. I will ride back to Sud and await your messenger. I know that this is no small matter for you. I thank you for having taken the time to listen to me." With that, he got up and left the general to ponder his words. Still the rain pounded down, but he felt sure he could find his way back to Sud alone. After all, he only had to ride on the paved roadway. Now everything was in the hands of this general.

"Curse this infernal rain!" Mikhailovich commented to his sister. The twins were huddled inside their hide skinned domed hut. Indeed, thousands of similar huts lined the land for miles around. Not even a fire could be kept burning in this downpour. For days now, no one had anything hot to eat. Mud was everywhere. The very land under their feet had given way to a sea of mud, trampled by the thousands of men and horses. At least they had the foresight to bring their huts with them; after all, the Galts were nomadic by nature. "The men are grumbling that this is an omen that we should retreat and head for home and the comforts of the soft snow. It's wintertime back home, anyway."

"Yes, our people see omens everywhere," Zdlenka absentmindedly replied, fingering her long hair, completely bored. She had been bored for days now, ever since this interminable rain had begun. "Should we head for home? We are way overdue."

"It's just that I hate stopping here. We are so close to Sud and Megalos that I can almost sense them. Besides, we have gotten very little treasure this trip, only a few of their gold mines have been found thus far. If we head home now, the men are going to complain bitterly about the total lack of treasure and rewards for these months of heavy fighting. Further, if we leave and come back next spring, I would put money on this General Lacerta rebuilding all these forts; we'll just have to repeat what we did this year all over again." He sighed apathetically.

"Surely, they can see that ultimately the greatest of treasures lies just ahead, can't they?" she complained. "Won't they understand that, because of the unexpectedly good defenses of the Centurions, we weren't able to get as far this year as we intended? Or do you suppose that the fighters will hold this against us? We women are far more understanding of situations than men, that's for sure."

Just then, several scouts arrived back before the Czar's hut. Their report was just what Mikhailovich desperately wanted to hear. This was indeed the last of the defensive fortifications. Once this one was eliminated, there was nothing standing between them and Sud or even Megalos itself! Emboldened by this news, Mikhailovich decided against stopping the campaign for the winter season. He held a brief conference with his many captains relaying the good news, and that once Sud was sacked, they would head for home, leaving the island kingdom for next spring. This way, every fighter was assured a reasonable amount of booty for their labors this fall. Once the rain let up, this last fortress would fall in a few hours. A couple days later, they would be sacking Sud. Advance scouts reported that Sud had none of the heavy fortifications similar to those that they had encountered in the Sea Prince cities. Mikhailovich had dreams of his men galloping throughout Sud, eliminating the last pockets of resistance. He fully expected to be heading for home in a couple weeks at the very most. All the Galts did, for that matter; it seemed a sure thing, once this rain stopped.

General Lacerta pondered the promised miracle of Yazi. He couldn't help thinking of the words that had appeared in his mind several months ago. "You will know when it is time to counterattack." *Could this be that sign? Should I launch an attack in this downpour?* All his training suggested no, but then his mind began coldly calculating. *If I attack them with all my cavalry and follow up with foot soldiers, surely I will gain the element of complete surprise. They are hunkered down in those silly-looking domed huts. If my cavalry can hit them without warning, for once, the odds would be on my side; we're on horseback and they're on foot. You know, this might be the time to strike back. Then what about this Yazi priest and his promised miracle? Theos, you old fool, you have never been particularly religious, now have you? Certainly, this all mighty God must know that anyway, so I wouldn't be lying. I never go to church. If I do this ceremony and a miracle does result, then maybe there is something with this God. Hum, could that message in my mind be from this God in the first place? I wonder. If it was Sol, then I'm likely doomed if I forsake Sol for this Jehosa fellow. Get a grip, Theos, when has Sol ever spoken to you? Never in all my years. Yet I swear someone or something did! Okay, I'll do it. If nothing else, it certainly can't hurt. Besides, no matter which way the battle goes, the Emperor will be pleased with my actions as well as all our citizens who now believe in this new god.* He called for messengers and rapidly wrote out several sets of orders.

"Yes, Sir!" a young scout saluted as he entered the tent of the general.

"Son, take these to my headquarters in Sud. Along the road you ought to catch up to that priest fellow, Yazi. Tell him to get back here at once. No matter what happens, I want these dispatches to arrive in Sud by tomorrow night at the very latest. Ride hard. Lives depend upon it."

"Yes, Sir!" he enthusiastically saluted and headed off in the pouring rain to carry out this vital mission.

It was night when Yazi returned to the fortification. General Lacerta offered him a pup tent for the night, saying, "Tomorrow you may conduct your ceremony. I really do not have much of a choice in this matter do I?"

"Oh yes, you do. It's a choice only you can make for yourself. Tomorrow will do fine," Yazi acknowledged.

"One detail, priest. I insist that you stay here at my side until said miracle occurs," General Lacerta added. If no miracle occurred, he wanted everyone to witness that absence, especially this upstart of a priest!

The next day after breakfast of cold dried foods, Yazi conducted the simple ceremony, and General Lacerta sipped the Holy Wine, symbolic blood of the Great Messiah. "That's all there is to this?" asked the General puzzled by the utter simplicity of this supposed conversion of faith.

"Jehosa is all-knowing. He is everywhere. He sees all. He has witnessed your conversion, and that is all that matters. Now you may expect your miracle."

"Tomorrow noon we attack the barbarians in this monsoon. I will silently approach with all my cavalry, ten legions of them. We should take them completely by surprise. For once, we will be the cavalry and they, the foot soldiers! My foot soldiers will follow to mop up the chaos we create. I want you to bear witness to the attack; you may position yourself just in front of the fortress walls here. From there you should be able to see it all. Mind you, we're going to need that miracle: a thousand cavalry and maybe slightly less that number of foot soldiers versus this Galt army of four thousand plus. It is all or nothing. If said miracle does not come, then you, priest, shall bear witness to its failure. If you try to leave before hand, I'll simply tie you to the fortress timbers so that you may see the action."

"Oh, I'm honored, General Lacerta that you think so highly of me that you would have me bear witness to this great miracle!" Yazi completely turned it around on him. "I wouldn't miss this Great Miracle for anything. I'm so glad that I don't have to sneak back here to watch it!"

The general looked completely befuddled. He thought this priest would just make a hasty exit. He scratched his head, rubbed his bushy stubble, and realized that he was long overdue for a shave. All his men were, for that matter. However, just to be certain, the general ordered a foot soldier to keep a sharp eye on this priest.

Late that night, five hundred cavalrymen arrived from Sud, tired and exhausted from the nearly continual ride to get here so fast. Their horses would need the night to recover from the exertion of this frantic ride in the monsoon. Following his orders to the letter, they had silently walked the last mile up to the fortress on foot, keeping the noise of their coming as silent as possible. Further, during the late night hours, fifty wagons also arrived. Each one was filled with a dozen foot soldiers. Now he had eleven hundred foot soldiers to back up his ten legions of cavalry. On a level battlefield, it was four to one against him, but with any luck at all, taking the barbarians by surprise should even those odds up substantially. Still, a miracle would be needed.

At dawn, the torrential rains lessened a good deal, though the sun still couldn't penetrate the heavy, black clouds. General Lacerta mounted his horse, drew his sword, and looked up and down the long line of his cavalry. Impressive, he thought to himself. Never in his long career had he actually fielded ten legions of cavalry! The eleven legions of foot soldiers, now armed with spears and short swords and wearing their traditional armor bits with large shields, stood tall just behind the line of horses. Every man here knew that, though their numbers looked impressive, they were still outnumbered four to one. Yet, they followed orders. General Lacerta gave a nod to Pope Yazi I, who stood before the fortress walls wearing only his sky blue toga, ignoring the rain. The Pope looked both holy and impressive standing there, the lone observer. The General motioned his sword forward and kicked his mare into action.

The Galts were just arising for yet another rain-soaking day when they heard the thunder of thousands of horses coming their way. Mass confusion resulted. No one suspected an attack, so most just stood and looked to see who was coming, more scouts perhaps. Mikhailovich crawled out of his hut to see for himself. He assumed a number of advance scouts were reporting en-mass. He stood beside the tall pole before his hut, which flew his flag of office to mark his location for all his men to see. After all, with four thousand men in similar huts, how was one to find the Czar?

By the time that the Galts and Mikhailovich realized that these Centurions were actually attacking and that somehow their cavalry had doubled over the night, they were set upon by the Centurions! Just as General Lacerta expected, the tables were turned on these barbarians, who were now afoot fighting attacking cavalry. The attacking horsemen quickly cut a path through the Galts. As General Lacerta, somewhat out in front of his line, neared the center of the encampment, he spied the unmistakable flag of the Galt leader. He headed directly toward Mikhailovich. "We're under attack!" he screamed to Zdlenka, who stuck her head out of the hut to see for herself. But Mikhailovich reacted swiftly. Untying his horse and using no saddle or bridle, he leapt bareback and rode out to meet General Lacerta personally, waving his magical blade before him.

He sent back to Zdlenka, *I'll eliminate this General personally. That should break the back of this surprise attack.* The two men charged toward each other.

High above the clouds, using an infrared scope, cold black tentacles adjusted some controls. The outlines of the two charging men were clearly visible in the rangefinder. The timing had to be perfect; there was no other acceptable outcome. At just the right instant, another tentacle pushed a red button.

Yelling wildly in true Galt fashion, Mikhailovich charged toward General Lacerta, who ignored the distracting noise, and concentrated fully on his actions, controlling his horse on the slippery, mud-covered ground. He could not afford the slightest miscalculation. The two men closed and their eyes met, like two immoveable mountains defying each other. Then, their horses brought them into striking range. Both blades swung out and toward the other man. Just as both blades were about to hit, Yazi saw a blue flash of energy beaming down from the sky above. The blue beam struck the magical blade of Mikhailovich. Instantly, his specially built sword shattered into a hundred small bits! General Lacerta also noticed that his blade did not actually make physical contact with Mikhailovich's blade. It had just shattered for no apparent reason!

Quickly, the general neck reined his mare one hundred eighty degrees and headed back to Mikhailovich just as fast as he could safely do in the slippery mud. His only intention was to finish off this barbarian leader while he had the miracle on his side.

Mikhailovich literally halted his horse and stood staring wild-eyed at the pummel in his hand, all that remained of his magically enchanted blade. He was in shock! This was never supposed to happen! Zdlenka, who had also watched this terrible stroke of bad luck, also looked on in just as much shock as her brother. She spied the general returning toward the back of her brother and instantly pulled out of it, screaming into his mind, *Behind you! He's returning!*

However, Mikhailovich was still in total shock over the destruction of his enchanted blade. Slowly he pivoted his horse as if to meet the general, but could only raise the pummel in his defense. In slow motion, he watched the general's blade cut a fine arc through the air, aimed straight for his neck. For the briefest of instants, he felt his body resisting that blade. Then, all became dark and black. He screamed for his sister; though no sounds could be heard, still, she heard that deafening scream in her mind, a scream that would torment her for the rest of her life. Then, a command came unbidden into his mind. *Return to the Appian Way.* Though he had no idea why, he immediately floated off, heading northwest toward that mountain range.

General Lacerta watched as his perfectly executed swing beheaded his longtime opponent. He watched as the head of Mikhailovich fell down into the mud, rolled off some ten feet and stopped with its face, now mud covered, staring up at the sky overhead. Suddenly, cries began echoing over the chaos of the battlefield, "The Czar's dead! The Czar's been beheaded! Flee! Run! Abandon everything!" These words were spoken in the Galt tongue, but the Centurions needed no translator to get the meaning of the cries.

Yes, the battlefield was one gigantic, chaotic mass of men and horses clashing with men sloshing around in the three-inch deep mud. True, some of the Galts managed to get astride their horses, mostly bareback, and were counterattacking both the Centurion foot soldiers as well as the cavalry. Yet at this time in history, please note that the Galts were highly independent clan oriented. Only the incredible will of Mikhailovich Strokova could make them work even slightly together as a team. That will had just been completely shattered. Combine that with the surprise attack and it is not hard to understand how quickly their morale broke.

Break it did. In less than a minute after all of the wailing cries relayed the horrible news of their leader's death around the huge encampment, the barbarian's morale completely shattered. Those already on horseback turned around, abandoned everything, and rode north as fast as they could gallop. Many others found a horse and followed suit. Those that could not reach a horse simply ran north from the battlefield. All were chased by General Lacerta's cavalry, while his foot soldiers raced this way and that throughout the huge encampment, attacking anything that moved! Here near the center of the assault, the bodies of over one thousand Galts lay dead or dying in the soupy mud.

Seeing the miracle route, General Lacerta finally relaxed for the first time in four years. Over the din of the ongoing slaughter and route, he signaled for a messenger. He ordered, "Ride at top speed up to Al Barq and then head along the coast to Zargarb. Once there, spread the word that the Galts have been defeated. Tell anyone you find to send what forces they can muster into Juda Arad to cut any stragglers off, keep them from reaching their homeland. Ride now!" The young man saluted and began to canter off, dodging fallen bodies as he went.

Slowly, General Lacerta retreated to the wooden fortress walls. A smile was on his face for the first time in four years. Pope Yazi I was also grinning from ear to ear. When they were within hearing distance, Yazi said calmly, "Jehosa spoke with a blue energy from the sky, shattering Strokova's blade. You, general, then did the rest. Please let me be the first to congratulate you on winning the battle and very likely the entire war!"

"You saw it too — the blue light? I couldn't see from where it came, though. My sword never did touch his. His just shattered for no reason," the general attempted to analyze just what occurred.

"Behold yet another miracle from Jehosa, general. Such was promised. Not only have you saved Megalos from certain destruction, you have also earned your place in history," Yazi spoke what he knew the general wanted to hear.

The general just stared long and hard at this Arad man, dressed in the soaked but still impressive sky blue toga. His opinion of Pope Yazi I had just grown immensely as well as that of his new religion, Jehosanity. He said, "Well, I guess you can say that the war is won. Still, we must drive them all the way back into the Northern Steppes. There is likely much fighting to do, though without their leader, I suspect the barbarians will not regroup as an effective fighting force, although they still have the numbers with which to defeat us — three to one odds at least. I release you from your watching position. You are free to return to Megalos, Pope Yazi. I will send dispatch riders to the Emperor later today, once the full story on the battlefield is known. Perhaps one day I will be able to return to Galantas and see our new church."

"You're most welcome anytime, general. Thank you again for saving our entire country." Yazi bowed, then turned around, and left.

The General watched Pope Yazi I walk back behind the fortification walls before turning his attention back to the battlefield. Never once did the thought of just why should the God of the Arads help him, previously their sworn enemy, appear in his conscious thought. It ought to have.

Yazi's teeth were chattering involuntarily; he was freezing, dressed only in the light toga and completely soaked to the skin; he was sure he would catch a cold. Nevertheless, he felt supremely confident and sure of himself, for nothing now stood in the way of any of his plans. The sky was the limit now. He went into the small tent, dried off, donned dry clothes, his rain gear, mounted his horse, and headed south toward Sud. He dreamed of a long, long hot soaking bath, then a huge warm meal, and then sleep!

Zdlenka stared in utter horror as her eyes riveted upon the rolling head of her brother, the only person in the universe for whom she cared. For what seemed an eternity, her mind kept expecting the head of Mikhailovich to reattach itself somehow. When it didn't but with open eyes staring up at the sky, she exerted forth a tremendous effort to stop time and roll time backwards, undoing this. Then, like the sounds of far off sea gulls on a summer's day, her mind heard the men calling out "The Czar is dead! Flee! Run! Save yourself!" Continuing to stare at the ghastly remains of her brother, Zdlenka was unable to move or speak. Men, slopping through the mud, rushed passed her on either side; a few yelled for her to retreat and save herself. Still, she could not take her eyes off her brother. Shock gave way to grief. Her eyes watered, and Zdlenka began crying heavily, as she had so often done as a very young child, when it was just her and her brother against the rest of their clan.

Just then, a Centurion on horseback came riding towards her, intent upon spearing her next. As the cavalryman attempted to thrust his spear into her heaving chest, at the last instant, she dropped face down into the deep mud and did not move. The rider mistakenly thought that he had slain this woman and passed on towards the next hut. Though totally overcome with grief, still her sense of survival kicked in. She raised her mud covered face and glanced about. In a few minutes, the line of foot soldiers would get to where she lay, and they were uniformly making sure each body was dead. Carefully, she slithered through the mud, not rising more than a few inches so as not to attract the attention of any nearby Centurions. She continued heading eastward, moving past hut after hut, sometimes moving around a dead Galt.

Finally, as she neared the eastern edge of their encampment, she turned around to see if anyone was following her. None was. Further, she could not see her horse anywhere. Worse still, she could not see any other Galt horse anywhere around her; they had all been ridden off by her routing countrymen or had been spooked off by the attack. She, the Czarina of all Tarra, was forced to crawl off the battlefield on all fours, completely covered in a reddish-brown mud. For several minutes longer, she crawled out of fear that some charging Centurion on horseback would spy her and come after her.

Finally, when she was far enough away, the darkness and light rain of the dim day hid her from the battlefield. The still moving cavalrymen seemed like small darkish forms. Zdlenka finally got to her feet and began running,

running eastward for her life, crying heavily as she ran. After a minute, she found that she could not both run and cry, so she ran and ran, heedless of anything. She felt that she was already dead. Yet she ran, trying to run away from that awful battlefield and more importantly, to run away from her awful memories from just a few minutes before, which were still vivid in her mind. She ran and ran until she could run no more and finally collapsed, exhausted, out of breath, and in an apathy.

She awoke shivering uncontrollably. The monsoon rains had lightened appreciably, but she was still soaked and cold; it was nighttime, pitch black out. Intensely hungry and thirsty, she had brought nothing with her, save her dagger in her boot. Out of desperation, she began to try to run eastward once more, though more than once she stumbled over unseen obstacles, landing hard onto the ground. Sharp pains now fought for her attention over her shivering body, yet her numb mind blotted even these out. An image of her brother's head sat frozen before her; that was all that she could see in her mind. Dark as it was, she could not see the world with her eyes, and thus she continued to see nothing but Mikhailovich's head staring up at her. In panic, she continued to run, stumble, and fall, only to get up and continue her dash across the land in the near total darkness.

Finally, she didn't get up after yet another collision with an unseen obstacle. Exhausted, she fell into a deep sleep, still staring at her brother's head. Time passed. Now she felt warmth upon her back. Zdlenka opened her eyes to a bright, sunny day. From the height of the sun in the southern sky, it must have been around noon. What day, she had no idea. The pain in her empty stomach and parched throat fought for her attention, yet she had nothing to quench her thirst or hunger. She was in misery. The only good thing was that the sun blocked out the horrible image of her brother in her mind.

There was nothing else to do but rise and continue walking, either that or just lie down and wait for death to come. While Zdlenka was many things, she was still a survivor. Her childhood had taught her that. No one would ever look out for her, except her brother and now he was gone. The mere thought of this caused her to begin crying once more. Still, she continued walking. If she were a horse, she would have had plenty to eat. A low grass covered most of the rolling lands here, though small boulders occasionally cropped up. She realized that these must have been what she kept tripping over during the nighttime runs. Finally, when she thought she could walk no more, she heard birds chirping and the babbling sound of running water!

She quickened her pace. Just over a low hill, she saw a small creek merrily flowing eastward down to the sea. She ran down the hill and collapsed at the brook's edge, gulping the cool water as fast as she could swallow. Her thirst quenched, she felt her vitality returning somewhat. As she sat up, she perceived more of her surroundings. Now she heard a sound that she had heard last year when they were in the cities of the Sea Princes, the sound of the ocean waters thrashing upon the shoreline.

Once more, she got up and began walking. Just over the next hill, she saw the vast panorama of the ocean meeting the Southlands. Magnificent white sandy beaches stretched in both directions as far as she could see. Waves moved onshore, ebbing and flowing, unseen by any eyes but hers. Not another living person was anywhere around. Transfixed momentarily by the unexpected beauty, she stared up and down the beach. Finally, she walked the short distance down to the pristine white sands. Caked in semi-dried mud, her hair one huge mass of tangles and dried mud, she felt filthy, dirtier than she had ever thought possible. Only one thought entered her mind. Zdlenka ran out into the warm waters of the ocean for a much-needed bath.

As she splashed in the waters, layers of mud began dissolving. At last, she gave in and carefully took off all her clothes, placing them carefully on the sand, just out of the water's flowing reach and returned naked to the deeper water. It took her over a half hour to get the last of the mud off her; yes, most of that time was spent on her hair. Satisfied that she was finally free of the mud, she then methodically washed her underclothes and then her outer leather garments and boots. Unfortunately, her waist length beautiful hair was now one enormous mass of tangles. Without even a rudimentary comb, she could do little with it and so just tied it back into a long ponytail for the time being. All these actions, by the way, she did more out of habit, methodically, rather like a robot. Her mental state could not accommodate anything more complex right now.

She had nothing with which to start a fire, so she laid everything out to dry in the late afternoon sun, and she laid down letting the warm rays dry her as well. When the sun reddened, her hunger awoke with a vengeance! Her under garments were mostly dry, so she put them on and went to forage for something to eat before the nighttime came. She found only some berries.

Once the sun set, she found herself shivering once more. She had to stay warm somehow. She retrieved her still damp outer clothes and dagger and went in search of some place to sleep. She found a suitable indentation in the hillside. Next, she gathered a large number of small branches and proceeded to use them as a covering over the top of her indentation. Once she crawled inside, she found that the makeshift shelter did keep the chill off, and her body heat kept her from chilling. But the night was horrible for her. Once the twilight had passed, she could see nothing once more, and the horrid image frozen in her mind again became vividly real to her. She cried and cried, finally falling asleep from exhaustion once more.

When day came, she put on the dry outer leathers, which were quite stiff from having been so wet. Again, she took a long drink from her bubbling creek and then surveyed the land. She saw no one and no signs of any nearby village. What to do? Images of the crude maps that they had confiscated from some of the Sea Prince cites came to mind. Based upon where they last were, a hundred miles from Sud, she estimated that she was at the eastern edge of the ocean. The tall, imposing mountains that formed the impassable Kathas Range should begin hundreds of miles north of here. Some six hundred miles of the Southlands lay between her and Juda Arad. She could hike close to the seashore and very likely avoid all Centurion towns. Still, once at the border of the Arad, she still had another several hundred miles to travel before the Northern Steppes and home. She had no horse, no food, no water, and no money — nothing but her dagger and the clothes that she wore. Further, she could not speak one word of the Centurion language, if she did manage to meet anyone.

She sighed and began slowly walking northward. Soon, she found a small branch that with the help of her dagger managed to become her walking stick. At least, the daytime was her friend now; images of the countryside overwhelmed that horrid image frozen in her mind. She just walked more or less aimlessly northward, taking advantage of anything she could find to eat, primarily late season berries.

Chapter 29 Motherhood

In late November 589 AH, Antonio Pazzio came down from Paese di Dio with his flock of sheep and goats to spend the winter with the Sisterhood and the children at North Point. Here in this system of remote caves, the Sisterhood in Zargarb raised their children — a place where young mothers could be safe, as well as their children. No one could find them to cause trouble. Rosalita, who had now resumed her post as Fighter Group Leader for the Sisterhood, managed to find some excuse to also visit North Point. Ever since she had spent the entire month of July up there in the high country in Antonio's company, she found herself longing to be with that simple shepherd! She had never before felt this way about a man, ever. She was too embarrassed to speak openly about what she was feeling to her other Sisters. Rosalita just did not know what to make of the fact that this man's face always seemed to be in her mind and heart.

When she arrived at North Point and the other Sisters and children came out to greet her, she felt a great warmth in her heart. Yet, when Antonio came out after them, her heart nearly skipped a beat! Yes, several Sisters gave her a strong welcoming hug, but when Antonio also gave her a hug, she felt that her legs might not hold her up! She held onto his arm for support as he said, "I'm so glad you could come by for a visit. You must see how we have fixed up the caves for all the sheep and the children. They just love helping me with the flock." He was truly a happy man; all traces of his sins had evaporated, just as Simon had predicted they would.

While Rosalita got a guided tour of how the Sisters accommodated Antonio for the winter, a messenger arrived with an urgent message for Rosalita. Sister Ali exclaimed breathlessly for everyone to hear, "The Galts, they have been defeated by the Centurions. Something about a miracle of Jehosanity. Their general has beheaded Mikhailovich! Can you believe that! The Galt army is in a rout and is expected to be heading up through the Arad soon. Their general sent a message for all forces that can be spared to intercept them and finish them off as they pass through the Arad. Even the High Council has reacted by sending a few hundred of its new soldiers into the Arad. Isn't that just the most fantastic news?"

Everyone began talking at once. Rosalita was just about to re-saddle her horse and race back to the Sisterhood ranch, when Antonio pulled her aside for a private word. "Rosalita," he said in a very worried tone, "what about the children? I mean yours and Mikhailovich's? Their father is now dead. You are their mother. What will become of them?"

Strange how unexpected circumstances can rekindle long suppressed ideas and concepts. Rosalita had successfully repressed all motherly feelings toward the two children. To keep the Sisterhood from being destroyed by the Galts, she had bargained to provide him two children, rather like two potatoes.

Since from the beginning, he planned to take them back to the steppes to raise, she had stifled any feelings of motherhood she had. It had worked; both children were not upset when leaving with Mikhailovich. Now — now he was dead! Suddenly the plight of two small children left alone among relative strangers hit Rosalita like a heavy brick upon her heart and her mind.

She cursed, which was a rare thing for this woman. Without realizing it, she exclaimed, "I've got to go rescue the children! Lord knows what will happen to them if I don't! The Galts might even try to kill them to keep them from following in their father's footsteps."

Antonio replied, "Wait a minute, Rosalita. I doubt that they would outright kill his children. His sister might look after them."

Sister Ali interrupted, "She's probably dead too, though there was nothing in the message from the Centurions about her. She was always at his side, so she is probably gone as well, don't you think? Isn't this just incredible news?"

He went on, "No matter, think about it. If you go riding into their land and just outright take the children, might that cause the Galts to attempt to retake them back from us by force, bringing the barbarian cavalry back down on the Sisterhood once again?"

She sighed; resuming her logical voice tone, she said, "Antonio, you are a wise man. Yes, you're right. I can't go in there openly and just take the children back. That would almost certainly bring down their wrath upon the Sisterhood. However, now would be an excellent time to get them, I will admit. Look, all their fighters are away to the south, admittedly probably frantically trying to get back home to the steppes. So if I went to their village right now, probably there are only women there, few real fighters, would be my guess."

"I agree. It would seem to be an opportune time to rescue the children, Rosalita. Do you know where their village is located? I know that the snows have come, so your passage would leave a clear trail for anyone to follow, anyone of them who might want to follow you to get the children back. If only it had come before the snows fell, then you might not leave such an obvious trail."

"Er, no," she said more than a little perplexed. "I have no idea where their village is located." She fussed with her sword, trying to cover up her small fib. "Horse passage through the snow would be a dead giveaway, that's for sure, but there must be a way." Her voice trailed off as she pondered the situation and these strange, new feelings that had awakened within her.

"Where there is a will, there is always a way, I always say," Antonio said, trying to sound helpful. "Let's think about it some."

"Well, even if we know where their village is located and how to get there, I can't do this alone. It is going to take two to bring both children back; they can ride double with us. However, if I take a group of fighters, this could easily be misinterpreted as being a war party. No, it has to be limited to me and one or two other people," Rosalita thought aloud.

"Ah, yes, that is a good start. Now, as far as tracks are concerned, if you could time it right, why, you could return, say to the Paese di Dio, and have a new snowfall completely cover your tracks. I know that happens; I've had much experience with winter snows up there. Even familiar landmarks become hidden in deep snow. It is almost like a different world in the wintertime. With some luck, traveling through a storm will hide all traces of our passage."

"Say that is clever, but wouldn't we get lost as well? Well, I guess that is okay too," she chuckled. "They won't know where we've gone, and neither will we!"

"It'd be okay as long as we bring along enough food and blankets to keep warm," Antonio explained. "I've toughed it out up there in the deep snow many a time, but you've got to have enough food or it is miserable and life threatening. What I don't see is how will we ever find the right village and find it undiscovered?"

Rosalita flushed and squirmed her boot on the ground; she was suddenly very embarrassed. Her eyes refused to meet his. "Okay my pretty fighter, out with it. You know you shouldn't withhold it. What is it?" he said in a playful, almost teasing manner, designed to disarm her feelings that she should not say anything about it — that it was acceptable to say it to him.

Her eyes finally rose and met his; his reassuring grin broke down her embarrassment. "Two weeks ago, I was in Florintine Junction checking up on how things are going in the town. A number of traveling merchants from the steppes were there. I do speak a little Galt now, you see. I just had this incredible urge to know where the children were at, you know, where were they, how were they doing, were they adapting to their new life, that sort of thing. I never thought I would feel that way; I've tried so hard to stifle motherhood. I don't know what came over me, but I just had to know. Anyway, I met one of those merchants at an inn and got him very drunk. I kept the wine flowing and soon his tongue wagged. I don't know if anything that he told me was supposed to be a secret or not. Probably not. I heard the children were alive and well. I think I can find their village. It seems that every clan now has so much gold and treasure that they can no longer migrate around as they used to. They are pretty well stuck where they are currently encamped. Certainly, with all their fighters off down south, the women aren't going to be moving the camp around. I probably can find it, given enough time."

He replied, "You know, you will make a good mother. I was wondering all summer long whether you would be thinking about your children. After all, they are half yours. Now that he is dead, you have a rightful claim to your children."

Rosalita blushed. No one had ever suggested that she would be a good mother. It was not something commonly discussed with the Fighter Group Leader. She quickly said, "Their camp is about seventy miles north of the Arad border and nearly dead center east-west in the steppes. However, I'm not certain that we could travel all that distance without encountering other Galts. What would we say to them when we are challenged upon entering their country? How do we get the children from their caretakers? Those seem insurmountable problems without actually fighting our way there."

"The first is easy. We take along a couple bags of treasure. If we are challenged, we say we are bringing a bag of tribute to Mikhailovich. If all else fails, we can say we wanted to visit with the children and see how they are doing. After all, he did stop by here several times to check on them before he took them away. As for the other question, we can figure that out when we get there. Maybe by then we will have thought of a good idea. What say you?"

"Good thinking. I think that ought to work. Okay. I shall do it. I wonder whom I should ask to go with me? Probably a good fighter, don't you think?"

"You are taking me, Rosalita. You can't take another Sisterhood fighter. We're trying to keep the Sisterhood out of this completely, remember. Besides, we aren't trying to take them by force. If we need fighting ability, why, we've already failed, for surely we would then be bringing down the wrath of the Galts. No, stealth is needed, and someone who is wise with the weather, that's me. You and I, Rosalita, we're going to go rescue your children. We should leave yet today. Time is going to be our worst enemy. We have to pull this off before all the routing Galt fighters get back from down south. That can only be a few days at most! According to Sister Ali, their rider came at once, so we only have a very few days here at the very most."

"I can't ask you to risk your life for me and the children, Antonio. I just can't," she pleaded. "You don't owe me anything."

"No you can't. However, Rosalita, you're one of the finest people I have ever known in my entire life. Admittedly, I haven't known that many people, especially women. I care deeply for you, and I would never be able to live with myself if I let you go off on this all by yourself when I could be of help to you. If you don't let me come with you, then I'll just follow behind you. No matter what, I'm going with you, and that is settled. Now let's get packing. We need to take a lot of food and blankets. We should dress in many layers of clothing; it's going to be very cold out there on the steppes in winter. Let's get going quickly; time's a'wasting!"

She gave him a very loving hug. Here was a man doing something for her solely for her benefit, asking nothing in return. Antonio was so unlike most other men that she had met. "Thank you," she said softly. Then, they both set to work putting together what they would need.

Via Sister Ali, Rosalita sent word back to Sister Aminia concerning what she and Antonio were about to do. She knew perfectly well that by the time her boss heard the news, they would be long on their way and could not stop them. Further, she borrowed a hefty bag of gold and gems from the Sisters here at North Point, sending word to Sister Aminia to send by return messenger an equal amount from Rosalita's treasury bag kept back at the ranch. An hour later, with two saddlebags strapped behind two mares along with a number of blankets stowed in sacks, the two mounted up and quietly rode out of North Point.

Antonio suggested that they head up to the Paese di Dio and from there ride due east until this high plateau ended where the giant's teeth began, the natural barrier between Juda Arad and the Northern Steppes. From there, they could swiftly cross the Arad and then ride the some seventy miles north to the encampment.

In an hour, they were up on the high plateau of the Paese di Dio, riding through six inches of snow. By evening, the moon was full, and they were able to continue riding slowly for most of the night without overtiring the horses. Only in the wee dawn hours did they stop to rest the horses and eat a cold meal.

The next day, they crossed into the Arad, and the temperature warmed considerably. Juda Arad is a semi-arid desert land. The snow quickly disappeared, leaving only the dry sandy soil of the Arad. They encountered almost no people at all here in Juda Arad. What had once been a thriving section of the Arad with mining, smeltering, and weapon smithing activities was now deserted; ghost towns dotted the land here at the far north of Juda Arad. All the Arads had long ago been killed or fled. For the past few years, the Galt army had continually passed through this area, either going or coming, to say nothing of all the treasure wagons and supply wagons for the massive army. No Arad citizen wanted to be anywhere around this area. However, Rosalita figured that once the Arads learned of the defeat of the Galts, they might resettle this land once more.

Hence, they made good time. Several nights later, they arrived at the ruins of Al Dun, and the end of the Centurion paved roadway, there at the north-central edge of Juda Arad. Without a word, the two headed north into the steppes. Once they crossed the barrier teeth, snow covered the landscape. At first, the tall grasses held only a light dusting, but quickly, the snow grew deeper and deeper until the snow nearly covered the grasslands, matting the tall grass down.

They had not gone but a few miles north when Rosalita was startled by a voice appearing in her head. *Rosalita, Sandy here. We heard what you are trying to do. We want to help you get your children back safely. We have a plan. Where are you now?* So startled was she, that she completely stopped her horse, staring in all directions, raising Antonio's concern that trouble was somewhere just beyond his view.

"I'm here, Sandy," Rosalita spoke aloud, forgetting that she only needed to think her thoughts for this druwid to hear them. She saw Antonio's frantic look on his face and said, "It's okay; someone is talking to me — in my mind."

"We are here, just inside the border of the steppes, due south of where I think their camp might be. Antonio's with me," she continued speaking aloud.

Say, it's surprising that Antonio came along. Did you ask him? Sandy asked.

Rosalita's face flushed; she remembered now that she only needed to think her thoughts and was glad that she didn't have to vocalize them now. *No, he just insisted that he come along with me.*

Well, that's a good sign, Rosalita. He is a nice man, Simon told me about him. Now here's the plan. We are sending one of our Guardians to help you. He is a Judger, like Simon, and a master of illusions. Well, maybe not as good as Simon, but he knows the Galts very well and how best to handle them. Trust me on this one. His name is George Wainthrope, and he is on his way to join you. If you retrace your route into the steppes, where would you be when you get back into Juda Arad? We need to set up a rendevous in safe territory.

Al Dun, it's a ghost town now; no one is there. The place is a ruins. Will that do?

Perfect, George knows where that is. Give me a minute to see how soon he can be there to meet up with you two.

Meanwhile, Rosalita looked at Antonio's face; he had no idea what was going on and felt very ill at ease, as if some dark trouble was looming nearby and he couldn't see what it might be. "A very good friend of mine from the Greenway is sending us help. We are supposed to head back to Al Dun and wait for him to join up with us. Sandy thinks he'll be able to help us get the children back safely. Come on; let's head back to that ghost town."

"But how can she tell you all this? I don't see anyone around here for miles?" asked Antonio, completely baffled.

"She can talk into my mind, Antonio. I don't know how she does this, only that she does. Come on; we should do as she asks. I've never known her to be wrong on anything. She is a legend among the Sisterhood." Slowly, the two retraced their rather obvious passage back toward the Arad. Both grimaced at the very distinctive trail through the snow that they had left already. Antonio knew they would need the cover of a snowstorm to hide their tracks from the Galts.

George will join you in thirty-six hours, Sandy placed in Rosalita's mind. *Keep low and keep out of sight in case some of the routing Galts pass by your position. Any questions?*

She couldn't think of any, so Sandy broke her connection. Rosalita and Antonio returned to Al Dun and found a good hiding place, just inside one of the mine tunnels. From here, their horses couldn't be seen, and they had a good view of the internal courtyard. The view, however, was not pretty; most of the buildings were in bad repair, ransacked and torched by the barbarians years ago. The two made themselves comfortable and began their long wait. At least one of the two needed to be awake to keep guard, so they each took turns sleeping, leaning against each other.

Spooky and lonely were their descriptions of spending a day and a half in this ghost town. The only living things they saw were rats, many rats, plus the occasional field mouse scampering about the courtyard. During the times they were both awake at the same time, they chatted about their lives and their hopes for the future. Both kept each other from speculating about the fate of her children. Worry would do no good.

Late the next evening, a lone rider came into the ghost town, entering as they had, from the north. This they took as a good sign. They watched as the rider dismounted and began looking around. At last, the stranger whispered, "Rosalita? You here? George here. Where are you at?"

She stepped out of the shadows of the mine entrance and caught his attention. "Over here," she whispered. The man led his horse over to the mine. Because the two were in the dark, he chanted briefly, and a blue light shown from his hand, dimly illuminating the pair. Rosalita, now convinced, said, "Welcome, George. I'm Rosalita; this is Antonio. I'm glad you're here."

He smiled, "Are you ready to leave? Time is of the essence. We must get there before any of their clan fighters return. We ride night and day."

"Sure thing. Give us a minute," she replied, noticing that George probably wasn't even twenty-five yet, the youngest druwid she had seen. Without wasting any time, the two saddled their horses and followed George out of the mine. Soon they were once more heading north. Even in the moon light, she could clearly see the trail he had left coming here. He had come from the northwest. Though her knowledge of geography beyond the Zargarb sector was limited, she estimated that had he come directly from the Greenway, he should have taken much longer to reach Al Dun. She looked at George now more closely, and he sensed her probing.

"Yes?" he prodded, making it acceptable for her to inquire.

"Correct me if I'm wrong, but the only way you could have gotten here so quickly is if you already had been nearby here in the steppes. Your clothes look almost like those of the Galts, though I haven't seen any of them in their winter gear."

"How'd you know all that?" asked Antonio, rather surprised with her observations. "Oh, I see. How could he get here so fast? He must have already been nearby. I see."

George chuckled, "You have keen eyes, Fighter Group Leader Rosalita. Yes, for many months I have been traveling around the steppes gathering intelligence on the Galts. We feared that they would sooner or later attempt to invade the Greenway, probably from our eastern border with the steppes."

"And no one has challenged you?" asked Antonio, who wondered just why this man had not been captured as a spy long ago.

George's answer was simple, "People see what they want and expect to see. Here in the steppes, you only see the Galts. I just help that expectancy along a little bit. I've been in a dozen villages or camps as the locals call them, and they just see another Galt. Actually, that's why I am here. Here's the plan. We will ride in to the camp where the children are. All there will see just three normal Galts, a trader, a mother, and a guard; I'm the guard. I'll say that we are under orders from Mikhailovich. He fears that the other evil brother of the Snake Demon is now walking the steppes and has ordered us to get his children to safety up north. We get the children and head north before we attempt to head back to Zargarb. How's that sound?"

"You think that they will just hand the children over?" asked Rosalita, a tone of worry in her voice.

"Yes, the plan will work as long as word of Mikhailovich's death has not reached them. If they already know he is dead, then I'll improvise," he replied with confidence in his voice.

"What is this Snake Demon thing?" asked Rosalita. "Are my children in any danger?" For the first time ever, she had just referred to them as her children. Antonio smiled; he definitely noticed that subtle change. For the next half hour, George told them the lengthy tale of the Snake Demon. He'd heard it from various villagers he'd met during his spying trips.

"Fortunately, Mikhailovich killed this decrepit, insane man before he could threaten your children, Rosalita. However, Mikhailovich did say that there were two crazy men that day in Florintine Junction. I will just be altering things a tad. The cover story ought to be readily believed. Here, we need to veer a little to the west. Their camp lies less than a day from where we are. I should like to time our arrival so that we get there at dusk. The illusion will be easier to perform in the dim light, and the children will have been fed and ready for sleep. We can then ride all night, putting some distance between us and the camp, should anyone have second thoughts. Thus, we can take a few hours break tonight. Besides, I need a little more time to work on the weather."

"What do you mean work on the weather?" asked Antonio, now more than a little curious. Weather was one thing of which he had years of constant observation. "What we need is a good snowstorm to hide our tracks; that's what I was telling Rosalita. Can you make it snow? From the cloud pattern way to the west, a storm is coming within days, I estimate."

"Yes, given lots of time, we can make the weather come to our aid. Nature respects little nudges here and there. If there wasn't a storm coming, I don't have the skills to create one; but I do know some who could make a storm appear when there is none. I can just nudge it along a bit. You're quite right, Antonio; a good snowstorm will hide our obvious passage."

They rode on for several more hours. In the wee hours of the morning, they halted to rest the horses and eat a cold meal. Rosalita and Antonio also caught a few hours' sleep as well. Just before she fell asleep, she saw George standing facing the far distant storm, muttering something softly to himself.

The next day, the storm clouds appeared much closer, which all took to be very encouraging. They rode steadily all the daylight hours. Finally, as the sun set behind the ever-growing cloudbanks, they spied many smoke clouds twisting and turning into the cold sky. The signs of the Galt camp could be seen long before the actual domed huts appeared nestled in a small valley. They had timed it perfectly. Perhaps a hundred domed huts dotted the landscape. Several rows of horses were tethered in long lines. Numerous campfires dotted the trampled snow covered grasslands. Here the snow was nearly a foot deep. Without the slightest hesitation, they rode straight into the camp.

Rosalita was now very glad George had come along. Entering the camp of the enemy was suddenly almost more than she could face without panicking. George rode in and slowly dismounted as if he had done this a thousand times. As planned, neither of the other two dismounted. Speaking in the Galt tongue to the couple older guards who came out to greet him, George delivered his rehearsed speech. "I come from Mikhailovich. He has news that the brother of the Snake Demon may have entered our lands in search of his children. For their protection, we're to take them way up north. Please bundle them up; we've a long ride ahead of us. Also, he suggests that you double your guard here in case he is right about this Snake Demon's brother."

Rosalita only knew a few words of Galt from her association with Mikhailovich. Thus, she only caught a bit of the conversation. She was most impressed that one guard entered a domed hut to fetch her children. Not in a million years would she have just turned her children over to total strangers. Now one of the other guards was speaking, she tried to follow what he was asking. "So how goes the war down south? He is very late in returning. Winter snow has already come. If he doesn't return soon, we will all miss the winter festival."

"He is very nearly to their southernmost huge city of Sud. It is not barricaded like Zargarb was; he expects to return here shortly, heavily laden with treasures," George improvised, combining the few facts that he knew along with a reasonable prediction.

"It's not like we really need more gold," one older man grumbled. "We can't even move what we got. It's not like the old days anymore."

"Ah, you can never have too much gold," George replied. "Think of the women!" All the guards, except the older one, chuckled and agreed. Just then, the original guard came outside the hut, holding it open for two women, who were carrying the children. Rosalita leaned over to take her littlest one, Lenkova, who was still very much a baby, only a year and a half. Her two and a half year old son, Illanovich, was given to Antonio. Both were heavily wrapped in blankets so they could stay warm on the winter's night ride. She thought that both women appeared somehow relieved to be handing the children over to them. Perhaps they were afraid what might happen to them should the children in their care be harmed.

George slowly remounted, saying, "Mikhailovich thanks you for all you have done on his behalf. Please be very alert for the brother of the Snake Demon." All the guards chorused that they would double their guards from on, as well as spread the word to the neighboring clans. Slowly, George led the trio northward from the camp. So far so good, thought Rosalita, but she dare not look back. Instead, she held her breath, concentrating on holding firm her young daughter and controlling her horse.

At last, the camp disappeared behind them as they entered the next valley. By now, it was quite dark. Though the moon was nearly full, dark storm clouds nearly completely hid it. Yet nothing can hide smells. Lenkova, though still half asleep, smelled the distinct odor of her mother and called out, muffled by the blankets, "Mommy?"

Finally, Rosalita spoke; she was grateful for the darkness so that the men would not see the tears trickling down her cheeks, "Yes, it's mommy. I've come for you. It's time to go back home."

Hearing the familiar voice, Illanovich twisted and turned to get a view of her. Poor Antonio could barely keep a hold of him. In his young voice, he said, "Mother, is you?" She nudged her horse closer to Antonio's before replying.

"Yes, silly boy, it's me. I've come to take you both home. Now quit struggling so or Antonio might drop you." He stopped squirming and smiled inside all the blankets.

Their progress was very slow because of the darkness and the slippery, snow covered grasslands. Then, Rosalita felt something cold and wet land on her nose. Snow. The storm had finally begun. At once, George stopped and got out a two ropes. He explained, "Going to be a blizzard soon, and we won't be able to see anything. Can't risk being separated. I'll tie my horse to Antonio's and his to yours, Rosalita. This way, we can't possibly get separated."

"Once the snow becomes really heavy, are you going to head west?" asked Antonio.

"I want to get at least ten miles north of here before we turn west. Then, if I can somehow keep a straight course, yes, west to the foothills of the Appian Way. Once there, we follow them on down into the Arad, and then you can take it from there. Probably will be slow going, though, take at least five days, maybe more, if the snow gets deep. I did bring along one small pup tent. It is normally big enough to hold just me, but in this case, we can all snuggle up close to stay warm. I don't want to risk an open fire; it could give away our position, should anyone become curious. It is my fondest hope that the Galts will come to believe that the children and us fell victim to this winter storm. That way, they may never come looking for them. We can hope anyway. Just in case, I will spread some rumors to that effect later on once you are all safely home."

They rode on as the light snow turned into a much heavier downfall. Soon Rosalita could no longer even see Antonio's horse ahead of hers. She wondered if Antonio had been scared by these blizzards all those years he had spent alone in the high country. By midnight, the winds picked up, and the blizzard began in earnest! George decided it was time to head westward, straight into the fury of the storm. Their progress became slower and slower, as the biting winds whipped heavy snow straight at them, stinging their exposed faces. George paused so that each of them could wrap cloth wrappings around their faces, leaving only their eyes exposed. Then, he continued, but said, "I know it looks awful out, but I do have an uncanny sense of direction. Trust me; let's put some miles behind us, if we can. Yell if you get too cold. We can't afford to get frostbitten. Rosalita wondered what that was and what the symptoms were. She ought to have asked.

This was the first experience Rosalita had ever had with major snow. True, light snow did fall in her country, but it was always light, never accumulating more than an inch at most. This was something foreign to her. By the time that dawn came, she was nearly frozen to death. George halted at the edge of a patch of trees, insisted that they setup a camp, get some rest, and warm up somehow. Her hands were so cold, that she couldn't even unsaddle her horse, let alone do anything useful. Even her teeth were chattering uncontrollably.

Antonio, on the other hand was a master at survival in winter conditions; he'd lived for years up on the Paese di Dio, where often the snow cover could be measured in feet. He knew just what to do to help setup their small camp, making suggestions, which George readily accepted. They put up George's small pup tent, unloaded the horses, covered their tack with a blanket, tied the horses to nearby trees where they could still find some grass beneath the snow, and crawled into the tent.

Inside, space was at a premium to say the very least. Worse still, Rosalita had managed to check on the children and discovered, not unexpectedly, that both needed their diapers changed. She moaned to Antonio, "Of all the things to forget, I forgot to bring diapers!"

"No we didn't. I stuck some in one of these sacks," he replied and soon found the right sack. Since Rosalita was still shaking badly, Antonio volunteered to change both children. His actions were rather bumbling and awkward. He had never changed a diaper before. He'd never been this close to children for that matter. She talked him through the procedure, all the while marveling at just how thoughtful this man really was. Once the children were handled and fed, George laid down on one side of the tent, Antonio on the other. Between the two men, Rosalita and the children snuggled. This was a very wise move indeed, for the three, being so close together, were actually able to warm her up and keep the children warm as well. Soon all were sleeping soundly, while the blizzard now raged just beyond their canvas cover.

By that evening, George stuck his head outside to check on things before it got too dark to see. From the howling of the wind, he knew it was bad. Even he was very surprised; he could not see much of anything. Deep snow blanketed everything. The horses had put their rears to the wind and were now heavily covered in snow, but otherwise resting nicely. Still the blizzard raged. Antonio took a quick peek and commented, "I don't think it would be wise to travel just yet."

"That's an understatement," George teased. Together though awkwardly in the incredibly confined space, they rummaged through the food packs and fixed a cold meal. The children were now fully awake and alert, but confined to this very small tent, they were rapidly becoming bored. While Rosalita fed the children, she explained to them what was going on, that their father had been killed. Most importantly, she carefully explained that they would now live with her back at North Point. Both children were more than happy with the arrangement, though the smallest, Lenkova, probably didn't fully grasp what she was saying. An hour later, they all laid back down to try to sleep some more. In such a confined space, they could do little else.

When dawn came again, the brunt of the storm had passed. While Rosalita did the domestic duties, the men went outside to dig out the tack, which had become completely buried and see to the needs of their horses. "Me thinks me over-did the storm, Antonio," George commented as he waded through over three feet of snow to the horses.

Laughing, Antonio said, "I've been in worse up in the high country. If we go slow and let the horses go at their own pace, we should be fine. If we had sheep, it would be a disaster. However, we won't cover much ground, and we'll certainly leave a clear trail."

"I've thought of that," George replied. "We're heading west still. I know a place where we can light a fire in complete safety. There is a cave complex in one of the valleys. We can rest up there before we head south. Usually after a big storm, the temperatures drop and a big blow comes. I'm counting on the wind to hide our tracks."

Three agonizing days later, they entered a narrow valley at the edge of the Appian Way range, the beginning of that range of mountains there in the east. Almost unerringly, George led them to a concealed cave, which opened to the south and was invisible unless you knew just where to look. Once inside, Antonio and Rosalita were surprised not only with the sheer size of the complex but also with the large pile of firewood and well-stocked pantry. It was obvious that the druwids had used this cave on numerous occasions. Illanovich loved it because he could crawl around all over the place; he had his freedom of movement back. For the first time in a week, they ate a hot meal and warmed completely up, most satisfying. The group spent two days here before tackling the next leg of their journey.

Once more, they were lucky. During those two days, the winds were strong and blew snow into great drifts. The byproduct was a complete covering of their passage into the valley from the steppes. George was satisfied that no one could follow their trail, even if they had wanted to do so. Rosalita was very relieved to hear that encouraging news.

They still had a hundred miles to cover to get back to Juda Arad. However, the going now was substantially easier because George kept them close to the Appian Way range all the way south. Here, the volume of snow was drastically smaller, though the cold wind that blew down from the peaks was bone chilling. They made good time and finally arrived at that point where the range touched the northwestern tip of Juda Arad. It took five days to reach it.

Interestingly enough, Juda Arad had also received part of the snowstorm, a real rarity in this semi-arid land. True, it was barely an inch deep and nearly melted by the time that the travelers arrived; still it was snow. Here George bid them farewell and both thanked him profusely. They watched as he retraced their route. He suspected that he would first return to the cave complex. From there, they could only speculate.

Antonio now took the lead and had them quickly up onto the Paese di Dio and on familiar ground. The land was spectacular, even in winter. Snow a foot deep blanketed the region, contrasting sharply with the deep blue sky and the magnificent, snow covered, tall peaks of the Appian Way. Again, Rosalita could see why this was called "God's Country."

Four days later, the pair rode into North Point and home. She had seen more than enough snow to last a lifetime, and she now far better appreciated Antonio. Until recently, he had spent the winters up in this snow-covered land with his sheep, coming down into a valley only when it got too cold or the snow too deep.

When they arrived, both got a very warm welcome from the Sisters and mothers. Rosalita merely commented with a deep conviction that she did not know she had had, "I got my children back!" Such finality was in her voice that all were impressed.

Later that day, both she and Antonio spied Illanovich playing with some of the other children. He had made some friends before his father had taken him away. Now he was very happy to be back on familiar ground and among his small friends and their furry sheep. Rosalita knew completely that her children would adapt just fine. She also knew that she was way overdue to report back to Sister Aminia and fully expected to get chastised or worse for having gone off like this. So she put off heading back to the ranch for a couple more days, claiming she wanted to get the children settled.

The evening before she left to report for work at the ranch, she and Antonio stood just outside the cave complex in the low walled yard that served as a playground for the children. Her arm found its way around his waist and he reciprocated. At last she said solemnly, "This is probably not how it is done, Antonio. Please don't take offense at my boldness." He looked at her wondering what she was talking about.

Taking a deep breath, she said, "Antonio, let's get married. I want to marry you, if you will have me. I know I now have children that are not yours, but. . ." She did not get to finish her sentence.

"I love you too, Rosalita. You would make me the luckiest man in the world if you married me! I promise to be a good father to the children, always. I was afraid to ask you before now because I sort of thought that Sisters never got married or something."

"Of course we do, silly, only it is rather rare, all things considered, if you know what I mean." That ended the talk; both embraced each other, lovingly doing what both had been dreaming of for some time now.

After a while, Antonio said, "Have you given any thought to the well-being of our children? I mean, as they grow up, other children are very likely to tease them about their father, who tried to conquer the world and got his head cut off. Or some who have lost fathers or other family members or even who were somehow affected by the Galts — they might try to shift some blame for it onto the children, you know how vicious some kids can be."

"As usual, you are way ahead of me," she teased. "I suppose you are right. I have seen other children picking on each other, kids games, I thought. Now I see that it can be a very vicious thing, particularly considering who their father was. What should we do?"

"Well, we will just consider me to be their dad. You know, their last name will be mine. We just will not go around telling others any different. Few outside of the Sisterhood knows anything about this whole affair. So if we just say they are ours, why, that might hide it from others."

"You would do that?" she asked incredulously.

"Sure, they look like good kids to me. Of course, one day the children have to know who their real father was and all that. I'll not be a party to actually hiding that fact from them. However, that day is far into the future, when they are old enough to understand matters and when it will not adversely affect them. How's that sound?" She answered by giving him a loving kiss.

Footnote: Antonio and Rosalita Pazzio were married in a simple ceremony in late December. Things worked out well for them, Antonio spent much time caring for the children at North Point, while she was off on Sisterhood duties. As the children grew older, he often took them with him up onto the Paese di Dio to help him herd the ever-growing flock of sheep.

From all this, Rosalita learned subjectively a lesson that she had not fully known: motherhood is a strong bond, one not easily broken. She appreciated the other mothers at North Point more than ever before.

Chapter 30 Retaliation

Come midnight of the day that Mikhailovich Strokova was killed on the battlefield by the sword of General Lacerta, a grey shape flew high in the sky out over the Red Desert. Only one studying the stars that night could have detected its form momentarily blotting out the distant starlight. It was flying fast and over twenty thousand feet above ground level. Straight toward the three tall pyramids located out in the east-central section of that desert of death was its path.

Three of the giant mantis creatures were attached to the sides of one of the pyramids, operating some machinery. A tall metallic pole radiated energy waves; spiritual beings, who only hours before had had their bodies slain on the battlefield, were now lined up for their turn at the pole.

Large grey elongated, spindly fingers manipulated some controls and pushed a black button on the complex console. An energy wave or force field shot out toward one of the pyramids. When it connected, a huge clap of thunder-like noise echoed throughout the desert. The pyramid was instantly reduced to a gigantic pile of crushed, pulverized stone, no longer recognizable as having once been a stone pyramid!

More importantly, the ground all around this area shook violently, as if a great earthquake had struck, jolting the very earth itself. All three mantis creatures were knocked off the other pyramid, but instantly took flight to avoid the harm of hitting the ground. The same grey finger pressed another button and spoke into a transducer, whose electronics converted it into another language, "You have been warned." That was all that was said. Just as suddenly as the flying ship had come, it was gone, flying back north toward the Appian Way.

Four druwids who were studying the stars that night noted both its coming and going. The information was eventually forwarded to the All Greenway Circle. However, the earthquake did far more damage.

Chapter 31 When Gods War

Come midnight of the day that Mikhailovich Strokova was killed by the sword of General Lacerta, deep underground in the Red Desert, the Moon People were fast asleep, safe in their underground chambers. These people have pale bronzed skin and fair complexions, likely distant relatives of those who lived in Megalos.

The surface of the Red Desert contains a fine dust which glows faintly red in the dark. If any of that dust get on one's bare skin, he or she comes down with the "rotting sickness" and dies within a few weeks. Instead, these people live in hundreds of underground chambers, seldom venturing out upon the surface of the desert. When they do have to travel from one chamber to another, they wrap themselves completely in layers of cloth wrappings so that no skin shows and travel only at night, when the moon is not full so they can see the faint reddish glow and thus avoid those patches of sand. Hence, the dark skinned natives of the Southlands call these people the Moon People.

As you may recall, I first encountered these people in my last lifetime, when I was the Wid of our Lightning Circle. These people speak a language that is much like that of Megalos, save it is far older. When we first encountered these people, we discovered that to the last person, they always mentally recited the same passage:

> Wash thy feet before entering. Expose no flesh out of doors. Touch no one save thy mate and then only after both have bathed. Be cautious of strangers for they may bring sickness. Eat no offering that grows upon the surface save that that lives under waters. Stay ever alert for the winds of Atlas for they bring the sands of death. Accept in trade nothing that comes from the land's surface. Thus sayeth the Holy Defense Code of Amin, messenger of Sol.

It became obvious this code serves as a constant reminder of the terrible danger in which they constantly live.

From the surface, these underground chambers are completely hidden, except for a single entrance door usually half buried under sand dunes. These doors swing open effortlessly, opening to a pool of water about six inches deep into which one had to step if he or she were to enter. In this manner, all traces of the poisonous dust are washed away before entering the chamber proper. From this small entry pool, one then moves down a long tunnel that is about six feet tall and six wide. The main tunnels can run straight as an arrow for more than a mile! The sides are stone, perfectly cut and polished so that light shines off its surface. Every ten feet a light fixture hangs from the ceiling. These are no ordinary light fixtures; from what we could tell, they appear to be made of some kind of transparent glass with the source of light encased within the glass. A small metal pipe runs along the ceiling, connecting to each of these light fixtures. Each of these chambers was at one time home to over five hundred people.

Every so often a metal side door appears. Behind these doors are amazing rooms, tall and expansive. Some house huge gardens where they grow grain and fungi, their staple foods. Others house playrooms for the children. Still others, house public baths, kitchens, and pantries. Yes, there is a special room for the High Priest or Priestess who runs the Chamber.

The entrance doors to the High Priestess's room are usually especially large double doors, elaborately carved with two doves sitting upon two vines with many leaves. Inside a pale blue light fully illuminates these chambers, each of which is approximately thirty foot square with the entrance door squarely in the middle of one side. The sides rise upwards to seven feet but the ceiling is really a dome, rising from the sides to a lofty twenty feet above the floor. Ringing the joint between the walls and the bottom of the domed ceiling are long glass tubes that provide the pale blue glow, which illuminates the room. The ceiling is painted black with stars as though one is looking at the nighttime sky. Every foot of the walls is covered with painted frescoes or paintings, realistic looking scenes of life. Yes, these underground living chambers are indeed a wonder to behold and operate using completely unknown technology.

Here was where I first met Galentia, the High Priest of the Edhessa Chamber. She was then perhaps thirty years old, though now she is sixty. She stood nearly six feet tall, with very long black hair and the brownest eyes I have ever seen, contrasting sharply with her completely pale-bronze skin. According to Galentia, they are the children of Amin, for it was he alone who saved their ancestors after the angry, fiery outburst of Angibus, who scorched the land turning it into a desert of death. Galentia explained, "Our legends say that most of our original people perished either in the fiery blast or from the rotting sickness that followed shortly thereafter. But father Amin invented the Code and all those who chose to follow his code survived. To this day, we, the faithful, still follow his Code, for failure to do so results in the rotting disease and death."

"Long ago, Amin brought his faithful here to these underground chambers to survive. Still today, we, his children, still live, holding strong his Codes in our hearts. Here in the chamber we have everything we need to live. Everything is recycled to give life to the future. When one of us passes away and goes to join Amin, his earthly body is placed into the compost room, where it decays and returns to the earth from which it is made. The only exceptions are those who die from the rotting disease; those we bury outside the chamber according to the parables of the Code."

In each of the Priest/Priestess chambers, the frescoes depict their history. In one painting, Angibus is seen casting down fires from the sky, creating the Red Desert. You can see a green land with stone buildings much as those in Megalos. Then, people are running in all directions from the flames as the buildings crumbled. It is not a pretty fresco. In the top portion, a disembodied hand seemed to be causing the flames and destruction. Angibus, no doubt. In the next fresco, Lord Amin is shown leading the faithful into the Chambers. You can see a white robed man leading a scant number of people into an opening just like the ones you enter today. Behind them, the scenes of destruction are smaller in relief, giving a sense of hope to those fleeing underground.

Galentia shocked us all by showing us another fresco. "Legends speak of the coming of the Outsider — one who comes unlooked for during a time of great need. She comes bearing a gift of life, asking nothing in return. Here you see the prediction. She is the white robed lady with her hands opened wide. Here, she is healing the sick." Shocked beyond words, I stared at the frescoes and the white woman. It was frightening for the white lady closely resembled me!

If you recall, Sandy, our Healer, did find a cure for the rotting sickness and gave it freely to these people. However, their life-threatening problem was their grain seed. After inbreeding for so many hundreds of years, it had begun dying out. They were more than desperate for new seed grain, which we supplied by the boatloads.

Additionally, when asked why they had not abandoned the Red Desert and moved out into the world to find a new home, the answer was reasonable. She explained it this way. "In the beginning, we believed the destruction so massive that one could not survive outside long enough to leave. That is what we believed at least. As for now, that is simple. We, none of us, have the knowledge or skills with which to survive elsewhere. Yes, we all could leave the safety of the Chamber, but once outside, then what? We have occasionally monitored our black-skinned neighbors across the river, building dwellings, cooking, and even hunting once. None of us knows the first thing about these things. Surely we would all starve long before we learned."

Yet, in another fresco, these Moon People are seen going out into the world once more. That was again where the druwids came to their aid. As Wid, I had ordered a number of our druwids to travel to their land and to begin helping them learn the skills necessary to survive in the outside world. Of course, my druwid body was killed long before I knew the results of that endeavor. Only recently have I learned that for thirty years now, druwids from the Greenway have been helping the Moon People learn the skills needed to survive above ground.

On the opposite side of the river which separates the Red Desert from the Southlands, under the constant supervision of the druwids, four large towns have been constructed as of this time, each housing some two thousand people. All have adapted as well as can be expected from such a complete life-style change — from living underground to surface dwelling. In fact, at this particular time, sixteen of the chambers closest to the south central border with the Southlands have been largely emptied. Only a few guides remain there to assist others who are slowly migrating down from their northern chambers. Yes, it is a controlled migration of their entire population.

In case you are curious about how the druwids accomplished this transformation, here is the basic plan they followed. The Circle works with one chamber's population, that chamber which is next scheduled to migrate to the surface. After spending many months in basic education, they then lead the entire group out onto the surface and assist in getting them established. Homes are constructed; gardens are planted; fishing boats are built, and so on. However, the existing sixteen groups who already have successfully made the transition are also helping. Thus, the rate of progress is escalating rapidly.

Come midnight of the day that Mikhailovich Strokova was killed on the battlefield by the sword of General Lacerta, deep underground in the Red Desert, a tremendous earthquake awakened the sleeping Moon People. The hardest hit chambers were those closest to the epicenter, where the three, make that two now, pyramids are located.

One of these chambers, the Decagon Chamber, was especially hard it. Here, sleeping bodies were physically bounced several inches into the air by the tremendous jolt. Even more terrifying, all of the eternal lights went out. The entire chamber was suddenly and inexplicably pitch black, frightening even the hardiest of souls! Some even said the end of the world was at hand. Panic set in, especially when bits of the ceilings fell down on top of the inhabitants, who, in the total darkness, were petrified. Men, women, and children began screaming and moving about in the blackness, smashing into objects and each other in their panic.

The violent shaking of the earth subsided within a few minutes, though the shrieking only grew louder. Nothing in the Defense Code of Amin dealt with this situation. No frescoes on any wall told of this occurrence. Hence, the panic of the residents of the chamber. Dax, the High Priest, attempted to calm his people from his opened doorway, but his voice could not be heard over the screams of his people. Quickly, he ceased trying to out-shout them. "Use your mind, Dax," he said to himself aloud, partially to help drown out the screaming voices.

Feeling his way about his room, he headed straight for one cabinet in a corner, bumping into other furniture and planters along the way. He fumbled about until he felt the familiar square box of an Eternal Light of Amin. A moment later, his groping fingers found the on-switch and light poured out of one end. "Ah, much better." Using his lantern, he made his way back to the doorway, noticing bits of the ceiling now littered his floor. He hoped that the damage was not serious. Loss of the starry dome overhead would be difficult to accept.

Flashing his light up and down the long hallway caught people's attention. Their panic quieted, and he called out, "Remember the Eternal Lights of Amin. Everyone who has one or knows where one is stored, please get them and turn them on. Meanwhile, everyone bring some blankets from your beds and follow my light to my room. I think it best if we are all together in a couple of rooms, which have some lights."

Within five minutes, six other lights were now in operation, and the five hundred plus people were now gathered into seven rooms, all near the High Priest's room. "There now, this is not yet the end of the world. We can see. Nothing can stop these Eternal Lights, so there is no cause for panic. Perhaps the lights will come back on later on, but for now, I suggest that we try to get some sleep. In the morning, we can decide what to do next."

Leaving the lantern near the doorway as a night light, he stepped among those now lying on his room's floor, consoling this one, comforting that one, yet always making sure none was physically hurt. Once everything had quieted down, he walked out into the hallway and gathered his dozen leaders — those who were in charge of the various daily activities, such as gardening, cooking, outside travel, and so on. He held a quick council out in the mile long hallway so as not to disturb his people.

"First, are there any serious injuries?" The others shook their heads no. "Okay, then I think it best if one of us takes a lantern and inspects every inch of our chamber for damage. That should be our first action." The man in charge of the garden rooms volunteered, borrowed the lantern from the Dax's room, and headed off down the corridor. "While he is gone, I'm open to suggestions about what we should do tomorrow, if the lights don't come back on."

The chief replied, "If the lights don't come back on, then all the growing plants will die, and there goes our food supply. We'll starve to death."

"I noticed that the water is no longer flowing as it is supposed to," commented a tailor.

Within a few minutes, the Dax realized that should the lights not come back on in a reasonable period, they'd have no choice but to wholesale evacuate the Decagon Chamber. Where to lead his people was another matter entirely. It would take several nights to move this many people safely across the Red Desert just to the next chamber. What if its lights were out as well? How could a thousand people live in a chamber designed for five hundred? He had many unanswerable questions.

In a half hour, the man returned. Other than the lighting and water systems, there seemed to be only superficial damage to the chamber. All were relieved to hear that piece of good news. Dax then asked the outside travel man, "Is it too late for you to go outside to the nearest other chamber and see if they are in the same plight as we?"

"If I hurry, I should be able to get to the one south of us. Should I try? I can't get back until late tomorrow night."

"Yes, but if the one south of us has also lost their lights, then keep heading south, night after night, until you do come to one that still has lights. Tell them of our plight and seek aid. If nothing else, find those from the Greenway. Perhaps they can help in some way." The man bowed to his priest and backed away. The gardener leader carried the lantern down to the exit chamber so he could see to put on his wrappings. In a few minutes, the gardener leader returned with the lantern. There was nothing else that could be done, so they also retired for the remainder of the night.

The next day the magnitude of their plight became apparent to everyone. The cooks reported that none of the ovens now worked. Water became a scarce commodity; the wells no longer bubbled up life giving water from somewhere underground. However, the pantry held enough food for them to get by for at least several weeks. Harvesting some of the fungus slightly early would extend the period even further. However, once that ran out, they would face slow starvation. Everyone waited anxiously for their outside man to return that night, he did not. In fact, he did not return for over a week. However, several other men came from neighboring chambers looking for aid for their own groups. Dax quickly learned that several nearby chambers were also damaged by the earthquake. Now he was very glad that he had given his man orders to keep going south in search of help.

Five days after the quake, word of the calamity reached the southernmost chamber, the Edhessa Chamber, now the headquarters of the druwid training center. Here in this last chamber next to the river, they trained an entire group for life above ground. When the group was ready, they led them outside, across the river, and to their new homes in the nearby villages. Currently, they were training their seventeenth chamber group of five hundred.

Wid John Henry Penton quickly called for a meeting of his Moon Circle, the name they adopted. Incidentally, John Henry was the eldest son of my dear friends, Raphael and Sarah Jane. All had extensively trained specifically for the task of aiding these people. "We know that at least two chambers near the north-central section of the desert are without power. My guess is that earthquake we all felt here a few days ago has somehow damaged more than just two. We need to determine which ones are without power. Planner Lilly Elizabeth, do you have our rough map of the chamber complexes?" She did and proceeded to open the wide scroll and spread it out on the table. "Ah, here are the two that we know are in trouble." He placed a red mark on the two whose runners had arrived last night with the news.

Planner Lilly Elizabeth, the eldest daughter of Thomas and Thallia Wilkins, commented, "The first action we should do is to send out a lot of runners to the whole central area and find out the total extent of the problem. It may be only a few chambers are in trouble, but then it could well become a disaster. In our favor is the fact that sixteen chambers have been emptied already. Against us is the fact that they are the furthest from here. Our grand scheme of slowly migrating everyone south to here, one chamber at a time has just developed a significant problem, if many of the ones in the center are now not usable for any length of time."

"Ellen Sarah, how close is this chamber to being ready to move out onto the surface?" asked John Henry. Ellen Sarah Randell Stanton, my daughter, was their Healer and kept accurate records of each chamber's progress.

She replied, "If we need to move them out, we probably can, though I think that several of us should stay with them for another month, just in case."

"I'll volunteer for that duty," put in Robert. His name was Robert Roy

Randell Stanton, my eldest son, their Protector.

"I will too," added Misty Simone, the eldest daughter of Sandy and Simon. "As Communicator, I can keep you all informed of their progress and any troubles that may arise." She did not need to add that besides, she wanted to be close to her husband, Robert.

"Count me in as well," offered Henry Alabaster, their Judger and son of Sandy and Simon.

"Where do you want me?" asked their Loremaster, Ellie Ann, the daughter of Raphael and Sarah Jane. "I would be more useful going to the surface with them."

"Wait a minute; you all can't go top-side! Ellen Sarah has to stay here. Who knows how much her healing skills are going to be needed. Ellie Ann, you probably should go to the surface with them, your skills are more useful there. Henry, I think you should stay here and help organize things. Sorry, I know you just can't wait to get out of these underground chambers, but I really need you here," Wid John Henry decided.

He continued, "We should send out the runners at once. Lilly Elizabeth and I will attend to it now. While we look for the most optimum routes on which to send the runners, the rest of you get cracking on getting this chamber group ready to go to the surface." The Circle disbanded to begin their tasks.

Footnote: the day that I learned of the existence of the Moon Circle, its members, and its duties — that was one of the proudest days of my life. My children from my marriage to Roy last lifetime — my children and those of my dearest Circle friends — all of them had followed in our footsteps, becoming powerful druwids and Guardians in their own right! Further, they were here helping to save an entire people. Yes, I felt elated the day I learned of this from Sandy, but that is getting ahead of the story.

It took nearly a week before a fuller picture could be had. More messengers for darkened chambers made their way to the Edhessa Chamber as well as those that the Moon Circle had sent out. Planner Lilly Elizabeth and Wid John Henry marked all the results on their makeshift map of known chambers. Lilly commented, "Well, this makes the nineteenth chamber emptied with forty-one more to go, assuming that we have found all of the chambers and no one reports yet another chamber to us."

"Yes, and eight are now dark, all centrally located ones. This is playing havoc with our controlled evacuation plans," John Henry replied. "Looks like there is only one narrow route left open for us to use to get the more northern chambers moved down here. We'll have to let all the Chamber Priests know the precise route they are going to have to follow."

"What are we going to do about the eight groups in dire trouble right now?" Lilly asked. "They've shown an incredible resilience to panicking; they have been trying to survive in almost total darkness now for at least a couple of weeks."

"I've been thinking on that Lilly," he answered thoughtfully. "If we start issuing orders to have some chambers back up to chambers they previously occupied, they are certainly going to feel like they are being cheated out of their turn. They have all been educated on the sequence of the planned evacuation and to date have followed it. However, to make room for the eight that went dark, we'd have to shuffle not only the eight chambers of effected people, but also nearly every other chamber, just to back up and give them room to move out. I just don't see how we are going to coordinate such a huge amount of simultaneous movement of populations. Besides, every time a chamber moves its entire population, some invariably get the rotting sickness. If we move so many at once, we could have an epidemic of rotting sickness with which to deal."

Lilly played with her long hair a moment, as she always did this while pondering alternatives, just a nervous habit. At last, she volunteered, "John Henry, we've got eighteen chambers, make that nineteen now, moved out onto the surface. Crops are growing, homes built, and all have adapted well. Perhaps it is time to see if those people can help. How about bringing out seven more chambers worth of people with no training at all. Divide them up among the four towns; let their own people train and educate them. We can at least see how it goes, and all of us can help as needed. If it succeeds, then we can multiply our rate of evacuation by at least eight times and finish this drastically sooner."

"Yes, but what if there are adaption problems? You are talking thirty-five hundred people undergoing a crash course in life all at once. If anything goes wrong, we are in deep trouble," he countered.

"Well, we can always ship food down here from the Greenway and boat it up the river from the east coast of the Southlands. I should think that they wouldn't starve. Building enough homes — that will be a challenge on such short notice, but I was thinking of having each family unit take one of the new arriving families into their home. That way, housing would not be a critical, immediate problem. They can learn the ropes this way in a non-hostile setting, among others who have already made the transition."

"You are cleverly avoiding my question, Lilly Elizabeth! I agree. Food will not likely be a problem. What if they have mental problems adapting to such a huge, dramatic change in the way they live? As we discussed years ago, they are experiencing a total change in the way they live their lives. This could be quite a shock to some of them. Then what do we do?"

She grinned; she had been caught. Often, she would play this game with John Henry called "see if he can detect that I'm not really answering his questions." Invariably, he won. It was hard getting anything past John Henry. "Okay, any that have trouble we can bring back at once to this chamber here and educate them as we have been doing. How's that?"

He yielded to her plan, since after all she was the Planner. If she thought it was doable, then he couldn't afford not to try it. If it worked, years could be trimmed off this huge relocation problem. In fact, they were trying to relocate an entire civilization. Via their Communicator Misty, John Henry explained his decision to try it. The Moon Circle's consensus was that the four towns needed at least a week to prepare for this sudden influx of people. That would not be a problem, for it would take longer than that to get the first chamber moved here and then on out onto the surface and to the town.

Now the two spent an hour working out the details of which chamber would move to where and when. It had to be a well-orchestrated action so that no chamber suddenly found itself trying to house more than it could hold. This was indeed a challenge in mass-movement, particularly so now that their main central chambers could no longer be used. Further, once they had worked out a proper evacuation sequence, they then had to send runners to communicate the information to the respective High Priests of the impacted chambers. They controlled the actual population movement activities. Always before, they only moved one chamber at a time. Now, however, due to the severity of the problem, eight chambers would have to move simultaneously out of the darkened, useless chambers and soon. That meant all the chambers further south had to be evacuate just ahead of the new arrivals. It was a coordination nightmare, worthy of a Planner and a Wid.

A month later, the move was finished. Thirty-five hundred people now resided in the ever growing towns. The entire operation had been a success. Only a hundred people caught the rotting sickness, and Sarah Jane's cure worked miracles on them. However, Ellen Sarah, their healer, made an interesting observation as she cared for those that were stricken. Every single case of the rotting sickness was a very mild one. Comparing notes with Sarah Jane back in the Greenway, Ellen's opinion was that something significant had changed. Either the people had suddenly developed immunity to this disease or some other factor was now in play to lessen the impact of the disease. One theory she proposed was that over this lengthy time, perhaps most of the red dust had become deeply buried in the sands, so that all exposures were now mild ones. There was some supporting evidence for that idea; the reddish glow had become vastly more difficult to see. No one could now travel between the first and third quarters of the moon, for there was just too much moonlight to see the reddish glow.

During the winter months, the Moon Circle continued training another group who had arrived in the Edhessa Chamber during the great shuffle. When spring came to the Southlands, the Circle carefully evaluated how moving that large a number of people out without any training actually fared. While there were small problems, overall it worked well. In fact, those Moon People who actually took on the responsibility of training their fellow people were highly enthusiastic about it. To the person, they felt elated that they could actually help in this desperate resettlement project. Thus, during the early spring months, a fifth town was built some five miles further downstream from the other four, with enough houses for another four thousand people. Volunteers to live there came from all of the other four towns.

Thus, in the early summer of 590 AH, the Moon Circle attempted to move ten chambers topside, only one of which had been educated and trained. Now, only twenty-three chambers remained occupied underground. So successful was this move, that by fall yet another town was built and occupied, so that near the start of winter time, another ten chambers were emptied, only one of which had been trained.

Finally, during the summer of 591 AH, the last of the known, occupied underground chambers had been moved to the surface. All the High Priests held a final closing ceremony from the banks of the river overlooking the tiny village where the Lightning Circle had first encountered the Moon People. The highest praise was heaped upon the Moon Circle and their predecessors for such a fantastic job. Not a single person had been lost during all these years, and the entire known population of Moon People, close to forty thousand, had been saved. They had been taught all skills needed to survive on the surface, knowledge that none of them had before the druwids came. Yes, this Circle felt that they had really done something of great worth and value and had every right to feel proud of their achievement.

Still, they stuck around until the fall, when a replacement Circle arrived from the Greenway to continue to watch over the seven towns. Indeed, the druwids fully intended to keep at least one Circle permanently located here to help as they would in any town back in the Greenway. In late September, the Moon Circle mounted up on the spare horses brought by along the Distant Circle, when they arrived earlier. It took several weeks to ride down the length of the river to where it emptied into the ocean on the eastern shores of the Southlands. There a Sea Prince boat was lying to, awaiting their arrival, ready to take them home to the Greenway.

Planner Lilly Elizabeth thought that a port town ought to be constructed here at the mouth of the river. She intended to bring that issue up with the All Greenway Circle, when she got home.

Chapter 32 The Death of the Great Messiah

In mid-May 588 AH, Jes hopped a Sea Prince ship for the mainland, Velona in particular. At this time, only Velona remained unconquered by the barbarians from the Northern Steppes. His supposed goal was to bring as many dislocated Arads here to our new town on West Reach. Though he did not say it, I suspected he thought that he could persuade tens of thousands to immigrate here.

Per our agreement, each night, once the children were put to bed, he mentally joined with my mind and we shared. I enjoyed these times immensely. Further, because of the roundabout route his ship followed, Jes visited Calgary in the Greenway! Oh, did I envy him. I forgot how much I missed my former homeland and friends! Because he didn't speak the local language, Jes stayed aboard the ship the few days it was docked, unloading and loading its cargo. Thus, it was early June before he actually landed in Velona.

The situation in this last unconquered Sea Prince city was chaotic, preparations for the almost certain war were everywhere in the city. The chaos Jes avoided by getting a guide to lead him straight to the Arad sector of town, where our people grouped together, forming a small subsection of Velona. Jes estimated at least a couple thousand had immigrated here. Because he wore West Reach clothing and because of his more clean-shaven appearance, no one recognized him as their Great Messiah. Further, he called himself, Josh Azir.

Uniformly he found most were very worried about the coming invasion of the Galts, though they would not likely arrive here until the following spring. Many ears listened to Jes's description of the new lands in West Reach. Two months later, more and more of these people did actually begin arriving in West Reach in search of our new town. Yes, at first, Jes was successful in slowly building up our population, out of the reach of the barbarians.

After spending a month at this, he learned that some Arads had settled in several outlying towns and villages. Naturally, he told me he intended to go visit each of these. I was greatly relieved when he followed my advice. Banditry was commonplace in these areas closer to the main city. My suggestion was to hire a couple of the Sisterhood fighters to escort him to all of the places he desired to visit. I knew that he had taken along sufficient funds to cover just such an expense. Besides, I could actually sleep nights now, knowing that he was under the protection of the Sisterhood during his travels about the countryside.

He was far less effective in gaining new immigrants from these more remote areas. Our people had settled in nicely with the local indigenous population and were reluctant to relocate again. In fact, many had reports from the other Sea Prince sectors that the barbarians mostly ignored the smaller outlying villages. Upon this, people based their hopes for the future.

Next, he decided to travel on to the Barcella Sector just ahead of the barbarian invasion. Again, he traveled under the protection of the Sisterhood, thankfully! Perhaps he didn't want me screaming into his mind about his safety all the time. Well, I certainly would have, had he not made good use of these terrific fighters. I found it extremely frustrating to have my husband traveling around like this without my presence and knowledge of the local situation. I was very familiar with the circumstances in the Sea Princes. Okay, I longed to be with him as well, I'll admit it.

He was successful in part in Barcella. Many were fleeing the city just ahead of the barbarian invasion. It wasn't hard to convince them to flee to Velona and purchase passage to West Reach. Thus, for many months, a steady stream of Arad immigrants trickled onto the soil of West Reach and then to our town. By fall, the construction of our sister town some five miles distant on another perfect hilltop began. During the early winter, people began moving into the new wooden cabin homes. Once more, we built a wooden fortress wall around the hilltop, providing protection from any raiders. All winter long, we continued to see growth in our numbers.

Jes managed to leave the city just ahead of the invading Galts, much to my relief and the Sisterhood guides as well. I know that he was most curious about these Yellow Butchers and probably wanted a way to observe them firsthand. Via the Sisters who guarded him, we learned much of what had happened during the previous two years, including the self-sacrifice that Rosalita had made to safeguard the entire Sisterhood. Thus, under their protection, Jes did get a few opportunities to observe these barbarians in action, though from a safe distance.

However, Jes is a sensitive man, seeing the wanton destruction of lives and property eventually weighted heavily on his mind. Sometimes, he was so moody that he deliberately did not make contact with me at night, fearing to upset me with the gory details he had witnessed that day. While I missed his mind touching mine, I accepted his rationale. Perhaps I should not have, because, as I later concluded, it gave him a valid excuse to "miss" some of our nightly mental sharing. In truth, I was now very busy trying to run two towns at the same time: working out all the new construction details, planning the spring crop plantings, exploring additional trading opportunities — the list went on and on. Some nights, I was so tired from the day that I fell asleep and didn't even know if he had tried to contact me that night. Again, I probably shouldn't have gotten so complacent about it. As is said, hindsight is easier than foresight.

October 15, 588 AH, Jes made contact with me for the last time. *Bethany, these grey creatures — something has to be done about them. I've watched for weeks now as they seem to relish literally sucking in all the poor beings whose bodies have just been slain on the battlefields, scrambling their memories, and sending them off to move into a new baby body. Some days, there has been a veritable line up of spiritual beings just waiting to get mind washed! This has to stop! My love, you were entirely correct about these* creatures — *they are diabolical, perhaps Evil Incarnate. I swear they are trying to control ordinary people's lives. Perhaps they are responsible for convincing an immortal spirit that they are a body instead of a being, but I'm not wholly convinced of this. It sure seems that way on the surface of it.*

Jes, please don't do this! These things — they are so incredibly powerful compared to us! Even at a distance, their devices just seem to suck one into their mind scrambler. Remember, I told you I almost was sucked in once. Please don't do this alone; you'll just get yourself killed! I realized how silly this plea from the heart sounded. *Okay, you won't get killed, just your body, but you might get your mind scrambled. We need you here, our children need you, and our town needs you.*

Bethany, you believe in the Seven Aspects of Life. This is something I must do for all mankind; perhaps this is why I was sent here in the first place — these creatures are entrapping Jehosa's children. Us — you — our family is just one of the seven aspects. This is something I must do for all. Please understand. If I do not succeed, promise me that you'll not come looking for me, that you'll take care of our children and even Josh's, so they may one day be fit to be kings and queens — I beg you, don't let me down on this, please, dearest Bethany.

I promise, but why not wait and muster a large army and attack them outright? Alone, they are too powerful; they are like gods themselves.

Ah, but am I not the Son of Jehosa?

How do you argue against religious beliefs and teachings? I never could. I tried my best along the only avenue I thought might reach him. *But why not get some help? Don't try this alone!*

I can't endanger the lives and mental states of others, that's why. These creatures are incredibly powerful. If I brought an army against them, I'm sure the entire army would be wiped out. I've watched them for weeks now' and I believe I have chosen the right time and place to attack one of them. I'm only going to go up against them one at a time. I'm not rushing into this, Bethany. I have it all worked out. Oops, here comes the one I have targeted. I have to go now and see if my strategy works. No matter what happens, remember always, I love you more than anything else on Tarra.

Abruptly, he broke off our telepathic connection. Giant tears swelled up in my eyes. "How could he do this to us?" I wailed aloud to myself. "He'll just get his body killed and himself zapped like the other poor folks." How long I cried I couldn't say. Then something inside me kicked in, *Bethany, you fool, get him some help!* But who? The only person I could think of who could possibly help was Alabaster himself!

I hadn't heard from him since this body was around five years old. I had no idea where he was or what he was doing. Yet, I had to try. Wiping the tears from my face, I concentrated. At first, my grief was still too strong to concentrate effectively. Minutes passed and then my mind reached out across space. I felt the distinctive presence of Alabaster. Certain spiritual beings have a distinctive presence, at least, that is how I describe it. I made contact with his mind.

Alabaster, Bethany here. I need your help immediately. Jes has gone after the grey creatures. He is trying to stop them from mind zapping all these beings. He won't listen to me. You've got to help!

Ah ha. So that is who that is. Yes, I see them. Maybe the two of us can overpower one of them. Watch through my mind. Suddenly, mentally I could see what Alabaster was seeing. Far off in the distance near the tunnel where the creature eluded the Lightning Circle so many years ago and high in the Appian Way, I saw Jes's tiny form trying to battle single grey creature, who towered over him like a giant. For a spiritual being without a body, moving across distances takes very little time at all — I saw one giant swish and blur of motion. Alabaster had moved from miles away right into the thick of the action! I watched and observed; there was nothing else that I could do, whether or not I wanted to — I was connected to Alabaster's eyes instead of my own, only he didn't have any physical body or eyes.

Jes attempted to hack at the legs of the grey giant with little success. Alabaster took a moment to study the creature. I could see that it had something resembling a loincloth about its waist held firmly in place by a metallic looking belt with some kind of small, red blinking lights on it. My initial panic slowly began to subside, due in part to Alabaster's calming influence. He had that way with me. At last, I could just observe, which I now realize was Alabaster's full intent. Whether or not he knew what the ultimate outcome would be, he certainly wanted me to gain as much knowledge about our opponent as possible.

From the strikes Jes made, I could tell that the creature had some kind of force field around him. The sword just bounced off the creature a few inches before it would have struck its leg. The invisible barrier appeared to extend about six inches from the surface of its skin. However, I noticed that the lights blinked rapidly just after Jes struck this invisible barrier. Conclusion: the belt thing had something to do with making the creature impervious to physical blows. Corollary: if nothing changed, Jes was doomed to complete failure.

Alabaster summoned a bolt of lightning, aiming for the belt contraption, hitting the creature from behind so as not to hit Jes by mistake. The invisible shield wavered; the red blinking came fast and furious, as the energy was shunted on down into the stony ground. Alabaster paused and thought a moment, while the creature swung it huge fist toward Jes, who nimbly dodged out of the way, narrowly avoiding getting pulverized.

With Jes now some distance away, Alabaster brought down an even more powerful bolt, only this time he made the connection at the very top of the creature's head. Electrical energy sparked and flashed all down the outside of the invisible shield, outlining it and making it quite visible for a moment. The rate of blinking crescendoed and became so fast that it was nearly a continuous light and then suddenly went out. Alabaster placed the thought, *Now!* into Jes's mind.

Jes, now back on his feet, closed the distance and swung once more.

This time his blade found its mark, slicing into the grey hide or skin of the creature. Ah, it bled, if the greenish ooze that seeped out of the cut was its equivalent of blood. The creature, quite startled and in pain, cried out an unintelligible language and began a very hasty retreat back up into the mountains towards their base of operations. Now I could see why it had eluded the Lightning Circle some thirty years ago. The grey giant was incredibly fast moving. Jes had no chance to strike a second blow.

I hoped that Jes would now see reason, that Alabaster could somehow talk him out of doing this. Unfortunately, Jes was now so fired up with apparent success that he dashed off on up the narrow rocky valley after the slightly wounded creature. Alabaster had no choice but to follow behind. Soon, they came out on a high small plateau near the peak of the tall mountain. I could see the familiar vertical pole contraption that they used to ensnare so many free brings. Now the grey creature was no longer alone; two more appeared walking out of a cavern entrance that I hadn't seen before. Evidently they lived deep inside and perhaps even had the equipment stored in there. Interesting, I thought.

Jes closed rapidly on the wounded creature and attacked him once more, cutting into his other leg. That did it, the creature dropped down to both knees in pain. However, wounded, it was still more than a formidable opponent. Before Jes could get in another swing, it swung its fist and knocked the sword from Jes's hand, while its other hand smashed into Jes' head. My husband's face was no longer recognizable! Instantly I knew that blow had killed his body, that I would indeed never see Jes alive again. I watched as, completely unfazed, Jes moved out of his body, attacking the grey creature, this time using an energy flow similar to our lightning bolts. I never knew that he could do that! He was creating electricity, whereas we were just borrowing it from the storm clouds. Without the protection of his belt contraption, the grey creature died on the spot, his giant body jerking in massive convulsions on the ground.

However, the other two weren't idle. Somehow, I did not see how, they activated their electronic pole contraption; waves of energy came out from it. I watched in horror as the waves flowed over Jes; naturally, he began resisting it and slowly was forced to move closer and closer to the pole! I knew what they were experiencing. Memories of having almost been sucked into the mantis's pole out in the Red Desert thirty years ago came flooding into my mind. I mentally screamed to them, *Don't resist it! Don't fight that pull.* So hard was Jes concentrating on fighting it, that I couldn't get through to him. He had forgotten all I'd told him about my experiences with it.

Even Alabaster was being affected by the sucking energy, though not nearly as much as Jes. A moment later, Jes hit the pole and clung on to it. Now I could see his mental memories swishing, swirling into view. Like all the other beings I had seen get sucked into the pole, his entire memory bank was being scrambled, turned into an incomprehensible mess of dis-related images no one could ever sort out!

Alabaster then began to move toward the pole, in a vain attempt to try to free Jes before it was too late. However, at that instant, Alabaster focused my attention onto a critical detail. There was some kind of cable running from the bottom of the pole across the rocky plateau and on into the dark cavern. I picked up his intention; an electrical strike on that unprotected cable might just disable the pole sucker. Alabaster had no time to concentrate to pull down said bolt. I realize now that he was priming me for the future, showing me one possible avenue of attack later on.

As he too became entrapped while trying to rescue Jes, he sent me a very clear message; his last words rang out in my mind. *Bethany, if I don't contact you for thirty years, you must come and find me wherever I'm at and help me, because I will not have been able to help myself by then.* Then I saw the contraption attempting to scramble his memories, but he stopped creating them, and the pole appeared to have little other effect upon him, though he slipped into unconsciousness. I wondered how a spiritual being could knowingly stop creating his memories. However, at this point, my contact with him evaporated. I was left sitting petrified upon my bed, sweating profusely, my body rigid as a board.

Worse still, I felt the probing senses of one of the grey creatures attempting to come after me. It had obviously discovered that I was watching through Alabaster. Its intention was quite clear: it wanted to get me sucked into their machine along with the other two. I felt its tug upon my mind and being. No way was I going to get sucked in there after them! I focused my mind, relaxed my body, and concentrated on the floor beside my bed, dimly illuminated by an oil lamp that was nearly spent. I forced myself to relax and not resist. Just when I was about to panic, I felt the creature's attachment to me suddenly fade away. I grinned. If you don't offer resistance, then it has nothing on which to latch and grab you. I filed that away for future reference. Then, I panicked!

I slipped on some outer clothes, grabbed a coat, and dashed out of my house. I ran towards Josh and Milla's house, a block away. It was 2 am, cold and dark outside. As I ran, I began to slow down. Just as I reached their door, I began to think once more. What was I going to say to them? That I had just watched giant grey creatures smash Jes' head in, saw him sucked into the pole thing, and watched as all of his memories got scrambled? They would think I had gone mad or crazy. They wouldn't understand or comprehend any of it. Slowly, I withdrew my hand. I did the only thing that I could think of at the moment: I went for a walk around my town.

For security at night, we always posed three guards to watch the outermost gates. I ambled down to where one was at and chatted. He was most surprised to see me at this hour, though, and asked me if everything was okay. I muttered something like, "Can't sleep." This he could grasp and smiled knowingly back at me. Just now, I didn't really want to be alone, so I asked him if he would accompany me around the grounds. Together for an hour, we walked and walked. Jeremiah, was his name. He kindly didn't speak nor did I.

After that time, I felt more relaxed, thanked him, and went back to my darkened home, dead tired, and ready for sleep.

About seven the next morning, Josh and Milla knocked loudly on my door, waking me. This was highly unusual, I thought as I opened the door, feeling the cold blast of air hit me in the face, along with the blinding light of a new day. Both had the most morose looks on their faces that I have ever seen. "Come in," I managed to say.

Once inside, Josh, in a shaking voice, said, "He's dead, isn't he?"

Startled, I muttered rather clumsily, "Who?"

"Jes! Last night I had a terrible feeling that something horrible happened to my brother. Milla felt it too. He's dead isn't he? Surely you felt it too."

So they too had somehow sensed the calamity! "Yes, I am certain of it. I came over to your house around two in the morning, but thought better of waking you. I have no proof that he is dead. I decided against scaring you."

Somehow having me validate what they had sensed made all the difference to the two. Both now relaxed, confident that they were not just imagining it. Milla spoke quietly, "We will have to tell the kids, won't we?"

"It is only fair, but I'm not sure what we can really tell them — we don't know the details," Josh answered.

"I agree, Josh. We need to break the news to them. Know this, both of you: he died trying to save us all. In the end, one man was just not enough to defeat them, whoever 'them' is. He sent me a little information: that he was trying to put a stop to some great evil on our behalf. He failed, though. He was somewhere in the Land of the Sea Princes when he was killed." I left it at that, hoping that they wouldn't try to get me to explain more fully.

Whether or not they would have, I never found out, for as I finished, their suppressed grief finally surfaced. Both began crying. I did too. My grief now surfaced, swallowing me whole. There in my living room, we three cried and consoled each other for some time, until the children came down to see what was going on and for their breakfast. While Milla and I wandered into the kitchen, Josh did the explaining to his brother's children. I think that they also sensed that their father had died and wouldn't be returning in the spring. However, children are so resilient. Yes, they were sad, but only for a short while. Soon they wanted to go out and play before their lessons with Brother Jackal. After they ran outside, we three hugged each other, and they left to go tell their children the news of their uncle's death. I was very grateful Josh told my children the horrible news. I know I would have broken down had I had to do that.

I went back into my bedroom and sat down, mechanically brushing out my long hair. Now for the first time that I can remember, I felt completely, totally, utterly alone! Alabaster was gone. Jes was gone. The two men on which I had always depended — both were gone! I had no one in whom I could confide my thoughts, no one with which to discuss the horrid situation or even make plans. I think in my years here on Tarra, this was my darkest hour to date. I mechanically did my duties for the day, rather like an unfeeling robot.

Only after the children were sent to bed that night and I was once more alone in my bedroom did I regain some sense of humanity. Perhaps it was the simple action of brushing my hair, I don't know. I remembered that there was still one person with whom I could discuss these things, one person who might be able to help me, if only to talk with me and not think I was crazy. Sandy!

I didn't know if she still had the same body anymore, if she were still a druwid, if she still remembered me. Once, thirty years ago, she and I were very, very close friends. She first showed me how to use telepathy to communicate. Did she still have that skill? I had a thousand reasons for not trying to contact her. Still, in the end, I decided that there was absolutely no one else I could turn to for help. I checked on the oil lamp, crawled upon my bed, sat comfortably cross-legged, and relaxed my mind. I knew that this action I was embarking upon would take all of my telepathic skills. I hoped that they would be sufficient. I was long out of practice with them, except with Jes.

Slowly I expanded my mind. I expanded my awareness outward, touching upon my children in a nearby room. Soon I was aware of the outside of my house and our town. I reached out further toward the Greenway. Spatial distances are nothing to a spiritual being, but sensing a specific being takes a lot of concentration as well as a familiarization with that person. I got a vague sensation of the presence of thousands of beings in the Greenway. I was looking for one particular being, Sandy, dearest Sandy.

After an hour, I finally sensed her presence; she appeared to me much as she had some thirty years ago, a vibrant being surrounded with a yellowish glow. Step one, accomplished; I had located her. Now came the hard part, actually to place a thought in her mind without startling her. *Sandy? This is Bethany. Remember me? Can we talk?* I tried to keep it as simple as possible, remembering how awkward she and I had been at this when she was still learning how to do it. After all, she might have gotten a new body and not even be a druwid now. Thirty years is a long time. Still, I startled her terribly. I know, she shrieked aloud!

She was lying in bed snuggled up with Simon when I contacted her. Naturally, Simon was just as startled as well. *Bethany! Is this really you? No, now is fine. I'm just lying here with Simon. How are you? Gosh, I thought we'd never hear from you! Alabaster told us you were on a secret mission and never to disturb you. Can Simon join us?*

I felt Simon's presence as he joined with Sandy; those two still are inseparable. *Yes, it's really me. I've missed you all so terribly! I'm alive and well physically. But right now, I really, really, really need you guys. Secret mission has ended in a total, complete disaster. Even Alabaster is gone now too!* My grief once again overwhelmed me, and they sensed it as well. I felt Sandy's soothing song in my mind, much as Willow had done for me so many years ago, calming me after I had gone berserk with the massive lightning bolt attack on the cavalrymen who tried to kill my family and Ellen. Soon, I felt serenity flowing over me and could talk further.

Guys, I have to tell you all about this, beginning with when I got my body killed trying to reach King Randolf, that's when Alabaster gave me this mission. If I don't, none of what is going on now is going to make any sense to you. I spent an hour relating my adventures with the Great Messiah and how it related to what Alabaster had wanted me to find out for him. I placed much emphasis on these grey creatures and their meddling in the spiritual freedom of the peoples of the northern lands, ending with what I had witnessed last night. I made sure that all the observations I had made were duplicated by these two, just in case something happened to me. That way, the valuable, hard-earned information would not die with me.

After that hour, I felt an incredible relief. I'd told others all about it, and I had a sort of release from purgatory, one might say. Okay, Sandy's constant humming also helped keep me feeling serene as well. When I finished, Simon jumped in, *We all thank you, Bethany, for all you have done. We'll see that this information is broadly known among the Guardians. You're right in not wanting it to get lost. One day, we may be able to find a way to defeat these Evil Creatures. Just so you know, after you got killed, er, I guess you didn't get killed, rather, your body did, gosh words are so hard with this, I mean, Alabaster came to us and explained everything to us, easing us over our grief too. However, he said that he sent you on a secret mission into the Arad and that we weren't to try to contact you, even in an emergency. He was most insistent. So many times we wanted to contact you, but in the end, we honored his request.*

Now Sandy jumped in, *Now that the mission is over, there's no reason we can't all chat as much as we want. I'm dying to tell you tons of stuff!*

Oh, please, please do! Any time is fine with me, though early evenings just after the kids are put to bed is best for me. I'm getting really tired. Can we connect tomorrow night, same time?

I won't miss it for anything! Sandy replied. *I have to admit, doing this much has gotten me really tired. Can you believe it, Bethany, I'm an old woman, grey hair and all! I get tired so easily nowadays. Yes, tomorrow is perfect! Shall I contact you or you, me?*

I'll contact you, that's best for me — I'm running two whole towns now over on West Reach, but I'll tell you all about that tomorrow. We said good night and I let the contact break. My oil lantern was once more nearly out, so I pulled down my covers, blew the light out, and crawled into bed. Finally, I could sleep the sleep of babies once more. I still felt serene when morning came.

Here in 588 AH, my body was now twenty-nine years old. In comparison, Sandy was forty-three, one year older than I would have been had my body not been killed by the Galts and King Randolf. During the course of our nightly chats over the next week, I learned that she and Simon had just returned from a two-year visit to the Sea Princes and that they had seen all our old friends, which we had made when the Lightning Circle had visited that land so long ago. They had returned hurriedly because Roy, my husband in that life and their Protector, had recently died in a construction accident. Sandy explained that ever since I had been killed, well my body that is, he could never forgive himself. He'd been moody and morose ever since and never remarried. She pointed out that raising our children had been the only thing that had kept Roy going. "Children often give we parents something to live for," Sandy had told me.

I found it elating to hear how my children had turned out. Two belonged to the Moon Circle, Robert Roy, a Protector, and Ellen Sarah, a Healer. Robert had married Misty Simone, so that made Sandy and me mothers-in-law, though because of their assignment in the Red Desert, they had not yet had any children. However, I would have been a grandmother. My youngest son, Al Helmut, had become a blacksmith, married a Sue Ellen, and now had four children. They lived in Calgary proper, and he had a thriving business.

I also learned that my Lightning Circle had a very hard time replacing me after I had been killed. For the next five years, they were Wid-less because everyone felt that this topmost Wid in the hierarchy had to have great wisdom and knowledge. Finally, they accepted a young man, John Small as their Wid; he was now barely thirty. For at least five years, the Circle had to educate him, instead of the other way around. Yes, replacing me had given them a terrific challenge.

Later in the week, John, via a Sandy Mind Join, was able to speak to me personally. *Do you have any idea how **hard** it has been trying to fill your shoes let alone Alabaster's?* He was both teasing me and telling the truth, funny. He had me repeat entirely what had happened to Alabaster and Jes. I gave him my full report on the Great Messiah and his teachings. After all, I felt it was my duty to get this data back to the Guardians.

I finished by saying, *While I'm still no closer to knowing how he does it, I can definitely say that Jes is, or rather was, on our side. It's just that everyone misunderstood how he intended to help his people escape the domination of the Centurions. He really could perform great miracles, and he really could get a spiritual being to move out of their body, even when they were normally stuck in one. He could move headers out! Unfortunately, I never learned how he did this.*

He asked probably the most important personal question, both for himself and for me, *Are you planning now to return here to the Greenway?* I could sense that he suspected that his position as Wid might be in doubt.

Honestly, I can't. I have given my word to Jes to raise our children. Also, I have made a solemn pledge to help all these people get started on a new life here in West Reach. I need to see it through. However, I would like to perhaps come for a visit and see everyone, especially my grown children sometime.

Even though we were communicating telepathically, I could just hear his sigh of relief. I wasn't planning to return and resume my position as Wid of the Lightning Circle. Men, always worrying about their positions!

I did work out a trade agreement between my two new towns and the Greenway. In addition, I learned a bit of what had been going on in my homeland these past years. The Centurion roadway was fully built, and each major town now boasted hot and cold running water bathhouses! Once the construction had been finished, about five hundred were stationed along the border with the Northern Steppes. Only a handful remained elsewhere in the Greenway. When word of the Galt invasion of the Sea Princes arrived, all but fifty Centurions returned to Calgary and then left for Velona. Now, all fifty were in Calgary guarding the Governor, who did little governing. Thus, our solution to the Centurion problem had been a very good one for all concerned.

I did get Wid John to begin an active discussion among the Guardians on what to do about these Grey Creatures in the Appian Way. He promised to keep me fully informed and to ask for my opinions and input. I believe he now considered me the only remaining authority on these creatures.

I learned that our Lightning Circle fortress on Mont Blanc was now a wonder to behold. Raphael, our Planner, had built dozens of magnificent stone buildings, which were the envy of all who visited them. I was glad to hear that this was now the most defensible position in all the Greenway.

At the end of the week, I got a complete surprise. Sandy joined the whole Lightning Circle into one giant Mind Join, and everyone chatted with me. I felt very sad that Roy had passed away; I really had wanted to talk with him. Their gaiety and enthusiasm soon had me forgetting all about Roy's absence. I can't find the words to describe how wonderful I felt chatting with these dear friends after so many years had passed.

Finally, we discussed the impending Galt invasion of the Greenway. Most were of the opinion that Sandy and Simon had been successful in getting Mikhailovich Strokova to delay any assault on the Greenway until after he had conquered Megalos proper. Also, they were still evaluating the consideration that the Galts believed that there were Evil Witches in the Greenway, that is what they called us Guardians. If so, somehow that fear was going to be used against them. I was encouraged to form up an army to send to the Greenway should the Galts finally invade. I promised I would do what I could, though in truth, I didn't see how I could create an army from my two towns.

Rather what interested me most was the impact that these Grey Creatures were having on our peoples. More and more that winter, I found myself thinking about them and their mind scrambling activities. Yet, it was a fruitless pondering. After all, if Jes and Alabaster, the two strongest, most powerful beings that I had known had failed completely, what could the rest of us possibly do? Somehow, I knew deep inside my mind that this was by far the most important problem on Tarra to solve! It could be that these creatures were wholly responsible for the condition we called headers: namely, a spiritual being stuck inside his or her head, unable to get out, and believing wholly that they are the body and not a spiritual being.

During the winter of 588 AH, Josh and I shared preaching duties. Due to the ever-growing size of our two towns, four wooden churches had been built. Because of the local traditions here on Cymry, the accepted Holy Day was Sunday. Thus, we had changed our day of community worship and prayer from Saturday so we would blend in better here in our new homeland. However, neither one of us alone could minister to four churches in the same day. Hence, we split them. Josh took the two churches in our sister town, while I took the two here at home. He insisted that I shouldn't be traveling so much with my daughter, Sarah Elizabeth, being only one year old.

Further, since many of the more traditionalist Arads refused to have a female pastor, those went with Josh. Yet, every Saturday night, Josh and I conferred upon what we would discuss during our services the next day. I did try to stay with their traditional Arad preachings as told by Jes, but often I found myself adding my own slant or truths to my sermons. I didn't like standing on the high altar preaching to others, but I felt I owed it to Jes. In my own small way, I was attempting to try to undo what the Grey Creatures had done, to convince everyone that they are a body not an immortal spiritual being. Thus, in less than a half of a year, Josh and I became the spiritual leaders of our towns.

However, disaster struck again in late December. Josh took the three boys and Ros a few miles downstream to Cairn Pond to go ice fishing. When they hadn't returned by late afternoon, both Milla and I became worried. At last, leaving our babies behind, we, accompanied by Jackal, rode off in search of them. When we arrived, we knew instantly something was very wrong. I will say this: our children had done a commendable job. The ice wasn't as solid as Josh had thought. It had given way under his feet, and he'd fallen into the freezing waters. Rather than panicking, our children began to invent ways of rescuing him. The children knew that time was critical, so they tried to rescue him instead of wasting time going for help that would arrive too late.

They'd tried reaching him with long branches, but he'd lost so much feeling in his hands that he couldn't hold on to the branches. Next, they had tried to make a prone human chain on the ice so that Hadid, the strongest, could reach him with his outstretched hand. Amazing, they had the sense to lie prone on the ice to distribute their weight. When that failed, they next tried to lasso him with a rope to pull him out, but Josh had slipped under the icy waters by this time. Just as we rode up, they were debating whether Hadid should tie the rope to himself and dive into the waters to try to pull his father out.

Milla was horror stricken. Jackal, unused to such cold weather, had no ideas. I, on the other hand, knew from my lifetime in the Greenway, that Josh had already passed away. There was really nothing we could do for him now, except to try to fish his body out of the pond. After carefully validating the children on having done everything that I would have done to save him, I then decided to try to contact Josh. I found him floating above the ice, grief stricken. Can you imagine how awful he felt having spent an hour watching as his children tried valiantly to rescue him even after his body had died from the cold waters?

I had a deep suspicion that their failure to rescue him might make an indelible mark on their psyche; this I had to avert at all costs. I relaxed and joined my mind with Josh's. Next, I spoke softly to the now crying children. First, I helped each of them locate Josh, who was still floating just above the hole in the ice. Next, one by one, I brought them into the Mind Join. At last, I added Milla as well.

Josh had an opportunity not only to say goodbye to his children and wife but also they got to share their final thoughts with him. Josh heaped tons of praise upon the children for maintaining their presence of mind to rescue him. It didn't matter that it had failed; rather they had done everything humanly possible. For my part, I stayed quietly in the background, maintaining the spiritual connection between all of them.

When they had finished about a half hour later, I helped Josh move off toward town to go in search of a new baby body. At first, I was terribly worried that he too would be commanded to go back to the Appian Way and get his mind scrambled. Indeed, just as I saw that forceful command starting to appear in his mind, I zapped it with an even more powerful suggestion to just go back to town and pick up a new baby body. This he did. For the first time, I realized that this commandment to return to the Appian Way, which had somehow been instilled in these people, could easily be overridden if one got to the person in time!

Then we all went home. The next day several men from town were able to extract his body from the pond, and we held a simple burial service. These were the basic details. However, I learned something of tremendous importance from this. By interceding and allowing the family members to be in a final communication with one another, the horror, shock, feelings of guilt, shame, and blame were totally gone. The children realized it was just an accident, that Josh hadn't been sufficiently observant of the ice thickness, and that it was his own carelessness that had caused the accident. The children knew that Josh knew that they had done everything possible to save him, including everything that Aunt Bethany would have done. The closure was complete and no one had any regrets or feelings of blame or shame. Everyone could go on with their lives without having mental repercussions so often found in others.

Yes, Milla was in grief for days, but she too had benefitted enormously from having this final sharing of words with her husband. I kept a very close eye on all of them for the next few months, but all recovered far above what one might have expected from such a traumatic experience. Hence, I made a vow to implement this fully in our two towns.

At the next Sunday Service as I went between all four churches, I announced that from now on, when anyone died, they were to summon me immediately. I would perform the Last Holy Communion for the deceased. Of course, I had to explain this new ritual. "We are all immortal spiritual beings.

Only the body has died, not us, the personality. When a loved one had lost their body, I will attempt to join that spiritual being with the remaining loved ones for a final sharing."

Okay, I admit that I was improvising. There was no such ceremony in the Jehosanity religion for this or any precedent for it. Yet, in the years to come, every time I performed this ritual, the results were uniformly the same: fantastic. The sharing of last thoughts between the deceased and their loved ones made a huge impression on all sides, allowing a full closure between all concerned. Further, in nearly all these cases, I was able also to circumvent the implanted orders of the Grey Creatures to return to the Appian Way. So in a small way, I was beginning to have an impact on undoing what these Evil Creatures had done to these people!

By spring of 589 AH, I was incredibly busy! I found myself being the sole spiritual leader of two ever-growing towns, as well as being their primary planner, their unchallenged leader, and their healer, to say nothing of trying to raise my own three children and help Milla with her three. Coping was the only thing I could do, while I desperately attempted to establish some organization.

First, I appointed an official town mayor, whose first duty was to arrange general elections for a town council of seven members. After a period of four years, each town would be free to elect their own mayors. The mayor and town council are charged with running the daily affairs of the town, bringing only more important matters to my attention or those that they couldn't resolve amicably.

Next, I appointed Jackal and Missa the task of forming an official town protection force, which would respond first to outside attack, most likely from the Axemen. I wanted cavalry to patrol our outlying crop fields providing a measure of security as well as advanced warning of attacks. I also wanted sufficient archers to defend the fortress walls should an attack come. Finally, I wanted some footmen to act as guards, particularly at night. I left the organizational matters of said forces up to those two to work out as they thought best.

Two men had shown great promise in designing and building our towns and fortresses. Naturally, I chose these two to be Town Planners. I gave them the dual assignments of working out what each town needed to build next as they expanded and to draw up plans for a third town that hopefully would be located at most five miles from one of the two existing towns. I fully expected that we would need to expand rapidly and knew that I could not handle this many details personally. I had to get others working on not only our current needs but also those in the not too distant future.

Unfortunately, the healing arts here in Cymry were primitive at best. Thus, I alone performed all the actual healing. As our numbers grew, I knew I'd eventually become overloaded with healing requests. My idea was to create a network of nurses, people trained to aid the sick and injured, as well as helping with births. Initially, I converted one small out building to serve as the infirmary for both towns. Here my volunteer nurses stockpiled supplies we might need, bandages, herbs, water, and even firewood. Cleverly, they installed a dozen beds so that we might handle twelve at once. This turned out to be a very wise action; I had forgotten that when attacks came, we would need many beds for the injured. That I forgot this point is an indication of the extreme cope that I was undergoing.

We had built our first town out in the northwestern section of the wilderness of Layamon so we owed no allegiance to any Duke or Earl. New Jerilum, or Nuadilan, as the locals call it in their language, now held twenty-five hundred people. Sitting atop a magnificent green hill, we can see the surrounding forests and grasslands for miles in all directions. It is located about fifty miles north by west of Bregia on the coast. Most new Arad immigrants arrived in Bregia. Nearby New Jerilum flows the river Daneas, ambling on down to the ocean not too far from Bregia.

Our second town, Bedwyn, lies five miles nearly northwest of New Jerilum. On a clear day, it can easily be seen from New Jerilum, and vice versa. Bedwyn already is home to another two thousand folks, with at least a dozen or so new arrivals each week. Each of these families had to be housed and grooved in on what was wanted of them here in their newly adopted town. Thank goodness for the town councils! My guess was that by fall we would need to either greatly expand either of the two existing towns or begin construction of a third.

Sundays I wore the hat of religious teacher for both towns. I conducted three morning services in Nuadilan before eating a quick lunch and riding over to Bedwyn to deliver three afternoon services there. However, many of the Arad immigrants were devout worshipers of Jehosa in the traditional ways brought with them from Juda Arad. Tradition held no female prophets or priests. I knew that if I just unilaterally took over, trouble would instantly arise. After thinking the situation over very carefully that first week, I met midweek with a dozen men that Josh and Jes had helping them run their services.

"Gentlemen, both Jes and Josh have ordered me to continue their teachings. Yet, I do not want to be a Priest or Priestess in any way. I'm not qualified to hold that position and never will be." You can't imagine the relief that swept like tidal waves over their faces when they heard my opening remarks! I knew instantly that I had made the wisest decision. "Gentlemen, Jes and Josh would want you to set up a primary priest to run each of the four churches we now have between the two towns. Be aware that we will likely be adding more by fall and will need additional priests. My role will be that of Religious Teacher. I will give two services at my church on Sunday morning and one later that morning at Josh's church. Then, after lunch, I will ride over to Bedwyn and deliver three there. Since our small churches can hold only about three hundred at a time, obviously not everyone can be serviced with just six services — at best, less than half of our people could hear me on

Sunday. Besides, many wouldn't even care to hear me, but they should hear your preachings. Thus, your priests will conduct as many additional services on Sunday as you see fit so all who want to pray can have the opportunity to do so. The only restriction is to permit me to hold my service as I get them scheduled. Obviously, I will be on a tight schedule on Sunday. How does that sound to you?" Yes, this was one of my finer moments; I had come up with a very workable system of religious worship that would satisfy everyone. They leapt at the opportunity I gave them. However, I had not the foresight to see what the situation would become in ten years, but that is getting ahead of events.

What did I teach? Every Sunday, I drilled into those who came to hear me, the truth of our existence. Each of us is a spiritual being, immortal, not made of flesh and blood, and not composed of anything found on Tarra. Each inhabits a fleshly body, whose life cycle is birth, growth, decay, and then death. Upon body death, we then find a new baby body and start the cycle over once more. I taught them about the Seven Aspects of Life, yes, a druwid principle. I taught them how to choose a right action over a wrong one, by asking whether or not an action helped more of the Aspects of Life or not.

Further, I began implementing my Last Holy Communion for the deceased. Little did I know just how important this seemingly last act of kindness would turn out to be. Within six months, I discovered this action left the surviving family members with a solid reality on the fact that they were indeed immortal spiritual beings! Suddenly my Sunday teaching began to take on vastly more important meaning to these people. By fall, my services were standing room only, and I had to ponder how I might squeeze in a fourth service for each town. I was extremely gratified to discover that I had come across a way to begin to undo the mind scrambling of the Grey Creatures.

Although the extreme coping finally subsided somewhat by fall, I was still more than fully occupied and loving every minute of it all.

Chapter 33 The Choices of Zdlenka Strokova

It was November 25, 589, nearly two weeks after her brother had been beheaded on the battlefield. Her long beautiful black hair was a matted mass of tangles. Her light moccasins now had more holes in them than soles. Her face and hands remained dirty and stained from the late season berries she could find to eat. Her light leather garments provided the only protection from the cold winter nights. By day, she wandered aimlessly around the Southlands, always staying close to the shores of the ocean just above the island of Megalos, never traveling too far from the small streams that flowed down into the ocean, her source of drinking water. She was in the lower foothills of Kathas, the impenetrable, tall mountain range that ran straight south, to the ocean itself. By day, she wandered and explored, always searching for something to kill her intense hunger pains. Armed only with her dagger and a walking stick, she fared very poorly.

Days ago, she had estimated that some six hundred miles of the Southlands lay between her and Juda Arad. Even if she could hike close to the mountains to avoid all Centurion towns, once at the border of the Arad, she still would have another three hundred miles to travel before the Northern Steppes began and home. She had no horse, no food, no water, and no money — nothing but her dagger and the clothes that she wore. Now her shoes failed her as well. Further, she could not speak one word of the Centurion language, if she did manage to meet anyone.

However, every night when the daylight failed, that horrid image frozen in her mind reappeared. Repeatedly, she watched her beloved brother's head fall off his body and roll across the ground, coming to a halt with its eyes staring up at her. After a long pause, the sequence of images would begin once more, un-abating. She tried covering her eyes with her hands, literally forcing them into pain, but to no avail; the images continued to dominate her mind, her being. In desperation, she tried slicing her arm, hoping the wound would suppress these horrid images. She could barely feel the pain of the cut. She couldn't even sob herself to sleep.

Besides, while there was yet no snow at this elevation, the nights grew colder and colder. Hence, she continued to return before dark to her bungalow, as she now called it. She had found a hollow in the ground and had covered it with branches, twigs, and such. Once inside the tiny hollow, she at least didn't freeze to death. Even her matted, tangled hair served to help keep her body warm at night. She wrapped herself in it as if it were a blanket. To say that Zdlenka was miserable would be an understatement.

It had taken nearly two weeks of this near starvation situation for the horrible shock of her brother's untimely, unexpected death finally to release its tenacious grip over her entire being. During this time, her shoes had given out. If snow should come, she knew her feet would suffer badly. Yes, higher up in the mountains, the snows had already fallen; she could see the white peaks in the daytime. She figured it wouldn't be long before it reached this lower elevation. Then her meager berries would be gone, and she would starve to death, if she did not freeze first.

This night, she realized that the shock had finally subsided, though not those awful images in her mind. She could feel the aches and pains in her body once more, to say nothing of the nearly continuous growl in her mostly empty stomach. "What do I do?" she wailed to the moon from under her shelter, as its beams filtered through tiny cracks in the covering over her. "I should just die." Suicide — suddenly she realized what she was saying. "Yes, I wish I could just die." She wiggled about to get her dagger out from its sheath. She could just barely see the reflection of the faint moonlight off the cold steel blade a few inches in front of her face. She slowly moved its sharp point over her chest and heart, touching the cold steel to her bosom. Even through her leather shirt, she could feel its uncaring coldness. "One good plunge and I will be at peace," she rationalized, but her hand did not move.

How long she laid there with the dagger ready to plunge into her breast she could not say, but now she could clearly see the dagger. The sun's redden rays poked just above the distant horizon out over the ocean. "I can't even kill myself," she wailed in complete hopelessness and broke down into heavy crying. "I am such a total coward! I do not even have the guts to kill myself and put myself out of my misery!" She cried and cried, until nature kicked in. She just had to urinate and her stomach hurt terribly. Slowly, she put the dagger away and ventured out of her crude shelter to face the day.

As usual, she wandered first to the small stream and drank as much water as she could, hoping to squelch the hunger pangs; it never worked, though. She also felt very weak. More importantly, she felt completely and totally alone, something she had never felt before in her life. True, she had been orphaned at a very early age and had no real memories of her parents. Yet, she had always had Mik there. They had been inseparable; she had never been truly alone until now.

Once she had finished drinking, she sat back and absorbed the warming rays of the rising sun. Tears of grief trickled down her face, leaving streaks among the dirt on her face. Finally, she just had to find something to eat and began her daily wandering in search of anything edible. As she moved more or less aimlessly about the rocky land, she felt utter despair flood over her entire being, a despair so whole, so complete that nothing could ever move her out of it. All was more than totally lost! Suddenly she thought she heard the sound of horses! Her despair instantly gave way to a fear almost bordering on terror! What if the Centurions were closing in on her? Would they rape her? Behead her like her brother? Perhaps they would make her into a brothel slave. Wild imaginings flooded her mind.

As the sounds faded away, her fear gave way to violent anger. She cursed the Centurions loudly, vocalizing every known curse in her language, wishing unspeakable deaths to all, and especially to that vile general who had killed her brother! Her anger eventually subsided or gave way to pain and then hostility toward the Centurions. She found a new berry patch and began to eat ravenously. Her hunger slightly satiated for the moment and her face and hands re-stained, she felt antagonistic. "How dare that general kill my brother!" she called out to the heavens above, raising a clenched fist toward the sky.

She began wandering again, still muttering about the uncivilized barbarians of the south. Soon, she found that she was completely bored with everything and sat down at least to enjoy the warmth of the noonday sun. While she was basking in the sunlight, she began to think more clearly than she had for the last couple of weeks. "I've got to get shoes, food, a horse, clothes, and a comb, for god's sake! I need supplies and I need them now! And I don't have a coin with which to buy any. Don't see a store around here, though," she began to laugh, imagining herself walking into any one of the hundreds of towns and villages she had helped conquer, walking into a store, and taking all she desired. For a moment, she stood and whirled around, holding an imaginary dress up to her bosom as if to check its size and how it would look on her.

A sea gull flew overhead, circled around her, watching her wild antics for a moment. Then, it flew on out over the ocean. Her eyes caught sight of its outward flight, and for an unknown reason, she began looking back the way the bird had come, back toward that horrible battlefield. Suddenly she knew where she could find the store she so desperately needed. Half running, half walking, she retraced her route here as best she could remember. Her flight was one big, foggy memory, short on any real details; she had been in a complete state of shock when she had fled the battlefield weeks ago.

Time passed, day into night into day, still she forced herself to walk, to recover from a painful stumble and move westward. She forced her mind to concentrate on finding that hellish battlefield by day. By night, she whimpered like a baby as the fixed images continued to roll by in her mind endlessly. Then, she found a discarded, worthless boot and knew she was drawing near. Now fear dictated caution. She laid down and crept forward, eyes searching everywhere for the enemy, the Centurions. Finding none, she crawled forward once more, to the great relief of her feet. She stopped as she noticed their throbbing. Looking at her feet, she gasped, they were bloody and bruised beyond belief! She had no other recourse except to crawl into this general store.

In a few minutes, she realized from the telltale signs all over the ground that she had entered that battlefield. No one was in sight. Somewhat ahead of her, she made out the paved roadway of the Centurions. Now she began her searching in earnest. The ground for a mile around her was littered with the remains of the great battle. A shoe here, a broken blade from some sword there, the shaft of an arrow stuck in the mud over there. Like a child who finds himself in a candy store for the first time, she began collecting everything she could find, amassing her new possessions into an ever-growing pile.

Suddenly, she came across a discarded food pouch, the kind her cavalry would carry with them on horseback. She tore it open as her stomach suddenly sprang to life, screaming for food. She found dried meats and stale, slightly moldy bread, which she ate as fast as she could gulp them down! By the time that she had the presence of mind to think to ration herself on her newfound food supply, the pouch was empty. Still, she could feel the impact of the first real food in two weeks as it hit her system. It felt very good.

Embolden by her successes, she began her diligent crawling search once more. Then, she came upon the area near the wooden fortress walls, which now stood like silent sentinels out here in this nearly flat land. "Where did all of those treacherous pits go?" she wondered aloud, remembering all the diabolic trouble those pits had caused her cavalry. Where they had been were now small mounds of earth, she observed. "Where did all the bodies go?" she spoke aloud. Then, she answered herself, "I bet they threw them into the pits and covered them up!"

She crawled over to one and began digging with her hands, pulling the loose dirt out of the top of what had been a pit. Soon she felt a body. Normally, she would never consider digging a person out of a grave, let along with her bare hands! Now she felt that she was in a giant general store, going shopping. She hastened her digging, revealing the remains of a Galt cavalryman. More importantly, the man had clothes and boots! Even more critically, she discovered the remnants of a blanket. She hastily stripped the man and wrapped her precious finds in the blanket.

Slowly, she crawled to the next pit and repeated her actions. Only when it became too dark to see did she finally stop. She had uncovered a half dozen food bags and untold clothing and boots! However, the night brought unrelenting cold down on her. Cleverly, she wrestled, tugged, and finally got the last buried man out of his pit. She grabbed all her blankets and food and crawled into the empty pit, piling her newfound wealth over her. Tonight, she would stay warm indeed! She ignored the stench. Just as soon as darkness came, those horrid images in her mind could no longer be blotted out by the light of day. Whimpering, she tried to sleep as she had for weeks now.

The next day, she ate well once more, but discovered that her feet were swollen nearly twice their normal size. Undaunted, she continued her search and discovery mission. For six more days, she scoured the battlefield for anything that would aid her survival. Lady Luck was on her side. She came upon the remains of a wagon of theirs. After a day of trial and error, she managed to make a makeshift, two-wheeled pushcart out of the broken bits. Now she could load her precious wealth onto the cart and take them with her. She spent another day sorting out just what to take. Yes, the dozen food pouches would have to go, along with the dozen blankets. She added several sets of leather outer garments, all way too large for her. "I can bundle up against the cold," she rationalized. Also, she took several different sizes of shoes. Now that the swelling in her feet began to subside, she found that she could wear a pair of the largest size. She calculated that as her feet recovered, she would need smaller and smaller shoes, hence the assortment.

She also added two dozen intact arrows and one bow that were still useable. Now she could hunt for fresh meat. She had two tinderboxes, containing rock, steel and dried grasses with which to start a fire, though she dared not light one this close to the Centurions, wherever they may be. The only item that she really wanted but could not find was a comb or brush for her hair, but she shrugged that off as a vanity item for now.

During these days, she had had two scares. Twice now, riders had come galloping along the paved roadway. Each time, she had heard them long before she could see them. Thus, she quickly crawled into a pit, hiding by piling stuff over her. Thus far, no one noticed her on the abandoned battlefield.

On December 1, she set out to the northeast, pulling and pushing her cart, which was loaded with her newfound treasures. Only a few days later, she was back beside the ocean and just in time to see the first snowflakes begin to fall on these foothills. Winter snows come late to these northern Southland foothills of Kathas.

Now in the relative comfort and safety inside her covered hollow in the ground, she began to weigh what she should do next. The first day, she carefully repaired the three water bags. All had holes or tears in them. After sewing them up as best she could, she used a bit of her precious tinderbox to light a candle, allowing the melted wax to make a water-tight seal. Once it had cooled, she filled them with water from the small brook. She tested them and found that if she were careful, the patches would hold water. Now she could move away from here; she had both a little food and some water.

In the late afternoon sun, which shone brightly on the half inch of snow, she suddenly saw her reflection in the calm brook's waters. "Oh my god! Is this really me?" she cried aloud in shock and disbelief. She saw an utterly filthy woman, dressed in layers of tattered, oversized men's leather clothing, wearing boots too big for her that were also the worst for wear. What had been her pride and joy, her beautiful long black hair that flowed to her waist was now a giant tangled mass of hair; bits of leaves and twigs were enmeshed in the lengthy mat of hair. Her face was stained and filthy, as were her hands. The person she saw in the water's reflection was about as far from her idea of herself as anyone could possibly imagine! She cried tears of sorrow and self-pity, crawling back into her makeshift shelter in the hollow in the ground, hiding from the world around her. Gone was her elation over her survival treasures; stark reality stared her squarely in her face, and all she could do was whimper and cry a little.

This new memory of just what she now looked like appeared nearly life-sized in her mind; for a time, she could see nothing but this horrible image of herself. All of a sudden, another memory, another picture flashed by her consciousness. She remembered those two Arad men in Florentine Junction, who had stared wild-eyed at her and her brother when they rode victorious through that town years ago. She now recognized their gleeful laugher at that time for what it was, insanity. "Did they undergo what I have?" she wondered aloud.

Sometimes, the dark curtain of lies is pierced by a tiny inkling of the truth. It is up to the person to pull on that thread. For over a year, she had been haunted by the mental image she had of those two men on that day. Now she remembered once more that one of those two had turned into the Snake Demon, as vile and filthy looking as she now was, and he had terrorized the Northern Steppes for over a year, stealing the newborn babies and eating their brains. That horrible episode came fully back into her mind.

She pulled on the thread of truth a little harder. *Both men were from Juda Arad. I'm certain of that — their clothing and skin color give them away. What had happened there? I don't remember ever seeing them in the Arad when we conquered all those towns. Did they lose their wives, children perhaps? Oh yes, I remember now, we were positive that there were Evil Witches somewhere in the Arad. Our men were under orders to kill any suspected women who might be an Evil Witch before they could cast their diabolical spells upon them. Could our warriors have maybe killed their wives and children? Oh my god!*

Suddenly, the magnitude of what she had done over the last four years flooded through her consciousness, like a tidal wave of disjoined pictures. Every town — every battle — she saw all the men, women, and children that had been killed, lying upon the ground just as she had come across them after the battles were finished. Thousands of them. Image after image flashed by her consciousness, a seemingly endless parade of their victims of their war of conquest.

"Oh my god, what have we done?" she screamed, at last finding her voice after the gusher of images finally subsided. Startled by the loud noise of her shrill scream breaking the eternal tranquility of this desolate shore of the ocean, several gulls took flight in a mad rush to get away from impending danger. Reality had struck home to her. Now, another seemingly endless stream of images swept through her mind, but these were all her own imaginings, done of her own volition. She pictured the surviving family members of all their thousands upon thousands of victims: a mother with no husband, children with no father or perhaps no mother to care for them. Yes, Zdlenka finally grasped the brutal, savage, raw truth of what she and her brother had actually done for the last four years. It was not a pretty sight.

She felt sick at her stomach and quickly vomited green bile over her clothing, cramped as she was inside the tiny hollow. Fumbling around, she found a water bag and took a small sip. Though she was not physically cold, she began shivering and rocked back and forth while holding her head in her hands. Her mind was now a complete blank for several minutes.

Then, she realized that her mind was blank, completely blank. Gone were those horrible images of her brother being beheaded on the battlefield! She closed her eyes, testing that they really were gone — that when it was dark again, they wouldn't reappear as they had done every night since he had been killed. Nothing appeared. Hesitantly, she tried to see if she could remember her brother being killed. Yes, she could see those horrible memories, those images in her mind. That is, they were still there in her mind, but when she no longer desired to look at them, they were gone.

She took a deep breath and uttered, "Thank you, Centurion general, for finally putting a stop to our barbarism, our wanton destruction of human lives. We had to be stopped. There, I've said it aloud." Speaking to the world at large, she added, "I was just as wrong as that Snake Demon fellow. I just didn't consider all the others to be people like myself. But we are all people — all of us on Tarra. War can't exist unless you consider the other side to be less than human. What must the world think of us now? History will record us as the worst barbarians of all time, and rightly so. We have been. We've brought the uttermost disgrace upon the heads of all our people."

Then she found an additional thread. "For years, anytime that our people ventured out of the steppes for whatever reason, we were attacked and driven back into the steppes. I feel somehow like the Centurions and those in the Greenway were not letting us have or see or visit the rest of the world. That certainly made a good justification for us to fight our way out of the steppes. I guess I'm not totally to blame; it isn't all just my doing."

She thought for a moment and realized another detail, "Then there was that strange, cold, alien voice that sometimes appeared in my mind, urging us to conquer the neighboring lands. I wonder who that was? Well, whoever was doing that, they definitely helped push us to go to war as well. Still, I do see exactly what my part in it has been. I was the ultimate planner of this immense tragedy. A flood of images of all her own actions in the entire affair rapidly passed by in her mind. Each of these, she accepted as they came into view. Then finally, her mind became silent once more.

It was dark outside; she closed her eyes and saw nothing. She began to listen to the waves lapping onto the shore not too far from where she lay in her hollow. It was the first time that Zdlenka actually heard the ocean lapping onto the shore, and she slipped into a calm, restful sleep.

Sunlight filtering through the makeshift matting over her hollow woke her up to a new day. She crawled out, stretched, and ate a little from her meager rations, ignoring the mold. She sighed, "Okay, now what do I do, Zdlenka?" After a moment, she answered herself, "I don't know. I guess I could try to find a Centurion, turn myself in to them, and let them execute me for my crimes against humanity. It would be more than justified." She fell silent for a time.

She countered herself, "What would one more death accomplish? Nothing, really. My death will not bring back to life even one of the thousands we have tortured and slain. They can only say, 'Well, we killed his sister too,' that's about all. If I were a victim, that really wouldn't bring me any real comfort."

Presently, another idea struck her, "Well, I could give back all the treasure we've stolen." Quickly she countered that one too, "Now Zdlenka, how on Tarra could you possibly do that, huh? We kept nearly nothing for ourselves; the clans took the vast majority of all treasure as payment for their services. So in reality, I have nothing much to give back, even if I were back home in the steppes. And there is no way on Tarra that I could make all the clans give back what they stole. Not even Mik could have accomplished that feat. Besides, if I were a victim who had lost my spouse and gold, getting my gold returned to me would be the least of my desires. I suppose that I could go on some kind of crusade in the steppes to convince the clans to return some of the treasure. Still, treasure is so meaningless, compared to a living person." Again, she fell silent.

Perhaps a half hour later, she spoke once more, "Well, I guess at this time I really do not know how I can make amends for my vile deeds. I can at least be alert for any opportunity that comes my way. How does that sound?" She then answered herself, "I like it. Keep alert; perhaps one day there will be something that you can do to atone for your treachery, Zdlenka." She seemed satisfied with her answer.

"Okay, Zdlenka, now what do you do? You can't stay here much longer. It's certain that you can't go east; the ocean is there. If I go south, I enter the heartland of the Centurions. It serves no purpose for me to become captured and forced to spend the rest of my days as their slave, though I probably deserve it. Still, if I let them do that to me, am I not perpetuating inhumanity to man? Darn right, woman! No, I shouldn't let them capture me. So heading south is out."

"West lies the unknown. I remember now that our advance scouts reporting all manner of strange beasts and landscapes. Oh yes, and even people whose skin is actually black. I wonder if they really have black skin? If they did, I certainly wouldn't fit in there; mine is rather yellowish. No matter what I did there, I would always be singled out as being of a different color. Besides, I have had more than enough new lands with new customs and people and animals for one lifetime. I think I shall not go west."

"Silly woman, that only leaves going north, but it is hundreds of miles before I even get to the Arad. Just what and where are you going to go once you get out of the Southlands? Who knows the answer to that one, Zdlenka? But you have got to get there first." She thought for a while in silence.

"One thing is for certain, I cannot return to my homeland! I have helped get so many of our people killed that I wouldn't be remotely welcomed. I'm certain they'll have already reverted to our traditional clan ways. Once more, I would have no standing at all, maybe even be forced to wed someone of their choice. Knowing our clan members, they'll not treat me kindly at all, if I should one day return. Zdlenka, you cannot return to the Northern Steppes that is for certain!"

Now she remembered the Sisterhood in Zargarb. All at once, tears began to flow; she at last fully appreciated those women and their struggle for life. Her thoughts drifted to Rosalita, that incredibly brave and valiant woman who had agreed to bear her brother's children just so that the other women of her Sisterhood would be spared the might of the Galts. She saw Rosalita in an entirely new light; she couldn't help but wonder how that woman felt now, knowing that the Galts had finally been stopped, far to the south. She recalled that Rosalita had told them that she had killed her husband after taking much physical abuse from him. Zdlenka finally understood Rosalita and felt a strong kinship with her. "Maybe I could go there and beg to be allowed to join their Sisterhood, if they would have me." It sounded like a plan anyway, the only one she had.

"Pull yourself together, Zdlenka, you are drifting into idle thought. Hundreds of miles lie ahead of you before you even get to the Arad, let alone to Zargarb. First, you have to get there somehow. You'll never get there if you continue to stand around talking about it!" At last, she began to take action. Within a few minutes, she had her precious cargo stowed on the rickety cart. She paused a minute to look over her special place here, before heading north.

As she walked slowly along, she recalled all that she could remember of the land from when they rode south with their mighty army. They followed the paved roadway for the most part. She knew that most of the small towns and villages lay within a few miles of this road. Thus, she would somehow have to avoid the way they had come. She couldn't risk falling into the hands of the Centurions. Besides, if she could walk into one of the towns, she couldn't speak a word of their language. How could she tell a shopkeeper what she wanted? Further, how would she pay for said supplies that she so desperately needed? She had absolutely nothing of value, except her body. And that she would never sell!

For only a fleeting instant did she think about trying to sneak in at night and rob a store to get what she needed. "No, Zdlenka, you have stolen the last things you are ever going to steal for the rest of your life! If I've learned one thing, it's to resist the temptation to steal what isn't mine. No, I'm going to have to do this totally on my own somehow or die trying."

At last, she saw her path. "I must head further up into the foothills of Kathas. Probably no one lives up there. I ought to be safe from the Centurions, and besides, I am used to heavy snow. Only food is going to be the major problem. I'll figure something out. If I can stay high in the foothills all the way north, I should make it without being discovered." Determinedly, she changed her course a little east of north.

Soon she spied a rabbit and remembered her newly acquire bow. She stopped and went hunting for the first time in her life. After several misses, she finally caught it. Late that afternoon, she built her first fire in weeks, feasting on roasted rabbit. She saved all she didn't eat; the outside temperature would preserve the leftovers for at least a day or more. She also saved the pelt, though she was not too sure why. By the time the sun was setting, she began to look for something that would serve as a makeshift shelter. Again, she found a concealed spot between two large boulders. Using the cart and her supply of worn-out blankets, she constructed herself a simple shelter for the night.

Days passed and turned into weeks as she trudged slowly north. Her supplies of food ran out, but she was able to keep the three water bags filled. She was forced to spend more and more time each day hunting for what small game she could find, but the finding rapidly became more challenging, because more and more snow fell. The snow base was at least a foot and a half, making walking difficult, let alone trying to pull the cart behind her. Her strength was beginning to fail her.

She stank terribly; her period had come and gone, and she had nothing with which to clean herself up. Besides, the clothes stank of the dead, which they covered before she had taken them from the graves. Yes, she felt about as miserable as she thought imaginable. To make matters worse, her hunger had returned. Daily, she had less and less to eat. Hiking through deep snow burned lots of energy; yet she was eating more and more poorly. Finally, she had to spend one entire day just foraging for food. She managed to shoot a fair number of rabbits and next spent hours trying to find some wood with which to make a fire. Another hour passed as she struggled with nearly frozen fingers to make a fire. In the end, she ate well that late afternoon and felt she could go on her journey the next day with enough meat to last her a couple days.

Weeks turned into months. She was down to her last arrow. All the others had broken. She was out of food; her drinking water had frozen. Further, her worn out clothing was beyond repair, and she was now wearing the last pair of boots that she had salvaged. She was perpetually cold, dangerously close to having her fingers and toes frostbitten. She knew the telltale signs of that danger well. Even worse, she knew that a winter storm was coming shortly; she could tell by the intense dark clouds moving her way. She was physically too weak to panic as the first snowflakes fell melting on her nose.

Within minutes, she knew that this was no ordinary snowstorm like those she had endured in the past many weeks. This one was a real blizzard. Winds howled around her, chilling her to the bone. Soon she could no longer even see where she was walking, concentrating solely on putting one step in front of the other, tugging and pulling the broken down cart behind her. She realized she could not pull that cart one more step. Thus, she wrapped herself up in all of the remaining blankets, which helped her regain some warmth. With little other choice and wrapped like a mummy, she began forcing her way through the deep snow once more.

All around, her the storm raged its violent fury, drifts grew rapidly, and soon they were over her waist. Several times, she became almost stuck in an unexpected drift. Starving and weak, she was no match for the brutal storm. Mentally, she no longer thought about anything; she had become numb to the world. She did not even ponder the significance of her dying, freezing to death out here in the middle of nowhere, being buried by the pure white snow. No, Zdlenka had no thoughts at all. She was just completely numb to the world and to all existence, blindly attempting to push her body further northwards. Gone was all hope of survival. Gone was all hope of anything. She thought of nothing at all, except for peace. Her aching body yearned to just lay down and sleep, but her numb mind could not give her body even this thought, this command. Instead, like a robot, her body kept thrashing its way forward through the ever-deepening snow.

She did not even see three of her blankets fly off her when her fingers got too cold to hold onto them anymore. Now the cold bit into her with a vengeance, attempting to claim what was left of her life. Stung by the bitter cold blasts, she finally relented and let go of her body. Immediately it collapsed into the snowdrift, ready to fall asleep, and let nature take its course.

Still no thoughts appeared in her mind; she had not the energy to think. Her eyes closed and snow began freezing her lashes together. Finally, she had a thought, "I am at peace with myself." She sighed slightly and relaxed, accepting her fate.

But her nose was not yet frozen. A familiar smell whiffed in on the strong winds. Slowly her mind tried to recall what that smell meant. "Smoke," came a distant recognition into her mind, "Smoke, a fire burning near." She tried to open her eyes to see if she could see from where it was coming, but her eyes were frozen shut. She struggled to her knees and flailed her way through the snow, sniffing her way toward that fire. It seemed a slow-motioned eternity before the smell grew pungent and close. Finally, she banged into something solid, collapsed, and fell into a deep unconscious sleep, her last energy spent.

A pair of strong hands picked her up and carried her inside the warm stone home. "Mother, come here; we seem to have picked up a surprise guest. I think it is a she, can't tell for sure. Nearly dead from the storm that's for sure."

"Goodness, is that a woman?" came a surprised middle-aged voice. "Strangest outfit I ever saw. What is she doing out there anyway? Town's twenty miles away. Gosh, what a horrid stench!"

"It's still alive; it's breathing," the man said. "Come on; help me get it to the fire. We have to get it warmed up fast. You are right. It stinks something awful. But no matter, first we must get it thawed out."

"Can we see too?" chorused a pair of young boys in their very early teens. "Awful smell. Can we help too?"

"Okay, guys, you know the drill. You get plenty of water warming up on the kitchen stove please," the father said. To his wife, he said, "I'll start removing these awful, tattered clothes. What a foul, stinking mess this is." He began peeling off the layers of half-rotten leather outer garments. "Might be a woman, awfully long hair."

"By Sol, I've never seen hair in that bad a shape!" she commented as she gingerly picked up the rotten clothes and stuffed them into a sack. She wanted these foul smelling tatters out of her home as fast as possible!

Within a couple of minutes, both knew their guest was a woman — that was abundantly clear when all of her clothing had been removed. None of the clothing was remotely salvageable. "Poor woman," the mother said, "she's the most pitiful creature that I've ever laid eyes on — wonder who she is? Skin has a yellowish tint to it under all that grime; at least I think so. Probably not from

Megalos. Arad maybe? Don't they have yellowish skins?"

"I don't know; never seen one. Guess you must be right. Can't be from Megalos or from the Southlands. She must be from the Arad way up north. Since she is a woman, perhaps I ought to turn her over to you?" His sense of propriety returned.

"Yes, move over. You get me plenty of soap and water. Go fetch some of my old clothes from that large box under our bed. She's going to need everything. While you are at it, tell the boys to give us some privacy."

It took her an hour to get Zdlenka cleaned up. While she managed to get her hair washed and the bits of leaves and twigs out of it, she let the tangled mat go until later. With the help of her husband, she managed to get Zdlenka re-clothed. Next, the four of them carried her into their spare room and onto the small bed they used for the rare guest. Soon Zdlenka was tucked into a warm bed. The boys lit a fire in the fireplace and presently the room was quite warm. They kept asking, "Who is she? Where do you suppose she comes from? Why did she come here? Why did she stink so badly? When is she going to wake up? How long do you think she'll stay here?" Yes, visitors were so rare here that the boys had an endless sea of questions, while their father had not a single answer.

"Safe bet the poor thing is half-starved, malnourished would be my guess. Look how skinny she is," his wife pronounced. "I'd better get some nourishing chicken and lamb soup a'cooking." She headed directly for the kitchen. Meanwhile her husband and the boys cleaned up the mess and tossed out all the rotting, stinking clothing. A half hour later, the family gathered around their kitchen table for their evening meal. Of course the conversation centered around their surprise guest, but no one had any answers, only mysteries. "I'll sit up with her for a while in case she wakes up. When I get too tired, I'll wake you, and you can spell me," she declared, ending the boy's speculations. Secretly, they had hope that their mom would let them take turns watching over their guest until she woke.

Around eight pm, Zdlenka stirred and awakened. She felt warm and cozy for the first time in many months. Better still, that horrid stench was gone; her skin felt like it had been scrubbed. Gone were the awful smells she'd grown used to for so many months. She heard the crackle of a warming fire to her left and slowly sat up to find herself in a small room. Two sides of the room were built of grey stone blocks, while the other two were wooden. She heard words, turned her head, and saw a middle aged woman sitting in a chair near the fire, sewing something.

The woman spoke, "About time you woke up. You were darn lucky you found our house. You were nearly frozen to death when Gregorio heard something outside and found you on our doorstep. You are one lucky young woman." Unfortunately, Zdlenka didn't understand a single word the woman was saying! Her worst nightmare had come true; she had fallen into the hands of Centurions.

She suspected that one word might be a name, so she repeated it uncertainly, "Gregorio?"

"Ah, yes, that would be my husband, Gregorio Yiros. I'm called Thessa. What is your name?"

Zdlenka thought rapidly and made a good guess that this woman's name was Thessa. She also guessed that she was asking for her name, so she pointed to herself and said "Zdlenka," before she realized that perhaps it wasn't wise to use her actual name. However, she had already blurted it out.

She made some eating gestures, and Thessa replied, "Oh yes, you are probably half starved. One minute. I've made you a nourishing soup." She hurried out the door and returned carrying a steaming copper bowl of her soup. Zdlenka found her body barely functioned. It was weak beyond belief. While she ate ravenously, Thessa chatted away, "Well, you certainly surprised us, appearing on our doorstep, so to speak, and in the middle of a very nasty blizzard to boot! Slow down; don't eat so fast. There's plenty more." Suddenly, Thessa finally realized Zdlenka didn't understand anything she was saying. She tested her theory. "How come you are a man?" It got no response save a sort of questioning look from Zdlenka. "Doesn't this beat all? By Sol, she must be from the Arad. That would explain everything. Now don't you worry; I'm going to wake up Gregorio." She quietly left to rouse her husband.

In a couple minutes, wiping the sleep from his eyes, Gregorio followed his wife into the spare bedroom. Zdlenka noticed him behind her and presumed that he must be Gregorio. So she questioned, "Gregorio?"

"Yes, I'm Gregorio. Can you understand me?" he replied. She looked at him with a look that told all. She didn't. Twisting his mouth as if that action would help him think, he tried the only thing he could think of at the moment, "Arad? Juda Arad?"

Zdlenka understood those words and nodded, repeating them several times. She tried pointing to herself and saying, "Juda Arad." She hoped that they might assume she was from there. At least that was where she was trying to go.

Both Gregorio and Thessa smiled approvingly. Nodding his head and smiling, he said, "Yes, she must have come from Juda Arad. Now we're getting someplace."

"Ask her if she is married, Gregorio. Maybe someone is out looking for her in this storm. Maybe she has some children that are still outside. She was in an awful state when you found her; maybe she was held captive by the barbarians and escaped them. Ask her if there is someone we should try to contact and tell them she is alive and well."

"Thessa, how do I ask her all those things? She doesn't speak our language," he protested.

"Oh, like this," she exclaimed. "Zdlenka, you have a husband?" she said while gesturing at herself and then pointing to Gregorio. She pointed the Zdlenka, made a questioning gesture, and then pointed to herself and Gregorio.

Zdlenka figured out that she was asking if she had a husband. "No," she said, shaking her head to communicate it to her rescuers. As an afterthought, she frowned slightly and looked a bit sad just to make sure they understood.

Thessa nodded, "See, she isn't married. Probably no children either. Well, she should get some rest. We should too." She was trying to imagine what needs her houseguest might have while they slept, and she thought of the chamber pot. "If you need to go during the night, here is the pot." She slid it out from underneath the bed and showed it to Zdlenka, who looked completely puzzled. So Thessa pretended to squat over it. Zdlenka's face reddened slightly, finally understanding the use of this pot. In her country, one just got up and went outside. In this blizzard, this method was far better. She nodded that she understood. Thessa dimmed the lantern light, and both left to go to their rooms in the upstairs balcony, closing the door behind them.

Zdlenka laid back on her warm bed and relaxed fully. She was warm, full, clean, and cozy. These people, obviously Centurions, had taken her in without the slightest hesitation or concern and cared for her desperate needs. It hadn't mattered that her skin was yellowish while theirs was bronze. It didn't matter they couldn't speak the same language. She had been closer to death than she'd ever been in her life. This family had taken care of her and seemed happy to have done it. "Boy, did we ever blow it," she whispered to herself. "These are really nice, honest people, and we were robbing them, raping some, pillaging their possessions, and even burning their homes. We were incredibly wrong. How could we have ever thought what we were doing was right, honest, and just? Well, that is now in the past. I'm in the present, and I need to use their pot." She got up to use it, but discovered just how incredibly weak her body actually was from her long ordeal. Only with great difficulty did she manage to accomplish this minor task. Once she was snugly back under the warm covers, she fell into a deep sleep at once.

The next morning, Thessa introduced her two boys to Zdlenka, "This is Arnos, the older one, and Beltas, my youngest." Both boys were in their early teens and had begun to look at girls. However, out here where they lived, women were scarce. Thus, they both took a keen interest in their new houseguest, staring at her constantly when their mother wasn't looking.

Zdlenka repeated their names several times, and said hers for their benefit. They grinned and repeated hers. Then, Thessa told them to go bring her some breakfast, and they raced to see who could be the first to serve her. "Boys will be boys," Thessa laughed. Zdlenka smiled as well, guessing at the young boys' motives.

Once she had eaten, Thessa had her set up on the edge of the bed. She brought out her scissors, a hairbrush, and a comb. From the delight on Zdlenka's face, Thessa knew she was doing just the right thing at the right time. The two exchanged the words for these items, Zdlenka repeating them many times to make sure she would never forget them. These seeming trivial items were worth their weight in gold to Zdlenka. She'd been without them for months. However, she was still too weak to do much on her own.

Thessa pulled up a chair and set to work on Zdlenka's hair. As the hours flew by, she chatted away, it didn't matter that Zdlenka probably did not understand much of anything. It was just her way. "Well, this is one fine mess. Don't recall ever having seen such a mess. How on Tarra did your hair get into such a fine mess anyway? Ah well doesn't matter. So long it is. My, I'll bet you have never cut it in your life. Well, I bet your hair used to be your pride and joy. Well, we'll try not to have to cut out much, if we can. Probably take us all morning to get it untangled, mind you. Not much else to do anyway, what with the blizzard still raging outside. You know, you are much like the daughter I once had. She was my first born, but died when she was six. She got awfully sick and died on us before we could find a healer. I tried to have another daughter to help with chores around the place, but as you can see, I had no such luck. All boys after that. Now I am too old to try again. Ah well. But now you come along. So if it is alright with you, I'm just going to pretend that you are my daughter for a little while. No harm in that." On and on she chatted while she worked on Zdlenka's hair. In turn, Zdlenka chatted as well, though not as much. This was a woman's ritual that transcended language barriers.

Around noon, Thessa had finished and Gregorio had just come inside. He'd spent all morning tending his huge flock of sheep safely penned up inside the cave complex behind his small farmstead. Zdlenka finally felt human once more, her long hair glowed down her back, and she radiated her thanks, hugging the older woman for what she had done. Next, Thessa helped steady her on her feet, as they walked out into the large central room, which served as their living room, dining room, and playroom.

The boys had gone ahead, fixed lunch for everyone, and had the table all set. All three men gaped at Zdlenka when she walked into the room and sat down at the place Thessa indicated. "Wow, you are really quite stunning!" Gregorio stated the obvious.

"Now don't you go getting any ideas," she played with him. He flushed, but his sons could not keep from staring at her. She was the prettiest woman they had ever seen. In their eyes, she looked radiant, like a goddess.

"Thank you all," Zdlenka said and meant it sincerely. All four readily grasped her meaning and smiled. Then, they ate lunch. When they had finished, Zdlenka wanted to help Thessa with the cleanup chores, but she still was too weak and unsteady on her feet.

"No you still have recovering to do, Zdlenka. You just sit there with the boys. Say, why don't you to show her how to play that game you are always playing, chess." She chatted on, carrying the dishes and left overs off into the kitchen. The boys needed no encouragement. Both rushed to get their game board and pieces. Zdlenka smiled as she watched them.

The boys sat opposite each other and rapidly set up the game. Next, they tried to show her how the game was played. Quickly, they found language to be a barrier. Zdlenka came to the rescue by picking up a piece and gesturing which way it could go. They caught on fast and soon she had the basic idea. She watched the two brothers play a game and saw how it was won, when the leader piece was threatened and could not block the attack or escape. She realized that this kind of game she had been playing all of her life, only it had been for real, not just a game.

When they had finished, she took turns playing each of the boys. To their utter amazement, she won both games in short order. This brought a lot of conversation between the boys and their parents, none of which she understood. Since they were all smiling and grinning, she assumed that everything was acceptable, that she had not done the wrong thing by winning the games. "Dad, you've got to play her. She is really good," Arnos kept insisting. Eventually, Gregorio gave in, gesturing to Zdlenka if she wouldn't mind playing him.

Since everyone was laughing, smiling, and grinning, Zdlenka took up the challenge. As the game progressed, she discovered that he was a far better player than his boys were; he'd probably been teaching them how to play. She realized that this was a good pastime to occupy the long days when going outside was hampered by the bad weather. It took her nearly three-quarters of an hour to finish him off in a grand style that left all five of them laughing and patting her on the back. Gregorio swore that she was a genius at this game.

From this time on during her stay, every day she took some time out of the day to help each of them improve their game. Yes, the boys loved every minute they could spend with this beautiful, young woman. Even Thessa was grateful for her taking the time to help keep the boys occupied. During these weeks when the weather was so bad, the entire family was mostly house bound. Finding something the boys could do to occupy their time was a blessing.

Zdlenka saw that during the long afternoons, Thessa worked on spinning sacks of wool into yarn and then yarn into cloth. She felt that she just had to find some way to pay these people back for their kindness and generosity. Hence, she insisted on having Thessa show her how to do it, and soon Zdlenka began making yarn. Of course, with some time freed up, Thessa began to bake more bread, flooding the home with the delicious odors of yeast-rising bread.

At least once a day, Gregorio and his boys would don heavy clothing and trudge the short distance to the caverns. There they cared for the sheep, the few goats, and dozens of chickens, usually returning with a fresh supply of eggs and sometimes, fresh goat's milk. One morning, when her strength had returned, Zdlenka convinced them to take her with them so that she could get a better understanding of how these people were surviving out here in the foothills of the tall mountains.

Drifts over three feet tall dwarfed everything outside, turning the world into a surrealistic scene. However, the men had beaten a solid path to the cavern's entrance. The mouth was only about six feet wide, but inside, it opened into a huge area at least a hundred feet across or more. Gregorio had built wooden pens in which to keep his herds. Chicken coops lined one side wall, while a special pen housed the seven goats. She could only guess at the total number of sheep he had, perhaps a hundred.

On the southern side, a side cavern opened up. In here, a vast amount of dried grasses was stored, though just now, the room was only about one quarter full. She watched as the three made efficient work out of the chores. Beltas gathered the eggs while he put fresh food out for the chickens. Arnos proudly showed Zdlenka how to milk the goats, assuming that she had never seen goats milked before. However, she had done this back in her homeland, especially when babies were plentiful; they had to be fed. Much to the chagrin of Arnos, she began milking the goat next to his, smiling at him. He grinned back. Meanwhile, Gregorio did the heavy work of cleaning out the sheep pen and carrying large amounts of the grass into the pen for his sheep to munch. Of course, as soon as the four re-entered the house, Arnos called out to his mother, "Hey, she already knows how to milk goats!" His mother grinned back, thinking what woman would not know how to do that.

All told, Zdlenka stayed with the family for six weeks, until the spring snow melt was in full swing and the heavy drifts had partially melted. She now understood and could speak fairly simple sentences in their language, which greatly aided them all. One day as she was making yarn with Thessa, she said, "You know soon I will be able to leave and head north once more. You all have been so kind to me, feeding me, clothing me, everything. I really want to pay you back somehow. Only I don't have any money, not a single coin. How can I possibly repay my debt to you?"

"Oh dear child, you have more than paid us back. It has been a joy for us to have you stay with us. You have brought us more fun during the long winter months than I can ever recall having. You help with anything you can do. I really hate to see you leave, but I know you must; we all know that."

"But I feel I owe you so much. I'd have been dead if you hadn't rescued me," she protested, certain in her mind that she hadn't done nearly enough to thank them.

"Well, maybe sometime in the future, someone will land on your doorstep that needs a helping hand. Think of us and help them. That way you are passing the kindness of Sol onwards. How's that?" Thessa answered with her pat religious reply she often gave when asked advice.

"Surely there is something you need?" Zdlenka continued pressing the matter.

"We've got everything we need out here," she replied mechanically, "except perhaps some young women, for the boys, you know. They are starting to look at women now," she grinned knowingly at Zdlenka. She grinned back. "You don't happen to have a few young girls around, do you?" Both women chuckled.

Gregorio, who had just come inside, heard part of their conversation. "Out here, Zdlenka, we have to be totally self-sufficient or we would perish during the long winters. So we have all that we need. Well, with the boys growing up, we could use another horse. I only have Roxy and she's getting rather old. You don't know where we might get a horse, by chance do you? We can trade wool cloth for it, if you know of someone who might have one they could spare."

Horses! Had it been that long? How could they have known that she had been a breda back in the steppes, a breda of wide repute? No they couldn't know; she'd even forgotten about that herself. Breeding horses was perhaps the only real skill she knew, and right now, she didn't even have a horse to ride. "No, but I will see what I can do," she answered him.

On April 1, 590 AH, Gregorio began packing supplies into several large sacks. Curious, Zdlenka asked him what was happening. "It is time I moved the penned-up sheep out into the high country where they can eat the fresh green grasses that have begun to grow once more. I always lead them out to pasture about this time. Want to come along? Always we can use an extra hand moving this many sheep at one time. You can see the magnificent countryside and see why we, Thessa and I, have chosen to live up here in the foothills, so far from any villages." She didn't need any further push! Under his guidance, she packed herself a pack of food and several blankets. They would be gone for several days and would have to camp out at least a night or two. Both boys were elated she was coming along with them, naturally.

She was handed a shepherd's crook and told what to do. Soon, the hundred plus sheep were being guided out of the caverns and out across the open lands. Now Zdlenka could get a far better picture of this homestead. Gregorio pointed out their huge garden plot, explaining that once the sheep were out to pasture, they would plow the garden and plant this year's crops. Slowly, the full picture of their existence became clear to her; she saw that they had to be very industrious indeed in order to create enough on which to survive.

Then the magnificence of the green foothills dispatched all other thoughts from her mind! Nestled against the snow-covered high peaks of the Kathas mountains to the east, these rolling, rocky green hills looked spectacular, a paradise of the gods. She knew that if she had any choice, she would love to live out here in the foothills, and she made just such a decision.

The next day, as they got the herd to the first of the many pastures they used during the year, everyone was startled to see a small herd of six horses grazing not too far from where they stood. "Well look at that!" exclaimed Arnos. "Horses, wild horses. We've never seen horses in the wild before. Too bad we can't catch them."

"Wild horses are not tame like Roxy, Arnos. It takes a master horseman to tame a wild horse. But they sure are pretty. I guess we will let them share the pasture with our sheep. I'm sure the sheep won't mind."

Zdlenka stared at the horses and could not believe her incredible luck. Not just any horses, she recognized these at once. They were from the Northern Steppes! She recalled how so many of their horses had been scattered when the Centurions made their surprise attack. Some had somehow survived the heavy snows of the winter and had wandered here, obviously because of the abundant grass.

"Will you excuse me for a while, please?" she said. "I want to go fetch those horses. It looks like you will get your wish for a few new horses."

"You can't just go walking up to wild horses, Zdlenka. They won't let you get remotely close to them before they will spook and gallop off," Gregorio answered.

She just smiled, "You all stay here. I will bring them back down here. Watch." All three stared at her in complete wonderment. Zdlenka was full of surprises, in their minds, anyway.

She took off her pack and picked up a few handfuls of grass. Then, she began walking slowly across the hills toward the small herd, speaking softly to herself in her own tongue. Yes, Zdlenka had a way with horses, for she was a breda and a good one. She knew horses and their minds, perhaps better than she knew men's minds. It took only a minute for her to spot the key horse, the one that was acting as the herd boss. Only this one needed her attention. What that one did, the others would follow. Ah, it was a stallion; so much the better, she thought, easier to handle. She slowly approached it with her hands holding out the grass before her, speaking softly all the way. Yes, it helped that these were Galt warhorses by training. The stallion sensed the approach of another Galt horse-person and didn't spook or bolt. Rather it stood there wondering why the Galts had taken so long to come and find them. He had to fend for himself all winter. It saw the offering in her hand and let her get close. When she was within his reach, he eagerly took her offering. She, in turn, began petting its back and long neck, comforting him as only a breda can. "Where have you been, Big Fellow? I've missed you. I see you have been looking after the others. Some are mares. You thinking of mating with your little harem? Well, that is okay with me, big fellow. You have earned the right to have some pleasure. Come with me, and I'll take good care of you. I like it here with all this grass. How about we stay up here where there is a lot of good grass? No more fighting for us. How does that sound big fellow?"

She chatted on in a similar fashion; all the while, she carefully inspected him for any signs of damage, infections, or worse. Finding none, she looked him squarely in the face, made eye contact, and asked, "Okay Big Boy, you going to let me ride you for a while now? How about a frolic around the hills?" He seemed to understand, whinnied, and nuzzled her. She touched her head to his. Then, grabbing a hold of his long mane, in one leap she was up on his back.

Normally, she would have had a bridle and saddle. Normally, the Galts used what you call a hackamore for their bridles. That is, nothing goes into the horse's mouth; rather a loop goes around its nose instead. No Galt would ever consider placing anything into their horse's mouths. Lacking a bridle was not a problem, Zdlenka, as well as any Galt horseman, could totally control their mount using only the pressure of her legs on its sides. Zdlenka urged the big stallion into a canter. Soon, she felt the wonderful breeze flowing across her face, hair flying behind her. Oh, how she had missed this and her horses. She galloped carefree about the hills, several of the others followed behind, enjoying the playful romp. Finally, she directed the horse back to the speechless men, who had watched her in compete disbelief!

She slid off perfectly and patted her thanks to the big boy, who nuzzled her once more. He had accepted her; she, him. "Well, here come the others. I think one or two of the mares will work out perfect for you. A couple are relatively old and probably will adapt nicely to your needs. Big boy here and at least two of the mares are going to be way too much for you to handle, I suspect. They are full of life."

"How — but — how did, I mean, can you — you just walked up to them. You rode without a saddle or a bridle. How is that possible?" Gregorio fumbled, completely at a loss for words. His boys were equally stunned.

However, Arnos recovered the quickest, "That was incredible, Zdlenka! Can you teach me to ride like that? How can you stay on? How can you tell the horse what to do without any reins? How do you do that? Is it hard? Dad sometimes lets me canter away, but not often. He thinks I will fall off and break something."

She replied, "I love horses. You know all about sheep and goats. You've been around them all your life. It's that way with me and horses. I guess you can call me a horsewoman. It's the only real skill I have, raising and training horses. It just takes a lot of practice. First, you need to get the horse's agreement to let you ride him. Once granted, why, even the horse will help keep you aboard, if you let him. You tell him what you want him to do with your legs, along with how you sit or lean. Horses are really very smart animals."

Gregorio made an astute observation, "It is good to see you really come alive, Zdlenka. It's plain to see that horses and you are, and should be, inseparable. May you never be parted from these noble beasts again. Your eyes are radiant; your cheeks, full of life. Praise be to Sol that you came with us. Just to see you come so alive really makes my day. Wait until Thessa hears about this and sees your glow. You are a horsewoman, that is for sure. This land really needs good horse breeders and trainers. Good horses are a real rarity here in the Southlands. If you wanted to go into business raising and training horses, why, you could become a very wealthy woman, no doubt about that. However, the day is ebbing; we'd best get the sheep moving on a little further. There is a good camping spot just ahead. Will the horses follow us or you rather?"

Beaming with a large smile, she replied, "Thanks. Yes, Big Boy here will follow and the others will follow him. Lead on, guys." An hour later, they stopped for the night in a relatively sheltered, narrow valley. A crude one room, drafty, stone cabin was Gregorio's home away from home. He'd built it several years ago.

A week later, Zdlenka said her farewells to this incredible family, thanking them profusely for all their help and generosity. They did likewise, for they were now the proud owners of two new mares. She promised to return and visit them later on, once she was settled. She'd tied the three mares into a string to lead behind her stallion. Using another bit of cord, she had fashioned a simple hackamore bridle for Big Boy. Thessa had kindly provided two sacks of essentials, food, water, and even one of her old brush and comb sets. Most of the snow had melted, and the day was bright and sunny, illuminating the vibrant green grass, the deep blue sky, and the stark grey mountains as she slowly rode off from their small settlement.

Yes, to her, their place looked like a small settlement — one large stone home surrounded by stone walled gardens, an orchard, a cavern complex, and more. She felt totally at peace and very much alive as she rode slowly north and slightly east, following the foothills. "Big Boy, I somehow feel like I have been reborn. Part of me has died and passed away, but what is left is more alive than I have ever felt before. You are part of that, you know." The big stallion nodded its head and snorted as if it understood her words.

After a few hours, Zdlenka began thinking aloud once more. "You know, Big Boy, I bet that there are lots of others like you now wandering alone up here where the grass is good. When we came south last year, we brought perhaps five thousand of your kin with us. Many of you are now masterless, wandering about the land trying to survive on your own without our help. I know you all can do just that, but, you know, most were used to having a master and right about now, they might feel just a little bit lost. What say you to seeing if we can find some more of your kin and help give them a good home once more — one that does not involve fighting and combat?" Big Boy neighed.

During the next few weeks, she and her Big Boy did just that. Together they roamed about the high country in search of lost horses from the Northern Steppes. Occasionally, she would sell one at a village she encountered for supplies. She now had a Centurion style saddle and bridle for Big Boy as well as a number of packsaddles for her ever-growing supplies. By the time she actually approached the river that separated the Southlands from Juda Arad, she led a string of horses that numbered well over a hundred.

At the river's edge, she paused for a time. "It's decision time, Big Boy. Where should I go now? To Zargarb, to the steppes?" As if in answer, Big Boy began to cross the river, followed by the huge string of horses. Curious, she let him continue to lead the way, wondering if he was going to head back home to the steppes. But no, once across the river, he veered more to the east, heading up into the grasslands of the high foothills. "Ah you want to stay around here where the grass is good and there are no fighters. Well that is just fine with me. Let's see if we can find a valley to call home." Together they rode out onto the grasslands of the high foothills. She knew that in the northeastern portion of the Arad, these hills were often filled with shepherds tending large flocks of sheep. Here in the extreme south, she saw none.

Besides, Big Boy was climbing even higher into the foothills, taking her farther from the civilized portion of the Arad. A day later, she came upon the ruins of some ancient hamlet or village, long abandoned. Built of grey stone blocks, the building's walls still stood, but their wooden doors had long ago fallen into dust. The village was at the end of a lush valley that ran east-west, and just behind the village, the Kathas mountains began climbing steeply up.

She was as close to the tall mountains as she could get. "I think we have found us a home, Big Boy," she commented as she dismounted to examine the desolate ruins. She unloaded the horses and let them wander free about the long, wide valley. The grass was good here and a small bubbling stream carried some of the snow melt down from the high peaks behind the ruins.

She counted ten stone buildings all told. Most were similar in size and shape, probably they once held an extended family. Their roofs were gone, and from the rubble, she suspected the roofs had been either wooden or thatch. She found a centrally located well or cistern, she could not tell which. She lowered a cup tied to a rope to test its waters and found it refreshing and pure; she assumed the water came from the mountains behind the ruins.

Further examination yielded a large corral, or rather what she could use as a corral. Three-foot tall stones carefully placed formed a rectangular area next to the ruins, and a very large stone building occupied the side closest to the mountains. Perhaps this was once a stable or a barn, she thought. Of course, if she were going to make this her home, she had a tremendous amount of work to get done. Every building needed a new roof as well as windows and doors. She would have to store up enough hay for the horses to winter here as well as food for herself. Firewood would have to be hauled in from somewhere or else a large supply of charcoal or peat found to provide heat and a cooking fire.

"Look, I can talk all day about the difficulties in making these ruins livable once more, but that won't accomplish a thing, Zdlenka. You will simply have to find the nearest town and hire some workers, that's all. Probably trade a few horses to get the work done."

The next day, she left her small herd of horses to graze in the valley while she rode Big Boy in search of the nearest town. As she looked back, she felt certain that her herd also liked this location. None attempted to follow the two. Now her problem was to find civilization, and she had no idea how to do that. She was wholly unfamiliar with this part of Juda Arad.

She rode a searching-style path, twenty miles north, then due west for five, then due south for thirty, and then west again, in continuous sweeps. She saw no telltale smoke clouds circling in the sky, a sure sign of a village. She saw no roads or paths, save those used by some deer herds. However, she managed to round up another dozen stray horses, to both her and Big Boy's delight. On the fourth day, she finally found people, though they were not what she was expecting.

She crested a rise and halted. Down in the valley below her was a large convoy or caravan or group, she could not tell exactly what they were. Hundreds of sheep were being moved out ahead of the people, several distant figures were driving them before the mass of people. Behind the sheep walked at least fifty people, a few men, lots of women, and a fair number of children. Most were heavily laden with packs and sacks, while several were pushing or pulling small carts brimming with sacks and packs. If she were in her homeland, she would conclude a clan was migrating to a new camping location, but she wasn't. Yet the more she watched, the more they did give the appearance that an entire village was indeed moving. Since they were coming her way, she sat motionless on Big Boy watching them, the other dozen horses she had picked up grazed behind them. It was nearly noon and the sun was directly behind her as the group slowly made their way toward her.

She continued to ponder what she was seeing. "As far as I know, the Arads are not nomadic, as the Galts. I don't ever recall seeing a migration," she spoke to Big Boy. She waited and watched.

Finally, the six shepherds, two men and four youngsters, were close enough to see her. Their reaction startled her. Every one of them stopped and stared at her, mouths gaping, eyes wide, as if they had seen a ghost or something. She flushed, "Do they recognize who I am or rather was?" She began to panic slightly. Wild thoughts flickered through her mind. "Do they know I planned the invasion of their lands? If so, will they want to kill me? I deserved it, though. Maybe they remember seeing me passing through one of their towns when we were conquering their lands. No, Zdlenka, look at them, that look is not one of recognition of a despot, but rather one of awe. Well, maybe they have never see a woman riding bareback on a large stallion before. Yes, that is more like what they must be thinking."

One of the young shepherds, a girl about ten, suddenly ran back toward the main group, shouting and pointing toward Zdlenka, though she could not hear what the girl was saying. She noted to whom the girl was speaking; that young man must surely be their leader, Zdlenka thought to herself. Now she was sure of it; the man began moving rapidly toward her, accompanied by the shepherd girl.

As he approached her, he too looked upon her with what she thought might be awe or perhaps reverence, although why she should command reverence was beyond her. Perhaps he was merely displaying the usual male reaction to her youthful beauty. Zdlenka was used to turning all the heads of men her way. However, those were Galt men, and she had her brother at hand to keep their attentions at bay. She decided to stay mounted just in case she needed to flee.

What the young man did when he arrived near her took her completely by surprise! He knelt down on his knees, bowed reverently to her, and muttered a brief prayer. "All praise to Jehosa! His visions have come true. Well met indeed my Lady of the Blue! I am your humble servant, Prophet Emil Al Amir, descendent of the Great King who long ago led our people out of Anuir during its destruction, as I am leading my people out of the destruction of the Arad."

Well, he had manners and seems to be well spoken. I am wearing the blue dress that Thessa made for me. Looks like my knowledge of their language is going to get me by; I think I understand what he is saying. Since he paused, she took that as a sign for her to reply, "I am Zdlenka, Horse Friend." She did not want to use her Galt title nor other words that might get them to conclude that she was from the steppes originally. "My command of

Arad is not perfect, so please speak slowly."

"You are just like I saw in my vision, a young beautiful woman dressed in the blue of the sky, sitting tall upon a brown horse against the green of the hills! All praise to Jehosa. We have been searching for you." This was not what she had expected to hear. Visions? How could anyone have visions of her out here? Were they looking for the leaders of the invasion, her brother and her? She'd only gotten here a short while ago and had not even known beforehand that she would be here. Zargarb had been her first choice of possible destinations. She blushed. He was a very handsome young man, probably her age; she was now twenty-seven.

By now, everyone else had drawn close to the pair and formed a semicircle around Zdlenka and Prophet Emil. Uniformly dumping their heavy loads onto the ground, they all sat close enough to hear every word. To the last person, they gawked and stared at Zdlenka, as though she were some kind of goddess! Her reaction was that of extreme nervousness; she had no idea what was going on and was considering just galloping away.

Prophet Emil recovered his presence of mind first. Noticing that they were actually spooking their long sought savior, he sat down, and said, "Let me explain our situation. You may sit on your horse if you prefer." Zdlenka saw no real danger here. Since the others were sitting, it did look a bit strange for her to remain mounted, looking sharply down at them.

Quickly, she gracefully dismounted in her usual manner, touching the grass lightly as her feet took her weight. She raised a finger to indicate she needed a minute. She took off Big Boy's bridle so that he could graze unencumbered. "Go eat some grass, Big Boy. I'll call if I need you," she spoke softly to the big stallion, which nodded and wandered back to the new mares they had recovered during the last couple of days. She sat on the soft grass opposite him, noticing that everyone watched in fascination her every move with her horse.

"We are mostly all from a village about fifty miles that way," he began by indicating a northwesterly direction. "During the last few years, our lives have become a living horror. As you probably know, the Galts from the Northern Steppes invaded and conquered Juda Arad. They carried off most anything that was of value, leaving us paupers. In truth, we were not doing all that well under the many years of the Infidel occupation, that is, the Centurions as you probably know them. Also, many of our village's young men were killed during the last few years. Life has only gotten tougher. We've heard that the barbarians from the north were roundly defeated by the Infidels down near their home island last winter. Still we are not free of them; many came and still are coming through the Arad heading north, stealing anything they need, particularly food, this time. Small bands of them are still passing through the Arad. If all this weren't bad enough, now there is a new threat, the Old Man of the Mountain."

Zdlenka fought back the urge to let her tears flow. She fully realized just how wrong she and her brother had been. Now she was facing the terrible truth of its impact on normal people's lives. Her eyes watered anyway.

Prophet Emil continued, "The Old Man of the Mountain's messengers come to our village and tell us what we are to give them. If we do not give them what they want, one of our village leaders is assassinated, usually in less than a month! Just four months ago, we lost the one man who had kept the village going throughout all these troubled times. From what we have learned, this Old Man of the Mountain is doing this same thing to all of the villages throughout the Arad. No one knows who this man is or where he is located. The assassin is always someone from that village who just goes up and kills the victim outright and then stands there waiting to be killed in turn. It just gets too weird to believe."

"So now, many of us want to start over, to form a village where we can live in safety, free from wars and strife and assassinations. Naturally, they looked to me as one of the few remaining Prophets of Jehosa still alive for guidance. I could not turn them aside. I prayed to Jehosa for guidance. Finally, after months of prayer, one night I had a vision, which could only be sent by Jehosa. Yes, it is true; we prophets are known to have visions, often of things to come. In my vision, I saw you, well someone who appeared as you did. She was dressed all in blue and riding atop a large horse. Incidentally, there are almost no horses remaining in all the Arad these days. This Lady in Blue was beckoning to me, telling me to lead our people to her; she would provide us a safe place to live, a place that is all grey with lush green grass underfoot, something the Arad is not noted for. At the Grey Place we would be able to establish our religious retreat and live in peace to strive to become worthy of re-entering the Holy Realm of Jehosa when our fleshly bodies die at last."

"I told them of my vision, so you can imagine everyone here was rather surprised when you did appear as was foretold. I think that they may not have quite the faith that I do. We are a peaceful group who are in dire need of a new place to live. That is our story. Can you help us?"

Zdlenka thought for a moment. *Perhaps this is just what I need, but then what is this religious thing?* "I have only recently arrived from the Southlands," she began, careful not to divulge more than was prudent or safe. "I, too, am looking for a new start on life, a place where my horses and I can live in peace. I have found just the place several days ago. There, we would all be safe. However, I have been searching for a village where I could hire enough workers to help rebuild the Grey Haven." She just made up the name. She had to call it something, and Grey Haven seemed appropriate at the moment. "The walls are solid stone but the roofs, doors, and windows have long ago turned to dust. I left in search of both workers and the necessary supplies to rebuild it. I have no money, but I do have many good horses. I intended to swap a few horses for the supplies and to pay for the workers to rebuild it."

Zdlenka continued, "What can you tell me about your religion? Your beliefs? I'm afraid I know nothing of it." She knew she at least had to have some idea in what these people believed. There were Evil Witches about somewhere, perhaps even worse.

Prophet Emil was more than willing to discuss their religion. In fact, once he started, he talked for a very long time. "Our Great Messiah, the fleshly son of Jehosa, has preached that we are all immortal spiritual beings, trapped within these fleshly bodies. Jehosa has given us the Holy Decalogue, which if we follow it, will one day set us free. We hope to be able to practice this in our new village. These are our guiding principles." He recited his version of the Decalogue.

There is no god but Jehosa.

Do not worship any other god but the One God, Jehosa.

Set aside the Holy Day, Saturday, from your labors and worship the Lord that day.

Respect and serve thy mother and thy father, for they have labored long in your raising.

Do not kill another.

Do not steal from another.

Do not commit adultery.

Do not lie to another.

Do not desire another's house or possessions.

Do unto men, women, and children as you would have men, women, and children do unto you.

(Note to the reader: Again, note the changes to the Decalogue as modified by Prophet Emil.)

He talked on at great length, but soon Zdlenka, with her feeble command of their language, began to miss too many words, and his words rather became background noise in her mind.

Finally, she interrupted him. "Excuse me. I'm not able to grasp all the words you're saying. My command of Arad isn't sufficiently good just yet. I've reached my decision. I'll grant your desire for a new place to stay for as long as you desire under certain precise conditions. First, it is my obligation to help all people of whatever nationality or color of their skin that need assistance and are willing to accept my help. Do not ever ask why I do this or why I live with such an obligation. Realize that I may grant sanctuary to a person from the Southlands, from the Sea Princes, from the Arad, or, yes, even from the Northern Steppes. Never ask why I do this. Just know that the person will be in great need, and I am able to assist him or her. Second, never ask about my past. Third, I'll be raising a large number of horses, so there will always be horses around in quantity. Fourth, through my horse herd, I'll provide for all our needs for as long as you desire to stay at the Grey Haven. Fifth, it would help us all immensely if you could lend a hand with helping to rebuild the place and helping to make us self-sufficient. When winter comes, I expect the snowfall will be heavy. We'll be completely isolated from the rest of the world. By then, we must be able to survive on our own. These are my only conditions. Are they acceptable to you?"

"Your generosity, your kindness is indeed godlike. There is no way we can ever repay you for your help, though I detect that none is needed. However, your fifth condition is indeed the critical one for us. We must be allowed to contribute as we can toward your survival and ours. If you would not let us help as we can, use what skills we do have, we could not accept your offer. We would be humiliated if we could not help."

Turning to face his group, he called out, "Do we all accept fully her conditions?" As expected, everyone shouted out their complete approval with no dissension. Turning back to Zdlenka, he said, "There you have your answer and our pledge. May Jehosa be praised for leading us to you, our savior." Everyone cheered in celebration, embarrassing Zdlenka slightly. She was not used to being the focus of such reverence. Yet, she felt warm inside, a feeling she had rarely, if ever, felt before in her life. She began to trust that inner feeling now.

Quickly they decided the best course of action would be to get everyone to their new home, the Grey Haven. Then, the men and women could best determine what needed to be done and how best to accomplish those tasks. Shortly, she began leading them slowly to her special place. More than once, she and Big Boy rode off to gather up another stray horse. Each time, the Arads were more than a little amazed to see her just ride up to the stray horse and then without seemingly doing anything physically to the horse, have that horse fall in behind her and join the ever growing group of horses. They had never seen anything quite like this done before or heard of such happening before. In their eyes, she loomed large, like a Blue Goddess.

By the time of the first snowfall, the Holy Order of the Blue Servants of Jehosa at Grey Haven was fully operational, led by Prophet Emil Al Amir and the Blue Goddess. Word had begun to spread throughout the Arad that anyone looking to keep the Holy Ancient Ways was welcome here, as well as those in dire need, spiritually, mentally, or physically. True to her word, Zdlenka now had a sizeable herd of over three hundred-fifty horses and had begun their controlled breeding; at least fifty foals would arrive with the spring. Her horses provided for all the sect's major expenses. From this point onward in her life, she always wore simple, homespun, blue dresses, never anything fancy, as a constant reminder of her salvation.

Footnote: just before the heavy snows virtually blocked all passage in the foothills until the spring thaw came, she made a quick trip south to visit Gregorio Yiros and his family. She brought them a new wagon loaded with supplies that she knew they could use including some seed grains and blankets.

Chapter 34 The Price of Success

Fifteen years have passed me by here in West Reach, or Cymry. It is early summer, 603 AH. I have been just incredibly busy all these years. Unfortunately, I have never taken the time to go back to the Greenway to visit my dear old friends. For several years, Sandy and I exchanged mental messages, but then she passed away of old age, at least that is what I assumed. She was my main contact person in the Greenway, telepathically. Thus, for the last many years, I have been mostly out of direct communication with the druwids. I still exchange letters via the infrequent mariners who visit West Reach to trade cargos.

Expansion is the key to life and survival; that is a key druwid principle, which I put into action every day. Our towns are not only thriving, but have also become some of the largest settlements on the entire island! Here in the northwest section of Layamon, about fifty miles northwest of Bregia on the coast, New Jerilum, or Nuadilan, as the locals call it, now has reached a population of well over seven thousand, and it is still growing, though I'm at my wits end trying to figure out how to make the town grow physically in size to alleviate the cramped quarters we currently face.

Our second town, Bedwyn, lies five miles northwest of New Jerilum. Likewise, it holds at least another seven thousand people. Thus, whatever solution I can work out for Nuadilan can also be used in Bedwyn. However, we've added two more towns already. Across the river Daneas from us lies Brea, home to another six thousand. Southwest of us is Amathon, our fourth town, which has five thousand people. Yes, we are thriving, boasting some twenty-five thousand people all told. What I find fascinating is that immigrants from the Arad account for slightly less than half of our people! That so many of the local inhabitants of this large island would move to our towns speaks highly of our success.

Our crop fields lie scattered in a roughly circular perimeter nearly twenty-five miles in diameter. Yearly, we send large caravans of trade goods south to Bregia and from there by ship over to the Greenway. On their return trips, we have received a large quantity of metal farming equipment, seed grains, cloth, and yes, even weapons. Our towns have set new records for profitability, unmatched by any other town or village. Though I have long ago delegated the responsibility for the daily operations of the towns to the people who live there, not a day goes by when I'm not asked for an opinion or guidance on some matter. It has been a near constant barrage of "Can you help us on this little matter?" Usually, it is not a *little* matter.

On Sundays, I still wear the hat of religious teacher for all four towns. I'm now down to conducting only two services in each of them. Still, it makes for a very long Sunday! However, we have been very fortunate indeed. Several men who moved into town were stone workers. Though it took these men several years to accomplish it, each of the four towns now boasts a huge stone Cathedral to Jehsoa and Nature. These are the largest buildings in each town and can hold nearly a thousand worshipers at one time, although in very crowded conditions. Their name is a compromise worked out between Josh, the traditionalist Arads, and myself, as you might have guessed. I will say that the locals are quite akin to my teachings, as they are also believers in Nature. Yet, we all get along very well; nothing that any of us preach contradicts the other in any significant way. It is a reasonable union of beliefs.

Every Sunday, I continue to drill into those who come to hear me, the truth of our existence that each of us is a spiritual being, immortal, not made of flesh and blood, not composed of anything found on Tarra. Each inhabits a fleshly body, whose life cycle is birth, growth, decay, and then death. Upon body death, we then find a new baby body and start the cycle over once more. What is the point of this cycle you may ask? The answer depends upon your faith. According to Jehosanity, it is purify one's spiritual being so that he or she may once more be worthy of re-entering the Holy Realm of Jehosa. According to the Cymry faith, your task is to triumph over evil, temptation, and travail so that you may gain the Holy Realm of Gwynfyd, a purely spiritual kingdom close to God. Me, I have and preach no specific answer to that question.

However, reflecting back on the whole time period, I now realize that probably the deciding factor in my success with the locals as well as the immigrants was my Last Holy Communion ceremony for the deceased. Whenever someone passed away, using my telepathic ability, I would perform a Mind Join with them and their loved ones so that all could say a final farewell and such. Invariably, those for whom I performed this ceremony became instant converts to our church and community; so strong is the taste of truth! Looking back now, I see that this little action did much to convince them that they were indeed immortal spiritual beings. Whatever the reasons were, more and more people kept moving into our towns.

On a sadder note, we laid to rest Jackal and Missa as well as Brother Jackal several years ago. I sorely miss them, especially right now. However, that is once again getting ahead of the story.

Politics. I really hate to go into politics, but we must a little if you are to grasp what all has transpired here. As you might expect, our smashing success has made us some jealous enemies in the eyes of nearby Dukes and Earls. Only the Duke in Bregia is wholly on our side, because all our trade off-island goes through his port, and he makes a handy profit as a result. Over the years, more than one Duke or Earl has brought a small force to attempt to take us over by force. Naturally, they were soundly defeated each time. Our children took note of this and have taken their own actions to counter this constant threat.

Four of our children are of age and have long ago moved out on their own. My sons, King Ahmad and King Emil are twenty-two and twenty-one respectively. Milla's two older children are King Hadid, twenty-three, and Queen Ros, twenty-two. King of what you ask? Well, our four older children decided those details for themselves. They agreed that Ahmad would be King over Nuadilan and Amathon, while Emil would be king over Bedwyn and Brea. Hadid wanted to expand outward; he formed up a small band of fighters and took control over the wilder lands between Layamon and the highlands of Ruaden with its many moors. He always had a pioneering spirit of conquering new lands, so I guess it has been a fitting decision.

What about Queen Ros? Well, to keep the peace with the highlanders next to King Hadid's territory, she married the Earl of Aine, the southernmost town of the highlands. She immediately changed his title to King of Aine. Yes, I thought her marriage to a somewhat older man, he is thirty, was just a political move. However, she seems more than happy with her life there and in many ways seems to be heavily influencing her husband's actions.

Oh yes, I'm now a grandmother. I have four grandchildren, or rather babies. The eldest is only a year old. Just before the older children decided to go their own ways and just after the births of the grandchildren, I took them into the stone church in Nuadilan and showed them the secret hiding place behind the central altar. Concealed beneath the stone floor is a hollow chamber. In it, I had placed a watertight stone box. In that box, I placed the scrolls that Jes, Josh, and I had written, outlining each child's heritage or lineage, back to the original King Amir. Each agreed to maintain this family treasure and pass its knowledge along to heirs, sons and daughters. Theirs is the direct bloodline of the original King Amir. King Ahmad swore to protect this church with his life. Thus, I had done all that I could to preserve their lineage for the ages, just as Jes and Josh had wanted. I hope that this will be enough.

Our two remaining children, Sarah Elizabeth, and Milla's Mac Dez, both sixteen, still live with us. In fact, Sarah and Mac have just thrown a fortieth birthday party for me. I suspect Milla had a hand in it, though. Neither of these two children had really known their fathers, since they were only about a year old when they lost them. Neither of these two had any desire to become a king or queen. Mac was more interested in becoming a farmer, much to Milla's frustration; she kept trying her best to convince him that he should aspire to be a king of men. In the end, he would have none of it. This year, he has made his own farm and gotten his crops planted; thus, Milla resigned herself to the fact that Mac is going to be a farmer.

Sarah takes after me. As she was growing up, she constantly followed me everywhere, learning everything that she could or that I or anyone else, for that matter, would teach her. When she was eight, I relented, seeing an awful lot of myself in her. I began training her in earnest. When the guests of the surprise birthday party had left our house, she and I sat staring at the mess, drinking a cup of tea. To my surprise, instead of talking about the mess in the house, she said, "Mom, have you given any thought to your eventual replacement here?" I nearly choked on my tea! Replacement? I am only forty. Still, this was a very adult comment, and one that I had been completely ignoring all these years, though deep inside, I knew that I should not have. It would nearly prove fatal.

"Who is going to preach to our people when you are gone? Surely not the Arad priests! They really don't know what you are talking about most of the time, I swear. Who is going to conduct the Last Holy Communion ceremony for the deceased? No one other than you that I know about can do what you do. Mom, you are completely irreplaceable!"

I smiled, "Yes, I do seem to be involved in a great many things around here."

"Probably more than you know, mom. I've been counting. Do you realize that you are now averaging about a dozen major healing actions per week? Completely ignoring the minor ones. Do you realize that you are doing about two Last Holy Communion ceremonies each week? And many of those are for folks who do not actually *live* in our towns. Honestly, mom. If anything should happen to you, the hole that your absence would leave here is enormous!"

I stared into her beautiful blue eyes and long black hair and smiled. "Sarah, you are absolutely right. I've been so caught up in all the things I'm doing here, that I rather placed such thoughts out of my mind. Do you realize that this is the first night this week that we have some peace and quiet here and time to chat?" She grinned back at me; perhaps this quiet time was also her doing. I wouldn't put it past her.

"Mom, I can help, if only you'd let me. I know I can't do the Last Holy Communion ceremony, that's for sure. However, I've heard your Sunday sermons since I was a baby. I know them all by heart. I could easily step in and deliver some of the Sunday sermons. You're dead tired every Sunday night. Honestly, mom, two sermons at four churches takes the entire day from dawn to dusk. Let me do half of them for you, please. I want to help."

Okay, she knew the magic words that melted me, "I want to help." I know just how powerful that urge in human beings really is, how vital, how important helping others is to a person. Smiling, I replied, "You win. You're more than right. Honestly, Sarah, I'd really appreciate the help. It's becoming so draining to deliver so many sermons on the same day, to say nothing of riding all that distance in great haste to get there in time. I never dreamed that it would become so large an event here. Thank you, dear."

She glowed with happiness, as I knew she would. I added, "If something should happen to me, we do need a healer here and someone who can run our Last Holy Communion ceremony. I'll arrange for someone tomorrow."

"Does that mean you'll get some druwids of the Greenway to come here?" she exclaimed excitedly.

"You bet," I grinned. "Yes, it probably will take a pair to handle both the healing and the ceremony, although they might just fine the right person who could handle both."

"Do you suppose that it would be a young man?" she asked eagerly. Now I saw her line of thinking. I had noticed that she paid scant attention to all the younger teenagers here in our towns. Often she had said they were not worthy of her. I had assumed that she meant because she should be a queen. However, I saw that all along she had her heart set upon a druwid. It was my doing; all these years I had talked incessantly to her about them.

"Okay, okay, I'll ask for a handsome, young, unmarried man to come," I grinned.

For an instant, she couldn't tell if I were serious or if I were teasing her. "Whoopee!" she exclaimed when I insisted I meant it. The next day, I wrote out a lengthy letter, sealed it, and arranged for it to be sent to Calgary and the All Greenway Circle. That turned out to be a vital action on my part.

Midsummer's Sunday night, Sarah and I met, as we were both riding back to Nuadilan from separate towns. We had finished the last of our Sunday sermons, and as usual, we met a couple miles west of Nuadilan and rode home together. We both enjoyed the nighttime rides and the freedom we both felt out in Nature. She and I were a lot alike.

We chatted about the day's events as we rode carefree slowly home. Suddenly, I felt very uneasy; she picked up my feelings at once. Our eyes darted about; we even turned around to peer into the darkness behind us. We saw no one. That cold fear feeling continued to grow; we picked up our pace. Could it be some Duke or Earl planning a nighttime raid on our towns?

Then I spied something or rather the lack of something. Sarah did too. Ahead of us, some of the stars were gone! Looking closer, no, some huge, black thing was blocking the starlight. That something was moving. "Mom, what is it? It is moving our way!"

Fear turned to terror. I suddenly grasped what it was. "Ride, ride like the wind! They are after us or me! Ride for your life!" We both instantly forced our horses into an all-out canter, hooves thundering upon the green grass, throwing bits of sod up as they raced along the narrow path. The black ship turned to follow us. We were both certain of that as we kept one eye staring at it. However, it moved slowly and deliberately following us. I cursed and swore as I rode.

"Mom, what is it? What do they want?" Sarah cried, just as terrified of this flying thing as I was. She had a right to be; only she did not know it.

Soon it became clear that we couldn't outrun it. I began coldly calculating what it might do or try to do to us. For once, I was right. "Rein in, Sarah. We can't outrun it, and I need to be stationary if I think what is going to happen actually happens." At once, we stopped, horses panting, well lathered up. "Here take my reins."

No sooner had I freed myself from the reins than the first attack came. I detected the telltale signs of an energy beam or flow coming directly down from the ship straight at me. In that split second, my lessons, so many years ago when Alabaster had fired lightning bolts at me and I had to deflect them, came back to me. I spotted the leading edge of the beam and just barely had time to push it slightly to my left. It struck the ground with a thunderous blast, sending piles of grass, sod, and rocks flying in all directions. The horses spooked and bolted from Sarah's hands, knocking her onto the ground.

Hovering over us, the ship tried to blast me once more. Again, I deflected the bolt to the right this time. Sarah was just screaming and staring at me and the ship. I knew she was terrified out of her wits, but I had to keep my full attention on the ship or else be killed in the next energy blast. However, I got mad instead. They were endangering my daughter. Something in me triggered. *Never mess with a mother!* The next beam began forming; I just twisted it and turned it back on itself. The beam struck the ship! Sparks of energy, not unlike lightning, darted like a spider web across the dark ship overhead, a sparkler on the 4th of July in your world, I'm told.

I don't think it did any real damage to the ship. However, once the fireworks stopped, the ship instantly took off at a very fast speed heading due east and was soon out of sight. Satisfied it was gone, I helped my daughter to her feet, brushing off the debris that had covered her. "Wha — wha — what was that?" she finally managed to utter.

"I'm not certain, but I think I know who it was, not what it was," I said seriously.

"How, how come the lightning didn't hit us? They must be incredibly bad shots," she added.

"Come on; let's get walking. We still have several miles to go on foot now," I replied before I answered her. "I deflected the first two shots or I would have been fried. I got really mad after that and reflected the third blast back their way. I don't think it hurt them, but I think they got the message that they're not going to kill me this way, and they then left."

Sarah looked at me as if she had never seen me before. I knew I had a lot of explaining to do. "Mom, there are a lot of somethings that you haven't told me!"

I replied, "Come on; out here isn't the place to discuss this. When we get safely home, I'll tell you all about it, if you want to hear it." We nearly ran all the way home, okay, jogged is more like it. It felt good to exercise off the fear of that attack.

Safe inside our home, Sarah made us both a cup of tea. I was very winded and quite thankful for her assistance. At forty, I wasn't as fit as I was when I was twenty; I was beginning not to like growing old with these fleshly bodies. When Sarah sat the cups down along with some biscuits, she pulled up her chair close to mine, the signal that I should start explaining things.

I began, "Sarah, what I am about to tell you should never leave this room. Promise me that you will speak not a single word about this, save perhaps to Milla, and then only in a dire emergency. She has a feeble knowledge of these matters, feeble at best. Promise me."

She did eagerly, so I continued. "High in the Appian Way mountains, far from any people of Tarra, live what I call the Grey Creatures. Their bodies are giants compared to ours. One stood at least three times as tall as your father was. Yes, your father died while fighting these evil creatures. They have three toes, weird. Anyway, how many they number, I have no idea. I have only seen three of them at any one time. At their mountain top location, they have some kind of pole contraption that entraps spiritual beings. From what I have learned, when a person's body dies, they have been implanted with an order to return to this pole area. So strong is this implanted command that none can seem to ignore it. I've seen the beings head off there at incredible speeds."

"Once there, the Grey Creatures activate their contraption. It sucks the person into the pole. Next, the pole thing literally scrambles all the person's memories! When they are done, the person's mind is the most confused mess of memories you could ever imagine. Then, they are given the command to go find a new baby body and report here when that body dies."

Sarah looked at me with shock and fright in her eyes and demeanor. "Yes, these creatures are attempting to control us. Perhaps their actions are keeping everyone from realizing that they are a spiritual being and not just a body. I just don't know. I first came across these creatures last life, when I led a druwid Circle past their area by accident. I had been observing that peoples in the Greenway and the Sea Princes were uniformly all heading to this area in the Appian Way shortly after their bodies died. A number of years ago, I also spotted that the Arads were doing the same thing and told all of this to your father."

"He then did his own observations and found that I was entirely correct. For him, this was a hideous problem, one that operated directly opposite of his goals for being here, to help his people realize that they were immortal spiritual beings. I guess I knew deep down that eventually he would take some kind of action against them. I now suspect that was the primary reason why he left here and went to the Sea Princes. When he discovered one of them alone high in the mountains, he did a Mind Join to me to tell me what he was doing. He believed that he could kill these creatures, if he could attack them one at a time. I knew that he couldn't; they are just too powerful."

"In terror, I contacted the only person on Tarra who might be able to help Jes, good old Alabaster Benjamin Crowley, the founder of the druwid movement. He still had not yet picked up a new baby body and had been also spying on these creatures. You see, they are working directly against the goals we druwids as well have for all people. He did a Mind Join with me so I saw everything that happened. I have only told my druwid friends about what I saw. Not even Milla knows this; please don't tell her this part. I watched as Jes battled the single giant creature. Only with Alabaster's help was he able to lower the defensive screen that the giant wore. I have no idea what to call it, except defensive screen. It made him impervious to any sword strike. Jes did wound it in its leg and it ran off."

"I pleaded with Jes to stop, but there was no stopping your father. He dashed off after it, intent on killing it. Alabaster followed as I watched through his eyes, though he didn't have any physical eyes. Next thing I knew, Jes was near the pole, and two more came out. Jes manage to wound it in its other leg, whereon the creature lashed out with its fist, totally caving in Jes' head. His face was no longer recognizable as human; these creatures are incredibly strong. His body died instantly. Next, the pole thing turned on, and Jes was sucked into it. I watched in horror as all his memories were completely scrambled! Alabaster tried to pull him out of there, but was caught by the pole thing himself! I lost my two closest, most powerful companions that day."

"Worse, the creatures recognized that I had been watching the whole affair, and they attempted to suck me right out of my body here in West Reach and right into the pole! However, they didn't succeed. I know how to fight back. The secret is not to resist that pull in any way. It can only pull one into it, if that person resists its pull. I escaped."

Sarah's face was white as a sheet. Tears trickled down her cheek as she learned of her father's last moments. However, I was not through; Sarah had to know the full truth. "It is far worse than this, I'm afraid. Down south across the Med Sea lies the Red Desert — you know, the one with the poisonous sand that causes the rotting sickness, where the Moon people live their entire lives underground? Well, when I led my Circle through that land, I discovered there is another group of even weirder creatures operating much the same way there. They suck in and scramble the memories of all the beings who dwell in the Southlands and Megalos, where the Centurions live. These creatures are like giant praying mantises. My best guess is that their bodies are fifty feet long, truly monsters in every sense of the word. My group fought them using fire, ice, and lightning. None of these had any real affect upon them. That's why I was so afraid for your father to attempt to openly challenge them."

"During some battles when the Centurions were in the process of conquering the Sea Princes, I watched in horror as the Sea Prince fighters died and were sucked into the Appian Way, while the few Centurions who died were sucked up by the mantises. My conclusion is a ghastly one. Perhaps these two groups are controlling history on Tarra. Perhaps they are the ones fomenting all the wars for their own petty reasons. Certainly, they are totally interfering with all the spiritual beings on Tarra. Sarah, your father died trying to do something about this, the greatest evil on Tarra. I know that he would want you to know this."

Sarah was only sixteen. I know I was dumping a hideous situation on her. Yet, she had seen their aircraft tonight. She had to know the truth. In spite of her fear, panic, and yes, terror that I knew she was feeling, she shocked me. There are times when even your own children can surprise you. She said, "Mom, I bet I know why they are after you after all these years — your Last Holy Communion ceremony! Most of the time, you have been successful at preventing those that have died, I mean whose bodies have died, from returning back to these Evil Creatures for more of their hideous brainwashing. How many has it been all these years, mom? At least several hundred. They have probably noticed that they are getting far fewer beings reporting in from West Reach and figured out that you are responsible."

My mouth opened, but no words came out. For the first time in a very long time, I was entirely speechless. My own young daughter had drawn precisely the right conclusion! I beamed with pride in her. Finally, I was able to say, "You amaze me, Sarah. You are very likely correct. I should be listening more to what you have to say! I promise to pay far more attention to you in the future. Can you forgive me for not taking you as seriously as I should have?"

My response wasn't what she expected either. We stared at each other for a moment, and then she hugged me tightly, and I, her. Then, her mind began to race with corollary thoughts. "Mom, how do they know you're here? They must have some spies around that report on our comings and goings, don't you think? How else can they know so much? How else could they know that you ride back from Bedwyn on Sunday nights? Do you suppose that they have a spy right here in Nuadilan, right under our very noses?"

"Sarah, I have to believe that they don't have a spy here. These creatures are so utterly foreign, so monstrous looking, that no person I have ever met would have anything to do with them."

"But couldn't they have somehow taken control of someone's mind, forcing to do their bidding?" came her speculation. "How could they possibly know you always ride home at night alone? Surely that information had to have come from someone who is familiar with your routine."

I thought for a moment before replying, "I just don't know. If these creatures have the mental capabilities as Jes, many druwids, and I do, they could locate me by sensing my presence. They have encountered me now on several occasions. Yet, you are right. How did they know precisely where I would be and when? Further, they used some kind of air ship to get here. Obviously, they had to come at night, because in the daytime, everyone between here and there would have seen their ship. They would instantly lose their secrecy. They would have become exposed to all Tarra or at least to a huge number of people. So Sarah, you may well be right in suspecting they have a spy here in our town."

"But you're safe as long as you stay inside our house here, right?" she asked her burning question. I could tell that she was very worried about my safety. She didn't want to lose her mother too.

I knew she wasn't going to like my answer. "No, this house is absolutely no protection from their weapons. If their ship were directly overhead right now, they could blast me as I sit here drinking my tea. The only thing we have going for us is our ability to detect their coming, Sarah." She gave me a total blank look. "Remember just before we first saw their strange air ship. Remember, we both felt ill at ease and quite fearful. We were even looking back over our shoulders. We can sense their coming. Their presence is so foreign, so antipathetic to us. We can use that to tell when they are near. Right now, I don't sense them. How about you?"

She had to admit that she did not and that she had felt a real fear just before they attacked us. Hence, she had some relief from her worries. At least, she might have a minute's warning of their next attack.

In typical teenager fashion, she then cheerily said, "Okay, mom, so what do we do about them? How do we fight them? What's next?" Ah, the optimism of youth!

"You know, I've just had another thought. Something you just said. Suppose that they can influence the minds of normal people. Suppose further that they have been on to me ever since your father died. Could it be that all the attacks on our town by the dukes and earls have been their doing? Ideas implanted into the unsuspecting minds of the dukes and earls? It follows then that since all those attempts failed and now we have the four Kings protecting the towns, they must try a different tactic. If that tactic is to risk exposure of themselves by flying a strange air ship that is sure to attract the total attention of anyone who should see it fly overhead, then surely they must be getting rather desperate. The only conclusion is that since that failed, they will take even more drastic an action, whatever that might be."

"As to what we can do, in actuality, when one faces a problem, a calamity, a threat such as this, only one of five choices present themselves. First, we could openly attack them, as you suggest. That option is totally out of the question. Your father and the most powerful person I know, Alabaster, both failed completely attacking them. Surely, tonight's episode should convince you that we can't openly attack them. They are way too powerful for us; we would only get bodies killed and beings further entrapped with their minds scrambled. No, the first choice is completely out; we can't attack them back."

"A second choice would be to completely ignore them and hope they forget about me. That is so foolhardy that I won't comment further on it. A third possibility is to just lie down and give in, let them kill this body and entrap me, that is, just give up, for they are so powerful, and I'm so weak compared to them. Sorry, but that I can't stomach! The fourth possibility is somehow to bypass or go around them. If we encountered a wild boar on our path, it is easy to avoid it by going wide around its location; hence no problem. With these creatures, I don't see how I can go around them, since they are finding me where I am at."

I noticed that Sarah was writing these choices to a situation down on a parchment. I knew she was very happy to be learning this bit of wisdom and would later make good use of it. She looked up as she finished writing, "So what's the fifth one? Surely that is what we have to do here."

"Flee. The last thing one can do is to flee from the danger, from the problem. Ordinarily, I would say this is likewise not a good thing to do. One cannot run away from his or her problems and troubles; they follow you."

"So then there is *nothing* that we can do?" she asked forlornly, if not exasperatedly.

"Flee might be my only choice, Sarah," I said and drifted into thought. She tugged my sleeve to regain my attention. "I was just pondering all this, Sarah. Suppose that we are right — that they have chosen to escalate their attempts to get rid of me. Suppose this is actually the truth of the situation. Where does that logically lead?" I paused in true druwid fashion, hoping my adept would reach her own conclusion.

She thought for a moment before answering, "Well, if they are escalating their attempts to get you, why, maybe they will blast the town to smithereens. Can they do that? If not, why they might recruit a huge army to conquer Nuadilan by force." She rattled off wilder and wilder actions that these ultra-powerful creatures might take. I let her invent away for quite some time before I interrupted her.

"Very good, Sarah. Now take your pick of any one of those actions you have dreamed up. Ask yourself who endures the worst of it? Yes, I get wiped out, but who else gets hurt in the process?" Now I knew I had her; I was patient.

"Oh my god! All of us — the townsfolk — our friends — all the rest of us!" she replied shocked at her own conclusion.

I simply said, "Flee might not be such a poor decision after all, mightn't it?"

"But mom!" she protested, "You can't just leave; you are indispensable here! Everyone will miss you utterly. You're the one who is keeping everything running perfectly! You can't just leave."

"If my staying brings down death and destruction to our people and towns, then I simply cannot stay. I could never live with myself if my actions brought such hardship upon everyone. I think you can understand that, even if emotionally you reject it." I gave her time to let her emotions subside and her analytical thoughts regain control.

After a few minutes of silence, she looked up at me determinedly and stated, "Well, you can't go away alone! I'm coming too." I knew that this was coming and was prepared for it.

"For one, whoever I take with me, they are likely to be killed as well, if only because they also saw these Grey Creatures slay me. Whom do I choose to come and die along side of me? Secondly, I can't just abandon all that we have worked so long and hard for, not at all. You have already shown me that you are more than capable of replacing me as our religious teacher. If I go, I want you to continue teaching our people, so that these ideas don't die with me. Your task is perhaps one of the most crucial factors of all; keep our spiritual concepts alive and intact."

Tears welled up in her eyes, yet she knew I spoke true. "Well, then take Ahmad or Emil with you, please."

"You would have your brothers killed?"

Sobbing, she said meekly, "No, but . . ." Her voice trailed off.

"No, if I go, I go alone. However, I can't go until I can get word of a replacement for me in the areas of healing and our special ceremony. Certainly, these are having a noticeable impact on the Grey Creatures. Hence, it is our main line of attack: to educate people and do what we can to prevent them from following the implanted orders to return and get mind-washed when their bodies die. No, I can't go until I get word on whether the druwids will send someone to replace me and keep our attack going. With luck, the Grey Creatures will not have the slightest idea who is following my example, and the towns will remain safe with me out of the picture. But come, Sarah,

462

we've had one intense Sunday night. I'm dead tired. Let's get to bed." I led her to our bedrooms. Tonight, we chose to sleep in the same bed, side by side. It was the least I could do for her, knowing that my days with my daughter were numbered.

The next day, I sent another dispatch to the All Greenway Circle in Calgary, outlining what had occurred last night. We both knew that it would take quite some time for it to get there and for any reply to return. Hence, we had time to spend together and we did. Sarah insisted that I not leave the town, and she took over my Sunday sermons at Bedwyn.

It was August before an answer arrived back. Sarah looked over my shoulder as I carefully opened the dispatch. "Mom, it's all gibberish. They aren't even words," she commented. I had taught her the basics of the language spoken in the Greenway, and yet she could not read the letter.

"It is in code. The Centurion friend of mine, Niccolo, worked out this code. Sandy figured it out. See, it is just a simple letter transposition," I explained. Hastily, I began writing the translated words on to another parchment, with Sarah reading over my shoulder.

Dearest Bethany,

We concur with your analysis of the situation.

Too risky to send just one.

Vastly too important to neglect.

So sending the *young* Hedgehog Circle by next boat.

My prayers go with you,

Wid John Small

"What does it mean? He didn't say much," commented Sarah.

"It is still rather cryptic on purpose, should it fall into the wrong hands. Look at the seal on the dispatch pouch. Remember how I examined it first before opening it?" She nodded. "The seal was broken, which means someone tried to read what was in the dispatch. Likely, the code probably did its job. Still, even if the code were broken, as it might in time by a clever mind, the contents are still cryptic. He is saying that the druwids believe everything that I told them and that what we are doing here represents a powerful attack on the Grey Creatures, undoing partially what they have been doing, and that the druwids want to keep on doing it. Hence, he is sending an entire druwid Circle of seven. Not only do you get a top-notch healer, but seven healers. One will be a Communicator, who will take over the ceremonies when someone's body dies. One is a Protector who will be responsible for keeping the others safe from harm." I carefully explained the purpose and special training that each member of the Circle would be bringing to our town. "They will probably be arriving within a couple weeks. Finally, the word 'young' is underlined and that is a special note to me. He is indicating that they are all going to be about your age, and some will not yet be married. Just promise me that you will marry for love and no other reason." Sarah blushed, but I could tell she was ecstatic over the possibility of meeting some young men whom she could totally respect and trust. Mothers worry about these sorts of things, you see.

"I guess we had better figure out how I'm going to leave the town. Do I dare just disappear?" Sarah and I then began a lengthy discussion. In the end, my daughter had the best plan.

"Mom, we spread the word that you are going on a vacation. You haven't had a break from your duties since you began. Everyone will accept that because it's the truth. We'll say that you're going up to the highlands of Ruadan to see the moors and the breathtaking beauty of the landscape there, stopping briefly to visit your niece, Ros. However, you go to the green hills of Tewdwr instead. Stay close to the coast, because, by all accounts, it is always very foggy and hard to see; it rains nearly every day there. That should make spotting you from their air ships much more difficult to do. Then, when it is safe, you can return. Besides, if I get too lonesome, I can always wander over to Tewdwr for a visit."

Her plan made good sense to me and was adopted. While she spread the word about my impending vacation, I began arranging things and packing. I had hoped to delay my departure until the Hedgehog Circle arrived and I could groove them in on the situation and duties. That would ensure a clean transition of power and maintain some continuity for everyone. However, that was not to be.

On Saturday, five days after the letter arrived, around noon, Sarah, face white as a sheet, came running into our house. Out of breath from running as fast as she could, she exclaimed, "Mom! You have to go now! It's here. Remember how we could sense their coming that night? Well, I was down by the outer gates chatting, when a stranger walked in from the road. He spoke with a funny accent to the gatekeeper, which is why I took notice of him. The man looks like just another man, like us, but it is just a disguise. I feel that heavy fear emanating from him. I think the Grey Creatures can somehow disguise themselves somehow — I don't know how, but he was asking directions on how to find you, called for you by name even. Gatekeeper gave him some confusing directions. I think the gatekeeper was just as scared as I was by this guy's presence. You've got to get out of here fast; use the north gate." She finally ran down.

"You go saddle my horse, and I'll meet you by the north gate! Guess I'm leaving sooner than I expected." I frantically began stuffing things almost at random into my sacks. Finally, carrying three large sacks of gear, I headed out of the house and went straight toward the north gate. Well, the layout of our town is such that there is no direct path from my house near the center of town to any gate that leads outside. Rather, we built a wooden stockade wall entirely around the original town when it was small. As we grew in size, another concentric circle of stockade was added, only the entrances were offset from those of the inner circle. Now, we have seven circles of stockades. This way, should we be attacked and the outer wall fall, we still have six more stockades to protect the rest of the town. Further, you cannot ride in a straight line from one of the outer entrances into the next circle; rather you must follow the circular road until you come to the next entrance, offset by forty-five degrees from the entrance you entered. Today, I found the added defensive measures exasperating for I was trying to get out of town just as fast as I could go. I relaxed finally when I realized that the creature would be making far slower time trying to navigate its way up to the top of the hill at the very center of the town where our stone church dominated the skyline.

When I reached the gate, Herman, the keeper, commented, "Ah, Ma'am. I see you are taking your vacation earlier than expected. Rightly so, I says to the misses, you deserve some time for yourself."

"Yes, yes I am, if only my daughter hurries up with my horse. You take care of yourself, Herman and your wife too. Ah, here she comes now." Riding rapidly through the crowded streets, Sarah pulled up just outside the gate. I think she overshot on purpose so we could speak privately before I left.

"Mom, do stay in touch with me please," she begged, as she helped me tie the sacks onto the mare.

"No matter what happens, Sarah, remember always that I love you and I respect you. You are a terrific person. If I can, I will Mind Join with you at bedtimes. If I can't, please don't fret about it. I may be involved with something else just them. Goodbye for now." We hugged each other tightly, and then I mounted and cantered off down the north road heading for the river Daneas and our northern town of Brea. Within minutes, I reached the river. Here, the hills completely hid our town from view. A thin line of oak and maple trees with some very tall sycamore trees followed the river as it snaked its way through the rolling hills of Layamon. I moved into the cover of the trees and headed west, following the river. Out here, I was not too likely to run into any people except for any lumber crews cutting wood for our needs. I tried to remember the various town councils' advance plans for timber cutting so I could avoid those areas, but as shook as I was, I couldn't think of anything, except these Grey Creatures and the safety of Sarah.

With me out of the way, Sarah should be perfectly safe. After all, she could really do nothing more than recite my teachings. No, the Hedgehog Circle was going to inherit my dangerous mission, particularly with the Last Holy Communion ceremony. I was grateful for the wisdom that John, the Wid of the All Greenway Circle, had in sending an entire Circle. Seven would be a lot harder to defeat than one single person.

An hour later, I cleared the known lands of our extended set of towns. Now I was in unsettled countryside, for the most part. Sure, one could occasionally find an extended family living by themselves, and there were a few small hamlets this distant from the main portion of Layamon. However, of what lay in the Tewdwr sector, I had no direct knowledge, never having been there. From others, I had heard that it was sparsely settled, primarily for two reasons. The coastline was rugged and nearly always fog bound. It rained there nearly every day — snow, of course, in the wintertime. However, it was supposed to be a very beautiful land of rolling green hills that sloped ever downward from the Ath mountains in the east to the seashore.

After riding hard for three hours with no signs of pursuit, I began to relax and enjoy myself. I felt elated to be getting away from the constant workload I had been handling for so long now. This was personal time for me, though I wished more than once, I had someone with me with which to share the adventure. However, I sensed that if I had brought someone along, it might well be a death sentence to them. In spite of appearances, this was not a pleasure trip, rather one of trying to survive these Grey Creatures.

Ah, I'm overlooking a vital fact here, I suddenly thought of the plainly obvious. I, too, had sensed its coming, though far fainter than had Sarah; she'd been dangerously close to the creature. *They can take man-form; that is what is critical. They are definitely giants compared to our bodies. Yet, they can take man-sized forms. How? Ah, illusion, I'm forgetting our own druwid skills! Simon could make the Centurions believe they were looking at a woman instead of him. If we can do it, surely these creatures can as well. I bet anything that it was really a giant who entered the gates, casting the illusion that it was just a large man. That's terrifying! They can walk among us with impunity! I must relay that to the Hedgehog Circle, but I bet they will also reach the same conclusion once Sarah has filled them in on what has happened.*

I rode on, constantly alert for danger, but none came my way. At night, I camped out near the southern edge of the Ath mountains where they gradually faded into the rolling hills of Layamon. Their craggy peaks formed a natural barrier separating the highlands of Ruadan from the green hills of Tewdwr. Tomorrow, I would officially enter Tewdwr. As I settled down for the night, I relaxed and expanded my perceptions, focusing on sensing my daughter, Sarah. She was very easy to locate. She had participated several times in Mind Joins and so knew mostly what to expect. I regretted not having telepathically communicated with her many times before now. I guess you can say that I use this gift sparingly.

She reported that the creature had finally gotten to my house only to find out from the neighbors that I had already left for my vacation. From the neighbors, Sarah said that the creature seemed very upset, growling, and grumbling to himself. Since the neighbors also felt so ill at ease with this stranger, they didn't offer additional information. Sarah, rightly so, had stayed away from our house all day, choosing to practice her spying skills. She finally located the creature as it was working its way out of town following the route I had taken. She'd followed from a safe distance all the way to the north gate and then watched it walk off on the trail that led to Brea. She was certain that it had taken our bait. I felt a little relieved; we had bought me some valuable time to make my get-away.

I didn't see much difference in the scenery until early afternoon the next day, when the skies grew steadily overcast and light rain began to fall. The lands about me turned the most magnificent shade of emerald green! The sheer beauty of this land was overwhelming. A closer inspection of the ground also showed large patches of moss and ferns that grew nearly four feet tall in the lower valleys. Here was Nature untouched by the hand of man, a Garden of the Gods. All afternoon, I soaked in the magnificence of the countryside as I rode along, entirely forgetting the dangerous situation in which I was involved.

By nightfall the next day, I had reached the coast. Foggy, absolutely. I nearly rode off a cliff and fell down into the ocean far below! Here, the coastline was full of jagged rock outcropping; the thunderous roar of the ocean waves smashing their way onshore drowned out all other sounds. The cliff rose about a hundred feet from the shore. Only in those places where the occasional bubbling brook cut a passage could one ride on down to the coast proper. This was a spectacular coastline indeed. I camped with the roar of the ocean lapping onto the rugged coastline echoing in my ears.

The next morning I awoke to a foggy daylight. Visibility, poor. "Well, I guess I can hide more easily here," I commented to my mare as I saddled her up once more. I was at the coast of Tewdwr, but now what was I to do? I decided that because of the fog, it would not be too safe to continue to ride along the cliff tops. One slight misstep and over we would go. As if reading my thoughts, my horse began to follow the small bubbling creek down through the cut in the cliff side. Now the gently rolling water turned into a voracious torrent. As if sensing the nearness of its goal, the waters fought with a tenacity to reach the ocean below. Water slammed this way and that down the narrow cut. I let my mare have her head, trusting to her instincts to get us safely down. Instead of trying to control her, I concentrated on staying on her without forcing her off balance.

Once down on the white sands of the beach, I looked back through the fog at the way I had come. Stark white chalk cliffs loomed like surreal carvings of gods through the swirls of grey between my eyes and the near vertical wall. Yes, there was a breathtaking quality about this land. On the seaward side, great boulders loomed like giants only partially seen through the mist, like gods licked by the white foam of the ocean's caress. Caught up in the spectacular beauty of Nature, I dismounted and walked slowly northward, following the ebb and flow of the pristine white beach.

By noon, the fog had lifted revealing dense low clouds. It would rain soon. I was not disappointed. The afternoon rains were warm and gentle, as if Nature was gently touching this land. So far, I was amazed by everything about this land of Tewdwr. It was a wonder that more people didn't live here. I found a settlement by late afternoon, however.

A small break in the giant stones created a small natural harbor perhaps a half mile across. Cradled between the water and the cliffs lay a small fishing village of perhaps a dozen stone buildings. I spied several small fishing boats moving inland in the harbor as well as a number of men, women, and children in the streets. Actually, near the dock, the village had a large open plaza. The children were playing ball here, as I walked into the village, leading my horse. Absolutely everyone stopped what they were doing and stared at me; I felt more than a little uncomfortable.

I glanced about to see if I could spot an inn but saw nothing recognizable as such. As I approached the first person, an old man sitting beside a stone building and fixing a fishing net, I asked, "Good afternoon. What is the name of this village and is there an inn where I might spend the night?"

He grinned, revealing a nearly toothless mouth, and said in a very thick accent, "Cuch Glyn we'th be'th. Don'na have'th an inn, miss'eth. Try'th Goewin down'th there. She run'th 'ur pub. Might'th 'ave a place fer'th ah night."

"Thanks!" I replied and continued walking to the stone building to which he had pointed. A simple sign above the main door showed a ram's head with two beer mugs on either side. I tied my horse nearby and entered, acutely aware of all the eyes watching my every motion. Conclusion: this village seldom had any outside visitors.

Inside, the pub was filled with the traditional tables and chairs one expects to see in a village gathering place. Just now, only one older woman was inside, she was wiping off tables and setting the chairs, most of which were sitting on top of the tables, back on to the floor. Evidently, she was getting ready to open for the evening. She looked up at me. At once, she stopped and moved closer to me, "Caught'eth me bit soon'th. Thee be'th a stranger 'round here'th."

"Yes, I am looking for Goewin. A gentleman said I might be able to get a place to stay the night here."

"Aye, that be'th ol' Demna. I be'th Goewin. Sure got'h a spare'th room. Don'na get'h man'ie stranger'ths 'round here. Be'th welcome 'ere at Ram's Head. 'Ere on business'th?" Her accent was quite thick, but then I realized mine must seem that way to her.

"Thanks, I could use a room for the night. No, actually, I'm from down near Bregia in Layamon. I'm here on a holiday, just passing through and seeing the sights of this beautiful countryside. What little I have seen of Tewdwr thus far, it is just a breathtakingly magnificent land." My comments seemed to put her more at ease. She was about fifty years old and weighted perhaps just under two hundred pounds. Goewin was a heavyset woman well suited to running the pub and keeping things under her control.

As she led me to the spare room, she commented, "T'is unusual for t'us t'get alone'th woman — by'eth thyself, eh? Well, no matter'th. I be'st by'eth mie'self'th too — ever sin'th Erwin drown'th co'ple years ago'th. 'Ere how'eth this?" She showed me a corner room with a single tiny window too small to crawl out of in a pinch. It had a narrow bed, a small table, and a chair. Boxes of stuff lined one wall completely; evidently, this room was more frequently used for storage. I liked its rustic charm and next arranged for the stabling of my horse. She asked for three copper coins, but I gave her a gold one instead, insisting that I might eat and drink a lot. She laughed and graciously accepted it. I think she now completely liked my company, at least my coin, anyway.

She then explained that the fishermen would be docking shortly and, after the catch was unloaded and the men cleaned up, the entire village would go to their church for evening services. Once the short service was over, everyone went home for dinner, and then on to her pub for an enjoyable evening of drinks, songs, and conversation. "Since'th thee like'th our land, thee be'st welcome'th to come'th to our service'th." I agreed, chose to wash up, and then a short while later followed her to the church.

Their church, otherwise to my eyes, was indistinguishable from the other twenty grey stone buildings, save for an ornate, intertwined and interlocking set of carved circles on its front door. Inside, the main room was filled with wooden pews, just as ornately carved as the symbol on the door. I admired the craftsmanship and loving care that had gone into their making. About fifty people filed inside, most stared at me before turning their attention to their Priestess. Her name was Naessa, Goewin whispered to me.

Naessa was approximately thirty or so years old and definitely pregnant, nearly due, I estimated. She had long flowing yellow hair and a fair complexion. Rather than let you fight with her thick accent, I will translate her words. "We Annwn, the Children of God here in Cymry, give thanks that we have once more been allowed to experience life to its fullest, triumphing once more over evil, hardship, and travail. By experiencing life in its completeness, we continue to strive for our spiritual purity of being. Another successful day has ended, and we are now one day closer to being able to leave our fleshly bodies behind and move into the realm of Gwynfyd with God. Thank you all for your triumph over temptation and evil of this day. Go now, partake of your well-earned dinner, and enjoy the simple conversations of the night, knowing that once more, the morrow will bring a further test of our spirits over temptation and evil. We have with us tonight a traveler from afar here on a holiday; let us make her welcome."

One by one, as the villagers filed out, they all smiled at me and bid me "Good'th ev'n." I figured this was their custom and allowed each to do so. Naessa signaled me that she wanted a brief word with me, which allowed me to stay, while the others passed by me with their greetings.

"We don't often have visitors here, even more rarely a lone woman, but you are welcome nevertheless. I am Naessa, the village Priestess, my husband, Godwin, is a fisherman. He's gone home to tend to his catch and awaits me."

"Yes, I'm traveling alone, sort of a holiday for me. I'm the Priestess for my towns back in Layamon. I was impressed by your service tonight. We hold many beliefs in common, though I'm originally from Juda Arad many years ago. Is this your first child?"

She chuckled and smiled, "No, it is my third. It's due in about six weeks, if all goes well. Ah yes, your skin tone adds to your strangeness among our villagers." Her deep blue eyes looked deeply into mine. What she said next shocked me; I wasn't prepared for it. "Ah, Bethany, you're running from a great evil. I see a great evil following you." How could she have known? I nearly panicked.

"Well, that is true. I'm indeed trying to elude a very great evil. I promise only to spend this night in your village. I don't want to bring this evil down upon your people, but I am on a holiday, nevertheless. My daughter, Sarah, and I have decided that, if the evil should at last catch up with me and slay my fleshly body, I want to have at least seen the magnificent beauty of Tewdwr. From what I have seen thus far, it is more than spectacular. If my body is to be slain, at least I'll have seen great beauty beforehand."

"Thank you for being honest with me. We shall keep this between you and me. Tomorrow, I'll have my son, Garth, ride a ways with you to show you some of the marvelous sights where the Hand of God has touched Cymry near our village. You'll see. Come. I'll walk you back to the pub. Goewin probably has your meal waiting for you. Mind you, her pub can be really noisy until about eight at night."

She was and it was! Around six, her pub filled up with most of the adults of the village, though not all. Naessa was noticeably absent. They chatted some with me, but mostly they drank, sang songs, and played their traditional music. Music! I had forgotten all about just how much I enjoyed music and dancing. Their musicians played several kinds of stringed instruments, a flute, and a drum. The night passed altogether too swiftly from my point of view. I found out that this merrymaking went on every night. These were a lighthearted people, that's for sure. I really began to enjoy their company, but not their thick accents. For a few hours, all thoughts of my doom evaporated entirely. When I laid down that night, I relayed to Sarah all that had happened to me this day. Sarah told me, "See, you are having a wonderful holiday!"

The next day, Garth showed up in the early morning. "Mom's told me I'm to show you God's Back and God's Teeth. I'm ready whenever you are," he said in his thick accent. He was about ten years old, tall and lean, but full of life and very eager to show me these sights. We left in about ten minutes. I led my horse as we walked out of the village. As I departed, absolutely everyone, including the children waved goodbye to me, quite unlike my initial reception. I really liked these people.

We walked along the white sands draped in a dense fog for perhaps a mile before heading up the stream gorge to the top of the cliff. Another mile inland and the fog lifted, revealing God's Back. For miles in all directions, the land was barren, but stony brown bumps completely covered the land. These were uniform and square-shaped, as if the hand of God used a cookie cutter to carve out cookies of stone. Such a sight of Nature I had never seen or heard about — I was more than a little impressed with the magnificent sight. Garth, too, was pleased that I was so pleased.

He led me further inland, walking over the hard stone cookies, for several miles. Around noon, as we neared the edge of a deep gorge, he proclaimed, "Behold, God's Teeth."

Below me, rushing water from the distant Ath mountains had cut strange rock formations in the valley. Giant needles of stone protruded skyward from the valley floor. I was once more dutifully impressed with the sight! He explained that we could not enter the valley from here. If one wanted to wander down there among the needles, he or she would have to enter the valley from its eastern side. Then, Garth took his leave, saying that his mom had given his strict orders to return before the later afternoon services. I shook his hand and thanked him generously for taking the time to show me these wonders of Nature. He was quite pleased with my praise and began skipping over the cookies heading home. I watched him until he was out of sight, then turned once more to look at the impressing stone pillars they called teeth. It was not hard to see how they got their name. I imagined being high in the sky looking down at this elongated valley. Indeed, it would look much like a mouth, the right curves anyway. The pillars would seem to be teeth. I marveled at these sights for quite a while.

That's when I sensed it! Evil! That same foreboding sense of evil that I felt that night when Sarah and I were returning to town, and it was drawing closer to me! Quickly, I mounted up. I couldn't go further east; the only real avenue of exit was back the way I had come. I intended to get back down to the coastline and hide in the fog, which should be rolling in soon. It didn't help matters that it began to rain gently once more. Over this stony ground, I couldn't ride fast for fear of having my horse lose her footing. It took an endless hour to get back down onto the sandy beach. There was no sign of Garth, so I felt relieved that I hadn't placed him in any danger. Still I sensed the Grey Creature getting closer to me. I cantered northward along the coast at top speed, as the fog began closing in around me. In a half hour, I had to slow down because I couldn't see where I was going; the fog was that thick.

Then, I realized the stupidity of my entire hypotheses that I could hide in the fog. Look, I'm a spiritual being, and I can locate other spiritual beings at a great distance. If I can do this, surely these Grey Creatures can do the same. Fog, just as distance, was not a barrier. I couldn't hide from them in a fog — just go slower myself! "At least, I got to see some incredible wonders of Nature," I said to my mare, which seemed to understand.

Now, I sensed that the creature was very close. I pivoted in all directions trying to see it, but the fog blocked my vision. I didn't panic. I knew that I wasn't going to try to fight this creature. I didn't even have a useable weapon that could harm it. Suddenly, I smelled a foul odor to my right. As I turned, a huge fist appeared out of the fog, slamming straight into my face. The universe momentarily went completely black. My body had been killed in the same manner as my husband's had, of that I was certain. Yet, in that brief contact, because I was so aware, I observed a fact that I hadn't known — a fact that would later prove to be invaluable. The Grey Creature was highly allergic to the odor of burning sulfur!

Now my vision returned, only I was seeing in three hundred sixty degrees as a spiritual being sees, not when focusing through the tiny viewpoint of a body's eyes. Only everything was a dim grey; the fog was incredibly dense, and the sun had just gone down. Still, I was completely stunned by the unexpected blow, staggering might be a better description, if a spiritual being could be said to be staggering. Just then, I heard a mechanical click and felt a slight tugging pull on myself. I instantly recognized what was happening. The

Grey Creature was trying to suck me into some kind of portable trap! He was trying to do to me what he had done to Jes and Alabaster! He wanted to scramble all my memories and instill some demonic subliminal commands!

The hell you are! I declared to myself. I concentrated on not resisting that pull, and slowly backed away from him and the diabolical device. This he didn't like one bit. Suddenly, I picked up its thoughts. The creature had just realized that it couldn't entrap me! It changed tactics and suddenly blasted me with a massive bolt of energy. I wasn't prepared for this and took the blast full in my spiritual face — look, there are no words to describe this, please accept my analogy. I flew off out to sea in an uncontrolled swoosh. I sensed that, in effect, I was actually getting away from this evil creature, so I went along with the recoiling motion. Only now with my senses mostly numbed from that blast, I was slow in seeing the second blast headed my way. At the very last instant before it hit me full on, I recognized it and dove under the water, heading down, down, down into the incredibly black depths, holding my breath to keep from drowning! Again, a silly thought.

The original blast that I took had shrunk my space and awareness down to a mere three feet around me. No longer could I sense the creature. I pulled in my senses even further, trying to shrink myself into an unidentifiable dot, all the while holding my breath. Finally, I hit something solid, the bottom of the sea. There I froze, motionless, thoughtless, and senseless. I continued straining my utmost to hold my breath and waited. I could wait, yes, that I could do. If I waited lifeless and silent long enough, perhaps the evil creature would depart believing that I was dead. Wait a minute. How can an immortal spirit be "dead?" Okay, perhaps a better way to say this is I would be an inactive spiritual being, no longer any threat whatsoever to these creatures.

It was black. I thought no thoughts, made no motion, made no attempt to sense the universe around me, and in short played "dead." Still I kept holding my breath, concentrating, focusing my attention on not breathing this deep underwater, knowing if I did breath, why, I would drown long before I could reach the surface. In such a state, the universe time passes. Yet, without any observable changes in the environment going on by which to monitor it, you can't say how much time is elapsing. Rather, it appears to one that no time is elapsing.

Finally, I ventured a thought. *I must stay like this until I'm sure the creature is long gone.* Sometime later, I thought, *I wonder how long that will be?* Then, I had another thought; *I'm getting so tired holding my breath. I don't know how much longer I can hold my breath.*

Suddenly I burst out laughing! Okay, a spiritual laugh, since I had no fleshly body with which to laugh. Still, I laughed harder than I could ever remember laughing. An immortal spirit does not breathe! Bodies have to breathe. I was still acting as if I had brought my body way down here to the ocean's floor! I found that so incongruous that I had a fit of belly-laughter even without having a belly!

Now I could see that I was indeed on the bottom of the ocean. It was dimly illuminated. Several fish swam nearby and one actually swam through me before sensing me and bolting away in a flash. I hazard a slight expansion of my awareness, searching for the presence of the evil creature. I sensed nothing and so became sufficiently brave and confident to rise slowly to the surface, where it was indeed daytime. A light shower pinged upon the waves around me. Still no sign of the creature. Emboldened, I ventured up in the air and floated slowly toward the beach. Still no sign of my opponent. I took a deep spiritual breath and expanded my awareness outward a good distance, perhaps a mile in all directions, save downward. Satisfied that the creature had indeed gone away concluding that it had zapped me into oblivion, I now began to think what I ought to do next.

First action, acquire a new baby body. I'd dearly love to get one in the Greenway, but perhaps that is neither wise nor safe at this point. I would hate to bring down the wrath of these creatures upon all the Circles! I could never live with that. No, I can't yet return to the Greenway. That is out. Let's see, what are the requirements I need most? Gosh, I have an awful headache. Ah, that was from that energy blast. It's still with me. I need time for the new body to grow to adulthood in complete safety before I can get back into the action. I ought to be as far from the Appian Way as possible. I thought about this for some time.

Suddenly, I started laughing once more. *You idiot, Bethany, right here is just perfect! Naessa is just about to give birth, perfect timing. She at least holds nearly the same spiritual values as I do. Perfect. I wonder how close she is to having her baby? I'd better go and see.* I began floating south toward Cuch Glyn.

Presently, I floated over the tiny fishing village. It looked peaceful and tranquil just as it had when I spent the night here. I found the church and shortly Naessa. To my complete shock, she looked much older and not nearly as pregnant! If I had to guess, she was perhaps only five months pregnant! How could this be? I floated into her home as she returned there after giving the evening service and closing the church. I saw her dishing out supper. There was her husband; I recalled meeting him. At the table sat three boys and one girl!

All at once, I realized what had happened. I had been underwater for quite some time — perhaps over a year or more. She had already had her baby, probably the girl who appeared to be perhaps three years old. Naessa was pregnant with a fifth child. Time had indeed passed while I was more or less unconscious underwater. I felt a great relief just then — this meant that the evil Grey Creature was now very long gone. I didn't have to worry about it anymore.

Besides, I would only have to wait a few months for this new baby body to be born. I could watch over the village and even perhaps learn their language or their thick accent anyway to pass the time. Once more, I reviewed my complete line of reasoning and found it still to be sound and probably the optimum course to follow now. Satisfied, I just hung around the village and my mother-to-be, Naessa, waiting for her time. Mostly, I pondered how I could get Naessa to name me Bethany. I really liked that name, though it was definitely not Cymry in nature. This would be quite a challenge if I were to keep my name, which I loved.

It never dawned on me that she might give birth to a baby boy!
The End.

Other Books by Vic Broquard

Without Warning (fantasy)

The Trident Series: (fantasy)
> Volume 1 The Trident and the Book
> Volume 2 The Trident and the Scepter
> Volume 3 The Trident and the Resurrection

The Adventures of Elizabeth Stanton Series: (science fiction)
> Volume 1 The Evolution of the Path
> Volume 2 The Great Messiah
> Volume 3 Of Kings and Queens and Troubadours
> Volume 4 Chaos in the Aftermath
> Volume 5 Power Plays
> Volume 6 Age of Exploration
> Volume 7 Abducted
> Volume 8 The Emperor and Empress
> Volume 9 A Job Worth Doing
> Volume 10 Degradation
> Volume 11 The Second Crusade
> Volume 12 When Worlds Collide
> Volume 13 Dark Ages

The Lindsey Barron Series: (fantasy)
> Volume 1 The Rod of the Apocalypse
> Volume 2 The Board of Governors
> Volume 3 The Crown of Moses
> Volume 4 Dominus for President
> Volume 5 The National Health Care Program
> Volume 6 States Justice
> Volume 7 Cross and Double-cross

Zoran Chronicles Series: (fantasy)
> Volume 1 A Dragon in Our Town
> Volume 2 Dragons, Power, Courts, and War

Planet of the Orange-red Sun Series: (science fiction)
> Volume 1 When Kingdoms Fall
> Volume 2 Dark Ages
> Volume 3 Age of the Towers
> Volume 4 Difficillis Exitus
> Volume 5 Age of the Lords
> Volume 6 The Renegade Tower
> Volume 7 Rebellions

The Return of the Wizards: Twelve Companions – The Making of Wizards (fantasy)

www.ingramcontent.com/pod-product-compliance
Lightning Source LLC
Chambersburg PA
CBHW080719020726
47502CB00009B/2468